The

ROUND
PRAIRIE
WARS

Aden Ross

ISBN 978-1-66786-168-5
eBook ISBN 978-1-66786-169-2

To Denny who knows all the truth and all the lies,
the beginning and end of this story

ACKNOWLEDGMENTS

I OWE ENORMOUS GRATITUDE TO A CIRCLE OF friends and supporters without whom this novel would never have taken shape. Rob Terry, Professor of History, provided numerous insights and research suggestions for the period, especially the Red Scare; Dr. Michaela Mohr helped tremendously, both with the history of psychiatry and of Germany just after WWII; and Anne Decker, theater professional, characteristically assisted with the subtleties of narrative and characterization. Early readers—Raymond Soto, librarian par excellence; Betsy Burton, owner of The King's English bookstore; and Kimi Kasai, watcher of the cosmos—each generously loaned me a part of themselves for this project. I am particularly indebted to my old friend and former colleague William E. Smith, Professor of English, who started as my staunch advocate and, in effect, became my literary agent.

To my dearest friends, of course, I owe the deepest debt. Without the unflagging belief and support of Susan Fleming, Ric Collier and my brother, Dennis Ross, I couldn't have survived the last few years, much less finished this book. As for Puck and C. O. D., you know exactly what you did.

Thank you, thank you all.

CONTENTS

CHAPTER 1

BACK TO BACK

"MAYDAY! MAYDAY!" SAM WHISPERED AS LOUDLY as he could without waking up the folks at the other end of our trailer house. Mama hardly slept at all because she was afraid we would be gassed in our sleep by the Communists, who already controlled the minds of every gas meter man in Round Prairie. Grandma Strang—her own mother—called her *paranoid*, but Papa said Mama just had an overactive imagination. People said the same thing about me, so Mama couldn't be actually crazy.

Every Sunday morning I crept into Sam's bedroom and slid shut the elevator-like doors. By day, this was the trailer's living room, and his bed was a sofa, but made into a bed, it was the perfect size for the cockpit of a fighter plane engaged in dog fights or bombing runs. Every time we bombed Germany, our B-17 was riddled with bullets, three of our engines had flamed out, everyone else on board was killed, and we were both wounded. Sam hated to let me fire the machine guns in the nose turret because my girl's voice didn't sound fatal enough, but with the rest of the crew dead, he had no alternative.

He never let me be the pilot, never let me make the big life-and-death decisions, not because I was nine years old and Sam was eleven, but because he was so much smarter than I. *Exponentially* smarter, he called himself. It took me five minutes to learn how to spell that word but two weeks to understand what it meant. At least, to understand it as well as Sam pretended to. Even as a self-designated genius, he knew better than to try to stop me from doing something because I was a girl. That insult was a declaration of war, mostly in the form of Indian leg wrestling.

"Mayday!" He sounded more desperate at the plane's radio. "Can anybody hear me?"

Today we were returning from a mission over the Pacific in a crippled Douglas SBD Dauntless, a two-man dive bomber. Sam was both the pilot and radio man, his two favorite roles, while I sat in the rear cockpit, facing the airplane's tail and manning the thirty-caliber machine gun.

Sam looked over the plane's nose at the sputtering engine, now throwing out ominous sparks.

"Captain!" I called into my oxygen mask. "We have to open the canopies to let the smoke out of the cockpits!"

"Roger!" Sam whispered hoarsely. It took all our remaining strength to slide back the damaged covers. The wind pulled on our shoulder harnesses.

He pretended to shout, "I don't know how much longer I can keep us up!"

Sitting cross-legged and back to back on his bed, we echoed each other's movements as our plane pitched and rolled.

"Zero at three o'clock!" My specialty was adding catastrophes to already hopeless situations.

Sam instantly rolled our plane so I could nail the enemy with my few remaining shells. "Ek-ek-ek-ek-ek," My shoulders shook with the gun. "Ek-ek-ek-ek-ek."

I felt Sam wince, since he could duplicate the soundtrack for an entire war movie, complete with bombs, howitzers, exploding flares, ricochets, flak, and even the whistling German Doodlebugs as they dropped on London.

In spite of my pitiful ek-ek-eks, I nailed the Zero, which spiraled down in smoke, its target-like paint spot spinning in and out of view.

"Got 'im, Banshee!" "Banshee" was the Army's version of our Navy plane, a name I had already recorded in my journal of imaginary horses, in this case a wild black stallion with a white mane and tail.

"Will we make it?" With no trouble at all, I could work myself into a pretty realistic terror. If Sam decided to ditch the plane, he would order us to bail out as soon as possible, but I would heroically insist on riding it all the way down, straight into the ocean, even though I couldn't swim. In my opinion, a happy ending was always possible, no matter how unlikely.

Sam responded with a dip so sharp it pulled my hands off the machine gun. "We've got one try," he said grimly, as we both spotted the carrier on the choppy ocean below.

"What about the hurricane that's moving in?" I tried to sound like Gregory Peck's rear gunner.

Magnificently, Sam recreated the sputtering roar of a disabled dive bomber on its last-chance landing on a rolling aircraft carrier in high seas. "Rumn-rumn-rumn. Brace for a crash landing!"

He and I lurched violently, one way and then the other, until we felt our tailhook catch the arresting wire and jerk us to a stop.

Around us, the ship's crew began cheering. By radio, they had learned how we single-handedly sank a submarine and bombed the command tower of a Japanese battleship.

We sat there for a long moment, exhausted, while Sam shut down our crippled plane which had been held aloft by sheer grit, by two fighters who would never give up regardless of the odds, two buddies who fought every battle together, back to back.

CHAPTER 2
THE DAY THE EARTH STOOD STILL

EVERYBODY CALLED IT THE INAVALE DRIVE-IN movie, although it was actually the two-story wall of the Inavale Hotel facing a vacant lot. Built of Nebraska limestone, the hotel glistened creamy white, the perfect outdoor movie screen except for the windows breaking the surface. Every Friday night, people from neighboring farms and towns gathered there and spread blankets on the ground or built makeshift benches from cinder blocks and planks to watch the free movie sponsored by the hotel owners. They brought potatoes, corn, or garden vegetables to share with anyone nearby. Always hopeful for store-bought cookies, which almost never appeared, Sam and I at least maneuvered to sit near the cold storage apples rather than the carrots or leaf lettuce.

I didn't know where the projector was, but suddenly the roaring lion or the lady with the torch would magically spread across the hotel wall and, from somewhere behind us, the soundtrack would scratch and crackle, turned up too high for the speakers to handle.

Sam, halfway through his Electricity merit badge, explained, "It sounds like mismatched impedance to me."

I responded, "It sounds like a loose nut to me."

"That's why I'm the Boy Scout and you're not."

Sam always wanted to find out how things actually worked, unlike me, who was happier inventing explanations. My method took less time but required more imagination.

The owners asked the people staying in the hotel to close their shades to create as smooth a screen as possible, but someone would always open their window and look out—right in the middle of Claudette Colbert's eye or the starched bib Ingrid Bergman wore as a nun. Sometimes the hotel residents would close their shades but walk back and forth behind them, creating a silhouette show appearing in the canvas of the covered wagon stranded on the prairie or in the middle of bombs dropping from a Flying Fortress like fish eggs.

If the movie were thrilling enough, I could momentarily ignore the tiny, shadowy strangers appearing in the folds of Ginger Rogers' swirling skirt, but life in the hotel windows usually intruded on moments of greatest crisis or intimacy, predictably during the ever so hesitant and whispery kisses for which I waited through many a stupid grown-up movie. At any kiss on screen, Sam would groan the way boys were required to do, complete with bared teeth, but never so disgusted as when a previously dependable cowboy like John Wayne, back at the fort after a day killing Indians, suddenly grabbed and kissed Maureen O'Hara.

I relived any kisses for days afterward, replete with the billowy gowns and shiny ringlets, while Sam groused about the unrealistic blood which wouldn't fool a fly. Since everything was black and white, I told him to color the blood himself. Mama told me in secret that she always saw movies in color and encouraged me to do the same, to envision not just the ladies' gowns in turquoise or crimson but also to see Barbara Stanwyck with purple hair and Loretta Young with green cheeks, in other words, how she saw them. I finally got the courage to ask if she saw real people that way, or only fake ones in the movies.

"I see everybody's true colors," she answered.

This was not very helpful.

"Just because nobody else can see what you see doesn't mean it isn't true," she insisted.

Did her actual eyes see these things, or her overactive imagination? If I couldn't see what she saw, was something wrong with me? Could she be lying, my own mother? Sometimes you have to stop asking questions because there aren't enough answers to go around. Papa often said that, but possibly just to make me quiet.

Better than the kisses were the reunions on screen, reunions between long separated lovers, the slow, loping, striding, leaping across fields of flowers, the camera flicking from the lady hopping like a deer in from the left to the man loping in from the right, closer and closer until WHAM they met and he twirled her in his arms. I daydreamed that Sam and I were separated from Mama and Papa by war, wind and flood; after endless agony and heartache, we saw them from afar and began running in slow motion, leaping across vacant lots full of weeds until we all collided in a happy little tornado, spinning in each other's arms.

By the end of the Inavale movie, the people inside the hotel windows had created miniature, alternate movies embedded in the bigger one. In effect, we watched four or five movies of different sizes in different dimensions, simultaneously. Mama said a double feature couldn't hold a candle to it. I liked to make up lives for the people staying in the hotel: traveling salesmen became mad scientists developing secret weapons, construction workers were actually FBI agents investigating enemy spy rings on surrounding farms. Deep down, I knew that the real lives of the hotel people never ended with kisses or reunions, never ended half as happy as the gigantic, flat fiction surrounding them. But it could happen. Meanwhile, I would be happy if just once I could see June Allyson's perfect cheek unpocked by some tired trucker smoking a cigarette out his window.

We heard that tonight's movie was called "The Day the Earth Stood Still." On the drive to Inavale, Sam pointed out that the earth was spinning on its axis, orbiting the sun, and racing through the Milky Way for a total of half a million miles an hour, day and night, forever.

"If the earth ever stood still," Sam continued solemnly, "people on the sun side would immediately incinerate and people in the shade would freeze solid."

"It's a metaphor," Mama explained.

"Meta-what?" Sam asked.

"It says one thing, but means something else."

"Like a lie?" I was thrilled at the prospect of using a new word much more sophisticated than *fib*.

"No, like a poem," she answered. "A skull can be a metaphor for death."

When Mama wasn't cleaning the trailer, she spent all of her time reading poetry or the encyclopedia. She had already started Volume 2 of the Funk and Wagnall's we bought at the grocery store, one volume every month.

"How do you—"I began.

Before I could finish, Mama spelled, "M-e-t-a-p-h-o-r."

Oh boy. I loved words which had a 'ph' for an 'f,' like *philosophy*, which did it twice.

The audience never cared what movie was showing, given any break from hard work and sweltering heat. This late June night, sticky as warm honey on my bare legs, word went around the crowd that tonight's show was almost new, unlike the ancient episodes of the Three Stooges or Buster Keaton we usually saw. Most of the hotel windows stood open to catch any moving air even after the title flashed on the screen, accompanied by a high-pitched, quivering moan preparing us to be scared witless.

Right away, a flying saucer landed in Washington, D. C., but when the spaceman, Klaatu, stepped out to give Earthlings a present, he was gunned down by the surrounding Army. Typical. Immediately, a huge robot named Gort melted all of their weapons just by staring at them, his eyes a terrifying beam of light focused through a slit in his metal head.

Except for Earth, the whole universe had evolved beyond using violence to solve problems, but space-traveling civilizations realized that humans had atomic bombs and could not only destroy ourselves but also harm other planets. When the Earthlings couldn't agree even to meet at the United Nations to hear the warning from outer space, Klaatu demonstrated his power by cutting off all electricity in the world except for hospitals and planes in flight. He was pretty considerate for an alien.

At the exact moment when the Earth was standing still, someone opened their hotel window smack in the middle of Gort's smooth metal chest and shook out a long rug. All the grown-ups laughed, but not us kids.

In the end, Klaatu warned that, if Earthlings continued to use violence, especially nuclear war, Gort's race–the universe's designated executioners—would annihilate our planet and everything on it. The spaceship blasted off to woozy strings and Frankenstein organ music.

Wow. We all clapped, then people began gathering their seats, blankets and children.

Sam complained, "The Earth didn't exactly 'stand still.' It was just a massive power outage."

"Yeah." Whenever it didn't cost me anything, I agreed with him. "But that would be a pretty dumb title: 'The Day the Earth Had a Power Outage'."

"It would've been better if the aliens used mind control, too," he continued. "If Gort's race had evolved that far, they could certainly control the minds of us puny Earthlings."

"If they could control our minds, they could've stayed home and done it from there," I argued. "Of course, then there wouldn't have been any movie."

"That is so stupid," Sam picked up a pop bottle to see if anything was left in it, then tossed it back on the ground.

"It's just logic."

As the expert in logic, Sam looked momentarily crestfallen. To cheer him up, I pointed out, "There were some pretty good explosions, though." Explosives of any kind always made Sam feel better.

We walked slowly toward the highway with the crowd, the grown-ups all shaking hands and cracking jokes, while the kids jumped back and forth across the temporary plank benches. Mama and Papa were leaning against the car, both with tightly folded arms, the sign of a Serious Disagreement.

Papa handed us each a penny and asked, "Does anybody need a jawbreaker?"

Stunned, Sam and I raced across the deserted two-lane highway to the little grocery store which had a whole shelf of penny candy. The old man at the counter said wasn't it remarkable that just for tonight jawbreakers were on sale for half-price, and he gave us each two. Cradling a red and a yellow one in my palm, I thanked him three times.

Sam could make his jawbreaker last all the way home, continually licking his fingers and taking it out of his mouth to show me the various colored layers, slowly exposed, until it was just a little seed. I knew that the same colors were also magically appearing and dissolving in my mouth, but I chomped at mine until my jaw ached, finally splitting it into shards I could crunch and swallow.

On the drive home, Mama leaned into the hot wind through the open car window and lifted her hair off her neck. "I'm amazed the Communists let that movie pass."

"Edie, Communists had nothing to do with it."

"Don't kid yourself. If the film industry isn't full of Communists, why is McCarthy interrogating every movie star and writer and director he can get his hands on?"

"Because he's a sick little man conducting a witch hunt with the help of other political idiots and cowards. If McCarthy sees purple cows, they see purple cows. Never mind the fact that his delusions come out of a whiskey bottle."

Mama snorted. "You can't see the nose at the end of your face."

"I've only got one eye, remember?"

"Oh, you see what you want to see and ignore anything you don't like. I never knew anyone who could look right at an impending disaster and not see it. Bury-your-head-in-the-sand-Frank. Until the Communists come to bury the rest of you."

"Add that to the list of things I don't do right." The steering wheel almost jerked out of Papa's hands as we hit a chuckhole.

I couldn't stand it. "Papa, you do a lot of things right."

"Not according to your mother."

Mama calmed down a little. "The movie said outright that the rocket ship was the work of the Russians."

"Flying saucer," Sam corrected her. "They're a lot harder to get airborne than rockets."

"I'll tell you who will be airborne in a minute," Papa warned.

"You gotta admit, that flying saucer was neat." Sam attacked one of his hands with the other, like spinning plates. "Battle of the flying saucers. Bzzht. Bzzht."

"There was only one flying saucer," I corrected him, suddenly sticking to the facts.

Papa tried not to argue with Mama in front of us, but tonight he persisted, "The point of the movie is that we have to live together peacefully, or we'll all be destroyed."

"By the Communists."

I continually asked but never got an answer, "What's a Communist?"

Papa flashed our headlights at an oncoming car which was blinding us with its high beams. "Nothing a little girl needs to worry about."

"Don't lie to her." Mama turned in her seat to talk to me. "Communists are evil people who live all around us. Trying to destroy us every way they can—-infiltrating the schools, brainwashing, poison gas."

I had a million questions but chose one. "What gas?"

"They're all in cahoots with the gas company," Mama gave one of her typical non-answers.

Sam's flying saucer hands crash-landed in his lap. "I thought Communists were Russians."

"They are." Mama turned back to look at Papa. "But they're here, too. Hastings . . . Hebron . . . Round Prairie."

"Wow. Who's one in Round Prairie?" I asked. "I have my suspicions," she answered, "and I'm not alone."

Papa asked quickly, "What did you like about the movie, Jeb?"

I recognized Papa's attempt to change the subject, so I went along with it. Maybe he would explain the gas problem later. "The little boy everybody thought was lying."

"I'll bet that did sound familiar," Papa answered.

"And Gort. I wish I had a robot like that." An armored friend nine feet tall would be very useful when school started.

In a rare humanitarian moment, Sam pointed out, "Gort only destroyed weapons, not people. Zzzzht." To his inexhaustible supply of war sounds, tonight Sam had added extraterrestrial combat. "Zzzzht. There goes a machine gun. Zzzzht. There goes a tank."

Mama insisted, "If we're not surrounded by Communists, why does the news keep saying we are?"

"Because Hoover and his gang have control of the radio and newspapers."

Mama tossed her head. "And you accuse *me* of conspiracy theories."

"I don't accuse you of one damned—"

"You don't need to swear." She sighed. "Hoover and McCarthy are trying to protect us."

"Protect a bunch of sheep who stampede to their own slaughter. This country deserves exactly what it's getting. We've created the monsters."

"I hope you don't talk this way at work. You in a government job."

"The Communists can't hurt us nearly as much as we can hurt ourselves."

"You are so gullible, Frank. Exactly the kind of person the Communists can brainwash."

I wasn't sure what "gullible" or "brainwashing" meant, but to stop their fight from going on past bedtime, I tried a red herring. "I thought Hoover was a vacuum cleaner."

Mama poked Papa's shoulder with one stiff finger. "I know. What I know."

"Klaatu barada nikto," Sam said quietly.

"What's that, son?" Papa asked loudly, above the dark wind.

"It's Klaatu's magic saying to keep Gort from killing everybody." Sam glumly looked out the window at the fingernail moon pasted sideways near the horizon, sucking his jawbreaker through all its changing colors down to its tiny heart.

CHAPTER 3
MAPS

I LEARNED A FEW THINGS OUR FIRST SUMMER IN Round Prairie, but nothing held a candle to what I learned from Sam working on Boy Scout merit badges. Since we lived in a trailer house and moved every year, Sam was my only friend, which meant that I either helped him with his projects or played by myself. When I pointed out that the Boy Scouts acted like an army of midgets, he asked if I would rather embroider dish towels and weave potholders with the Brownies or learn Morse code and build fires. Given a choice, I preferred anything to do with horses to anything else, but he was right. Besides, I hated little girls. From the get-go, I played hooky from Brownie meetings and lied to Mama about it—two major sources of blackmail for Sam to use against me.

Round Prairie, like the other towns where we lived in southern Nebraska, was short on horses and long on wheat. Flat, unfenced wheat fields spread for miles in every direction, broken only by occasional farm buildings or cottonwoods along the twisty Republican River. Papa told us that Nebraska was the bottom of an ancient sea, which seemed awfully unlikely in this country full of dry farms and dry stream beds and the dry chaff exploding out of combines during harvest. But he wouldn't lie.

Papa also warned that the slow, friendly Republican River could suddenly go insane, slice whole houses off their foundations like a knife under a layer cake, and slide them downstream, stranding them miles away in someone's field like a huge practical joke. Mama's kind of joke. She sneered that floods could turn anybody's house into a mobile home, then laughed with a sound like one high note played fast on a piano, faster and faster until one of us called out her name. Instantly, her laughing changed to hoarse whispering about how a person could either laugh or just go nuts, nuts, nuts, nuts, nuts.

Working on a huge Bureau of Reclamation project, Papa helped build dams along the Republican, but as soon as one section of it was under control, it would flood somewhere else. So we migrated with the river—the reason we lived in a trailer house. Well, one of the reasons. We sold our real house to finish paying for Papa's doctor bills when he almost died of burns before Sam and I were born. Papa's burns topped the list of Topics the Wilder Family Did Not Discuss.

As soon as the trailer was hooked up in Round Prairie, I scouted every horse within bicycle distance along the gravel roads marking the county into a grid. As soon as I spotted a horse, I named it from my journal, which recorded my favorite words as well, words like *ukulele, archaeology* and *conundrum.* I dubbed one sway-backed horse Billy Batson with no real hope of transforming him into Captain Marvel, but you never knew. It could happen. Near Billy's pasture lived the most beautiful work horse I had ever seen. He was my third favorite color, dappled grey, which immediately transformed him into an Arabian stallion, galloping around the field and rearing on his hind legs on a nearby hilltop. That there was no hill anywhere within miles and that it would take a crane to lift his front feet off the ground didn't slow me down. It never hurt to dream. Mama always said so, although with that tilted look she had, as if she were talking to someone standing behind me. I gave the big grey horse a name I had been saving–Alberta Clipper, after the winds which howled down the prairie all the way from northern Canada to Texas. While Clipper was obviously no racehorse, he looked strong enough to pull our trailer house, which would have been handy, since the old Buick broke down every time we moved. Last time, Papa called it a *vapor lock* but never explained how vapor could lock. I kept trying to imagine it, transforming the steam into something solid as clay, shaping it into an old padlock with an hourglass keyhole in its front. But then I couldn't figure out a key to unlock my own invention.

Papa told stories about the Alberta Clippers which pulverized farmland into the Dust Bowl and which still ground snow into ice particles fine enough to suffocate cattle left out in blizzards. He survived the Dust Bowl on a dry farm but insisted that his family wasn't nearly as bad off as those miserable Okies, to which Mama would reply that there wasn't *always* somebody worse off than we were. Then she would point out how he had just fixed somebody's radio or stove or car for free when we needed the money. Whenever the conversation went the money direction, I would ask something I knew was idiotic, like who invented long division, anyway. Or Sam would toss out an impressive fact like how to make the gas which smelled like rotten eggs.

Any reference to chemistry stopped everybody cold, especially as Sam started to work seriously on his Chemistry merit badge. In private—and not to sound intentionally stupid—I asked him what chemistry was good for, anyway. He replied, "To blow things up." After that, my interest in chemistry increased exponentially, and led, ultimately, to the formula, which led to the fort and the broomcorn wars and, well, everything else that happened that year, the year I was in fourth grade and Sam was in sixth.

* * * * *

For Sam, nothing held a candle to a map. He could stand smack dab in the middle of a road he already knew to study the map without noticing the tractor bearing down on him in a cloud of dust. He wanted to know *scientifically* where he was just so he could seem smart and give orders, part of what he called his "natural leadership," but what I called "natural bossiness." Whenever Sam stopped to determine our current location on some map, I spent the time imagining events that had happened right under our feet—Indians on painted ponies chasing buffalo, farmers running for cover from a thunderstorm, little kids walking to one-room country schoolhouses. Of course, as the B-17 pilot who got one fleeting glance at a map of the German city we were about to bomb, Sam needed to calculate precisely where we were headed, but to require knowing the distance in tenths of a mile between the city limit signs of Hebron and Round Prairie seemed excessive.

Mama maintained that it took a lot more than a map to know where you were. To prove her point, she would describe some poem about catching tigers in red weather or thirteen ways of looking at a blackbird and recite lines like, "It was evening all afternoon" or "The blackbird is involved in what I know." Frankly, her poems left me just as confused as Sam's compass calculations. Papa, on the other hand, always knew where he was through landmarks like a particular windmill or a Model T rusting beside someone's chicken coop.

So when Sam discovered he could earn a Surveying merit badge, he was ecstatic, especially since Papa could borrow some government equipment from the dam site to help him. For this badge, the almost biblical Boy Scout Handbook required mapping a half mile of road, including a "gradient" and 440 yards on each side. As Papa set up the little telescope, he cautioned me that one person stayed at the plane table and drew the map, while the other one did the "leg work" across the actual territory. I was an experienced leg man from Sam's earlier projects, but legging it had never meant dragging a wooden pole eight feet long over every inch of a square half-mile of prairie.

Papa often teased, "Never touch a tool with a long handle, since that means real work." I was holding the world's longest handle with no tool attached at all. It wasn't called an idiot stick for nothing.

To be fair, Sam always taught me the basics of the task at hand, in this case letting me look through the scope with cross hairs like a rifle that he would focus on a tiny, faraway me, tiny as Alice after drinking the potion to grow small. The telescope was called a *level*, one of my favorite types of words, spelled the same backward and forward, like *racecar*. But as usual, Sam glossed over the specifics of who would be the brains and who would be the brawn in the operation. Because he always made all the decisions, I naturally assumed that he would play the Lone Ranger, but in this case, I couldn't even play Tonto. I was the pack mule.

All morning I dragged the pole and walked back for the chain and unkinked the links and dragged the pole again and walked back for the chain again. And again and again. Why was I doing this? If I couldn't answer my own question, who could?

"Straighten the chain!" From across the gully, Sam was half lost in heat waves rising from the weeds. In his cowboy hat, he looked like one of the bad guys in "High Noon," my favorite movie of all time. That would make me Gary Cooper, which meant that I had to kill him. I couldn't possibly do that, although if the situation were reversed, Sam would shoot me in a heartbeat, allowing his superior role as sheriff to outweigh loyalty to his own little sister. It didn't take a genius to know where I stood with Sam. On principle, I absolutely refused to be Grace Kelly, not because she was beautiful, peace-loving or religious, but she was yet another timid and dutiful movie female. Much to her credit, she did turn killer at the end.

"Straighter!" When I squinted, Sam now looked more like Yosemite Sam, especially when he waved his arms and shouted.

How much could I jiggle the surveyor's chain without stirring up the red anthill nearby? I already had several bites on my bare legs. Papa said if you don't bother somebody, they won't bother you, a version of his primary rule: Don't Rock the Boat. This rule usually worked around Mama, but not always. And it certainly didn't apply to red ants, which would attack for no reason. For me, Don't Rock the Boat naturally became Watch Out for Red Ants. Every time Sam could accumulate extra gasoline, he poured it on red anthills and lighted them on fire–a skill probably not required for the Firemanship merit badge.

"The chain is straight!" I called out. A few little kinks wouldn't matter.

Leaning over the surveyor's table, Sam wrote something, then yelled, "Stick!"

I lifted one end of the heavy wooden pole and walked my hands along it until it stood upright. I had two slivers in my right palm and had broken the strap on my left plastic sandal. I was shocked that Mama had bought them at all, even during the half-price sale at Hested's Five and Dime. Now she would either be furious or cry. I could face her fury but felt helpless when she cried. Couldn't I take care of anything? Did I think we were made of money? Yes, no: any answer I gave was wrong. With Mama, I could never win.

All morning, I dragged the chain and idiot stick, moving out in ever-widening circles from Sam, who remained stationary and scientific at the plane table. We continually stretched the chain between us, connected by the beautiful and strange links, a mix of metal sticks and rings, at once solid and loose, measuring inches in this huge landscape, turning the actual knolls and gullies into the flat paper map under Sam's pencil.

The ants found me again, at first tickling my feet. I stomped from foot to foot, waving the idiot stick like a cavalry flag just before my horse was shot from under me.

Sam shouted into the hot wind, "Hold! Still!"

Knowing that he was helpless without me, I decided this was a good moment to rebel. I was no simple slave. "Do it yourself!"

"Vertical!" He yelled. "Inches! . . . Off." Did he say *inches* ? Let us not forget, I wanted to say, that he was surveying a dirt road which *already existed*. How did the Boy Scouts dream up this stuff? I was missing something here, except the usual fate of the little sister.

Sam waved his hand back and forth until I held the pole the way he wanted, meanwhile balancing on one foot while fighting the attack of the red ants with the other. I seriously reconsidered casting myself as Gary Cooper. Sam could fend for himself.

Farmland stretched as far as I could see in every direction. The wheat, which wouldn't turn gold until the Fourth of July, flickered from a silver sheen to pale green, smooth as fur petted by the wind. Nearby towns were marked by their characteristic water towers: Round Prairie's flattened orange basketball on spindly legs, Gilead's tall tube with red stripes running around like a peppermint stick, and Deshler's big teapot without a handle. Overhead, clouds puffed irregular spots and streamers like Indian smoke signals.

To my far right, off the map we were making, a grove of cottonwoods surrounded an odd house, more like a mansion out of a storybook than a Nebraska farmhouse. I must be dreaming. At the same time, I heard ghostly cries on the wind, then realized Sam was shouting and motioning me back to headquarters at the plane table. I couldn't drop the idiot stick fast enough.

Limping back to Sam with my floppy sandal, I remembered our family's drive last Sunday to Lebanon, Kansas, the geographical center of the continental United States. Sam the Mapmaker had gone on High Alert, using fancy notations like west-by-south-southwest for everything from telephone lines to highway signs. It drove him completely berserk that the distance on the highway sign from Round Prairie to Lebanon going south read 19 miles, but the same distance from Lebanon back to Round Prairie going north read 20 miles. Papa joked that it was always quicker to leave home than to return.

Sam had asked, "How did they figure out Lebanon is the center of the country?"

I could make up an answer for anything. "They drew a bunch of lines from the furthest points of the United States, and where they crossed each other was right here."

"Jeb, don't make things up." Mama could see right through me.

Papa answered, "She has a point, Edie. I think they calculated longitude and latitude and whatever else, but I like your system better, Jeb."

"Don't encourage her to lie, Frank."

Too low for Mama to hear, Sam defended me, "It wasn't a lie, exactly."

Sam avoided direct confrontations with Mama, while I tended to charge right in. With her, neither strategy worked.

Papa continued, "Why use math, when a drawing will do?"

"I wish I could draw," I said, watching the telephone poles pass.

Mama pounced. "You can draw. Who said you can't draw?"

"Mrs. Meyers."

"In Hebron? What does a third-grade teacher know?" Mama gave Papa a Significant Look. "You know what I think about Mrs. Highfalutin' Meyers?"

Papa looked at the road ahead and didn't answer.

"Her political affiliations . . . " Mama glanced over her shoulder at Sam and me in the back seat. "I have my suspicions . . . ."

"You always have your suspicions."

Mama snapped back. "I know what I know."

Just outside Lebanon, on the exact pinpoint center of the United States of America, someone had stacked a tall pile of rocks. Since that didn't seem celebratory enough, nearby they built a little chapel from plywood containing four tiny single-chair pews and a varnished plywood podium. Papa and Mama had to duck to get through the door, and when they sat down, their legs were folded funny, as if they had eaten Alice's cake to grow big. Sam and I fell silent, not knowing if we were in the world's smallest church or the world's largest dollhouse.

Behind the podium was a plywood cut-out map of America, painted with a U. S. flag, with stars covering the state of Washington, and red and white stripes covering the rest of the states. Bisecting the country from North Dakota to Texas was a cross. At its intersection–covering most of Nebraska—was a plywood Valentine heart. In a wooden banner over the map were the words "PRAY AMERICA."

Papa began to chuckle.

"What, may I ask, is so funny?" Mama had looped her arms around her knees, her slender body forming curves just like the waves in her hair. She always looked most elegant when she didn't even try.

"I wonder if that's a suggestion to pray *for* America or a threat to *pray, you Americans, dammit.*"

"Is it patriotism or religion that makes you feel the need to swear?"

"Both."

Turning America into a wood map was quite inventive, but I preferred the maps in school which rolled up like window shades, imagining each time that all the towns and farms and people were flattened and rolled up inside, then how funny we looked unrolled and how long it took us to pop back into three dimensions.

Back outside, Sam and I scrambled up the rock pile. I stretched out my arms and slowly turned in a circle, imagining America streaming from my fingertips: Maine, Florida, the tip of Texas, California, Washington. Although I had never been anywhere except the Kansas-Nebraska borderlands, I knew about mountains, but today the whole earth felt smooth as the prairie, a huge ball spinning slowly through the universe. If we didn't hold on to each other, we could all roll off into space.

When I reached the surveyor's plane table, Sam pulled our sack lunch from his Army surplus backpack he had stashed in the square of shade under the table. Sam peeled an orange with Mama's oldest paring knife and handed it to me.

"What I wouldn't give for an official Boy Scout knife." The holes in Sam's straw cowboy hat made little freckles of sunshine move around his face.

"What I wouldn't give for a candy bar," I answered. As usual, I had finished my Halloween haul by November 2nd and wouldn't see any candy for five more months.

He started peeling an orange for himself. "We're about a quarter done, Jujube. Not bad."

I liked it when Sam called me Jujube, although it was the only candy on earth I didn't like. Scratching my red ant bites, I tried to sound innocent. "You could make up the rest. Just look at the countryside ... and draw what you see."

Why did we have to eat oranges instead of peanut butter and jelly or even baloney sandwiches, which Mama packed in Papa's lunch?

"That's cheating. It's a good thing you're not a Boy Scout."

"If the Boy Scout dragged the idiot stick around awhile, he might feel like cheating, too." I sucked on my orange and pointed a sticky finger toward the mansion in the trees. "Did you see that house?"

Sam squinted toward it. "Wow."

To make up for the fact that he hadn't discovered it first, he Took Charge. "Hurry up," he indicated my half-eaten orange. "Let's check it out."

"I'm not done eating."

Sam threw his backpack under the plane table and started walking. "Suit yourself." He knew I would follow him, even if I starved.

In Tornado Alley, partially destroyed farms, houses and towns littered the prairie. A month ago, just after we moved away, Hebron had been half leveled by a tornado. Grandma Strang, Mama's mother, and her brother, Uncle Ralph, still lived there but had escaped. Grandma wrote that people were still deciding which houses to save and which to finish demolishing and were trucking off rubble day and night. Many towns on the plains contained heavily damaged but still beautiful buildings, like the old hotel in Lebanon with a staircase leading to the open sky, or they were bordered with grain silos twisted like Chinese finger puzzles. Often all that remained of a farm were a chimney rising from an empty basement and a line of trees twisted off halfway up their main trunks.

This huge, two-story house was wedged among four trees which had grown up tight around it. The front wall had blown out, and the house had long been abandoned to finish its slow collapse. The central part of the house was wood and had intricate carving hanging like wooden icicles from the roof corners. Like bookends, rooms built of Nebraska limestone protected the more fragile core.

"What would it be like to live in a house like this?" I could only dream of living in a real house, much less one with two stories.

"Breezy," Sam answered. Then, to make up for his smarty response, he added, "I'll bet our whole trailer house would fit in its living room."

"I mean, when it was new– "

Sam actually considered it a minute. "Pretty lonesome out here."

A crow flew through the missing wall, landed, and began pecking the splintered floor.

I backed up. "Okay, if it were in town–"

"But it isn't. It's demolished and in the middle of nowhere."

I didn't want realism, I wanted him to join my daydreams, just as I joined Mama's, although hers weren't very happy. In my opinion, she spent too much time reading books about prisoners and dying ladies and headless horsemen and not enough with cheery characters like My Friend Flicka. But, unlike most grown-ups, she did play make-believe. And really well.

Years ago, a massive limb had crashed through the roof and top story of this house and had bowed the living room ceiling halfway to the floor. In turn, that floor was sinking into a dirt basement littered with bottles, soggy cardboard and, in one corner, a pile of stiff and muddy rags.

Along the back wall of the living room stood the remains of an upright piano, decayed beyond recognition except for the keyboard jutting out. The wood had turned to grey, weathered fur, and the keys, swelling with age, had grown together. A few keys still had splinters of surface ivory, but the hammers wiggled out of the open cabinet like broken, dead fingers.

In the wind, loose shutters waved slowly and creaked, giving the house a pale, spooky life. Suddenly, a shadow passed an open doorway and a ghostly face briefly appeared in a broken window upstairs. From the collapsing parlor came faint piano music, a honky-tonk tinkling, sad and slow.

"Did you see that?" I sucked in my breath sharply.

"What?"

"Or hear that music?"

Sam answered with an impatient groan.

With enough time and concentration, I could create all the missing pieces, could rebuild the walls and roof, reassemble the house and its memories like a gigantic, complex puzzle.

Sam folded his arms–his gesture of Sizing Up the Situation. "What a great hide-out," he said, without conviction.

"Somebody's using it already." A simple explanation was usually the best. I deliberately turned off the piano music.

"Maybe so, maybe not." Big brothers couldn't give little sisters too much credit for observation.

As we circled the house, Sam stopped and held up his hand like Henry Fonda halting the cavalry. "Look!"

In the back yard was an open cement staircase leading underground. Most houses and farms on the plains had storm cellars where the family could run from tornadoes. In Hebron, Grandma Strang used hers as a root cellar, since it stayed cool year-round.

When Papa was a little boy, a tornado had touched down near their farm. When she saw the funnel cloud, Grandma Wilder had grabbed him and his sister and raced to the storm cellar a little ways from the house. While Grandpa let their work horses run out of the barn, where they would have a better chance of surviving, Papa was terrified the whole time–until his dad jumped into the storm cellar and pulled the door shut overhead just in time. Papa, the bravest man in the world, remained deathly afraid of tornadoes all his life, especially now that we lived in a trailer house, always the first building to blow apart in any strong wind, much less a twister.

This storm cellar was a slice in the earth with cement steps leading down, more like a tomb than a shelter. The door lay open on the ground, rickety but too heavy for Sam to lift alone, and I wasn't about to help. I remembered stories of people buried in storm cellars when trees blew across the closed door—one of my recurring nightmares of being trapped underground, in the dark, hopelessly calling for help. Often my nightmares would wake up everybody in the trailer.

"Follow me." Sam crushed the tumbleweeds filling the stairway as he started downward.

The sweat on my back turned clammy. "What if there's–?"

"Chicken." From the darkness below, he used the single insult which always catapulted me into action, usually followed by disaster.

I gingerly reached the bottom step, the tumbleweeds tickling my bare legs. Inside, the earth smelled damp and cool, like a fresh, open grave. While my eyes adjusted to the darkness, I heard Sam rustling around, then silence.

"Sam?"

In the dark, I heard a scuffle with someone or something in there, then Sam's voice in a clipped yell, as if he were being strangled.

"Sam!" I stumbled toward him in the dark.

Suddenly, a flashlight shone in my eyes, temporarily blinding me. I screamed.

Sam erupted with laughter.

I lunged for him and the flashlight. "You creep!"

"Look at this stuff," Sam immediately diverted me by shining the flashlight around the inside of the cellar.

In neat piles on the floor we saw a patched coat, overalls, a pair of old, cracked work boots and some rusty crescent wrenches and screwdrivers. Obviously, someone had been hiding here.

I looked at the coat, looked again, then picked it up, dumbfounded. "Sam, this is Papa's old coat."

"Yeah, sure." Sam was rummaging through the tools.

"But it is. I watched Mama patch the elbow." I showed Sam the plaid flannel we had used. "These were your old pajamas."

He looked more closely at the patch. "She must have thrown it away, and somebody found it."

"There's too much wear left in it," I said, echoing her. "Papa's been here. Or someone stole it from him."

"Why? And why bring it here?" Sam never bought my theories.

Just then, someone's shadow passed the open doorway. I thought it was my imagination, except that Sam instantly clicked off the flashlight.

My heart thumped hard. Whoever it was could shut the door and trap us down here.

Sam grabbed my arm tightly, as if I would make a sound under these conditions.

The person passed the open doorway again. This time we could see the bottom of his legs, old boots and frayed overalls ending above his ankles. He paused, obviously deciding whether or not to come down. I wasn't particularly religious, but I prayed that he would go away.

"Anybody down there?" A boy's voice called out.

Sam shook my arm to keep me quiet. He could order me around without saying a word.

"Hey," the boy called out again.

What would we do if he came downstairs and discovered us? Jump him? We stood there, clammy and silent. To my horror, I heard him lift the door lying on the ground to close it. I started to call out, but Sam clamped his hand across my mouth. His hand smelled like dirt and greasy metal. Overhead, the boy hesitated, then let the door thud back to the ground, but I had the distinct feeling he knew we were down there. Otherwise, why didn't he come down and check his things, if they were his?

Sam and I waited a long time until we couldn't hear anything but the wind in the cottonwoods.

"The coast is clear," Sam decided. He led the way up the cellar stairs, peered around at ground level, than ordered, "Run for it."

We crouched and scrambled from tree to tree, not even pretending we were avoiding machine gunfire. When we reached open country, we ran all the way back to the surveyor's table where Papa would pick us up.

"It could make a great hide-out," Sam gasped for breath.

"Somebody's already hiding there," I choked. "That was him at the top of the stairs."

"We'll call it the Inavale House."

Inavale was the nearest little town, closer than Round Prairie. Obviously, Sam had already decided my future as well as his, which he did all the time.

"It's a long ways from the trailer," I objected. "Besides, it's creepy. Terrible things have happened in that house and storm cellar."

"Starting with a tornado."

"I mean . . . death. Multiple deaths. Murder."

"You and your imagination," he huffed. "You're always hearing things or seeing things and making stuff up."

"Some woman," I continued, "went crazy and . . . locked her two children down there . . . until they starved to death." I added details from one of Mama's poems. "She was . . . driven mad by the bells, the bells, the tintinnabulation of the bells—"

"You're making that up," Sam snorted.

"I am not."

"There's no such word."

"Wanna bet? Money?"

Sam knew then that I wasn't bluffing.

"It's from a poem named . . . " I couldn't remember the title but took a stab, "'The Bells.' Mama recites poems every time we clean the trailer or sew. The same guy wrote another one about—"

"Jeb." Sam interrupted what he knew could go on indefinitely. "Whatever might have happened in that storm cellar, we've got to have a hide-out somewhere."

Every time we moved, we never felt at home until we had a hide-out. In fact, the hide-out *was* home.

CHAPTER 4
THE CHAMBERED NAUTILUS

PAPA HAD FOUND A PLACE TO PARK OUR TRAILER IN the deep shady yard of an old farmhouse near the edge of town. The house, two stories tall with a wraparound porch, belonged to an old man named Charlie Whitaker, although grown-ups called him Spud, the food he lived on and fed any animal that strayed into his life. He let us park in his yard in exchange for Papa helping him out, which Mama said would prove very expensive in "real money." Even if we had paid cash rent, Papa would have helped him anyway, so Mama let the argument go.

Our trailer, a Prairie Schooner thirty-three feet long, was parked between the farmhouse and a barn with a broken backed roof, a survivor of the tornado two years ago which had clipped that end of town and flattened two farms further west. In the barn, Papa parked our old Buick and set up his shop to work on radios, fiddle with electrical appliances, turn lawn mowers into boat motors and, generally, to fix things for everybody but us, Mama said. The hayloft still held a few bales of moldy straw and instantly became temporary headquarters for Sam and me until we could find a real hideout. For now, the storm cellar at the Inavale spook house would have to do.

The rest of our block was a fallow broomcorn field bordered by cottonwood trees and a wobbly picket fence stuffed with tumbleweeds like dirty straw batting. The day we moved in, Sam and I performed *reconnaissance*, a word he had just taught me and which I instantly recorded in my Favorite Word Journal. Tricky spelling, too. The field was full of dry broomcorn stalks, about five feet long and jointed like bamboo but lighter weight. Mr. Whitaker told us in the Olden Days his family would harvest and sell the ripe corn tassels to the Deshler Broom Factory, while some people used the dry stalks as lath in plaster walls. Sam and I quickly discovered that the stalks were the perfect material to sharpen into spears and immediately began to stockpile our secret weapons in the hayloft.

Directly behind Mr. Whitaker's farmhouse was a weedy, overgrown garden, which prompted Sam and me to debate Wilder Family Rules concerning other people's property. Obviously, fresh concrete anywhere was off limits. If a field didn't contain a living crop and wasn't posted against trespassing, it was open season for us kids, so the broomcorn field clearly passed the test. But we needed to ask Mr. Whitaker about the garden. Asking grown-ups' permission amounted to a loss of face and was always a last resort. Generally, our unspoken motto was, "What grown-ups don't know won't hurt us," a subtle variation on the Boy Scouts' motto, "Be Prepared."

Clearly, Sam and I had a summer of worlds waiting for us in the barn and broomcorn, but Mama had other ideas. Every time we moved, she enrolled us in something free and horrifying like community projects, art in the park or, worst of all, vacation Bible school, where we could make "new little friends." It never worked because we never stayed in a town long enough to keep them. In fact, Sam, who could solve an arithmetic problem faster than I could eat a Jujube, had plotted the graph of the "little friends" project: in one summer (91 days) and one school year (274 days), it took at least 60 days to move in, an additional 75 days to clarify the battle lines, an overlapping 170 days to win or lose the major fights, a variable 40 days to negotiate miscellaneous terms and the remaining 24 days of relative peace before we moved again.

Instead of trying to make little friends, Sam and I knew that the best use of our summer was to make money. A Kool-Aid stand was reliable for hauling in pennies, but the Whitaker place stood pretty far off the beaten track, to the extent that Round Prairie had a beaten track. The other problem was getting Mama's permission, not to mention commandeering the Kool-Aid, a luxury item. For a special treat, sometimes Mama froze Kool-Aid in the ice cube tray, but the trailer's refrigerator was so little that the ice cubes were the size of dice. Nonetheless, we didn't look a gift horse in the mouth and praised the effort, knowing that if weren't Grateful Children, we could kiss Kool-Aid dice good-bye forever.

Theoretically, Sam and I could have cashed in some allowance for a Kool-Aid grubstake, but allowance was a tricky topic in our family. Every Sunday night, Mama recorded our allowance on the same piece of yellow graph paper, adding a nickel for work we had done that week beyond our required chores. The extra work, like helping wax the car or run clothes through the wringer, transformed into tiny numbers, intricate additions in our mother's perfect handwriting. The nickels existed, and they didn't. By an Unspoken Rule, we never collected our allowance or even mentioned it, knowing our parents had no money for us and not wanting to embarrass them. Instead, we kept sacred that bursting sense of hidden riches, imagined spending a whole dollar at a time on the little bronze horse with keychain reins or the bags of marbles in the window of Hested's Five and Dime. So our allowance became a tacit agreement, like so many other things in our family, a creation of the family's collective imagination, an agreed-upon lie far more real than actual money. Allowance ranked in the top ten topics Wilders Never Discussed.

To explore other income sources, Sam and I had already asked Mr. Whitaker if we could weed and harvest his garden. He had laughed at the word "garden" and had asked us our current rates. We settled on salvage fees: what we could earn by selling the soft and pithy radishes the size of small baseballs. From his back porch rocker, he said to go to it and wished us luck.

Next day, Mama decided to attend the Methodist's Women's Society, not because she felt religious, but to make new big friends. When Mama dressed up these days, she always asked me if she were wearing enough

rouge, pushing her face close to mine and holding out the flattened miniature puff the size of a half dollar. I really wanted to wipe off the rouge
she was wearing, since lately she had started rubbing a bright clown spot
on each cheek, making her face look even thinner and paler than before.

"It looks fine, Mama," I lied. Lies to save peoples' feelings didn't count.

She pulled on cotton gloves, which I never understood in summer,
warned us to behave like a lady and gentleman, and left.

As soon as she was out of sight, we scrambled for the barn, where
we had stowed Mr. Whitaker's radishes in our wagon. Sam pulled out his
printed crayon sign saying "VEGTABLES 5cents."

"You misspelled 'vegetables'." I loved to spell and particularly liked
to point out misspelled words in newspaper headlines and professional
signs. A misspelled billboard cheered me up for a week.

"No sir." He inspected his sign.

"It's missing an *e*."

"It already has two *e*'s." He added defensively, "That's enough."

"Lots of words have more than two *e*'s."

"Name one."

"*Eerie*," I pulled out of somewhere, inspired.

"I'll bet you can't think of eight more words with three *e*'s," Sam
challenged as we rattled the wagon along the dirt road. Except for Main
and Center Streets, which were paved with red bricks, all the roads in
Round Prairie were gravel, and almost none had sidewalks.

"*Eyeglasses*," my brain started galloping, "*one-eyed*—"

"In thirty seconds." He looked at his wrist as if he had a watch.
"Without using 'eye'."

A few blocks from the trailer, we saw three boys ambling toward
us, idly throwing rocks at the tires of parked cars, occasionally hitting the
fenders as well. Suddenly, the tallest one spotted us and stopped like a stray

dog which has just smelled raw hamburger. He elbowed one of the shorter boys, and they all speeded up. Sam and I stopped, stiff and wary.

As they came nearer, I pasted on my best saleswoman smile and called out, "Want to buy some radishes?"

The tallest boy had red hair shaved close to his scalp and one ear which stuck out more than the other. The shorter one had a scar holding his upper lip together, and the third boy, wearing a John Deere baseball cap, I had seen in the yard across the street from Mr. Whitaker's.

"Whadda ya think yer doin?" the tall one said in a voice as if he had been looking at nasty pictures.

What did he think we were doing, the moron. If I could talk fast enough, we might not need to prove ourselves, at least not so soon, and could start life in Round Prairie on a peaceful note. Using my brightest fake-friendly voice, I said, "Selling vegetables." I stood tall because Papa advised meeting trouble face to face. My face reached the tall boy's middle shirt button.

"Who said ya could?" He sent his sidekicks a mean smile and looked back at me.

With strange boys, I always felt more dread for Sam than for myself because they ignored me, at least until they experienced my deadly kick. I heard Sam start to breathe funny and quickly offered, "Since you're our first customers, we'll give you a free sample."

"Free sample," he sneered in a baby voice, and his friends laughed nervously.

The boy in the baseball cap said, "They live in that trailer."

"'Zat so?" The tall boy turned on Sam. "You deef an' dumb?"

I knew Sam was calculating our odds, which, given their size, were worse than three against two. "I'm Sam. This is Jeb," he said.

The boy with the split lip looked at his tall friend, then imitated in a baby voice, "I'm Sam. This is Jeb."

The tall one suddenly grabbed our crayon sign out of Sam's hand and tore it in two. "This is my street. Get outta here."

His street, my foot. "We're not doing anything—"

Before I knew what was happening, Sam lunged at him.

"Wait!" I called, too late.

The boy with the scarred lip kicked over the wagon and punched me in the arm, which momentarily distracted Sam. The big boy shoved Sam so hard he lost his balance and fell backwards onto the grass. All three boys laughed too loud and too long, pointing at the wagon, the scattered radishes and Sam on the ground.

I primed myself to kick the boy who had pushed me, but Sam stopped me with a shout, "Jeb!"

"C'mon, guys," the big one turned and led them sauntering down the street with exaggerated nonchalance, tossing rocks over their shoulders in our direction, then continuing to throw rocks at car tires.

My knees gave way, and I sat on the grass beside Sam. Even his freckles looked a little pale.

"Why do we always have to fight?" I asked. "Every time we move."

Sam pulled grass blades one at a time near his knee. "It's their territory."

"They don't own it. They just live here. Anyway, why fight about it?"

"They started it. We were minding our own business."

True. Another instance of Papa's Don't Rock the Boat rule or Watch Out for Red Ants.

"Why do you think some kids just go around looking for a fight? For no reason."

"That's the way it is." Sam sounded like Papa.

"Is, schmiz," I sounded like Mama. "If we ever had our own territory, I wouldn't fight over it."

"I would."

I began pulling grass like Sam.

"I'll get even," Sam vowed. I knew he would, too. In some spectacular, scientific way.

"Am I too late to buy some radishes?" came a voice way over our heads.

There stood Mr. Whitaker. He wore a pair of overstuffed bib overalls and a shirt so old the plaid was almost worn off. "At least it was a short war."

Sam and I slowly stood up, since we were trained to stand in the presence of adults.

The old man was the size of a bear on its hind legs. He gave a little snort. "It's just a phase. Bobby and Leon will grow out of it . . . in twenty or thirty years. Probably in the State Pen. The Hartsock kid's not such a bad egg. He lives across the street."

With an oof, Mr. Whitaker stooped over to pick up a radish. "How much are you charging for these beauties?"

"You can't buy your own radishes," Sam said.

"Whose rules?" The old man's cheeks hung down in folds, with freckles which had grown into dime-sized brown spots.

"Mr. Whitaker—" I began.

"Call me Spud."

Sam and I said, almost in unison, "Our folks won't let us—" which Sam finished, "—call grown-ups by their first names."

"It's my nickname. Don't count."

Past Mr. Whitaker's shoulder, I saw Mama hurrying toward us. Her ankles were wiggling, probably because of her dress-up shoes. I wished she would wear really high heels like Mrs. Meyers in Hebron, but Mama called such things putting on airs.

"WHAT . . . ," she breathed hard, "on EARTH are you doing?!"

"S-selling . . . radishes," Sam began.

"What radishes?" She kept opening and closing her purse as if she wanted to buy some, then changed her mind. Snap, snap. Snap, snap.

"Mrs. Wilder—" Mr. Whitaker intervened.

"So now we're selling . . . vegetables? On the STREET?"

"I can explain—" The old man weighed the radish in his hand like a baseball player about to pitch.

"What will people think?! Let's just tell the whole world how poor we are."

"The kids–" Mr. Whitaker started again.

She looked around the ground in contempt. "Did you give them these . . . these . . ."

"They weeded my garden, and I figured they could have some fun–"

Mama was really angry when she wouldn't be polite to other grown-ups. With a twist in her voice, she turned on Sam, "Have you? Had fun? Tell Mr. Whitaker how much fun you've had."

Sam wouldn't stand up to Mama, but I usually took a stab at self-defense. "Nobody saw us, Mama . . . ." I reconsidered: no use wasting a lie here. "Except three boys."

"Who will go home and tell their parents . . . what? That the Wilders are—"

Mr. Whitaker interrupted, "I wouldn't worry a'tall about what the Clawsons or Troxels think, if I were you."

"Well, you aren't me."

Mr. Whitaker tossed the radish he was holding into the wagon with a thump. "Did Frank get rid of that rash on his arms?"

"It's just the heat," Mama snapped.

"He coulda gotten into milkweed down by the river. It's nasty stuff for some folks, especially with all those scars he's got."

"He's fine."

Papa's burn scars twined up his arms and around his neck like vines of extra skin. He told us kids that scars didn't let you keep any sweat glands, so he preferred Nebraska's violent blizzards to summer heat that wrapped around your neck like wet wool.

"Frank should see our new doctor in town," Mr. Whitaker continued. "A woman. Ain't that somethin?"

"I've heard about her."

"'Course some folks don't trust a lady doctor."

"I don't." Mama pointed for us to clean up the scattered radishes. "Sam. Jeb."

"Doctor Mary. Says she's gonna settle here, not just visit twice a week."

"Probably nobody else will hire her."

"Tall, strapping girl. Nice as the day is long."

Mama looked at him a minute. "They always are."

"Who's they?" Mr. Whitaker asked.

"You know exactly what I'm talking about," Mama answered.

Clearly, Mr. Whitaker didn't know and looked at me for help.

"Communists," I answered.

"Who?" Sometimes Mr. Whitaker's cheeks shook instead of his hands.

I clarified, "A lot of people. In Hastings and Hebron, too."

Mama turned to walk away, stiff-backed. "Sam, finish cleaning this up. Jeb, come with me."

Long ago, Sam and I had learned not to protest punishment or to question who was selected for it, since keeping Mama calm was far more important than kid stuff we could sort out in private. In my view, the punishment didn't need to match the actual crime, since Sam and I had broken so many rules our folks didn't know about that it was only fair to pay in general once in awhile. In this way, we created our own justice system, not what Mama or anybody else imposed.

Sam, of course, had a more elegant theory. When you threw two dice, he explained, there were more ways to roll a seven than a twelve or a two; in other words, the *probability* of rolling a seven was higher. We were bound to get caught for crimes we committed most often, the "sevens." But the bigger crimes, the "twelves," had a lower probability of getting caught, which left us still far ahead of the game. I didn't completely understand Sam's explanation, but I wouldn't admit it. Besides, I liked the word *probability*. If they had a Gambling merit badge, Sam would have cleaned everybody's plow.

"Do I get to help this young man?" Mr. Whitaker called after Mama and me. "Or is that also against the law?

The trailer stayed cool inside because Papa had transformed parts of a broken house furnace into a window air conditioner over the sofa where Sam slept. I waited for Mama to take off her gloves and put her purse in the folks' bedroom at the other end of the trailer. When she was this mad, it was best not to say a word, just to ride it out and let her run down.

She collapsed on the footstool. Her dress-up dress was starched cotton, butter yellow with lace trim Grandma Strang had crocheted. She was so beautiful, she looked like a tulip.

"Jeb." Her worst voice: I could stand her being mad forever, but not sad.

"I'm sorry, Mama." Sam and I always apologized with the vague hope it would make everything better. It never worked.

"Your father and I work so hard . . . to be decent and clean and . . . respectable, in spite of . . . ," she waved her hand vaguely around the trailer.

She sighed in two parts, a little sigh which wasn't deep enough, followed by a big one. When she stood up, I automatically sat on the footstool, the traditional scene of my most dreaded punishment: to sit without a back rest, absolutely silent, for as long as Mama designated. If I made a peep, she would add fifteen or even thirty minutes.

Mama looked at me and shook her head hopelessly. "One hour."

A whole hour for selling radishes. What was the probability of that? Sam owed me big time.

The footstool, an old, cracked leather cube, squatted in front of a lopsided chair which folded out into my bed— a narrow bedspring with a thin mattress. Papa joked what a bargain it was–an unusable chair by day and a back-breaker by night. But I didn't mind it. Sleeping in the living room meant that I could stay up until everybody went to bed–Mama and Papa behind the closed door at one end of the trailer and Sam behind the sliding doors at the other. That left me with the kitchen, the rest of the living room and the kerosene furnace by the door all to myself.

As I shifted my weight, the footstool wheezed its familiar greeting, my jail cell door closing. I would have been thrilled to get a spanking or a switch across my bare legs—anything except being condemned to absolute silence and immobility.

"Settle down," she warned from the back bedroom, and I stared into the next interminable hour like William Holden, the prisoner of war in "Stalag 17."

From the footstool, I could see most of the trailer: a smooth and rounded wooden tube with a small kitchen alcove, our table which folded into the wall, and the folks' pride and joy—a compact piano sixty-five keys long. They were paying it off over time. Papa had fixed someone's circular saw in trade for the clock above my chair-bed, a tiny log cabin with a stiff smoke ribbon coming out its chimney, wagging back and forth with the passing seconds. Until today, I hadn't considered the solid smoke a form of vapor lock. If I concentrated hard enough, I wondered if I could speed up time by forcing the smoke ribbon to wave faster. On the other hand, if I stopped its swinging altogether, would the earth stand still, if only for a moment? Better not chance it until I knew for sure.

On the kitchen counter stood the radio, its lemon-colored case shaped like a miniature trailer house, and beside it, the cookie jar, a white ceramic cat wearing a pink bow and a permanent wink, as if teasing me for being empty. Mama used to make cookies out of graham crackers filled with home-made frosting, but recently she had lost interest in that, as well as other things. Papa said we needed to be patient, and that the lack of cookies was the smallest of our problems. We didn't ask about the biggest ones.

Papa was the most patient person I ever met, more than all my teachers put together, and that's saying a lot. I think it was because of his burns.

Sam and I never knew how much of Papa burned. We never saw his legs bare and saw his arms only in deep summer, when the heat forced him to roll up the sleeves of his heavy khaki work shirt. Every evening, when Sam and I flanked Papa on the sofa while he read the newspaper out loud, I traced the scars that twisted up his arms like white snakes. Papa joked that he had been chewed up and spit out by other accidents—being blinded in one eye and losing fingers on his left hand—but the explosion was a major subject our family Did Not Discuss, along with the Hebron tornado and my dead baby sister, Janet. On top of the list was Mama's nerves, probably the reason for the list in the first place. The Wilder family had whole catalogs of explicit rules, but underneath them lay the Real Rules, a minefield of tacit agreements and complex silences Sam and I could ignore only at our peril. In spite of Sam's warnings, I tested the unspoken rules much more than he did, always with catastrophic results.

Years before Sam and I were born, Papa was working for the WPA along a river bank, dredging out the channel. One July 3rd, he was standing near a pile of gunpowder when he happened to look up at the bridge overhead and saw a man lighting a firecracker. Before Papa could run or even shout, the man threw the lighted firecracker into the gunpowder, which exploded in a ball of flame instantly encompassing Papa. He ran out of the fireball with his clothes and hair in flames but managed to dive into the mud along the riverbank, which saved what skin remained on his body.

For four days, the little hospital in Hebron didn't even give Papa a room because they said that no one could survive such burns. They kept telling Mama to give up and go home, but she refused. At her pleading, they finally put him in a room where, slowly and excruciatingly, Papa returned to life. The only help the nurses could give was to lay bandages soaked in Vaseline and Merthiolate over his burned arms and legs. They were afraid that he would get addicted to morphine, so they gave him very little painkiller. Papa was the bravest and strongest person most people would ever meet, but Mama said that when they changed his bandages, she could hear him scream from home a block away.

For three months, Papa lay there and healed. And didn't turn mean. And didn't turn bitter. And, as soon as he could talk, joked with the nurses. Two days before he was scheduled to go home, he picked off his last scab, got blood poisoning, and almost died. That close, and almost died. After that, he signed up as a volunteer fireman because, he said, you face what scares you, or you'll never face anything.

The sheriff eventually found the man who had thrown the fire-cracker. He didn't know Papa, said he did it for a joke, and was never punished. Not one bit. Ever. Sometimes, when I needed to break the silence rule and Mama was out of earshot, I would ask Papa why *anyone* would do such a thing, try to kill a total stranger. If Papa answered at all, he would say, "If it hadn't been me, it would've been somebody else."

But it wasn't somebody else. That maniac was still loose in the world, hurting innocent people for no reason. Why wasn't he in jail? I couldn't understand it.

Papa usually added, "If you want to worry about somebody, worry about our poor soldiers in Korea."

I didn't want to worry about our soldiers in Korea. Instead, I dreamed, over and over, a ball of flame, then a man's black silhouette running out of it, silently flailing his arms. Not until he ran close to me did I see it was Papa–Papa!—and his clothes and hair were on fire and his skin was peeling off in ribbons and patches. I chased him and tried to keep the skin on his body, to hold the patches on, but they disintegrated in my hands like ashes.

Those nights, I would sleepwalk, would stand in the middle of our trailer house, or sit on the edge of Sam's bed and stare at him, or wander in and out of the folks' bedroom asking muffled questions.

Everybody said I would usually ask, "What's burning? I smell something burning."

Papa and Sam would ignore me, but Mama would say she smelled it, too. Mama could smell the fire in my nightmares.

"Jeb!"

On the footstool, I jerked and quickly looked around to see if Mama saw me move. She was standing with both hands on the kitchen counter, looking in my direction, but her eyes were focused on something over my right shoulder.

Using her poetry voice–faraway and serious—she began reciting,

"Build thee more stately mansions, O Jeb,

As the swift seasons roll!

Leave thy low-vaulted past!

Let each new temple, nobler than the last,

Shut thee from heaven with a dome more vast,

Till thou at length art free,

Leaving thine outgrown shell by life's unresting sea!"

She was like a teacher, but with only her and me in the classroom. "Do you understand that?"

I had no idea what she was talking about, but I was pretty sure the poem didn't have my name in it. I was also afraid to speak because it might add to my time.

Sensing the reason for my silence, she added, "Your time is up, Jeb."

How could that be? Maybe she had reduced my sentence for good behavior. No: the log cabin clock said one hour had passed.

"Do you know what that is? That poem?"

I shook my head.

"It's called 'The Chambered Nautilus,' by Oliver Wendell Holmes. It's about a conch, a spiral seashell. Do you remember the big seashell Grandma Strang has on her dresser in Hebron, the one in which you can hear the ocean?"

Still afraid to move, I barely nodded yes.

"The little creatures in those shells build their homes from some material inside themselves, build bigger and bigger rooms to live in as they get bigger. They make their own houses to grow with them as they grow up."

I knew that Mama was trying to tell me something important, but I was too stupid to understand. She always created new ways to disappoint her, new opportunities for failure. "And then what?" I asked quietly.

"Then?" She paused and looked straight at me. "They die." Mama threw back her head and laughed, laughed her note high and fast. If I didn't stop her, would she ever quit?

CHAPTER 5

ROUND JOHN AND BOSTON CHARLIE

MAMA MUST HAVE READ SOMEWHERE THAT being a Methodist, unlike being a Catholic or Presbyterian, didn't have any requirements, because the first Sunday after the trailer was hooked up in a new town, we had to attend a Methodist church. Papa mildly objected, saying that God, like Santa Claus, could find anybody anywhere—except in church, where, as far as he could tell, God never darkened the door.

Mama gave him a Bette Davis look—beautiful but deadly. "Did you need to say that in front of the children?"

"In a thirty-three-foot trailer house, we can't say anything that *isn't* in front of the kids." Papa poked me in the ribs. "Keeps us all honest."

I was wiping off my shoes with a rag. "If God came to church, he could see my Sunday shoes." They were black patent leather with a strap across the top, but they always looked greasy because Mama smeared Vaseline on them during the week so they wouldn't crack. The Vaseline never wiped off completely but left swirling patterns, like how-to-dance diagrams on my toes.

Mama tied a nickel into the corner of my handkerchief so I wouldn't lose it and handed one to Sam for his pocket. Going to church was bad enough, but paying for it added insult to injury.

"Do you know how long it takes us to earn a nickel?" Sam practiced palming his coin like a magician.

Imitating something I had seen Sam do with rags tied to heavy bolts, I threw my hanky up and let it fall to the floor like a parachute. "I don't understand what we're paying for."

Papa joined in. "Jeb has a good idea. Why don't we see how much the sermon is worth, and then pay what we feel like?"

Another Bette Davis look.

After the congregation sang all four verses of "My country, 'tis of thee," Number 489 in the Methodist hymnal, we settled into yet another interminable service.

Church, like the footstool, created its own kind of time, like a gas which leaked out of the organ pipes, snaked around the carving on the pulpit, and wound around our ankles under the pews. To speed things up, our minister in Hebron had provided some spectacular words for my journal, like *reciprocity, nemesis* and *lex talionis*, which weren't even English but could be the perfect name for the right horse.

"The Communists!"

I snapped to attention. Maybe Reverend Harkin would say something interesting after all.

" . . . many faces and many names, but we know who they are."

Next to me, the brim of Mama's hat tipped up and down in agreement. We all got new dress-up clothes on Easter and wore them every Sunday the rest of the year. Mama spent part of her allowance on a hat, this year a pink upside-down basket.

Reverend Harkin was the only Methodist minister we ever had who wore a robe, today one of blood-red satin. "How can we stop them?" he asked the chandelier.

Papa began to tap his knee with his left hand, the hand missing his whole ring finger and half of his middle one. Years ago, he had mangled his hand in some gears, a result of what he joked about as his "wild, misspent youth," but he could still play the piano by "faking the bass." Unbelievably, he could play the piano without any music, ever, and could play a whole song after hearing it just once. I couldn't play Beethoven's "Für Elise" with the music smack dab in front of me.

"The very fabric of our society is being threatened by godless Communists. Only Christianity can destroy them!" He slapped the pulpit with an open palm. That must have hurt.

What I couldn't do with that robe. From an old curtain, Mama had sewn a skirt for me to play dress-up, but with those swishing acres of red satin, I could look like Queen Elizabeth, who had just been crowned. With real diamonds and emeralds, I might add. I saw her picture on the cover of *Life* magazine in the library.

"Only Christianity can grind Communism to dust. Can wipe it from the face of the earth." His fat hand rubbed and rubbed the top of the pulpit. "Clean. Clean. Clean."

Sam had managed to sneak one of the stubby pencils from the holes drilled into a rack next to the hymnals behind each pew. He had also smuggled an offering envelope, so he could write during the sermon, no doubt secret chemistry formulas or plans for a bomb. When I slowly, ever so slowly reached for a pencil, Mama clamped her hand around my wrist. Wilder Rule: no squirming in church. She ignored what Sam was doing, which wasn't fair, and Papa didn't care what we did as long as we were quiet. Mama kept a closer eye on me than Sam because he seemed to obey her, but he was actually much more dangerous. My little secret. Good blackmail material.

"We must PRAY . . ." Yippee! Church must be over because Methodists never prayed except at the end of the sermon or as a last-ditch effort.

"Our soldiers in Korea . . ." False alarm.

Along the oak floor and pews slid warped rainbows made by the stained glass windows. In the rays of light hung millions of dust particles which randomly milled around each other, sometimes shooting straight up for no reason, at other times spiraling slowly downward. What if each particle were a little planet, containing whole civilizations like Earth? Dust People. I blew lightly on the dust, creating miniature tornadoes, throwing their universe into chaos. What if Earth were a dust particle in somebody else's unimaginably huge church, full of mega-mega-mega giants watching us, ready to destroy us like that? I leaned forward to signal Sam about the dust universes, but he was busy writing something next to his leg, sliding his eyes around the sanctuary with the forced casualness of a spy.

"Amen."

The minister said Amen!

"Please turn to hymn number 280: 'Onward, Christian Soldiers'." Oh: not done. At least we could stand for a minute. Since my feet didn't reach the floor in the pew, my legs went to sleep every Sunday. "Onward, Christian Soldiers" had a great marching tune but the words didn't make any sense for a church hymn:

"Christ the royal Master,

Leads against the foe;

Forward into battle,

See His banners go!"

Last Sunday, I had asked Papa why Jesus appeared in war songs, since he loved peace even more than Grace Kelly in "High Noon." Papa had said that was an excellent question and I should ask the minister. Papa always told me that, if I didn't agree with a song or speech, I should object, or at least substitute my own words. In this case, I chose the song Papa played on the piano every Sunday after dinner and sang under my breath:

"Cruising down the river

On a Sunday afternoon;

With you I love, the sun above,

Waiting for the moon."

The words didn't quite fit the tune to "Onward Christian Soldiers," but it was certainly more peaceful than Jesus's army "marching as to war."

We sat back down in the pew, and Harkin cleared his throat to enter his full drone mode. "President Eisenhower . . . ."

Eisenhower started out as a General and, in fact, looked better as a General, mostly because of the fancy cap which covered his bald head. In his General's outfit, he looked like an old version of Gregory Peck from "Twelve O'Clock High," a war movie we had seen in Hebron that Mama said was too old for us. She used that phrase whenever a movie showed swimming suits, too much blood, or weird behavior, not in science fiction but in real life. Because of the war, Gregory Peck suddenly went crazy, not berserk but *catatonic*, a word I looked up later and added to my word journal. Until then, I didn't know anybody could stay completely motionless for days, apparently without getting bored, a useful technique for the footstool, but pretty extreme. What did catatonics think about?

I looked on the floor at my feet and—oboy oboy!—saw a fan someone had dropped. Bending over, I nearly fell out of the pew but managed to snag it in spite of Mama's yanking on my blouse.

The size and shape of ping-pong paddles, the cardboard fans had a full-color religious picture on one side and an advertisement for some local business on the other, like two worlds pasted back to back, as unaware of each other as the people in the Inavale Hotel living inside an Abbott and Costello movie. Some fans showed the little boy Jesus wearing an outfit nobody could play in, while others pictured the grown-up Jesus resting on a rock trying to get a kid to sit on his lap. This fan showed Jesus praying in Gethsemane, backed by an ad for the funeral home:

Harkin's funeral parlor all sizes caskets & coffins in oak or fancy woods

Marvin Harkin, the minister's brother, owned the mortuary and must be religious, but it didn't seem right to advertise embalming on the flip side of Jesus's final hours of life. With my finger, I drew a horse looking over Jesus's shoulder, my version of Man o' War, fastest horse in history. If a donkey could show up at every Nativity, a horse could appear in Gethsemane, when Jesus, wearing only a robe and sandals, needed a fast getaway.

The organist struck up the Doxology: church was nearly over! As we stood up to sing, I noticed an exotic woman at the end of the row in front of us. She wore a black pillbox hat and dangly earrings which looked like diamonds, but no one would waste diamonds on earrings instead of brooches or rings. The lady also wore rings on top of her gloves, something I had never seen—big, colored stones which were obviously fake.

"Praise God from whom all blessings flow," I sang and wondered why, if all blessings flowed from God, he needed my nickel.

Standing in the aisle and blocking our way to the exit were Marvin Harkin and the organist, his totally blind wife, Maxine. Besides being the mortician, Marvin was also the Scoutmaster and, if that weren't creepy enough, had a completely bald head like a worm. Sam said I didn't like him because I couldn't be a Boy Scout.

"Hey, Tenderfoot," he said to Sam but winked at me as if we shared some secret, then squeezed my shoulder. Yuck. His glance flicked around, always landing on women's faces, then dropping to their chests. Marvin stood beside Maxine, telling her who was shaking her hand, while her milky eyes focused about a foot over everyone's head. He could have been lying to her the whole time, but she had to trust him to tell the truth. Her smile never relaxed, as if her face had settled into one expression for the rest of her life.

Her hand wasn't much bigger than mine and felt cool. "Please call me Jeb."

"Next time I see you, I'll remember that."

It would be impolite to point out that she would never "see" anyone, exactly.

While Sam and the folks talked to Marvin, I was left trying to make conversation with Maxine. Mama had told me that Maxine played the piano by memorizing every single note in Braille. Instead of mentioning that, I blurted out, "My father is blind in one eye." With horror, I instantly considered the consequences of what I had said. Wilders never let family secrets out of the house. I added hastily, "But don't tell my mom."

Maxine leaned down and whispered near my ear, "She probably knows."

The minister stood guard at the door, not letting anyone out without shaking his rubbery, sweaty hand. We fell into line behind the exotic lady, who wore a black suit with a skinny waist, spike heels and blood red lipstick.

Reverend Harkin stopped us to make introductions. "All of you are newcomers: This is the Wilder family–Frank, Edith, and their children, Sam and Judith. Mrs. Greta Keindorf. Mr. Keindorf is our new dry cleaner and Mrs. Keindorf teaches piano, in case you know of anyone.

I did. Me. I practically raised my hand. I was starting my fourth year of piano and hadn't resumed lessons in Round Prairie yet. Up close, her rings looked real, but whoever heard of emeralds or rubies the size of gumdrops?

Without moving her head, Mama looked Mrs. Keindorf up and down while Papa shook the minister's hand, saying, "Thanks, Reverend."

Thanks for what? Taking two nickels from Deserving Children and a whole dollar from our parents?

We had barely left the church steps when Sam exploded. "You know how they electrocuted those people? The Rosenbaums?"

"-bergs," Papa corrected.

"Not now, Sam." Mama was smiling faintly and nodding at the other people coming out of church.

"They attached the wires to little sponges on their head and legs, then zapped 'em with 2,000 volts!" Sam had already overstepped the bounds of his electricity merit badge. During church, he had probably designed his own electric chair.

"Shhh!" Mama scanned the crowd, which stood in little groups laughing and talking. "Don't you know anybody here, Frank?" She snapped her purse open and shut, open and shut. "I need to meet some people, make some friends."

"There's Lee McCormick from work. You met him last week. The old bachelor? With the beard?"

"I mean more women. Or couples. Anybody. Just to socialize a little . . . . Have coffee or . . . I get so lonesome . . ." Mama trailed off.

"Go introduce yourself," Papa suggested, "Walk up, shake hands . . . ."

"I . . . I can't. You know I can't do that." Mama looked at him like a terrified little girl. "Help me, Frank. I'm asking you to help me."

"The only person I know is Lee." Papa turned away to wave at the man from work.

Looking at Papa's back, Mama let out a deep breath and looked at the ground.

Walking beside me, Papa held out his chewed-up hand because he knew I liked to hold his one-and-a-half good fingers in my fist, which fit exactly into the space where his finger was missing. Mama never touched us unless she couldn't avoid it. Sam explained that was because Grandma Strang had raised her that way; besides, we were too old for holding hands or hugging. I didn't feel too old.

"Electrocution raises their body temperature to 140 degrees. That fries their brains!" Sam continued.

"Sam." Papa could silence either of us just with the way he said our name.

I liked to walk down Main Street and listen to the rumble and thump of passing car tires on the red brick road. Sam and I hung back to look in the window of Hested's Five and Dime, where the toys never changed but did move around: piggy banks, plastic typewriters, harmonicas, glider airplane kits and two metal dump trucks. Today they featured Magic Slates on which you could write with a perpetual pencil, then lift the page to watch your writing disappear. Because the backing kept a faint imprint of what you had written, your words both existed and didn't exist, all at the same time. Better than that, you could keep changing what you had written and deny any version somebody called a lie. At the top, one Magic Slate showed Donald Duck with Jiminy Cricket at his shoulder and Goofy in the background scratching his head.

I blew a kiss to the little bronze horse with the keychain reins, currently named Alibi because I liked words ending with an 'i' and colored like a palomino, although I was considering changing him to a buckskin. I never asked to own him because I didn't want to cash in any fake allowance or subtract credits from the Big Ask—for a real horse.

This Sunday in Hested's window stood a gallon jar full of marbles with a sign:

WIN THIS
GUESS THE CORECT CORECT NUMBER of MARBLES

Even better than accidentally misspelled signs were ones which were corrected wrong.

Overdramatically, Sam dropped his jaw like Wile E. Coyote who has just put his finger in a socket.

"I can do it! I can figure it out!" His mathematical genius brain started to work.

"You can! You can!" I cheered.

Papa put one hand on each of our heads to quiet us down.

Next to Hested's, the hardware store window contained an old sign with blurred letters:

ROOM FO RE UPSTA R
Utils. Includ d

As Mama studied the sign, I felt it was safe to confide, "It's probably a message left for spies. Sam and I find them all over Round Prairie."

"Good for you. What do you think it says?" she asked.

"Well, backwards, one of my best decoding techniques, it spells 'Rats Puer Of Moor'." I considered for a moment. "That doesn't make much sense."

Sam interjected, "It's obviously a foreign language which could take months to translate."

"It could be an anagram," Mama suggested. One day while we were ironing, she had taught me how to make anagrams, changing *eat* to *ate* and *tea* and rearranging *rebate* to *beater*. "Yes," she decided. "It says 'Test for Reds'."

Papa shifted his weight and tried to move us on.

"Or," Mama continued, "Better Dead Than Red'."

Anagrams were supposed to use all the letters, just in a different order, probably not a good idea to mention now. But I had to point out, "There isn't a 'b' or an 'h' or—"

Sam stared. He hated not knowing everything that I knew in addition to everything he knew.

Papa shook his head to make me quiet. "Edie, do you think we should talk to that Mrs. Keindorf about piano lessons? She's new, might not be too expensive . . ."

Mama snorted, "As if she needs our money. Did you see that outfit? Who does she think she is?"

Still staring at the signs, Sam ventured, "She's sure pretty."

"Sure*ly*," Mama corrected him.

"She looks like a movie star," he added. "Don't you think, Papa?"

"I'm not dumb enough to enter a dog in that race."

What race?

"If you like a painted woman, which your father does."

I was growing more confused. "What's a painted woman?"

"Someone who wears all that lipstick and rouge," Mama answered through closed teeth.

"You wear rouge," I pointed out.

"Mama's is a different shade of red," Papa clarified.

"That's typical, Frank. Make a joke out of everything."

I hadn't heard any joke.

"Your mama doesn't need any of that stuff." Papa tried to put his arm around Mama, but she spun away from him. "She could have married any man she wanted, including every lawyer who walked into the law office."

"People aren't dumb," Mama said. "Did you see how everyone ignored her in church?"

"They ignore us," I offered helpfully.

"It takes little towns awhile to accept strangers—" Papa started.

Mama interrupted, "Everyone suspects she's a you-know-what."

"What?" Sam stopped working on his own anagram.

"What?" I echoed.

"A German," Papa filled in the blank with the wrong word, I was sure.

"Posing as a piano teacher," Mama continued. "That's how they infiltrate, infect the youth."

I had heard about youth being infected but hadn't seen any yet.

"Germans?" Papa used his testing voice, lower than the one for starting an argument. "Like eighty percent of Round Prairie? And all your relatives."

"She's probably a Lutheran to boot," Mama added.

Papa had a little smile. "Trying to pass as a *Methodist*? You know what the Catholics call Methodists?" He paused. "Blue-collar Presbyterians."

"I know what I know."

Sam pointed imaginary six-guns at the bank across the street. "Electrocution doesn't always work the first time, and their hair catches on fire, or at least you can smell 'em burning."

"You know what else will be burning in a minute?" Mama warned.

Sam gave her his look of innocence unjustly accused. "It's scientific fact."

"Fact, schmact."

Papa added quietly, "At least, the Rosenbergs died fast. I still think they didn't have any real evidence against Ethel–"

"They wouldn't execute an innocent woman," Mama insisted. "Not in America. If anybody deserved the electric chair, those two Communists did."

"Pow! Pow!" Sam blew the smoke off the ends of his gun barrels and re-holstered his Colt .45s.

"Hey, Mr. Wilder!" A boy walking across the street waved. He looked about sixteen years old and wore clothes and boots caked with mud.

Mama frowned. "Who on earth is that?"

"Will Hankins. His family lives in the motel behind the trailer court." Papa waved back. "Migrant workers. Will came out to the dam looking for work. Poor as church mice."

"That's no excuse–"

"Your family was just as bad off," Papa objected.

"My mother wouldn't let us out the door looking that reprehensible. You can be poor and still be clean."

"Not if you just finished helping some farmer irrigate. From what I've heard, Will works harder than most full-grown men."

We were passing the Pawnee Hotel, but I didn't have the nerve to watch myself dance past in the glass, not with the whole family along. I always imagined the exotic people inside, some who lived there all the time. How romantic. Even better than living in a real house. I had heard that one woman was a retired opera singer, and I had already made up an entire life for her, including tragic love affairs, a bad car accident and boxes of jewels. People said that another woman tried to kill herself by sticking her head in the oven, but the gas was blocked somehow and instead blew off her back porch. I had consoled her with a voyage around the world, during which she blossomed into a completely happy woman, sometimes mistaken for Greta Garbo. Some man in the hotel supposedly made his fortune breeding chihuahuas. I hadn't been able to do anything with his life yet.

Mama pointed at the streaks on the lobby window. "Look at that filth."

Sam suddenly asked, "What's Korea?"

Papa sighed. "The last thing any minister should be talking about in church. It's a wonder he didn't have us sing 'Yankee Doodle Dandy'."

"Korea is where the war is right now." Mama answered Sam with her teacher's voice. "The Reverend wants us to pray for our soldiers."

"So the Koreas are the enemy?" Sam asked.

"Koreans," Mama corrected. "Yes. Well, no. Well–"

"Half of them are," Papa explained, working on his deadpan look.

"Which half?"

"The *North* Koreans. They're the bad guys." Papa voice sounded thick, as if he were trying to swallow a big bite.

"North Koreans are Communists," Mama explained coldly. "Evil people."

"The *South* Koreans are the good guys," Papa was grinning. "We're supposed to pray for them."

Sam was trying to work out the map in his head. "But it's all the same country, right?"

"Yes," Papa smiled broadly now. "It's like praying for Kansans against Nebraskans."

"That's enough of that," Mama decided.

"Hey, everybody–"

"Don't say 'hey,' Judith Beatrice," Mama reserved my whole name for lessons in etiquette or proper grammar. "You sound as if you were raised in a barn."

"Guess what, everybody," I started over. "I discovered I don't believe all of the Apostles' Creed."

Papa coughed. Sam stopped practicing his quick draw and slowed down to listen.

Mama re-pinned her hat with her fake pearl hatpin. "When did you come up with this bright idea?"

"Today. I actually listened to the words I was saying and realized. . . ," I paused for dramatic effect, "I was lying." Even though they pinched my feet, I loved to watch my black patent shoes flicker in the sunlight. In these shoes, my feet belonged to Ginger Rogers.

"I don't like to lie, especially in church." I added coyly, "I wasn't raised that way."

Papa coughed again.

"Do you have something in your throat, Frank?" Mama asked with a Help-Me-with-the-Children look, more Ma Kettle than Bette Davis.

He suggested gamely, "Just say . . . the parts you do believe."

"What don't you believe?" Sam pounced like a spy.

"Are you going to report me to the Boy Scouts? I'll tell them you don't say all twelve Boy Scout laws."

Sam paused. "You believe in God, right?"

"You always leave out 'Clean and Obedient'."

"How about God?" Sam insisted.

"Not the 'Father Almighty' part. He's not my dad. I've got Papa."

"What about 'Maker of heaven and earth'?" Sam pressed. Obviously, he had also thought about this. "You know, if you study the scientific explanation–"

"And you're the expert on that?" Mama could ask questions which sounded more like threats.

Sam defended himself. "I'm thinking of doing an Astronomy merit badge, and, besides, Uncle Ralph said the universe came from a huge explosion." Uncle Ralph, Mama's brother, always wanted to be an astronomer.

"Ralph," Mama sneered, "has an overactive imagination."

"It's a darn shame Ralph couldn't go to college," Papa interjected. "He's plenty smart." Papa had gone to a few years of college before the Depression hit and he had to go back to the farm to help Grandpa Wilder.

Mama's voice was tight. "College takes more than being smart. It takes money and more money and more money."

Mama was smarter than Uncle Ralph, I was certain. "If you could, would you have gone to college?" I asked. It had never occurred to me that she wanted to be more than our mother.

"Fat chance," she said. "It was all I could afford to work my way through stenography classes." Mama had worked as a legal secretary before she married Papa.

Sam returned to his interrogation of me, "Do you believe in Jesus Christ?"

Papa added, "Who is second in power only to God–and Uncle Ralph. Ask Grandma Strang. In fact, Ralph's the only man on earth worth a plug nickel." He looked sideways at Mama, "Including yours truly."

"Frank, you look like a hick with that weed in your mouth."

"I should look like a hick who can't wait to get to his cigar at home." Papa bought five cigars a week with his allowance.

"I don't like the 'only Son' part," I answered. "What about girls? Maybe God had a daughter."

"You've got a point, Sugar. It would be a very different world if we believed in God's only daughter."

"Frank," Mama warned again, and Papa took the weed out of his mouth.

Sam was growing increasingly excited. "The part I don't get is 'who was conceived by the Holy Spirit.' What does that mean?"

"Your mother will explain."

Mama hesitated. "Some things . . . you should say . . . on faith, even if you don't . . . understand or . . . . believe them. Yet."

"We should say things we don't believe?" I had a brand-new defense in the Lying Department, one based on church, no less. Added to *metaphor, faith* was a gold mine.

"A Boy Scout can't do that," Sam said from his high horse.

Papa egged me on. "You understand 'born of the Virgin Mary'?"

"Jesus's mom was Mary," I explained. "I don't know why she's called 'Virgin.' But you know what? In Bible School, Joe Clary thought 'Silent Night' said 'Round John Virgin'."

Mama smiled and Papa laughed out loud.

Sam reminded me, "You used to think it was 'Deck the halls with Boston Charlie'."

"That's when I was a little girl."

Sam explained, "Her first name is 'Virgin'."

I couldn't believe that I had never thought about this before. "So her last name is Mary?" "It's Jesus's last name, too."

Jesus Mary. I'd heard some Catholic kids at school say in-a-row 'Jesus Mary and Joseph.'

Sam decided to check, "Right, Mama?"

Exasperated, Mama said, "Jesus doesn't have a last name."

"Why not?" I asked.

Quickly changing opinions, Sam answered me. "When you're famous, you don't need a last name. Like Einstein."

"Einstein is his last name," Mama tried to redeem the conversation. "His first name is Albert. Like my cousin."

"Who is no Einstein," Papa interjected. "Edie, did I ever tell you about the day your cousin said to me, 'Not everybody can be as smart as George Einstein'?"

Papa threw back his head and laughed. Mama didn't.

We were rounding the corner by Mr. Whitaker's house, so I had to hurry. "If we're Methodists, how can we believe in 'the holy catholic church'? And I don't understand the 'resurrection of the dead'."

Now completely straight-faced, Papa explained, "Reverend Harkin is living proof of the resurrection of the dead."

"Frank!"

"And somebody judging the 'quick and the dead.' Who are the 'quick'?"

Sam had already thought this through. "They're the opposite of the slow ones. If you aren't quick enough, you'll be dead."

CHAPTER 6
THE DATE STAMP

"DO YOU HAVE ANY BOOKS ON SUB-MACHINE guns?"

The librarian's mouth stayed open, a puckered rim of dark red lipstick you could barely see. Sitting behind her desk, Miss Reynolds took off her glasses and let them rest from a chain on her bosom, a shelf which stuck out almost straight. The chain alternated heavy gold rings with pearls the size of gumballs. It must have cost a fortune.

"*Sub*-machine guns. Let me think. Do you want to . . . order one from Montgomery Ward? Find the nearest stock-pile? Or build one?"

"It's for Sam."

"Sam should be in here, getting his own books. He's probably wasting time playing baseball."

"His Scout troop is working on emergency preparedness."

"Oh. So they need sub-machine guns right away. Maybe Hoover's right: the Boy Scouts *have* been infiltrated by the Communists."

"I don't think that—"

"I'm teasing you, Judith."

I fingered the pile of books I was returning, trying not to sound disrespectful. "Miss Reynolds, would you please call me Jeb?"

"Certainly not. You have a wonderful name. Do you know who Judith is?"

"Grandma Wilder."

"In legend, child. Judith was a great warrior. A real heroine."

Why hadn't anyone ever told me this?

"When her people were under siege, she sneaked behind enemy lines and killed their general. Decapitated him."

"Wow."

"But she never used the word *wow*, which is a vulgar colloquialism unworthy of anyone named Judith." Without her glasses, Miss Reynolds' eyes looked like hard raisins surrounded by creamy folds of fat. "At least, you could go by Jude. Patron saint of hopeless causes." She opened her desk drawer to search for something. "My personal favorite."

"Mama says only Catholics use saints. Are you Catholic?"

When she laughed her whole body jiggled up and down in her chair. "Heavens no."

"L-Lutheran?"

"No. Presbyterian, no. Baptist, no." She answered in-a-row, as if people asked her this all the time. "I don't go to any church."

I stopped myself from saying *wow*. "That would save a lot of time on Sundays."

"It does."

"And you wouldn't have to lie by saying the Apostles' Creed."

She jiggled again, this time without sound. "Now *that's* an advantage I never considered."

Like Mama, Miss Reynolds had trouble putting on rouge, not by rubbing on clown spots but by making one cheek bright red and leaving the other one white, as if she lost interest halfway through the job. Her hair was held in tiny reddish brown tubes with lots of bobby pins. Mama said it was a wig, but I thought wigs were supposed to be prettier than normal hair.

She picked the top book off the pile I had brought in. "How did you like J. Edgar Hoover?"

"I started it, but you know, that was Mama's book."

"*Persons in Hiding*," she said, as if she had run out of spit. "Can't keep it on the shelf."

"Papa kept covering it with the newspaper. I think he didn't like the picture of the guy."

"*Man*," she corrected me. All grown-ups in my life were frustrated English teachers.

I pointed to the photograph on the book's cover. "His head looks like a basketball blown up too tight."

"He has the brains of a basketball, too." Miss Reynolds stealthily looked over her shoulder. "Do I dare criticize the Director of the Federal Bureau of Insult to Intelligence? They'll haul me in for a Communist yet."

Papa and Mama argued a lot about Communists but never told me what they were. Maybe she would. "What's a Communist?"

Her tiny eyes seemed to focus all her power into killer vision, like the robot Gort. "In Round Prairie? Anyone who doesn't fit in. Who dares to think for themselves. Or stands up for their own convictions."

Was it possible? "That's me. I could be a Communist!"

She looked at me, assessing, then decided, "You're too short."

"You didn't say anything about short."

"That's the way they play the game. They keep changing the rules."

I looked over my shoulder as she had just done and whispered. "Are you a Communist?"

"I'm a liberal, which, McCarthy tells us, is the first step toward becoming one. It's no wonder he was named after a ventriloquist's dummy."

I wasn't sure what she meant, but I recognized *ventriloquist*, a lovely word.

She tried to fold her arms over her huge bosom, but could only touch her elbows. "Unlike Hoover and his goons, I have actually read *The Communist Manifesto* and understand what Communism is. And no, I am not a Communist, in spite of what people call me behind my back." She looked out the tall window behind me. "Mostly crazy. But if normal is what most people are, who wants to be normal?" She looked back at me. "Is that what you want on your tombstone, Judith? *She was normal? She fit in?*"

With all the time I spent in cemeteries, I had never thought about my own tombstone but probably should get cracking on it. "I . . . don't know. What do you want on yours?"

"*I'M BORED ALREADY.*"

"You know who else doesn't fit in? Mrs. Keindorf. She goes to our church."

"I'll say she doesn't fit in. She's educated, urbane, genteel and beautiful to boot. Now which of these characteristics would prevent her from fitting into Round Prairie?"

"How do you spell *genteel*?"

"G-e-n-t-e-e-l. Have you heard a word I said?"

A brand-new word with three e's. Oboy.

"Unfortunately, people who have no refinement tend to distrust those who do. Greta Keindorf has more culture in her little finger than most people have in their whole body." Miss Reynolds patted her thighs. "In my case, that's saying something."

"Is she your friend?" I tried to make my spying sound like polite conversation.

"She came into the library to get a card almost as fast as your mother. Checked out our ancient copy of Montaigne's *Essays*, one of three books we have in French." She chuckled. "I couldn't interest her in *Madame Bovary* or Rabelais."

"I haven't read any of those."

"You'll have time enough. A whole lifetime to read. Lucky you." She shivered a little, although it wasn't cold. "Let's check in some books."

She flipped open each book to see if any were overdue, which was pointless, since she had just checked them out to Sam and me a week ago. It was probably a job requirement. I handed her the list of books I was to bring home, all penciled in Mama's neat handwriting on the back of a used envelope.

She turned the list over. "Where are the sub-machine guns?"

"They were a last minute addition."

"I'll see what I can do." She waved me away. "Go read."

Soon after we moved anywhere, Mama walked Sam and me to the library to meet the librarian and to get cards. I especially loved the library in Round Prairie, a small square building of red bricks sitting high enough so the basement had windows, too. Surrounding the main floor the windows were tall enough to require long poles to open and close them, poles which Sam saw as perfect spears and I envisioned as stick horses, complete with a brass curl at the end for a tail. The oak floors were worn into ridges and smelled like oil with dirt rubbed into it, like the floors in school. This library made you feel you could read every single book in it, a task I decided to put off until I turned twelve.

"Do you want any suggestions?" Miss Reynolds called to me in the Young Adult section, where I knew I would find *Black Beauty*. The library's copy had a ragged binding and broken cardboard cover, but a picture of a shiny black horse on the front, although its ears curled unnaturally inward, more like horns. I opened it carefully, reading the familiar inscription in elaborate, scrolled handwriting: "To George E. Menke from your Aunt Tillie Daubendick, Dec. 25th 1913." I looked at the pictures only at the beginning and end, since I couldn't bear to see some of the cart horses whipped.

"If you want a good book, read *Black Beauty*," I called out to Miss Reynolds, "but parts of it are very, very sad."

"I cry every time I read it," she answered. I suspected she was lying, but you couldn't say that to a grown-up, and certainly not to Miss Reynolds.

I petted the book. "When I come to a section I don't like, I rewrite it—like the death of Ginger, Beauty's friend. I rewrite church, too."

She called out from her desk, "I would love to hear your version of the Methodist service sometime."

"First, Reverend Harkin would explain important things like how Jesus was conceived by the Holy Spirit."

"Good start!"

"He wouldn't talk about war or Korea, and he'd let Maxine Harkin play anything she wanted on the organ. He could also throw in a joke or two, like Papa would."

"Your father would need to give him lessons. Better yet, Frank should just run church."

"We would all stand up more to keep our feet from going to sleep, and we'd sing better songs, like 'Tea for Two' instead of 'The Old Rugged Cross'."

"Let me know when your version happens, and I'll be on the front row."

I carefully slid *Black* Beauty back into its slot. "I wish this was my book."

"You wish it *were* your book," she called out. "Subjunctive mood for statements contrary to fact or expressing a wish."

"What kind of wish?"

"Any wish. What do they teach you children in school nowadays?"

Contrary to fact could be a very useful concept. "The sub-what . . .?"

"Subjunctive."

With *metaphor* and *faith*, I now had three brand-new defenses for my version of the truth, all elegant.

As I walked out of the stacks, she was slipping a little card into the pocket in the back of each book.

"You should be an English teacher, Miss Reynolds." This was a great compliment, since I loved English.

"I would have been, except I hate children."

I knew lots of adults who hated children, but I had never heard one admit it. "Really? I do, too."

When she leaned her arms on her desk, fat hung over her elbows. "I knew that you and I would be good friends." She pointed to the stack of books I had returned. "What did you think of *The Little House on the Prairie*?"

"It was pretty boring."

"Boring?"

"I had to make up a lot of episodes. Like coloring black and white movies."

She objected, "But the Ingalls family nearly drowned in their covered wagon, almost died of malaria and finally lost the house they worked so hard to build."

I turned the book over like a pancake. "They deserved to lose it. They were squatters on Indian land, which the government kept stealing from the Indians, anyway."

"What episodes did you add?"

"An Indian counter-attack, for starters. In the book, they performed the war dance but never got organized enough to fight."

Miss Reynolds put on her glasses. "You run a tight ship, Judith."

"But no book holds a candle to *Alice in Wonderland*."

"I emphatically agree."

"It's my favorite book of all time. You can't add a thing to it. Whatever you could think, the guy—man—has already thought it, and stranger than you could imagine, anyway."

"Lewis Carroll." She squared up the stack of returned books. "I'm afraid a little house on the prairie is no match for Wonderland."

"I liked Sam's Tom Swift novels, but they're pretty predictable. Sam says Tom's inventions aren't feasible."

"*Feasible?*"

"That means possible or likely to happen."

She smiled. "I know." Her teeth were so perfect that they must be false. Mama and Papa both needed false teeth, but we couldn't afford them. Sam and I had never been to a dentist.

"Sam uses *feasible* to defend his crackpot ideas. Which, you might want to know, aren't feasible. I like the word, though. I keep a journal of names for horses and my favorite words."

"Good idea! What's your favorite word?"

"Currently? I'd say . . . *lugubrious.*"

She laughed, one big, single sound like a shout. "You have real style, Judith." She stood up slowly, using the arms on her wooden chair to push herself up, and walked around her desk, leaning heavily on a closed umbrella.

"Can't you afford a cane?"

With her teeth clamped, she answered, "I don't need a cane."

Miss Reynolds walked around the library, gathering books from my list which she handed to me to carry. Sunlight wiggled through the slag glass windows, making everything look wavy, as if it were underwater.

"Did you find any horse books I haven't read?" I already knew the answer.

"One on equestrian gaits and one for veterinarians. Better than J. Edgar Hoover, but not exactly scintillating prose."

What a word! I was ready to ask her about it when she continued, "But yesterday the Book Mobile delivered a brand new book that I ordered just for you."

With my arms full, I followed her to the storage closet, where she put on my stack a book titled *Brighty of the Grand Canyon*. "He's not a horse, but evidently, he's a big-hearted burro. I'll expect a book report."

Burros had almost nothing in common with horses, but I didn't have the heart to tell her that.

She sat down with a pumph, barely fitting between the chair's arm-rests, and put on her glasses. My favorite part of checking out books was the tall, mechanical book stamp with the changing rubber dates. Sam was intrigued with how it inked itself, but I liked the way the days, months and years rolled on rubber wheels like miniature tractor treads. All dates existed at the same time, so you could make it any day you wanted, could roll it back or ahead, keep it on good days, like your birthday, and avoid Sundays altogether. I loved its sound, too: a carink halfway between a stapler and a cash register.

She checked my pile of books against Mama's list. "Let's see: *Tom Swift and His War Tank* and *Tom Swift and His Electric Rifle*, plus *Ordnance Went Up Front* for Sam. It's the best I can do for machine guns. The poetry of Edna St. Vincent Millay for Edith, and a shop manual for Minneapolis-Moline tractors for Frank. Looks as if your father's working on a different emergency."

"He's fixing our neighbor's tractor."

"If it's a Minneapolis-Moline, it's Ernst Dagendorf, that cheap old buzzard. He's almost blind, you know. Shouldn't be driving at all, let alone a tractor."

I had held out as long as I could and, knowing it was impolite, still blurted, "Are those real pearls on your necklace?"

"If they were, I wouldn't be working in the Carnegie Free Public Library in Round Prairie, Nebraska."

"Where would you be?"

Miss Reynolds stopped with the book stamp in mid-air. "I haven't thought about that for . . . . I don't know how long. Some place . . . with a magnificent public library. Maybe Chicago. New York City . . . but Chicago would be . . . . more feasible."

"My mom says if you want to do something, you should wish upon a star. You know that song Jiminy Cricket sang in 'Pinocchio'?"

She shook her head no, but she might have been fibbing, since she knew just about everything.

My voice has never been one of my strong points, as even Mama would admit, but I wanted Miss Reynolds to hear the song. In the library, my voice sounded thin as a wire and way too high, like the ladies who sang solos in church:

"When you wish upon a star, makes no difference who you are, anything your heart desires will come to you."

Miss Reynolds looked at me, her x-ray eyes dark and furious. Maybe there was a rule against singing in the library. If so, she should have told me ahead of time. But she needed to hear the last stanza:

"Like a bolt out of the blue, fate steps in and sees you through; when you wish upon a star, your dreams come true."

She looked at me for a long minute, then cleared her throat. "The stars gave up on me a long time ago."

CHAPTER 7
LITTLE GIRL BLUE

PAPA HAD COME HOME FROM WORK, HIS SHIRT stained down his back and under his arms, dead hot and tired, and Mama had made macaroni with Velveeta cheese, one of my favorites, and we were eating knee to knee around the fold-down table, and it was a hummy time, when my glass suddenly slipped out of my hand, hurling milk into my lap and across the linoleum Mama had just scrubbed and waxed, even splattering the piano legs. Everyone was paralyzed, as if time had cracked open, momentarily suspending us between seconds, where the accident had happened and it also hadn't. As long as no one moved, we could step back half an instant and the glass would miraculously fly back to my hand, sucking the milk with it, leaving the piano clean, the floor shiny and my dress ironed, leaving Mama and Papa talking about their day and Sam and me eating our steamy macaroni and cheese.

"JEB!" Mama jumped across the gap in time so fast that she knocked over her chair. Although she never hit us, she raised her hand to slap me, then dropped it. Papa grabbed my glass to save what milk he could, and Sam puckered his face as if he had just eaten something sour.

Mama threw a dishcloth in my lap to sop up what I could. "WHY WHY can't you get through a meal without spilling something!" She was on her knees frantically wiping the floor.

"I'm sorry, Mama." Nothing I said would help.

"Sorry, schmorry! Who buys the milk? Who waxes the floor? And what do you do? Make a mess! All you can do is make a mess! Do you think we're made of money?!"

Papa bent down to help her, but she screamed at him, too. "Get away from me! GET!"

Papa's whole face sagged. "Sugar, you've got to hang onto things tighter."

"I try, Papa," I didn't dare look at him anymore.

"Try harder." His defeated voice was the worst punishment he ever gave.

An Unspoken Family Rule required us all to be as still as possible until Mama cleaned up a spill. I would have licked it off the floor if I could have restored the evening to where we started. Sam carefully pulled *Tom Swift and His War Tank* off the piano, hid it on his lap and began to read.

"Put that g. d. book away!" Mama snarled at him as she finished wiping up the milk and hopelessly looked at the smears across her once perfect floor. "Books books books books books."

I pushed my macaroni and cheese around the milk pooling in my plate and knew I deserved the footstool for a whole afternoon for this one. After we silently finished our cold, rubbery macaroni, Mama carefully divided out to everyone except me chocolate pudding and vanilla wafers. I kept staring at the dishcloth in my wet lap and pretended not to notice.

That evening, when Papa unfolded my chair-bed and tucked me in, he didn't give me my good-night kiss. Since I only got seven kisses a week, I couldn't bear to miss one. Maybe he would kiss me twice tomorrow. Asking him wouldn't help, I just had to wait and see. As Sam walked around my bed on the way to his bedroom, he stuffed something under my pillow. When all the lights were out, I pulled out a vanilla wafer and nibbled it in squirrel bites, carefully sweeping up and eating all the crumbs. If Mama found out, we would both be in trouble.

In the dark from their end of the trailer, Mama and Papa argued for a long time, shouting then hissing whispers, loud, soft, loud again, interrupted by the sounds of drawers screeching open and shut.

" . . . trailer house!" Mama accused. "The neighbors—"

"They don't give a—"

She snarled. "Just because you can't see . . . ."

"I see exactly—" The rest of Papa's answer was lost in something slamming.

" . . . joke, joke, joke, make a joke out of everything, that's all you ever do . . . . Don't ever DO something!"

". . . a little humor . . ."

There was a long pause, then Mama shouted, "Frank! Look at me! Here I am. What do you see?"

". . . too sensitive—"

"*Crazy!* Call me *crazy!* That's what you mean."

" . . . don't tell me what I mean . . . so goddam high-strung . . ."

"I'll show you high-strung: you . . . you . . . idiot!"

"Smart enough to put food on the table," Papa shot back.

"Macaroni?! Where are the pork chops? Huh? Huh?"

"Still on the pig."

There was another pause.

Papa said more quietly, "We're both doing what we can—"

". . . paying the bills with no money . . . . You try it: bills, bills, your doctor bills . . . "

"Throw that in my face, why don't you?"

"Doctor, doctor . . . " Mama started sing-songing, "who's got the doctor? Mary, that's who! Doctor Mary—"

Papa said, "The kids—" and their voices dropped.

"Doctor Mary, *quite* contrary."

What did Doctor Mary have to do with anything?

Papa tried again, "Settle down. The kids—"

"Kids, schmids. . . . Wake up and die right!"

I could tell Papa was trying not to shout, but he couldn't stop himself, "Die right? You'd like that, you and your mother—"

"Leave my mother out of this!"

They grew quiet again.

"Sam?" I whispered to his closed sliding door. The streetlight shining through the trailer window transformed the cookie jar and radio into little aliens hunkered down, waiting to attack. "Are you there?"

"Yeah," he said in a hoarse voice.

"Thanks for the cookie."

Suddenly, a light went on in the folks' bedroom, the door hurtled open, and Papa stalked out.

"To hell with you!" he shouted over his shoulder at Mama.

In five steps, he was out the front door and slammed it behind him. The trailer bounced a little as he jumped off the bottom step. It took a lot to make Papa mad, and he had never walked out before. I pulled my sheet up to my nose, again trying to will time to back up and start over. A few minutes later, Mama walked out in her bathrobe, the bedroom light behind her making long shadows across my bed.

Nothing could make me cry, really deep down cry, except family arguments. Knowing I couldn't stop once I started, I kept swallowing.

Mama waved toward the front door. "Now see what you've done."

"Wh-where'd P-Papa go?" My stomach was heaving.

"Who knows? Stop sniveling!" she warned. "You're such a crybaby."

I wasn't a crybaby, but this was no time to argue. "Are you . . . are you . . ." I hiccupped with crying, "going to get . . . to get . . . divorced?"

"Ask him. He's the know-it-all," she snapped. "I never know one g.d. thing."

Whenever they argued, I always asked the divorce question, but before this she had always said "no." I let go and began to wail. What if Papa never came back? Just like Mama's father deserted her family when she was a little girl? What if they got divorced? Sam and I would be orphans, the worst thing in the world, worse than not having food, let alone a house. I could probably survive without Mama or Papa, even if we were orphans, but without Sam, I would die. That, or kill myself.

Sam pushed open the sliding door to his bedroom and squinted into the light. "Jujube?"

"Now look!" Mama screeched at me. "You woke up Sam."

Sam sat heavily on the piano bench next to my chair-bed. His pajamas had cowboys riding bucking horses, waving their hats and smiling. I wanted cowboy pajamas, too, even Sam's hand-me-downs, but for me, Mama sewed flour sacks printed with daisies or bluebells.

Mama paced up and down the slash of light from her bedroom door to the kitchen, about eight steps each way, reciting some poem. "'Not only underground are the brains of men eaten by maggots.' Maggots, maggots, maggots." She tiptoed as if she were walking on maggots, whatever they were.

Sam kneeled on the floor and pulled a cigar box full of small toys from under my chair-bed where it was stored. Two of his toy cars, a green coupe and a blue Studebaker sedan, were cast from pot metal with rubber tires, but a third was a small dome of tin painted to look like a convertible. From the top, you could look inside at the painted seats and steering wheel as if it didn't have a solid, smooth roof, completely convincing even though you knew it was fake. Somebody could make a curved piece of metal look like empty space. They could paint air.

"You want the convertible?" he asked.

I always wanted the convertible, but I was still in bed, hiccupping and trying to stop crying. Sam pushed the convertible and his little blue sedan along the floor, then jumped them to my covers, hill-climbed my bed and ran them across my ankles.

The sedan stalled in a gully in my sheet, and Sam raced its engine with a quiet "vroom vroom" until he could dig out with a high "screee."

Mama watched him for a minute. "Not maggots. Toys. It's toys." She used her poetry voice but wasn't really talking to us:

"The little toy dog is covered with dust, and the little toy soldier is red with rust.

She dreamt of her pretty toys.

And as she was dreaming, an angel song awakened our Little Girl Blue,—

Oh, the years are many, the years are long, but the little toy friends are true!"

Mama's hair was bobby-pinned into flat curls the size of quarters all over her head so that it would fall in waves tomorrow. "Who is my little girl blue? Hmmm?"

I knew it was my dead sister, Janet, but didn't want to say so. Before Sam and I were born, Janet was born too early because Mama crashed the car in a thunderstorm. Mama and Papa had her name ready, just waiting for her to live in it. Janet was part of our family, dead and not dead, the one who would remain a baby forever. Every Memorial Day, we put flowers on her grave in Rose Hill Cemetery near Hebron, an unmarked patch of grass because tombstones cost too much.

"Where is Little Girl Blue?" Mama stood over my bed, her eyes glittering strangely in the light from the street.

I knew the right answer to the test, "With the angels." I still sucked air in little sobby packets. Mama and I both knew that Janet would not spill *her* milk.

"Wrong! Underground. Underground, eaten by maggots. That's where."

Mama paced again, mumbling more of the poem:

"Her toys wonder, waiting these long years through,

In the dust of her little chair . . ."

I crawled out of my sheet carefully, since I didn't want to disturb Sam's race course.

He held the cars in place while I slid down beside him on the floor. He quietly reminded me, "Don't forget: the convertible has a bad clutch."

We whispered our car racing sounds, which slowed down the race. Even though I had the more powerful car, Sam beat the first two rounds, but he let me win the third. He mapped the race course on my covers and changed it every lap, so I lost a lot of time driving into walls he built with his free hand just as my car arrived. He always decided the rules, usually at the last second, and changed them at random. The word for this was *impromptu,* a musical word, a good-looking word, beginning and ending with vowels and balanced in the middle with two p's.

Mama watched us. "What has become of our Little Girl Blue since she kissed her toys and put them there?"

Just then, the trailer door jiggled open. Sam held my arm so I wouldn't throw myself on Papa and cry again.

"Does anybody in here need a car ride?" Somehow, Papa had gotten dressed. The log cabin clock said 11:25.

Sam and I jumped up, looking at Mama, who pushed her bobby pin curls into place.

"Edie?" Papa asked warily, still standing outside.

She tied her bathrobe tighter, and we all crept outdoors and across the yard, barefoot and in our pajamas, and climbed into the old Buick.

We often took car rides late at night when Mama couldn't sleep, but we had never done it to stop an argument. We drove the thumpeta thumpeta red brick of Main Street, lined with dark buildings. Tonight Round Prairie was like a giant hotel on its side, only with individual houses instead of rooms, each house holding its own story like the people's lives in the Inavale Hotel drive-in. Where would the movie screen be for the whole town? A huge sheet spread on top of our heads? What big movie was being projected onto our real lives? I could almost see the movie flickering in the alleys as we drove by.

If Miss Reynolds were still awake, she was reading, but I was sure that Mr. Whitaker was asleep and dreaming, probably about cookies. I wondered if other parents fought like Mama and Papa, and if other kids were afraid of being orphaned. Sam said we had bigger things to worry about, but I couldn't think of one bigger thing. Did anybody think the thoughts I did?

The whole town was dark except for a single light shining in the lobby of Harkins Funeral Parlor. People must bring dead bodies to Marvin Harkin in the middle of the night. Then what did he do with them, the dead people, cold and stiff? At some point he would have to take off their clothes and handle them. Naked. Even ladies. Did Maxine, his wife, help him? That would be a good time to be blind, when Marvin was handling naked ladies right in front of you. As the Shadow said on the radio, the dead don't talk.

On the highway toward Inavale, we didn't see any other cars, and our headlights moved slow and dim through the prairie night. In the distance, yard lights marked farms where families and tractors and chickens and horses slept.

During car rides, our whole family could snug down together and nobody could see us or bother us, which settled Mama down. The Buick smelled like old cotton batting, but it floated over bumps and didn't jerk when it changed gears. Papa called that "Dyna-flow."

He turned on the radio, and a voice sang, "Brylcreem, the gals'll all pursue ya; they'll love to get their fingers in your hair. . . . ." He moved the marker across the dial, a shiny pointer capturing invisible signals from places far, far away. "Welcome back," somebody said, "to K-triple-X radio in beautiful Colby, Kansas." The static whirred and crackled, tearing up the words like confetti, until a serious voice said confidentially, " Last episode, the aliens had just poisoned . . . ." Papa dialed through more static until he hit an excited voice shouting above cheers, " . . . served up a fat one! First run for the Braves! . . . eleven to one in favor of the Dodgers . . . ."

"Must be that double-header in Milwaukee," Papa tried not to sound interested. Over his shoulder, he said to Sam, "Looks like Warren Spahn won't save the Braves tonight." He glanced at Mama and tuned past the game.

I liked the name "Braves" better than "Dodgers." What were the Dodgers dodging, anyway?

Sam said quietly, "I got a baseball card of Warren Spahn while the Braves were still in Boston. I traded an extra Micky Mantle for him."

"Be sure to keep that one," Papa answered. "It'll be valuable someday."

Baseball cards came with Topps bubble-gum, but I never saw the gum. I wondered what Milwaukee looked like, what people were thinking as they watched the baseball game, shouting and eating peanuts and Crackerjacks—just like in the song—while our family was driving a straight and silent road among wheat fields. Mr. Whitaker said that wheat ripened even in the dark.

Sam put his head out the window into the warm wind, craning to see the stars.

Another radio voice said, "... are meeting for armistice negotiations, but students from nearby Panmunjom are demonstrating against the pull-out of ...."

Mama waved away the news broadcast, her first motion since we left home. Papa finally found a crackly station playing music which I recognized as Glenn Miller.

"Remember that, Edie? 'In the Mood'? Haven't heard that for a long time." He began tapping the steering wheel in time to the music.

"I used to love hearing you play that on the trumpet with your neighborhood dance band."

I vaguely remembered seeing a trumpet in the closet in Hebron, but I had never heard about Papa's dance band.

In the light from the dashboard, I saw Papa smile. "With Bob Wilkerson on sax. What was that guy's name? Our drummer?"

"Old Bill Wade." Mama began nodding in time to the music. "Couldn't keep the beat to save his soul."

"And I couldn't keep my old trumpet in tune. What a band. We only hit our stride when we could stop playing and shout 'Penn-syl-va-nia six five thousand!'"

"Remember Doris Talbot—" Mama began.

"Oh lord."

"How she loved to dance." Mama was now nodding hard enough with the music to make her bobby-pin curls bounce.

"Couldn't stop her, and fat as a butcher's dog ..." Papa looked quickly in the rear view mirror to see if we were listening. "I mean—"

Mama finished for him, "I swear, you could feel the high school gym floor bounce when she did the two-step."

The music sounded so happy. If band members felt miserable and played as if they were happy, was that a lie?

The music lulled us all, and I felt my head slipping toward Sam's shoulder. Normally, he would push me away, but tonight he was too tired to care.

The next thing I knew, I woke up in my chair-bed in the quiet and dark trailer, in complete disbelief that Papa had carried me inside and put me back to bed, all without my waking up. This wasn't like sleepwalking and waking up in the folks' or Sam's bedroom. When I walked in my sleep, some part of me stayed awake enough not to stumble or run into things. Somehow, one Jeb stayed awake while the other slept. But tonight was different. Papa had lifted me out of the car seat and carried me into the trailer and put me in bed and tucked me in. He had hugged me the whole time, and I had missed it. I couldn't afford to have important moments in my life happen while both Jebs stayed asleep. But how could I fix it?

Maybe it was all a bad dream, I told myself. Maybe this whole night didn't happen. But as I turned over, Sam's little cars bounced to the floor and slowly rolled across the smeared linoleum, driven by tiny people, although gigantic compared to the Dust People.

CHAPTER 8

CHESTY PULLER IN NEBRASKA

T**HE VERY NEXT MORNING, SAM CALLED A SUMMIT** meeting in the hayloft, where we had hidden the longest and strongest broomcorn stalks, already sharpened into spears. I had tied La Cheetah, my stick horse, outside and now sat Indian-style on the straw bale, watching Sam map our future. Sunlight sifted through the cracks between the wall boards and fell in dusty slits through the air. I wanted to tell Sam about the Dust People I had invented in church but didn't dare swerve him off the path to a Great Idea. The sneezy smell of old hay mixed with the smell of grease embedded in the dirt floor of the barn stalls beneath us. Originally Papa meant to park our Buick there, but the space was currently filled with Mr. Dagendorf's tractor, an orange beast the size of a baby elephant, named Minneapolis-Moline. I had already listed that name for an imaginary rust-colored work horse who did all the heavy work but was ignored the rest of the time, like a fat Cinderella.

"Jeb, we're approaching a crisis."

We had heard that a lot on the radio, a word which looked equally serious forward or backward–*sisirc*–as opposed to *peril*, which was *lirep*. When you added *red*, it became *der lirep*, pretty silly.

As usual, Sam wore his tattered straw cowboy hat and the empty holster set we found in a garbage can in Hebron. "The summer's half over, and we still don't have a hide-out. The Inavale house–"

"Is haunted." Anytime I let myself, I could hear those furry piano keys playing.

"I meant the storm cellar—"

"It's already being used," I interrupted again. I was pushing my luck.

"–is pretty far away. In case of an air raid–"

"The Boy Scouts will save us." Sam appreciated my sarcasm except when directed against the legendary BSA.

"Here's my idea. Brilliant, I might add." He often graded himself "brilliant." He walked back and forth across the creaky floorboards. "We dig a fort. For trench warfare."

"We don't have a shovel." Long handle, real work.

"And the best part: We'll be close to home, but hidden."

"So's the hayloft." Ready-made, no shovels.

"Under siege, we'd be trapped up here for days. We'd starve."

Any reference to food instantly changed the terms of the discussion. He pushed his cowboy hat back from his forehead like Roy Rogers. "A dug-out . . ." he paused for effect, "in the middle of the broomcorn field."

"In plain sight? We're trying to *hide out*."

"People see only what they expect to see–in this case, a deserted field. They won't even notice our fort."

I would not grade this idea brilliant. "That sounds like Marvin Harkin."

In my opinion, only the Scoutmaster was stupid enough to have such an idea and powerful enough to get gullible little boys to act on it.

"It's scientific fact."

Sam believed he could float any plan with some reference to science, however oblique, and it usually worked.

He continued, "People ignore the obvious. Scientific experiments have to worry about this all the time."

I felt like the only person who was *not* ignoring the obvious, an unusual position for me.

"When we aren't using the trench for war, we'll disguise it as an ordinary ditch under a pile of branches."

"That shouldn't be too hard." My scorn was lost on him.

Sam practiced a quick draw, fanning an imaginary gun out of his real holsters. "Pow. Pow." I could practically see the wood splinter from the rickety barn wall.

Digging on a hot July day sounded like as much fun as dragging around the idiot stick.

"Remember the trenches in 'Sergeant York'?"

I objected, "In the movie, a whole squadron of Marines dug the trenches."

"Army," Sam corrected.

"I'll bet movie people dug them. Part of their job." I never knew when I would be hit with an attack of realism. "Besides, Mr. Whitaker—"

"—already said we could."

Sam never lied except under extreme pressure, so I had to believe him. I did see the beauty of having our fort close to water, an indoor bathroom, and an occasional sneaked cracker, not to mention the advantage of easier digging in a field already plowed.

"We have a ready-made battlefield which can double as an airstrip, all the dirt clods we could ever need for ammo, and an unlimited supply of broomcorn stalks." Sam holstered his imaginary Colts decisively. "You must admit, this is beyond feasible."

Sam had clearly decided our future, but I could try one last strike. I wanted to mention *probability* and *archaeology*, but I couldn't work them in fast enough, so I settled on, "Bet you can't spell *feasible*."

"Are you kidding?" Of course, he knew better than to try.

Mr. Whitaker loaned us a shovel with the longest handle I had ever seen, called a road shovel. As he squeezed into his rocking chair on his back porch, he said, "I'd help you two, but I'll have more fun watching. Especially at 94 degrees, with who-knows-what humidity. What kinda fort you gonna build?"

"A trench," I answered. "To defend ourselves from the enemy."

"Who's the enemy?" Mr. Whitaker's hands always shook, as if he were trying to flick something sticky off them.

Sam furtively looked around before answering, "Communists."

"Oooh." He rocked back, "I keep forgetting the Reds in Round Prairie. And where you gonna dig this?"

"Smack in the middle of your field," I offered, noticing too late Sam's hand signals to be quiet, but secretly hoping that Mr. Whitaker would object.

Sam reluctantly added, "That way, the enemy can't sneak up on us."

"That's for damned sure. I mean, darned sure. Or you could be attacked from all sides at once. One of the advantages of livin' on the plains--you can always see what's comin' at ya." He chuckled. "You jes' can't do anything about it."

Had Sam considered that?

Mr. Whitaker pulled out a hanky the size of a dish towel from his overalls and blew his nose. "You kids know about Chesty Puller in Korea? Him and his Marines were trapped at Chosin Reservoir, outnumbered ten to one, and you know what he said? 'The enemy can't escape this time. We're completely surrounded'." Mr. Whitaker shook his head and clucked. "What a man."

I didn't think I heard right. "Chesty Puller?"

"Most decorated Marine in history."

A fine horse's name.

He stuffed his hanky back. "You kids got everything you need? Knife? Flashlight?"

Sam had asked for a Boy Scout flashlight for two Christmases in a row, but with no luck. Of course, he hadn't tried wishing on stars. "N-no, but–"

"How you gonna dig at night?"

Sam looked newly inspired.

"Tell you what." His rocker creaked under so much weight. "In the barn there's an old metal tool chest which has a coupla rusted jackknives and a flashlight. Your dad's using my trouble light to work on Dagendorf's junkheap, so he won't need it."

I started to say 'wow,' then remembered Miss Reynolds.

"Wow," Sam said. "Thanks."

"Be careful. You know, if you dig too deep, you'll hit China."

I liked grown-ups who teased kids in a friendly way, not a bit mean.

"Thank you, Mr. Whitaker," I called over my shoulder as Sam ran for the barn, dragging the shovel. If I were a Boy Scout, I would demand that Mr. Whitaker be appointed the Scoutmaster instead of somebody who handled dead bodies. If Maxine Harkin weren't blind, she could see how creepy Marvin was.

Pretending that he had a plane table and surveyor's level, Sam told me to walk around the field and use the road shovel for an idiot stick. Just as I was growing hot and impatient enough to object, with his foot Sam drew a line in the dirt parallel to the alley, utterly random.

"This is it," he announced.

"That's what?"

"We'll dig here."

It wouldn't have helped to ask the point of the surveyor's game or why he had just ordered me to drag the idiot shovel around the broomcorn field. The reason was always the same—for Sam to be the Boss, to make the decisions for everybody else. He had always been this way, but the Boy

Scouts actively encouraged it. Too bad they didn't have a Leadership merit badge. I had read up on the closest thing—the Salesmanship badge—even stupider than Farm Layout and Building Arrangement. While Sam certainly could "influence buyers" and "overcome their selling resistance," his couldn't sell "more than ten dollars" of merchandise. The radish episode had proven that.

I sighed loudly. "How long do you think this will take?" Whatever Sam answered, I knew that I could double it.

"Couple of hours." He started digging a furrow about an inch deep along his imaginary map, then handed me the shovel. "Your turn."

Just because a field looks plowed up doesn't mean that it isn't solid as concrete. No matter how hard I jumped on the shovel—even with my heavy school shoes—it kept skidding along the surface. Halfheartedly, I backtracked down Sam's row and managed to pile a little dirt beside the trench. Over and over, he followed my track, and, in turn, I followed his, making progress inches at a time.

During one of my turns, I looked up and saw Mama's head in the trailer kitchen window. I waved, but, instead of waving back, her face screwed up tight as if she were screaming at someone in the trailer. Who? Nobody ever visited. As I stared, her face inflated like a balloon until it completely filled the window. I blinked. She became one huge eye crammed in the tiny window. Maybe I was seeing part of the big movie projected onto Round Prairie from overhead.

I decided to double-check with Sam. "Don't look now, but do you see something weird in the kitchen window?"

From the other end of the trench, he answered, "How can I see anything if I don't look now?"

"Okay okay. Look now."

He scanned the trailer. "What?"

I looked again, and Mama's huge eye was gone. "I thought it was . . . a big head . . . ."

"You are so nuts. Stop daydreaming and concentrate."

Had Mama done this to herself, or had I? Could my imagination make someone else grow huge? One thing was certain: Mama and I never needed to eat Alice's cake in Wonderland.

"Heatstroke," I shouted, hardly fibbing, and pried free a few more little clods with the shovel.

How did the sodbusters do this, when they had to dig up prairie grass? Papa said when he was a little boy, their farm still had a few patches of big bluestem which stood over six feet tall, taller than Grandpa Wilder. They had used two work horses and a plow and still had a devil of a time breaking it up. Grandpa Wilder had died before I was born, but Grandma Wilder died when I was six. In a blizzard, she fell on the ice near her back door, and nobody found her before she froze to death. You might expect that to happen on a farm, but not in Belvedere, the town where she and Grandpa had moved when they got old. Papa said, knowing her, she was too proud to shout for help. My first name, Judith, came from her, but my middle name, Beatrice, came from Grandma Strang, nicknamed Bea, Papa said, for bee in a bonnet.

"How deep are we going to dig?" I hoped that whatever Sam answered, I could cut it in half.

"I was thinking four feet, but maybe it should be two."

He sounded open to compromise, so I suggested, "You know, it'll look deeper if we pile dirt along the top–"

"Yeah. And add branches and sticks and other stuff." This was code for "good idea," a compliment never openly allowed little sisters in the Unwritten Laws of Big Brothers.

"Oh oh," Sam said and tilted his head toward the alley, where Jim Hartsock was walking slowly, kicking a can and pretending not to care what we were doing. Jim lived across the street and was in Sam's scout troop. He always wore John Deere baseball caps because his father worked for the farm implement store and could get them for free. I liked Farmall tractors better because of their barn red color, but it would be impolite to tell him that.

"Hey," I called. With the odds two against one in our favor, I could afford to be nice to anybody, even after his role in the radish episode. Besides, I needed a rest.

Sam hissed, "What are you going to say we're doing?"

"He won't ask." I dropped the shovel.

"Whatcha doing?" Jim asked, stepping over the old furrows and broomcorn stubble toward us.

"Helping Mr. Whitaker plant potatoes," I lied. For a diversionary tactic, I asked, "Where are your friends?"

"Who? Bobby and Leon? They're not my friends."

This was good information for determining who might be For Us and Against Us in Round Prairie.

"I know how to dig," he said, half as an offer, half defensively.

Go to it, I was ready to say, when Mama called us from the trailer.

"Sam? Jeb? Dinner." What would normally have been a deplorable interruption of an important task turned into a stroke of luck, since the potato pretense couldn't last long.

Unfortunately, Mama's voice sounded tinny and too enthusiastic, which meant either that she had chores for us to do or had been reading something disturbing in the encyclopedia. At Hale's Grocery, she had just bought Funk and Wagnall's Volume 3, which might go all the way to Communism. Sam and I always watched our step, since we never knew which mother was waiting for us.

"We gotta go," Sam answered Jim. "Maybe later." Sam picked up the shovel and carried it toward the trailer.

We left Jim beside the shallow trench, trying to match what he saw in the dirt with any version of potato planting he had ever seen.

I had imagined our fort would be like Sergeant York's WWI trench, deeper than I was tall, safe and well-equipped with weapons and provisions to outlast any bombardment. Instead, it ended up as a shallow ditch about four feet long, two feet wide and less than a foot deep, counting the sides banked with extra dirt and broken concrete. It took us a week to dig it, and only one day for someone to find it and throw broken bottles and garbage into it. The war had found us.

CHAPTER 9

LULLABY

BECAUSE MRS. KEINDORF WAS THE ONLY PIANO teacher in Round Prairie accepting new students or at least ones who lived in a trailer house, Mama agreed to let me take lessons from her. I was thrilled.

Mrs. Keindorf lived in the new section of Round Prairie with real sidewalks smooth enough to skate without catching a wheel in the cracks or staggering over heaves made by tree roots. Her house stood in a row of houses which looked fancy to me, but Sam compared them to toy cars like his convertible—stamped out of tin into the same shape, only painted with different details. In his view, fake. Sam and I often disagreed, but when it came to style, I insisted that girls were born with an innate sense of elegance. I also pointed out that these were, after all, *real* houses with bathrooms bigger than closets, chairs that didn't turn into beds, and normal pianos.

Our piano, with sixty-five keys instead of eighty-eight, worked fine for me, but whenever Papa played it, he constantly thumped the wood at both ends of the keyboard. He laughed and said that his brain knew the keys were gone, but his hands didn't. Papa wanted to be a professional piano player and started out as a pick-up musician for shows traveling through Nebraska before he mangled the fingers on his left hand in the open fan blade of a hot rod he was building. Unlike his burns, he would tell and re-tell that story of the Olden Days, along with the motorcycle accident which blinded him in one eye. Papa told his stories differently every time—a form of creativity, not lying.

Mrs. Keindorf lived all the way across town, past the Methodist Church, past Bessinger's Small Engine Repair, even past Lincoln School, where Sam and I would begin 4th and 6th grade in less than a month. Along the way lived two terrifying dogs, a low-slung German shepherd and a Doberman pinscher like the one which had bitten me when I was five, so every time I could blackmail or bribe Sam to walk with me, I did. Reminding him that a Boy Scout should perform one good deed every day had no effect whatsoever, but offering to take an extra turn drying dishes did the trick, particularly if he felt that lethargy which overwhelmed even kids when both the humidity and temperature passed 95. Last week, Mrs. Dungan, the cook at the Home Plate Café, had fried an egg on the sidewalk, a summer tradition in every town where we had ever lived. Sam quibbled that it took two hours, which was no real measure of the heat trapped in concrete. She suggested that Sam measure the heat himself by standing there barefoot for two hours.

By my fourth piano lesson, I was growing less shy with Mrs. Keindorf, although nobody would ever call me shy. Since I changed teachers every time we moved, Mama warned me not to get attached to them, but with Mrs. Keindorf I couldn't help it. She looked as lonesome and exotic as a movie star, even plucking and re-penciling her eyebrows and wearing her long, wavy black hair parted in the middle exactly like Hedy Lamaar.

When I gushed about her, Mama told me to control my enthusiasm because it interfered with learning the piano. "Emotional outbursts" around Mama guaranteed a reprimand, if not the dreaded footstool, a major reason not to cry or even laugh around her. I realized that Grandma Strang raised Mama the same way, but I got tired of her threats to give me "something really to cry about." Actually, the trailer had room enough for only one person's outbursts, and Mama used it all. Mama said I should feel like a Very Lucky Child to take lessons at all, considering what they cost, instead of getting all wrapped up in my piano teacher. Knowing this was true, I fell silent, imagining a hundred better ways to spend my piano lesson money. For starters, on a pony.

From the beginning, Mama and Papa disagreed over Mrs. Keindorf. One Saturday when I was practicing Bach's Prelude in F in my John Thompson book, I overheard Mama and Papa outside the open screen door.

"They must have barely escaped Germany in time," Papa was saying. "Among the last refugees."

"With all her fancy-schmancy clothes? *I* should be such a refugee," Mama retorted. "Snooty, nose in the air . . ."

I couldn't stand it, I had to stop playing to defend her. "No, she's not," I called out. "She's the nicest lady—"

"Lady!" Mama shouted back. "Hussy! Her and her high-falu-tin' attitudes."

"She's the best piano teacher I ever had."

"If you think that will save her soul, you've got another think coming."

Save her soul? From what?

"She's a Methodist." I knew this wouldn't save her soul, but it was worth mentioning.

I heard Papa chuckle.

"You just practice and quit eavesdropping." She lowered her voice, "And her hubby the rich dry cleaner."

"Not so rich, Edie," Papa objected.

"Bought his own building on Main Street—didn't rent, mind you—bought it. That takes money. Money money money. Just to show the rest of us how poor we are."

"I heard Keindorf was a banker in Germany."

"Judith, I don't hear you practicing," Mama called out. "Frank, you work ten times harder than that . . . that Nazi."

"They aren't Nazis. Don't even say that word."

Mama could change her story as quickly as Sam could. "They're worse. How did some Germans come out of the war so rich? Huh? They throw it in everybody's face how some Germans got rich by losing the war."

"I wouldn't call anybody rich who barely escaped with their lives," Papa insisted.

"Who knows what deals they made with the Russians to get out?"

"What do the Russians have to do with—?"

"You think now the war's over, we can forget the Russians?" Mama often changed nursery rhymes to coded messages only she could decipher. "Rubies are red, and so are the Keindorfs."

"You shouldn't talk like that, Edie—"

"In front of Jeb?" She raised her voice, "Who isn't prac-ti-cing." To Papa she added, "Jeb's in loooove with the Keindorfs."

Papa insisted, "You know how rumors spread. The Keindorfs have enough on their plate—"

"They certainly do," Mama spit out, "and it isn't macaroni." She paused, listening for the piano. "Jeb!"

I resumed playing Bach's prelude so loud and fast no one would recognize it.

Mrs. Keindorf owned my dream furniture, a sofa and chair with wooden wagon wheels under the arms and plastic upholstery which pretended to be cowhide with cattle brands, horseshoes, and cowboy boots burned into them. The paddle arms were wide enough to hold small plates of cookies. When I admired her cowboy furniture, Mrs. Keindorf said tightly that it had come with the house and she would burn it if she could. Then her plump movie-star lips curved into a smile, not at all fake.

"I am naughty to say," her voice sounded like a wink.

I had to admit, the cowboys didn't go with the pictures on her walls. One showed a general with a droopy mustache and heavy medals on his bandolier, like a Boy Scout sash with huge jewels for merit badges. She told me her grandmother had lived in Vienna and had personally met this man, Archduke Franz Somebody. She added that the gas meter man had looked in her patio window and thought it was a picture of Stalin, if I could imagine, then she shook her head.

I shook my head the same way and couldn't wait to ask Miss Reynolds who Stalin was. Meanwhile, I took a stab. "Was he a Communist?"

"The worst of all," she answered, suddenly dark. "Head of the Party— for thirty-one years. He just died, you know. I think he was poisoned."

"Me, too," I answered. Wow. If you paid attention, real life sounded more like a movie than the movies did.

Over Mrs. Keindorf's blonde spinet hung a picture of a magic city full of castles and palaces, turrets and spires, probably a picture from a child's book. Sometimes I pretended that I was performing for the people who lived there, exotic people like princesses and ballet dancers and anyone else who rode in horse-drawn carriages. Every week, I added new palace intrigues, assassination attempts, love affairs, stolen jewels. Anything could happen in that city.

On top of the piano sat a mechanical metronome, a little wooden pyramid with a weight on a rocking arm which she could adjust from dead slow to speeding bullet. It felt as if the metronome didn't merely slice up existing time but actually controlled how fast time moved. You could slow happy times down to *largo* and race through bad times with *prestissimo*. While Miss Reynolds' date stamp controlled the days, months and years, Mrs. Keindorf's metronome determined minutes and seconds. Between the two, you could create just about any time you wanted.

Unlike my other piano teachers, Mrs. Keindorf dressed up for my lesson as if she were going to church. This made me feel guilty, since I suspected I was her only student. I always wore school dresses, although freshly starched and ironed. Today, her black hair was pulled up on the sides with jeweled barrettes and fell down her neck in lush curls. She was wearing a blue skirt , a powder blue silk blouse, and even blue high heels, which I had never seen on a real person, but only on a mannequin in the Brandeis department store in Omaha.

Even when you've practiced your music the same day and think you're ready, there's always something Terribly Wrong with your lesson. But Mrs. Keindorf invariably found at least one good thing, often as tiny as following the fingering she had penciled on my music. A teacher really had to care to notice such details.

Also unlike my previous piano teachers, she asked me to bring in music I wanted to learn to play, as if I should enjoy the piano. Unfortunately, all we had at home was the Methodist hymnal, some old sheet music with Shirley Temple on the front, and a volume of really hard honky-tonk music like "Kitten on the Keys," which Papa could play brilliantly with only half a left hand. From the hymnal I had taught myself "A Mighty Fortress is Our God," with noble words by somebody named Martin Luther. Sam said Luther was famous for more important things than writing song lyrics, but he didn't have time to tell me the whole story. In other words, Sam knew just enough about Luther to lord it over me. As our church organist, Maxine Harkin seldom played "Mighty Fortress," and never loud enough, although I kept requesting it. I told her it would bring in more money than the Doxology. At that, she raised her cloudy eyes to the ceiling and laughed a sound as soft as an organ note from the small wooden pipes.

Today Mrs. Keindorf sat on a separate chair beside the piano bench, adjusted her barrettes behind her perfect ears, and crossed her arms and long thin legs, a signal to begin.

I easily dispatched my scales and Hanon exercises, but my fingers tied in knots during Bach's Prelude in F.

THE ROUND PRAIRIE WARS | 97

She uncrossed her legs. "Why are you racing through Bach? Where is the house fire?" She rolled her r's like Ingrid Bergman and half swallowed the name Bach. Thrilling.

"I didn't want you to notice my mistakes."

She smiled. "Do you think your ruse worked?"

"What's a ruse?"

"A trick."

Another great word. "No."

I wanted to ask her if you played a song too fast, so it took only half the time it should, was it the same song? Or if you played it four times too slow? Did a piece of music exist in a particular block of time, which you shouldn't compress or stretch out, because then you might not be playing the same song? More than that, when Papa faked the bass, was it the same piece of music? How much could you change something without changing its real, deep-down self? I didn't know how to ask Mrs. Keindorf these questions. I didn't even know how to ask myself.

She played with her ring, a huge blue jewel, obviously fake, but one which matched her outfit. "What is the purpose of music, Jeb?"

Oh oh. This lesson was going from bad to worse.

Fortunately, she answered herself. "Music is a . . . bastion."

After *ruse*, I didn't dare ask her what a bastion was.

"That isn't the right word?"

I nodded yes, figuring it wasn't a lie to agree with someone if you had no idea what they were talking about, anyway.

Her voice thickened, as it did with Bach's name. "When the whole world is coming down on your head—is that the word?—music will protect you."

"Like a fort?" Now this was new.

"Fort? N-no. Not to fight someone." She chewed her lower lip. "They can bomb churches and schools and art museums and . . . people. But they can't kill music."

I didn't know what to say.

Fortunately, she gestured with one of her delicate hands. "Let's try Bach again—aiming for 'Moderato' instead of 'Presto'."

I aimed for it, but the way she smiled meant that I had missed.

While Mrs. Keindorf wrote my next lesson on a full-sized piece of linen stationery, once again I fell in love with her bony fingers, bony as Grandma Strang's, although she wasn't even as old as Mama. On her wedding ring finger were stacked five gold bands. When I asked Mama earlier if Mrs. Keindorf had been married a lot of times, she explained that in the Old World, women wore all the family's wedding rings which had survived—longer than the marriages, she added ha ha ha. On her right hand, Mrs. Keindorf wore different rings, like today's milky blue stone surrounded by little glass chips.

"Do you have any questions?"

I tried to sound nonchalant. "What is your ring?"

Obviously pleased, she extended her hand. "It's called a star sapphire. It's rare to find one so pure." She slipped it off her finger and held it out to me.

I jerked back as if it were hot. "Oh no. I might drop it." I had never heard of a star sapphire, but it sounded real.

She smiled her broad lipstick smile and closed my hand around it. "You couldn't hurt this ring. It has survived a great deal."

Still warm from her finger, the silver filigree held the smoky stone high, a mound the size of a large gumdrop.

"Catch the light on top of the stone and move it around. See that little star?"

I held a star in my hand and made it move. Magic. "How do they get a star into a stone?" I asked, halfway between panic and wonder.

"Sapphires develop that way; they merely polish them. I also have a star ruby, which I'll show you next time."

I had heard about rubies. Handing the ring back, I tried unsuccessfully not to say, "Wow. I'll bet you have real diamonds, too."

She slid the ring back onto her finger. "These are little diamonds circling the sapphire."

I sucked in my breath. Real diamonds the size of bb's. Although Sam was interested in telescopes right now, he would be impressed with the star sapphire information.

"If you like jewelry, someday I'll show you my collection. I have some beautiful emeralds—rings and earrings—and some loose stones. She paused. "My father was a jeweler in Germany." Her eyes went unfocused a little like Mama's. "It was all I could save when . . . Helmut and I . . . left . . . ."

"Did your mom and dad leave, too?"

"They, uh . . . " She cleared her throat. "They're dead."

I learned early, when people are dead, you should stop asking questions.

"For fun, would you like to learn a song you already know? Brahms' 'Cradle Song'." She paged through my new Fourth Grade book, stopping on page 72. "Why would they transpose it into six flats?"

Why was there such a key as six flats, I didn't ask.

From a stack on her piano, she pulled out a piece of sheet music. "Here it is. In the original key. E-flat."

She sat beside me on the bench and played a short, beautiful waltz. "Recognize that?"

I shook my head no.

"Of course you do." She played it again and sang along:

"Lullaby and good night, thy mother's delight,

Bright angels around, my darling, shall guard."

"I've never heard it."

"Maybe you heard different lyrics. They translate the German in different ways. Brahms' words actually say, 'Tomorrow morning, if God wills, you will wake again'."

I shook my head. This I would remember.

She insisted. "It's how your mother sang you to sleep when you were a baby."

I felt embarrassed and incomplete, as I always did when grown-ups talked about Mama. "She never sang it to me."

Mrs. Keindorf stood up and hugged the sheet music, frowning at me. "Really."

Quick and defensive, I added, "Mama sings other songs, like 'Gold Mine in the Sky' and 'Only a Shanty in Old Shanty-town' and 'Ain't We Got Fun?'"

Clearly Mrs. Keindorf didn't recognize any of these titles.

"But mostly Mama recites poetry. Like 'not only underground are the brains of men eaten by maggots'." Of all the things I could have said, I was sorry the maggot poem popped into my head.

Mrs. Keindorf kept watching me and listening, even though I had stopped talking.

"Actually, more like 'Somebody said it couldn't be done . . . .'" I trailed off.

On my shoulder, she put her hand, the one with all the wedding rings. "If your mother never sang Brahms' 'Lullaby' to you, then you *must* learn it." She paused. "So you can sing it to yourself."

When I got home, Sam was in the barn under Papa's trouble light, studying diagrams of different telescope lenses.

"Why don't you work on a useful merit badge, like Geology," I suggested with my most practiced offhand manner.

"What's so great about rocks? Except to throw?"

"Mrs. Keindorf has a sapphire ring which reflects a six-pointed star, no matter how you turn it."

"You're lying."

"Why would I make that up?" This was a good argument. "I *couldn't* make that up." This was an even better argument.

"I'll bet it's fake."

"Fake, schmake. I know what I know."

In two weeks, not only could I play Brahms, but also I could sing it in the original German. I began to love German because it often crammed several words together, like *Christkindleins*. One afternoon, I was singing Brahms' "Lullaby" to La Cheetah while we practiced figure eights, a very difficult maneuver for a stick horse:

"Guten Abend, gut' nacht, Von Englein bewacht,

Die zeigen in Traum, dir Christkindlein's baum."

Mama flew out the trailer door and shouted loud enough for Mr. Whitaker to hear. "Where did you learn that?!"

La Cheetah was startled, but I reined her in. "M-Mrs. Keindorf–"

"How dare that woman . . . ?!"

"It's to sing little babies to sleep," I defended myself. La Cheetah was positively dancing around.

"I know that." Mama's cheeks were shaking, she was so mad.

"You never sang it to me." For some reason, I felt like defending myself. "Actually, it's a poem—"

"Don't you sass me." Mama tried to grab my arm, but La Cheetah shied away.

"Why are some poems okay to say, and others aren't? Who decides?"

"Stand still, you little heathen."

Today all the unfairness fell on my head. Why was I always being accused of things I didn't even understand? Out of nowhere. Sometimes, you just have to put your head down and charge, even though you know your nose will get flattened. Like pouring more gasoline on Sam's anthills.

"I'm not a heathen," I insisted, although I couldn't say for certain what a heathen was. If Sam were here, he would have shaken his head and used Boy Scout hand signals for "halt" and "take cover."

Mama tried to grab my arm again, but La Cheetah wheeled around and galloped off.

"That's the end of that!" Mama screamed after me.

For several nights, Papa argued to keep Mrs. Keindorf as my piano teacher, pointing out that she was the cheapest teacher in town and the only one taking new students. Or would she rather have Jeb not take lessons at all. And after we'd paid all that money for the piano. And you always said that you wanted Jeb to learn music since you couldn't. And and and.

Mama finally relented.

In private, Papa suggested to me, "When you learn a song just for yourself, you're probably the only one who needs to hear it."

CHAPTER 10

KANSAS, 1 – NEBRASKA, 0

"PHILLIPS CARLIN REPORTING ... HISTORY IN THE making!" The radio announcer, usually a zombie, was practically shouting. "Today marks the end–I repeat, the *end*—of the police action in Korea! We'll have a full report following this important message."

The NBC chimes played what I now recognized as C – A – F.

The war was over! Oboyo boy!

Now Mama could stop worrying and she and Papa would stop arguing and everybody would sleep better and Reverend Harkin would have to preach about something religious for a change, although he would probably spend one more Sunday talking about how prayers for war were answered.

"I have a question," Sam talked fast, since we weren't allowed to interrupt the ten o'clock news.

Papa fine-tuned the radio dial around the flying saucer whistles to get better reception. Several women sang,

"You'll wonder where the yellow went when you brush your teeth with Pepsodent!"

A man's voice added with such fake enthusiasm you could tell he was lying,

"Brand new formula with IMP, for teeth much whiter, you can see!

And irium to fight tooth decay!"

Over the singing, Sam tried to be heard. "Why do they call it a police action and not a war?" He climbed into his sofa-bed. "That isn't fair. All those guys were killed."

Papa answered, "Truman didn't want to declare war officially on China. He just wanted to stop their aggression against South Korea."

Lying in my chair-bed, I crooked my finger signaling Papa to come closer and whispered, "Who won?"

He leaned over my face, smelling like Ivory hand soap, and whispered back, "We did: the U. S., the United Nations and South Korea."

Since the South Koreans were like Kansans, that meant Nebraska lost.

"What're you whispering about?" Mama asked from the folks' bedroom at the other end of the trailer. She had the hearing of a school teacher.

"I asked what irium is." I scared myself at how fast I could make up a lie to keep the boat from rocking.

"What irium?" Sam asked, incredulous.

"In the toothpaste commercial." I was so glad about Korea, I could practically see yellow disappearing from America's teeth.

Mama answered, "It's a fancy name for salt or sugar."

"You mean, it's a lie?" I asked, delighted.

"No," she clarified. "Commercials make up things all the time."

"What's the difference if–"

"That's enough, Jeb."

The announcer returned. "If you just tuned in, officials in Washington today declared the cessation of hostilities in Korea. Syngman Rhee has not yet signed the peace accord, but he is expected to do so imminently–"

"Peace, schmeace. He'll never sign it." Mama raised her voice. "Just ask Ralph."

"The expert on everything," Papa said under his breath. Papa wasn't best friends with Ralph because Grandma Strang thought Ralph was perfect and Papa wasn't even good enough to marry Mama.

"Although we have all been eagerly waiting for today," Carlin continued, "this conflict has claimed the lives of more than 36,000 American and United Nations forces, with more than 90,000 wounded, and an additional 15,000 estimated missing in action or prisoners of war. North Korean losses are inestimable but could approach *one million*. Stay tuned for the latest developments from your local NBC station throughout the night."

The news man now sounded so serious that I had to ask, "But the Communists lost, right? They're all dead."

"Don't be silly, Jeb," Mama called out. "They're all over the world: Russia, China, America. The more we try to destroy them, the stronger they grow. Attacking North Korea was like bashing a hornet's nest. It just scattered the Reds and gave them an excuse to retaliate."

Papa sighed, then pulled the sheet up to my neck. "It's nothing for a little girl to worry about." He tucked the sheet around my shoulders.

"If America won, why isn't everybody celebrating? You said at the end of World War II people danced in the streets and the fire sirens went off and— "

Papa kept his voice low. "Korea's been a different kind of war, Sugar. No Hitler or Pearl Harbor, just an invasion of a tiny country halfway around the world. I think a lot of people don't know why we fought it or what we've won, if anything. The most we can hope for now is an uneasy kind of peace." Papa looked tired.

Sam used his change-the-subject voice, which often came in handy. "Did the Braves win the double-header last night?"

Papa sat down on the edge of Sam's sofa-bed. "The Dodgers beat 3-2 and 2-1. 'Course, they had the home field advantage."

"The Braves are gonna lose the pennant, aren't they, Papa?"

Sam's favorite team of all time was the Braves, which had moved this year from Boston to Milwaukee. Papa said their new stadium in Wisconsin held 35,000 people, three times the number of people who lived in Hastings. All sitting in one place. I couldn't imagine.

"Well, the Dodgers have PeeWee Reese, Roy Campanella and Jackie Robinson. That's a tough combination to beat."

"We've got Warren Spahn," Sam said hopefully.

"It's never too late for the Braves, son. Not until the end of the very last game of the season. You know the old saying: 'The game isn't over 'til it's over'."

As I began to blur into sleep, Papa and Sam drifted away, murmuring about designated runners, pinch hitters, hit-and-runs, but why wouldn't every hit be a hit and run, and drag bunts and suicide squeezes and Texas leaguers . . . . All good horse names but I was too sleepy to get up and write them down.

If America's prayers were answered in Korea, then the enemy's prayers were ignored, so who decided whose prayers were answered, which was the same as who decided which side won the war. That must be God's job. But why would God be more in favor of Kansas than Nebraska? Did God decide whose house blew down in a tornado and whose stayed up? Did He decide that Papa would get burned in the first place, then live through it? But Baby Janet would die?

Grandma Strang believed in God's Plan, which no human could understand, but God had it all figured out down to the number of hairs on your head. Did that include how many M&Ms I would get for Halloween and who would win the World Series? Shouldn't God stick to big decisions like war, even if he seemed pretty arbitrary?

Who could answer my God questions? Reverend Harkin was no smarter than Marvin and almost as creepy, Miss Reynolds didn't believe in God but would be happy to gossip about him, and Mama's theories about God grew stranger every day. She and I now listened for his voice in the kitchen drain. Sam would answer with something about dice and probabilities, rolling . . . sevens and snake eyes. Maybe Mr. Whitaker . . . could help . . . and blind Maxine . . . would know a thing or two . . . .

"Good night, Kids." Amazingly, Mama called out from the bedroom.

I woke up enough to say the traditional Wilder family good-night, "I love everybody." I waited for some response, but no one answered.

CHAPTER 11

THE GLOBE OF DEATH

"**D**ID YOU HEAR THOSE STRANGE SOUNDS IN church last Sunday?" Mama asked above the wind coming in the car window, happy Saturday morning wind.

"You mean, Harkin droning on about how blessed are the meek?" Papa answered. "I'll bet that's his family motto. My dad always said, 'If you can't do anything useful, be a preacher'."

"Marvin shouldn't be the Scoutmaster, either," I chimed in.

"You don't know anything about Scouts," Sam loaded a rubber band onto the clothespin on his home-made wooden pistol. He had wrapped the handle with Papa's electrical tape, both to hold the clothespin and to look more like a pistol grip. Sam squinted his aim at me, then suddenly turned and shot the back of Mama's car seat.

"Pow," he spit, quickly adding a ricochet "ching" as the rubber band bounced back and hit him in the chest.

He pointed the empty gun at the doll on my lap, a monkey Mama had made from two of Papa's old work socks. She had wanted one like it when she was a little girl, but Grandma Strang ran out of men's work socks after Grandpa abandoned the family when Mama was only five. Wilder Rules prohibited any mention of Grandpa Strang, but we could talk about Grandpa Wilder until the cows came home.

I stuffed the monkey under my left arm and mouthed, "I'll scream." The Unwritten Code for Little Sisters required you to squeal if the brother attacked anything of yours, even if, deep down, you didn't really care. Sam changed tactics, balancing his blue Studebaker on the car seat long enough to strafe it with machine-gun fire from his right hand, now probably a P-38.

"Why do you say that about Marvin, Sugar?" Papa asked, looking at me in the rear view mirror. Only in a mirror did I notice Papa's artificial eye because it was on the wrong side of his face. It was hand-made from glass and exactly matched his good eye, right down to the little gold flecks around the blue iris. It was like wearing jewelry under his eyelid.

Mama answered, "He's a Communist."

"He's an undertaker." Remembering the church fans, I added, "That's a conflict of interest." I had heard that phrase but didn't know what it meant.

For some reason, Papa laughed as he navigated the Buick through the jog in the highway near Blue Hill, a little town on a hill nobody could find, let alone a blue one.

We were driving to Hastings for the first of the neighboring county fairs, my favorite events because almost everything was free, including samples of Kool-Aid, invented in Hastings in the Olden Days.

"I mean the banging in the basement during church." Mama wiped her neck with a hanky Grandma Strang had embroidered with bluebirds, "bluebirds of happiness" Grandma called them.

Sam reloaded his pistol and waited for the next sniper to jump from behind a passing telephone pole.

"Maybe they were fixing the plumbing," I offered, my hand sneaking toward the toy convertible Sam half hid under his leg.

I liked to ride in the Buick and in Sam's convertible at the same time. Especially when the Buick glided along smooth roads, Sam would squeal the toy car around imaginary hairpin curves, climb steep mountainsides, even jump across rivers where the bridge had flooded out. Unlike Papa,

Sam was a wild driver. He wouldn't let me drive with him as a passenger except in an emergency, he said. We hadn't hit an emergency yet.

"On Sunday? They weren't plumbers," Mama insisted. "They were Catholics."

"Maybe Catholics make better plumbers," I suggested. Sam slapped my hand away and stuffed the convertible further under his leg.

"Frank?" Mama didn't buy my explanation.

"I didn't hear anything," Papa slowed down for the turn at Ayr.

"All that hammering and sawing? I could barely hear the sermon. Just because you don't hear them doesn't mean they don't exist."

"I didn't hear anything, either," Sam added, letting his clothespin gun rest in his lap, although still loaded.

Mama turned in her seat to look at me. "Jeb heard them. Didn't you, Jeb?" She had let me spread out the rouge on her thin cheeks before we left home. She was growing thinner every week, thinner even than Mrs. Keindorf.

Sam shot me a look that warned me to be quiet.

"I heard something." I pushed the muzzle of Sam's gun away from me.

Triumphantly, Mama turned back to Papa. "See?"

Disgusted, Sam said, "She's lying."

I flared. "How do you know? I could have heard it."

Mama continued, "I know what the Catholics are doing down there, and it rhymes with gas."

Gas. *Mass*? I thought, wondering again why Catholics called church *mass*. "They have their own church, Mama," I reminded her. "Why would they use ours—"

"They wouldn't manufacture gas in their own church. What if it blew up?" Mama lifted her hair, limp with humidity, from her neck.

Sam instantly went on alert. "Blow up? What kind of gas?"

Papa used his hold-everything voice. "Everybody calm down."

Mama objected, "That's always your solution. Calm down. Calm calm calm. Don't rock the g.d. boat—"

Papa interrupted, "We're going to the county fair and we're going to have a good time."

Near Hastings, we passed the State Hospital for the Incurably Insane, which people called the Insane Asylum. Until I heard that, I always thought an asylum was a safe place, like a fort. The hospital had several three-story buildings arranged around grassy parks full of big trees. It looked like a school, except for the bars dividing the windows into tic-tac-toe squares. In a few of the squares I saw round white faces looking out like Mama's face at the trailer window.

"Frank," Mama pulled at Papa's arm and the car swerved a little. "Didn't Cecil Hauser put his wife in . . . .?"

Papa's jaw clamped and he nodded yes.

"What excuse did he give them? Besides the fact that he didn't want to be married to her anymore?"

"It's nothing for you to worry about, Edie."

"Just ignore the problem, and it'll go away. Right? RIGHT?"

Just in case Mrs. Hauser was one of the faces, I wiggled my fingers hello. What did people do all day in there? I didn't dare ask.

Although we could park for free on the fairgrounds, Papa paid a nearby farmer ten cents to park in his field, because everybody knew wheat prices were way down this year. Mama shook her head but didn't say anything.

We began in the building exhibiting the tallest cornstalks, the heaviest pumpkins and the most perfect home-canned tomatoes. Mama walked me through the prize-winning quilts, pointing out how tiny and regular the stitches were, as if they were done by miniature people. I wanted to tell her about the Dust People, but that would make her more nervous.

In another building, we watched a man who said more words per minute than I had ever heard except for an auctioneer, all while polishing a car hood with no car attached to it, using something called Like Nu 4 Cars. Papa asked him if this weren't just plain old pumice and he answered ono ono. When the man offered him a free trial, Papa laughed, "If I used that stuff on our Buick, it wouldn't just go through the paint, it'd go through the metal." People standing nearby laughed.

Next to the man with the car hood was a woman wearing slant-eyed glasses and a ruffled apron which Mama said wouldn't last five minutes in a real kitchen. She was demonstrating a magic solution which could clean anything in your house and "kill germs at the same time," as if everybody had germs. With sparkly eyes, Mama watched her scrub copper pans and marble sinks and toothbrush holders and other things nobody even owned, but it would work miracles if you did own them. Sam asked the lady what the formula was for the magic solution, but she answered with a smirk which said, in effect, she didn't know and wouldn't tell Sam if she did.

Outdoors, we admired the brand-new, magnificently red Farmall tractors, one of which was named "M," a rather subtle name for a horse. "G" would work, too, I made a mental note. The dealer let kids climb on the older models, but when we asked Mama if we could, she answered that, just because we were in Hastings and not in Round Prairie, we didn't have to act like heathens.

As we walked toward the small, traveling carnival on the edge of the fairgrounds, I saw more and more people eating cotton candy. My head turned with each color—pink, turquoise, pale lavender. Cotton candy was my one true dream food, even better than ice cream.

Sam, who could always read my mind, warned me under his breath, "Don't even ask."

We had eaten the sandwiches Mama packed but might get a treat later in the afternoon if we watched our p's and q's. Wilder Rules worked unpredictably: if you asked for something, you wouldn't stand a chance of getting it, but if you didn't ask for it, you might. Or might not. It took awhile to figure this out, in the same way that *yes* often meant *no* and vice versa, but not always.

Along the midway, people of all ages were throwing dimes into dishes and rolling balls up inclines into holes, all in hopes of winning bright green stuffed dogs or wide-eyed sequined dolls dangling from sticks. People were clapping and laughing, while somewhere a calliope whistled in the background. Papa asked me if he should try the shooting gallery. He felt pretty sure he could win a long-haired pink bear, and it only cost a nickel to try. Since Papa used to help feed his family during the Depression by shooting deer and rabbits on their farm, he was a crack shot. Sam and Mama waited for my answer.

"I think it's a trick, Papa," I answered. Sam agreed and Mama looked relieved. I didn't admit that I hated bears which were fake colors, especially pink ones.

Behind the shooting gallery, I nearly fainted. A sign wired to a temporary corral read

PONY RIDES 10 ¢

Inside were four real Shetland ponies, outfitted with children's saddles and bridles tied to a merry-go-round. Silently, I gave awards to the smallest horse, the one with the cutest mane, and the most unusual color, saving for the end the one I wanted to ride: a stout paint with stiff legs and a mind of its own. But riding cost a dime, which might as well have been a dollar, and probably required talent. I had never even sat on a horse and was so enthralled at the prospect that I didn't notice the family had walked on.

When I turned to catch up with them, a tall clown with purple hair blocked my way. His cheeks had big green target spots and his lips were painted all the way to his ears. He rocked from side to side with a fake chuckle and stretched his wide red mouth with his hairy fingers.

"Hey, little darlin'," he wheedled with a Tweety Bird voice.

I tried to sidestep him, but he stepped in my way again.

"I'm not your little darlin'." I didn't have to be polite to strangers. I looked past him to find Sam, now half a block down the midway.

"I'll give you a sucker if you let me kiss you," he twittered. He held a sack of candy in his cartoony glove.

"I don't like suckers," I lied.

He bent his face close to mine, and I could smell his breath, a mixture of kerosene and cigarette smoke. "Every little girl likes . . . s-s-s-suckers." His spit landed on my cheek.

Again, I tried to get around him, and he giggled. Suddenly, I saw Mama half running toward me, big and mad. I was going to get it for staying too long at the pony ride.

As Mama reached us, to my astonishment, she shoved the clown hard, my skinny Mama against a full-sized clown. "Don't you touch her!" She pushed him again, harder.

The clown staggered backwards in his cartoon boots, three times the size of normal shoes.

"Get away! Get!" She screamed at him like a dangerous dog.

People turned around to stare at Mama, which they always did when she shouted in public, but I didn't care a bit. Mama's arm had looped around my shoulders, if only for a moment.

"Thank you, Mama." As we walked back to Sam and Papa, I skipped to stay in step with her. I, Judith Beatrice Wilder, was walking beside my mother, who had just saved my life. Nothing could hold a candle to that.

At the end of the midway, a banner stretched between two poles with the sign:

THE GLOBE OF DEATH
Two Motorcycles Defy Death in a Cage!

Days Since Last Accident: 10

Someone had pasted the "10" over some other number.

Now it was Sam's turn to faint. "Can we watch? If it's free? Can we?" Last year, the Phillipsburg Fair had a free demolition derby, which had inspired Sam to wreck not just his bike, but Kenny Freeman's as well.

Then we heard it: a high-pitched buzzing like ten saws going at once. As we rounded the last booth, in an open field we saw a spherical cage containing two motorcycles which had evidently been racing each other inside. They were now stuttering to a stop, rocking up and back the rounded sides of the cage. People around the cage were clapping, shouting to them, shaking their heads.

"It's free!" Sam started to run so fast he nearly tripped, and I was close behind.

Inside a steel sphere about three times as tall as Papa, were two men on motorcycles which were idling, black smoke puffing out their tailpipes. For some reason, there was also a young woman standing in there. They were talking, trying to hear each other over the crowd and the mumble of their bikes.

Suddenly, each motorcycle revved and reared up a little way inside the cage wall. The lady stepped aside to miss them each time they returned to the center. What on earth was she doing in there?

Then, on some unspoken signal, both motorcycles screamed and began to chase each other, gaining speed until they were horizontal, whining like a thousand mosquitoes, while she still stood still at the bottom of the cage. The crowd cheered them on. As if this weren't enough, one motorcycle veered off its horizontal course to circle the cage over the top, so its rider was upside down half the time. This bike came within inches of the lady standing there, deathly still, as if she were part of the cage itself. Faster and faster, like frenzied bees.

By now, the crowd was gasping in disbelief, screaming with excitement, shouting at each other and the motorcycles. I couldn't watch and I couldn't look away, terrified for all of them, disbelieving what I saw, like a bad dream or hallucination, but I knew it was real because Sam was pushing me, shouting, leaning one way then the other as if he were riding, too.

I hadn't noticed that Mama and Papa had come up beside Sam and me until I heard Mama scream. As if she were hypnotized, she watched the cage, breathing fast and hard. "GET!" she shouted. "OUT!"

Papa was trying to talk to her, but she was in some kind of trance. "They CAN'T!!"

Papa pulled on her arm with no effect. Her eyes were moving in circles with the motorcycles. "GET . . . OUT!" She turned to Papa with tears in her eyes. "They won't! Let them out!"

By now, I was watching Mama more than the Globe of Death, although the scream of the motorcycles was deafening. Burying her fingernails in Papa's scarred arm, Mama pleaded, "They'll put me in there! Frank! Don't you see?"

Papa was now pulling her away from the crowd, which was fixated on the motorcycles. Anguished, Mama cried, "YOU! Lock me in there?!"

The motorcycles began to slow down, then, again rocking up and back down the sides of the cage, came to rest, one on each side of the young woman.

In spite of his sunburned face and neck, Papa had turned pale. He patted Mama's hand that was clawing his arm, then linked it through his arm and stumbled with her away from the Globe of Death.

To Sam, still mesmerized with the steel cage, Papa said, "Sam, meet us at the Ag Building, the first place we went. Watch out for Jeb."

Not until they rolled the motorcycles out of the cage into the cheering crowd did Sam notice the folks had gone.

"Do you know what we just saw? What it takes . . .?!"

I didn't know, and I didn't care. I was just staying glued to my brother.

When we met the folks in front of the Ag Building, Mama was drinking orange Kool-Aid from a paper cup but looking skittish. Sometimes a cold drink calmed her down.

"Does anybody need an ice cream cone?" Papa fished two nickels out of his pocket.

Sam and I looked at each other in disbelief and ran toward the ice cream booth, but before we got to the window, Sam stopped and held out the nickels in his open palm. He could be reading my mind. He puffed out his cheeks, causing his mouth to twist sideways, always a sign of Deep Thought.

"We should ask the folks, Jeb. About a pony ride. We shouldn't do it without asking."

If he hadn't offered, I might have tried to bribe and wangle, and I knew I might live to regret it, but I said no.

He instantly said, "Great!"

It was the best chocolate ice cream I have ever eaten, then the best strawberry. We switched cones halfway through.

As we left the fairgrounds that evening, Sam and I walked ahead of the folks across the trampled grass, watching grasshoppers gather in circles under each yard light, feeling the heat plastering our clothes to our backs.

Still dumbfounded, Sam sputtered, "Do you *realize*, Jeb? Gravity and . . . and . . . the forces at work? One tiny engine failure, one miscalculation in speed, one tire blow-out . . . "

We drove home a different way, skirting the Insane Asylum. Mama stared out the car window at the last remnants of sunset under the twilight line, clouds pink as Easter ribbons, fluttering under a blue-black ceiling. Her eyes kept closing and jerking open in the wind, still hot.

"Papa?" Sam asked quietly, not to disturb Mama. "What's the name of that force that spins stuff away from the middle of a circle?"

"Centrifugal force," Papa answered softly.

"And the one that pulls things in?"

"Centripetal force." Papa used his let's-all-be-quiet voice.

I would ask later how to spell such scary, powerful words.

*   *   *   *   *   *

For days afterward, Sam could talk of nothing but the engineering of domes and spheres, the construction of steel netting, two-stroke engines, forces and counter-forces and how they all related to speed. I encouraged him because, unlike the demolition derby, I knew that even Sam Wilder couldn't build a Globe of Death.

Meanwhile, every time I let it happen, I could hear those motorcycles screaming, could see, paralyzed and silent in their midst, the young woman staring straight out of the cage, by sheer force of will trying to keep gravity and every other law from dropping on her head and crushing her.

CHAPTER 12

PRELUDE

WHEN SAM LEFT FOR HIS PATROL MEETING, HE told me to perform reconnaissance, since our war maps of Round Prairie were woefully incomplete. On a hot July afternoon, I would normally have ignored his orders, except I liked both the words *woeful* and *reconnaissance*. Besides, I didn't have any friends or anything else to do. In Mama's words, business as usual.

I pulled my bicycle from under the trailer where we stored big things, a space Papa jokingly called our storm cellar. Last year, Papa had salvaged junk parts to build a bicycle for me, just as he had done for Sam when he turned eight. In his shop in Hebron, I had watched Papa flip down the Gort-like metal mask, spark the flame for the welder, cut through scrap steel tubing with fire and sparks, then heat and bend it into curves. The handlebars had been in some bad accident so Papa couldn't fully straighten them, but he said learning to ride with bent steering gear would not only slow me down but also teach me Valuable Lessons for Life.

"What lessons?" I asked.

"I could only tell you mine. You have to learn your own."

I could never tell if Papa were teasing me, but he did know almost everything, and this sounded feasible.

He wanted to paint it, but I liked the color of the plain steel pipe, especially the rainbows embedded in the welding at the joints. Mama told me to keep my eye out for rainbows which, I found, popped up everywhere you seriously looked. It helped to sing "Somewhere Over the Rainbow" while pretending to dance in Judy Garland's sparkly shoes. I rode my bike everywhere, but frankly, it wasn't very reliable. While my stick horse, La Cheetah, couldn't go nearly as fast, she could stop on a dime, never hit a missing gear tooth, and never had a flat tire. I hated to do it, but I had no choice: I named my bicycle Maybe.

Any reconnaissance mission had to start with my daily visit to Hested's window. Recently, I had renamed the little bronze horse Bunker, but Pinch Hitter also sounded good. Long ago, I had saved up enough fake allowance to buy it, but I wasn't sure how $2.35 in Mama's handwriting would translate into real money. In any case, I needed to name the horse first so it would recognize me and not go home with a stranger. On the Magic Slates in the window I pretended to write my new favorite words, *centrifugal* and *centripetal*, almost as fun as actually writing with the perpetual pencil and lifting them to disappear. This way, my writing couldn't be traced, a huge advantage for a spy.

The sign in the hardware store window next door was still missing letters. If I broke the anagram rules like Mama and added an 'n,' I could create important messages like "Send More Food" and "Include Donuts."

From the hardware store, I rode down the sidewalk on Main Street, where I might meet Miss Reynolds or someone else to talk to. If I felt desperate, I could always strike up a conversation with one of the friendly old farmers hanging around the front of the Home Plate Café. Mrs. Dungan, the cook, might come out to chat if she weren't busy.

When I reached the Pawnee Hotel, I dismounted so I could walk by slowly enough to watch my reflection in the huge window and catch glimpses of any people inside, as if I were simultaneously outdoors on the sidewalk and inside crossing the lobby. Sometimes I stopped smack still, pretending to inspect the geraniums in the window, but actually peering between them to see if the lobby were empty. When no one was around, I shaded my eyes, pushed my nose close to the glass and marveled at the cavernous lobby with the magic stairs (stairs!) behind the oak counter. Along the counter spread pads and blotters and shaded lamps, a huge old type-writer and—best of all—a wall of wooden cubbyholes for residents' keys and letters. The very best job in the world would be running the Pawnee Hotel and keeping all the newspapers and geraniums and tablets of paper and cubbyholes in order. That, or being a librarian. With my own date stamp.

People with Colorful Pasts lived in the Pawnee Hotel. I hadn't yet seen the chihuahua man, but I had actually met the opera singer. She must have been fat once, because now she looked like a deflated balloon, with her skin hanging almost off her face and chin. When she talked, her voice wheezed like an organ pipe which couldn't get enough air. On cool mornings, she dragged a lobby rocker to the sidewalk where she could smoke cigarettes and watch people pass. I never heard her sing, but I imagined that now she would sound like Mrs. Anderson, who sang solos in church with a high, vibrating warble which ran all around the notes but never hit them square. Every time Mrs. Anderson sang, even Mama covered her mouth with her hand.

Also in the Pawnee Hotel lived an old man who people said shot his crazy wife years ago when she was trying to drown their little girl. In the worst way, I wanted to find out if the wife went to prison, if the daughter survived and what she was like now. But try asking that about anybody in a small town, especially if you're new, you live in a trailer, and you're nine years old. For all I knew, this family had lived in the Inavale spook house. It could happen.

Mr. Whitaker said the new teacher in town had just moved into the Pawnee, and he thought she was the fourth-grade teacher, *my* teacher. Wouldn't that be something? To have my own teacher living in a romantic hotel bedroom with a bathroom down the hall, in a place smaller than a trailer. People who couldn't afford a hotel at all, like carnival folks and migrant harvesters, stayed in the trailer park north of town, some of them in tents. Mama and Papa forbade us kids to go anywhere near there, moving it to top priority for spy missions.

Across the street from the Pawnee Hotel was Eddy's Bakery, which had displayed the same wedding cake for months, actually a stack of cardboard drums covered with brittle gray-white frosting and faded crystallized sugar flowers, topped with a plastic bride and groom who would nicely fit in Sam's convertible. I hadn't yet gathered the courage to walk inside and pretend I was shopping, then casually ask for a sample of something they didn't need, like stale cookies. If Mama found out, she would cheerfully kill me. And she would find out. She should have a job with the FBI.

As I turned the corner, in the vacant lot behind the bakery I saw three boys shouting and chasing two others, who dived into the ground—*into the ground*—suddenly and miraculously invisible. I quickly parked my bike, plastered myself against the bakery wall and walked sideways, spylike, as Sam had taught me so I wouldn't attract attention.

The boys appeared and disappeared like prairie dogs, standing up unexpectedly, shooting real cap pistols and dropping back down into what must be a complex of tunnels and trenches. Near the back door of the bakery stood a machine which looked like a cement mixer. Its white enamel had rusted in places, but you could still read the sign:

Majesty Dough Mixer

The words were peeling off in blue ribbons. A boy's head popped up in the opening and ducked back inside. It was the most perfect ready-made hide-out I could imagine, even if its cave-like opening faced the street. If I hadn't seen kids in it, I would never have known this fort existed.

Near the abandoned mixer stood rusting metal cages, originally used as cooling racks for bread. Beside them was a 50-gallon barrel like most people in Round Prairie used for garbage. Suddenly one boy ran around the corner to the barrel, pulled off several handfuls of rubbery white material, and climbed inside the mixer. Close on his heels was a boy chasing him, screaming an admirable war cry and shooting caps at his back. The first boy instantly reappeared in the mixer opening and threw a small wad of the white stuff about the size of a ping-pong ball. Then he ate the rest of the wad. *Ate* it. It must be discarded bread dough. Brilliant! Whatever ammo didn't kill somebody you could eat.

I pedaled home wildly, hid Maybe in the tumbleweeds along the back fence, uncovered the branches from our fort and jumped inside to think. How many more secret forts existed in Round Prairie? Ours, exposed and isolated as John Wayne's outpost in "Rio Bravo," didn't qualify as secret or feel remotely safe like a fort should. Hardly a *bastion*, to use Mrs. Keindorf's word. No matter where we lived, kids always built forts— out of mud, dirt, scrap lumber, anything. Our fort in Hebron had been a cardboard refrigerator box, a perfect disguise.

I imagined myself on top of Mr. Whitaker's barn, from where I could see the fort behind Eddy's Bakery and tagged it with a target like the Boy Scout merit badge for Marksmanship. Ascending like a kite, I imagined seeing little targets scattered all through town, then across Webster County and nearby towns. There were thousands of them, just in Nebraska. Clearly, the war was much bigger than we had imagined. Round Prairie might look innocent to a casual observer, but now I knew it was riddled with escape tunnels, weapons stockpiles and even war rooms disguised as dough mixers.

Suddenly, a dirt clod sailed close to my head and pulverized behind me. Sam shouldn't be home yet, and even for a joke, he wouldn't aim at my head. I carefully peeked over the rim of the fort as PFFZHT! came another clod close to my ear. I ducked too fast to see who had thrown it, but it came from the alley.

How did they know I was here? Should I stand up and identify myself? Usually boys didn't attack a single, unarmed girl, but this was a new town, possibly with different rules. Maybe they saw me spying on them at the bakery fort, or they might be the kids who kept filling our fort with garbage. No matter what, I couldn't let them think I was chicken. Although I could throw only half as far and half as hard as Sam, the enemy needed to see a Wilder Show of Force. Gathering a handful of small clods from our supply, I quickly stood up, heaved them in their direction, and ducked back down. At least, I created a cloud of fine dust, in the windless day remaining suspended like a curtain.

Things stayed quiet for a moment. I didn't even hear the clod that hit me in the shoulder, exploding across the front of my dress. That stung. Another flew past and buried itself in the dirt. Well, I wasn't about to sit here like Deborah Kerr in "Quo Vadis" tied to the pole waiting for the Romans to kill me while Robert Taylor was tied to a matching pole in the stands near Nero. Too bad I hadn't yet taught La Cheetah to gallop over when I whistled for a quick getaway. Too bad I couldn't whistle.

I selected a short, fat stalk of broomcorn as my cavalry sword, took a deep breath, and did my best Errol Flynn leap out of the fort. As a precaution, I kept yelling "SHAZAM!" as I stumbled through the plowed earth, zigzagging as Sam had taught me to avoid machine gun fire. Dirt clods flew at my head.

Over my own shouts, I heard someone else's war cry. O lordy, how many of them were grouping for a counter-counterattack? Just then, I saw Sam running up the alley, scooping up rocks, cans and anything else he could throw. Reinforcements at three o'clock! When I reached the alley just ahead of him, I dropped my broomcorn sword and, like him, picked up small rocks. Sam could throw on the run, which I hopelessly admired. I ran beside him and at least went through the motions, looking good, I might say, even if I couldn't hit the broad side of a barn.

As I watched three boys running away, I recognized Leon Troxel, the boy with the scarred lip, and two others I didn't know. We chased them to the end of the alley, where we slowed down to a walk.

Panting, Sam asked, "What'd you do to them?"

"Nothing. I was just sitting here, waiting for you."

"They attacked you? With no provocation?" Obviously, he didn't believe me. I had been known to strike first, then neglect that detail in the retelling. Omitting details wasn't technically a lie, I felt.

"They could be from the bakery fort, the boys I spied on."

"Bakery fort?" Sam was loosening his Boy Scout kerchief. The folks could only afford to buy parts of the B. S. uniform—the kerchief and the bandolier for his merit badges.

"Or the kids who threw garbage in our fort."

"What bakery fort?"

We sat in our trench, both of us hot, sticky and covered with dust, while I debriefed on events of the afternoon. When Sam concentrated, his mouth turned into a straight line. He looked like Sergeant York as a boy, only smarter and without the funny helmet.

"You know what they're after, Jeb?"

I shook my head no. We didn't own anything that anyone else would want, including the Buick, the trailer and our home-made bicycles.

"They want . . . the formula." Sam drew lines in the loose earth with a short broomcorn stalk. "And they'll do anything to get it."

I had no idea what he was talking about, but the word *formula* sounded magic backwards as well—*alumrof*–just like *fort* and *trof.* "Sounds feasible to me," I agreed.

"Oh man," Sam kept repeating. "Oh man." I could tell that Sam was miserable–not because I had discovered the secret bakery fort without him or had been attacked by the enemy alone—but because he had missed the beginning of the first official battle of the Round Prairie War.

CHAPTER 13

CONSTELLATIONS

ON SUMMER NIGHTS, SAM AND I DIDN'T NEED TO bicycle far to find an isolated pasture where we could look at stars. All around us, lightning bugs silently glowed on and off, on and off, as if they were trying to compete with the stars winking overhead. The Big Dipper and the smoky ribbon of the Milky Way looked close enough to touch.

Who could see all that sparkle without making a wish or singing a song? Sam, that's who. Especially while he was working on his Astronomy merit badge. Mama said that the universe was full of creatures looking back at us, which provided me with some pretty unusual friends and fascinating conversations, but Sam relegated extraterrestrials to movies, unscientific theories and figments of my imagination. Nobody could suck the romance out of a situation faster than Sam. Honestly.

Over the coming year, Sam needed to identify ten "conspicuous constellations" and eight "first-magnitude" stars. Tonight, I needed to watch the meteor shower which happened near my birthday, the world's way of giving me hundreds of chances to wish on falling stars. Sam insisted that falling stars were actually dirt clods dropping from space in a fiery journey through the earth's atmosphere. I insisted that everybody else called them stars, including Jiminy Cricket and Frank Sinatra, who would not sing about falling dirt clods, I might add.

Sam spread out the star chart he had borrowed from the library and, using Mr. Whitaker's old flashlight, tried to match the flat map to actual stars in the shimmering dome overhead. I had never seen a map of the sky, just like a map of Nebraska, but substituting Orion and Scorpio for Valentine and Scottsbluff. Tonight, Sam began by outlining Sagittarius the Archer, his little boy finger drawing a connect-the-dots picture across the heavens. I could only see a square and a triangle forming a little teapot.

Irritated, Sam pulled me to him so I could sight up his arm. "Look harder. He's a centaur."

That was the problem. "What's a centaur?"

"A man with a horse's body. See him?" Sam's finger conducted a silent tune against the scattering of glitter overhead.

"What kind of horse?"

He dropped his arm. "Who cares?"

"How can a man have a horse's body?" This was definitely worth looking into.

"Who knows? Sagittarius was in ancient astronomy books, that's all. Like Pegasus." In the light breeze, Sam kneeled on two corners of the star map to keep it flat.

Pegasus, the flying horse, I had seen on Mobilgas signs. "Where's Pegasus?" Even I couldn't miss a flying horse.

"He's not up yet."

"When does he get up?"

Sam hit the flashlight to make it brighter, but it blinked off and back on, a dangerous sign.

"How would I know?"

"You're the Boy Scout, authority on the universe."

While Sam concentrated on the star chart, I tried to find anything resembling a centaur. "You know, just because some crackpot sees a pathetically deformed horse in the sky doesn't mean we have to. Who makes up this stuff, anyway?"

"You're mad you can't find it."

I counter-attacked, "If we lived *inside* Sagittarius, none of the constellations would look like this, anyway. Right?"

Trying to find a first magnitude star named Vega, Sam answered in exasperation, "In case you hadn't noticed, we're Earthlings—at least everybody but you—and this is how the stars look from Earth. Who cares what they look like from Sagittarius?"

"I just wanted to remind *somebody* that the stars don't form *real* pictures. Somebody *else* just dreamed them up and is forcing us to see what they saw. Figments of their imagination." Two could play the figment game. *Figment*, one of Mama's favorite words, reminded me of Fig Newtons, Sam's favorite cookie, which Mama never bought. We had to eat home-made cookies.

"Centaurs are myths," Sam added, as if this clarified something.

"Myth, schmyth," I said, remembering too late what Mrs. Meyers, my third grade teacher in Hebron, had taught us. Now that I thought about it, *myth* could be another useful defense for fibs, like *faith* or the *subjunctive*. It would not help, however, when push came to shove about my playing hooky from Brownie meetings. Brownies might be subjunctive but were definitely not mythic.

"That's gotta be it," Sam pointed directly overhead. "See that big bright star? Vega. The cluster of stars around it is named Lyra."

I saw an immense eye looking directly down on us. "Wow. It should be called the Eye."

"You are hopeless."

"The Eye of the Universe. That sounds better than Vega."

After that, I began building my own constellations, random and irresponsible as an astronomer or Boy Scout. Besides the teapot, I found a pentagon, a pyramid and several kites. If I strained, I could turn the Little Dipper into a tricycle.

"There's Cassiopeia, the Westinghouse 'W'." Sam added it to his tally on a scrap of paper on his knee.

This gave me an idea. Instead of sketchy diagrams of maimed animals, we could find letters in the sky. Or whole words. Instantly, the sky was crammed with L's, T's, and I's, U's, V's and M's, which spelled "mom," "lit," "wow" and "tilt" right off. It could take quite awhile to create something interesting like "metaphor" or "conundrum."

"Guess what else about Sagittarius?" Sam asked, his flashlight growing dimmer.

Who needed more than a horse with a man's head and arms?

"If you look through it, you're looking toward the center of our galaxy." Sam pointed to the star map. "You know where that puts us?"

"In a field outside Round Prairie, state of Nebraska, country of the United States, continent of–"

"In the Milky Way, Dumbo. The Milky Way is a wheel, and we're a third of the way down one of its spokes."

"How do you know the Milky Way's a wheel?"

"Mr. Harkin said so. But I'll be able to prove it when I finish my Astronomy merit badge."

"Marvin the Carver is an undertaker. He doesn't know about anything except bodies. Dead bodies and yucky stuff."

Sam sometimes sounded like Mama. "I don't know what you have against Mr. Harkin."

"Papa says that being related to a preacher is three strikes against him. Besides, he's dumb."

"Papa doesn't care if somebody's dumb." Sam folded up the star chart. "That's why he likes you."

"Papa doesn't like people who pretend to be something they aren't. Marvin pretends to be sooo nice, but he looks at . . . ladies . . . . and treats Maxine . . . creepy."

By now, a star was falling about every minute, sudden sparkling marks against the background glitter. They vanished as soon as you looked at them.

"Quick! Make a wish," I reminded him.

"You cannot possibly believe there's *any* connection between the wishes of some dinky little girl and the motions of the stars. Or in this case, falling rocks."

"I can't afford to pass up any chance for getting a horse." Lately, I had come down several notches to wishing for a saddle. As a last resort, I would try for a horse blanket. But not until Christmas.

"Isn't that a first-magnitude star?" I pointed to a particularly bright one. "You can wish on normal stars. They don't have to fall." I neglected to add it should be the first star you saw that night.

"That's not a star. It's a planet."

"How do you know?"

"If it doesn't twinkle, it's a planet."

"You're making that up."

"It's reflecting light, rather than burning itself. Mr. Harkin said so."

I looked again, and sure enough, it didn't twinkle. I had been wishing on planets for years. No wonder my wishes weren't coming true.

*　*　*　*　*　*

The next day was my ninth birthday, and we drove to Hebron to visit Grandma Strang and Uncle Ralph. I had hoped we could stay home and split four ways the cake Mama had made: a two-layer spice cake with vanilla frosting and nine blue birthday candles. But Good Girls shared their cake. This Good Girl could only hope that everyone hated spice cake or at least recognized that I needed cake more than they did, especially since my cake was also my only birthday present. Neither of these hopes came true.

Drives to Hebron always grew stickier the closer we got. I didn't know why, except Grandma Strang didn't like Papa much, and that made Mama mad, and she took it out on us kids, and Papa defended us, and then they argued over money and Communists. Sam counted telephone poles the whole way, even though he had memorized the number long ago.

"Hey, everybody."

"Don't say 'hey,' Judith," Mama warned.

"We could all sing Happy Birthday."

Sam rolled his eyes toward the roof liner of the Buick.

In the lengthening silence, I realized I had to sing it to myself, as Mrs. Keindorf had taught me to do with Brahms' "Lullaby."

"Happy Birthday to me," I started softly but grew louder with each repetition. "Happy Birthday to me. Happy Birthday, dear Je-e-eb . . ."

"That's enough," Mama snapped.

I practically shouted, "Happy Birthday to ME."

If I had known the words, I would have sung it in German just to make Mama even madder.

Uncle Ralph built basements where he lived until he could finish building the rest of the house overhead, which he sold and then moved into the next basement he had already finished. I liked his houses best when they were still almost flat with the ground, with only the stairwell and back door sticking up like a big periscope. As his houses progressed, I liked to play in the skeletons of rooms, sometimes pretending the empty frames were solid walls I could sail through like a ghost, at other times transforming them into prison bars from which I had to escape like a prisoner of war. In the three months since the tornado, he had built houses all over town but not his own house.

Uncle Ralph wolfed down his piece of my birthday cake in seven bites. "The other day Stutz Johnson called me a goddam prairie dog for living underground, but nobody who's ever been down here bitches about the heat."

Both Mama and Grandma Strang winced at the words *goddam* and *bitch*. Wilders weren't allowed to talk like that.

"They laugh now, but, by God, when the Big One happens, they'll be laughing out the other side of their mouths."

I wondered where the other side of someone's mouth was.

"What Big One?" Sam asked.

Papa was mashing the last of his cake crumbs with his fork to gather them up. He didn't like sweets, the only trait about Papa which made me doubt we were related. He had eaten the spice cake out from the frosting, leaving a perfect empty shell of his layered piece like a miniature bookcase on its side made from frosting. I couldn't take my eyes off it.

Mama went to the kitchen, and Papa stealthily traded plates with me. Boyo boy. I could feel Sam's gaze, hot as Gort's, practically melting the frosting until I divided it and scraped half onto his plate, repayment for the vanilla wafer he sneaked to me the night I spilled my milk. Under the table, he lightly kicked me, Sam Code for "thanks."

"Edith's getting screwier every day," Uncle Ralph raised his voice so she could hear him. "The Reds hiding in the woodwork in Hebron or Round Prairie aren't the problem."

Coming from the kitchen with coffee, Mama answered, "Just open your eyes. You'll see them everywhere." She didn't notice the extra frosting on Sam's and my plates.

"If you wanna really go crazy, Edith, don't worry about the goddamned Commies and Catholics and poison gas. Worry about the H-bomb." Uncle

Ralph leaned back on two legs of his wooden chair, also against Wilder Family Rules. He had the same pale blue eyes as Mama, and his hair was also thick and wavy, although his didn't need to be dyed brown.

"Let's don't start that again," said Grandma Strang. She was so thin you could see every bone in her arms. Even in summer, she wore three dresses on top of each other to warm up and pad herself out.

Ralph insisted, "If Eisenhower's so gung-ho about defending us from the Reds, he should dump Hoover and McCarthy and play poker with the hydrogen bomb."

Grandma Strang had almost no lips and a tight smile which barely covered her false teeth. Her teeth were loose and clacked when she talked. "You children go outside."

This seemed a good time to ask, "Grandma, can I walk over to your house to visit your nested dolls?" I was secretly hoping that if I strategically mentioned them, she might give them to me for a birthday present.

"What on earth are you talking about?"

Mama intervened. "You remember those painted dolls from Russia? Five or six of them fit inside each other. The Sturdevants gave them to you one Christmas."

The Sturdevants were rich people who paid Grandma to do their ironing in the Olden Days.

"What's a hydrogen bomb?" Sam was riveted at the mere mention of explosives.

"Stuff and nonsense." Grandma Strang pointed at the stairs leading up to the outdoors.

Strictly against the rules for Respecting Our Elders, Sam argued, "Children need to know more than anybody. We're the next people to take care of the world."

I tried a new tack, "After you eat a person's cake, don't you think you should sing Happy Birthday?"

"Kids should keep their mouths shut," Uncle Ralph snapped.

I looked from Mama to Papa for defense, but they stared at the tablecloth. Sam glared at Ralph.

The louder Ralph grew, the quieter Papa talked. "It's all scare tactics, Ralph. If Hoover and his thugs keep us scared enough, they can do anything they want, and people are dumb enough to go along with them."

Uncle Ralph snapped, "The H-bomb isn't some goddam scare tactic. It's the most powerful weapon ever created."

"What's an H-bomb?" Sam tried again.

Uncle Ralph lurched forward on his chair and banged the table for emphasis. "The U. S. tested one last November. It was *seven hundred times* more powerful than the A-bomb we dropped on Hiroshima, for Chrissake. Now tell me I'm crazy."

Papa rolled up his sleeves another fold. Above the sunburned scars on his forearms, his skin was white and soft. "That doesn't mean the Russians have one."

Uncle Ralph almost spit. "Don't be stupid."

I flared. "Papa's the smartest man in the world."

Uncle Ralph ignored me. "You think the Commies have the A-bomb and not this one? Everybody knows they're gonna test one. Any day now."

"Nobody's calling you crazy," Mama added quietly.

"People call me crazy all the goddamned time." Uncle Ralph threw his head back to finish his coffee and gestured vaguely at Grandma. "Both of us, Edith. Nuttier'n goddamned fruitcakes."

Grandma Strang suddenly stood up to gather dishes, and Papa followed her into the kitchen with cups and saucers. I took this chance to go to the bathroom, where I knew I could spy on them.

While Papa stacked the dishes, Grandma asked quietly, "Is Edith sleeping any better?"

"I think she catches up in the middle of the day."

"You've got to keep a closer eye on her."

"How am I supposed to do that from work?"

"She's getting more peculiar every day. Doesn't make sense half the time."

Papa answered, "Everybody's nerves are worn out. Now we've got McCarthy and his Un-American Committee . . ."

"All I know is, people are beginning to talk. Even in Hebron."

"Hebron's famous for that. One reason I wanted to get out of here."

Behind the bathroom door, I felt the urge to sneeze but clamped my nose shut.

"What will you do if she gets worse?"

"Well, I won't walk out, if that's what you mean. Not like some men we know."

"Throw that in my face, why don't you? Edward had no reason—no reason on earth—to leave me and the children except his own selfishness."

It took a lot to stir Papa up, but Grandma could do it. "He was an inventor, Bea. Something you wouldn't understand."

"You always defend Edward. You weren't with him, day after day, him sitting around, doing nothing, daydreaming . . ."

I heard a pan drop into the sink, then Papa's voice. "He could listen to a strange machine with his eyes closed and tell you what was wrong with it. Then invent some way to fix it—with stuff he found laying around. That's genius."

"—deserted me with two children and another on the way. No wonder I lost the baby . . ." Grandma began the familiar refrain in the voice she reserved for this story, a chant no one listened to, like the Lord's Prayer.

For a minute, dishes chinked, and they stopped talking altogether.

Finally, Grandma sighed. "Bring her home, Frank."

"She is home. Home is where our family is."

"In that miserable trailer house. When I think of you moving Edith all over God's green acres, never knowing where she's moving next, it's no wonder her nerves are . . . ."

They were both silent. I didn't even hear dishes moving. Papa quietly answered, "It's all we can afford right now."

"She should never have married you."

"When have I heard that before?"

"She could have married the richest men in Hebron."

"She must have loved me more than money."

"Love," Grandma sneered. Finally she said, "She needs a doctor, Frank. Hebron's got Doc Perry or Doc Zeigler."

"A chiropractor and an obstetrician, both pushing eighty. They should be a lot of help. Besides, Round Prairie just got a new doctor. General practitioner."

Grandma snorted. "A woman. Worse than useless. Let me take care of Edith."

"You've taken care of her enough to last a lifetime, thank you."

A cupboard door banged. "The druggist—you know Henry Duncan—told me about this new medicine. It's for sleeplessness and general . . . mental problems."

Through the crack in the door, I saw Grandma hand Papa a flat brown bottle with a peach-colored label.

"It's called Miles' Nervine." He tried to hand it back, but she pushed it at him. "At least, have her try it. It can't hurt."

Suddenly, Uncle Ralph shouted from the living room. "The horse is outta the goddamned barn. Korea's just the beginning, the Reds'll see to that. And it won't be poison gas or secret elevators. Brainwashing isn't science fiction, Edith."

Papa and Grandma walked back to the table, and, a minute later, I followed them.

Sam ventured, "The North Koreans are the same as the South Koreans." I was always proud of Sam. Even with grown-ups, he held his ground.

"What the hell do you know? You're a goddamned kid," Uncle Ralph sputtered.

I jumped in with reinforcements. "Papa said they're like Nebraskans and Kansans–"

"Your father's full of . . . beans." Ralph glanced briefly at Papa, then looked away.

I stood beside Uncle Ralph, which put me eye to eye with him, and said, "You can't talk about Sam and Papa that way."

"The hell I can't. This is my house." His hair was falling in his eyes, but he wouldn't look at me.

"You're not our dad." I added, "You're nobody's dad."

"It's a goddamned good thing." Uncle Ralph's face was so red I thought his eyes would explode.

"Jeb!" Mama warned in her footstool voice. I didn't care.

Papa decided, "It's time somebody went outside to play."

Sam reluctantly asked, "Uncle Ralph, can we look at your observatory? I'm working on my astronomy–"

He waved us away angrily.

From the stairs out of the basement, Papa turned back to say, "You know, Ralph, we could get that telescope working again. I've got plenty of spare parts, an old electric motor–"

"Frank drags around enough junk for four people," Mama sighed. "Believe me."

More to himself, Ralph answered, "What the hell did I think I was doing, building that damned thing?"

"You're an astronomer," Papa answered.

"Yeah, an astronomer who lives underground half the year, building cheap houses over his head in a podunk town in the middle of nowhere. I'm sure gonna set the world of astronomy on its ear."

Papa answered, "Why can't you just look at the stars and enjoy them?"

"Because any halfwit can look at stars. Astronomers find something new, make a contribution to the field."

We picked our way cross the vacant lot full of dead grass and tumbleweeds toward the observatory, a stucco cube with a half dome on top. The dome had a wide slit covered with rotting canvas, and its door hung on one hinge. After the cool basement, the sun pushed down on our heads like a giant hand.

"Why is Uncle Ralph always mad?" I ventured.

"He sure swears a lot," Sam added.

"Sometimes what sounds mad is actually something else. Everybody's on edge right now." Papa kicked some dirt away from the observatory door. "Jeb, you know you hurt Uncle Ralph's feelings. You'll have to apologize before we go home."

"He hurt our feelings," I shot back. But, since Papa never scolded me without a reason, I backtracked. "When?"

"When you said he was nobody's father," Papa continued.

"It's true," Sam defended me.

"Ralph wanted to be a daddy. In the worst way."

"He could've gotten married like everybody else, and . . . and . . ." I didn't know exactly where to go from there.

"Yeah," Sam echoed.

Papa pushed and pulled on the observatory door, trying to free it from the dirt which had piled up both inside and out.

I floated the usual reason. "Are we too young to know?"

Papa answered slowly, "Grandma Strang . . . needed him around . . . to help her."

"Grandma Strang doesn't need help. She's tougher than whang's leather." I didn't know what whang's leather was, but I had heard Mr. Whitaker use this expression.

Papa laughed. "I must admit, she's doesn't seem very helpless."

Sweat trickled between my shoulder blades. "I'm sure glad Grandma wasn't my mom."

"She was awfully hard on Edie, that's for sure." This was a new level of admission from Papa, the perfect opportunity for me to push.

"Was it . . . about a lady? Was Uncle Ralph in love?" I would make up stories as long as nobody stopped me, running as fast as I could in any direction until I hit a fence. "And Grandma Strang . . . hated her and had her . . . sent away—"

"Papa," Sam warned, "Jeb'll go on all day." He yanked on the broken door.

"But I'm right, aren't I?" I squinted at Papa through eyelashes twinkly with sweat.

"Close enough."

This cast Uncle Ralph in an entirely new light. I had never thought of him as a romantic hero, but here he was—right in my own family. He might be good for something after all: I could make up alternate lives for him indefinitely.

Inside, the observatory smelled dry as a feed store, suffocating with dust and heat. Sunlight filtered through the dirty windows and the canvas slot in the roof, dropping to the dirt floor littered with mice droppings and scrap metal. Spider webs draped everything like gauze bandages. Unlike the Inavale house, there were no bottles, rags or other junk, as if nobody cared about the little building enough even to invade it.

In the center of the room a metal stand held a complex arrangement of gears, handles, and shafts, which Papa touched like fine china. He loved mechanical things, especially if they were hand-made for some unique, complicated task. His tool box at home was full of wrenches and crowbars he had cut up and re-welded to do a single job, like to remove a bearing from deep within a tractor wheel. Mama often complained that Papa would rather waste half a day inventing a new system or tool than actually fixing the thing itself.

"Where's the telescope?" Sam asked Papa.

"It was probably mounted here," Papa slid his hand over a flat metal plate. "All Ralph needed was a little motor–like from a sewing machine— to run these gears. He must've used those tractor gears over there to move the dome."

I looked overhead. "The whole dome? Why?"

"To follow the moving stars, Dumbo," Sam said. "Stars don't stand still."

"Who are you calling that name?" Papa asked in a voice that made you want to stop talking for the rest of the day.

Sam retracted, "I meant 'Jeb'."

"I knew you did," Papa answered.

Lifting the yucky spider webs with a short piece of lath I had found, I unearthed a metal tube among shards of glass. It looked like the surveyor's level Sam and I had used earlier, but the tube was scratched up and slightly bent, as if someone had hit it hard against something.

"What's this?" I asked.

Papa took it from my hands. "By gosh, it's Ralph's telescope. Good detective work, Sugar."

Papa's praise was my second birthday present this year, almost as good as my cake.

"Do you think he destroyed it on purpose?" Sam asked.

Papa polished the tube on his trouser leg, then turned it over and over in his hands. "It sure looks that way."

Sam asked, "Why would he do that, after building his own observatory?"

I could imagine living in an observatory, more magical than a real house.

"Maybe he got tired of looking at things so far away," Papa sounded sad.

"He had to grow up without a dad," I pointed out.

Sam added, "That'd be horrible."

"Your Grandma would be a hard woman to live with," Papa said quietly.

"That's for sure," I agreed.

He continued, "But no matter what kind of genius inventor you are, no matter how trapped you feel, to desert your pregnant wife and two little kids is pretty cowardly."

"You wouldn't leave us, Papa." I wanted to add, 'Would you' but I didn't dare.

Papa remained silent for a minute. "What Ed Strang did to his family is completely understandable . . . and utterly despicable."

Just then Mama called from across the vacant lot. "Frank! It's time to go."

"Then your grandma lost the baby." Papa looked around the observatory, a jumble of metal Pick-up Sticks, and shook his head. "It's all a darned shame."

Sam took the broken telescope. "Can we take this home and try to fix it?"

"Ask Ralph. And Jeb–"

"I know. Apologize." As they pulled the observatory door shut, I added, "For telling the truth, I might add." It didn't seem fair to get punished for lying *and* for telling the truth.

At the car, I touched Uncle Ralph's sleeve to get his attention. "I'm sorry." This was a *true lie*.

"For what?" He frowned.

"For being sassy."

"Everyone gets to be sassy on their birthday."

I was amazed. At least he remembered whose birthday cake he had wolfed down.

"I have a question," I said to Ralph while looking at Sam. "Why don't planets twinkle?"

"Why in God's name would you want to know that?" Uncle Ralph barked, but underneath he was pleased, you could tell.

"Because Sam's Scoutmaster said–"

"–that they reflect light, rather than burning themselves," Uncle Ralph finished my sentence.

Sam looked at me triumphantly.

"Which is hogwash. Planets don't twinkle because they're so large with respect to us, so close that we can see the whole disk–which never 'goes out' all at once."

Sam's eyes were not twinkling as he listened.

"Stars are point sources of light. Because they're so far away, their light takes multiple paths through our atmosphere to our eyes and seems to be 'blinking' due to the interference of light waves."

I hoped that Sam understood that, because I certainly didn't. But Uncle Ralph had just scientifically proved that Marvin Harkin was full of ... beans.

* * * * * *

We never left Hebron without visiting our family graves at Rose Hill Cemetery. Walking across the brown grass, Sam quietly sang "Happy birthday dear Jeb." By telepathy and our own unspoken rules, it didn't seem quite right to sing the birthday song very loud in a cemetery.

"Thank you thank you." He really could be the best brother.

"The stuff about planets was great." That was Sam's way of thanking me back. We both knew he would get a lot of mileage out of that information with every Boy Scout, not to mention Marvin the Shark.

After we all stopped at the graves of different shirttail relatives, Sam and Papa set out to look at the oldest tombstones, tiny marble tablets with pictures of angels or hands with one finger pointing skyward. Many were children who had died in the 1918 influenza epidemic. It was always my job to go with Mama to visit my sister's unmarked grave, a little indentation in the grass next to the Stoetzer family tombstone. Stoetzer was Grandma Strang's maiden name.

To avoid Mama's sadness that they couldn't afford a tombstone for Janet, I asked,

"Did you ever play in Uncle Ralph's observatory? It would make a perfect fort."

"He built it when we were in high school, but he often showed me the stars." She slowed down as we approached Janet's grave. From Rose Hill, farmland sloped away in every direction, huge squares of pale wheat stubble alternating with plowed earth and dry pastures dotted with windmills. The clouds moved in little puffs, as if the dead were blowing smoke rings and watching their breath the way we did on cold mornings.

"Ralph loved to record stars and search for new ones. He's very smart."

"Not as smart as you are."

Mama smiled. "I'm so dumb. It's a shame Ralph couldn't be a scientist."

"Did you search for stars, too?"

"I spent my time making wishes on them."

"Oh, Mama. Isn't that remarkable? That's exactly what I do with Sam." I desperately wanted to hold her hand but knew she would shake me off, even on my birthday. "Did your wishes ever come true?"

Mama stopped walking and looked at something far away. For a moment, I was sorry that I had asked a question which let her escape through that door which only she could see. But this time, she looked back at me. "Yes. When I got my two little children."

"And Janet. Makes three."

Mama sighed. "Janet was a wish that didn't come true."

We looked down at the grassy indentation. Without Mama, I could never find the dead Stoetzers, let alone Janet.

"You know, Janet died on my birthday. I was driving in a thunderstorm when the old truck skidded off the curve at Ayr."

I knew this story, but Mama herself never talked about it.

"Born alive. If the county hospital had owned an incubator, Janet would have lived." Mama was starting to drift into the sadness. "Grandma Strang held her. Said even three months premature she had . . . red . . . hair."

I tried to pull Mama back. "If Janet had lived, maybe you wouldn't have wanted me."

Mama talked to a phantom standing behind me. "You're right. I only wanted two children."

"You mean–" I began swallowing the hot wind. "You would've had Janet and Sam and then quit having babies?"

"Yes."

I had to make certain I understood. "And I never would have been born?"

Mama remained silent, a long, loud silence in the wind blowing the tall cottonwoods surrounding the cemetery.

I had never thought of this before, never considered my existence as dependent upon chance, a chance thunderstorm on Mama's birthday so many years ago. I had never thought of my life as an alternate to someone else's. It was *either* Janet *or* me, but not both.

I managed to choke out, "Then wh-who would have been my mom and dad?"

"You wouldn't exist. You would have been somebody else."

I suddenly felt like crying. "There wouldn't have been any Jeb Wilder in the universe? Anywhere?"

"No. It took Papa and me to make you, exactly as you are."

How could she say that, and so calmly? My knees gave way and I sat down hard on top of Janet's grave.

Mama looked down at me and at the small depression under which Janet was buried, smiling her empty smile, then slowly glided off like a ghost.

How many Janets were in the cemetery? How many children were like me, alive only because somebody else had died? What if the dead ones were better people than the ones who lived?

I petted the brown grass on Janet's grave like hair, brushing it first one way and then the other. I didn't want to think what that tiny red-haired baby looked like now. My whole life I had resented Janet for being the perfect absent child–Little Girl Blue on some extended vacation in an exotic place, living in a fancy house–beautiful and smart, with store-bought clothes and maybe even a pony. I had never thought of her as a tiny skeleton with some strands of red hair, buried in the cold earth, in darkness forever.

I kept swallowing back tears but finally managed to whisper, "I am so sorry, Janet. You were such a tiny little baby and didn't have a chance. It wasn't fair, I know. But, Janet, thank you . . . for . . . dying. So I could live."

CHAPTER 14

VISIGOTHS

"DO YOU BELIEVE IN CENTAURS?" I ASKED MISS Reynolds. She had tiny dots of sweat on her upper lip. With two high ceiling fans barely turning, the inside of the library felt sleepy and bored in the late summer heat.

"You always ask me something unexpected, Judith—one of my favorite qualities in a friend." Today her glasses hung from a silver chain decorated with small ruby buttons, part of her wardrobe of expensive necklaces for her glasses.

Watching my eyes, she added, "They aren't rubies. Or even garnets. Just glass."

What a mind reader. I started over. "Do you? Believe in centaurs?"

"*Belief* isn't quite the right word. They certainly exist in literature and myth, but—"

"I was hoping for a simple yes or no."

"Don't get snippy with me, young lady."

"I'm sorry."

"You should be."

I was feeling guilty because, once again, I was playing hooky from Brownies and would need to invent a fresh, new lie when I got home. Someday my Brownie lies would all come home to roost, but for now, they allowed me to create all kinds of imaginary friends, including a kindhearted Brownie leader, and even to describe the houses where we met. I left out the treats I didn't eat because that would cost me dessert at supper. When Mama discovered all these lies, I would spend the next ten years on the footstool, after which they would move me to the state pen.

"The most interesting questions can't be answered with a simple yes or no." Miss Reynolds put on her glasses, as if she had to see me before she could talk to me. She folded her arms across her huge bosom and leaned back in her shrieking chair. "Where did you see a centaur?"

"I tried to find one in the stars, but it didn't pan out."

"Sagittarius. Sam must be working on a merit badge in astronomy."

I reluctantly admitted, "To me he looked like a teapot."

"You told me that stars were to wish upon."

"Isn't that the truth." I slid into the wooden chair across from her and picked up the heavy date stamp with the rubber rollers. I rolled it back to my birthday.

"How has wishing on stars worked out for you, Judith?"

"Not very well. But I haven't lost hope. Papa always says to hope for the best, but prepare for the worst."

"Ah, the voice of experience."

"Why would anybody make a centaur out of a horse?" I envisioned all sorts of horrid surgeries attaching a bleeding human torso to a headless horse's body.

"People were less concerned with the horse part than the human part. It's a metaphor for being half man and half beast. Congress is full of centaurs."

She looked at my face, then asked, "Do you know what a metaphor is?"

"A special kind of lie used in poems."

"Close enough. We'll talk more about them later."

I continued, "Like a skull for death or movies where the earth is supposed to stand still." I rolled the date stamp to Mama's birthday, which was also Baby Janet's. And her death date. I was fascinated that all dates were present on the date stamp: all time was there, all the time.

Her hard little eyes squinted at me. "What's the matter, Judith Beatrice?"

I always felt nervous when grown-ups asked me a personal question and actually waited for an answer. "Mama thinks I'm at a Brownie meeting."

"Why aren't you?"

I kicked my feet back and forth in the tall chair, as if I were running on air. "We can't afford a Brownie uniform. I don't know what the stupid assignment was, since I haven't been there all summer." I looked up at her. Clearly, she wasn't convinced. "I hate Brownies."

"As a bunch of screaming little girls? Or a paramilitary organization?"

"The girls hate me, too."

When Miss Reynolds sighed, her whole, large upper half raised and then dropped a bit. "I know exactly how you feel." She slapped both hands on her desk. "Let's find you something to read. The library is full of people who don't hate you."

"But they're not real."

"Real people have very little to recommend them. For one thing, fictional people use larger vocabularies."

As she stood up and limped around her desk, I asked, "Would you like me to get your umbrella?"

"It broke."

"You know, Papa can make tricycles and bicycles. He could make you a cane so fast it'd make your head swim."

"I'd rather have a bicycle." As we walked into the stacks, she asked, "How is your mother?"

"Fine." *Fine* was a hidden lie, since it seemed to say something but actually said nothing. Except in piano music, where it meant "the end." "How's your mother?"

"Actually, mine's been dead for . . . seventeen years. Come October. Best seventeen years of my life. Thank you for asking, Judith."

As we walked, she ran her hand along the smooth library tables as if they were her pets.

"My mother was crazier than a hoot owl: religious fanatic, spoke in tongues." Miss Reynolds had a sideways smile. "My first exposure to a foreign language."

I desperately wanted to ask what happened to her, since I had spent hours and hours imagining Miss Reynolds' private life, including her possible murder of a close relative. I was ready to testify at her trial.

In Adult Fiction, Miss Reynolds pulled out a book. "I think you're ready for Willa Cather. She wrote about places around here, but changed their names."

I could not imagine writing anything interesting about Round Prairie.

"She might be a little hard for you."

"Harder than *Alice in Wonderland*?"

"Good point."

"Sam'll help me read if he likes the book. Are there any muzzle-loaders in it?"

"Tell Sam that the world's greatest literature is not about war and weapons." She thought for a minute. "Except *War and Peace*." Miss Reynolds swayed and grabbed one of the book shelves for support.

"You could put your hand on my shoulder," I offered. "I wouldn't tell anybody."

To my surprise, she did, leaning heavily on me as we walked back to her desk. Compared to her fat, white arm, her hand was unexpectedly small, as if it belonged to a child.

As she checked me out with the revolving date stamp, she said, "Take this book to your mother. It's Edward Arlington Robinson. She likes him."

"Is there a poem in there longer than 'The Prisoner of Chillon'?"

Still a little out of breath, she asked incredulously, "Lord Byron's 'Prisoner of Chillon'?"

"I don't know whose it is, but it only takes Mama seventeen-and-a-half minutes to recite it, and I need something about thirty minutes long."

"From memory? Edith recites it from memory?"

"Yeah. I mean, yes. She knows jillions of poems by heart. She punishes me by making me sit on the footstool in total silence for thirty minutes. But one day she recited 'The Prisoner of Chillon,' and the time went a lot faster."

Miss Reynolds smiled so broadly all I could see was her perfect teeth. "Maybe I should start her on *Paradise Lost*."

This seemed like a good time to customize my order. "Is that a funny poem?"

Miss Reynolds barked her laugh. "Only if you're God."

As long as we were on the topic, I might as well push my luck. "Do you think God has a Plan?"

She clamped her hand on the poetry book as if it would get away. "If he does, it's certainly inscrutable."

"Inscrut—?"

"Incomprehensible. As in arbitrary, unjust and vicious. Like my mother, now that I think about it."

"Grandma Strang says God counts the hairs on our heads." Immediately I remembered Miss Reynolds' wig-like hair and regretted my example. "But I think God should spend his time on big problems like wars."

"He does a pretty wretched job with war, too, wouldn't you say?"

"Is that a trick question? That can't be answered with yes or no?"

"Exactly." She smiled and leaned across her desk. "Judith, if you require a plan, at least think up something more creative, more humane—and certainly more reliable—than God."

"So Grandma Strang is wrong."

"She's not alone. Millions and millions of religious people around the world agree with her. Different gods, different plans, but they all answer the same need."

I was beginning to think that Miss Reynolds shouldn't just be a teacher, she should be a Methodist minister.

"Do you know the word *teleology*?" she asked.

"No, but I like *—ology* words."

"We'll look it up on your next visit. It's a hard word, but a good one."

"And *inscrutable*."

"That, too. They go together, actually."

We finished checking out Robinson's poetry and a novel named *My Antonia*, in which Miss Reynolds couldn't recall any horses but wasn't certain.

As I pushed open the oak door to leave, a lady walked up the steps. Even on this hot day, she wore a pale green suit, a ruffled blouse and lace-up shoes with blocky high heels.

Miss Reynolds called out, "Oh, Mildred, how serendipitous."

What was *that* word?

"Judith, come back in here and meet Mrs. Dahlke. She'll be your fourth-grade teacher."

I tried not to gasp. It was bad enough to see your teacher outside school, but much worse in the summer, especially before you had met her officially. I was certain she could sense my guilt about the Brownies. I might as well have been staggering out of My Wife's Place, the beer joint in Round Prairie.

"Mildred, this is Judith Beatrice Wilder, my short friend I've told you about."

Her hair was fuzzy and white as lambs' wool, and she wore thin silver glasses, but her face was as smooth as a young woman's. "I'm very glad to meet you."

I didn't know what to say, so I held out my hand, which she shook. "I guess teachers have to read the whole library, huh."

Behind me, Miss Reynolds chuckled. "Mildred's read everything except a few farm journals and fashion magazines."

"I wouldn't bother with the farm journals, if I were you." I added, "Unless you're trying to repair something like a Minneapolis-Moline tractor."

She smiled down at me. "Well, right now I'm between tractor repairs, so I'll take your advice." On her lapel was a starburst brooch with emeralds that matched her suit.

"Your pin looks like Queen Elizabeth's."

Miss Reynolds gestured toward the periodicals, "The Queen's on the April cover of *Life*, one of the official coronation portraits."

To Miss Reynolds I asked, "Don't you bet her crown cost millions of dollars?"

"No."

"How about the pin on her bandolier? That couldn't be cheap."

"I'll be certain to look at it," Mrs. Dahlke said graciously.

On my way out the door, Miss Reynolds called, "Tell your parents I said hello."

As I passed the back door of the library, I ran smack dab into Bobby Clawson and Leon Troxel, two of the boys who had pushed over our wagon full of radishes. They looked hot and bored, ready for trouble.

"Looky, looky," Bobby sneered, "at what they let out today." He had a black eye swollen almost shut. Somebody must have gotten even for something, but they had to be pretty big to hit him like that.

He stood in front of me, while Leon stayed at my back, sniveling, "She carries books around so folks'll think she can read."

Bobby picked up the chorus from Leon. "Whadda ya do with books? In your traaay-ler house? Build a fire, so you can cook rats?"

I hugged my books tighter. "Leave me alone."

Leon shoved me from behind. "You're on our sidewalk. Huh, Bobby."

"It's not your sidewalk. It's a thoroughfare." I had run into this problem in Hebron and was ready to define terms on the spot.

Bobby, at least a foot taller than I, bent down to push his face into mine. "Tray-ler trash . . . . Tray-ler trash." He tried to pry open my arms, but I managed to hold onto the books.

Leon pushed me again from behind, causing me to lose my grip, and Bobby grabbed the books out of my arms.

"Try'n get 'em." He held the books way over my head.

Leon chanted, "Tray-ler, tray-ler—"

As I made a final lunge for the books, to my horror, Bobby threw them into the brick street, where they landed open, face down. I could almost hear the characters inside screaming. This idea knocked the wind out of me, so when Leon pushed me again, I fell to my knees on the sidewalk.

"Lookit her crawl," Leon hooted.

Just then, the back door of the library opened, and Miss Reynolds emerged, carrying a full wastebasket. The boys started to run, but the way she said "HOLD IT!" sounded more like a sheriff than a librarian. She instantly transformed into someone else, as if her fat had turned to steel. "WHAT is going on here?"

Bobby tried to look bored, while Leon snuffled and cracked his knuckles. He couldn't close his mouth because of his scarred upper lip.

She looked down at me, then saw the books in the street and demanded, "Who is responsible for that?!"

Leon pointed at me. "She started it." He stuffed his hands into his pants pockets.

"Miss Wilder threw her books at you? From a kneeling position on the sidewalk? She should pitch for the Yankees."

Bobby Clawson scraped the back of his hand across his nose.

"Do either of you know what a Visigoth is?" Looking from one to the other, she answered herself, "Of course not. Come inside, and we'll do some research. They sacked Rome in 410 A. D." With a little twisty smile, she added, "They couldn't read, either."

Bobby shuffled from one foot to the other. Leon scratched his leg from inside his pants pocket.

She continued, "Or you can continue on your present course, trying to lay waste to any sentient matter smaller than you are, until you meet sentient matter larger than you are, which will strike back, possibly with lethal consequences. It's your choice, boys." She paused for breath. "But if I ever catch either of you abusing books again, I will personally march you down to Sheriff Westergaard. *Comprendez-vous?*"

Looking with disgust at Leon's hands in his pocket, she huffed, "And Leon. Don't ever. Handle your private parts near me again, you nitwit."

She looked at them again, hard. "You may now improve the situation—by leaving."

Bobby punched Leon in the arm, his signal to leave. They sauntered off together.

I stood up and dusted off my dress, thankful that the blood from my knees hadn't gotten on it. My knees were always in some stage of fresh blood, grit, scabs and scars since girls didn't wear pants except wool snow suits. Farm girls could wear overalls even to school. Lucky them. "Are there still Visigoths?" I asked.

"Metaphorically. Like the poor, the Visigoths are always with us. Bobby Clawson and his crowd rank among their leading families."

"Is he poor?"

"The Clawsons are one of the richest families in Round Prairie, but intellectually they are impoverished."

Impoverished meant *really* poor.

I picked up the books from the street and dusted them off. "I'm so sorry about the books, Miss Reynolds."

"Books will survive, Judith, as long as we keep fighting for them." Changing her tone, she asked, "Are you all right, child?" To my amazement, she put two fingers under my chin and lifted my face. "Good for you," she said. "Never let them see you cry." She looked in the direction Bobby and Leon had gone. "*Never.*"

CHAPTER 15

ARMS RACE

FROM THE RADIO CAME THE FAMILIAR CHIMES OF NBC.

"Good evening, ladies and gentlemen. Phillips Carlin reporting."

He paused.

"Breaking news: PRAVDA, the official state news agency of the U. S. S. R., today announced the detonation of Russia's first hydrogen bomb. As far as our sources can tell, it's in the five-to eight-megaton range."

Mama stopped putting dishes away and smiled triumphantly at Papa. "Just like Ralph said. It's not my imagination."

Sitting at the table, Papa stared at the radio as if he could change the news.

"— described as 'somewhat surprising,' although the Defense Department has been expecting a test like this for some time. The hydrogen bomb which the Army tested last November near Bikini Atoll was ten megatons. A high-ranking Defense official, who spoke on condition of anonymity, said that the U. S. is now developing a 'significantly more powerful' hydrogen—"

Again Mama interrupted, "Thank God somebody sees the handwriting on the wall."

Playing Pick-Up Sticks on the floor, Sam and I stopped with our hands in mid-air. He purposely jostled my hand while it hovered over a delicately balanced stick, knocking several of them galley west, then pretended it was an accident. He better watch out: two could play that game.

"— following today's test, PRAVDA announced that Russia is already developing a hydrogen bomb in the 50-megaton range. 'We seem to be entering a full-blown arms race with the Soviet Union,' our source said, 'and it is a race we cannot afford to lose.' Stay tuned for—"

Papa snapped the radio off, and Mama looked at him in surprise. "We were listening to the news."

"And now we're not." Papa rubbed his eyes. I always wondered how his glass eye felt when he pushed on it.

"What's an arms race?" I asked. I knew it had to do with war, but it sounded like arm wrestling, which Sam had taught me—another useful skill not even mentioned in the B. S. Handbook.

Papa wiped his face with both hands, then looked at me sadly. "It's a race between the two most powerful countries to see which one can kill everybody on earth."

"But if everybody's dead—" I protested.

"Exactly. We barely understand the atomic bomb or radiation, and now we want to drop a bomb ten times worse—"

"Seven hundred times worse, Papa," Sam couldn't resist bringing up a fact, especially one he had just learned. "Uncle Ralph said—"

"Then we'll be seven hundred times more dead."

Mama snapped, "Ralph's right. Just because some of us choose to bury our heads in the sand—"

"Ralph's always right," Papa snapped back. "Him and your mother."

"Leave my mother out of this."

Whenever Sam and I saw a fight coming, we tried diversionary tactics.

"I thought the war was over," I knew this wasn't the right diversion, but it bought time for Sam to come up with something better.

"With Communists everywhere we look?" Mama said bitterly. "You sound as naïve as your father."

Sam stood up, kicking Pick-Up Sticks across the floor. "How do you make a hydrogen bomb?"

"Clean those up," Mama warned Sam. This was good. She was easily diverted by our making a mess, although this one looked like an accident.

"I don't know," Papa answered, "and I don't want you to know, either, Sam." He encouraged us to learn everything we could, so this must be Very Serious.

"Uncle Ralph said they used fusion of atomic particles, instead of fission."

"Sounds like you already know more than enough."

Sam gathered the Pick-Up Sticks into bundles before dropping them into the can. "I'm doing research for my Chemistry merit badge and need more information for a report to my Scout troop."

I always admired how Sam could create half-truths, which were also half-lies, without grown-ups smelling a rat.

"I smell a rat," Papa said. "What are you up to in Charlie's basement? Maybe it's time I had a look."

Mr. Whitaker had agreed to let Sam perform chemistry experiments in his basement, assuming that would be safer than the barn. Nobody but I knew that Sam was actually trying to make bombs. He had started scavenging gasoline and storing it in a rusty five-gallon can we found at the city dump. From the big can, currently hidden in the Inavale storm cellar, he would occasionally pour a little into a jar to drench red anthills so he could light them on fire. While these attacks created large, satisfying whooshes of flames, they didn't qualify as bombs.

In the first week after we moved to Round Prairie, Sam had built a real, honest-to-goodness pipe bomb with all of the store-bought gunpowder he owned—almost a pound of it— tightly capped into a pipe with a fuse trailing out a hole in the side. After I swore absolute secrecy, he let me help him half bury it under a section of the picket fence bordering the far side of the broomcorn field, then he ordered me to crouch in a nearby gully. I thought he was being overdramatic until I saw him light the fuse and race as fast as he could toward me, barely sliding into my gully before it blew.

BLEW! Dirt, fence pickets, pieces of pipe all exploded upward, higher than a barn roof, as high as the steeple on the Methodist Church. I had plugged my ears to look like a soldier in the movies, but nothing could muffle that KA-BOOM! More than a sound, it felt as if someone hit my chest and tried to knock out my breath.

Dirt clods and pipe shrapnel fell for what seemed like minutes, some pieces of pipe within a few feet of where we crouched. Sam and I looked at each other wide-eyed, powdered with dirt fine as flour.

"Wow!" we said simultaneously, but not exactly with delight.

The next day Mr. Whitaker asked Papa what could have blown such a deep hole in his field and destroyed twenty feet of perfectly good fence.

It took Papa five minutes to find Sam and ten seconds for Sam to break down completely under interrogation. Not exactly a model spy.

"What in God's name were you thinking?!" he shouted at Sam. "You could have lost an arm or a leg or been blinded. Sam! Do you hear me?!"

Sam kept looking at the ground and cringing, although Papa would never, ever hit us.

"Are you an idiot?! You could have killed both you and Jeb. *Killed*."

Sam nodded but stayed hunched up.

"If I ever hear of you doing anything like this again . . . " Papa's threat hung over us.

I had never seen him so furious.

Then Papa turned on me, of all things. "Jeb, why didn't you do something? At least *you* have some sense. Why didn't you stop him?"

Me? I was dumbfounded. Me? The powerless Little Sister, the mere Assistant to the Genius, stop her big brother from doing *anything*, including blowing up the world? In Papa's gaze, I felt like Bugs Bunny staring down the barrel of Elmer Fudd's shotgun.

"I . . . was only—"

"What? A bystander? Just watching? While Sam tried to kill both of you?!"

"I . . . I didn't know . . . " I stammered.

"She didn't, Papa," Sam gallantly tried to save me.

But Papa kept looking at me. "Well, now you do know. And to make sure you remember, you'll help Sam rebuild the fence."

I was amazed that Papa didn't ask Sam where he got a whole pound of store-bought gunpowder. It would have been my first question. Sam would never tell me, even under threat of torture or exposure or both. The source of that gunpowder was Sam's most closely guarded secret.

For the fence, Papa cut the new pickets and helped half bury the upright posts, but the nailing and painting quickly convinced Sam and me that some jobs were even worse than vacation Bible school. The cost of the new wood and paint wiped out our allowance for the past year, making it feel real instead of tiny numbers in Mama's ledger.

Although this pipe bomb was louder and more destructive than Sam had ever imagined, it only increased his determination to build an even bigger, better one. But he had used all of his good gunpowder and now needed to try and make his own out of sugar, burned wood and exotic chemicals like sulfur and saltpeter. Sam had extorted enough cash from fellow Boy Scouts by selling overpriced comic books and duplicate baseball cards to buy bomb materials at the Rexall, but he lacked the imagination to tell Mr. Keefer, the druggist, continually new lies about why Papa or Miss Reynolds or Mr. Whitaker needed more saltpeter and sulfur. For this, he needed a "front man," another name for a leg man.

"You're the perfect person for the job," he confided to me.

Earlier, he had argued that I could lie since I had more practice, was more creative and didn't have a perfect record for truth like him. As a Boy Scout, he couldn't lie, but it didn't hurt if I lied for him. There was something wrong with this logic, but I hadn't figured it out yet.

"Like I was perfect for rebuilding the fence you blew up?"

"You have the *finesse*." Sam started with compliments which I knew would soon turn to innuendo, then straightforward threats. "How would you like to be promoted from Assistant to Accomplice?" he wheedled.

Now this was a new approach, promising more equality if not more prestige. Besides, *accomplice* was a lovely word.

"No risk, no glory," Sam outdid himself.

I was in.

Mr. Keefer's eyebrows jerked up and down every time he spoke, so I couldn't tell if he believed my lies or not. Maybe he considered me an innocent little girl or simply grew tired of my questions about the drugs on his shelves. I was especially fascinated with the iridescent green-red of mercurochrome and the opium listed on the label of the paregoric. Mama recited a poem which had something to do with opium. In any case, the ruse worked, and I left the drug store every week carrying little sacks of yellow powder and tiny white crystals.

My resupply runs for bomb ingredients gave me endless blackmail material on Sam, so we both benefitted from the arrangement. Whatever other people thought about my brother, I knew he was a mad scientist. Truly. He made Tom Swift, Wonder Boy Inventor, look like a piker.

CHAPTER 16

THE FORMULA

"**A** MUMMY IS STILL A HUMAN, WHICH IS AN ANI-mal," I objected.

Sam always won Twenty Questions, because he dreamed up objects which were incredibly obscure or which could be two things at once, like dry ice or Clark Kent, then chose the part I hadn't guessed. He also specialized in pieces of things, like the hydrogen atoms in the hydrogen bomb or the gunpowder packed in a 50-caliber machine gun shell. I had finally won the argument that he couldn't use abstractions such as Time or Methodism, although our log cabin clock or the Methodist Church building was okay. We spent hours quibbling over items like a dirty paring knife, primarily mineral but with a little vegetable thrown in. Unlike me, Sam never made up objects, which I routinely attempted but was always caught.

Today, we were arguing over the mummy we had seen in the *National Geographic* in the library.

"Ask Marvin the Creep. He's the expert on dead bodies," I taunted.

"A mummy is more vegetable, because it's decomposed," Sam insisted. "If you knew chemistry, you'd know that."

I couldn't defend myself against chemistry references, because by now Sam had earned the equivalent of ten chemistry merit badges through the gas and pipe bombs he was secretly concocting in Mr. Whitaker's basement. To beat Sam, I needed to trot out genuine facts, which went against my principles. Facts were so boring, providing the same answers to the same questions, day after day. Papa's variations on his stories of the Olden

Days drove Sam nuts, but I looked forward to the revisions as much as the stories themselves, wondering which motorcycle Papa would be racing or whose hot rod he would be souping up or who might get hurt this time.

I took one last potshot. "You still didn't win, because the picture of the mummy isn't the same as the mummy itself."

"I meant the picture," he instantly landed on his feet, "which is vegetable, even in your screwy logic."

He had me. Sam and I argued plenty but seldom physically fought. His half-nelsons and neck locks would incapacitate me, unless I could twist around enough to kick him. The most useful fighting technique I learned from Sam was to bluff as long as possible, to go limp, to pretend to give up, then suddenly to employ deadly force. The surprise element alone usually worked, even in Indian leg wrestling, although Sam considered surprise moves cheating unless he was using them himself.

"Logic, schmogic," I resorted to Mama's vague insult.

I had consciously tried to forget the *National Geographic* mummy, a small bundle of bones with real jewelry laid across its chest. If I let myself, I could hear it speak, although I didn't understand the hummy words pushed through its rotting teeth. How could any human being, one who jumped rope and played the piano and ate macaroni and cheese, ever turn into a little pile of rags and rotting bones?

When the Bureau of Reclamation finished building the previous dam and was about to flood a nearby town for the rising reservoir, Papa had helped move the cemetery. He said that all those people, even their coffins and clothes, had decomposed into little shovelfuls of very dark and rich soil. It seemed odd that they were trying to save some towns from flooding by purposely flooding other towns. Whose Plan was this? The government acted like God, arbitrarily choosing winners and losers— granted, for floods instead of baseball games or wars.

I wondered if Baby Janet were just dirt now, but I wasn't about to ask anybody *that* question. How long does it take for a human being to turn into dirt? After you're dead, when do you stop being a person and start being dirt? Did some of the dirt clods which fell to earth in a meteor shower start out as some living creature out in the universe? What if the dirt clods Sam and I threw had ever been part of a person? This was a strong argument for using balls of bread dough for weapons as they did in the fort behind Eddy's Bakery.

The *National Geographic* said its mummy was an adult who had died from a hole in its skull, "probably a wound incurred in an ancient battle." I knew war started a long time ago, but when was the very first official war, not just some local fight over dinosaur meat? I needed to ask a grown-up. Papa had enough to worry about without the beginning of all wars. Mr. Whitaker wouldn't know but would talk for hours about World War II and Korea, Miss Reynolds would deliver an impromptu lecture on ancient wars, Mama would start in on the Communists, and Mrs. Keindorf would know but wouldn't be able to talk about it. I gave up worrying about the beginning of all wars on earth. But I did add *incur* to my list of interesting words.

Sam and I were walking up the alley toward the fort when he suddenly stopped and used Indian sign language for "hungry," followed by "sleep." Clearly he had forgotten the right signals from his Wolf Cub Scout manual, so I froze in position and went on the alert for spies, his most likely message, however garbled.

"Did you see that?" he whispered, looking furtively toward the barn. Every morning, Mama slicked his hair down, but as the day wore on, it spiked in every direction. He jerked his head without looking again, "Over in the junk pile."

Immediately I ambush-crouched like him and surreptitiously surveyed the pile of broken tabletops, jagged pieces of concrete, and half-burned tree branches behind Mr. Whitaker's barn.

"What is it?" I mirrored his actions, creeping bent over, stopping when he did, trying to make no noise.

"A flash of light. We've intercepted a signal from the enemy."

If we were in danger of imminent attack, I needed to remind Mighty Mouse that we were standing in the open, completely unprotected, and might thereby incur unnecessary casualties. "Shouldn't we take cover?"

"Too late. Rush 'em. One . . . two . . . THREE!"

Rush who? Where?

Sam whooped a bloodcurdling Indian yell, far more effective than my pale "SHAZAM!" and jumped on one corner of the junk pile. When I leaped after him, a branch gouged into my knee. A bottle which had been caught in the branches fell out.

"Don't touch it! It might explode."

It looked like the small, flat whiskey bottles we occasionally found behind My Wife's Place Saloon, but it could be a bomb. You never know.

"Cover me," Sam said as he kneeled over the bottle.

I automatically created a rifle with my empty hands and turned slowly in a complete circle, scanning the barn, Mr. Whitaker's house, the broomcorn field, and the back yards bordering the alley. All I saw was Tag, the Geigers' black Lab lying in their marigolds, a black silhouette against the lemon-colored blossoms.

"Do we need our gas masks?"

"Good idea." Sam fumbled at his empty neck, pulled imaginary straps around his head, then picked up the bottle between his thumb and index finger.

I suddenly realized what we had found. "It's Mama's medicine bottle. The one Grandma Strang gave Papa."

I had told Sam everything I had overheard in Uncle Ralph's kitchen, but he had never seen the bottle and probably hadn't believed me, anyway.

The peach-colored label said in big brown letters across the top:

DR. MILES'
NERVINE

ACTIVE INGREDIENTS
Each Teaspoonful (1/8 oz.) Contains:
Sodium Bromide 4 ½ gr.
Potassium Bromide 4 ½ gr.
Ammonium Bromide ½ gr.
Adult Dose: 1 teaspoonful in ½ glass of water.
If necessary, repeat but do not exceed a total of 4 teaspoonfuls in any 24 hour period.
If symptoms persist or recur frequently, see a physician.

Beneath that was a drawing of a human head with two faces pointing opposite directions.

"What's a bromide?" I asked.

Sam pulled off his gas mask to read the label

A Sedative for the Following Functional
Nervous Disturbances:
Nervous Headache, Nervous Irritability,
Excitability, Sleepless and Restlessness

We stared at the bottle for a full minute. These words might characterize some sick person, but they didn't describe our own Mama.

"What's a sedative?" I asked quietly.

"I don't know." Sam looked at the bottle as if it were a map of enemy territory. "Why is it on the junk pile instead of in the trailer garbage?" He whispered even more softly, "Do you think . . . Mama . . . drank it all?"

We were both silently calculating how many days the bottle should last at four teaspoons per day. I knew that my answer would be very important, because when Sam was this quiet, he was desperate enough to listen to me.

I thought for a minute, then whispered, "Someone . . . sneaked into the trailer . . . and stole it."

Sam's eyes flicked to mine, his squint more perfect communication than sign language or our experiments in mental telepathy. He let out his breath in a low whistle and hugged the bottle to his chest as if to hide it. "Yes! They thought nobody would find it."

I continued, "They dropped it . . . on the run . . ."

" . . . from the enemy," he automatically embellished, "the . . . Communists." His eyes widened as he looked at me directly. "Who will kill to get it back."

"Because it's . . . so powerful," I added.

"It's the Ultimate Weapon. This can . . . destroy the world as we know it."

"In the wrong hands," I emphasized.

He added in his best Shadow voice, "That's why it's our job to protect it."

Sam held up the bottle so we could both look through it toward the sun. The greasy glass bent the sun's rays, throwing wavy slices of light across Sam's upturned face like the reflections from a pond. A little bit of brown syrup coated the bottom and sides as he tilted it back and forth.

Like Papa, I wanted to add some hope-for-the-best while you prepare-for-the-worst. "But in the right hands, it can also save the world."

"Y-yes."

"As a deterrent." I didn't know exactly what that meant, but I had heard it on the radio.

Sam experimented thrusting the bottle like a knife. "It can protect us from . . . the future."

I took the bottle and held its amber warmth in my hands. "Can it protect us from the past?"

Sam took it back. "Don't be stupid. Who needs protection from the past?"

"How about Papa's burns? If we spread some Formula on them—"

"It won't cure old things, like wounds or scars. It can only prevent future . . . catastrophes."

Catastrophe was another of my favorite ph – for f – words. "Could it . . . help Mama?" From Sam's grimace, I instantly realized that I had gone too far. We never talked about any Wilder needing help, especially Mama. To cover my mistake, I suggested, "Let's smell it."

"Okay, but we can only have the cap off for a few seconds."

Even before Sam fully unscrewed the cap, the smell escaped, a mixture of rotten bananas and rancid milk.

"It smells more like poison than medicine."

"This," Sam screwed the cap back on, "is all that remains of . . . the Formula."

"That can save the world." I reminded him.

"Or destroy everything. That's why we have to figure out what chemicals to add to expand it and not dilute its power. The world needs all of this it can get."

Sam sounded like John Wayne, if John Wayne appeared in science fiction movies.

"We must protect it with our lives." I tried not to sound like Gabby Hayes.

He looked at the bottle as if he were about to taste it. "We have a huge job ahead of us, Jeb."

"Hu-u-uge," I echoed.

"We have to take an oath."

Oaths always seemed unnecessary to me, since we would be skinned alive for almost everything we did if the grown-ups ever found out. But, as long as we didn't put up three fingers like a Boy Scout, I would go along with the ritual.

"Repeat after me," Sam said, holding the Nervine bottle in one hand and putting his other hand over his heart. "If I ever tell anybody about the Formula . . . C'mon."

"If I ever tell anybody about the Formula . . ." I repeated half-heartedly.

"I hope to have my eyes poked out," he finished.

Having our eyes poked out was our most solemn oath, given the fact that Papa's eye was poked out when he was a teenager and Maxine Harkin was totally blind, probably through no fault of her own.

" . . . eyes poked out," I repeated, almost overwhelmed by the gravity of the proceeding.

"Now we add our blood to the Formula."

Blood oaths were outside our usual rituals and light years beyond the Boy Scout Oath. Sam found a piece of glass under the trash pile and stabbed the soft underside of his forearm. Yuck. He swiped the bright red blood with his finger, stuck it down the neck of the bottle and swabbed it around inside. "Your turn."

Happily, I remembered my gouged knee and picked off the scab that was already forming.

Sam objected, "You have to scuff it up to get enough blood to count."

I took his piece of glass and scraped the wound, not enough to hurt but enough to pass Sam's inspection.

"Now our secret handshake."

We tapped each other's initials in Morse code on the other's palm, then shook hands overhead like the gladiators in "Quo Vadis," since the Romans were more serious about oaths than, say, Hopalong Cassidy.

We spent the rest of the day determining the safest place to hide the Formula, finally burying it in some loose dirt along the picket fence at the site of Sam's pipe bomb. On a scrap of grocery sack, Sam drew a map to its location in our private hieroglyphics.

When I sarcastically asked how we could forget its burial site, he said, "To keep the enemy from finding it, we're going to move it every other day—in rain, wind and storm."

I thought he was joking, but he wasn't.

CHAPTER 17

THE PLANES OF DEATH

THE DOG DAYS OF AUGUST HAD ARRIVED, THE LAST week before school, with cricket racket full tilt day and night, too hot even for a dirt clod fight. The whole town seemed to be waiting for something to happen—a stranger to walk down Main Street, Hested's Five and Dime to announce a sale, the opera singer to emerge from the Pawnee Hotel. Of course, a Crime of Passion would be asking too much, but a harmless car accident would relieve the general lethargy. If the earth ever really stood still, it would happen in Nebraska in late August.

Sam was even growing bored with chemistry experiments. When Mr. Whitaker chuffed down to his basement to ask what Sam had killed in order to create such smells, Sam explained everything honestly, right down to the chemical formulas, which made Mr. Whitaker shake his head faster than usual so it looked as if he agreed. Then he wished Sam luck, told him not to murder anyone except Joseph McCarthy (who didn't live in Round Prairie), slowly clomped back upstairs, and never breathed a word to our folks. The folks thought Sam was innocently making ammonia or various chemicals for testing drinking water. Nobody but I knew how far he had progressed in perfecting gunpowder or about the fuse wire and dynamite caps he had found at Papa's dam site.

Mr. Whitaker should have been a dad, or at least somebody's uncle. I felt so sad that the great influenza epidemic had left him an orphan, which you remain the rest of your life, no matter how old you get. I offered to give him Grandma Strang, but he said he was getting by all right, thanks anyway. I always went out of my way to hug him, although I could only reach halfway around his waist. With a shaking hand, he daintily patted my shoulder, knowing exactly how to treat little girls without ever having one of his own.

One day when time had come to a dead stop, Sam suddenly remembered the Globe of Death at the county fair and decided that he should test his physics research.

What physics research, I wanted to ask, but instead asked why the Boy Scouts didn't offer a physics merit badge, since gravity was a branch of physics, and gravity kept everyone from flying off the earth. How could the B. S. Handbook jump from Photography to Pigeon Raising, bypassing physics altogether? Not to mention, why pigeon raising in the first place? Who was making all the decisions for this outfit?

With growing excitement, Sam said he had invented the most successful money-making scheme of our careers, combining maximum spectacle with maximum danger. He intended eventually to build his own Globe of Death, but for now, he would settle for a small-scale operation, a crowd-pleaser using local talent–a.k.a., him and me.

Whenever Sam said the word "danger," I automatically cut the risks for him in half and doubled them for me. Every Sam idea had its idiot stick, and I always dragged it. At this point, my only hope was a preemptive strike before his idea developed into a Great Idea.

For a surprise attack, I tried a fact. "You don't know anything about momentum."

Sam stopped walking and looked at me suspiciously. He hadn't expected *momentum* out of my mouth, a word I could also spell. "'Course, if you're chicken–"

I tried not to take the bait.

He pretended to find a nickel on the ground, but we both knew it was a bottlecap. He pocketed it, anyway. "I'll give you equal billing and half the take. That's my last offer."

"What was your first offer?"

"No fame, no money."

"I'll think about it." So much for my preemptive strike.

Next day, instead of handing me his list of books, Sam bicycled to the library with me, a startling indication of turning a New Leaf: equal work for equal fame. I jogged along beside his bicycle because Maybe had two flat tires.

With practiced nonchalance, he asked Miss Reynolds, "How would a person research the trajectories of heavy objects launched from ground to air?"

Her eyebrows shot up over her rimless glasses. "More like a mortar round or more like a hand grenade?" She was so smart, I felt proud to know her.

"Uh . . . um . . . ," Sam fumbled.

"You know, I have to report covert military operations in Round Prairie to the FBI."

Covert: what a word! But I didn't dare interrupt.

Sam's legendary casualness vanished. "More like . . . jumping a motorcycle . . . off a ramp."

I hadn't heard about this particular physics problem.

"Oh." Today Miss Reynolds' cheeks matched each other, but her hair rested lower on her forehead, suggesting that her tight and perfect rows of red-brown curls could be a wig after all. Mama might be right.

"Whose motorcycle and what ramp?" Miss Reynolds paused. "Notice, Sam, that I'm not asking the key question, *Why?*"

"I'm just doing research. General principles."

Miss Reynolds leaned forward, folding her hands on her desk, pulling the date stamper out of my reach before I could move time back to my birthday. "Are your general principles thinking of riding a motorcycle up a ramp and sailing through the air?"

Sam barely missed a beat, but I could tell that he was impressed. "Actually . . . a bicycle."

This seemed like the perfect time for me to ask, "What does *covert* mean?"

Keeping her eyes on Sam, she answered me, "The opposite of *overt*. The opposite of everything you are, Judith Beatrice. Look it up: c-o-v-e-r-t."

She continued speaking to Sam, "You understand, your trajectory depends upon the angle of the ramp and your speed."

I had said all along that Miss Reynolds would make a better Scoutmaster than Marvin the Moron, and now I had evidence to prove it.

On her desk, she built a ramp with a book and a clipboard and demonstrated with a stapler for a bicycle. "Obviously, the lower the ramp, the lower your trajectory. Your point of impact depends on how fast you pedal."

"Is that momentum?" I asked.

Still looking at Sam, she answered me, "The point of impact is where Sam's general principles land, feeling remarkably like a squashed bug."

Sam slid two more books under the clipboard ramp and took the stapler. "So the steeper the ramp, the faster I pedal, the higher the arc . . ."

"–and the more spectacular the fall," Miss Reynolds finished.

"We're creating a daredevil show," I blurted out. As soon as I said the words, I knew it would happen. Our family had an unspoken agreement that if we didn't mention things, they weren't true–like Mama's nerves or Grandpa Strang deserting Grandma or Papa's burns. For me, the opposite also worked: Saying something was true made it so. Other people called this technique *lies*, but I called it creativity. It hadn't worked yet for a horse.

Sam looked at me in shock, but instantly recovered, accustomed to my reading his mind. "We're calling it . . . 'The Planes of Death,' but nobody knows about it yet."

"I. e., your parents."

I asked Sam, "Shouldn't Miss Reynolds take an oath of secrecy?"

She looked dead serious. "No need. Librarians follow a Code of Confidentiality like doctors with patients or priests with confessors. They'll have to torture the information out of me."

"That's good enough," Sam decided and elbowed my side, the signal to leave.

Then she added, "But I warn you: I have a very low tolerance for pain."

* * * * * *

Since school would start in a week, Sam and I frantically prepared for the show, scavenging an old door and a broken wooden chair for the ramp, continually pumping up our bicycle tires with the wheezy hand pump Papa had found, and planning our stunts. I liked the word *stunt*, although I didn't understand how the same word could mean a performance, a con game, and something to stop an event, like candy *stunting your growth*.

Sam planned the order of our acts, building to the most dangerous trick, which he still hadn't described to me. He said we shouldn't practice any of them because he wanted the show to look impromptu. In an unguarded moment, he also admitted that he didn't want us to get injured ahead of time. Injured? Since he needed time between tricks to re-set the ramps, he told me I had to entertain the crowd by jumping rope or playing the piano loudly from inside the trailer or anything else I could think of. Except singing.

To prime the crowd, I wanted to hand out free cookies, purchased with money borrowed against future income, because our theoretical allowance hadn't recuperated enough since we had to buy the lumber and nails to repair the picket fence. Sam instantly rejected the idea as eating into our profits. Discouraged, I told Mr. Whitaker, who said he knew Eddy at Eddy's Bakery and promised they would donate food for the event.

All that was left was advertising. I decided that lovely hand-made posters could double as programs, supplemented with a few direct invitations to special friends. Sam pointed out that we didn't have any friends but agreed to tell his Boy Scout troop. I asked him to offer free admission to sisters, partly as a gesture of camaraderie, but mostly as a forlorn hope they could pass for the Brownies I had lied about meeting all summer. He said okay but wouldn't go lower than 1¢ per person through the gate, which existed only in our imagination, anyway. We settled on 1¢ for sisters, 2¢ for Boy Scouts and other kids, and 5¢ apiece for grown-ups, all to be kept in a pickle jar Mama scrubbed for us. As a cashier, Papa would be too friendly, Mama would be too proud, and Mr. Whitaker wouldn't notice who paid or didn't. We settled on Miss Reynolds, who was accustomed to catching sneaks in the library and terrifying them into doing the Right Thing.

Behind Hale's Grocery, we found some used butcher paper with eye-catching blood spatters on it, which dramatically enhanced the effect of my artwork. Using the black crayon stub I hoarded in my own cigar box, I made one poster for Sam's approval before producing the rest.

THE PLANES OF DEATH
performed by
THE FLYING WILDERS

SEE Bodies Fly through Thin Air!

SEE Death-defying Stunts Never Seen Before!

SEE Nonstop Thrills and Chills!

SMOKE! FIRE! SIRENS!
PHYSICS IN ACTION!

Days Since Last Accident: 0

In disbelief, he said, "What smoke, fire and sirens?"

"In advertising, you don't have to tell the truth. Remember the *irium* in the Pepsodent commercial?"

When Sam wrinkled his nose in disagreement, his freckles bunched up and looked darker. He grabbed my crayon stub and, with a flourish, crossed out *Physics* and replaced it with *Psychics*.

"There's no such word," I protested.

"That's how you spell *physics*, Dumbo."

"Don't call me Dumbo. Who left the third 'e' out of *vegetables?* And who's the authority on words with – ph's that sounded like f's?"

We finally resorted to Mama's dictionary, which proved me right, but we also found the word *psychics*.

"We could do *psychics* too–" I said excitedly.

"This is not a magic show." As a Big Brother's acknowledgment of my being right and his being wrong, Sam threw me a crumb. "Maybe next time."

* * * * * *

The evening of the daredevil show finally arrived, so humid that mist thickened under the trees, a perfect evening for me to walk the neighborhood at the last minute, luring people off their porches with the promise of free cookies and the performance of a lifetime.

It wasn't until the crowd started to gather on Mr. Whitaker's front lawn that I began to feel nervous. Sam's Boy Scout friends rode in on bicycles, as well as a few girls my age, possibly their sisters. Joe Clary, the Round John Virgin boy from Bible School, showed up with Jim Hartsock from across the street. In the park, we had met Will Hankins, the older boy whom Papa knew and who agreed to help us with the last trick, sight unseen. Grown-ups came, too, which surprised me, except for Jim's mother,

Mrs. Hartsock, and Ernst Dagendorf, the owner of the Minneapolis-Moline tractor. I saw Mama talking to the opera singer from the Pawnee Hotel and—heaven forbid—Mrs. Dahlke, my future fourth grade teacher. Miss Reynolds knew every single person and shook the pickle jar in front of them until something dropped inside. Fortunately, Mr. Whitaker had talked Eddy's Bakery into numerous sacks of free cookies, including ginger snaps, my personal favorites, which they couldn't have known.

As usual, Papa was friendly to everybody, even Leon Troxel and Bobby Clawson, who hung on the edges of the crowd. Standing at the very back, I thought I glimpsed Mrs. Keindorf but couldn't be certain. I had invited her at my last piano lesson.

Sam quieted the crowd with a slightly quivering voice. "Thank you for coming. And thanks to Mr. Whitaker, for supplying the cookies."

Mr. Whitaker, who had spread on his lawn anything that could pass for a chair, waved from his rocker to the appreciative crowd.

"Trick Number One," Sam called out. "Bicycle with two riders."

Thus we launched the Flying Wilders in The Planes of Death.

I took my cue and sat on his back fender like a side saddle. Bumpy ride around the yard, into the road and back. My bottom already hurt. People politely clapped.

For Trick Number Two, I sat on the frame of his bike between his seat and the handlebars while he pedaled into the ditch in front of Mr. Whitaker's house. People didn't seem very impressed.

"Trick Number Three," Sam called out more loudly. "Bicycle with two riders, a high man and a low man."

This was the last trick we had actually tried before. Sam pedaled standing up, while I stood on his bicycle seat, keeping balance by holding on to his shoulders. Inspired, I let go of him for a few seconds and teetered precariously. He stopped just in time. The crowd clapped more loudly.

While Sam and Will Hankins leaned a 2 X 6 against the broken chair for the next act, I single-jumped rope, planning to build to more elaborate entertainments. People were more interested in talking to each other than watching me, anyway.

"Trick Number Four: bicycle and a ramp." Sam started pedaling a ways down the sidewalk, hit the ramp squarely, sailed in the air a short distance and landed, wobbling but upright. Everyone clapped, and I tried to sound anonymous with my cheer.

"Trick Number Five: bicycle with a high man, a low man and a ramp." Sam gave me last minute instructions, which were actually first minute. We circled the yard while I now stood on his handlebars, facing him and holding onto his shoulders. He gathered speed and pedaled madly up the ramp. We were airborne! Then we weren't. I came down hard, straddling his front fender. Wow, did that hurt. The crowd, which had been silent, let out a hearty cheer, so I dared to look at Mama. She sat on the front row, her head tilted sideways, nodding and talking to some invisible child sitting on her lap.

While Sam and Will raised one ramp and built a second one with a low stool, I performed a few double-jumps, in spite of my legs hurting.

"Trick Number Six: Two bicycles, two ramps." I knew this was coming, but I hadn't known enough to dread it.

"Stay with me," Sam said quietly as we rode our bicycles side by side, gathering speed in the gravel road. As we approached the ramps, they seemed to shrink to about two inches wide. "C'mon, Maybe," I urged my bike and pretended I was jumping a horse. Miraculously, Sam and I both hit the ramps at the same time, flew about the same distance, and landed standing on our pedals so our knees could absorb the shock. Behind us, the ramps had flown apart.

Sam looked at me, his face flushed, with a grin so wide it showed the gap between his front teeth. We barely heard the crowd clapping.

When I passed Miss Reynolds to exchange my bicycle for my jump rope, she looked positively pale and silently handed me a ginger snap. Over her shoulder, I saw Bobby and Leon teasing Joe Clary, flicking his hair, which was almost white. Mrs. Keindorf, dressed all in cream, even her shoes, walked over to stand between them and Joe. That certainly sobered them up.

While Sam re-set both ramps, I performed double-doubles, twirling the rope twice between jumps. I was too tired to finish the twenty I had promised myself.

"And now for the last trick," Sam called out loudly. "Never before attempted by human beings, the 'Double-Shazam.' For this stunt, the Flying Wilders will be assisted by Mr. Will Hankins." Tall even for a fourteen-year-old, Will was lanky but muscular, obviously raised on hard knocks, as Papa would say. Pimples covered his cheeks, his overalls were too short and his shirt was almost worn through.

Sam and Will put a long two-by-four across the back fenders of the two bicycles, and I climbed up on the plank, balancing myself with one hand on each boy's shoulder. Sam was riding Maybe because his slightly larger boy's bike fit Will better. The crowd grew still.

The ride up to the ramps was so bumpy the board almost chattered off the fenders, but I managed to keep my footing. Pedaling faster and faster, they hit the ramps about the same time and speed, but as we three flew into thin air, something went terribly wrong. I felt each boy's shoulder turn away from me, while the bikes separated in opposite directions. That left me and the two-by-four hurtling straight forward. I felt as if I were trying to run in mid-air, like Wile E. Coyote just before he drops off the cliff. I don't remember seeing the ground rushing to meet my face, but I knew when I hit it, skidding along on my right cheek. Bloody knees were the least of my problems. I couldn't catch my breath and lay there, gasping little donkey hee-haw sounds.

Time tried to catch its breath, too. Unlike the night I spilled my milk, I wanted time to race forward, not to back up.

A slow, faraway cry went up from the crowd. Also on the ground, Will slowly turned his head to look at me. Blood ran from his nose, but he was grinning. Crookedly grinning. Sam moaned and extricated his torn pants and bleeding leg from the nut holding Maybe's back wheel on the axle. Out of the corner of my eye, Papa, who was already standing, started taking giant steps toward us. Mama smiled into the space in front of her where time never happened.

Sam and Will slowly got to their feet, and Sam stiffly walked over to offer me a hand. Still catching my breath, I shook my head. For just a minute, I wanted everyone to think I had broken my neck. At least Mama.

"C'mon, Jeb," Sam said softly. "You're not hurt that bad."

I slowly got to my knees, then to my feet, so we could all bow awkwardly, on some silent cue, together. Papa stopped where he was, near Mr. Whitaker. The crowd went wild. We had done something no one had ever tried in the history of the world.

After determining that we would live, people gathered in small groups, eating cookies and talking to each other in the deepening twilight. Mr. Whitaker loaned Will his huge hanky for his bloody nose, while talking to him non-stop, probably about some war. Will kept dipping his head, very respectfully. Jim Hartsock and two other Scouts gathered around Sam, imitating our stunts with their hands: Zoom! Flight! Splat!

Mrs. Keindorf waved at me from behind the crowd, then walked quickly down the alley behind Hartsock's house, a short-cut to Main Street. Maybe her husband was working late, or maybe she was just shy. I had wanted to introduce her to everybody I knew.

Leaving Mr. Whitaker, Will Hankins limped over to Sam and me and held out his hand. "Real gud," he said with his Arkansas accent.

Sam fairly twinkled and shook his hand like a real grown-up. "Yeah, we did," he mumbled.

Just in time, I remembered. "We'll bring out your share of the money."

"I don't need no money." Will shook out the bloody hanky before he stuffed it into his overall pocket. "Look what Mr. Whitaker give me." He grinned as he walked off, rhythmically swinging his right leg. I had tried to find out if he had been injured during some harvest or if he were born with one short leg, but you can't exactly ask somebody that to their face. Since he didn't have a bicycle, he must have walked all the way from the trailer court into town. Mama watched him until he was out of sight.

Miss Reynolds talked to Mama for a long time, her body so large and irregular that the hem of her dress hiked up in front. Mama, rouge-spotted and thin enough to fit twice into Miss Reynolds' dress, tilted her elegant head sideways then suddenly looked straight into Miss Reynolds' eyes and nodded at something she said.

Eating my seventh ginger snap and walking among the people, I heard little snatches of conversations, like distant radio stations, in and out of range.

"Without the Billy Mitchell bomber—" Mr. Whitaker had cornered some old man.

As I passed, Papa patted my head and continued talking to Ernst Dagendorf, "— the glow-plug, and you'll have to replace—"

Mrs. Hartsock and a woman I didn't know said "House Un-American Activities—" but fell silent until I walked past.

As I approached Mama and Miss Reynolds, Miss Reynolds looked down at me over her bosom. "You," she said, shaking her head. She loomed taller than usual, looked hard at me, slightly raising her chin. "You," she grimaced at my face. "How's your cheek?"

I saw with astonishment a real, two whole dollar bills in the pickle jar she was holding. "Is that *ours*?" There were also nickels and dimes galore.

"You and Sam made a killing." With a tight voice–maybe she was trying not to laugh–she added, "You almost made three killings."

"Did you see me, Mama? Did you?"

"I saw you making a spectacle of yourself. Foolishness." She sounded like Grandma Strang.

Miss Reynolds said in her quiet library voice, "In my opinion, Round Prairie could use a little more spectacle."

"Well, that's your opinion," Mama responded, then pointed at my dirty dress and the gravel embedded in my scraped cheek. "Have you ever gone for two days in your life without bloodying yourself up? What if that blood gets on your dress?"

I got tears in my eyes, not because my leg hurt.

Mama's response was instantaneous. "Don't you cry around me, or I'll give you something to cry about."

It didn't matter what I did, Mama would never, ever notice me, let alone care. She only cared about invisible children, figments of her imagination. If Miss Reynolds hadn't been standing there, I would have said it out loud, regardless of the consequences.

Mama vaguely gestured at the scattered programs. "Clean up this mess. And tell Sam to help Mr. Whitaker with the chairs."

As Mama turned away, Miss Reynolds frowned briefly at her back, then smiled at me, a smile big enough almost to make her eyes disappear. "You do us women proud, Judith. It was a triumph."

Well, maybe not a triumph, but it was grand. It was fame. It was laughter and free cookies and real bloodshed. Sam and I belonged to the brotherhood of daredevils, flying cyclists who defied the laws of physics in a sleepy little town smack in the middle of the country on a still, thick and misty August night.

*   *   *   *   *   *

Sam and I counted our proceeds–actual hard cash–at least twenty times. We had each cleared $1.65 and gave Will 50¢, which was all he would take. You would have thought it was fifty dollars.

At dinner the next night, Mama asked, "How did you children meet Will Hankins?"

No matter how few friends Sam and I had, Will Hankins still might not qualify, I quibbled, "We were, uh . . . riding our bikes one day . . ."

I looked to Sam for help, but he was staring at his beets. He hated beets more than I hated canned spinach, which broke all other records.

Papa grew interested. "Riding where? Sam?"

"On the highway." He mumbled and stabbed a beet.

As usual, I tried to reduce the growing tension by obscuring the truth as much as possible, which did not qualify as a lie in my book. "It was the day of that big thunderstorm, when we barely got home before the tornado siren went off, and–"

"Highway 81? Which direction?" Papa used the voice that meant look at him, but Sam still didn't.

Mama burst out, "Toward the trailer court?" She turned to Papa, "Didn't you say the Hankins are migrant harvesters? From Arkansas?"

Papa nodded yes.

Mama turned on Sam, "We told you not to go out there."

"We had to give Will his share of the money from the daredevil show." I wanted to add, the same daredevil show *you* spent talking to some invisible child.

Instantly Mama turned on me. "Did you—or did you not—hear us forbid you to go out there?"

Since my first ploy had failed, I tried its opposite–to make the situation worse. Sometimes I just couldn't stop myself. "Why can't we?" I contested.

"Trailer court people—"

"We live in a trailer." I was on such a roll that I didn't even care if I broke another Wilder Rule: Do Not Challenge Grown-ups.

Sam subtly drew his finger across his throat, an obvious signal for me to be quiet.

Mama's neck was turning red, a bad sign. "They are NOT like us. They don't work half the year, their children don't go to school . . . . And that old motel at the back of the trailer court . . . ." She looked sideways at Papa. "Who knows what goes on in there."

"Will Hankins works," I said defensively. "He drives their pick-up, and he's only fourteen."

Papa quietly intervened. "Will's a good kid, Edie. He gets piece-meal work all over town—repairing asphalt, cleaning out septic tanks, even digging graves—dirty, hot work nobody wants to do. He keeps showing up at the dam, but the Bureau doesn't hire day labor. I suspect he's the only breadwinner in that family."

"Family." Mama sneered.

I couldn't resist one parting shot. "Just because they're poor and live in a trailer doesn't mean they aren't a family."

Papa straightened in his chair. "That's enough. You kids know that the trailer court is off limits. I don't want you going near there again."

Unlike Mama, Papa laid down very few rules, and we obeyed them unless circumstances absolutely required breaking them. For that reason, I wanted to clarify the terms. "By the 'trailer court,' do you mean the part inside the fence where all the trailers are . . ." I glanced at Mama and added, "and the old motel, even if it isn't inside the fence? Or do you mean a big-ger area?" I paused. "The highway is a thoroughfare, and anybody can go—"

Papa seemed to be chewing on his tongue. "You should become a lawyer, Jeb."

"Boy, that's the truth," Sam agreed. He was being nice, because he always won arguments with me with his famous logic.

Concentrating, I continued, "Because there are some great places to play along the river *near* the trailer court but not *in* it." I was thinking the Inavale house with the furry piano couldn't be more than a mile away.

"What places?" Mama asked suspiciously.

I saw Sam shake his head once, violently. "We'll keep a mile away from the trailer court," he concluded in a voice to shut me up.

Papa stood and began clearing the dishes.

I loosely calculated, "If you keep us a mile away from the trailer court in every direction, we can't play anywhere in town." As a zinger, I added, "In fact, we can't even live in town."

"You know exactly what I mean," Papa warned. "Just stay away from there."

"And those people," Mama added, now stacking dishes in the tiny stainless steel sink.

"I dibbies drying the silverware!" Sam beat me to the easier job of helping with the dishes.

CHAPTER 18

NEMESIS

SUNLIGHT SLANTED ACROSS THE WOODEN SCHOOL desks connected to each other in rows like little trains, all carved with decades of students' initials and dirty words. Some of those students were probably dead already or at least in jail. The old oak floor, like the floor in the library, smelled like Chuck's Garage, dirt embedded in oil. On the wall above Mrs. Dahlke's desk hung the universal picture of George Washington flanked by our penmanship exercises and cut-out silhouettes of May baskets like faded paper tombstones from last year's fourth grade. There must be a teachers' manual, like the Boy Scout Handbook, requiring every student in the United States to cut out the same Lincoln heads and autumn leaves, valentines and shamrocks.

Something pelted my cheek, and I instantly knew where it came from. Straight across the aisle sat Leon Troxel, who had dumped his 48 brand-new Crayolas on his desk and was systematically stripping off their labels, then breaking them into pieces. Was he completely demented, a nice way of saying "insane"? He flipped a little chunk of burnt sienna at my arm, which I retrieved from the floor and added to my 8 basic colors. Up close, the jagged scar holding his upper lip together always looked inflamed, as if he were trying to chew it apart.

Leon now attacked his flesh colored crayon, biting off a piece when it wouldn't easily break. Several days ago, I had wistfully described Leon's overflowing pencil box to Mama and complained that the Troxels must be rich. She snapped that everybody was richer than we were. I argued with her silently: not Will Hankins. He was *impoverished*.

All the boys called Leon "Harelip," even his gang buddy Bobby Clawson. Papa said he would cheerfully kill me if he ever heard me call anyone that name, much less someone born with a cleft palate. This put *harelip* into the category of Immensely Desirable Words to be used only in an emergency or when no other word could medically describe the person. After helping me research cleft palates in the library, Miss Reynolds said that even J. Edgar Hoover shouldn't be called *harelip*, although *harebrained* would be appropriate, since it designated someone with the brain of a rabbit.

While we were paging through the library's lovely, fat dictionary, we also looked up *bromide*, which meant a *platitude* or a *cliché*. This didn't explain the words on Mama's Nervine bottle, but it inspired Miss Reynolds.

"Hoover and his gang spout bromides all the time, since they have nothing original to say." She looked at my face and realized that I needed more help. "They talk about our patriotic duty and keeping America safe, when they actually want us to spy on our neighbors and grow more paranoid every day."

"So a bromide is a lie?" This could be more useful than I thought.

"Not exactly."

"A half lie?" I was thinking of the brilliant ways Sam could avoid actually lying, often using me to lie for him.

"More as if it's false—and true—at the same time." She smiled sideways.

Oh dear. I needed to think about this more and probably shouldn't wait until I was twelve.

"Judith," Mrs. Dahlke called out, snapping me back to the classroom. "Are you finished with your art project?" Today she wore a pale rose suit with my favorite pin on her lapel, a little peacock studded with rubies, emeralds and diamonds.

"Yes, Ma'am," I mumbled and turned my construction paper face down, my required drawing of "home and family." At least the trailer was easy to draw: a metallic bread loaf, navy blue on the bottom and grey on top, with two black wheels on each side. Everybody else in class drew white houses with pointy roofs surrounded by tiny Christmas trees, all fake, because Round Prairie didn't have any of those, and certainly none with smiling sunbursts overhead. The farm kids could add barns and corn silos and haystacks without cheating. Easy to draw, authentic and pretty to boot. Enviable.

Mrs. Dahlke walked down the aisle holding a sheaf of papers and stopped between Leon and me. "May I see your drawing?" she asked me quietly.

Embarrassed, I handed it to her. Art was the only subject in which I never earned an "A."

She looked at both sides of the paper, then bent down and whispered, "Where's your family?"

"Inside the trailer." I pointed to the bloated face pushed up against the kitchen window. "That's Mama."

She looked at it for a minute, then shuffled my drawing under her sheaf of papers and handed me a page off the top. "You can start working on tomorrow's subtraction problems."

I liked subtraction, because you could re-add the problem on the spot and find out if you were right. Subtraction was an exact science if there ever was one, and even reversible. Naturally, Sam liked long division better and could hardly wait to learn algebra and who knows what after that.

In front of Leon sat Jane Englehardt, whose thick braids reached all the way to her waist. She was a Jehovah's Witness—in Mama's view, the only thing worse than a Catholic. On the first day of school, I had complimented Jane on her hair, but she had turned and run away, a typical reaction to the Girl from the Trailer House. Since we were both outcasts,

I kept trying to make friends with her, but she always reacted the same way. Soon I learned that Jane didn't talk to anybody unless she had to, not to teachers, not even to the other farm kids who rode on the same bus. She didn't have any brothers or sisters, either. What must her life be like without a brother, living with only her parents out in the country where she couldn't even walk to the library to make friends in books or enjoy a chat with Miss Reynolds?

I loved school but hated recess. Hated it. The teacher on guard duty routinely suggested that the girls include Jeb the Newcomer. I dutifully killed them at one round of jacks or hopscotch, then sauntered off. Doreen Cavin and her stupid friends wore Brownie uniforms to school on meeting days, huddled in small groups and whispered all through recess. Regardless of where we moved, it always worked this way. Girls were just as unfriendly as boys, but instead of throwing rocks at you, they giggled behind your back.

During recess, the clique of farm kids gathered along the cyclone fence like calves waiting to be loaded into the school bus from midday onward. Joe Clary, who lived in town, stood near them but always alone, his fingers hooked into the metal fence. He had almost silver hair and eyes the color of milk chocolate and looked as if he would fall over if I blew on him hard. I was dying to ask if he were sick or something, but even I wasn't that nervy. He was so shy he choked when we talked, although I could tell he liked me. Over the school year, maybe he and I could become friends.

When no one was looking, I would shimmy up the fire escape, a long metal tube running from the ground to a second-story window, an enclosed slippery slide about twenty feet high. During fire drills, teachers helped kids one at a time hop out the window to slide down the metal tunnel. In summer, Sam and I often climbed all the way to the top barefoot, but wearing school shoes, I could only scramble a third of the way before sliding helplessly back down, feet first and on my stomach.

Across the playground, I watched Sam play touch football or dodge ball, always including a few quick, illegal punches the playground teacher didn't notice. Sam absolutely forbade me to approach him at school, threatening me with Geronimo's Curse if I broke his rule, meaning he would cover me with honey and stake me out on a red ant hill, to be eaten slowly hair by hair, finger by finger, leg by leg, in the burning sun.

In spite of what awaited me at recess or even home later with Mama, I loved walking to school with Sam, when we could create imaginary maps of Germany or the Pacific for our next Saturday morning bombing run or could figure out new hiding places for ammo. We fought the Round Prairie War at least twice a week, either at our fort or in various alleys around town, progressively hiding an impressive arsenal of broomcorn spears and dirt clods near potential combat zones. Even with Jim Hartsock and a few of Sam's Scout buddies fighting on our side, the Clawson-Troxel gang outnumbered us. Worse than that, they cheated, completely ignoring the Unspoken Rules of Engagement for kid wars. Any day now, I expected to see real jackknives appear in their hands. Needless to say, the boys defending the fort behind Eddy's Bakery were almost useless allies, offering only dough balls for ammunition and, therefore, pretty weak military training.

On the way to school, Sam and I also negotiated additions to the Formula, which by now contained a little ketchup, lighter fluid and Bon Ami. I was currently lobbying for scraps of music, discreetly torn from "A Mighty Fortress" in the Methodist hymnal. Sam wanted to keep it chemically balanced with saltpeter and sulfur but hated to use up those chemicals before he could perfect gunpowder. The Mad Chemist was also working on something called *nitroglycerin*, so Top Secret he wouldn't even let me record it in my journal of favorite words, in spite of its delicate spelling and unstable look on a page. Some words just dance.

As we entered the school yard, we renewed our oath of silence about the fort, the formula and Sam's bombs, completely unnecessary since we were both headed for the electric chair, anyway. Once we climbed the steps and pulled open the massive oak doors with the scratched windows, Sam raced down the hall ahead of me. I didn't know if this instant strangerhood happened because I was ugly, a girl, or his sister. Probably all three.

In contrast, my walks home from school ranged from tolerably nerve-wracking to downright terrifying, depending on chance. Every time I could, I followed Sam and his boyfriends to a Scout meeting or tailed a group of girls walking in my direction, but sooner or later, I always ended up facing Leon Troxel or Bobby Clawson alone. The suspense and dread of their unpredictability were almost as bad as the ambushes themselves. No matter what streets I avoided or what alleys I crept along, eventually a calm afternoon would erupt in Leon's screaming leap out of a bush, Indian rope burns, threats with broken glass, my Big Chief tablet and schoolbooks flying, and my sitting, exhausted and dirty, in some stranger's driveway. Fighting back with kicks and punches, I could survive Leon's attacks relatively intact.

Bobby Clawson was a different story. Thank goodness, he was in seventh grade and had to walk several blocks out of his way from Clayton Junior High to hunt me down. No avoidance tactics, no tricky spy maneuvers helped, since he didn't even bother to hide. Facing Bobby wasn't "High Noon" or any other lopsided movie gunfight. This was Doom stalking me head-on. As soon as I saw Bobby looming ahead on the sidewalk or in the alley, my nebulous panic began to dissipate into calculations about the distance to a safer, open place like the middle of the street, where his attack might not last so long and I had a remote chance of encountering a grown-up. This never happened, but I never gave up hope.

The chase was always short and predictable: a puppy against a wolf. Once he caught me, he wouldn't let go, bending one arm up behind my back while locking my neck in the crook of his other arm. With my free hand, I scratched every part of him I could reach—with luck, his face—and tried to kick him backwards, causing him to yank my trapped arm until it felt as if it would break.

Worst of all, his hot whispers wormed into my ear, filthy words for going to the bathroom and for body parts and for naked ladies.

"Say it!" His breath smelled like rotting hamburger. "Say . . . 'I'm a titty'." He tightened the lock on my neck. "Say . . . 'I am a piece of –'" and he would fill in some new dirty word each time. I didn't even know what his words meant, but if I wanted to escape, I had to repeat them. Worse than calling me names, he made me call myself names, and all of them lies. I didn't fit Bobby's words any more than Mama fit the descriptions on the Nervine bottle.

For my own sake, like writing on a Magic Slate, after saying each of his horrible words, I silently erased his and replaced it with one of my own—*reciprocity, lex talionis, centrifugal, ubiquitous*. I took special comfort in thinking *Nemesis*, the goddess of retribution for evil deeds, especially seeking out people who committed crimes with apparent impunity. Mrs. Meyers had taught us about Nemesis in third grade mythology, but Miss Reynolds had added that a nemesis could also be the recurring agent of your personal suffering. When I asked her if Nemesis lived in a particular place, like in church, she answered that your nemesis wasn't necessarily somebody or some force outside yourself. It could be something within you. I definitely decided to postpone thinking about this until I was twelve and started to read the entire library. Nemesis felt like something, as Papa would say, a little girl shouldn't worry about.

I didn't tell Sam about Bobby because it would have been worse to have him along, since he would never give in and real blood would flow. I didn't tell Papa because he had enough to worry about and couldn't do anything, anyway. And telling Mama would have thrown gasoline on every fire and start some new ones to boot. No, I had to figure out a solution by myself.

The first time I walked past Bobby Clawson's house, he said he would sic his dog on me if I used his sidewalk again. No idle threat. Bobby's dog, a Doberman pinscher chained to a stake in his back yard, barked incessantly and bared its teeth when it growled. All the neighbors complained, even the Methodists, about how vicious it was. One day when I was riding by on my bicycle, I saw Bobby teasing it with a two-by-four. The dog held one end in its teeth while Bobby thrashed it back and forth. Wasn't it getting slivers in its mouth? Why didn't it let go?

Since a dog had bitten me when I was five, I was afraid of most dogs, anyway. Papa maintained that dogs could sense my fear, so I should smile and talk sweetly to them because, evidently, they can't sense lying. He did warn me not to turn my back on them, just like bullies. But Papa could make friends with a snake and wasn't afraid of anything, I think because of his burns. Once you live through that, everything else was easy. But how does a nine-year-old girl grow that brave without getting burned almost to death?

CHAPTER 19
THE SHADOW

THE SHADOW'S VOICE
Who knows what evil lurks in the hearts of men?
[Melodramatic organ music.]
The Shadow knows.
[Insane laugh.]

I NEVER KNEW WHY THE SHADOW LAUGHED IF HE knew what evil lurked in the heart of man, but it was one of my favorite radio programs, partly because Sunday evening was my favorite time of the week, when the family sat around our little kitchen table, eating Neapolitan ice cream and crackers for supper, and listening to the radio.

At the right moment, Mama would announce what we all knew was coming: "I scream, you scream, we all scream for ice scream." Lately she would add, louder and louder and faster and faster, "I scream, I scream, I SCREAM—" until one of us interrupted her, and she stopped.

In its lemon-colored plastic case, our radio hissed and spit static like a caged space alien, constantly threatening to drown out the programs. Nonetheless, on Sunday nights we listened to every thirty-minute show in order, practically without moving– "Amos 'n Andy," "Jack Benny," "Our Miss Brooks," "Fibber Magee 'n Molly," and the very best, "The Shadow."

COMMERCIAL VOICE
[In a frenzy.]

Quaker! Puffed! Oats! And Quaker! Puffed! Rice! The only cereal shot from guns!

[More intimately.]

At the Quaker plant, big guns are lined up to puff the rice and oats to sixteen times their normal size. Puffed cereal allows our bodies to "trigger" into the nutrition more easily.

[Sound of guns exploding.]

Children, next time you're at the grocery store, ask your mother to buy both, so you can eat Quaker Puffed Rice one day and Quaker Puffed Oats the next.

Fat chance. Sam and I knew better than to ask Mama for anything so silly or expensive as Quaker Puffed Rice, since we couldn't even have Post Toasties. For breakfast, we were condemned to food like bacon and eggs, with occasional pancakes or French toast with homemade tomato preserves.

NARRATOR'S VOICE

The Shadow, who learned from an ancient shaman how to cloud men's minds so that he's invisible—

[Melodramatic organ music.]

The program always told us the same background on the Shadow, in case you were one of five people in the entire country who didn't tune in every week.

NARRATOR

[Trying to sound like a newscaster.]

For three days and nights, the city has been enveloped in a black fog, almost complete darkness. Cars are crashing into each other, doctors in hospitals can't see to save children's lives—

WOMAN'S VOICE

[Terrified.]

What will we do?! What will we do?!

LITTLE GIRL'S VOICE

I'll protect you, Mother! I won't let them hurt you!

Caught up in the action, I imagined the little girl wearing a brown-checked dress just like the one Mama had sewn for me for school this year. I grabbed Mama's hand across the table and said, "I will, too, Mama. I'll protect you!"

She yanked her hand away. "Don't be stupid. That's a man's job."

"But you named me after Judith, the lady warrior."

Papa dug into the strawberry section of his Neapolitan ice cream, my least favorite. "I'd trust Sugar to save me."

Sam agreed, "When Jeb's mad, she can be scary." No doubt referring to my well-practiced kick, he added, "And she doesn't fight fair."

Papa repeated what he often said, "When you're outnumbered or really in danger, you don't have to fight fair."

Although I had taken his advice many times, it didn't help much with Bobby Clawson. The first time I came home scuffed up from a fight with him, Mama went through the roof, but Papa asked what the other kid looked like. I appreciated this no end.

NARRATOR'S VOICE

Earlier, Dr. Heath had created a dark fog to protect the city from air raids, but now his machine is in the hands of the forces of evil. They threaten to inject a deadly gas into the fog unless the city pays them five million dollars.

[Quivering organ chord.]

Mama pushed her wavy hair off her forehead. "Deadly gas is right. The radio station knows what's what."

"It's only a radio program, Edie," Papa said quietly.

"But it's based on fact, and you know it. You heard his accent."

"The Shadow knows what evil lurks in the hearts of men," I explained while I carefully segregated my vanilla ice cream from the strawberry so I could eat it last.

THE SHADOW

I'll go to the criminal hide-out with you, Dr. Heath, in order to capture the madman.

DR. HEATH

But he's holding my little son captive—

THE SHADOW

Here's a gun. Use it only if he threatens you first.

NARRATOR'S VOICE

Meanwhile, the fog deepens across the city—

Mama insisted, "Don't pretend you don't know people in this town . . . ."

Papa stopped eating. "Who? Just exactly who?"

Sam and I strained to hear how the Shadow would fight this new Force of Evil. All of the good guys sounded as if they came from England, and all the criminals from Germany, saying "Yabul," whatever that meant.

"Mrs. Kein—" Mama nodded toward me with her head.

Papa challenged again. "What about her?"

"And Doctor Mary—"

"Doctor Mary what?" Papa threw his spoon down on the table.

THE SHADOW

Dr. Heath! Watch out!

DR. HEATH

It's so dark in here! Can you see my son?

[Sound of gunshots.]

"As Red as they come—"

"That's ridiculous, Edith."

Suddenly, Mama snapped off the radio and stood up. "That's the end of that."

"Wait!" I protested. "We've got to find out–"

Sam shook his head at me, which meant to be quiet, but I refused. "It's not fair! How will we know if they saved the city?!"

"Jeb," Papa warned.

Mama had left us all trapped in a dark room, quickly filling with deadly gas, and someone was shooting.

"Besides," I continued to wail, "the Lone Ranger is next." I could give up the ending of "The Shadow," but I couldn't miss a night imagining Silver, galloping with his noble rider to fight the evil outlaws.

By now, Sam's knee was jumping up and down under the table.

"What did I just say." Mama's voice was getting harder.

"Then 'Jack Benny'," I tried a show which made even Mama smile.

"That's. The end. Of that," she repeated.

"Sugar." Papa's warning closed all possibilities.

By now, Mama had practically thrown the dirty dishes into the kitchen sink. "Go outside and play."

I tried a reason which even I knew was silly. "But it's dark out."

"Then go in Sam's room."

Sam stood up and folded his chair. He had left half of his ice cream, the chocolate part now melting and sliding over the white part.

"Can we take Sam's ice cream into his room?" Why did I try to break a cardinal rule, and at the worst possible time?

"Food is for the table."

"I'm not hungry," Sam answered. "C'mon, Jeb."

I sneaked the rest of the crackers out of the bowl, which Papa saw and didn't say anything, and we retreated to the front end of the trailer. We slid the doors shut. Sam and I sat in the dark, waiting for the argument which was sure to follow. Mama and Papa stomped to the other end of the trailer and slammed their bedroom door, so we could hear only scraps of what they said.

"—would it kill you to charge people to fix—?"

"They can't afford—"

"... a g.d. trailer house? ... pay your doctor bills?"

Mama didn't use that argument very often. It must hurt Papa's feelings because his burns weren't his fault.

I couldn't hear his whole answer, " . . . I should've just died. Your mother would've liked—"

" ... the best she could do on nothing. Nothing!"

Papa said something, and Mama answered, " ... ironed for rich folks ... ten cents an hour!"

Papa said something about "the kids."

Mama stormed, "Oh, the blessed kids," but did lower her voice.

After that, their voices raised and dropped, shushed and shouted, like a musical duet with a complicated rhythm.

I handed Sam a cracker and whispered in the dark, "What'll we do?" Sam was always good for a back-up plan.

"Let's go outside and play Lone Ranger."

I nearly fainted. Sam would never play horse-anything with me. Maybe he relented because it was dark.

"I won't ride a stick horse," he added quickly.

"That's okay." Actually, I wouldn't let him ride La Cheetah. My wild stick horse was barely tame enough to carry me, much less a stranger.

As we stepped quietly into the cool darkness of late September, Sam remembered, "You be Tonto."

I was just ready to object, when he added, "Isn't La Cheetah a paint? Like Tonto's horse?"

I was so astonished that he remembered her markings, I didn't even argue.

CHAPTER 20

PLEDGE OF ALLEGIANCE

"*UNDER GOD.* CONGRESS IS CURRENTLY CONSID-ering adding these important words to our Pledge of Allegiance. Why are they so important?"

Oh dear. I had experienced churchy principals before this, but Mr. Sprecker took the cake. We were supposed to be working on our history lesson, and instead he was preaching to us about God and America.

Leon had ducked further behind Jane Englehardt to carve something into his desk with a straight pin pushed through a pink Pearl eraser.

"What makes America the most powerful nation on earth?" Mr. Sprecker paused, but no one answered. His hair was combed into black furrows, thick as road tar, which didn't move when he moved his head. His suit was so big that it didn't move when he did, either. Maybe he thought he would grow into it.

He answered himself. "We are the only country in the world with a special mission from God."

I bet there were lots of other countries with missions from God, although I couldn't name one right off. Finland? Poland? Iceland? I liked countries ending in "–land."

I raised my hand. "What mission? Like a spy mission?"

Mr. Sprecker's eyes shone like black glass.

Remembering the God business, I added, "Or more like a church mission?"

"What's your name?"

Uh-oh. Causing the principal to ask your name was a Bad Start for a school year. "Jeb Wilder."

"Jeb Wilder What?" He asked impatiently.

"That's all. Oh. Judith Beatrice Wilder."

"Judith Beatrice Wilder, *Sir*. Do we have to teach you manners, as well as everything else?"

Mrs. Dahlke smiled her fake smile, which anybody but an idiot would see through. "Class, Mr. Sprecker wants to lead us in the Pledge of Allegiance this morning,"

He folded his arms, badly wrinkling his oversized suit, and spread his feet further apart. "Stand up, face the flag and put your right hand over your heart," he ordered, as if we hadn't done this every school day for our entire lives.

Everyone stood except Jane Englehardt.

The principal frowned at her, then slowly walked down the aisle. He stood over Jane and rocked up and down on his tiptoes. "I said, 'Stand up'."

"Mr. Sprecker?" Mrs. Dahlke called from the front of the room. "Jane is a Jehovah's Witness, so I've excused her from saying the Pledge."

"Nobody in my school refuses to say the Pledge of Allegiance." His head revolved slowly, like a robot's, toward Mrs. Dahlke. "It isn't in your power to excuse anyone from their patriotic duty." He turned back to Jane with a voice like a hammer. "Stand up. Do you hear me?"

All the kids had turned around to stare at Jane. Behind her, Leon Troxel made donkey ears to her back. Mrs. Dahlke began stacking and restacking the same set of papers on her desk.

Jane's head hung so low her chin touched her chest.

Without warning, the principal grabbed Jane's arm and jerked her out of her seat. Her long braids went flying.

"Mr. Sprecker!" Mrs. Dahlke called out sharply. "May I speak with you in the hall? Right now."

Jane had gone limp, hanging from her arm. Mr. Sprecker shook her like a dog with a rag, then threw her arm away from him. She collapsed back into her seat, burying her face in her arms.

Mr. Sprecker strode to the door of the room and snarled at Mrs. Dahlke, "I will see both of you in my office after school."

"Jane will miss the school bus," Mrs. Dahlke quietly objected.

"I said, both of you." He slammed the door behind him.

Mrs. Dahlke's mouth clamped shut so tightly her lips didn't show.

The big clock above the door ticked five loud seconds, its hand jumping.

"Everyone please sit down." Mrs. Dahlke glanced briefly at Jane. "Take out your reading books and turn to page seventeen."

Reading? Evidently, we were skipping our history lesson today.

Doreen Cavin raised her hand. "Aren't we going to say the Pledge of Allegiance?" She always wore ruffles and ringlets, which I called R & R.

"Not today."

"We have to pledge the flag. My mother says." Mrs. Cavin ran the Brownie Scouts, probably cut from the same cloth as Marvin Harkin.

"Everyone: page seventeen," Mrs. Dahlke repeated.

We made it completely through reading before Jane Englehardt raised her head. She hadn't missed anything but the next brain-numbing episode about perfect children who lived in Hansel and Gretel houses. Jane swallowed a lot but didn't have any tears on her face. Good for her: she wouldn't let them see her cry, either.

* * * * * *

On my walk home, I detoured to the library to ask Miss Reynolds about America's special mission from God. I didn't dare ask the folks because God was a Touchy Topic at our house. Sam and I had to brace ourselves for whichever Mama was waiting for us after school—the one repeating words over and over, the one cooking supper, the one rocking back and forth in my chair-bed, the one muttering at the encyclopedia, the one searching for secret gas lines into the trailer—but mentioning God would certainly bring out the worst.

From her office at the rear, I heard Miss Reynolds' voice, tight with fury. "Sprecker can't do that."

At the mention of the principals' name, I went on High Alert and hid in the History and Biography aisle.

"He's *breaking the law*, Mildred," Miss Reynolds continued.

Mildred? Mrs. Dahlke must be in her office, too. Breaking the law? Oh boy. Maybe Sheriff Westergaard would arrest Mr. Sprecker in front of the whole school. I would help in any way I could.

Mrs. Dahlke answered, "Sprecker told me the Supreme Court ruled that school children were *required* to recite it–specifically Jehovah's Witnesses."

"They did, but they reversed that ruling in 1943. Sprecker's only ten years behind the times. It's one of my favorite court decisions of all time. They weren't protecting religious freedom, but ruled instead that 'the compulsory unification of opinion' violates the First Amendment. It's *against the law* to force everybody to think alike. Don't you love that?"

I heard Mrs. Dahlke sigh. "I can't tell Sprecker that."

"I can and I will. I've known that little sawed-off so-and-so since he was in diapers. He may still wear them for all we know."

"Don't do anything. I'm afraid—"

"Of what? He can't fire you."

"Of course he can. He can do anything he wants. His philosophy of administration is coercion."

Coercion? What did that mean? How was it spelled?

"From day one," Mrs. Dahlke continued, "he insisted that I was 'over-educated' for this job."

"That's because he barely made it through high school, and who knows how he graduated from the ag college."

"I just found out that he's re-checking all my references in Indiana to detect any 'political irregularities.' My last principal wrote to me, asking what's going on."

"That weasel is fishing for a socialist or a unionizer or a 'fellow-traveler'." I could almost see Miss Reynolds spit.

"He's certainly looking for evidence that I'm being insubordinate. Last week, he reprimanded me for 'not following the curriculum.' I wanted to show my students some real art, so I brought in my book of American landscapes."

For landscape painting, all I had ever seen was the Garden of Gethsemane on our church fans. I remembered Mrs. Dahlke's book, amazed that paintings could seem more real than if you were standing right there looking at real trees and rivers. How could a painting—a flat piece of paper—make you feel happy or sad or scared, just like an actual field of ripe wheat or Rose Hill Cemetery or the Inavale spook house?

"That's pretty subversive, Mildred, illustrating once again that you should be the principal and Clarence should be the janitor of Lincoln Elementary."

"A woman principal? Not in our lifetime. Oh, Thelma, did you hear about Naomi Schmidt in Minden? It's happening all over. One day a teacher has a job, and the next day nobody knows where they've moved."

"How long will Eisenhower let these witch hunts go on? I don't even recognize this country anymore."

"Neither do I." Mrs. Dahlke let out her breath. "Well, I have papers to grade and better get to them. Thanks for talking with me, Thelma. As always."

I heard both of their chairs scrape and ducked a little lower.

"No, Mildred: thank you. Just when my cynicism starts to weaken, I get new fodder from someone like Sprecker. Stop by anytime. Please."

I heard footsteps, then the front door opened and closed.

Since Miss Reynolds didn't know I was in the library, I figured I could wait until she went back into her office and quietly sneak out.

"Judith?" Miss Reynolds called out. "It isn't polite to eavesdrop. Unless you work for the FBI, where offensiveness is a job requirement."

I walked around the bookcase, trying not to look guilty. "I thought Jane Englehardt just didn't want to say the parts of the Pledge of Allegiance she didn't believe in, like me and the Apostles Creed."

"Jehovah's Witnesses can't pledge allegiance to anything except God. They consider it idolatry."

"But if God's in the Pledge—?"

"You're still pledging allegiance to a country and, worse, to an icon, its flag." She limped close enough to her desk to lean on it. "The great irony is that the original Pledge was written by a socialist and trumped up by a magazine marketer basically to sell flags." She chuckled. "How American can you get?"

"Why didn't Mr. Sprecker tell us that?"

"Clarence Sprecker has the cerebral cortex of a flatworm."

More wonderful words! But I had to stay focused.

"There are parts I don't believe," I confided, realizing this could be more serious than the Apostles' Creed. "Like the 'liberty and justice for all'."

"Why, Judith Beatrice," Miss Reynolds pretended to be scandalized. "Who doesn't enjoy liberty and justice in this best of all possible nations?"

"Papa says the Negroes, but I'd say the people living in the trailer court."

Miss Reynolds leaned on her desk with both fists and tilted her head, really listening.

"They don't even let Will Hankins go to school. And Mrs. Keindorf."

"Why do you say Mrs. Keindorf?" She was listening so hard, she squinted.

"Nobody's nice to her, either—even in the Methodist Church, where you'd expect liberty and justice for all. No one will sit beside her except Marvin Harkin, who just wants to stare at her chest."

Miss Reynolds coughed. "Do you know why she's suspicious? She's different."

She illustrated with her small, white hand. "Greta Keindorf has more culture in her little finger than most people have in their whole body. She has traveled all over Europe, is familiar with some of the world's greatest music and art, and is fluent in five languages, including Russian. Five. How do you think that goes over in Round Prairie, Nebraska, where people can't even speak English correctly?"

Miss Reynolds softly hit her desk with her fist. "Anti-intellectual, anti-cultural, anti-everything that makes life worthwhile. Don't you ever succumb, Judith."

I didn't know what *succumb* meant, but I wasn't about to do it.

Miss Reynolds was breathing pretty hard, so I suggested, "Maybe you should sit down."

To my surprise, she dropped into her desk chair.

"Should I get you a glass of water?"

"I'm fine. Thank you."

"I have another question."

"You always do. Fortunately."

"Mr. Sprecker said America has a special mission from God."

Miss Reynolds' eyes fluttered upward. "Do you remember what a bromide is?"

"Repeating everybody else's ideas." That didn't seem quite complete, so I added, "Instead of thinking your own."

"Close enough. In Sprecker's case, bromides have replaced original thought altogether." She shifted her body to squeeze between the chair arms better. "Life is so much easier that way."

"So America doesn't have a special mission from God?" If not, the principal lied, and to a class of innocent fourth-graders, no less.

She grinned. "What do you think?" She often answered me with another question.

"Papa says folks should leave God in church and just run the country."

Miss Reynolds played with her glasses chain, today the one with gumball-sized pearls. "Do you think your father would consider running for President?"

"He's . . . never mentioned it."

"I imagine not. He's too smart to get elected."

I turned to leave. "I have to go home and help Mama now, but next time can we look up *cerebral cortex* and *succumb* and *coercion?*"

Her smile widened so I could see her perfect teeth. "Absolutely. But you already know what they mean."

CHAPTER 21

THE GARBAGE DRUM FIRE

"**B**OMB SHELTERS!" CHARLIE WHITAKER SNORTED. "Our grandaddies invented 'em 150 years ago. Called 'em storm cellars."

Civil Defense warnings on the radio had inspired Marvin Harkin to send his boy army on reconnaissance missions to find potential bomb shelters near Round Prairie. The only excuse he could concoct from the B. S. manual was the merit badge for Citizenship in the Community, which required such skills as determining when a sewer was plugged, knowing how to report a car accident, and obtaining a dog license. Only Marvin Harkin would consider these abilities critical in combating an air raid.

To be fair, on page 469 of the celebrated handbook, I discovered that Community Citizenship also included researching local agencies which cared for orphans and aided the poor, services which would be useful rather long after the entire town had been strafed, bombed and burned. I swear, I was the only living human being who ever read the fine print in that silly book. Or, I might add, evaluated the design of the actual badges, in this case a decorative pointy church steeple and a fake house like other kids drew in art class. Utterly stupid.

It was early Saturday evening, the dishes were finished, and Sam and I were headed to Inavale on our bicycles. I suggested we first visit Mr. Whitaker sitting on his front porch holding a bowl which might contain jelly beans.

Mr. Whitaker blew his nose on his huge hanky. "Fer once, us farmers'll be ahead of the rest of the country. But bomb shelters? The guvmint must think we were born yesterday. Honest to God." He looked quickly at us. "I mean 'gosh'."

"Go ahead and swear, Mr. Whitaker," I offered. "Papa says you don't mean it, not like Uncle Ralph."

"I need to have a talk with your daddy. I do mean it when I swear. If I was gonna lie, I wouldn't do it by swearing."

Sam checked his bicycle chain, which never worked right after our crash in the daredevil show. "Papa doesn't swear. Well, almost never."

"And he's got the best goddamned reasons to swear of anybody I know." Mr. Whitaker wiped his mouth with the back of his shaking hand.

"Papa says swearing doesn't help, anyway," I added. "That's why it's called 'taking the Lord's name *in vain*'."

Mr. Whitaker laughed, his pillow stomach inside his overalls pumphing up and down, and held out the candy bowl. "Take a handful. Take two."

Everything he did proved that he should be the Scoutmaster.

*　*　*　*　*　*

Given its construction, Sam figured the Inavale storm cellar could double as our ultra-secret hide-out and a bomb shelter, so we had already begun to stock it. So far, we didn't have any food or water, but Sam had hidden gasoline, fuse wire, pieces of pipe and various versions of homemade gunpowder. From trash piles around town, I had scrounged a bent butcher knife, a broken axe handle, a bunch of candle stubs and a rusty cowbell. My smartest contribution was my treasured matchbook with the advertisement inside that "You, too, can draw!" You simply copied their silhouette of a person's head, and they would send you free drawing lessons. Sam asked what on earth was I thinking with the cowbell, since we were trying to stay concealed. I asked what on earth was he thinking with the gasoline and gunpowder in a confined space, since we were trying to stay alive.

Wrapped in rags in Maybe's bicycle basket was the Formula, which we were now hiding in a different place every day. In our last battle at the fort, Clawson's gang smashed five of our broomcorn spears, then attacked us with rocks embedded in dirt clods. This broke yet another silent agreement, universal among kids, about the use of Deadly Force while playing war. Since they were spying on us as much as we were on them, Sam was afraid they might find the Formula, a war crime of the first magnitude, not to mention a tragedy for the human race.

Today we had added key magical ingredients to the Formula—a few pinches of saltpetre, a swipe of Papa's Lubriplate grease and a little dog hair from the neighbor's black lab, Tag. I had torn a few notes from the John Thompson piano version of the "Pathetique Symphony" by someone named Tchaikowsky. They must have misspelled his name, as they certainly did "pathetic," but Mrs. Keindorf could write in the missing notes. The Formula still needed something from Mr. Whitaker and Miss Reynolds and, when we got the chance, a little dirt from Janet's grave. As the Formula grew more powerful, now nearly filling Mama's Nervine bottle, Sam's vigilance bordered on *paranoia*, a word grown-ups often used.

When we bicycled up the rutted driveway at the Inavale house, long shadows snaked across its back yard. Between the trees, the setting sun outlined inky clouds like ashes rimmed in fire.

Sam raised his cavalry halt sign, and we wobbled our bikes to a stop. "Somebody's been here."

We had closed the storm cellar door, which now lay open. Using his old Wolf Cub Scout hand signals, Sam indicated "moon" and "water," obviously intending "danger" and "nearby." I signaled back "true" and "listen," motions generally applicable to any situation. When you're becoming a Mad Scientist, I guess you can't be bothered with remembering old Cub Scout hand signals.

We rested our bikes against a half-dead cottonwood tree nearby and crept toward the dark stairs. I cradled the Formula and Sam brandished Mr. Whitaker's dying flashlight. We peered down the dark stairs straining to hear above the riffling of the cottonwoods. The setting sunlight seemed to stir the leaves.

Unexpectedly, Sam shouted, "WHO'S THERE!?"

I almost dropped the Formula. He never forewarned me when the rules of engagement changed from Creep-Up to Attack.

No answer. He motioned for me to cover his back as we climbed down. As clammy and dark as the cellar was, it felt safer than the house, from which I heard a baby crying. Was it about to be murdered? Sam called me crazy for "hearing things" unless he were also scared; then he called me "crazy as a bedbug" to cheer himself up. The druggist, Mr. Keefer, called Mama a bedbug when he thought I had left the drugstore with a fresh bottle of Nervine.

He made me so mad that I called over my shoulder, "Takes one to know one" and slammed the door especially hard. With my arsenal of words, I should have thought of a smarter answer, something involving *irium* or *nitroglycerin*. Nervine cost $1.50 a bottle, so it must be doing some good. But Mama seemed to be getting worse.

Inside the cellar, Mr. Whitaker's flashlight died, so Sam lighted one of our candle stubs with a paper match. In the jumping light, we saw that someone had piled rags and old coats into a makeshift bed. Strangely, they hadn't moved any of our supplies, not even Sam's gasoline. They had rolled up Papa's old coat for a pillow.

I pointed to it. "Sam–"

"Who's there?" a strange voice called down the stairs, making us both jump.

Sam blew out the candle.

O lordy, if it were Clawson or anybody in his gang, all they had to do was close the door and drop something heavy on it, and we'd never be found. Thinking as one person, which we often did under stress, Sam and I suddenly bolted for the stairs, willing to face anyone head-on rather than be entombed in here forever.

Hearts pounding, arms flailing, halfway up, we heard the voice again.

"Hey." Will Hankins was standing in the twilight outside.

I practically hugged him in relief. "Hey," I managed to choke out.

"Whatcha doin'?" His voice lilted with his Arkansas accent.

"Just hanging around," Sam bordered on a lie. Moments ago, we were preparing for a Russian invasion and World War III.

"'Zat yer stuff down there?" Will was almost as tall as a grown-up but much thinner. He was wearing patched bib overalls, which skimmed his boot tops, and a short-sleeved shirt so full of holes even Mama would declare it a rag. "I ain't bothered it none."

"That's fine," Sam said with the voice he reserved for grown-ups.

I would explode if I didn't ask, "Do you live here?"

"Sometimes I sleep out here, cuzza the quiet." His cheeks were covered with pimples, but his grin made some of them disappear. "You know, if you ever sleep here, make sure that door can't shut on ya."

I hoped beyond hope that Sam and I would never sleep in the storm cellar. My very worst recurring nightmare: trapped underground in the dark.

"That's good advice," Sam agreed. Where did all this courtesy come from? Not the Fifth Boy Scout Law, which Sam also couldn't remember.

"You two et supper yet?"

We both nodded yes at the same time.

He recouped. "You ever et frog legs?"

We now nodded no in unison, looking like twin ventriloquist dummies.

"My pappy gigged some frogs today and is gonna fry 'em up. Whyn't y'all come over?"

"Sure," Sam instantly answered, to my amazement.

"Right now?"

Sam and I didn't need to look at each other to agree. There was no way on earth we were going to tell Will Hankins that our folks wouldn't let us play with him, as so many kids said to us. Will helped Sam close the heavy storm cellar door, then showed us the bicycle he had built with his money from the daredevil show. The frame, fenders and handlebars looked a little ragtag, but it was strong and all the business parts worked. I was sure Papa had helped him build it.

I realized that the Formula would be safer here than on the road with us, so I pretended to fiddle with Maybe's tire while I hid the Nervine bottle in the bushes. Reading my mind, Sam chatted loudly to cover my actions.

And we were all on our bicycles before you could say Jack Robinson.

Sam led us along washboard back roads, widely circling town and adding about two miles to the ride, but Will didn't question him. He could recognize a precautionary maneuver when he saw one. By the time we dismounted at the entrance to the trailer court, twilight was deepening and the crickets had slowed down in the cool autumn air.

Walking our bikes like little ponies, we followed Will single file down the wide driveway. On both sides stood rusty trailer houses, some with flat tires, others looking as if they had scraped along a wall or even rolled over. People sat in front on sagging sofas and torn car seats or sprawled across stained mattresses in the dirt. They stared at us as we passed, and Will ducked his head to them. I couldn't tell if he were proud or embarrassed, but I felt like part of a circus parade, something from another planet. A freak.

"We live back here." Will gestured toward the motel, a low adobe building trying to look like a trading post from a cowboy movie. Most of the windows were broken out, and I couldn't tell if the floors were dirt or if dirt just spread over the missing thresholds. "Wisht we had a trailer."

Two dogs whose ribs showed under their matted fur barked at us, lunged and retreated, lunged and retreated. Knowing how dogs scared me, Sam walked his bike between me and them, for which I would owe him big time. Chasing the dogs with sticks were several barefoot children with ketchup smeared around their mouths and dirt on their faces. The old dress I was wearing, one Mama had sewn from flour sacks, felt like Queen Elizabeth's coronation gown.

At one end of the motel building, a few grown-ups loosely circled a fifty-gallon oil drum, rusted to lace and shot through with bullet holes. It belched smoke and sparks.

"Hey, Pappy," Will called out.

A man wearing a slinky shirt and rubber overshoes held a frying pan and squinted through the smoke with bleary eyes. "Whatchoo got there?"

I felt as if Sam and I were exotic animals which Will had trapped and brought home, like someone else might bring bluegills or squirrel. Will's father seemed to size us up for butchering, deciding how best to disjoint our knees and split our breast bones.

"Get yerselfs over here." When he grinned, I saw a silver tooth glint in the firelight.

Sam and I rested our bikes on their sides in the dirt, while Will pushed his behind the motel. As we walked closer, the smell of rancid grapefruit and burning eggshells mixed with a greasy, musky smell.

"Who's ready for a little Bugs Bunny?" He widened his eyes, clown-like, then laughed. He didn't have many teeth except the silver one. He looked around the circle, and two women held out their chipped dinner plates to catch the little drumsticks he slid out of the heavy fry pan. With blunt, dented fingernails, they stripped the stringy meat, then sucked the delicate bones. When they finished, they threw the bones to the yapping dogs.

Will walked out of a motel room carrying a large metal tool box. The grown-ups parted to let him through.

Eye-level to Sam and me, the bonfire flickered behind the bullet holes in the garbage drum.

"Now fer the real treat!" Will's father said. "Gigged 'em today. To . . . day." His tooth sparked in the firelight when he spoke.

From the box, he lifted long, skinless fingers, triple-jointed, smooth as snakes. One by one, he dropped the legs into the spitting fat, then moved the pan low enough for Sam and me to watch. A leg *kinked*. It had to be a trick. Then another leg kicked. From a *dead* frog.

I couldn't help it: I screamed and jumped back, but Will's father jabbed at me with the skillet, now full of squirming, leaping legs trying to escape the spattering heat. My legs tangled and I fell backwards in the dirt.

The grown-ups laughed.

Sam pulled me up with one hand and said to the grown-ups, "We better be going." His straight line stubborn mouth, which I usually dreaded, looked downright lovable.

"Dontcha want summit to eat?" Will's dad asked.

"We . . . already did," I managed to stammer.

"Thanks, anyway," Sam added.

Across the fire, Will waved to us and grinned as we picked up our bicycles and walked them out of the trailer court as fast as we could without seeming impolite.

From the highway, we looked back at the jumping, pumpkin-colored light in the center of the grown-ups' circle. Ashes, outlined in fire ruffles, floated up from the garbage barrel and swirled in heat spirals.

I wanted to ask Sam how something dead could seem so alive, but neither of us felt like talking. Maybe the frog legs were like the stars which still look alive to us, but are actually dead. Or maybe they were like Baby Janet, both dead and alive, at the same time.

CHAPTER 22
THE APOCRYPHA

I PARTICULARLY LOVED WORDS WHICH DIDN'T SOUND the way they looked. By the time I was six, I was devouring "-ough" words, playing with *through* and *thorough* and *rough*. In second grade, I went through a "y" phase, collecting *rhyme, synonym, rhythm* and *hysteria*, then falling in love with words which seemed to be missing a final syllable, like *piano, alibi, auto,* and *taxi*.

In Round Prairie, I began spelling and saying words backwards. Some were easy, like *nug* for gun, *trof* for fort, *odanrot* for tornado, *edoc esroM*; but I preferred harder ones—*tsidohteM* or *tsinummoC*. I was thrilled to meet words which spelled other real words backwards: stop – pots, strap-parts, tool-loot, dam-mad, raw-war. They were a special type of anagram, which I soon learned Mama had been collecting for years. She asked, why look at the world only one way when you could see it forward and backward at the same time?

My obsession with words finally irritated Sam enough to use one of his ultimate weapons: math. Knowing he couldn't stop me, he could considerably slow me down with what he called the Vowel-to-Consonant Ratio. Randomly, he would decide not to talk to me until I could find a word which had at least the same number of vowels as consonants. This at once taxed my imagination and bought him silence while he worked on gunpowder and nitroglycerin. *Footstool*, I immediately realized, had a 4:5 ratio. No good. *Raucous* (4:3) and *paranoia* (5:3) were good, and *eerie* (4:1) was the best yet, but I was soon driven to ask adults for help, notably Mrs. Dahlke.

My repeated requests somehow convinced her that I should train for the tri-county spelling bee. I never knew that people actually studied for spelling bees, much less stayed after school three days a week for the whole school year.

"It will be fun," she had insisted. "And it will be good for you." Grown-ups said that when they really meant it would be hard on you but good for them.

What did I have to lose? By October Sam already knew enough Scouts and even normal boys to play with after school, leaving me alone in the fort or in the trailer with Mama. Mrs. Dahlke couldn't possibly know I avoided being alone with Mama whenever I could.

"How is your mother?" she asked at the beginning of every session.

"Fine-thank-you-for-asking."

We had started with lists of words published on cardstock, the first one pale pink as a baby shower announcement. When I mastered that list, we moved to butter yellow and sky blue, containing increasingly difficult words. The print was half rubbed off, and the stiff pages were curled at the edges and oily from years of use. If the words in the county spelling bee came from these lists, why not just memorize them and be done, I wondered.

"Sometimes the contest words come from these lists," Mrs. Dahlke explained, "but not always. Last year, they surprised everyone with *isthmus*."

Isthmus slowed me down, even after I learned what it meant. "Then why learn these particular words at all? We could just take our chances with . . . *philosophy* or . . . *decipher* . . . or—"

"*Siphon* or *phobia*?" She certainly knew how to tease me. "If nothing else, we want to expand your vocabulary."

I mumbled, "Why?"

"The more words you know, the more ideas you will have," she continued. "You can't have ideas without the words for them."

Nobody had ever told me this.

"The more complex your vocabulary, the more complex your ideas will be." She raised her eyebrows over her delicate wire-rimmed glasses and smiled like a little girl.

I couldn't wait to tell Sam: Ideas came in words. Immediately, I tried to have an idea without words, but all the time I was saying to myself, 'I'm going to try to have an idea without words,' I was using words to have even that idea.

"So if you use simple words, you have simple ideas?"

She hesitated. "M-more or less."

"Is that what bromides are?"

"Bromides." She paused. "Where did you hear about bromides?"

"Miss Reynolds." Before I could stop myself, I added, "And Mama takes bromides for medicine."

"I see." Mrs. Dahlke said in the way that meant she really did see and wasn't just faking it.

Since the horse was out of the barn about Mama, I might as well chase it to the fence. "But I don't understand how a bunch of simple, over-used words can also be medicine."

Mrs. Dahlke looked at me for a long time, as if she were trying to guess my weight at the county fair. "I think that the name of the medicine came before people applied it to habits of speech. Bromides are sedatives. They dull the mind, sometimes putting people to sleep."

"So words that put you to sleep are bromides." I thought of Reverend Harkin in church.

She turned to erase the blackboard. We were both silent. The clock hand jumped to 4:17. We had been working for forty-seven minutes, and I was getting tired. I started doodling in my Big Chief tablet around today's words, which all ended in "-ious." I had brought in *lugubrious*, and Mrs. Dahlke had countered with *conscientious* and *dubious*.

Since today was Tuesday, she was wearing her robin's egg blue suit and the silky blouse with the floppy bow at her throat. Like me, she had five different outfits to carry her through the school week, but she always added stunning jewelry to vary them. On her lapel sat a little basket of blue jeweled flowers, my second favorite after her peacock pin.

"Are those real sapphires and diamonds?" I pointed.

"Of course not, Jeb. No one wears real sapphires and diamonds."

"Mrs. Keindorf does."

She stopped writing *conscious* on the blackboard. "I doubt that."

"She's my piano teacher."

"I know."

"She said they were real. She has star sapphires and star rubies and lots of diamonds."

Maybe I shouldn't be saying this. In a little town everybody knew everything about everybody else. Mama said the neighbors even knew the cost of our electric bill, which was "none of their g.d. business." Worrying about things like this kept Mama awake and pacing the trailer's living room, that is, my bedroom, at night. She didn't want to wake up Sam or Papa. Bromides weren't putting her to sleep, that much was certain.

"Well, Mrs. Keindorf is . . . " Mrs. Dahlke looked out the window for a word. "Extraordinary."

I vaguely felt she needed some defense. "Like a movie star."

Mrs. Dahlke continued talking to the window, but not like Mama, who talked to people nobody else could see. "Like a survivor. How they lived through the war no one will ever know." She shook her head. "Nobody wins a war. Nobody."

I didn't see how the war made Mrs. Keindorf extraordinary, so I tried a different angle. "Is Mrs. Keindorf a Communist?"

Mrs. Dahlke looked straight at me now, her blue eyes intensified by her suit. I always felt the urge to pat her hair, white and plush as lambswool. "That's a very dangerous word, Jeb, and you mustn't use it until you know what it means. These days, people call anyone who isn't like themselves a Communist, often with terrible consequences."

"Maybe they don't know enough complex words to have better ideas." For some reason I thought of Bobby Clawson's dirty mouth.

Mrs. Dahlke smiled broadly, something she seldom did. "How do you spell *transcendent*?" It was our own little joke-compliment.

We chanted in unison, "J-E-B."

This seemed like a good time to ask, "Is anybody getting tired?"

"I certainly am." I knew she was fibbing, but she started gathering her things to leave. "Mama says you're so smart you could teach college if you wanted to."

"I love elementary school. I remember when my own daughter was in fourth grade."

It never occurred to me that teachers had their own children, especially if they were as old as Mrs. Dahlke. "How old is she now?"

"She . . . she died. When she was your age."

"*Died*?" I didn't think that I heard her right. "In the fourth grade? We're too little to die."

She took off her wire glasses, pinched the bridge of her nose and put them back on. "I think so, too."

"How did she die?" If Mama heard me ask a grown-up such personal questions, I would sit on the footstool for an hour.

"A . . . farm accident."

I knew better than to ask any more. "That is so sad, Mrs. Dahlke." Then I did the unthinkable with a teacher–took hold of her old, spotted hand.

She patted my hand with her other one. "It was a long time ago."

"Do you still miss her?"

"Every single day."

"If anything happened to Mama or Papa, I would die."

For no reason, Mrs. Dahlke suddenly looked worried. "Bad things happen, Jeb, and you go on. If anything happened to your parents, you have many friends who would see you through."

As I put my pencil inside my desk top, she added, "Tell your mother I was asking about her."

"Okay," I lied. Mama didn't want anyone asking about her, much less a schoolteacher.

"Jeb, why don't you want to be called Judith? It's such a wonderful name."

"Miss Reynolds told me about the first Judith, the warrior lady who sneaked behind enemy lines and killed their general."

"Holofernes, the Assyrian. Her story is in the Apocrypha."

"The what?"

"The Apocrypha. Contains books which weren't allowed in the Bible."

More news for Sam. "Why?"

"Politics. As usual." She gave a little humph. "We didn't invent blacklisting."

How could the Bible–of all books–keep out religious stuff?

"Some religions consider the Apocrypha part of the official Bible."

"Do Methodists?"

"No," she began to smile.

So some religions used the complete version of the Bible, but not Methodists. Did Reverend Harkin know this? As Marvin's brother, he probably did, but he would lie about it if I asked.

"How do you spell it?"

"It's another Jeb speciality, a – ph for – f word." In perfect Parker method penmanship, she wrote on the board *A-p-o-c-r-y-p-h-a*.

"It certainly won't be used in the county spelling bee, but it's fun to have it for your own."

"Now I can have Apocrypha ideas. Very complex ones." What a startling day.

"Actually, the adjective is *apocryphal*. It means unofficial. Untrustworthy."

"Like a lie?" I asked excitedly.

"Fictitious, anyway."

Another way to say "fib" in an elegant fashion, along with faith, subjunctive, myth, advertising, metaphor and sarcasm. And straight from the Bible, no less.

Kept out, ruled out, blacklisted: *My* name should be Apocrypha.

CHAPTER 23

EYES

THAT SUNDAY, I SURVIVED CHURCH BY MAKING UP glamorous lives for a new family I had never seen, bland enough in their white shirts and gray dresses to appreciate my help if they had only known. I couldn't add anything to Maxine Harkin, already exotic, who played impossible Bach fugues perfectly with both her hands and feet. I could understand how her feet wouldn't need to see the music, but her hands had memorized every piece, including long preludes and postludes, by reading Braille. Papa played without music, too, but by ear, which he said was much easier because he made it up instead of remembering what was written down. He called Maxine brilliant.

Sam compared Braille to Morse code for blind people. One day, when Mama was starting to wind up about something, Sam whipped out information about the inventor, Louis Braille, a blind Frenchman who tried to help Napoleon's soldiers communicate silently and in the dark. In the worst way, I wanted to run my fingers over Braille music, but I knew that asking Maxine Harkin would be Highly Inappropriate and, potentially, a Punishable Offense. Miss Reynolds had already assured me that the library didn't stock any Braille music but was delighted I had asked.

If Maxine were brilliant, why was she married to Marvin? Did he keep her in his power through some mysterious, grown-up variety of blackmail, possibly involving her blindness? Today, the Shark scanned the congregation from the back of the sanctuary, the model of Boy Scout surveillance, while Maxine finished the prelude, her cloudy eyes staring at the tallest organ pipes. Anyone who didn't know she always looked skyward would think she felt divinely inspired. Marvin spotted Mrs. Keindorf sitting alone in a pew, as usual, wearing a forest green summer suit and matching pillbox hat. With her hair twisted into a French roll, she looked like a magazine model, and even from a distance, I could tell she was draped with real emeralds which everyone assumed were fake. Mama wouldn't let us sit with her, although I asked every Sunday.

Marvin slinked down the aisle and stood beside Mrs. Keindorf until she had to slide over to give him room. He looked around to make certain everyone noticed before he sat down, as if he were doing her a favor. All through church he sneaked looks at her lap and long legs and tried to share a hymnal with her so he could touch her hand. The Eagle Scout of creeps. Mama called Marvin Harkin a "Christian martyr" for marrying a blind woman. Papa asked if Mama were half a Christian martyr for marrying a half-blind man.

On our way out the church door, mere seconds from freedom, Reverend Harkin held Sam's hand too long and put on his Jesus-with-the-children smile. "I was worried about you and your sister last night when I saw you on the highway—"

Sam and I stiffened in unison.

"—leaving the trailer court." He looked up at Mama and Papa. "I wondered, my goodness, what were they doing there. And if I could help."

Help, schmelp. Round Prairie was full of spies, and some of them wore preacher's robes. According to Sam's theory of probability, our chances of getting caught at the trailer court were about the same as rolling snake eyes, which meant we had committed a Big Crime, not some common, high-probability-low-punishment event. Because this encounter involved a Methodist minister, I briefly considered the possibility that God's Plan might be working after all. Rev. Harkin could not have found us without help.

Just then, Mrs. Keindorf slipped behind me to get out the door. I squeaked, "Hello, Mrs. K—" all I could manage impaled by Mama's fingernails digging into my shoulder, signaling Hell to Pay as soon as we moved out of Public View.

All the walk home, Mama was like a pressure cooker with the weight dancing and spitting on top.

"Trailer! Court!" She made it sound like two coughs.

My black patent shoes flashed as Sam and I trotted to keep up with the folks, but even they couldn't help me now. Mama's heels clipped like Mrs. Keindorf's metronome on "Presto."

Characteristically, Papa made friendly conversation as Mama gathered force like an approaching tornado. "Will Hankins is only fourteen. And a hard worker. I feel sorry for the kid."

Mama snarled, "If you want to feel sorry for someone, feel sorry–"

I silently finished, 'For Sam and me.'

"—for decent people," she continued, "who don't shift from pillar to post–"

"For heaven's sake, they're migrant workers," Papa defended.

" –who drink up every dollar they make," Mama continued.

"You don't know that."

We practically ran past Hested's window with the jar of marbles and the little bronze horse, which I was considering renaming something more inspiring than Bunker, something along the lines of Luther.

Mama tossed her head. "I know what I know."

"You don't know what's in their cupboard, Edie."

"Why do you always defend every Sam, Dick and Harry, every shiftless—"

"Edie—" Papa used his calming voice.

"Holier-than-thou Frank Wilder. Who do you think you are? Christ on the cross?"

I thought only Catholics got to have Christ on the cross, but this was no time to ask.

As soon as Mama slammed the trailer door, she turned on Sam and me. Her spots of rouge looked redder than when we left for church. "I hope you're proud of yourselves, you little HEATHENS. Ralph and I grew up poor as church mice, but we were decent. We may have lived on potatoes, but we didn't act like it. Mom made sure of that."

I wondered how people acted who lived on potatoes.

She took off her straw basket hat and jabbed the hatpin into it. "I'll bet they had a heyday about you two after you left the trailer court. And Reverend Harkin got his eyeful."

Sometimes I got tired, all at once, of waiting on pins and needles for whatever Mama dished out, and deliberately kicked up the red ant hill. "You don't care about the trailer court people, you said so yourself. And Rev. Harkin is almost as creepy as Marvin. So who cares what they think?"

"Jeb!" Papa warned.

Sam squeezed his eyes shut.

"Don't you sass me, you little brat," Mama warned, but I could tell she was listening.

While Mama stomped into their bedroom to change out of her Sunday outfit, Papa sat us down on the sofa and talked to us quietly–far worse than Mama's tirades.

"Now why did you do that, Jeb?" Papa asked.

"Why does Mama always get her way?" I asked seriously, not whining. "Just because she's in a bad mood, why should we have to be in a bad mood, too?" I had never asked this question before.

"You know Mama's very . . . nervous. High-strung."

"Maybe we are, too." I didn't know what had gotten in to me. "What about us?"

Papa wiped his hand down his whole face, at the end pulling on his chin. Sam's eyes were still squeezed shut.

"Since we're so full of questions today, I have one for you. Why did you kids deliberately go to the trailer court, when you *knew* that would throw Mama into a tailspin?"

Mama was so far gone she might not come back today.

"We didn't think we'd get caught," I answered, unexpectedly overwhelmed by honesty.

Sam's eyes popped open.

"I don't doubt that for a minute. Worse than that, you broke your word. To me." Papa might as well have hit us.

Under attack, Sam always fell mute, while I packed as many words as I could into the time left before we were riddled with Indian arrows.

"Will's so poor and doesn't have any friends—not *any*—and everybody treats the trailer court people like dirt and, if *we* don't know how he feels, who does, and we don't need to be like the Cavins or—" Sam kicked me surprisingly hard from a sideways position.

Papa looked at me as if he could focus sunlight through his glass eye and start a fire. "I understand, Jeb. But was it worth causing Mama to fly off the handle and betraying my trust in you?"

"You would've done it," I tested.

There was a long pause.

"Why do you say that?" Papa asked.

I didn't know why I said that, so I refused to answer. My silence could be misinterpreted as sulking, but I didn't care.

"The point is that you both knew you were breaking your word and did it, anyway. Didn't you."

Technically, we hadn't *given our word* not to go there, and trusty Sam had actually started it all by saying yes to Will's invitation, which I wouldn't have done. Well, maybe I wouldn't. Actually, I probably would have. In any case, Sam and I always presented a united front to the folks and haggled out our own version of justice later.

"Yes," Sam answered for both of us.

I wanted to point out that Mama would fly off the handle regardless of what we did or didn't do. If it weren't this today, it would be something else tomorrow. Every day, she needed less and less reason to explode. Sometimes no reason at all. Like the man throwing the firecracker at Papa. Why couldn't I say all this out loud? Because of the Red Ant Rule: Wilders didn't Rock the Boat.

Sam said, "We're sorry, Papa." He sounded sincere, like the Boy Scouts really intended, not just some fake oath they recited without listening to themselves.

When I thought about it, though, he didn't have any right to include me in his apology. I wasn't sorry.

"I know you are, but that doesn't help much now, does it?"

In the bedroom, Mama began to cry in loud hiccups. The screams would be next, screams you could hear all the way to the Hartsocks across the street. Papa sat on the piano bench and stared at his folded hands, as if he had just discovered his missing fingers for the first time.

"I wish she'd just hit us, and get it over with," I said.

"She'll never hit you, Jeb. And neither will I. Hitting never gets anybody anywhere."

"Not even self-defense?" I pushed on, "Or to save Sam's life? Hitting—"

"Just ignore her, Papa," Sam advised and tried to shut me up with a look.

As tired as I was of the Round Prairie War, I wasn't about to stop hitting Leon or Bobby any chance I got, preferably before they hit me.

Mama's screaming didn't last as long as we expected. When she emerged from the bedroom, her streaked rouge made her look as if her cheeks were melting. Around her mouth was a thin molasses-colored line.

"Because! I could not stop for Death!" she barked, then frowned, momentarily lost. "What happened?" She scowled at Papa and Sam. "Huh? Huh?"

I blurted out the rest of the line from one of Mama's poems. "Death stopped for you!"

Papa and Sam stared at me the same way they stared at Mama.

"That's my girl!" Mama crowed and caught my neck in her arm like Bobby Clawson, except not so tight. She had never called me her girl before, but I figured that was far better than being someone else's girl, even in a neck lock.

Thinking that I might cheer up Mama and avert disaster with a happy poem, I quoted, "Somebody said it couldn't be done, but he with a chuckle replied—"

"No. No no no. Everybody said it *could* be done . . . but you two knew it couldn't." She pushed me away and said to Sam and me, "My very own Gingham Dog and Calico Cat." Her speech was slightly slurred.

"I got my news from the Chinese plate!

Next morning where the two had sat

They found no trace of dog or cat . . .

But the truth about the cat and pup

Is this: they ate each other up!"

She sighed, "That's Eugene Field, for anybody who gives a g.d."

Papa answered thickly, "We should know that by now."

"Then I'll tell you something you don't know. No dinner, no supper, and two hours on the footstool every day for a week, Jeb. For you, Sam-bo, I'll think up something spec-tac-u-lar. How's them beans?"

Papa looked as if he'd been slapped. He waited a few moments, then spoke more deliberately than usual. "How about . . . we eat dinner, since you fried that good chicken last night? Then skip supper?" He paused. "After Jeb's first two hours on the footstool, let's see how everybody feels. Sam: You'll do the dishes all by yourself this week."

Mama squinted at Papa , as if she were trying to re-focus her eyes. Her pupils were so big they made her eyes look black. "Dishes. Dishes. Chinese plates?"

Papa turned to both of us. "Since you're so fond of gadding about, you can do it on foot for a week–no bicycles." He looked closely at me and added, "Or tricycles or roller skates or anything else with wheels. Do you understand?"

We nodded.

"Do I have your word on it? Say it."

"We promise," we both said. Papa knew how to punish us, all right.

Knowing dinner was our last meal for the day, Sam and I ate everything in sight, even the mashed turnips and canned asparagus, two foods developed specifically to torture kids. After Sam finished the dishes, he and Papa went to Mr. Whitaker's to repair a leaky faucet.

The footstool wheezed under my weight.

Mama poured some Nervine into a glass, quickly swallowed it, washed the glass and put it away. She pointed to the log cabin clock. "At 3:35, you can get up." She walked into their bedroom and closed the door.

Something was making Mama worse, maybe the Nervine. The words on the old bottle holding our Formula now described Mama pretty well— mental disturbances, excitability and sleeplessness. I wished Sam and I could talk to Papa about Mama, but that was more Strictly Forbidden than ever. If she would only fall asleep today, I could read *Tom Swift Circling the Globe,* which lay on top of the piano beside volumes 1-6 of our new Funk and Wagnall's encyclopedia.

"I can see you through the door," she called out. "I can hear what you're thinking."

If anybody could, she could. She said that Communists read your mind, then brainwash you. Is that what she was doing to me? Normally, I liked words composed of two other words, like *flapjack*, *shindig*, and *shamrock*. But not *brainwash*.

I wished I had memorized poems like Mama, who always had one handy for company. "Paul Revere's Ride," or, better yet, "Evangeline" would really be useful right now. Maybe when I got older and didn't need to play so much, I could memorize poetry. Miss Reynolds had helped me find the "more stately mansions" poem, which was equally mysterious spelled backwards—"derebmahC sulituaN." Maybe someday I could recite the whole poem backwards: "Soul my oh, mansions stately more thee build."

Sun came through the Venetian blinds in slots of light suspending Dust People. They moved randomly up and down, circling each other in every direction, lazy and chaotic. Then I had a brilliant idea. Maybe I could move them just by concentrating on them. Since second grade, Sam and I had experimented with mental telepathy, but recently we had added *telekinesis*. He read that mediums could move objects with their minds alone, but that sounded like more Marvin Harkin drivel. Miss Reynolds would know.

I focused my gaze on the Dust People, like Gort on the Army, and thought, 'move up,' 'move sideways,' or 'retreat.' No effect. An order to 'move down' worked, but ever so slowly.

Only 2:00 according to the log cabin clock, an hour and thirty-five minutes to go. Maybe by concentrating, I could speed up the stiff smoke ribbon ticking seconds out its chimney, could make the clock hands move, like advancing Miss Reynolds' date stamp at the library or resetting Mrs. Keindorf's metronome to Presto. I stared at the clock really, really hard.

Suddenly, filling its tiny window was an eyeball, not like Mama's in the trailer window when we dug the fort, but like Papa's artificial eye, a glassy blue iris full of golden flecks. One day, when our family still lived in our house in Hebron, Sam and I were playing in the basement and opened a drawer in an old dresser. Hidden under some old pillowcases was a small jewel box. Instantly, I envisioned the folks' secret hoard of diamonds or at least a few emerald and ruby rings. Sam slowly opened the hinged lid and nearly dropped it in surprise. He snapped it shut, then slowly re-opened it. Nestled in black velvet was a glass eye, a smooth, tiny cup, white with hairline blood vessels surrounding the jeweled iris looking for all the world as if it were alive. Whether it was a spare eye or one which didn't fit any more, it felt as if Papa himself had become small enough to stare out from the little box. It didn't matter where we stood, it looked at us. Never until that day had I considered what Papa's blind eyeball must look like behind his glass eye.

To clear my vision, I blinked at the clock. And blinked again. Amazingly, the whole log cabin began to change shape, to breathe, and the hands sagged slightly.

At the same time, I felt myself lift off the footstool a few inches and begin to drift upward to the ceiling–a huge Dust Person. The clock left the wall and glided toward me, a cabin-shaped pillow with soft, droopy hands.

The trailer roof evaporated, and I floated outdoors, slowly spiraling up and outward. Now I could see our whole street: Mr. Whitaker's roof, the barn and the broomcorn field. Our fort, headquarters for the entire Round Prairie War, looked like a tiny pile of rubbish. Tag, a barking black spot, played with a knotted rope by himself, while a few blocks away, Clawson's Doberman sat chained in their back yard. The log cabin clock coasted past.

Soon I could see all of Round Prairie from overhead, our trailer house barely visible among the trees. On Main Street was the Pawnee Hotel, Hested's dime store and the library, with Miss Reynolds on the sidewalk, talking to a woman holding a sack of groceries. Near Lincoln Elementary, I tried to pick out Mrs. Keindorf's roof, but it looked like everyone else's on her block. I rose, light as the ashes from the garbage drum fire at the trailer court.

Main Street turned into the highway, with Round Prairie threaded in place between Hebron and Inavale with Lebanon, Kansas, to the south, while the horizon grew more and more curved. By now, Round Prairie wasn't even a pinpoint on the plains, and I started leaving the earth, which looked like the globe in Sam's 6th grade classroom. North America was still recognizable, but I could only guess where Nebraska was. Without Tom Swift's airship or Gort's flying saucer, I could leave the earth behind and head for the stars, dead or alive, dead *and* alive, like Janet.

What if I couldn't come back? If I abandoned the folks, would I be an orphan? Or did they have to abandon me? Just then, the log cabin floated into view. Stretching out, I grabbed the stiff ribbon of smoke wagging the seconds out its chimney and instantly fell downward. The harder I squeezed it, the faster I fell. Now worried that I might fall into an ocean, I loosened my grip on the smoke so time could move again and I could slow my descent. But where would I land? How would I find Sam?

The bedroom door banged open, and BANG I was back in trailer space and BANG I was back in log cabin clock time and BANG there stood Mama holding a dust mop and rags.

"Are you asleep?" she demanded.

I shook my head no. Or was I? I couldn't say anything without lying.

"I never knew anybody but Judith Beatrice Wilder who could sleep all night with their eyes open."

I was afraid to speak until I knew how much actual time had passed.

"On the other hand, I stay awake all night with my eyes closed." Her laugh sounded like a saw blade cutting tin. "We make quite a pair, don't we, Jujube?"

Only Sam could use that nickname for me. Wary, I watched her.

"Quite a pair. You can spend the rest of your footstool time helping me clean the trailer." She had washed her face and looked rested.

Anything was better than sitting still and staying dead quiet.

With fake casualness, she added, "We need to look for the new gas lines the meter man put in. He's in cahoots with Dr. Mary and Mrs. Fancy-Schmancy Piano Teacher."

I didn't try to defend Mrs. Keindorf. I wasn't up to another fight today, but as I scrubbed the already spotless pipes under the kitchen sink with Bon Ami, I wondered what kind of pair Mama and I did make.

CHAPTER 24
THEME AND VARIATIONS

MRS. KEINDORF SAID THAT MAXINE HARKIN played much more than notes: she played *music*.

She smiled her ruby red lipstick smile. "Debussy called music 'the space between notes.' Like the meanings in the silence between people's words." She paused. "Does that make sense?"

Not one bit. I nodded yes. Was a nod a lie of *commission* or *omission*? Mrs. Dahlke had been teaching me when to double consonants, but when it came to lies, the difference between these two words involved more than spelling rules. Something else to figure out.

"Good. Now," she pointed to my music, "Where have we heard this before?"

I was so flabbergasted by Mrs. Keindorf's fingernail polish that I couldn't concentrate on the notes under her index finger. Her polish exactly matched her ruby ring and her elaborately ruffled blouse. Her house always smelled like vanilla, which didn't go with the cowboy furniture, but neither did the pictures of the archduke or the city full of castles.

I was stumped. Since we were only on the second page of the piece, the answer must lurk nearby, but I couldn't see one repetition. Beethoven wrote altogether too many notes, even in John Thompson's simplified piano version of the second movement of his Fifth Symphony. Worse than that, this version was in four flats, which, in my opinion, didn't qualify as simplified.

Mrs. Keindorf patted my arm in encouragement. "Remember how 'Arkansas Traveler' varies the theme by putting it into the left hand?" She had let me jump ahead ten songs to learn a fun and easy piece when I first bogged down in Beethoven.

"Theme and variations." Today her hair was pulled up into a bun on top of her head, emphasizing her high cheek bones. "The basis of most music. Look right here." Her finger ran across a slew of eighth notes. "Same melody, different rhythm." They might as well have been black ants.

She leaned back and tilted her head. "It's one reason why we love music: we recognize the melody like a friend, but dressed a little differently each time." The way she rolled her r's, I would've agreed with anything, especially the way she said "Arkansas."

"When we're finished today, I'll play a little Rachmaninoff, and you'll see what I mean."

"We could finish right now," I suggested brightly. My brain was numb from playing scales, Hanon, and a silly piece called "The Juggler" before I hit big, bad Beethoven.

She wrote down my lesson. "All right, but for next week, I want you to mark all the themes and variations in both Beethoven and 'Arkansas Traveler'."

She stood, smoothed her straight black skirt and walked to the buffet which held her sheet music, phonograph player and records. "Rachmaninoff wrote twenty-four variations on Paganini's theme, but I'll play just one or two."

I now pretended that I was paying a social call and balancing a cup of tea on my lap. "How did you end up in Round Prairie?" I could understand if her husband were working on the Republican River dam, but he was the new dry cleaner.

For a moment, she looked at me as if she were sight-reading a piano piece. "Helmut and I first heard about Nebraska from my brother. He was a prisoner of war interned in the German camp in Hebron."

"Hebron, *Nebraska*? Where Grandma Strang lives? And I went to third grade?" I wondered who else knew about this. Sam didn't, or we would have played POW camp on the actual historical site.

"Yes." She pulled out several music books and replaced them. "There were camps all across Nebraska. A huge one in Atlanta and big ones in Fort Robinson and Holdredge. Thousands of POW's."

Why hadn't I heard this before?

"The farms were short-handed because all the men were fighting in Europe, so they let the German prisoners work on nearby farms. My brother said the farm wives often baked potatoes for them and even paid them a little."

"Weren't they afraid they'd escape?" I asked breathlessly. Real-life enemies from a real war had been imprisoned in my back yard, and I didn't even know it.

Mrs. Keindorf smiled. "Where would they go?"

"You mean, Americans soldiers went over to fight in Germany, and German soldiers came over here to do their farm work?"

She nodded.

"It would have saved a lot of trouble if everybody had just stayed home."

She sat in the chair with the cowboy boots burned into it. "Very true. Nebraska felt like home to the prisoners, since so many people here were originally German immigrants and even spoke the language. Johann's letters home told how much he loved the land and the warmth of the American people. He wanted to come back here to live. Quite a few did return, you know."

I felt as if I didn't know anything. "Did he? Come back?"

"He . . . never left." She tucked a few stray hairs behind her ears. "My brother miraculously survived the Wacht am Rhein, which Americans call the Battle of the Bulge. Tens of thousands were killed—on both sides. That's where Johann was taken prisoner. Then he endured the terrible forced marches across Europe and being wounded and nearly starving, and the horrible crossing on the ship here. His life in Nebraska felt like a godsend."

She twirled her ring around and around her finger.

"At the end, just as the prisoners gathered to board the train east, a fellow prisoner accidentally pushed him and . . . he fell backward off the platform and . . . ." She bit her thick lower lip. "Broke his neck." She held her thumb and index finger a quarter inch apart. "That close. To survive all that . . . just to die." Her hands dropped in her lap.

"That's so unfair," I protested.

"Nineteen years old. We couldn't ship his body home, so–" She shrugged. "He was buried here."

"Wh-where?"

"In Hebron. On a little hill outside of town."

"Rose Hill Cemetery?"

She looked surprised, "Do you know–?

"That's where Janet's buried!" I blurted out. "My sister."

"You have a dead?–"

"A long time ago," I brushed off the question. "Do you realize you have a brother and I have a sister, and they're both dead, and both are buried in the *same* cemetery?"

"That is remarkable, I must say."

"Where is he in Rose Hill? We go there all the time, and I could visit him."

"He doesn't have a marker yet."

"Just like Janet!"

We both sighed, slowly absorbing this coincidence. I wondered if she talked to her brother like I talked to Janet.

"Helmut and I moved to Nebraska, expecting people to be friendly and . . . ." She played with the ruffles at her neck. "They were so good to Johann. Sometimes the farm women sent him back to the camp with a loaf of home-made bread for the other men."

"Well," she shook herself and cleared her throat. "This isn't getting us anywhere with themes and variations, is it?"

She stood up and searched inside the buffet, carved into leaves and flowers from a dark red wood which didn't match the cowboy furniture. She pulled some music out of a pile and smiled at it as if she were greeting a friend.

"The eighteenth variation."

"On the same theme?" Papa joked that Reverend Harkin knew all about this technique.

The music was yellowed and torn on the edges, and she opened it tenderly. "He wrote twenty-four in all. My mother never let me play Rachmaninoff. Even though I was studying to become a concert pianist."

"Why?" I gasped at the injustices piling up in Mrs. Keindorf's life.

"He's Russian." Realizing I didn't understand, she added, "Germans have suffered terribly at the hands of Russians. And not only Germans." She closed the music. "Everybody's afraid of them. That's why America has this Cold War." She put the sheet music back and closed the cupboard.

What cold war? Where was it being fought? When did it start? Who was winning? I felt so stupid I didn't know which question to ask first.

"Russians, Americans, British, Japanese, Nazis, Communists . . . . It just goes on and on."

She looked so sad that I wanted to cheer her up. "Would you play that for me? The Rach– . . . variations?"

She cocked her head and smiled. "Thank you for reminding me, Jeb. It would be my pleasure." Nobody but Mrs. Keindorf could fill that word with so much pleasure, thick as ice cream.

I slid off the bench and sat in the chair where she always listened to my lesson. "Don't you need music?"

"Not for Rachmaninoff." She sat down at the piano, took off her watch and ring, momentarily glanced at the picture of the magical city, and began to play.

Played one of the most beautiful songs I had ever heard, ever. As her thin, elegant fingers danced up and down the keyboard, her music filled the streets of the magical city, rose to the top of the highest spires, filled each castle and palace and cathedral with light, and with life.

CHAPTER 25

RADAR

"DO YOU THINK TELEKINESIS IS POSSIBLE?" SAM asked Miss Reynolds.

She stopped shelving a book and leaned on her cart, a tall wagon with wheels.

Sam ran his hand along the spines of the books, in this aisle marked with tiny white numbers from 900-999. He loved the Dewey decimal system, a map for finding books, easier to use than a topographical map and more reliable than a star chart, since books didn't move by themselves. He had drawn maps for places where we hid the Formula until Clawson's gang stole our stockpile of dirt-clod ammunition. They didn't need directions to the Ultimate Weapon which could save all life on earth.

I explained to her, "Telekinesis means moving objects with your mind."

"I'm well aware of that, Judith. Can you spell it?"

"T-e-l-i-k-i-n-e-s-i-s," I rattled off. "You might have noticed, every other letter is a vowel."

"True. But you have one wrong vowel."

"Sam taught me how to spell it."

"That's a recommendation? Who's the scientist in your family?"

Sam frowned. "Me."

"My case rests. It's t-e-l-e-k-i-n-e-s-i-s."

Before she slid the book into its correct slot, I saw its title: *I Led Three Lives.*

"What three lives?" I knew about the three Musketeers, the movie "Three Faces West," three blind mice and the three gods of the Methodist Trinity. But someone leading three lives, possibly at the same time, was new.

Miss Reynolds answered all-in-a-row, "Citizen, Communist and Counterspy. Could be describing the Wilder children."

"We're not Communists," Sam defended.

"Or citizens," I added. I'd have to look into counterspies.

As she searched the row of books, Miss Reynolds turned to Sam. "Telekinesis would certainly help me shelve books. I could sit at my desk and merely think about it. Maybe that's what city employees are doing when four men stand around, leaning on shovels and staring into a hole."

Sam hitched up his holster set, empty because Miss Reynolds wouldn't allow guns in the library. "You must admit, we can't travel by teleportation until we master ESP and telekinesis."

Miss Reynolds continued shelving books, one about a man called Peter and another about a Caine mutiny. "Are the Boy Scouts launching a merit badge in parapsychology?"

"Seriously–" Sam tried again.

"Sam, I will not be serious about hocus-pocus. I personally forbid you to join the company of frauds and charlatans who rig up special effects, lie about their 'evidence' and publish their crackpot accounts for the ultra-gullible. Have you encountered Alexander Aksakof or Eva Carrière?"

Sam shook his head no.

"Look them up: certifiable lunatics."

"What else would you expect from Marvin Harkin?" I sounded like Mama talking about Dr. Mary.

She pretended to consider, "Maybe Marve wants to become a medium and hold séances. As an undertaker, he has a head start."

Sam pushed Miss Reynolds' cart back to her desk slowly enough for her to hang on to one side to walk. It would just be so neat," he continued wistfully, "to control things from far away, using only your mind. No . . . wires or . . . transmitters or . . . . "

"–incriminating evidence," Miss Reynolds finished his sentence and sat down hard behind her desk. I grabbed the date stamp before she could stop me.

"Look what Mr. Harkin handed out at our last troop meeting." From his back pocket, Sam pulled a plastic card showing six black silhouettes of airplanes. "This is a Russian bomber, the Bear F, and this one's a Bison. Here's my favorite–the MiG-15–the jet the Reds have used in Korea."

"In-cre-dible." When Miss Reynolds was being sarcastic, her mouth looked as if she were chewing something large.

Sarcasm, I had learned, was an acceptable form of lying, different from metaphor and probably closer to faith.

"What are you supposed to do with that?" she indicated the card. In addition to her silver glasses chain, she wore a tiny purple pendant which might be a genuine amethyst. It matched what must be a new dress, although it looked exactly like all her other dresses, a shapeless cotton shirtwaist with three-quarter length sleeves. Mama could sew her a much prettier dress if you could keep her attention long enough.

Sam answered, "Identify Russian planes flying overhead and report them to Sheriff Westergaard."

Now I was confused. "I thought the Russians were on our side." They certainly saved Sam and me from the Messerschmitts in Sunday morning bombing runs.

"That was the last war," Miss Reynolds said with fake sweetness. "Nine years ago. Seems like yesterday."

Sam carefully slipped the card into his back pocket.

Miss Reynolds folded her hands and leaned across her desk. "Sam, how far is it from here to either coast?"

I piped up, "Lebanon is only 14 miles away, and it's the—"

Without looking at me, Miss Reynolds asked, "Is your name Sam?"

I shook my head, but she didn't see me.

With my clue, Sam calculated, "The same distance to both coasts."

I had to finish, like a sneeze. "–center of the continental United States."

Again without looking at me, Miss Reynolds pointed toward the unabridged dictionary. "Judith, look up *fractious*: f-r-a-c . . . . Sam, how far it is to either coast?"

"About . . . two thousand miles?" he guessed.

"Good," she responded. "How many big cities, military bases and radar facilities would a Russian plane need to fly over, undetected and unscathed, before it reached central Nebraska?"

I called from the dictionary, "*Radar* is one of those words you spell the same forward and backward."

"Have you found *fractious* yet?"

"What comes after the *c*?"

"T – i – o – u – s. Sam, be logical: what are the chances of a Russian war plane dropping a bomb on Round Prairie? Literally in the middle of nowhere. Not to mention, how far away is Russia? And where would that misguided Russian pilot re-fuel?

Stopped by Miss Reynolds' irrefutable logic, Sam fell back on the unspoken Boy Scout Code—mindless allegiance to authority, even if he's a moron. "Mr. Harkin didn't exactly say they would bomb Round Prairie . . . . "

I hated to see Sam take the rap for the entire B. S. nation, so I called out, "It could be on its way to the Lincoln Air Force Base."

"Yeah," Sam took my cue excitedly. "Lincoln just brought in a bunch of B-29s."

Miss Reynolds continued, "Tell Marvin that we have much more to fear from people right here in Round Prairie than some pitiful Russian accidentally flying this far inland."

Sam suddenly remembered our mission in the library. "Oh. Mama wondered if you had a brand-new book called *Angel . . . Un— derwear.*"

"*Unaware,*" Miss Reynolds corrected.

I walked back to her desk and rolled the date stamp to Mama's birthday. "It's by Dale Evans, who, you might want to know, is Roy Rogers' wife. I don't know why they don't have the same last name."

"Show biz," she answered.

Helpfully, Sam explained, "Joseph and Jesus have different last names."

Miss Reynolds' mouth opened and closed slowly. She leaned back in her squeaking chair and folded her creamy arms across her giant bosom. "I eagerly await a completely new explanation of Jesus' extraordinary parentage. What do you think is Jesus's last name? *God?*"

"No, it's *Mary,*" I offered.

"Then Mary's name is . . . Mary *Mary?*" Miss Reynolds was starting to jiggle.

Sam explained, "No, she's Virgin Mary."

"What is Tom Harkin preaching at the Methodist Church?"

"It isn't Methodism, it's logic," Sam was one of the few boys his age who could use the word *logic* convincingly and against Miss Reynolds, no less.

"True: religion and logic seldom go together." Turning to me, she added, "By the way, his name isn't really Roy Rogers."

At the look of horror and disbelief on my face, she changed tone. "But we can talk about that another day."

Sam advised, "Tell us now; it will only get harder to take later."

I added, "Papa says, face the bad news first, when you have the most energy for it."

"Frank's right, as always: Roy Rogers' real name is Leonard Franklin Slye."

The one world I thought I could rely on—movies—suddenly started to fall apart as well. "That's just not feasible," I argued.

"No, it wasn't feasible trying to sell a movie star named Leonard Slye."

"How about Trigger?" I demanded. "What's his real name? Or Bullet?"

"The movie industry doesn't need to change the names of dogs and horses who don't pretend to act."

Sam was almost as upset as I. "Even if they did that to Roy Rogers, they wouldn't dare do it to John Wayne."

Miss Reynolds cleared her throat. "Even worse: His real name is Marion Morrison."

"That's a girl's name!" Sam protested. "This is all just . . . a lie, somebody's idea of . . . of . . ."

"A sales pitch," Miss Reynolds finished his sentence.

At that moment, who walked in the door but Mrs. Vince, Sam's sixth-grade teacher. Sam evaporated into the stacks so fast I didn't even see him move.

Miss Reynolds asked, "Did you find out what *fractious* means?"

"Yes, Ma'am." I felt the need to sound more polite in front of a teacher, especially the one who held Sam's fate in her hands. He would do the same for me.

Miss Reynolds explained, "Judith loves words."

"So I've heard from Mildred." Mrs. Vince would have looked a lot younger if she didn't always wear brown suits shaped like Army uniforms. She was very tall and thin and as old as Miss Reynolds.

"It means disruptive, disobedient, and unmanageable—a lot like *raucous* and *rambunctious*. Mrs. Dahlke taught me those."

The two women laughed, although I didn't find anything funny. "Why are there so many words that mean the same thing?"

Miss Reynolds answered, "To describe people like you, Judith. You started out rambunctious, soon turned raucous and now border on fractious."

I decided to let that pass and turned to Mrs. Vince, "Do you know *radar* is spelled the same forwards and backwards?"

Mrs. Vince smiled like a grandmother. "So are *level* and *racecar*. They're called palindromes."

Possibly Mrs. Vince knew as much as Mrs. Dahlke and Miss Reynolds.

She backtracked. "Well, technically, a single word can't be a palindrome, but it's close enough."

Miss Reynolds added, "Usually palindromes are whole sentences."

"I've always liked 'Madam, in Eden, I'm Adam'," Mrs. Vince said.

"Of course you have, Edna. My favorite is 'Dogma: I am god.' I'm trying to figure out how to work Hoover into it."

"They'll lock you up yet, Thelma," Mrs. Vince warned, laying two books on the desk to check in. On the cover of the top book was an old fashioned picture of a man in an army uniform with a decorated bandolier.

"Is that the Archduke Franz Ferdinand of Austria?"

"Judith Beatrice, you never cease to amaze me." Miss Reynolds took off her glasses and let them hang on her plain silver rope, her least showy but possibly most expensive chain. "This is a biography of Joseph Stalin. Where did you encounter the ill-fated Archduke?"

"Mrs. Keindorf has a picture of him on her living room wall. He was a friend of her grandmother. An actual archduke. The meter man thought he was that Stalin guy." I self-corrected, "Stalin man."

"Stalin! Why on earth would he think—?" Mrs. Vince said, exchanging glances with Miss Reynolds.

I had probably said too much. Maybe this was what counterspies did.

"Are you certain of this, Judith?" Miss Reynolds used her test voice. "It's not a subject around which to fabricate stories."

"I don't even know Stalin." I could tell from their faces that this was a good argument. "Besides, Mrs. Keindorf told me herself, and she wouldn't make up things. The meter man got mad and called her names and everything, even though she explained the picture was the Archduke of Austria."

Mrs. Vince looked very serious. "I hate to think what the meter man has done with this misinformation. The gossip—"

"Never underestimate the ignorance of the American proletariat," Miss Reynolds added.

Excited about the new word, I asked, "Are gas meter men proletariats? Mama says they're all Communists."

Miss Reynolds looked at Mrs. Vince for a minute before she answered me, "We'll talk about the proletariat another day, all right?"

In spite of Papa's constant warnings to mind my own business, I added, "Did you know Mrs. Keindorf's brother was a prisoner of war? In Hebron? Nebraska."

Very quietly, Mrs. Vince said, "I had heard—"

"She and Mr. Keindorf moved here because everybody was so nice to her brother."

Mrs. Vince said very quietly, "Oh dear."

Miss Reynolds added, "Ain't that the gods' truth, Edna? Haven't folks in Round Prairie always set the gold standard for *niceness?*"

At this moment, Sam walked out of the stacks in a hurry, very businesslike.

"Sam. What a nice surprise," Mrs. Vince said.

"I'm late for . . . a Scout meeting." He must have felt desperate to lie, and to his teacher of all people, but she stood between him and the door.

"What's your troop working on now?" Mrs. Vince asked politely.

Miss Reynolds answered, "A merit badge in the occult. Starring Marve Harkin as the medium."

"We're, uh . . . ," Sam trailed off. He was so awkward, he would never make a good liar. Honestly.

I stepped in, "Emergency preparedness." That sounded good, and it saved Sam.

With fake innocence, Miss Reynolds said, "Sam carries a card with the silhouettes of Russian warplanes. To warn us all in case of attack."

Sam explained, "Mr. Harkin thinks the Boy Scouts could be the town's first line of defense."

Miss Reynolds put on her glasses and just looked at him, then turned to Mrs. Vince. "Edna, did I tell you the latest absurdity? The city 'council'— for want of a better epithet— – has proposed using the library as a bomb shelter. Half the basement lies above ground, surrounded by glass windows. A glass bomb shelter. Isn't that rich?"

Mrs. Vince added, "Remember a few years ago, when they debated thirty minutes before deciding to shorten library hours on Saturday–"

Miss Reynolds finished, "After I had volunteered to work all day *for free.* The three stooges—Cavin, Clawson and Harkin."

Which Harkin, I wondered, although either would qualify.

"Better watch out," Mrs. Vince warned. "The walls have ears."

"Cavin was thrilled when McCarthy blacklisted Albert Einstein."

Mrs. Vince shook her head and let out a big breath.

Miss Reynolds continued, "HUAC needed a policy clarification–officially outlawing intelligence."

Starting for the door, Sam called over his shoulder, "The Russian planes could be heading for the Hastings ammo dump."

Miss Reynolds barked, "*Ammo dump*? With your extensive education in all things explosive, why would you use such a vulgar colloquialism?"

Mrs. Vince added, "Sam, it's the Naval Ammunition Depot. During World War II, the fourth largest munitions storage facility in the country."

Sam looked at her with drastically increased respect.

In her let's-educate-the-children voice, Miss Reynolds added, "In September of 1944, one of the buildings exploded. We heard it all the way to Round Prairie, forty miles away.

"Wow," Sam looked from one woman to the other.

"It killed nine people and injured fifty-three others."

I felt queasy, suddenly seeing my dream, Papa a running silhouette against a wall of fire. "Did somebody throw a firecracker?"

Mrs. Vince looked at me quizzically, then slowly answered. "No. They were smoking a cigarette."

Miss Reynolds added softly, "Edna's brother was killed in the explosion."

Mrs. Vince shook her head sadly. "Him with three young children."

What if Papa had been killed? What if Sam were ever killed? As usual, I suddenly felt the need to cheer everybody up. "I was born in 1944," was all I could think to say. "So you've lived my whole life without your brother."

Mrs. Vince smiled. "Thank you, Judith. Now I have a new way of thinking about it."

Sam pushed through the library door. "See you later."

I turned to follow him.

Miss Reynolds indicated the date stamp I was holding. "If you're finished playing with the date, would you please roll it to where you found it?"

"Why does the rubber year only go to1950? It's 1953."

"In his dotage, Seth Post took a knife and whittled off the years after that, figuring he wouldn't get any older, I guess."

"How long has he been dead?" Mrs. Vince asked.

"Three years."

For some reason, both women laughed. They were still laughing as I walked out.

CHAPTER 26
NEVER ODD OR EVEN

WHILE I LOOKED AS IF I WERE INNOCENTLY RIDing Maybe home from Hale's Grocery with a loaf of Wonder Bread and a bottle of Andersen's Milk in my basket, I was actually on a reconnaissance mission in an unfamiliar part of town, looking for enemy activity. Last Saturday afternoon, Jim Hartsock, Sam and I were attacked in the fort by five boys from their scout troop who wielded cap guns, had no discernible battle strategy, and fought as if they were fulfilling the requirements for a merit badge in playing war. Even the boys in Eddy's Bakery fort could beat these troops with dough balls. The scouts surrendered in our first counter-attack, instantly routed by Sam's blood-curdling Indian yell and our synchronized Musketeer leap out of the fort to capture them.

Jim told them they should join our side but, if they rejected the offer, advised them to become *guerillas*, which increased my respect for him tenfold, even though he pronounced it *gorillas*. He probably spelled it wrong, too. Jim had buck teeth, but he never looked goofier than when he wore his John Deere baseball cap backwards. Even worn frontwards, baseball caps had no point that I could see.

While we had prisoners of war, however briefly, I wanted to interrogate them. "Do any of you guys know Joe Clary?" I thought I sounded pretty nonchalant.

"He's a Cub Scout," said one of the captives, as if this qualified as useful information.

"Jeb wants him for a boyfriend," Sam snickered.

That was so patently untrue that I slugged him on the shoulder. "I wondered if he fights with anybody because he might join our side, too."

Jim Hartsock volunteered, "My mom said he's kind of sickly, part albino or something."

I was so flabbergasted, I overcame my pride to ask, "What's an albino?"

"They're all white, even their hair," Sam answered as if he knew anything, "but they have to have pink eyes." He wouldn't lie, but he could be making this up to impress our Scout prisoners with arcane information. *Arcane* was my latest favorite word—"requiring secret knowledge"—which Sam did all the time but didn't know the word for it. I liked the way he and I knew different things that, put together, made a complete picture.

I was still contemplating albinos on my bicycle grocery run when, up ahead, I spotted a hopscotch board chalked on the sidewalk, rare because most of Round Prairie had dirt paths instead of cement sidewalks. It could be a coded map leading to a stash of secret weapons or a message like the anagram sign in the hardware store window. On the other hand, a hopscotch board might simply mean that girls lived there. The house itself looked like every other one in this part of town, a rectangular white box trimmed with fake blue shutters, but it was a real house. A United States flag hung from a special holder like a metal hand beside the stoop.

My spy mission could wait. I dismounted, leaned Maybe against a tree, found a rock for a taw, and threw it into the first square. I hopped perfect rounds through square four, when I heard the front door of the house open. Giggling and squealing came from inside.

To my horror, out walked Doreen Cavin and her mother. Doreen wore a pink polished cotton dress and patent leather shoes, and her mother wore a white ruffled apron over a gaudy flowered dress.

"Is this where you live?" I asked incredulously.

"You can't play here," Doreen blurted out. She looked particularly ridiculous with a pink bow on top of her ringlets.

"I'm not playing. I'm . . . practicing."

Her mother wiped her hands on a starched tea towel she was carrying. "Well, today you'll have to practice somewhere else." She wore flashy wedding rings, silver filigree trying to look like diamonds. I knew what I knew.

"There isn't anywhere else." I kept one eye on Maybe, in case they tried to impound it or steal the groceries.

"Draw a hopscotch board in the park." Mrs. Cavin's smile was turning hard, like plaster. She could barely talk through it.

"This is my hopscotch board, and you can't play on it," Doreen bossed all the girls at school except the farm girls and me. We weren't worth the trouble.

I tried to sound like Miss Reynolds. "Sidewalks are public property."

"Not today," Mrs. Cavin used the adult sing-song voice reserved for babies.

Doreen sneered, "It's my birthday party, and only Brownies are invited."

I looked behind her at the doorway to the house and now recognized Alana Hofmann and Nancy Gillian. I had created a fictitious Brownie troop so convincing that I had forgotten a real one existed. Even though I didn't want to stay here any longer, I hated to let Doreen and her mother win without a fight.

"You don't own the sidewalk or, actually, any property between here and the street." Sam had proven this to me in Hebron.

Mrs. Cavin's plaster smile was cracking. "You don't want to be a troublemaker, do you?"

"I'm not the one defacing public property." Her snooty attitude forced me to be more of a smart aleck than usual and to ignore Mama's advice: Never stoop to arguing with a lowbrow no-account. It wasn't always easy to identify one, but in this case it was obvious.

Mrs. Cavin wiped her hands again on the fancy towel. "Well, aren't you the little lawyer?"

In a rare moment when I could use the line and mean it, I said, "I'm just telling the truth."

With her free hand, Mrs. Cavin straightened the bow on top of Doreen's head, like adjusting a pet dog to show at the county fair. "Has anyone ever told you that you're a little too smart for your own good?"

How could anyone be too smart for their own good, I wondered. "Better than being too stupid." I didn't know what else to say.

"Why, you little . . . . No wonder your mother's headed for . . . ."

"Wh-where?" Where was Mama going, and how could Mrs. Cavin possibly know?"And you're driving her to it. You go home. Right now."

I knew I couldn't win with a grown-up. Besides, Mama and Papa would take turns tanning my hide if they knew I had sassed Mrs. Cavin.

As I turned to get Maybe, Doreen sneered, "To your tray-ler." With her mother's hand on her shoulder, she hissed, "White trash."

"Doreen!" Mrs. Cavin tried to sound as if she disapproved, but I could tell she was secretly pleased.

As I climbed on Maybe, I considered my options. I could park my bike on the sidewalk just past their property and watch them, but they might think I wanted to be at their stupid party. I could ride to the fort and get a sack of dirt clods to throw on their illegal hopscotch board, but that would spend valuable ammo on silly girl stuff. Instead, I rode to the end of the block, crossed the street, and hid behind the bushes in some stranger's front yard to spy on the birthday party. About ten girls came running and shrieking outside, followed by Mrs. Cavin carrying a birthday cake with white frosting and Mr. Cavin with a card table and a camera around his neck. Each girl had a balloon.

Where was Mama going? How was I sending her there? Was Sam sending her there, too?

As I rode Maybe home, jolting the milk and bread each time my bicycle chain hit a missing tooth, I wondered about white trash. Sam and I had scoured every trash pile in town, where we had found some major treasures: a green kazoo that still worked, a blue rubber dog connected to a hose and bulb you could squeeze to make him jump, a miniature plastic hourglass filled with solidified sand, four bright red glass beads and—my favorite—a pair of turquoise sunglasses with one lens missing. Wearing them, I could be a pirate or a movie star or pretend to be blind in one eye like Papa.

Trash came in every color in the world, but never white. To make it white, you would have to imagine away all its colors in the reverse process Mama and I used to add color to black and white movies. But why would you? The red beads alone were like holding ripe cherries in your hand. Sam and I had immediately popped one into the Formula, where it lay at the bottom of the bottle, adding red magic to the dark liquid.

At supper that night, I asked, "What's 'white trash'?"

Papa stopped his bite of food in mid-air. Since we were having meat loaf, one of his favorite things in the world, I knew this was an Important Question.

He and Mama looked at each other, and Sam held his head perfectly still but rolled his eyes in a circle.

"Where did you hear that?" Mama asked, sounding more like a statement than a question.

"Doreen Cavin. Called me white trash."

"I hope you nailed her." Sam blurted. "You could deck her with one hand, Jeb."

"Just a minute, Sam," Papa warned.

"But she could." Sam sounded as proud of me as rules about Little Sisters allowed.

"I didn't know what it meant." I studied my carrots. "But it sounded bad."

Papa laid down his fork with a little meat loaf still on it. "It says more about the person saying the words than the person they're talking about."

"What had you done to her?" Mama asked.

"Nothing."

Sam defended me. "Doreen calls everybody names–except her whiney little girlfriends."

"She was having her birthday party with all the Brownies—" Oh oh. I had tricked myself into unintentionally saying the B-word.

Mama seized on it. "Why didn't she invite you? You're a Brownie."

Sam, who knew all about my fake life as a Brownie, jumped in to my rescue. "She probably invited only Brownies of a certain rank, like above a Tenderfoot."

Not necessarily a lie, and logical to boot. I could have kissed him.

"I know how you feel, Jeb," Mama said with unexpected tenderness. "When I was a little girl, nobody invited me to parties, either, no matter what I did."

"Why not?" I knew Mama had been raised like a lady and didn't fight with boys or have a fort or Formula.

Mama looked right at me, carefully tucking her wavy hair away from her eyes. "Partly because we were poor, but mostly because . . . I didn't have a father."

Mama so seldom talked like this that I didn't dare interrupt. All three of us sat as still as in church.

"Well, I had a father, but . . . when he deserted us kids and your Grandma Strang about to have another baby . . . people just, I don't know. Blamed us, I guess."

Papa kept looking at the table and shaking his head. I could tell her story still made him sad.

"I'm so sorry, Mama," I finally said. "Life without Papa would be horrible."

"Yes, it would, Jeb," she agreed.

Papa looked up at her in surprise, and she smiled. A real smile.

"It's true, Frank. Without you, I don't know what I would do."

"Me neither, Edie."

We were all quiet for a minute, then, unfortunately, Mama remembered my original question. "Why did Doreen call you that terrible name?"

"She said people who live in trailers are white trash."

"I hope you didn't lower yourself to her level." Good old Mama always said that. I loved it when Mama did what I expected.

I stabbed a carrot wheel, which stood out in bright orange against my turquoise Fiesta plate. "Frankly, I think people who live in trailers are interesting." *Frankly* was my latest favorite adverb, automatically reducing suspicions about lies.

Sam's face wrinkled up, as if he were trying to swallow something too big. Clearly, he couldn't believe I would even mention trailers, since the trailer court still ranked in the top priority of Topics to Avoid around the folks. And after he had beautifully engineered the supper conversation away from the Brownies.

"We live in a trailer," I pushed, without knowing why.

Mama picked up her yellow Fiesta plate and carried it to the sink. She looked out the tiny window toward the fort. "You can say that again."

Sam watched everybody without moving his head.

Since the migrant workers had all moved north by now, I felt it was safe at least to mention them. "You have to admit, Will Hankins is way more interesting than Doreen Cavin."

Papa smiled sideways and picked up his fork with the bite still on it. "I don't know Doreen, but Edie, you know her father, Tom Cavin. The used car dealer."

"Who wears those slinky shirts? Looks as if he works in a beer joint?"

"The very one." He glanced at Mama. "I'd have to agree with Jeb about who's more interesting here."

"And Cavin a city councilman," Mama said scornfully.

Papa answered, "My case rests."

Mama put a pan of home-made peach cobbler on a trivet on the table. "The Cavins are Catholics to boot. What can you expect?"

Then, to my drop-dead amazement, Mama bent over Papa's shoulder and kissed him on the cheek.

CHAPTER 27

SHAZAM

THE FIRST TIME I WAS TOLD TO REPORT TO Sprecker's office after school, I assumed the playground teacher had reported Leon Troxel and me for roughhousing during recess. While playing Red Rover, each of us would try to dislocate the shoulder of the other one by running flat out at their line and, at the last minute, raising one knee to drop our full weight on their clasped hands. Unfortunately, any innocent kid holding our hand was attacked as well. Finally, no one would hold my hand except Joe Clary, even when I warned him of his personal danger. He couldn't hang on, but that was all right, since he had tried. Like Papa, I valued that in a person.

To my surprise, instead of Leon Troxel, I heard Mrs. Dahlke's voice coming from the principal's office. I stood outside the door, slightly ajar, and eavesdropped.

"I monitored the room the entire time. You have absolutely no grounds—" She broke off. "Come in, Judith. Mr. Sprecker and I are finished."

"Mrs. Dahlke, you don't need to stay for this," Sprecker said in a loud voice designed to silence opposition. After such a long teaching day," he added lamely. His suit coat was so big I could see only half his fingers coming out his sleeves. He and Will Hankins should exchange clothes, since Will's sleeves ended halfway up his forearm.

"I don't mind," she answered. "In fact, I insist." Looking at me, she added, "If it wouldn't make Judith nervous."

"Nervous?" I asked with growing alarm. Was it legal for principals to beat up students they didn't like?

Sprecker never looked straight at anybody, or maybe it was just kids. "I want you to re-take the test your class took last month."

"Why?" I asked Mrs. Dahlke, who shrugged her shoulders in an exaggerated fashion. I had never seen her do that.

I turned to Sprecker. "Why?"

He lined up every paper on his desk along a perfect grid only he could see. "There was some . . . irregularity. A mistake . . . in the scoring."

From any other grown-up, even one of the Harkin brothers, I would have accepted such an obvious lie, but something about the principal drove me to resist, in spite of Sam's continual warnings to fly under the radar with both Mama and Mr. Sprecker. As Mr. Whitaker said, some people were born to throw a wrench in the monkeyworks.

"For the whole class?" I asked.

Mr. Sprecker waited for Mrs. Dahlke to answer for him. She folded her arms.

"I won't put up with your impertinence, little girl. Some people around here may allow it," he glanced at Mrs. Dahlke, "but I won't."

Mrs. Dahlke adjusted her wire rim glasses and looked back at him steadily.

I wanted to make him lie again by asking how many other kids were affected by mistakes in the scoring, but I settled on, "Just me?"

"Yes." He gathered the papers off the invisible grid on his desk. "Let's get this over with."

We walked to Mrs. Dahlke's classroom, where some of my double-"l" spelling words were still on the blackboard: *ballistic, surveillance, artillery, collision* . Sprecker unsealed a test packet like the ones issued to the whole fourth grade a month earlier. On my desk, he put a short yellow pencil, very sharp with no eraser, then looked at his watch, although the clock, bigger than a Buick hubcap, hung over his head.

"One hour." He began to circle the room, looking out the windows, stepping on the same squeaking floorboard each round.

Mrs. Dahlke sat at her desk grading arithmetic papers, looking annoyed each time he walked between her and the blackboard.

The warm afternoon sunlight yellowed the walls and intensified the smell of dirt and oil embedded in the old oak floors.

I don't know how long I took, but when I finished, I began kicking my legs under my desk, a Forbidden Act during class.

"Stumped?" Mr. Sprecker asked sharply. "Can't go any further?" I could tell that he expected me to break down in tears or something.

"I'm done."

He looked at his watch. "In thirty-eight minutes? You couldn't answer them all, could you?" His lips disappeared in a thin line, probably his version of a real smile.

"I did. I'm done."

He strode over to my desk and saw that I had penciled in the blank for each question. He pulled up his over-long sleeve to check his watch again.

I held out my answer sheet. "It was easier this time."

"Why is that?" he asked with a voice like hitting the wrong note in a piano piece.

"A lot of the questions were the same, so I didn't have to think so long."

He snatched my answer sheet and ran his hand over it as if it were written in Braille.

I clarified, "But the questions were in a different order."

Mrs. Dahlke curled her fist and covered her mouth. She must've been about to cough.

"Is that so." Mr. Sprecker's mouth looked as if invisible fingers were pulling it up at the corners.

"Can I go now?"

"Yes," Mrs. Dahlke answered before Sprecker could say anything.

I toyed with the little pencil. "May I keep this?"

"What if everybody did that?" Sprecker pulled it out of my hand and answered with his standard fake democracy argument. "It wouldn't take long for us to run out of pencils, would it?"

As he walked toward the classroom door with my test and the pencil, Mrs. Dahlke called to him, "I hope that you learned everything you needed to know." He walked out the door without looking back.

The air in the room suddenly expanded as if it had been holding its breath.

"Guess what, Jeb?" Mrs. Dahlke sounded just like me. She held out the pencil she had been using to grade papers, a brand-new yellow Dixon Ticonderoga 2/B with a perfect eraser. "For you. Our little secret."

Grown-ups were always asking me to keep secrets, but never one so sweet as Mrs. Dahlke's. I named my new, very own full-sized pencil Shazam on the spot.

CHAPTER 28
PAVANE FOR A DYING PRINCESS

HALLOWEEN WAS, NATURALLY, MY FAVORITE HOLI-day, created basically for children to acquire a year's supply of candy in one simple night's work. I should say a year's supply for people like Sam, who could make his candy last until his birthday in May, while I careened along the edge of sick until I had eaten it all–usually in two weeks, with a few pieces of stale gum lasting until Christmas, when I might or might not find candy in my sock. Besides the candy advantage, on Halloween you could legally run around in public pretending to be a hero, and nobody could turn you in as a liar or fraud. Miss Reynolds said that J. Edgar Hoover had invented Halloween so no one could distinguish the real devils from the ones in disguise.

"He gets more ubiquitous every day," she scowled. "Baby Hoovers are popping up everywhere–"

"Like the Communists?" I asked excitedly.

Miss Reynolds slowly nodded. "The Reds and the Red-hunters. A thug by the opposite name smells the same."

Just as Sam and I were closing in on a short list of Communists in Round Prairie, we now had to worry about Baby Hoovers. Maybe we should focus the power of the Formula on the thugs in Round Prairie instead of trying to save the world.

Miss Reynolds smoothed the unabridged dictionary page where we had found *ubiquitous*. "Proving, once again, that we should choose our enemies carefully, since we end up acting just like them." She paused. "To wit, the French Revolution."

To wit? Whose wit? What revolution in France? Was it still going?

"On a lighter note, Judith, you will appreciate the fact that I'm keeping the library open Halloween evening to distribute candy. Horehound drops."

I dared to say, "Nobody likes horehound drops except you."

"That's the whole point."

"Sam and I may not have time to drop by." On Papa's advice, I was working on being diplomatic, a weak and acceptable kind of lie.

"I'll give you a few drops ahead of time to prime your pump."

Sam and I had lived in Round Prairie long enough to know which houses to avoid trick-or-treating, knowing that the Clawsons and Cavins would cheerfully poison us if they saw through our disguises. From an old curtain, Mama had sewn me a princess's costume which looked more like Victor Mature's robe than Hedy Lamaar's gown in "Samson and Delilah," but I wasn't about to complain. To be a pirate, Sam needed only a wooden yardstick for a sword and the black eye patch Papa used to wear before the folks could afford to buy his fake glass eye.

On Halloween morning, a cold front suddenly moved in, dropping the wind chill to near zero. This was good news for Hearty Children who considered this a golden opportunity to reduce competition. It became bad news when we opened the trailer door to a chunk of air so cold it stood in the middle of the living room like a block of ice.

With his added pea coat and his bandit-scarf tied over his nose and mouth, Sam could still pass as a pirate, but what princess would wear a pile of sweaters and her grey school coat over her coronation gown? And still freeze, I might add. Papa hit upon the solution that I should wear his work coat—an Army surplus parka with coyote fur around the hood. When I put it on, it nearly reached the ground, as did the sleeves. How could I convince people I was a princess in this get-up, in spite of the real fur around my face? Sam studied me for a minute then bloomed with his Inspired Look.

"You can cover your face with cheesecloth and tell people you're an Alien from Outer Space."

Everybody loved the idea except me. Mama found a piece of cheesecloth in Papa's car polishing rags, cut two tiny eyeholes and pinned it all around the opening of the parka's hood. The cut-outs didn't quite match where my eyes were, but I could see enough: Papa trying not to grin and Sam choking on swallowed laughter. Even Mama smiled, so I went along with it. I could lose the vote even when nobody held an election.

Mama gave us each an old pillowcase for our loot, and out the door we stepped into air cold enough to stop a clock.

On the way across the yard to Mr. Whitaker's house, Sam instructed me. "Don't tell anybody that you started as a princess but ended up an alien. Introduce yourself with conviction."

Sam had earned his Public Speaking merit badge, the easiest and possibly the stupidest one in the handbook.

"Besides, you can convince anybody of anything. You're the best liar I ever met."

High praise from a boy who couldn't remember the first Scout Law, "Be trustworthy," and who routinely used me to lie for him.

I was still trying to navigate the night shadows through the cheesecloth veil when Sam called out "Trick 'r Treat" at Mr. Whitaker's front door.

He filled the whole doorway. "Well, come on in. Haven't had many takers tonight. Too damned cold. I mean, darned cold." He paused. "No, I mean damned cold."

He peered into Sam's face, still covered with the bandit kerchief. "If I didn't know better, I'd say it was . . . "

"A pirate," I helped him out.

Sam brandished his yardstick sword. "It's Papa's eye patch."

Mr. Whitaker turned toward me. "And here we have . . . "

Sam finished for him, "An alien from outer space."

He straightened up and put his hands on his wide hips. "Well, there it is." He walked toward a soup pot full of Baby Ruth candy bars.

"Are you going to give away all of those?" My cheesecloth mask blew in and out when I spoke.

"Nope. And I'm stymied about what to do with the leftovers." He dropped three candy bars into each sack. "Come back tomorrow and we'll figure out how to get rid of 'em."

"Thank you, thank you," we said as we left his porch.

"Watch out for the spooks," he called after us. His words froze in mid-air and tinkled to the ground.

We decided to start with Mrs. Keindorf's fancy neighborhood and work our way back home, hitting the Hartsocks and Sam's other friends at the end.

Mrs. Keindorf answered her door in a swirling, purple silk dress and opal drop earrings. Sam stared at her as if he had never seen her before, utterly mute, on the verge of some kind of collapse. She held a cut glass bowl full of Snickers bars. Incredible: two stops with full-sized candy bars in one night.

"Well. What do we have here?" she said in her breathy German accent.

"It's Jeb Wilder, Mrs. Keindorf. And Sam, my brother." I pulled my cheesecloth mask so I could see out of one eyehole.

With her free hand, she reached down and squeezed Sam's mittened hand. "I'm very glad to see you. Won't you come in?"

"We haveta . . . haveta . . ." Sam stammered.

"I thought you were dressing up as a princess, Jeb."

"It was so cold I turned into an alien from outer space."

"What a shame. Just for the occasion, I found some princess music for you–Ravel's 'Pavane'—but we'll learn it, anyway." When she laughed, her earrings sparkled back and forth. "I don't have any outer space music."

Behind her, Mr. Keindorf sat on the cowboy sofa reading the newspaper. He had bushy eyebrows and wiry grey hair. I had seen him through the window at his dry cleaning store but never at home.

"Hello, Mr. Keindorf," I called to him. He looked at me over his glasses, snapped the newspaper straight and continued reading.

Mrs. Keindorf held out the bowl. "Take as many as you want."

I heard Sam gasp, but I answered, "We wouldn't dream of it. You might run out."

"I doubt it. You're the only children we've seen all night."

Sam took four, so I didn't take any. One Wilder family representative had to remain civil.

We thanked her in unison and left.

At the sidewalk, I whispered, "Did you see her cowboy furniture?"

"Are you out of your mind? We could've had eight Snickers bars. *Eight.*" He wrapped the neck of his pillowcase around his hand. "You're not getting any of mine."

"Why would I eat your candy? I've got my own." However, I was already regretting the lost Snickers bars.

Mrs. Keindorf's neighborhood proved to be especially rewarding since everybody in that section of town was rich, and the cold decimated the Trick 'r Treater population. Every time a door whooshed open and flooded us with warm air, I spied inside as far as I could, building my dream house as we went along–a living room here, a fireplace or dinette set there.

Sam argued, "They're nothing special, just cinder blocks with different paint jobs."

Through my mask, I could barely make out the houses, much less the colors.

"The people are probably all the same, too. Booo-ring."

"Mrs. Keindorf isn't."

He paused, knowing that was true. "I'd rather live in our trailer house."

"I'd rather live in a real house."

In the cold, Sam and I amassed triple our usual Halloween loot in no time. We gathered so many Abba Zabbas, candy cigarettes, Sugar Daddys, and Nik-L-Nip wax bottles full of syrup that we could sound genuinely grateful for the occasional apple and home-made popcorn ball. Only two houses dared to hand out orange marshmallow peanuts and only one dispensed candy buttons stuck on paper tape. Yuck. But in the very next street, a lady gave us real wax lips and wax fangs. I was ready to gush gratitude when, to my amazement, Joe Clary appeared at her side in the doorway looking like a boy angel outlined in light. I prayed that he wouldn't recognize me.

"Hey, Joe," Sam suddenly turned talkative. "It's us: Sam and Jeb Wilder."

Why must Sam's Public Speaking merit badge belatedly take effect right now?

Joe squinted hard at my cheesecloth mask. "J-Jeb?"

I daintily lifted the hem of Papa's coat to reveal my curtain dress. "I'm really a princess," I croaked.

"Disguised as a space alien," Sam added.

Since I couldn't move, Sam took my elbow and led me down their steps.

"Thanks, Mrs. Clary," he called out before turning on me and imitating my squeaky voice, "I'm really a princess." Dropping it, he finished with, "Just cuz' Joe Clary has a crush on you—"

"Oh spit. He does not."

"Why do you think he traded me so many baseball cards for a few beat-up marbles?"

This was the first I had heard of that.

By now, our pillowcases were growing heavy and our toes were numb, so we decided to head for home, turning down the nearest alley.

As soon as we left the lighted houses and street lights, my cheese-cloth mask became almost opaque, virtually blinding me. No matter how I tried to match my eyes with the eyeholes, I could see only the blurred outlines of garages and sheds, which began to shift and wave, at times filling like hot air balloons, then collapsing altogether. Piles of trash rippled, hiding rats the size of dogs, and abandoned cars heaved and swelled, transformed into murky prison cells. At my feet, holes opened in the alley ruts, revealing tunnels which connected all the storm cellars in Round Prairie and the secret graves in people's back yards. Faraway organ music drifted out of the graves, and the sounds of people crying. Leaves fluttered up like bats, and shadows moaned.

"Sam?" I called out uncertainly. Obviously, he had speeded up in the alley. "Wait for me."

At my elbow, a wolf howled behind a fence, and I screamed. The fence mutated into matchsticks. What if the wolf jumped out at me? Or the fence lit itself on fire?

"Sam!" I tried not to sound desperate.

Just then, I heard him run up behind me, trying to scare me. I expected his yardstick sword on my shoulder, but instead, a silky curtain flew over my head while he yanked my pillowcase out of my hand.

"Sam! What?!" I yelled. He shoved me so hard I fell to the ground. "If you think you can scare me—" I was lying. I was already scared.

From the ground, through one eyehole, I saw someone in a flapping cape running away with my pillowcase. He turned back long enough for me to see a Dracula mask.

A few seconds later, I felt Sam's foot in my side. "Guard this!" He dropped his pillowcase and ran off.

Tangled in my princess costume, I struggled to my feet and ripped open the cheesecloth enough to see Sam chasing Dracula down the alley, swinging his sword overhead. I ran after both of them, stumbling inside Papa's coat and yelling, "Sam! Come back!" Sam wouldn't give up without a fight to the death, and all he had was a yardstick for a weapon. He could get seriously hurt without my help. Not to mention, I didn't want to be left alone.

At the first cross street, I caught up with him, both of us out of breath. Miraculously, I still held his pillowcase of candy.

"Was it Bobby Clawson?" I panted.

"Probably." Sam took two long breaths. "He was awful big. And Bobby could afford a store-bought costume."

We collapsed on the curb under a streetlight, warm from the chase even though the air felt like frozen meat clamped to our cheeks.

My whole year's supply of candy. Gone, just like that. And after I had worked so hard to get it, and Mama had even sewn a costume for me. I hated to cry, but Sam couldn't see my face under the torn cheesecloth. Then I remembered the missing pillowcase: what would Mama do about that? Not Taking Care of Things had always been a Punishable Offense in our house.

I dropped my chin on my chest and let the arms of Papa's coat drag in the gutter. Sam must have heard me sniffle, because he put his arm around my shoulders. A very rare event.

"Aliens don't cry."

"Deep down I'm a princess."

"They don't cry, either. They have to run their country."

I hadn't thought about that, fixated as I was on their jewelry and fancy gowns.

"Let's look for your sack. He may have dropped it somewhere."

Sam's face looked blurry through my torn mask. "Where's Papa's eye patch?"

He felt his face. "Oh geez. I must've lost it while I was chasing Clawson." He looked as miserable as I felt.

"You're a great pirate, Sam. Very great."

"I did hit him once with my sword." In the dim light from the street-light, Sam rifled in his pillowcase and pulled out a full-sized Tootsie Roll. "C-rations."

"Where did we get those?" I asked, riveted on the chummy wrapper.

"The house with the tire swing in front. We gotta remember that for next Halloween." He unwrapped the Tootsie Roll and twisted off a section for each of us.

"We won't be here next Halloween," I mumbled around the sweet, sticky bite. "We're never the same place two Halloweens in a row."

He twisted the package shut and dropped it into his pillowcase.

I thought of my lost Tootsie Roll. "I could go back to some of the houses and tell 'em what happened and . . . " Even I knew it was too cold to do that. Besides, they would think I was lying.

We stood up, and Sam helped me rip a larger opening in my cheese-cloth mask so I could see. "Let's look down all the alleys, just in case . . ."

Sam handed me his candy to carry. "Here's the deal: our plane has just been shot down over the North Pole, and we're stranded on an iceberg."

I took a deep breath and added, "And a huge storm is heading our way."

Halfway down an alley, I spied a large white rag on the ground. It was Mama's pillowcase, empty and smudged with dirt, as if it had been dragged on the ground, but it didn't look torn. As I looked around, I slowly realized that my candy had been thrown all over–in the alley ruts, under bushes, even on shed roofs. Why would anybody steal my candy and then just throw it away? I dropped to my knees to salvage what I could, stuffing a few pieces into Papa's coat pockets.

Sam remained standing.

"Maybe I could take it home and wash it and . . . " My eyes started stinging.

Sam's voice sounded thick and far away. He reached under my arm and pulled me to my feet. "C'mon, Jujube. We don't have to eat that. Let's go home."

We were both thinking the same thing: he could share his candy with me, but that wouldn't be right, especially since he had defended me. Without saying anything, we also knew we had to figure it out between us because the folks wouldn't be fair in our terms.

"How about if you take the bubble-gum cigars, the jawbreakers, and the Clove gum?"

"That'd be great," I fibbed about the Clove gum.

"We'll divvy up the rest later."

Sam was the best brother who ever lived. On a bush in the dark alley and so improbable that I thought I was imagining it, I saw a little black scrap. "Sam! Look."

One strap was torn, but Papa's eye patch was still intact.

When we climbed the trailer steps and walked into the warm, golden light, Mama and Papa looked at us and stopped playing Scrabble.

"What on earth happened?" Mama asked.

I waited for the storm to break.

Papa said, "If you two won, I'd hate to see the losers."

"They stole– They stole–" I began to hiccup.

Sam held up the dirty pillowcase. "All of Jeb's candy . . . scattered it in the alley and . . . your pillowcase, Mama . . . ."

"It was awful, but Sam . . . ." I broke into real sobs, the kind you can't talk through, that make your throat grab itself, and the harder you try to control it, the worse it gets.

"He knocked Jeb down," Sam continued, "but your coat saved her, Papa, with all the padding."

"I'm so sorry," Mama sounded as if she really meant it. "I know how much you two count on Halloween." She gestured toward the full bowl of penny suckers on the kitchen counter. "We didn't have any kids, needless to say, us living in a trailer. You two can divide these."

Next to Jujubes, I hated penny suckers the most but kept quiet. Maybe I could trade some for other candy at school.

"I fought him off, Papa," Sam's voice was sounding a little rocky. "But your eye patch got torn, and–"

"It's nothing we can't mend, Sam." Papa squatted down between us and put his arms around our waists. "It wasn't somebody's eye."

CHAPTER 29
NITROGEN TRIIODIDE

JUST AS SAM RAN OUT OF THE MONEY HE HAD earned folding church bulletins and stuffing pledge envelopes for Reverend Harkin, the dime store notified him that he had guessed almost the exact number of marbles in the jar and had won all 475 of them. Not only that, but they put a sign in their window, temporarily covering up Luther, the little bronze horse, but making Sam famous:

WINNER OF THE HESTED'S MARBLE CONTEST
SAM WILDER
CONGRATULATIONS!!!

Sam didn't care about the fame, but he could sell or trade the marbles for money to buy bomb materials.

"My goal," he told me seriously, "is to own unlimited supplies of nitroglycerin, TNT and dynamite, but that's a ways off."

"About the same time I own a whole herd of horses," I responded. Sam seldom caught my sarcasm, and never when he was contemplating strategic weapons development.

In the library, Sam and I paged through an old high school chemistry book. November sunlight rippled through the slag glass windows, spreading all the way to Miss Reynolds at her desk, pretending she wasn't eavesdropping on us. The fat around her eyes made it difficult to see where she was looking–a big advantage for a spy.

I pointed to a chemical formula. "What's that?"

I knew that the letters stood for elements, like H for hydrogen, and they came from something called the periodic table, a kind of map for chemicals. I didn't understand why they called it *periodic*, since the elements supposedly never changed.

Sam whispered, "I don't know, but it has ammonia in it." Sam's finding ammonia in those letters was like Mrs. Keindorf's finding the theme and variations in Beethoven. I was always amazed at how people saw things I didn't see, and not just Mama.

"The chapter's about chemical instability, so it must mean . . ." Sam's grin crinkled his freckles, "it explodes."

"Is that the same hydrogen as in the hydrogen bomb?"

"Why would there be two hydrogens, Nitwit?"

"There's more than one C on the piano." I moved my chair to stand up. "I'll ask Miss Reynolds."

He pulled me back down. "It's the same hydrogen. I didn't mean to call you Nitwit." He scanned the text with his finger. "This formula is for something called nitrogen triiodide."

I leaned into his shoulder to see better. What a thrilling word. *Triiodide* contained five vowels and four consonants, and even better, three of the vowels were i's and two of those stood next to each other. Very rare. Mrs. Dahlke would be excited, although *triiodide* would probably not occur in the county spelling bee. But it could happen.

Sam added in a quieter whisper, "They use it to make nitroglycerin." He pulled the book closer to his chest and looked shiftily from side to side. "Which is part of dynamite."

In Sam's hands, a Chemistry merit badge was the perfect cover for learning how to blow things up with the greatest anonymity and the lowest cost. He hoarded firecrackers like I hoarded candy. Unknown to Papa, the dam construction site had supplied Sam with dynamite caps, surplus electrical cables, and a small roll of genuine fuse wire. Somewhere in town,

Sam found a secret source for matches and gasoline, which he routinely used to fire-bomb red anthills, as much a diversionary tactic to camouflage his real weapons as simple revenge for ant bites. He still stored his most dangerous supplies in the storm cellar at the Inavale spook house.

In Mr. Whitaker's basement, Sam continued to experiment to perfect the right mixture of charcoal, sulfur and saltpeter to make gunpowder. He had "secured" a little black powder from somebody whose father reloaded rifle shells, but he needed much more. Now he could sell brand-new marbles to Joe Clary, Jim Hartsock and other rich Boy Scouts for cold, hard cash. Hence, the marbles arrived in the nick of time. Grandma Strang would call this part of God's Plan.

I was still Sam's front man buying iodine crystals, potassium nitrate and sulfur at the drug store, although Mr. Keefer was growing suspicious. He was as bald as Marvin Harkin, but clean bald, not slimy bald. Sam said that the hardest part of manufacturing gunpowder was making charcoal, for which he was currently using sugar. Long ago I had stopped asking how Sam's mad scientist experiments obeyed the Scout Laws, especially being helpful, friendly and kind.

"What are you up to over there?" Miss Reynolds couldn't pretend to work any longer and stood up in three jerky motions, bracing herself on the desk.

Sam closed the book and slid it under a pile of magazines on the table. "We're looking for . . . games."

Of all his fine qualities, I especially admired Sam's mastery of doublespeak, true and false at the same time.

"In the Science section?" Using the window pole as a cane, Miss Reynolds limped over to our table.

Several weeks ago, Sam had let slip that the Boy Scouts might need to use Molotov cocktails for the defense of Round Prairie.

"Do you know what a Molotov cocktail is?" she had asked sternly.

I had answered helpfully, "A pop bottle full of gasoline with a wick you can light. Then you throw it and it explodes."

"R-right. Do you know who Molotov is?"

This we did not know. Information like this fell under the category of History, which was always irrelevant.

"He's a Communist. The real thing. One of Stalin's thugs. He's killed millions of people." She had loomed over us, twice her normal size.

"Sam. Look at me. You could easily blow your hand off or blind yourself or even worse. These are not games or toys. Do you understand?"

I hadn't been able to stop myself. "With a Molotov cocktail, Sam blew out one wall of our fort." To be completely truthful, I had to add, "Accidentally."

"Does your father know what you're doing?"

We had remained silent.

Inspired, I answered, "Mama might know."

Sam had quickly agreed, "Yeah she might."

After that, Miss Reynolds' suspicions had increased exponentially. Would she tell the folks? Did her oath of silence about the daredevil show still hold?

Today, Sam studied his hands folded meekly on the tabletop. Miss Reynolds' glasses hung from her giant pearl necklace, as if her second pair of eyes were also staring at Sam's hands.

I sounded as innocent as I could. "We were on our way to the Games section."

"Good. It's right over there." She pointed the pole at the bookcases under the tall windows.

Sam slipped out of his chair and followed me.

We looked listlessly through children's magical tricks needing only rubber balls and coins, how-to books for making your own badminton birdies, and the ubiquitous walkie-talkies made with string and tin cans. How stupid did they think kids were? Attracted by its cracked leather spine, I pulled out the oldest book on the shelf, titled *The Young Folks Cyclopaedia of Games and Sports*. Published in 1899, it was even older than *Black Beauty*.

"This should be a good diversionary tactic," I suggested.

Sam glanced at the book. "Boooring." He wandered off, managing surreptitiously to re-shelve the chemistry book.

I checked out the beautiful antique book, mainly for the joy of watching the date stamp pounce inside the back book cover. No one had checked it out since 1933.

"That should keep you out of trouble," Miss Reynolds said with her straight-line smile.

A week later, I heard popping sounds, like a cap pistol, coming from Mr. Whitaker's basement. I could still smell the rotten egg gas Sam made yesterday.

Sam stopped me at the bottom of the stairs. "What's the secret knock?"

Politely ignoring the fact there was no door, I tapped out "S. O. S." in Morse Code on the wall.

"This book is a gold mine, Jeb. A *gold mine*. Look at this."

On page 442, in old-fashioned print, were the following instructions:

Powder some iodine fine, and put a very little of it {about as much as will lie on quarter of an inch of the small blade of a knife} into a small saucer. Pour in enough strong ammonia water to cover it, and let it stand for about 20 minutes. Then either stir the powder up, and filter it (see Chemical Experiments) or pour off most of the ammonia, and then pour the powder on a piece of blotting-paper. Place the filter-paper or blotting paper where it will dry in the sun. When it is perfectly dry, rub a stick on the powder, or even brush a feather over it, and it will explode with a crackling noise.

Though it has not changed in looks, the iodine has been made by the ammonia into a very explosive substance called Nitrogen Triiodide. The reason why so little iodine was used, is that otherwise the explosion might be dangerous.

"Nitrogen triiodide! We have in our hands the ultimate weapon." I could practically hear the Shadow's insane laugh from the radio. "You are looking at the most spectacular chemical demonstration Round Prairie will ever experience. My finest moment."

"What does it do?"

"Some day you will see," his voice grew dreamy and famous. "Possibly in the Avalon Movie Theater."

"Are you going to blow up the theater?" I had always suspected that bombing a building was Sam's greatest ambition.

"N-no . . ." he answered, then slowly added, "Not exactly."

In other words, a definite *yes*.

"Why don't you put this stuff into the Formula?"

He squinted at me indecisively. "It's too . . . precious."

I sensed a vague conflict of interest if Sam were simultaneously creating the Formula which would save the world and one which would blow up the Avalon Movie Theater.

CHAPTER 30

LOYALTY OATHS

NEWS ANNOUNCER

". . . threat to national security from betrayals of disloyal federal employees.

UNDER PRESSURE FROM CONGRESS, THE FBI AND the House Un-American Activities Committee, President Eisenhower has agreed to require loyalty oaths of all federal government employees. He cited as precedents the Hatch Act of 1940 and President Truman's Executive Order 9835 of 1947, calling membership in, affiliation with, or sympathetic association with 'named organizations' a sign of disloyalty. The Attorney General can designate specific groups as 'totalitarian, fascist, communist, or subversive' and 'dedicated to force or violence'.

Effective immediately, people employed in all branches of the federal government will be required to sign a loyalty oath."

Papa snapped off the radio so violently the little yellow plastic case almost skidded off the kitchen table. "First Hoover accuses Truman of being a Communist sympathizer, then turns around and uses Truman's own loyalty oath to test everybody's so-called patriotism."

Getting ready for bed, Sam and I were lobbing marbles off the piano bench in a mortar attack on a Lincoln Log house we had built on the floor.

Mama gently tucked her wavy hair under a heavy black hairnet, making her look like Ingrid Bergman the nun in "The Bells of St. Mary's," only thinner. "Ignoring the news doesn't make it go away."

Papa practically spit, "Loyalty oaths, my eye."

"Regardless what you think, they're trying to protect us."

I wanted to share my new word. "That's called a bromide."

"A what?" Papa asked, irritated more than interested.

"Saying they're *trying to protect us* is a bromide."

They all looked at me as if I were speaking Martian.

I clarified, "A bromide is a saying that keeps people stupid. But it can also be a medicine that . . . uh, makes them . . . stupid." I realized too late that Nervine might be a Particularly Forbidden Topic.

Oh-oh. Ticktock time stopped. The smoke ribbon from the log cabin clock froze, straight up.

"What. Medicine." Mama's butcher knife voice slashed time back into seconds.

Sam was looking at me like a genuine space alien, not just a Halloween princess disguised as one.

"What medicine?" Mama repeated. "Where did you hear such nonsense?"

"Miss Reynolds said—"

"Of course, Miss Reynolds," Mama interrupted. "Who sitteth at the right hand of God the Father Almighty."

Why was Mama quoting the Apostles' Creed?

"I'm sick of hearing about Miss Reynolds. God only knows how Red she is."

"She's not a Communist," I defended her, "but she knows what they are. She's read their handbook."

"I'll bet she has. Every g.d. word."

"What handbook?" Sam asked with sudden interest.

I pretended not to hear him so I could research its exact title and lord it over him at the perfect moment.

"She says people call her a Communists because she doesn't fit in. She thinks for herself."

"You can say that again." Papa tapped his hand with the missing fingers on the table. "Edie, Hoover's been FBI Director since Calvin Coolidge, for godssake. Congress gives him a blank check, and never asks how he spends it. Nev-er. I'll bet that he and his spies keep secret files on everybody in Washington."

Mama wiped off the kitchen counter, the fourth time since supper. "Who's sounding paranoid now?"

"That's rich, coming from you."

Mama threw the rag in the kitchen sink. "If you really believed what you say, you wouldn't bury your head in the sand. Don't-rock-the-boat-Frankie, ignore-the-wind-Frankie until the house blows down. Right? Right right right? Why don't you do SOMEthing, even if it's wrong? ANYthing."

"I will. I'll ignore their goddam oath." Papa never swore, so this must be a Very Important Conversation.

This seemed like a good time to change the subject. I randomly picked a strange word out of the news. "What's a fascist?"

"Oh Jesus." Papa threw up his hands and walked in little circles around the living room, accidentally scattering the half-bombed log house, in which Sam had secretly hidden a few toy cars. Surprise.

"The children don't need to hear you swear."

I wanted to give Papa a hand. "Mr. Whitaker says Papa has dam—darn—good reasons to swear."

"That's enough out of you. Talky talk talk talk," Mama warned. "Pick up that mess."

Sam pulled out two cigar boxes, one for the Lincoln Logs and one for his cars. "Is a loyalty oath like the Pledge of Allegiance?"

Papa began to unfold my chair bed. "At work, they call it the 'duck test': If it walks like a duck and talks like a duck, it *is* a duck."

This did not help me. "I don't get it."

"That's because you *are* a duck," Sam quacked his Donald Duck imitation, which I envied almost as much as his two-octave whistle.

"It's guilt by association, Sugar. If you have a friend somebody *names as* a Communist, that makes you one, too." Papa looked at Mama. "That's all the *evidence* they need."

"Birds of a feather." Mama stalked back to their bedroom.

Sighting down his index finger revolver, Sam silently picked off cowboys galloping across his pajamas. "So if you hang around somebody like Bobby Clawson . . . ."

"You'll be blamed for everything he does, whether you're involved or not."

That meant anybody who played with us could be called White Trash. I was trying to work *albino* into that description, with no luck so far.

Mama walked back into the kitchen in her pajamas, rubbing cold cream into her cheeks. "You have to take the oath. They said all government employees." She stopped rubbing her cheeks, shiny with grease. "If you're innocent, you have nothing to fear."

"It's not about innocence, it's about coercion."

Coercion almost rhymed with *inertia* and had a 4:4 vowel to consonant ratio. I helped Papa spread the extra narrow sheets Mama had cut and hemmed to fit my chair bed. She had run out of white thread, so they were stitched in red, like lacing around cowboy chaps and holsters.

"Is it like the Boy Scout Oath?" I asked.

If so, Papa had a lot of leeway in semi-lying about it. Sam had vowed to stay "physically strong, mentally awake, and morally straight." Neither of us knew what "morally straight" meant, but it smacked remotely of church, so he felt pretty well covered in that area. But he always forgot key Scout laws, a little like forgetting "Thou shalt not kill." Scout Law # 11 was "A scout is clean." How would they know? It gave me the creeps to think of Marvin Harkin checking his scouts to see if they were clean.

Papa answered, "They ask about your associations with the Communist Party and its 'front groups.' That list changes every day." He kept looking at Mama. "But the question that gets my goat is what I think about 'race relations' in the country. What do race relations have to do with the price of tea in China? They're trying to connect everyone who disagrees with them to some Communist plot."

Mama poured half a glass of Nervine and swallowed it. "For heaven's sake, Frank, you're not a Communist. Just sign the blankety-blank oath."

Every time Mama said that, I imagined holes in her sentence, like missing bricks in a wall.

"Just because Hoover's gang is turning America into a police state doesn't mean I have to cooperate."

"And when they cart you off to jail, what are we supposed to do? The children and I?"

"J-jail?" I stammered.

"They're not putting me in jail."

"They could fire you."

Papa paused. "I suppose so. But would you swear 'loyalty' in front of anybody who shows up, like Tom Cavin or anybody else on the City Council? That bunch has all the integrity of the south end of a north-bound horse."

Standing behind the kitchen counter, Mama began twirling the head of the cookie jar cat. "Maybe you aren't so innocent after all. Maybe you've been secretly meeting with Communists."

"Oh, for God's sake, Edith."

Mama squinted at Papa as if she were in bright sunlight. "I hear you've been seeing Dr. Mary."

"What are you talking about now?" Papa smoothed out my blanket.

"Charlie Whitaker told me."

"He thought she could give me some salve for my allergies."

Mama looked into the cookie jar cat's eyes as if it could hear her. "Why can't you go to Dr. Buchanan like everybody else?"

"Because he's a chiropractor. Eighty-two years old. And a border-line quack."

"And how, may I ask, are we going to pay for your little . . . doctor visits?"

"I used my cigar money." Papa gave himself an allowance just like us kids, except his was in real money. "Can we talk about this later?"

Mama puckered her mouth as if for a kiss. "Doc-tor Ma-ary. You can tell she's a Communist just by looking at her. A zombie. Brainwashed. And now she's brainwashing you."

"At least that would prove I have a brain, contrary to your opinion. Or your mother's opinion."

"You leave my mother out of this." Mama grew quiet. "I was never so happy to get away from anyone as I was to get away from her. And I have you to thank for that, Frank."

Everybody grew still for a few seconds.

"I'd do anything if I could make you happy, Edie."

Papa reached for her hand, but she yanked it away. I knew just how he felt. I could have told him not even to try that move.

To cheer everybody up, I suggested, "Maybe that's what's wrong with Marvin Harkin. He's been brainwashed. He looks like a zombie, and he's ordered the Boy Scouts to spy on all their friends."

Silent Sam finally spoke. "He did not. He said to keep our eyes open for suspicious activities. As part of being Citizens in the Community."

"What suspicious activities?" I wasn't about to let Marvin the Larva off the hook so easily.

"You know what Mr. Harkin brought to our patrol meeting? A microscope–a real microscope—and we looked at water. Regular tap water."

"What did you see, Son?" Papa asked.

"All kinds of things floating in it. Living in it."

"Ee-yew." My usual response to anything resembling a bug.

"We drink them every day, all the time," Sam relished.

"Like red ants?" My stomach lurched.

Mama straightened the cookie jar's head and patted its cheeks. "Dr. Mary and her Red pals have put them in our drinking water. It's just a matter of time until they poison us all." She slowly walked back to their bedroom.

"Papa, it's not–" Sam objected, but Papa shook his head to be quiet and motioned for Sam to climb into bed.

I lay down so Papa could tuck me in and I could get my good-night kiss. "Papa, you're not going to jail, are you?"

"Don't be dumb," Sam called from his end of the trailer in a lying-down voice.

Papa squatted on his heels beside my chair bed, a position he could hold for hours while he worked on the Buick. "If it's a good oath, I'll sign it; but I won't lie to anybody just to make them feel safer."

"How do you know if it's good or bad?" Sam called out again, infringing on my precious time with Papa.

Papa thought for a minute. "You have to figure it out for yourself. If something about a situation makes you feel creepy, don't go along with it." Up close, both his real eye and his glass one looked straight at you.

"What if you're scared?" I thought about Bobby Clawson and his dog.

Papa tucked me into the sheet so tightly that I could barely move, like a mummy or a papoose. I loved that, even in summer when I roasted. "Nobody can scare you unless you let them."

"That's easy if you're a grown-up."

"No easier than being a little girl."

I had decided long ago. "I'm not going to grow up."

Papa kissed me good-night, his beard stubble against my cheek, the best part of every day. "The alternative to growing up is pretty grim."

When Papa turned off the piano lamp, light from the streetlight spread across my bed. Janet never grew up, or Mrs. Dahlke's daughter who died mysteriously at my age, or Mrs. Vince's brother or Mrs. Keindorf's brother or all the soldiers who were killed in Korea and World War I and II and the French Revolution.

I decided that I'd better grow up, even if I didn't know how.

CHAPTER 31
THE JUMPER

MAMA AND I HAD LEFT THE TRAILER BECAUSE she smelled something burning, but she smelled it outside, too. At least it wasn't gas which, she said, had no smell at all.

November wind hurtled down Main Street, churning up dirt from the red brick road with bits of paper and straw into dust devils higher than the old two-story buildings. On the plains, the wind blew all the time, which made Mama nervous, while Papa joked about standing on our shadows so they wouldn't blow away.

As we walked toward the grocery store, I jumped across cracks in the sidewalk. Sometimes I wished that I had a broken leg or polio or were crippled so Mama would hold my hand to help me walk.

"Step on a crack, break your mother's back," Mama recited the old poem.

In our private game of talking through poetry, I answered in rhythm to my jumping, "There was a little GIRL, who had a little CURL, right in the middle of her FORE . . . head."

Instead of singsonging back, "And when she was good, she was very, very good," Mama started a new poem:

"Whenever Richard Cory went downtown. . ."

Oh boy. I had never heard a poem about downtown.

"We people on the pavement looked at him:

He was a gentleman from sole to crown,

Clean-favored and imperially slim."

A long time ago, Mama had explained to me that poems about men were also about women. It certainly described Mama— "imperially slim."

"And he was rich, yes, richer than a king,

And admirably schooled in every grace:

In fine—we thought that he was everything

To make us wish—"

Mama stopped when she saw a woman walking toward us, wrapping her coat tight against the wind.

At the last minute, Mama stepped right in front of her, making her stumble backwards. "What are you looking at? Huh? Huh?"

The lady clutched her purse tighter as if we were about to grab it. I gave her a big, lying smile and tried to catch Mama's hand to stop her, but the lady had already stepped off the sidewalk and circled us. In a real hurry, I might add.

"Always ignore people like that," Mama advised.

Like what?

Mama continued the poem:

"So on we worked and waited for the light,

And went without the meat and cursed the bread."

We quickly passed the library, the Pawnee Hotel and Eddy's Bakery, but I had to pause to whisper hello to Luther in Hested's dime store window. He whinnied every time he saw me now. They had taken down Sam's congratulatory sign.

Just as I slowed down, Mama's fingers dug into my shoulder all the way through my grey winter coat.

"Did you see that?" she whispered excitedly.

"What?" I searched Main Street, empty except for a feed truck, some parked cars and two men talking in front of the post office.

"In the sky." She looked up, pushing back a wave of her hair which the wind had blown across her eyes. Her eyes followed something flying overhead, her head dipping in rhythm. "Beautiful!"

"What?" I squinted harder but could see only small white clouds scudding across the blue sky. My eyes watered in the wind, blurring my vision.

"There!" She shook my shoulder, then looked down at me expectantly, smiling happily. "Horses!"

Horses? I glanced back at Luther in the window.

Mama was still smiling, but her dry upper lip was caught above her teeth. "I didn't think they'd send horses. Probably just for you."

I scanned the sky again, more carefully this time, anxious to see what she saw. I knew she wasn't pretending, and she never, ever lied. "H-Horses?"

"Flying!" she almost laughed. "Flying horses." She looked up again. "Wait. Where'd they go?" Her smile dimmed. "Gone. But you saw them, right?" She looked at me with her testing look, the test I always failed.

How could I lie to her face? But how could I not lie? "I . . . tried."

"You have to try harder."

At her disappointment, I added, "There's a flying horse on the Mobilgas sign."

"Don't be silly. That's Pegasus. Normal horses don't have wings. They don't need them."

Her eyes jerked back and forth, suddenly stopping on an empty two-story building across the street with tall windows framed by pillars, one of the oldest buildings in town. Sam had told me it was the original Harkin Funeral Home before they moved closer to the church.

"Oh my God." Mama focused on the ledge of the highest window. "Look. Look!"

Mama never said swear words, so something was terribly wrong. I couldn't see anything except the sky, the puffy clouds moving over the building like smoke coming off the roof. The clouds moved so fast it looked as if the building were falling toward us. Maybe that's what she meant.

"Do you see her? Standing there?" Mama nervously bunched the shoulder of my coat in her fingers.

Who? Where? I didn't dare ask.

"My God, that's a narrow ledge." Mama looked at me in terror. "She could fall." She looked back up. "Who is it? Can you tell?"

I wanted desperately to find the woman on the ledge. Why couldn't I? What was wrong with me? I could only see Mama and me, our tiny selves reflected in the street-level window, rippled by the old glass. Maybe she would love me if I could see what she saw.

"You see her, don't you?"

"Y-yes." I kept looking where Mama did, kept turning my head when she turned hers. I tried to look into her eyes, where I might find the woman reflected in her big, black pupils.

"Do you know who she is?"

"N-No. Wh-What should we do?"

"I think . . . it's." Mama's voice turned cold, colder than the wind, only still, solid. A block of space without time in it enfolded us both. "It's Doctor Mary. That's who. Doc – tor Maa-ry."

Mama looked down at me, her mouth as crooked as Leon Troxel's. "She wants . . . to . . . jump." Triumphantly, Mama looked back at the empty ledge. "Yes. Jump." Suddenly, she shouted so loudly I lurched backwards, "JUMP! C'mon, Jeb. Help me. Shout 'Jump'!"

I didn't feel like shouting anything, but Mama was frantic for my response.

"JUMP!" My shout surprised myself.

In a frenzy then, we both shouted, over and over, our screams echoing up and down empty Main Street, then I began jumping JUMP up and down JUMP on every crack in the sidewalk JUMP with the building looming over us JUMP leaning forward with the weight of the jumper on the ledge JUMP and screaming JUMP trying to scream JUMP loud enough to make it JUMP true.

CHAPTER 32
CIVIL OFFENSE

"TODAY, CHILDREN, WE'RE GOING TO PRACTICE A drill which could save your life." Mr. Sprecker's voice came over the loud speaker in Mrs. Dahlke's classroom, sounding as tinny and fake as the speakers at the Inavale drive-in. I wondered if it were Sam's fancy schmancy mismatched impedance or just another loose nut.

Across the aisle from me, Leon Troxel played with the tip of one of Jane Englehardt's long braids which rested on his desktop, but not enough for her to feel it.

"As you all know," Sprecker droned on, obviously reading something, "our country is in danger of air raids from the Russians, and we must all be prepared. Has your family located the nearest bomb shelter? What do we call this? We call it Civil Defense."

Miss Reynolds called it Civil Offense. Mr. Sprecker really needed to talk with her about the probability of Russian planes flying this far inland.

For no reason, Leon looked at me and stuck out his tongue. Since his mouth never closed completely over the scar on his upper lip, he looked like an ugly, hairless rabbit.

"By now, your teacher should have told you about nuclear bombs. First, you will hear the blast, then you will feel the heat, and last of all experience the radiation. Just remember: blast, heat, radiation. By taking cover under your school desks, you will protect yourself from these three harmful effects."

Jane must have felt a tug on her hair, because she moved her head, jerking her braid out of Leon's fingers.

"As soon as you hear the fire drill bell, remain calm, crawl under your desks, cover your head with your arms, and remain in that position until you hear the all-clear signal. Teachers? Are you ready?"

Mrs. Dahlke raised her eyebrows over the top of her wire glasses and forced a smile at us all. Today she was wearing a brown suit more like something Mrs. Vince would wear, and her lapel pin was a plain maple leaf, but probably pure gold.

CLANGCLANGCLANGCLANGCLANG!

Even when you're expecting it, a fire bell shocks you into action. In the confusion Leon and I bumped into each other in the aisle, which provided a rare opportunity for him to punch me and for me to back-kick him. We crouched under our respective desks, glaring at each other. I briefly looked at the kids around me. Joe Clary had scrunched his eyes shut and seemed to be holding his breath, Doreen Cavin was trying to keep her dress from touching the floor, while Jane Englehardt looked perfectly comfortable with her forehead touching the floor. Maybe Jehovah's Witnesses prayed in that position.

A few minutes later came the all-clear signal. CLANGCLANG, pause, CLANGCLANG, pause, CLANGCLANG.

"All right, class," said Mrs. Dahlke. "You can get up now." She hadn't crawled under her desk.

As Jane and Leon unfolded from beneath their desks, I happened to look over. To my horror, I saw Leon holding a pair of scissors, reaching for one of Jane's long braids.

A scream started in my stomach, but I couldn't push it out in time: "N-n-n-n —"

Like in a dream underwater, time gagged me and slowed my out-stretched arm, reaching for his hand holding the scissors.

"N-N-N-N-O-O-O-O!" my scream surfaced, just as his scissors sawed through her braid close to her neck.

"What on earth?!" I heard Mrs. Dahlke from far away.

"NO!" I screamed again, this time punching Leon's arm until he dropped the scissors, but his other fist was still clamped around the severed braid. He laughed like a jackhammer.

"Judith! Leon!" Mrs. Dahlke stormed down the aisle.

Only now did Jane realize what had happened. She felt behind her neck for her missing braid, then felt more frantically, her hand disbelieving that it was gone. In shock, she turned to look at Leon, her mouth open, soundless. He laughed harder. Her hands frantically felt both sides of her neck for her hair.

Mrs. Dahlke grabbed Leon's hand still dangling Jane's braid. "What have you done?!" I had never seen her so angry. Her cheeks were redder than Mama's rouge.

Leon's giggles blew out of his scarred mouth like cartoon balloons and hung in the air. I couldn't stand to look at him any longer. My hand instinctively curled into a fist, and I swung with all my strength at that grotesque, twisted mouth.

"HARELIP!" I screamed.

"Judith!" Mrs. Dahlke cried out. "Sit down and be quiet. Jane: you, too."

We both collapsed into our desks.

"Everyone!" She continued, "Take your seats. Right this minute. Open your reading books to Chapter Nine."

When she looked at Leon, the light ricocheted off her delicate wire glasses as if she could melt him with x-ray vision. She dragged him up the aisle like a rag doll. Jane held her stomach and rocked back and forth.

"Jeb!" Leon suddenly called out. "It's her fault. She dared me." He started to whine and wiggle as if he had to go to the bathroom.

Mrs. Dahlke yanked him out the door. Everyone was stunned into silence, then whispers ran around the room faster than one of Sam's fuse wires burning. Everyone craned to look at Jane and me, then turned to whisper to each other.

"Leave her alone!" I blurted to the class in general.

Joe Clary looked as if he were about to cry.

The clock jerked ahead several minutes, but no one opened their books. Suddenly, Jane jumped up from her desk and bolted for the door, running into Mrs. Dahlke, who said a few quiet words to her and let her leave. Mrs. Dahlke walked back into the room without Leon. It became quieter than church during silent prayer. Not a seat squeaked.

"Judith, report to Mr. Sprecker after school." She wouldn't even look at me. In my fury, I hadn't thought about how Mrs. Dahlke would react, much less about what she had taught me—that my choice of words reflected the quality of my ideas. To call Leon such a horrible name dragged me down to his level. White trash.

Mr. Sprecker was standing beside his desk, hitting Jane's severed braid against his thigh like a soft whip.

"Sit down." Mr. Sprecker tossed Jane's braid onto his desk. "How many times have I called you into my office already this year?"

I didn't know if he wanted me to answer, but I did, anyway. "Once for roughhousing at recess, and once to re-take my test."

He played with Jane's braid on the desk near my shoulder, the curly black hairs on his knuckles contrasting with her smooth and glossy braid.

With his free hand, he pointed to some red spots on my dress. "What's that?"

"I don't know," I answered honestly.

"It's blood. You split open Leon's lip with your hooliganism."

I looked at my knuckles, which were also bleeding lightly. "It was his fault. He–"

"This isn't about Leon. This is about you." He straightened the braid, aligning it with the edge of his desk.

"Jane had never cut her hair before, in her whole life."

"I don't care about Jane Englehardt. Do you know what we call people who punch other people in the face?"

My mind raced among possibilities, settling on what Miss Reynolds would say. "A Visigoth."

"Don't get smart with me." He rapped his knuckles on the desk. "You're a hoodlum, that's what. And a girl," he spit out in disgust.

"Girls are just as important as boys." Papa told me this all the time.

"That isn't the point."

"Leon deserved it."

"That's not for you to decide." He stood so close I could smell the front of his trousers. "You can't go around hitting boys for what *you* consider their violations of the rules."

"Leon never gets punished." I knew that I should throw in a "Sir," but I couldn't make my mouth do it.

Mr. Sprecker began rising up and down on his toes, up and down, growing creepier by the minute. He'd better not ask me to sign a loyalty oath.

From his desk drawer he took out a sheet of paper. "I'm sending you home with a note for your parents. If I don't hear back from them tomorrow, I will personally visit your house."

This was a threat worth paying attention to.

He began writing in jerky marks, not at all like Mrs. Dahlke's penmanship. "I'm telling your parents that you are becoming intractable. Not that you would know what that means."

"I bet it's like *fractious*. That's what other people call me."

He looked at me quickly, but his hair didn't move. How did he re-comb exactly the same greasy rows every day?

"Look up *intractable* in a dictionary." Under his breath, he added, "If you have one at home."

"We have a huge one."

"Really." I could tell he didn't believe me. He continued writing.

"My folks play Scrabble, and Mama always beats the tar out of Papa with words like *xi*."

"There's no such word."

Why couldn't I keep quiet, as Sam always did? Fly under the radar, don't kick up the red ant hill, then, in a surprise attack, blow them to smithereens. "Yes there is."

Mr. Sprecker folded the note. "I've had about enough of you and your disrespect for authority."

I tried to be meek, which never sounded genuine with me. "It's a letter in the Greek alphabet. If you have a dictionary, I'll show you."

"I'm warning you, I won't put up with insubordination, not from you or anyone else. I can have you expelled from school. Have you thought of that?"

I certainly hadn't thought of that.

He swept Jane's braid into his open desk drawer and slammed it shut. "You can be too smart for your own good."

Mrs. Cavin's exact words. They must have been talking to each other.

"Tomorrow I'll start posting lists at the front of every classroom with the names of Troublemakers, just like the government keeps lists of Communists and Fellow Travelers. From now on, anyone who breaks the rules will be put on that list." He smiled like James Cagney loading his pistol. "Yours will be the first name on it."

I knew that he was trying to scare me, but, as Papa advised, I had decided not to be afraid. If Mr. Sprecker really wanted to terrify me, he should hire Bobby Clawson and his dog.

"What about Leon?" In all fairness, my name should be second.

"You always want to be at the head of your class. Well, Miss Priss, now you will be."

Sam was waiting for me at the far end of the playground. Word of the Incident had spread like wildfire.

"Way to go, Jeb!" He was so jubilant he skipped around me in circles and walked me all the way home, asking for every detail, feeling hugely disappointed that he hadn't witnessed the fight in person. He particularly admired my bloody knuckles.

When Jane returned to school two days later, her other beautiful braid had been cut off, and her short hair fell straight and shiny like a cap.

Immediately, the other girls started paying attention to her, since she had lost the distinction of never cutting her hair. She could now fit in, look just like them, smirk and giggle like them. But Jane grew even more bashful, shying away from everyone like a stray dog, not trusting any luck, good or bad.

In my weekly offer of genuine friendship, on the playground I said, "I like your hair. I wish mine were straight like that."

"Leave me alone," she answered, panicked, the kind of leave-me-alone which will last as long as you both live.

So I remained the Kiss of Death, even for the outcast Jane. I figured I would be the Kiss of Death for my whole life. "Guilt by association," Papa had called it. If childhood were going to be like this, I might as well be a real Communist, not just a name at the top of Sprecker's list.

CHAPTER 33

TORNADO

*I*NTRACTABLE. THAT'S WHAT SPRECKER'S NOTE called me, all right. The timing couldn't have 2been worse, since Grandma Strang was coming from Hebron to visit Mama while Uncle Ralph bought construction supplies. Six months after the tornado, materials were still scarce in Hebron because they were rebuilding over half of the town.

Knowing it would only make matters worse, I still protested the footstool. Nobody else would defend Jane Englehardt, I told Mama. Leon Troxel would get off scot free. Even little girls could fight for liberty and justice for all. Think of the little girl on "The Shadow." Why had Mama named me Judith, anyway?

"Who do you think you are?!" Mama shook me until my head wobbled, although I wasn't fighting back. She wouldn't be touching me at all if I hadn't committed a Crime of the Highest Order.

"But Jane's hair . . . might be part of her *religion*."

"Jehovah's Witnesses?!" Mama kicked the footstool into Sam's bedroom. "Worse than Catholics."

"It was so *unfair*. If you'd been there–"

Mama's mouth sounded as if it had filled with saliva for a week. "I wouldn't act like a bully. Is that how I raised you? Fist fighting! In school! You can't fix anything, not one g.d. thing! Do you hear me? You aren't *God*."

Then Mama did something she had never done: she pinched my face between her fingers and thumb and twisted my head to look straight at her.

Today one of her cheeks had a tiny rouge spot, but the other was smeared red to her eyebrow. "Just because we live in a trailer doesn't mean we have to act like TRAILER TRASH." She threw my face away from her.

A knock came at the door.

Mama kicked the footstool into Sam's bedroom, pushed me down on it and took two deep breaths. "Coming," she called out.

She yanked Sam's sliding doors shut so hard they bounced. Mama was right, but not totally. And would Mrs. Dahlke ever speak to me again?

Through the closed doors, I heard Grandma say "Knock knock" and open the front door. "Isn't Judith in here?"

"In Sam's room. She's being punished."

"I heard you shouting. I'm sure the neighbors heard you, too."

"It won't be the first time."

Although their voices were muffled, I could understand them if I sat still. I had a lot of practice at that.

"I brought you more Nervine." I heard a sack rustling. "Is it helping?"

"Do you want a cup of coffee, Mom?"

I heard a cupboard door.

"You know, you could go to one of our doctors in Hebron–"

"I don't need a doctor."

"–or stay with me awhile, settle your nerves."

"Settle my nerves? With you? That's a joke."

"You've always been high strung—"

"I would be just. Fine. If people would stop . . . talking . . . behind my back, and . . . stop . . . stop . . . ."

"That's all in your head, Edith."

"... if the wind would stop ... the wind ...." Mama's voice grew softer, as if it had been blown away on a gust inside the trailer. "... enough to drive anybody crazy."

Suddenly, I couldn't breathe. Maybe I was having a heart attack. Mama would be sorry if I died in here. For company, I concentrated on Sam's Scout bandolier hanging on the wall, displaying twice as many merit badges as any normal boy's. Even though I complained about being his Leg Man, I was proud of him. I should tell him so before one of us died, which could be any day now.

I heard dishes clatter into the sink.

" ... tornado?! Has nothing to do with anything, Edith. Anybody who's lived more than five minutes on the plains has been through a tornado."

Too bad I couldn't warn Grandma: the tornado was the second major Subject to Avoid with Mama, Papa's burns being the first.

We had moved to Round Prairie only two weeks before the tornado hit Hebron. I remember sitting in our new church that Sunday before we knew anybody. Smack in the opening Scripture reading, when Reverend Harkin lowered his voice to sound like God, the most incredible event in my personal history inside a Methodist Church happened. Marvin Harkin, whom we had just met, began to walk toward the altar. At first, everyone tried to ignore him, then openly stared as he nodded to people on both sides of the aisle, like a bride at her wedding. He held up his hand toward the pulpit, a Heil Hitler signal to his brother, the minister, then, to our horror, stopped at our pew. Mama looked at him as if the tin rooster on the church weathervane had flown down the aisle to perch on Papa's shoulder. Of all things Mama avoided, Being Noticed in Church was high on her list.

Marvin's white Sunday shirt was tightly stretched across his stomach, causing him to bend stiffly from his waist while he whispered in Papa's ear. When he straightened up, he smiled broadly, basking in the most attention he had probably ever received in his brother's sanctuary. Papa looked worried. Before Marvin could ceremoniously march back to his seat, Papa said our family needed to leave church. Right now.

On the radio, Marvin had just heard that last night a tornado had almost leveled Hebron. Grandma Strang and Uncle Ralph might be hurt or homeless. We didn't even stop at the trailer to change out of our Sunday clothes. On the first half of the way to Hebron, the Buick danced on the washboard gravel road, then skidded, yipping, once its tires hit the hardtop section of the highway.

As we passed Deshler, we began to see tornado damage: trees twisted off their trunks, barns splintered into pick-up sticks, trucks on their sides in ditches. Metal grain elevators had folded as if a giant had punched them in their stomachs, and corncribs had unspooled like huge metal ribbons. Chickens with feathers missing or sticking every which way wandered into the highway, while the cows in the fields looked stunned and dreamy, as if they had forgotten how to eat.

"If only Ralph and Mom," Mama repeated over and over, "Ralph and Mom . . . ."

Nothing compared to Hebron itself. At the town limits, National Guardsmen, wearing full uniforms and carrying real guns, stopped all cars, letting through only residents and relatives.

Transfixed by one soldier cradling a machine gun, Sam whispered, "That's an M-1 semi-automatic rifle. Takes .30-06 ammo."

Mama called out the car window to a soldier, "What's this all about–?"

"Looters, Ma'am," he saluted her and waved us through. "Be careful."

"What kind of person would steal from people so bad off?" she asked.

"Somebody who's worse off," Papa answered grimly.

Papa drove around fallen trees, torn couches, pulverized glass, tables missing legs, cupboards still full of dishes, and everywhere, torn and muddy magazines and newspapers. Stray dogs pawed at piles of branches and trash. Several times, he eased the Buick over the curb and drove on someone's lawn to get around cars crushed by trees. One car was so flat you couldn't see into it with a flashlight. Bricks littered every street as if whole armies had thrown them at each other instead of dirt clods. Red rags fluttered from fallen power lines, and voices on megaphones continually blared about gas leaks and no smoking, broken water lines and raw sewage.

"If Mom just made it to Ralph's . . . ," Mama said to her lap, barely able to look at the devastation out the car window.

This must be what real war looks like, I thought. Some houses stood untouched between two piles of neighboring rubble, some were just free-standing chimneys next to basements full of bricks like bloody sugar cubes. One time, Papa couldn't figure out where we were in town, since all the houses and landmarks had been leveled.

Finally, he jammed the Buick to a stop in front of Ralph's basement house. He and Mama jumped out almost before the car quit moving. The outlines of rooms Ralph had built overhead were gone. Missing. His windows were blown out, but the periscope stairway leading up and out of the basement looked intact.

"Ralph! You here!?" Papa shouted and began to yank on the upright door.

On his second pull, Uncle Ralph was pulled out, his hand on the doorknob.

"Thank God!" Mama hugged Uncle Ralph hard. "Thank God. Is Mom–?"

"She's okay. I'll be goddamned if the twister didn't skip her house and completely flatten the McNeils next door. Damnedest thing."

Mama was so relieved, she was gasping for air. Papa put his arm around her shoulders, and she let it stay there.

"Mom's at the high school gym, where they've set up cots and are handing out food. I'll be damned if the Red Cross isn't good for something after all. The National Guard was here within two hours, checking house by house, every house–flashlights, searchlights, shouting. Must've come from Grand Island, Lincoln, Omaha, everywhere." As Uncle Ralph shook his head, his hair fell across his eyes. His voice sounded thick. "Who would've thought?"

"Was anybody—?" Papa didn't finish his question.

"I've heard of two people killed, somebody else said four, a couple at the old folks' home. Sixty, seventy injured, some critical. They're taking 'em to Geneva, Deshler, Hastings, anywhere with a clinic or–"

"Thank God," Mama kept shaking her head.

"It's a damned good thing you folks weren't here. That trailer would've been shredded. You'd be dead."

Papa and Mama both nodded. They looked sad even though that news should make them happy.

Mama slowly said, "I'm going to walk over and find Mom. You kids stay with Papa." "Be careful of the fallen lines, Edith. Power's off, but you never know," Ralph warned. "Frank, I heard your folks' old farm took a beating."

Grandpa and Grandma Wilder had moved off the farm to Belvidere a few years ago.

"The new owners would be safe," Papa answered. "That storm cellar saved our hide more than once."

After promising to touch absolutely nothing, Sam and I picked our way through the littered streets nearby. We saw three people wearing pajamas and one man just in his underwear, making us feel particularly stupid in our Sunday clothes. They stood in their wreckage, picking up broken radios or high chairs, putting them back down, picking them up again. How could they ever fit all the broken parts together? What do you do when your house was here last night and is gone this morning? Your whole house, *gone*? Where do you go?

At the high school gym, Grandma looked pale but held a sandwich in one hand and a can of corned beef in the other. From her storm cellar under her house, she had watched the tornado rip off the cellar door but she was fine-thank-you, along with all of her home-canned preserves.

"Always a silver lining," she tried to smile. "Ralph will have work for the next ten years."

Stories poured in from everywhere: a player piano sitting upright in the pasture beside the cemetery, a rowboat on top of the hardware store, pieces of straw driven through fence posts. At the Majestic Theater downtown, a huge tree trunk had rammed through the screen directly at the audience, right in the middle of the movie. The fire siren could only give about sixty seconds' warning, but the stores downtown had just closed for Saturday night, otherwise many more people would have been killed in the collapsing buildings. They said it was the second worst tornado in Nebraska's history. That was saying something, Grandma added.

I overheard that a Shetland pony had been lifted and tumbled over half a mile, then dropped through someone's front porch roof, dazed but otherwise unhurt.

"A flying horse!" I nudged Sam. "Like Pegasus."

"Pegasus had wings," he corrected me. "It didn't need wind."

Although I hadn't met that pony personally, I kept thinking about it. How could a tornado do that to a *horse*? People were one thing, but horses were innocent animals, with no warning. What must the pony have thought, transformed into a flying horse? Did its legs gallop on thin air? Would it have nightmares the rest of its life?

The miracle of the tornado, everyone agreed, was the Catholic Church. The entire building had been demolished except for the half-dome over the altar, painted with a huge Jesus holding out his hands.

Normally, he would be blessing the congregation, but now he was called "Christ Above the Ruins."

As we looked at the devastated church, Mama said, "Leave it to the Catholics."

"Pretty amazing," Papa countered.

"Actually," Sam had the last word, "a dome is one of the strongest structures and can withstand ten to twenty times more force than any other design. That's why Roman buildings are still standing."

Mama laughed. "So much for miracles." Amazingly, she gave Sam a quick hug.

On the way back to Round Prairie, we drove out of our way to see the Wilder farm where Papa had grown up.

"My God," Papa said as we turned off the highway and headed down the gravel county road. Half a mile away, we could see that most of the windbreak trees were snapped off, and the barn was gone. The windmill had buckled in half, its blades now resting face down in the water tank, and the chicken coop had been shredded to matchsticks. The house itself, a tall two-story box, looked like a huge dollhouse with its front wall missing, now lying flat on the ground. The rugs and furniture were in place, the pictures still hung on the walls, even the books remained lined up neatly in their shelves. Upstairs, a brass bed rested against the missing wall, as if it had slept through the tornado's fury.

"Thank goodness is all I have to say," Mama shook her head. "Your folks didn't have to live through this as well."

"Edith! Everybody's lost a baby," Grandma Strang said sharply.

I snapped back to the trailer. Oh oh. Talking about Baby Janet to Mama wasn't any better than talking about the tornado.

"But *why*. I want to know *why*." Mama sounded shaky.

"Why what?"

"And Frank. Those terrible burns." I could hear Mama starting to crumble. Grandma should leave her alone.

"It doesn't do any good to complain."

"I'm not complaining, I'm asking–"

"People go on. You do what you have to do."

Mama tried again, softer and softer. "Why. Why did Father leave us. Ralph and me, and you pregnant–"

"That. Has nothing to do with anything."

"Or Grandpa Stoetzer, seeing his father killed by a train, right in front of his eyes–"

Grandma answered, clipped and angry, "That's the way life happens. One minute, everything's fine, the next minute somebody's hit by a tornado. Or a blizzard, or drought, or the grasshoppers. Summer of 1895, the grasshoppers even ate the wash off the clothesline."

"It doesn't make any sense." Mama sounded as if she were about to cry.

"Doesn't do one bitta good to worry. It's all out of our hands."

"In God's hands," Mama sneered.

I heard Grandma stand up. "If you're going to talk that way–"

"*God's plan*. To throw the kindest man in the world into a *fire*. A practical joke. Of a madman. What a plan." Mama sounded as if she were strangling.

"You've always thought you knew everything, but you don't know one blessed thing."

"And you wonder why I scream. Scream. I SCREAM, I SCREAM–" Mama almost had the hiccups because she couldn't get the words out fast enough.

"Edith!" Grandma almost shouted, stopping Mama in mid-sentence. "Get hold of yourself. You're acting crazy. If you were a little girl, I'd wash your mouth out with soap."

"Well, I'm not, mother. Not." When Mama was extra upset, she repeated a word over and over, like a clock with a stuck second hand, jerking at the same time, over and over. "Not not not not not not not . . . ."

"I won't listen to such crazy talk. You hear me? Do you?"

I heard Grandma open the door and slam it behind her. Then silence.

I waited for several minutes, then carefully slid open the doors to Sam's room. "Mama?" I called in my littlest voice.

Mama was staring at the door where Grandma had just left. Sometimes she would go stiff and stare at the same spot for several minutes.

"Mama?" I almost whispered.

"Not not not not not not—" she stared at the door.

I put my hand on her arm, but she looked at it as if it were something dead.

"I know, Mama."

She looked up at me, as puzzled at my face as she was at my hand. "Not? Know what? Not." She asked in the voice of a little girl.

"You're not a little girl. You're my Mama."

She frowned as if trying to recognize me. "Mama?"

"Remember?"

She looked as if she were trying to piece me together, to fit fragments into someone she could recognize, or a place she had lived before.

"Can I get off the footstool now?"

"Footstool." she answered.

I didn't want to leave Mama by herself yet. I kept my hand on her arm until she yanked away from me, the sure sign she was back in her body.

"Can I go out and play?"

"Play," Mama said dully.

I took that as a 'yes,' slowly put on my coat and quietly left the trailer.

Now, besides everything else, I needed to figure out God's Plan. I doubted that Sam would understand it, smart as he was. Reverend Harkin didn't have the sense to come in out of the rain, Papa said, and Miss Reynolds just laughed at God. That left Charlie Whitaker, the oldest person I knew, and one who kept cookies.

Meanwhile, Sam and I needed to fix the Formula, because it wasn't working any better than Nervine. The problem was a lot bigger than we thought. Now it went all the way to God.

*   *   *   *   *   *

Until I could figure out God's Plan, I would implement one of my own. If I lived to be a hundred, no one could convince me that I shouldn't have punched Leon Troxel in the face for cutting off Jane's braid, especially since no one else would punish him. But I didn't feel good about it. Mama's fury, Papa's disappointment, even becoming a minor celebrity with Sam's Boy Scout troop didn't make me feel right.

A week later, the solution came to me when I cantered La Cheetah out to visit Alberta Clipper, the dappled grey work horse. So noble. The back roads had thawed and re-frozen so many times they were covered in wriggling shiny lines, unpredictable, icy ruts. As I watched Clipper stomp and snort little clouds of breath, his massive shoulders shivering with each jolt, I suddenly understood my problem.

I wasn't sorry for hitting Leon. I was sorry I called him Harelip. In a way it was worse than calling someone White Trash because Leon couldn't help being a harelip. Possibly he could help being stupid and certainly he could stop playing with his private parts, but he couldn't help being a harelip. He had done something horrible to Jane, *irrevocable* as one of my new words described it, but I couldn't bring her braid back. Miss Reynolds said you can't fix the world, but you can cultivate your own garden. Her friend Voltaire, who had only one name, had written that. Cultivating your own garden was minding your own business, I was quite sure. Maybe I should re-name Luther Voltaire.

As Clipper snorted and nodded his huge head up and down, making his mane fly like an Arabian's at full gallop, I thought of the perfect justice. Leave it to a horse to be smarter than a little girl.

Next day, I purposely walked out of my way to my piano lesson so I could pass Leon's house. Sure enough, he was in his front yard, practicing mumbly-peg, repeatedly embedding the point of his jackknife in the frosty dirt near his foot. When he saw me, his lip, still scabbed over, lifted in a snarl.

"Get outta here. This is my yard."

I put my piano music down on the sidewalk and began walking toward him, the unarmed sheriff facing the outlaw with two loaded six-shooters.

"Hey, Leon." My voice didn't even quiver.

"Get out." He stood taller and held his ground, his jackknife pointing toward me.

"I came to say . . ." If I didn't hurry, I wouldn't do it. "I'm sorry . . . I called you that name."

He wiped the dirt off his knife blade, closed it, and slipped it in his pocket, his eyes never leaving mine. "Huh?"

"I want you . . . to hit me back." I couldn't believe my own words, but I knew they were true.

"I don't believe you." As I got within striking distance, he took a few steps back, obviously confused, then searched up and down the street. "So yer stupid brother can beat me up?"

"It's just between you and me." I repeated, "I called you a bad name."

"What name? You're crazy." He sounded genuinely scared. Clearly, he had no idea what to do with me.

I stood in front of him with my arms at my sides. "I'm unarmed. I won't hit back. I promise."

More in an attempt to protect himself, he lashed his fist out at me, connecting with my eye so hard I saw little flashes of light and heard springs in my head, like Wile E. Coyote in the cartoons. As dizzy as I felt, I managed to stay on my feet and stumble back to the sidewalk for my piano music.

"You asked for it," Leon called to my back, uncertainly. He was completely confused, but I was in the clear.

By the time I reached Mrs. Keindorf's house, my eye was throbbing.

"Jeb?" Still in the doorway, she took my face in her hands and turned my head sideways to see better. "What happened?!"

I was feeling a little woozy. "Could I have a–?"

She sat me down in the cowboy chair and brought a glass of water. "Who did this?"

"N-nobody. I . . . hit my head–" This wasn't a complete lie. I petted the wide arms of the chair, flat wooden slabs resting on top of polished wagon wheels.

"If someone hurt you, it won't serve justice to protect them." She rolled the word *protect* around, but *justice* came out clear and sharp.

Then Mrs. Keindorf did the unthinkable. With her plushy red lips, she actually kissed my eye. That day, I could barely see Beethoven and didn't play even my scales worth a plug nickel. But it was the best piano lesson of my life.

CHAPTER 34

DIPHTHONG

I NEVER KNEW WHAT LEON TOLD OTHER PEOPLE about my black eye, but I stuck to my story that I had fallen and hit my head on a rock. Only Sam knew the truth, and he would be the last person to blow my cover, especially since he didn't agree with my version of justice. His version would have involved surprise attacks and a small explosion.

Mrs. Dahlke was another story. During our stiff and businesslike spelling sessions, I felt worse and worse and, finally, just faced it.

"I . . . shouldn't have called Leon that name," I tested.

She remained silent.

"Will you ever forgive me?"

"It isn't up to me to forgive you, Jeb." She erased today's spelling words from the blackboard. "You need to apologize to Leon."

"I did."

She stopped erasing the board and looked at me. "You did?" She sounded surprised. "And he gave you a black eye in return."

I nodded yes, without adding that I had asked for it, definitely a lie of omission..

She lined up the erasers in the chalk tray. "Did that fix anything?"

I had to admit that it didn't, but I couldn't explain why, either to her or to myself. Very confusing.

"Jane—" I began. "Of all the kids . . . it was so *unfair*."

Mrs. Dahlke walked to the window. "Jane has enough troubles without you or Leon or anyone else interfering. Living with her grandparents on that old dry farm . . . ." She squinted across the playground as if she could see the farm at its edge.

Lordy. What had happened to Jane's parents? Had they abandoned her? Were they dead? I didn't dare ask, but this information catapulted Jane into the category of the Most Interesting Child I had ever met. And she wouldn't even talk to me.

Mrs. Dahlke turned back. "Jeb, you can't mend Jane's braid or undo the damage Leon has done or mitigate Jane's situation in the long run. You'll have your hands full in this life just fixing the problems you create, let alone other people's."

Now I had to think about not only past problems but also future ones I would cause. And what did *mitigate* mean?

"If I was–"

"*Were*," she corrected me.

"Subjunctive," we said in unison.

"— your daughter, what would you do?"

We both knew her daughter would never have done something so terrible in the first place. She was perfect, like dead baby Janet. If they weren't born perfect, most people, and all children, turned perfect after they died.

Mrs. Dahlke fingered her lapel pin, the tiny peacock studded with rubies and sapphires, as if she were trying to pick one of its tail feathers.

"I would remind her that the quality of her language expresses the quality of her mind."

I knew it. "I really am intractable," I said miserably.

"Who called you that?"

"Mr. Sprecker. In his note to my folks."

The light danced across her delicate glasses. "Do you think that was fair?"

"Yes," I answered honestly. "It means difficult to manipulate and resistant to authority. I looked it up."

Mrs. Dahlke quickly looked away.

"If nothing else, hopefully you've learned that words can be weapons. More powerful than sticks and stones, or guns or bombs."

Words more powerful than broomcorn spears or Sam's pipe bombs. The words Bobby Clawson spit into my ears. Miss Reynolds' words against the Visigoths and Mama's scary poems. I had an awfully lot to ponder, and none of it could wait until I was twelve. Now that I thought about it, *ponder* was a good name for a horse. I would ask Luther what he thought.

Late afternoon sunlight came through the tall windows in perfect grids, but once in the room, zigzagged up and down over the desks like the rick-rack Mama sewed on aprons and pajamas.

After a moment, Mrs. Dahlke said, "I ran across a word for you the other day." In the area of the blackboard which was striped in dotted yellow lines for illustrating penmanship, she wrote

diphthong

She knew how I loved all words which substituted ph – for f-, but in this one the letters teeter-tottered with each other and backwards formed a maze: g-n-o-h-t-h-p-i-d.

"How would you pronounce it, do you think?"

"Diff . . . thong?" As difficult to say fast as crossing your thumb under your fifth finger in piano.

"Good."

I copied it in my Big Chief tablet.

"It means 'two sounds.' A *diphthong* is a word which starts out with one vowel sound but ends with another in the same word: for example, *oi* or *ei*."

"Like the word changed its mind in the middle?"

"More like a bend in the road. You thought you were headed one direction but came out somewhere else. A good example is *eye*. Say it slowly. Feel how your mouth needs to change shape to finish the word?"

Eye! Was also a palindrome. Such a tiny word, and so complex.

She now wiped the blackboard with a damp towel, signaling the end of my spelling lesson.

"Are you going home now?" I asked. If I could walk with Mrs. Dahlke to the Pawnee Hotel, I could prolong arriving at the trailer and legitimately walk into the hotel lobby for a minute. I had no hope, of course, of ever seeing her room, which must be staggeringly romantic, filled with papers and piles of books and little jewelry boxes.

"No, dear. I have some housekeeping to do here." She paused. "Won't your mother be expecting you?"

"Lots of times I stay at school and play." I couldn't admit that I avoided being alone with Mama whenever possible.

"How is your mother?"

"She's fine-thank-you-for-asking." Then, for no reason, I blurted out, "Do you know Marvin Harkin?"

She stopped loading papers into her briefcase and answered quietly, "The minister's brother? Who owns the funeral home?"

"He's the Scoutmaster, too."

"Y-yes."

I toyed with my pencil, Shazam, and swung my legs back and forth under the desk, separately, a scissors kick. "Do you think he's creepy?"

"Creepy?"

"The way he . . . hangs around . . . ."

Mrs. Dahlke snapped shut her briefcase. "*Creepy* isn't a very descriptive word, is it?" She walked to my desk and stood beside me, her long, white fingers lightly tracing the initials carved into it. "What, exactly, do you mean, Jeb? And where does he . . . *hang around*?"

I didn't want to tattle on somebody, but I figured grown-ups like him could defend themselves. "After our spelling lesson? Friday? I was playing on the swings . . . ."

"And?"

"He walked by on the sidewalk."

"Marvin Harkin," Mrs. Dahlke repeated, as if she didn't want to misunderstand me.

"Yes. He walked all the way to the end of the block, then . . . turned around and came all the way back, clear across the playground to where I was."

"Was anyone else around?"

"No." Being alone made it hard for people to believe you, I knew from experience. Mama had the same problem. "I'm not lying."

"I believe you." Mrs. Dahlke sat down in Leon Troxel's desk. Because she was skinny, she could fit in it sideways, so she could look at me eye level.

"He said he wanted to . . . swing me." I quickly reminded her, "'Cuz I was sitting in the swing."

"Go on." She crossed her arms and hugged herself.

"I said no." In quick explanation, I added, "Because I like to swing myself and not go too high and then drag my feet to slow down and quit when I want to. You know?"

Mrs. Dahlke wasn't even blinking. "Go on."

"Before I could jump out of the swing, he grabbed the seat from behind and pulled me way up high, then let go, but he kept pushing harder and harder, pushing on my bottom every time I returned, so I was swinging way higher than I would ever go, and I started getting sick to my stomach you know how that feels when you get to the highest point and start backwards?"

"Did you tell him to stop?" Mrs. Dahlke said without taking a breath.

"I didn't want to say anything because he's the Scoutmaster and I didn't want him to think girls were chicken, especially me, but finally I yelled STOP."

"Did he?" Mrs. Dahlke now talked without opening her teeth. Her mouth was a little tight line, her lips didn't show at all.

"He came around and stood in front of me. Which was weird because I could kick him every time I swung close enough . . . . Which I finally tried to do. Kick him. But I kept missing."

"And–?" She paused, then said sternly, "Jeb?"

"He . . . laughed. Then he said 'Kick harder'."

Mrs. Dahlke leaned back and covered her mouth with one hand. I thought she was about to laugh until she said, "Oh dear." She paused. "Then what?"

"Just then Mr. Sprecker walked out of the building and saw us. The Shark—Marvin—turned faster'n greased lightning to get away, but Mr. Sprecker yelled, 'Marvin! What brings you this way?' I dragged my feet in the dirt to stop swinging. Marvin said, 'Hey Clarence. I'm just having a friendly chat here with . . . with . . .' Mr. Sprecker had to tell him my name, 'Judith. Judith Wilder.' 'That's the one,' Marvin smiled his churchy smile."

"What did Mr. Sprecker do?"

"He told me to run on home. But he looked at me as if I had done something wrong. Then he folded his arms and turned toward Marvin and Marvin folded his arms so they looked like twins except one was bald and one had lots of greasy hair, and they were still talking when I turned the corner."

Mrs. Dahlke looked more serious than the days she handed out report cards. "Did you tell your parents about this?"

"Mama said it was my overactive imagination. As usual."

"And you father?"

"I didn't tell Papa."

Mrs. Dahlke clapped her hands flat on her lap and stood up. "I'll talk to him."

At the thought of Papa hearing all this, I began to doubt myself. Maybe Harkin wasn't that weird. After all, nothing had really happened, it was just icky. Maybe he was the normal one, and I wasn't.

"I don't want to get anybody in trouble—"

"Some people need to get into trouble. You did the right thing, telling me." She looked out the window across the playground and put her hands on her hips. "I think it's safe for you to go home now."

"The coast is clear," I translated to Samspeak. I gathered my spelling practice papers and slid out of my desk. "By land, sea and air."

"All three."

"The machine guns are covering us, the crew's on stand-by, the arresting wires are tight, the decks are clear." I paused. "That's our drill when Sam and I land our dive bomber on an aircraft carrier. We're always out of gas, you know, or on fire or riddled with bullets or something. If your tailhook misses the wire, there's a crash net that catches you."

"Hopefully we won't need that," Mrs. Dahlke smiled wanly. "But it's good to know we have it."

The following Saturday, I was helping Papa adjust the brakes on his government truck because the men in their shop didn't do it carefully enough. He said if your steering and brakes were good, you might not get where you thought you were going, but you'd be safe along the way. He was squatting on his heels beside the dismantled back wheel while I sat cross-legged on a piece of cardboard, holding the flashlight and handing him tools.

"See that lining?" He pointed to two wide strips held in a circle by springs. "How it's worn on one end? That means it doesn't completely contact the drum."

With his hand over mine, he pointed the flashlight to the exact place. "It also means that somebody didn't adjust the anchors right when they relined the brakes."

Even though it felt cold in the barn, Papa's sleeves were rolled up past his scars, which didn't stand out as much in the winter when his arms weren't sunburned.

"Do your burns hurt?" Papa and I had the best conversations when he was working in the barn. Lucky for me, Sam didn't care about fixing cars or other machines.

"Not anymore." With long-nosed pliers, he unhooked one end of a brake spring and held it tense. "They used to hurt. Nobody who hasn't been burned could know how much."

Papa never talked about this, so I seized my chance. "Did you just want to die?"

"Some days." He re-hooked the spring and ran his fingers around the lining. "But you know what? I loved your mama so much I couldn't stand the thought of losing a minute with her."

"Wow. You loved her?" This was exciting news. I'd never thought of my folks as romantic.

"Still do. More than ever."

Papa sat down, now cross-legged like me. "I wish you'd known your mama before . . . before she lost the baby. She was the most beautiful . . . sweetest . . . gentlest woman you could ever know. And smart? Way smarter than the lawyers she worked for. Could've married any one of them. As Grandma Strang reminds me every chance she gets."

He smiled crooked "I walked into Edith's life as a back-up piano player, half-blind, wearing an eye patch like a pirate. She thought I was *exotic*." He laughed out loud. "Did I ever tell you about the pork chops when I was courting her?"

"No," I lied. I loved this story and always looked forward to the variations Papa would add each time.

"Since Mama's family was poorer than church mice, they never had enough to eat, let alone good food. As soon as Edith began earning a salary as a legal secretary, she came to me and asked if she could buy a whole pig from my family's farm. I was overjoyed that I could finally do something for her. Then she said she wanted the whole pig cut into pork chops, her favorite food in the whole world. She didn't know that you only get a few pork chops from each hog—the tenderest meat along the spine. But I wasn't about to quibble. My dad and I slaughtered fifteen hogs to get Edith's pork chops, and he never breathed a word to her."

Papa searched around his knees for a different tool. "Prince of a fella, your Grandpa Wilder. And boy, did he love you. You'd crawl all over him like a puppy, pull his eyebrows, stick your fingers in his nose. And laugh? Would he laugh. He'd sit in his old leather chair, gather you into a little ball on his chest, and you'd both fall asleep in half a minute."

Why had I never heard this story before? I was thrilled.

"You were way too little to remember, but when he got so sick at the end, he asked me to put you on his chest. You fell asleep and . . . ." Papa cleared his throat, "Dad wouldn't let me move you. He . . . died with you asleep, curled up, with your ear right over his heart."

"I never knew that, Papa."

"I'll bet I've told you before. You always pretend I haven't."

"It's really true."

"Edie loved Dad, too, especially since she didn't have a father. In fact, I think she married me so she could have my dad." Papa's grew more serious. "Then I lost my fingers and any chance for a job in music and then . . . the burns and—. Your mama has stuck by me through thick and thin. Mostly thin. She's a wonderful woman. No matter how . . . upset she gets these days."

More and more to think about. "If you had died from your burns, Sam and I would never have been born."

"If I'd known you and Sam were waiting for me in the future, it would've been a lot easier."

"And Janet," I had to add.

He stood up, hooked the trouble light inside the fender, and squatted back down. "Some little ones make it and some don't."

"Is that God's Plan?" We had never talked about this.

Papa looked sideways at me with his good eye. "I think God leaves a lot up to us, and we can make a real mess of things. But I don't think he lets little children die on purpose."

This wasn't completely clear, but I knew Papa was explaining something to me without any tricks in it.

"At this point," he pointed with a screwdriver, "we'll adjust the anchor pin and the star wheel, and we'll be done." Papa's mechanic words always sounded like music. *Star wheel.*

"You can fix anything, Papa."

"Only the easy stuff. The really important problems are way past me."

As he tapped on the star wheel, Papa tried to sound offhand, but he couldn't fake anything. "Have you seen any more of Marvin Harkin?"

So Mrs. Dahlke had already talked to Papa.

I shook my head no.

He handed me the hammer and screwdriver and jiggled the brake assembly. "Don't ever be alone with him, all right? If he comes around and you're alone, you yell."

"Yell what?"

"Anything." He put his hands on his knees and stood up in two parts, like unfolding his carpenter's rule. "Do you hear me, Sugar? Yell as loud as you can. And take off running. Don't worry about what anybody thinks: just yell and run."

My creepy feelings must have been right. "Is he a Communist?"

"I don't know what he is, but he doesn't have any business with you."

"What about Sam? And the Boy Scouts?"

"They have all that self-defense training," Papa smiled a little bit. "And they stay bunched up."

"He's creepy, but he wouldn't really hurt me."

Papa stopped grinning.

"Papa? Do you think Marvin Harkin would hurt me?"

"He might."

I hugged the tools which Papa handed me. "What would you do if he hurt me, Papa?"

"I'd kill him."

CHAPTER 35

THE HOUSE OF YESTERDAY

THE DAY BEFORE THANKSGIVING VACATION, THE fourth, fifth and sixth grades went on a field trip to Hastings to the House of Yesterday, the Nebraska museum of science and natural history. Our family had driven past it before, but we had never gone in because it cost money. In front, Sam and I had played on the machine gun, which originally rotated and defended an aircraft carrier but was now encased in years and years of gray paint.

Just outside Hastings, the school bus stopped at the railroad tracks near the State Hospital for the Incurably Insane. I looked for tiny faces in the tic-tac-toe bars at the windows, but they were empty today.

"Cuckoo, cuckoo," a boy in the front of the bus sang out, stirring up choruses of "nuthouse" and "looney tunes." I heard somebody whisper "Mrs. Wilder," prompting Doreen Cavin to jump up from her seat, turn around and call out, "How's the Cuckoo Family, Jeb?" She sat back down and giggled with her friends. She had probably done it on a dare. Sam was showing Jim Hartsock and some other sixth grade boys a coin trick and didn't seem to hear her.

In the bus seat ahead of me, Vicky Lindquist told Elaine Welsh, "They have chairs in there like barbershop chairs but they're really electric chairs and they strap them in–"

Leon jumped from his seat. "They zap 'em WHAM! and the looneys turn into spastics–" He fell into the aisle, gurgling and pretending convulsions.

Roused from his pretended apathy, Sam scoffed, "That's not how the electric chair works. The Rosenbergs–"

"Leon! Get up this instant." Mrs. Dahlke called out.

Now everyone was talking, with Doreen in the lead. "My dad says they could kill the loonies if they wanted to, but they keep them alive . . ." her voice dropped to a ghost-story mumble, "to practice torture. So when they capture Communists they know what to do."

I tasted vomit at the back of my throat. Who put people in there? Why? How could they escape?

Mrs. Vince stood up. In her charcoal suit and heavy lace-up shoes, she looked more like an Army general than usual. "Everyone: get your coats and lunches."

Silence swallowed us all. She was so scary, she should have been the principal.

Once inside the museum, we scattered like ants at a picnic. I heard there was a real mummy like the one Sam and I had read about in *National Geographic* last summer. I headed straight for that, certain that no one else would be interested, but Joe Clary followed me. He peered into the glass case straight across from me, his moving reflection momentarily giving life to the little heap of rags and bones.

He walked around the case toward me. "Do you think that's a real person?" His chocolate-colored eyes always looked as if they were about to melt. I would have died and gone to heaven if I had brown eyes like his, but I was too bashful to compliment him.

"A museum wouldn't lie. Besides, without our muscles and organs and stuff, we turn into piles of bones." I added, "Like my dead baby sister."

"Where is she?" He looked around anxiously, as if expecting to see her in a nearby exhibit.

"In the Rose Hill Cemetery in Hebron."

"Oh."

I tried to make friendly conversation. "Your mom handed out the very best treats this Halloween. Wax lips and fangs are the best."

"I couldn't go trick 'r treating. Mother said it was too cold." He sniffled.

In fact, he was always sniffling. It never occurred to me that he might have asthma. Asthma was a horrible disease but a beautiful word, with its tall, silent 'th' in the middle.

Joe carefully laid his open palm against the glass case. It was an odd word to think about with a boy, but he was actually *delicate*. "Did you know downstairs, they have a wolf?"

"No kidding? Sam said, in the basement they have old fire trucks and even hearses."

"Wow. I'm going there." Joe ran off.

On my way to the wolf, I looked into a room with glass cases full of rocks and model dinosaurs ranging in size from a quart of milk to a small tricycle. All of them were gray and furry with dust, like abandoned toys. Sam said they used to rule the world, but that could be another Boy Scout myth.

Hanging on the wall was a huge painted clock face like I had never seen. It was called a Geologic Clock. A sign nearby said it scaled Earth's history of 4.6 billion years to one hour. Added to ticktock time, star time, footstool time and up-in-the-night time, geologic time was a gold mine, as Sam would say. Around the clock face ran poetic words like *Archaean* and *Proterozoic* and *multi-cellular eukaryotes*—incredible 'y' and 'z' words, also jammed with vowels. After the origin of the solar system (in 6 minutes) and atmospheric oxygen (after 27 minutes) animals appeared in the last 9 minutes. I thought they had made a mistake and left off humans, unless they counted us in with the other animals. Then I saw a colored sliver of time near 12 o'clock. The entire history of humans—called *hominins*—lasted one second on this clock. *One second.* From cavemen through all the kings and queens and all the wars right down to Jeb Wilder right now. One second. What could make a little girl feel smaller?

Outside that room, I stopped dead at the most amazing dollhouse I could even imagine. Someone had built a model of a farmhouse from 1900, missing one wall and the roof, like Papa's home place after the Hebron tornado. It was three stories high and crammed with perfect miniature furniture—carved dressers and fireplaces, tiny brass beds and delicate dishes and doors with oval glass windows. A petit-pointed rug lay at the bottom of the stairs, and on the bedroom floor were knitted socks half the size of my little fingernail. A miniature upright piano stood in one corner of the living room with little slivers of painted keys. The keys were too little to count, but there couldn't be more than ten or eleven. Much more compact than our trailer piano but still way too big for a Dust Person. If it hadn't been so noisy in the museum, I might have heard it play.

When I circled the exhibit, I saw Mrs. Vince talking to Mrs. Dahlke near the stuffed Sand Hill cranes. I would need to walk by them to see the wolf and the hearses. As I hesitated, I heard the words "insane asylum" and went on High Alert, retracing my steps to hide behind the dollhouse.

Mrs. Vince towered over Mrs. Dahlke, like a basketball player with her coach. Today Mrs. Dahlke wore a butterfly pin made from white pearls, possibly fake and not nearly as dressy as her usual jewelry. She probably wore it in honor of the animals and bugs in the museum.

Mrs. Dahlke was saying, ". . . poor Arlene—Cecil Hauser's wife?—was locked in there. You know, they lived north of Gilead, my home town, on that miserable dry farm. Not a friend to her name."

Mrs. Vince murmured, "Why . . . State Hospital?"

Mrs. Dahlke flashed out, "Do they need a reason? Arlene was skittish, a little odd—and no wonder. Living out there on the prairie with only the wind and dirt for company, trying to scrabble a living. Not two nickels to rub together. She lowered her voice. "Would Cecil Hauser need a reason to lock up Arlene? That skirt-chaser?"

Mrs. Vince bent her head over Mrs. Dahlke's. "Have you ever been *inside* that hole? I have a shirt-tail cousin I visited once. Mildred, they just sit and stare, haven't a thing to do. Up one side of the hall and down the other. And they're all filthy. *Filthy.* They don't feed them enough, either. They're just skin and bones. The screamers aren't allowed in the public rooms, but you can still hear them. Locked away who knows where. Or strapped down. It's enough to make a stone weep. You know, I grew up on a farm like you, and we wouldn't treat an animal like that, no matter how unmanageable it was. If you weren't crazy when you went into the State Hospital, you'd certainly go crazy inside."

Mrs. Dahlke put her hand on Mrs. Vince's arm. "What happened to your cousin?"

Mrs. Vince cleared her throat as if she'd been coughing. "When she went in there, she was the prettiest little thing. High-strung, but talented. Sang like an angel. A little too religious for some folks, but. When I saw her, she'd shriveled up, looked twenty years older, stared at the floor the whole time. And twitched. All over. Sometimes, she almost flung herself out of her chair. She never twitched before. I still have dreams about that poor thing."

"What did they do to her?"

"I can't even imagine. I heard rumors about ice baths and shots. They gave her electric shock treatments, but do those make a person twitch? Would the drugs?"

Mrs. Dahlke took off her glasses and cleaned them with her hanky. "I don't know, but folks who are put in there never come out again. It's worse than prison; it's a death sentence."

"Absolute disgrace. When will Nebraska do something–"

"Nebraska isn't any worse than anywhere else, from what I hear."

Suddenly Mike Letson ran out of the stairwell ahead of Leon. "Did not!"

"Did too!" Leon reached to shove him, but as he passed Mrs. Vince, she grabbed the neck of his shirt.

"Stop behaving like a hoodlum!"

"You're not my teacher." Leon tried to jerk out of her hands, but she was too tall and strong for him.

"It's a good thing. I'd hang you on a clothesline and watch you kick around."

Mrs. Dahlke stepped from behind the display. "Leon. You calm down, or you and I will spend the afternoon in the school bus. And your parents will hear about it."

I used their interruption as cover for bolting for the stairs. I had to talk to Sam right away. A field trip didn't count as school or recess, so he would let me talk to him. All I needed was one minute.

What if they tried to lock Mama in the State Hospital! Mama! Tied up and electrocuted and twitching like that. Sam and I had to do something to save her. Anything. Could he do something with explosions? Sam would have a plan. I jumped down the stairs two at a time.

On the next floor, I saw him in a group of boys peering down into a tall wooden box. I tried to get his attention with Boy Scout hand signals for "council" and "double-time," but he purposely avoided looking at me. I knew that it would break a Cardinal Rule, but I was so desperate I walked closer and called his name.

He turned on me furiously, then seemed to get an idea.

"Hey, Jeb, look at this," he said and motioned for the boys to part so I could look into the box.

Inside was a rattlesnake curled up on a little hill of sand. I could hardly believe the museum would keep a live rattlesnake. It didn't move, so I looked closer, bending over the case, my nose nearly touching the glass, when it came alive and rattled its tail. I screamed. Not a little girls' I'm-going-to-tell-on-you scream, but a true stopped-heart scream.

"She fell for it, she fell for it!" The boys jeered. Sam was laughing.

Joe Clary pointed to the side of the box and said, "It's a button. See?" He pushed it, and the snake rattled again.

I stumbled to the exit and out the front door. If I didn't have Sam, I didn't have anybody. Now he didn't care, either. Not about me or Mama or the State Hospital. All I had wanted was one minute. One. I sat at the disabled machine gun, making quiet ek-ek-ek-ek sounds.

On the bus, Jane Englehardt was sitting alone two rows from the back. Expecting her to tell me to go away, I decided to take a chance. Beside her, the seat was cracked, and foam rubber pushed out like fat from a deep cut which had never healed.

"Are you saving this?"

When she shook her head no, her cropped hair tapped against her thin cheeks.

Sam and his buddies shoved each other to sit in the front seats, but before he sat down, I saw him scan the crowd. I wished that I had hidden in the House of Yesterday until they closed it for the night so he would think I was locked in. Then he'd be sorry.

On the ride home, Jane and I looked out the window in silence.

"What was your favorite part?" I asked her half-heartedly.

Barely audible, she answered, "The dollhouse."

"Me too. Can you imagine living in a house that big?" I had to be careful not to say too much and scare her off. "I always wanted to live in a house with an upstairs."

"Our farmhouse has an upstairs," she answered. "But everything in there was so clean and pretty. They were rich."

She sounded so wistful I wanted to console her. "It was missing a wall."

"Doesn't matter. It was still beautiful."

"May I join you two?"

Mrs. Vince sat sideways in the seat across the aisle. Her suit smelled like vinegar and tree bark. She always pulled her hair into a tight bun, never a single hair out of place, but not a wig, either. She leaned over to look right at us through her rimless glasses.

"Did you enjoy the museum?"

"Yes, Ma'am," I answered, and Jane nodded.

Bending toward us like that, she was so nice. Tough but nice: what a great combination. With her as my teacher, I could survive sixth grade. If we still lived in Round Prairie, that is.

"I have a question."

"Fire away, Jeb." That's what Papa said.

"What if a mom is put into the Insane Asylum? What happens to her kids?"

Jane looked at me in surprise. "Yeah."

Mrs. Vince let out a long breath. "Sometimes their father can take care of them."

"What if he can't?"

"He might . . . send them to live with relatives."

Now Jane asked, "What if her parents are dead and she lives with her grandparents and they die?"

Oh lordy. Jane didn't have a mom or a dad. She was a real, live orphan.

"Well," Mrs. Vince stalled, "They put them into orphanages, where, hopefully, they will be adopted into good homes."

Mrs. Vince was trying so hard, I wanted to help her out. "Miss Reynolds told me about the orphan trains. How they shipped thousands of kids from back East and stopped in little prairie towns and lined the kids up and people in the crowd just . . . took their pick."

Jane made a funny sound.

"That was a hard, hard time. For everybody—the real parents, the adoptive parents and the children." Mrs. Vince smiled. "But a lot of those children had good lives. Some went to college, some became teachers and doctors. Two even became state governors."

Standing beside the driver of the lurching bus, Mrs. Dahlke asked, "Before we get back to school, are there any questions?"

Here was my chance. I raised my hand. "About the mummy? Is it an animal, vegetable or mineral?"

Without hesitation, she answered, "Animal, since it's still a human being."

I shot a triumphant look at the back of Sam's head, which I knew he could feel.

Near Blue Hill, Sam turned in his seat, pretending to look at something in the back of the bus, but I knew he was looking at me. I ignored him. He might be apologizing by telepathy. Or he might have just considered who his Leg Man was at the drugstore. Or remembered who had enough blackmail material to lock him away for the duration of his childhood.

Tired, we all lulled into silence. I wanted to ask Jane a hundred questions, but she rested her head against the window and pretended to sleep. Twilight was already falling, draining the color from the empty fields and isolated farmhouses, washing everything a uniform gray, even the thin layer of new snow.

CHAPTER 36
BABY JESUS AND THE BOY SCOUT KNIFE

EACH YEAR MRS. VINCE INHERITED THE TASK OF directing the Christmas play, which involved every sixth grader and anybody else who could follow directions. This year she had unearthed a Drama titled "Why the Bells Rang" about two beggar children who perform a miracle. Sam, who had advertised his Public Speaking merit badge in the wrong quarters, unintentionally landed the lead role.

I was safe until Mrs. Dahlke announced at the end of my spelling lesson that Mrs. Vince wanted to talk to me. For over a week she had worn a small Christmas tree brooch set with pinpoint emeralds and ruby chips.

"Are those–?"

Mrs. Dahlke shook her head.

"Maybe they're real jewels . . . which some G-man confiscated from a *heist*–" We had been studying 'i-before-e-except-after-c,' or when they're trying to trick you in the spelling bee.

"Just for you, Mrs. Vince has changed the role of the little brother to a little sister."

"My mother won't let me." This was true.

"She already gave permission."

I couldn't believe it. Having one, much less both, of her children Noticed in Public usually ranked dead last on Mama's list of priorities.

"If it's about a miracle, it shouldn't be allowed in school. There's a law against church and state." That didn't sound right. "Miss Reynolds said so." It sounded like her, anyway.

"Miss Reynolds has volunteered to help us."

"But she hates children. She told me so."

"That's why she's perfect for the job."

Miss Reynolds, it turned out, was surprisingly effective at keeping the troops in order, moving us stiffly into place by our shoulders, helping us memorize our lines, cracking jokes which most of us didn't understand. At one point, she offered to teach us "O Come All Ye Faithful" in Latin so at least something educational could come out of the project.

Mrs. Dahlke said that we were all having enough trouble learning English.

Hoisting her bosom with her folded arms, Miss Reynolds replied, "They might as well be thoroughly illiterate in two languages as marginally literate in one."

Mrs. Vince visibly stiffened and continued waving like a musical conductor at the tallest boys on the back row.

Off to one side, I confided to Miss Reynolds, "I thought only Catholics could use Latin."

"Nothing validates primitive rites and hocus-pocus like intoning them in a respectably ancient language." She hastened to add, "I don't have anything against Catholics *per se*. I'm equally vicious about all institutions which wage war in the name of peace, burn heretics in the name of a benevolent god, or divide the world into the saved and the damned. In American politics, that takes the form of Us versus Them."

A blizzard of words. When I grew up, I wanted to be just like her. Or like Papa, who didn't say much at all.

"What's a *per se* Catholic?"

Miss Reynolds threw back her head and laughed, which she had been doing a lot during play practices. "How did they con you into this, Judith? You're too short."

"Mrs. Vince rewrote the part for me."

"Agh. Show biz," she snorted.

My role required following Sam around the stage while we both dragged canes and pretended to be poor and hungry, until we wandered into a little town whose church bells hadn't rung for years and years no matter what the townspeople offered as sacrifices. Even the King's donating his crown didn't turn the trick. They were all *hypocrites*, a good example of a y-for-i sound, although with a terrible vowel-to-consonant ratio. In an unlikely plot twist, the beggar children placed on the church altar their last coin. Instead of spending it on food? I had objected. This unfeasible sacrifice made the bells ring.

During rehearsals Sam was having trouble understanding the logic, and therefore the motivation, behind the coin business.

Mrs. Vince suggested, "Tell me some physical object you value the most, which you can pretend to give to the Baby Jesus."

"A Boy Scout knife–you know, the kind with the Boy Scout insignia on it? If I had one. They cost a dollar, so I don't have one. If I did, that would be the most valuable thing."

"Good. Now imagine putting that on the altar," Mrs. Vince encouraged.

"But I wouldn't do it," Sam explained. "First of all, I don't have one. And if I did, I sure wouldn't leave it there."

From the sidelines, Miss Reynolds explained, "Someone might steal it. After all, they're in church."

Mrs. Vince ignored her.

I thought of a better reason. "Why would Jesus need a Boy Scout knife?"

Sam nodded violently in agreement. "Yeah. Why?"

Miss Reynolds added, "He's just a baby. Has no motor skills—"

"Thelma, if you can't control your tongue, I'll send you home," Mrs. Vince warned. She turned back to Sam. "If you had a Boy Scout knife, for whom would you give it up?"

Sam thought and thought. "For my Dad. Or maybe my Mom. If they were being held by pirates or something. You know, ransom."

"Or me," I called out. "If I were tied up by Indians."

Sam considered this, no doubt remembering the numerous times he had tied me up practicing merit badge knots. "I don't . . . think so." He decided, "No."

Looking alarmed, Mrs. Vince suggested, "For your sister? Of course you would."

"Jeb would give them so much trouble, they'd want to get rid of her."

Finally, the big night arrived, the night before Christmas Eve. The backdrop, repainted every year by new sixth-graders, portrayed a Heidi-like village on a mountaintop with a church hovering near collapse because it had ten spires. The cast members were disguised in whatever bath towels, aprons, dust mops and old curtains our mothers could spare. The high school gym, borrowed for the occasion, quickly filled with parents on metal folding chairs.

On Miss Reynolds' "Go," everyone but Sam and I trooped onto stage and, shuffling and re-shuffling to stand in the right places, managed to convey the long-standing problem with the silent church bells. Sixth-grade girls whined without conviction that their rubies and diamonds and baskets of gold were useless, and the King, Jim Hartsock, shouted that even his crown hadn't worked. In the wings, Miss Reynolds prompted forgotten lines without even looking at the script. She had memorized every part, if you can imagine.

On the cue of "two beggar children," Sam and I staggered down the center aisle of the audience, bent over with hunger and dragging our walking sticks. This wasn't hard, since both of us felt sick with nervousness. At the end of the first act, we were supposedly so exhausted that we fell asleep draped over a rock, actually our footstool from the trailer covered with camouflage material.

During the intermission, backstage was utter chaos. Kids ran everywhere, teachers were trying to catch them for last minute costume repairs, Mrs. Vince was calling out orders. Meanwhile, I actually fell asleep with my head on Sam's lap.

At the beginning of Act II, I was told later, Sam pretended to wake up, yawned, stretched, and walked to front and center stage to deliver his lines. Only then did he realize that I should be at his side. Still facing the audience, he walked backward in his own footsteps and punched my shoulder.

"Jeb!" he hissed through his teeth and a frozen smile. "Wake up!"

At this point, a little groan went through the audience, since they realized that nobody my age could act that well.

I opened my eyes to a very bright light and wondered if I had been sleepwalking and ended up here.

Sam whispered my line to me without moving his lips. "The Christ child knows–"

I almost shouted, "The Christ child knows! I want to worship him!"

A collective sigh rose from both the stage and the audience, but none so loud as Mrs. Vince's, and the play ran. And ran. Even Joe Clary, a last minute volunteer, delivered his line about candles and *poinsettias* without a hitch.

At the right moment, Sam looked wistfully at the quarter in his hand, a prop Miss Reynolds had donated, and put it on the altar, the Geigers' picnic table covered with a sheet. For just a moment, I saw him transform it into a Boy Scout knife, the best acting in the show, if I did say so.

And then the bells rang. Very loudly. Too loudly. Unknown to anyone, Mrs. Vince had arranged to have the churches in town ring their bells on her signal. So the play spilled outside, through the town, and all of Round Prairie rang with the miracle of children's gifts. More than that, the miracle of yet another Christmas play survived—with no accidents, enormous relief, and even some fun.

At home, Mama dished out ice cream in celebration, even though it wasn't Sunday night. Oboyo boy.

"The real miracle," she teased, "is that Jeb woke up and remembered her lines." She handed around a pale green Fiesta bowl of ginger snaps.

Sam said, "It wasn't a miracle. Jeb could say her part backwards. Besides, she could make up what she didn't remember."

Papa ate a whole ginger snap in one bite. "My dad always said, 'Never expect miracles, but always clear a little place for them'."

"Which he did," Mama added. "He was such a good man."

"Not as good as his son," Papa grinned.

Our tiny Christmas tree, the artificial one we used every year, stood on the piano. Each furry hollow branch ended in a colored glass tip, so one small light bulb in the base spread light through the whole tree, all the way to the tiny frosted star on top. Next to the tree, on top of my piano music, sat the family's Christmas presents—one from me to Sam and one from him to me. This year, Mama and Papa said they had everything they needed, so we should spend our allowance on each other.

"Guess what, everybody?" Mama sounded like me. "Let's open our Christmas presents tonight."

Sam and I looked at each other in disbelief and scrambled for the boxes we had been squeezing and shaking for a week. We were both masters of disguise, so neither of us had guessed what was inside.

"You start, Jeb," Sam couldn't sit still with excitement.

I carefully untied the ripple ribbon and slid my finger under the snowman wrapping we used from year to year. There, inside a shoe box three times too large and wrapped in newspapers lay the little bronze horse from Hested's dime store. Luther. My Luther.

"Oh Sam." I almost began to cry from being happy. "Thank you thank you thank you." I wanted to hug him but knew he wouldn't allow it. I held Luther with one hand and bounce-galloped him up my arm, until he could put his nose on my cheek, a little horse kiss. "You're the best."

"Now you, Sam," Papa fairly twinkled, knowing what I had bought.

Sam started to rip into the package, also in a shoe box, before he remembered that we needed to salvage the wrapping. Throwing open the lid and rifling through the wadded newspapers, he spied the little box inside. Reverently picking it up, he still wouldn't let himself believe what it must be. But it was: an official, insignia-and-all Boy Scout knife.

He looked at me, his mouth a little O, jumped up, and hugged me. Actually hugged me.

Maybe miracles could happen after all.

CHAPTER 37
WHITE-OUT

THE DAY STARTED COLD AND WINDY, LIKE MOST January days in Nebraska. At mid-morning recess, the eastern sky was steel blue, but in the northwest it was thickening like dirty lint. When the noon bell rang, Sam, bundled up almost beyond recognition, met me at our usual place inside the front door to walk home. The smell of baking cornbread and chili–the school's hot lunch–filled the halls. We couldn't afford school lunch and always ate at home, six-and-a-half blocks away.

I thought our Christmas joke might cheer us up. "Deck the halls with Boston Charlie.""Yeah," he said quietly, looking out the window in the door.

By now, snow was blowing so hard we could barely see across the street. Sam had buckled the earflaps on his plaid wool cap under his chin, which he hated, so I knew the storm was pretty bad. He told me to go back and get my leggings, which were so scratchy they drove me crazy, but I retrieved them off the coat peg outside Mrs. Dahlke's room. With Sam, I pulled the unlined wool pants over my bare legs under my dress and stuffed the cuffs down my rubber overshoes, which Sam kneeled down and buckled.

"Put on your mittens," he sounded like Papa.

"We could pretend we're on a forced march," I suggested for fun.

"We are," he answered grimly.

When he opened the school door, the wind yanked it out of his hands and banged it against the outside wall. It took both of us to slam it shut.

Fine ice particles swept off the school roof in long veils, dropped down our necks, and clogged our eyelashes. Blowing sideways, the snow plastered the sides of houses white, sweeping the ground bare in places while piling higher the drifts left over from the last storm. Parked cars were already re-buried under snow mounds with tops swirling off in smoky clouds.

Round Prairie hadn't had time to dig out of the last storm, so we couldn't see where the sidewalks ran. Even with Sam walking ahead breaking trail, I foundered through snowdrifts up to my knees and, in places, up to my thighs. My legs felt surprisingly hot and prickly, while my cheeks burned in the wind. It was getting colder by the minute, and my nostrils kept plugging up both from the snow and my freezing breath. I could breathe easier with my hand over my mouth and nose, but my wool mitten was soon caked with ice.

"Walk in the street!" Sam yelled over the wind.

We fell down several times but managed to climb over snowplow drifts to the road, which was rapidly blowing closed. By now, we could barely make out the outlines of houses in the spinning whiteness. I tried to remember how many blocks we had already walked, but through the snow, I didn't recognize one house. Maybe we had taken a wrong turn. I wondered if we could still go back to school to wait out the storm, or if we could head to Main Street for shelter in the library or Pawnee Hotel.

"Turn around!" Sam shouted.

I didn't understand until he seized me by the shoulders so my back was to the wind. He ducked down, using my body as a shield, and began walking me backward, occasionally looking around my shoulder to guide us. It was twice as hard to walk backward in the drifts, and we fell down about every ten steps, but it was a relief not to be facing the wind. Sam kept his head down so I could almost rest my chin on the back of his wool cap.

The snow swirled thicker and thicker, even between our heads, bent close. From nearby houses, we must have looked like the two-headed calf advertised at the Hastings fair. Each time we stopped to rest, Sam tried to figure out where we were. Like Papa after the Hebron tornado, he had lost all reference points, but I trusted Sam to find us. All that map training was finally coming in handy.

Shortly after we resumed walking, my back bumped into something. Sam looked around my shoulder in disbelief. Unknowingly, we had left the road, walked past unseen trees, climbed over a hedge and hit the corner of a house. We felt our way around to the front of the house so we could find an address or something recognizable.

"Should we ask them to help us?" I yelled, leaving my icy mittens off my mouth just long enough to gulp more blowing snow. Sam and I knew that asking strangers for help was against Wilder Rules and would have serious Consequences. Also, what if the house belonged to someone like Doreen Cavin or Bobby Clawson?

"I think!" He shouted. "I know about where we are!"

Resuming our shield and guide positions, we once again plowed our way into the street, although I was falling down backwards about every five steps now. Sam stopped. At that moment, the wind let up, lifting its skirt of snow, just long enough for us to get our bearings. There, in the wrong place and facing the wrong direction, was the back of Mr. Whitaker's farmhouse. For a moment, I thought the wind had twisted it on its axis but quickly realized we had overshot the trailer and had stumbled into the broomcorn field. Somewhere beneath our feet and deep snowdrifts lay the sleeping fort.

We beat on the trailer door, knowing that we couldn't go inside covered with snow. No answer. Sam beat again. What if Mama weren't home? What if something had happened—

Mama threw open the door and stood there, looking terrified. "Oh my God!"

Sam and I tried to brush the snow off each other and kick it off our boots, but Mama grabbed Sam by one arm and pulled him up the steps. "Oh my God," she said again, then pulled me in, too, snow clouds following.

"I went to Charlie's and called the school . . . When Sprecker said you had left . . . Oh my God." She didn't cry or laugh but sat on my chair-bed with her hands on her lap and watched us unwrap, dropping small sheets of icy snow from our wool coats and overshoes.

"Where should we put–?" Sam asked, knowing we shouldn't be tracking into the trailer.

"Just leave them on the floor." Mama's eyes were strangely sparkly.

"Does anybody want to feel my cheeks?" No takers. I put my own palms on my face. I could feel my cheeks with my hands but not my hands with my cheeks. "They're numb."

Mama jumped up. "You must be starved."

She had already put out bread, home-made syrup, and her canister of used bacon grease: my favorite lunch. As Sam and I spread the grease on the bread and poured Mapleine over it, Mama told us how she had tried to keep us safe in school. She had climbed through the snow to Mr. Whitaker's house to use the phone. When she finally got through his party line, then through the busy school line, she had talked to Mr. Sprecker himself.

"I asked him if you two could stay and eat a hot lunch at school." She clenched her jaw. "And do you know what he said?"

We both shook our heads no. Hoping she wouldn't see me, I ran my finger through a tiny pool of syrup on my plate and quickly licked it.

"Sprecker said, 'What if everybody did that?'" She imitated him so perfectly, I could almost see his road-tar hair and oversized suit. "What if everybody did that?" She repeated with a twist in her voice. "What if everybody, everybody, everybody–"

Sam stopped her with, "Mama, could we have some graham crackers?" Not only could Sam save my life but also he could bargain for dessert.

"You can have two apiece."

Did she mean two connected halves or two full pieces each, which would actually be four?

She looked at the trailer window, plastered and darkened with ice and snow. "And you know what else?"

Sam lifted the head off the kitty cookie jar and lifted out four connected halves.

"You two aren't going back to school today."

Sam and I stopped in mid-bite. We had never missed a day of school in our lives–not when we had colds, not when we had stomach aches, not ever.

"Or tomorrow. You're not going back to school until this blizzard's over."

Sam and I looked at each other, not knowing whether to be thrilled or terrified. Was that legal?

"And anybody who tries to make you?" Mama looked as triumphant as the picture of Joshua in Grandma Strang's Bible, except she was a woman. "Will have *me* to contend with."

We didn't know anybody who would voluntarily *contend* with our mother.

The wind blew harder, furiously pelting the trailer with snow, occasionally letting up, then returning with fistfuls of sleet like someone throwing gravel hard against the windows. The trailer shuddered each time and, in the strongest blasts, felt as if it were rocking up on two wheels. Inside, the trailer grew hotter and steamier, a pressure cooker, while the chaos and rage outdoors dropped the temperature further by the minute. I suddenly imagined Ice People the size of Dust People, swirled around in their own tornado. I didn't worry about Papa because he always spent bad snow days in the government shop doing paperwork which he hated, even though his desk stood near a very cute pot-belly stove. Miss Reynolds called this another example of government waste, not making men work outdoors when visibility was less than six inches.

Sam helped Mama sop up the melting snow and spread out our clothes to dry near the kerosene furnace. The wet wool smelled like a dead animal.

"Can you have tornadoes in the winter?" I asked, drying the last glass from lunch. For dessert, Mama had drunk Nervine. I was thinking of a human-sized one, not just for Ice People.

Simultaneously, Sam said "Sure" and Mama said "No."

Alone, Sam added, "No."

"I've been reading poems," Mama said with her skidding voice. "From a library book."

Sam pulled out his cigar box of Lincoln logs and began to build a little house, while I sat on the footstool and watched. As my fingers warmed up, they ached.

Without looking at any book, Mama recited, "There's some corner of a foreign field that is forever England."

I tried to imagine the map of England compressed into a corner of somebody's field.

"He's dead, you know." She twitched a fake smile. "We are the Dead."

Maybe Mama had Dead People for secret friends like I had Dust People.

She continued reciting, "Short days ago we lived, felt dawn, saw sunset glow. . . Now we lie in Flanders fields."

Was this the foreign field, and where was it? Was Mr. Flanders like Mr. Whitaker?

"Here's one Sam will like." She read from the book,

"Gas! Gas! Quick, boys!–An ecstasy of fumbling,

Fitting the clumsy helmets just in time,

But someone still was yelling out and stumbling

And flound'ring like a man in fire or lime . . . .

In all my dreams before my helpless sight,

He plunges at me, guttering, choking, drowning."

Mama clapped the book shut. "That's named 'Dulce et decorum est.' Latin."

Latin. It must be a Catholic poem.

"Gas gas gas," her voice started a slow climb Sam and I recognized. "In World War I, they learned how to use gas."

"Mama?" I didn't know what to say, only that I should stop her if I could.

"Chlorine gas." With her knuckles, she rapped Sam hard on the head. "Have you made that yet? What good is a Chemistry merit badge? Huh? Chlorine. Hideous death, but it works."

Sam pulled his head further into his shoulders.

"Mama?" I tried again.

"They used chlorine gas to make the flu epidemic, you know. 1918. Did I tell you that? The Catholics weren't in power yet. But they are now, by g-o-d."

Mama was cranking up, so I tried a sure-fire distraction. After Christmas, she had promised to help me make a pattern and to sew a stuffed dog. "Can we cut out the little dog?"

Mama hooked her two index fingers together. "And thick as thieves with the Communists. But now it's polio. They were just ready to arrest them with the flu, but they'll never get them with polio."

Sam frowned at his log house, trying to map out where to put windows and doors.

"Polio, polio," she nodded.

Polio was one of those words which sounded incomplete, like *zero*.

"I need to practice the piano." This ruse always worked. "And I need you to hold the cardboard over my hands." This was a direct lie, but lies to help your brother, especially who had just saved your life, didn't count.

"Polio, po . . li . . ," she slowed to a stop.

"In John Thompson, I have a hard song. The notes are way above the staff." This was not a lie. The song was "The Skylark," by somebody named Tchaikovsky, a wonderful name, but they would never ask it in a spelling bee.

Sam slid his Lincoln logs to the floor of his bedroom, where he could also read the comic books he stored under his sofa-bed. He had doubled his collection by trading marbles for them. Mama and I settled into position at the piano.

Mama looked at my music. "The notes really are off the staff."

"The 8 with the dots behind it means you play an octave above even that."

"I know that. How stupid do you think I am?" Her words slurred. Mama had played a year of violin in high school, but Grandma Strang couldn't afford lessons after that.

"I can't play that part," I said.

"Why not?"

"Because we don't have those keys on our piano." I thumped the wood at the high end of the shortened keyboard.

"What'll we do?" Mama asked fearfully.

"Mrs. Keindorf said I could play them an octave lower."

"Oh she did, did she?" Mama fanned herself with the cardboard. "I hear Mrs. Fancy-Schmancy has a picture of Stalin in her house."

Who told Mama this? She never talked to anybody, let alone the gas man. Miss Reynolds compared rumors to prairie fires that start small and suddenly explode, incinerating farmhouses and whole towns and any people who can't escape in time. How could we stop the Stalin lie before it spread further? Maybe an ad in the paper. Miss Reynolds would know.

I started to explain, "It's not Stalin. It's the Archduke–"

"Duke, schmuke. A Commie by any other name smells like . . . Mrs. Nose-in-the-Air." Mama laughed her single note, high and fast. "Let's bury *her* in Flanders fields."

I considered telling Mama about Mrs. Keindorf's brother buried in Rose Hill but decided instead to ask her questions about triplets and grace notes and rests, details I was certain she knew. When her attention began to wander, I asked her to count the time for me as well.

"Da-da-da, one, two, three; da-da-da, one, two three. Slow down, Jeb."

I did.

"Slower than that."

I played the notes so slowly that the log cabin clock ticked twice in the silence between notes. The song was unrecognizable at that speed. A different song.

Mama punched my shoulder. "I meant, go faster. Faster faster faster."

She counted so fast that my fingers couldn't keep up.

She hit my arm again. "Which is it? Fast or slow?"

I didn't care, as long as she calmed down. All at once, she threw the cardboard like a boomerang at Sam to get his attention.

"Where do you hide the gasoline, Sam-bo?"

CHAPTER 38

FAHRENHEIT 451

THE BLIZZARD LASTED TWO DAYS AND ONE NIGHT, nowhere near a record, although they closed school. Sam and I played outside as soon as feasible, building a snow fort on top of our real fort and arming it extensively with icicles and snowballs. With blocks of snow stacked waist high in a full circle, it was a masterpiece of attack capabilities and perfect protection for defense, much better than our dirt fort. We were finally and fully prepared for the next battle in the Round Prairie War. In the relentless wind and blowing snow, nobody showed up to fight.

I spent the rest of our windfall vacation in the library draped over the unabridged dictionary looking up the words ending in '-ious' Mrs. Dahlke had assigned. As usual, she wanted me not only to spell them correctly but also to know what they meant. This took much more time, clearly proving her philosophy that words are actually ideas. The suffix '-ious' meant "full of," which made no sense with *pious* or *impervious*—full of pie or imperv. I didn't have a handle on this yet, but I welcomed any word containing the vowels i, o, and u.

Scoffing at simple words like *contentious*, Miss Reynolds dropped a bombshell. "Do you know some words contain all five vowels? And in their correct order?"

I literally dropped my jaw.

"*Facetious*," she could barely contain herself. "And *abstemious*. There are others, but they usually repeat a vowel or two." Miss Reynolds knew everything, or at least as much as Mama and Papa.

"Wow." I corrected myself, "I don't mean 'wow'."

"You mean some precise and elegant expression of incredulity. You'll have to find your own."

She wrote *facetious* and *abstemious* on a piece of paper. It wouldn't do any good to lord this information over Sam, since at first he wouldn't believe me, then pretend not to care, and finally forget them. Numbers or formulas would be a different matter altogether.

"I have a question."

"Good."

"Mama got mad about Mrs. Keindorf having Stalin's picture over her piano, which means that somebody told her . . . ."

She sighed. "The small-town rumor mill is the only perpetual motion machine ever invented. Without gossip, what would people talk about? They can flap their jaws about anyone who makes them feel small or cheap or stupid. The Keindorfs are the perfect targets."

"How can we stop them?"

"There's an old saying: 'Trying to control a rumor is like trying to unring a bell'." She looked down the rows of library books, as if the answer were written there. "We can defend the Keindorfs every chance we get, but nobody listens to either of us. Of course, that never stopped us before."

I needed to think about the rumor problem more. "I have another question."

"About my necklace." In addition to her glasses holder, today she was wearing a separate necklace with one blue stone the size of a quarter.

"No. That's just a rock."

"Wrong. It's lapis lazuli. Semi-precious."

"Really?" I hurried around her desk to inspect the deep blue stone flecked with gold, startling as Papa's glass eye resting on her creamy neck. "It's beautiful."

I paused. "I want to ask you about . . . the State Hospital."

She leaned back in her chair, causing it to yelp.

I hurried on. "For the Incurably Insane? Do they have an electric chair where they strap down people and–"

"Judith." Miss Reynolds' voice had the snap of a ruler on a teachers' desk. "Where did you hear such nonsense?"

"The kids at school."

She blew out a huge breath. "Who skew Nebraska's average I. Q. downward. We're marginally functional as it is. Do you remember the Visigoths?"

I nodded. "The sack of Rome."

"We are surrounded by barbarians who thrive on hogwash. Do you know what hogwash is?"

I thought I did, but I didn't want to hazard a guess.

"Garbage. Fed to pigs. Although ignorance is the default human condition, it is incumbent upon you NOT to capitulate to it."

Since I didn't know *incumbent* or *capitulate*, I asked, "How can I not? Be. Do."

"First, by avoiding such unconscionable grammatical constructions. How can you *not be do*? Second, by thinking for yourself." She drilled her desk with a stiff index finger on each word. "Think. For. Yourself."

"Mrs. Dahlke already warned me not to think for other people, most of all for Jane Englehardt."

"So I've heard, although I wish I had been present for your face off with the sublimely witless Leon Troxel."

With my finger, I circled the spot she had just poked with her stubby finger. "All my good words failed me. I should at least have said he had the *cerebral cortex of a flatworm.*"

She barked my favorite laugh. "Actually, you don't need any advice about thinking for yourself. Just stay the way you are, Judith."

The front door blew open with a cold fist of wind, and there stood Mrs. Vince. She was wearing a forest green wool coat with a fur collar. Fur: almost as impressive as jewels.

"Hello, Thelma. How are you?"

"Spitting nails. How are you?"

"Cold." She pulled off her gloves and blew on her hands. "Jeb. What a nice surprise." She could sound delighted even if she weren't. I saw that happen time and again during our Christmas play rehearsals. "Mrs. Vince, what is that exotic fur on your coat?" I wanted to pet it in the worst way.

Miss Reynolds chuckled.

"It's honest-to-goodness, genuine squirrel."

I couldn't tell if she were teasing or not.

Miss Reynolds suggested, "Judith, go look up *unconscionable* so you can spring it on Mildred."

That was my signal to leave, although I could easily eavesdrop from the dictionary.

"Spitting what nails now, Thelma?"

"This just came in the mail." Miss Reynolds waved a piece of paper and deepened her voice to sound like Reverend Harkin reading the Scripture. "From the Staaate Deparrrtment."

Mrs. Vince took off her coat and sat down.

"Our beloved John Foster Dulles has joined the cockroaches." She began to read, "'The State Department will now impose an *outright ban* on books by any controversial persons, Communists, and fellow travelers.' Foreign service workers have started *burning* books. Listen to this: 'Senator McCarthy will purge the State Department's overseas libraries, which harbor thousands of subversive books by Communists, pro-Communists, former Communists, and anti-anti-Communists'."

Miss Reynolds slapped the paper on her desk. "Don't you love that double negative? I'm going to start calling myself pro-anti-Hoover."

"Thelma, loose lips—" Mrs. Vince nodded in my direction.

"Judith? She's as pro-anti-Hoover as I am. She said he has the brains of a basketball."

With Sam's teacher, I needed to keep the record straight. I called out, "I said, his head looks like a basketball."

"Same difference. Has the FBI contacted anybody at Lincoln Elementary about loyalty oaths?"

"I think it's mostly at the universities," Mrs. Vince kept her voice low.

"An oath! To what?" Miss Reynolds sounded like Papa. "To fight unfounded allegations with facts? To counter mass hysteria with critical thinking? To demonstrate in person that we don't all need to walk hunched over with our knuckles dragging on the ground?"

Mrs. Vince murmured something about "Mildred."

"Mildred Dahlke?!" Miss Reynolds yelped. "Did that s.o.b. Sprecker turn her in?"

Mrs. Vince tried to calm her down. "We don't know for sure. Somebody started rumors." Her voice dropped. "Added to the charges of insubordination, Mildred's very worried."

Miss Reynolds stood up and walked back and forth, steadying herself with one hand on her desk. "McCarthyism in microcosm: accuse innocent people of unspecified crimes based on your own prejudice and envy. Don't check for facts—because there are none—and pronounce them guilty."

Mrs. Vince added, "Remember what Erroll Flynn said? 'It isn't what they say about you that will destroy you. It's what they whisper'."

Miss Reynolds stopped pacing. "Edna, where will this country end up when Hoover's gone? Spies and lies: I'm afraid he's forever changed the political climate in America."

The louder Miss Reynolds talked, the more softly Mrs. Vince responded, like Papa with Mama. "Doesn't every generation feel that way about current politics?"

"Do you ever wonder what Hoover is hiding? Personally? You know, he lived with his mother until he was 43 years old. His *mother*."

"These are frightening times, Thelma, more than the war with all our boys killed overseas or the Depression." Mrs. Vince thought a minute. "I take that back. Nothing could be harder on ordinary folks than the Depression."

She stood up, a head taller than Miss Reynolds, and put on her coat. "Did the Omaha library send my book?"

Miss Reynolds handed her a book the size of a dictionary. "You had no competition for the fifth volume of Churchills' *History of World War II*."

Mrs. Vince hugged the book like I hugged Halloween candy. "There's only one more volume after this."

"Tragic. After a mere seven or eight thousand pages." I liked to hear Miss Reynolds tease someone else for a change.

"I can't help anyone who prefers fiction to history." Mrs. Vince shot back.

Miss Reynolds squinted hard at Mrs. Vince, her eyes almost disappearing in fat. "Fiction is a lie which tells the truth."

Did I hear right? An entire section of the library disguising lies?

"Who said that?" Mrs. Vince challenged.

"Find out for yourself."

"Thelma, even you can't quibble about Churchill. Last year's Nobel Prize winner. In Literature, no less."

Miss Reynolds slid a book from under the pile on her desk. "Look what just came in: hot off the presses."

Mrs. Vince read the title, "*Fahrenheit 451*. What's that about?"

"A future American society where reading is outlawed and firemen start fires to burn books. Four hundred and fifty-one degrees is the temperature at which books catch fire."

"Now you've stooped to reading science fiction."

"What's science fiction?" Miss Reynolds shook her head. "Once they start purging libraries overseas, their next target is right here." She poked her desk again with one finger.

"They wouldn't dare."

"If anybody comes through that door and tries to censor my books—" Miss Reynolds breathed harder when she got excited.

"You'll act like a rational person. At least, you'd better."

"My daddy, whom you remember well, left me his 12-gauge shotgun and the knowledge of how to use it. I can attest that its barrel is considerably shorter than when it left the factory. Has an impressive scatter pattern."

"You wouldn't–"

"Wouldn't I? Socrates versus the barbarians. At the end, when all the battles are lost, Winchester will beat hemlock all to hell."

CHAPTER 39

LA VALSE

I LOOKED AT MRS. KEINDORF'S PICTURES OF THE Archduke and the magical city over the full-sized keyboard of her blonde piano. They all looked larger today. The Archduke's head pushed at the edges of his frame, the beautiful city spread across most of the wall, and the piano keyboard stretched an extra yard.

On the way to my lesson, I had barely escaped Bobby Clawson and his ice-packed snowballs by transforming into the lone surviving cavalry officer riding my thoroughbred palomino pell-mell to the fort. Summer chases were so much easier when I could ride La Cheetah, but it wasn't safe for her to gallop in snow where she could break a leg.

Sitting on Mrs. Keindorf's piano bench, I kept stalling to catch my breath and to wait for everything to return to normal size.

"Why would Ravel compose a dance for a dead princess?" I loved his name. When I first saw it, I thought it was pronounced "ravel," as in "unravel."

"Ravel liked the pavane form, a processional dance popular in Europe in the sixteenth and seventeenth centuries." In Mrs. Keindorf's voice, I could see the dance.

"How did she die?"

"He wasn't thinking of a princess, he just wanted a Spanish flavor."

Especially since my Halloween costume had started the whole idea, I hated to exchange a real live dead princess for mere Spanish flavor.

"Wouldn't I play it better if I thought of a dead princess?"

Last lesson, we had talked about the pictures you see when you hear music. All week, I had tried to imagine what blind Maxine Harkin must see, and not just when she played music. Since I was a little girl, I liked to walk around with one eye closed to see what Papa saw.

Mrs. Keindorf put one finger across her lips, her signal for thinking. Today her star ruby ring matched her pale rose lipstick, her starched blouse, and the bow holding her pony tail. "What dead princess do you know?" She trilled "princess."

Mama had plenty to say about Queen Elizabeth's sister, Princess Margaret, but she was still alive and it seemed impolite to imagine her dead.

Mrs. Keindorf continued marking her copy of Ravel's "Pavane pour une infante défunte." We had come a long way from the fur in "Für Elise." The piece was in Volume 9 of her Scribner Radio Music Library, a set of red hard-backed books containing, she said, most of the musical masterpieces of the world transcribed for piano. When she suggested that my folks buy a set, I told her that we could barely afford the Funk and Wagnalls Encyclopedia Mama bought one volume a month at the grocery store. We had made it to Volume 11.

With the red book spread on her lap, her long legs stretched out straight, she was not only penciling in fingering but also crossing out notes.

I was amazed. "Can you do that?"

"What?"

"To somebody famous like Ravel?"

"I'm marking off notes which aren't on your piano keyboard at home."

How did she know which keys were missing?

"Isn't that against the law? Censoring someone's music?" I was certain that Miss Reynolds would object.

She touched the pencil end to her tongue. "Worse things have happened to Ravel. Once when he left a concert where someone had played this song, he told his friend it was titled 'Pavane for a Dead Princess,' not 'Dead Pavane for a Princess'." She laughed, a sound like a low flute.

She closed the book. "It's marked *Dolce e grave*. I know you can be *dolce*, but can you be *grave*?"

She could tease a person in French, Italian, English and German. Honestly.

"I'll think of dead Baby Janet."

"Oh. That must be so hard on your mother." Mrs. Keindorf folded her arms across her lower stomach. "I wanted to have children desperately." Her voice shivered. "But I can't."

I didn't ask her why, since this was a grown-up conversation, although I wanted to know in the worst way. I couldn't ask Mama or Papa or Charlie Whitaker or Mrs. Dahlke. That left Miss Reynolds, probably not an expert on children.

"Music has given me the children I couldn't have. Both in my students and the songs themselves."

Suddenly I understood something new about Brahms' "Lullaby." Mrs. Keindorf played it to her missing baby.

She and I settled into our usual pattern, starting with scales and arpeggios, continuing through my assigned skylark song and ending with my sight-reading Ravel's "Pavane." I had always been good at sight-reading, which Papa considered a version of thinking on your feet and which he had used as a boy to disguise his lack of practice.

When she had finished writing my new lesson on another page of her stationery, Mrs. Keindorf stood up. "Before you leave today, do you have time to listen to a record?"

"Oh yes. Papa is always saying, 'What's time to a nine-year-old?'"

With her pink lipstick, her smile looked sweet as bubble-gum. She opened her tweed suitcase record player and centered a 78 record on the spindle.

"This is also by Ravel. It isn't piano music, but you should know it if you want to be a citizen of the world."

I didn't know what that was, but if she were one, I wanted to be one.

"It's called 'La Valse'–his response to the First World War, but it holds true for any war." She motioned for me to sit in the big armchair opposite her. Nestling against the fake burned cattle brands, I briefly pretended I was visiting Dale Evans. Mrs. Keindorf was ten times more beautiful but probably couldn't ride a horse.

"Listen for the theme and variations. A waltz will keep reappearing, while the rest of the music will try to drown it out."

I was certain I wouldn't be able to hear all that.

But I was wrong.

Until that moment, I didn't realize that music could tell a story as vivid as a book. Right away, I heard long silk dresses swishing along marble floors, saw couples waltzing, men's tuxedo tails flying, women's necklaces flashing in the candlelight. The waltz was diamonds and chandeliers, faces flushed with dancing, all glistening and smiling. The music made me see it better than a movie. In the magical city over Mrs. Keindorf's piano, the windows flickered with life.

But then something started thumping, a heartbeat in the lowest strings, and some instrument sneering. The flutes fluttered in, slightly queasy, then definitely off-key, as if the musicians were sick but trying their best to play together. When the drums and cymbals rushed in to help out, the waltz would roar just right; but as soon as the violins had to carry the weight alone, they crashed into each other like wild birds trapped in a cage. Over and over, the drums stepped in and insisted that this was a waltz, after all, but some clippity-clop wood block would tell dirty jokes like Bobby Clawson behind everyone's back and the nauseous flutes would collapse.

Now the waltz started more seriously, an ocean liner in heavy seas, sliding all the dancers first into one wall, then the other. But they kept dancing, valiantly trying to ignore the terrible sounds rising beneath them, slowly but irrevocably. The harp ran up and down hysterically on the side of the horns, all ripping into the waltz, which could escape only for a measure or two at a time. It was so clearly a war in music. Near the end, the waltz started over and over, each time more frenzied, more panicked. The less power it had, the more insane it sounded, trying harder and harder as hope receded.

At the end came crescendos, something beyond music, different from anything I had ever heard: crash-silence, crash-silence, crash-silence, until the chaotic forces took over the music, ending in an explosion like a bomb. Then silence. In that silence, everything was destroyed, not like a tornado or a fire, but absolute obliteration, everything missing, gone.

Mrs. Keindorf quietly stood, picked the needle off the record and looked at me. "Do you understand, Jeb?"

I did, although I couldn't say it in words.

She suddenly looked sad. "They can bomb cathedrals. They can burn down art museums and universities. They can murder thousands and thousands of people." She paused. "But they can't. Kill. Music."

CHAPTER 40
PAVANE FOR A DEAD PRINCESS

"Wake up!"
Someone. Shaking. Shaking me.
"Jeb!"

MY EYES POPPED OPEN. "THE CHRIST CHILD knows!" I shouted before I realized I wasn't in the school play. The trailer was dark except for a light under the folks' bedroom door.

Mama leaned over me and kept pushing my shoulder. "Wake up! Hurry!"

I woke up all in one breath. What had happened? Was Papa–? Sam–? Had someone found out about Sam's bombs and were coming to arrest us? Sam's doors were closed. The trailer was still sleeping.

"Wh-Where's Papa? Is Sam–?"

"Hurry up. You don't have to get dressed."

"Where is everybody?" My heart started thudding, hard, in growing panic.

Mama pulled me out of my covers into the cold air of the living room. Why was it dark? "Come on." She pulled out the piano bench and turned on the little piano light over the music stand.

Now I could see the log cabin clock: it said 3:10.

"Papa?" I called out, half expecting to see blood oozing under their door.

His scratchy voice answered from the bedroom. "I'll be there in a minute, Sugar."

I let out a huge breath, not realizing I had been holding it in. "That's okay."

"Stay put, Frank. We're fine." In the piano light, Mama pawed through my music. "Where were we? What were you practicing?"

"Mama, it's–"

She pulled me to the piano bench and pushed me down on it, hard.

"It's . . . I'm. . . My fingers are–"

"Your fingers are fine. Wake up. WAKE UP." Half her bobby pins had come out, and her curls were springing around her face. "It's time to practice."

"I did. Yesterday."

"Well, now it's tomorrow."

Mama opened Mrs. Keindorf's red book. "What was it?" Her fingers riffled the pages. "Ravel something. A dead princess." She found it, pulled her cardboard from the pile of music and sat down on my chair-bed.

It was worth a shot. "We'll wake up Sam."

"He's outside playing in the fort."

I wondered if Papa had slept at all. "But Mama–"

"If you don't play, I'll tear up your music"

"It's Mrs. Keindorf's music."

"Her and her high-and-mighty money and the nerve of wearing all that gaudy jewelry to church and holier-than-thou. All the while having a picture of Stalin in her house."

"It isn't Stalin. I told you. It's the Archduke."

"What did I just say?'

To get Mama back, or at least get her off Mrs. Keindorf, I suddenly thought of a church hymn. It might lull her to sleep. It always worked with me.

"Let's play 'Abide with Me'." I hadn't told Mama that I was learning it for her, in spite of three flats.

"I hate 'Abide with Me'."

"You used to like it." I was glad to be off the hook, but she needed to know, "It's really hard to play."

"No one's going to abide with me, all right? Let alone GOD." She said "God" like a trumpet. "Let's hear this Ravel thing. The dead princess."

As soon as I staggered through the first page, Mama tore it out of the book.

"Mama! That's Mrs. Keindorf's music! You said if I played–"

"I lied." She began tearing the page into little pieces like snowflakes.

I helplessly watched my teacher's music disintegrate in my mother's hands. "It's Mrs. Keindorf's . . . she loaned it—"

Mama tore the music into smaller and smaller pieces, until only two or three notes were left on any scrap. When she had finished with the page, she began to slow down and to weave from side to side, her eyes half closing.

"I'm tired." Her eyes closed halfway. "I can't do this anymore."

"You can go to bed, Mama."

Her eyes popped open. "I can?"

"You can sleep in my bed."

She looked at me, confused, then at the confetti of music littering my covers and the floor.

"Humpty-dumpty," she giggled. "Just like me."

I would never find all the missing pieces, much less put them together again.

She slowly stood up and shuffled to the back of the trailer, where Papa was waiting in the dark.

CHAPTER 41

THE TIMING LIGHT

WHEN I TOLD PAPA ABOUT MRS. KEINDORF'S music, he talked to her after church, where she said that she and Maxine Harkin could reconstruct it from memory and not to worry. From memory, if you can imagine. Thank goodness for all the geniuses in the world, was all Papa and I could say. After the swing episode at school, Marvin had avoided me like the plague at church and even stopped hovering around Mrs. Keindorf. Was she guilty by association with me? Were she and I birds of a feather?

One evening a few weeks later I was sitting in the swing Mr. Whitaker had hung for Sam and me, twisting one way, letting myself go dizzy, then twisting the other way. Although he was a bit shaky on the step ladder, Mr. Whitaker was a grown-up you could really depend on.

From inside the trailer, I heard Mama and Papa arguing, which always made my stomach ache. I wished Mama had gotten mad at me instead, since she couldn't divorce me, although she could desert us all like Grandpa Strang.

Papa banged out of the trailer and swung his arm to slam the door, but caught himself in time and closed it normally. He stared at the closed door for a minute, shaking his head as if to clear it, before he saw me looking at him.

He readjusted his face. "What's up, Sugar? Why aren't you getting into trouble?"

"I don't feel like it."

"You're only nine for one year. Don't waste it."

"Sam's at a Scout meeting." I didn't add that Mama had lost interest in helping me sew my own stuffed dog or that I had finished all of my homework and, out of boredom, all of Sam's homework except math, or that I didn't have any friends and didn't even want any.

"How would you like to help me work on Mr. Big?" Mister Big was the name Mama had given to our 1949 Buick, which actually looked a lot smaller than our ancient Plymouth, the Gray Goose. Mister Big was only four years old and had a lot of chrome.

"I can't do anything." I trailed one shoe in the soft, thawing ground under the swing. The fort was now a small pond surrounded by mud.

Papa squatted in front of me and bounced a few times on his heels. "Are you talking about Jeb Wilder, ace mechanic?"

Already climbing out of the swing, I reminded him, "It'll make Mama mad."

"When did that ever slow you down?" On our way to the barn where the Buick was parked, he added, "I'll run interference for you. If you do the same for me."

Mama said that working on cars was "man's work," and the neighbors had enough to gossip about without my turning into a tomboy. I didn't know what they called boys who liked to do "woman's work." But next to playing with Sam, working on cars with Papa was still my favorite pastime. That, and talking to Mr. Whitaker or Miss Reynolds. I had already decided that I might be a car mechanic when I grew up and told that to nice grown-ups who cared enough to ask. Sam always answered that he wanted to be a nuclear physicist, which most people couldn't pronounce, let alone understand. Sam knew how to end a conversation before it even started.

As Papa arranged the tools he would need, he asked how school was going, a subtle technique both he and Mama used to check that we were really attending.

"Have you come across any interesting words?" He already knew the answer, but that's how polite he was.

"Guess what, Papa? There are words you can spell the same forward and backward, and they mean the same thing, like *racecar* and *level* and *kayak*. There are also words which do that but mean something different, like *tool* and *loot* or *raw* and *war*. They're called palindromes."

"Isn't that something?"

Not only could Papa fix anything, but also he could magically transform things like a broken washing machine motor into a room fan. One rainy Sunday when we were on our weekly drive, the windshield wipers quit. Since it was pouring, we either had to wait for the rain to stop, or Papa had to fix it on the spot, his head and shoulders shielded by the Buick's long hood. Half-soaked, he slid back into the driver's seat, explaining that he had pulled the vacuum advance hose off the distributor and hooked it to the windshield wiper motor. All the way home, every time Papa let up on the gas pedal, the wiper flapped like crazy, but when he tried to go faster, the wiper barely moved. In that way, we lurched home, constantly alternating between forward movement, perfectly blinded, and perfect visibility while slowing almost to a stop.

"You have to choose," he had tried to tease Mama out of a funk. "Do you want to see? Or move?"

"Typical," she had said. "Make a joke out of everything."

Every once in a while, Papa had to "time" our car. The first time he said that, I imagined racing the Gray Goose up and down back streets or taking it to the speedway and timing how long it would take to reach fifty miles an hour. But timing turned out to require standing still with the engine racing.

First I helped him clean the used spark plugs which Chuck at the Mobilgas station said he was just throwing away. Papa showed me how to clean the plug gaps with delicate emery paper, then lightly to tap the bottoms on a rock so he could test them with a wire gauge for the exact space.

"Guess what." Papa's good eye twinkled. "*Plug* is one of your words; backwards, it's *gulp*."

"Wow. I mean, wait till Mrs. Dahlke hears that."

Since his hands were greasy, he had me look in the *Chilton's Auto Repair Manual 1940-53*. "I think the Buick section starts on page 330." He knew this because we had checked the book out of the library so often.

On that page was a drawing of something taken apart and stretched out, down to the last bolt. Papa looked over my shoulder. "There's the carburetor."

"How do you know?"

"I could be wrong, but it sure looks like one. It also says so at the top of the page." He elbowed me in the ribs.

I traced the word c-a-r-b-u-r-e-t-o-r. "Is that a buretor for cars?"

Papa chuckled. "Good point. Except then every car part would need to start with *car.* "

I instantly began inventing, "Carbrakes, carradiators, cartires—"

He stopped me, "Try the next page. There."

Pages of numbers and tables followed, with magic names like 'Dimensions of Valves' and 'Wear Limit Tables' and 'Tension Wrench Specifications.' "What's 'a ligament'?"

"A what? Spell it."

"A-l-i-g-n-m-e-n-t."

Papa corrected my pronunciation. "*Alignment* means that all the wheels tilt in or out and line up just right. Otherwise, the tires wear unevenly and the car wanders all over the road. We don't have to worry about that yet. Keep going. There." He pointed his index finger, the one missing above the second joint. "Engine Tune-up Specifications."

I was dazzled with the amount of compressed information in this book, imagining how each number led to somebody's car and an evening just like this in somebody else's yard with a dad and a little girl or boy and with a Buick like ours, only not named Mr. Big.

"Read down the column until you get to 1949. Now read across and tell me what the spark plug gap should be."

I felt really nervous, knowing that Papa trusted me. "There's a 'point gap'–"

"No, that's for the distributor. Look under the spark plug heading. Or spark gulp," he teased.

"I'll never figure it out, Papa."

"Sure you will. Just relax and read it off to me." He was holding one of the cleaned spark plugs and waiting to measure its gap with a little bent wire, part of a set which fanned out.

"Here it is: 0-2-5, with a period in front of it."

"Good. That means point-0-2-5 inches. Twenty-five thousandths of an inch."

Thousandths of an inch? How big would that look to a Dust Person?

After the spark plugs, he cleaned and reset the points in the distributor, then we were ready for the fun. Papa showed me the paint spot on the engine's flywheel which we could watch just behind the fan blade. He hooked up a light that looked like a fat automatic pistol somewhere on the distributor and pointed it at the notch on top. Standing on my ace mechanic's crate, I leaned further over the fender while Papa started the engine.

If we had done everything right, he said, we would see magic. And we always did. Flash, flash into the notch: nothing. He twisted the distributor. Flash flash: oh. There was a little spot of white rushing past. He twisted some more. Flash flash flash. Suddenly, the little white spot froze in the light, apparently not moving at all, even though the engine was running and the spot was actually racing around the flywheel like a wild Ferris wheel ride. All that motion which looked absolutely still.

"Doesn't that make a little girl feel like singing a song?"

"Oh, Papa." Nobody ever asked me to sing because I sounded so off-key. Sam was right about a few things. "What would you like to hear?"

"How about 'Blue Skies'?"

"I don't know all the words."

He wiped his hands on a rag soaked in gasoline, then dried them on an old dish towel which had spots long ago washed into it. "Just fake it. If it's a good song, nobody ever notices."

So I did.

"Never saw the sun shining so bright,

Never saw things going so right.

Never saw the moon dum-de-dum-dum.

Never saw something dum-de-dum-dum."

Then Papa joined me on the chorus, even though he couldn't sing much better than I:

"Blue skies, nothing but blue skies,

Nothing but blue skies

From now on."

CHAPTER 42

THE JUMP

FAKING IT MIGHT WORK FOR "BLUE SKIES" AND PAPA, but it didn't work for Ravel and Mrs. Keindorf. I could read the minute and delicate notes she and Maxine Harkin had written by hand to replace the page Mama had torn up, but I was having a terrible time learning Ravel's "Pavane." My heart just wasn't in it. However, Mrs. Keindorf had been so kind at today's lesson—in a swirling pale green dress and matching jewelry called peridots—that I found myself half-skipping home to meet Sam.

The fort had finally dried out enough for us to re-dig the trench and re-stock it with the dried mudballs and broomcorn spears we hid in the hayloft last autumn. The Formula, wrapped in one of Papa's rags, had survived the winter at the bottom of Mr. Whitaker's junk chest in the barn, but we would soon need to replenish it and begin moving it daily.

Such a happy day: I didn't need to wear my heavy winter coat any more, Sam was designing an all-new Planes of Death to perform after Will Hankins moved back to town, and I had already memorized my spelling words. I didn't realize I was walking directly in front of Bobby Clawson's house.

I heard his dog barking, as usual, but also someone screaming. Normally, I would have started running for home, but I suddenly thought that the dog might be attacking someone and I could help. Cautiously, I looked between houses into Clawson's backyard and saw the Doberman chained up and Bobby playing with it. Some strange sound in Bobby's screams and the dog's yelps pulled me toward them.

Lashing out with a short two-by-four, Bobby was chasing the dog around the stake where it was chained. The dog kept trying to get away, running to the end of its chain, where it turned and faced him, snarling with its teeth bared.

"Goddam dog!" Bobby screamed, raised the two-by-four, and brought it down hard on the dog's back.

It yelped three times and tried to avoid his next swing, straining against its chain.

"I'll teach you!"

It was only then that I noticed blood on the dog's hip and its back leg strangely bent, sticking out sideways. It could barely stand.

As I was still trying to absorb what I was seeing, Bobby lifted the board and hit the dog's head as hard as he could.

This couldn't be happening. I must be imagining this. But I wouldn't imagine this. No matter how much I feared that dog, it couldn't deserve this.

"Stupid dog!" Bobby shouted. "Stupid goddamned dog!"

The dog was still standing but now quivering on three legs.

What could I do? I wasn't John Wayne fighting Indians, I wasn't Gregory Peck or Sergeant York or even Sam's rear gunner. I was a little girl named Jeb Wilder, facing a boy named Bobby Clawson in a fight which wasn't a fight.

I finally screamed. "STOP IT! STOP!"

Bobby wiped his face with his greasy t-shirt and looked at me but didn't seem to recognize me or even to realize that I was there, as if he were watching movies inside his head or as if I had interrupted him doing something dirty with himself.

For a moment, Bobby rested one end of the two-by-four on the ground, then he let out a superhuman scream. "AII-EE!" With a heave, he slammed the board against the dog's head one last time.

Time contracted. The Doberman's head swung away from the impact, its tongue flying out sideways, spitting blood exploding in little drops into the air, little rubies exploding from its head, sparkling in the afternoon sunlight.

I screamed, "NO-O-O!" but the word may not have left my mouth, as if I were being strangled in a nightmare. Bobby, the dog and I were trapped in a bend in time, a knot in a board. In slow motion, the dog fell gracefully, lightly on its side, tucking its broken leg underneath, and bounced once, blood now trickling from its eyes and mouth.

The taste of vomit rose in my throat. "You can't . . . you CAN'T . . . ."

The dog's legs began jerking as if it were running away, racing something while still lying on the ground. Its tongue licked the dirt.

"You have to . . . to . . . " I didn't want to finish the sentence with "kill it."

Bobby turned toward me as if seeing me for the first time. He licked sweat from the corners of his mouth. With slow, deliberate whacks, he pounded the ground near the dog's head, pounded, pounded some imaginary stakes into the ground.

His voice sounded queasy, slippery. "What," he said. "Do what." He looked at me without seeing anything, his eyes more dead than blind.

Neither of us moved. We stared at each other across the dog, which was still twitching.

I kept swallowing down the vomit taste. Now I was breathing as hard as he was. "I . . . saw . . . you."

"So?" He raised the board to his shoulder like a baseball bat. "You tell anybody, and I'll . . . " A smile leaked out of Bobby's mouth, spreading dark and sticky as tar across his sweat-streaked face.

The dog made little huffing sounds, yanking in a slow, terrible rhythm, as if it were gathering itself to jump a great height.

"You don't scare me." As soon as I said the words, I knew they were true.

"Izzat so?" Bobby began walking toward me, swinging the board back and forth like a bat, each time closer to my head.

I didn't move. I knew I could, but I chose not to. Somebody had to watch over this dog. "I saw you. I saw."

He began to laugh, fake and mechanical. "Nobody'll believe you. I'll tell 'em you did it."

He swung the board so close to my face that I felt a little wind from it. But I still didn't move. I looked straight at him, as if I wanted to remember every detail, registering the sweat and dirt on his face, his ears sticking out, a cut under his right eye, his smell of kerosene.

Either Bobby heard a sound or pretended to. He dropped the board, suddenly tired. In the worst way, I wanted to get out of here, but I knew better than to turn my back on him.

The dog had stopped jerking. For the first time in my life, I hoped something was dead. Maybe he had made the jump.

As I stood looking at the dog, Bobby walked away. "If you tell anybody, you're dead."

When I didn't move, he repeated, "You hear me?"

I don't know how long I stood there. How could that dog, always so terrifying, so alive, so full of rage and energy, of muscle and snarling, be so utterly still? In one second to go from being absolutely alive to being absolutely the opposite? No turning back, no calling back, just . . . gone?

The dog's eyes were still open but all the seeing had left them, a room where someone has turned off the lights, but the door stays open. I wanted to close its eyes, but I didn't dare touch it.

"Get outta here!" Bobby shouted from his back porch.

I looked up at him like a stranger. Something had ripped the space between us: a torn photograph which could never fit together again He and I no longer inhabited the same planet, let alone the same back yard.

Bobby feebly threw the two-by-four in my direction, but it fell short of both me and the dog, making a springing sound on the bare dirt The screen door slammed behind him.

Walking home, I swallowed faster and faster, but near the Methodist Church, I gave up, leaned over and vomited in the gravel road. I spit several times, then wiped my hands across my mouth, then on the church grass. If Mama saw me do that in public, I would have hell to pay.

I wanted to tell somebody. Anybody. Sam would listen and believe me, wide-eyed and furious, then start hatching a counter-attack. But telling wouldn't help. Revenge wouldn't help. I couldn't even imagine what would help. Most of all, I wanted this afternoon to be a nightmare, I wanted to wake up sitting on Mama's and Papa's bed, to wake up tomorrow morning and have Mama and Papa tell me that my eyes had been wide open, but I hadn't seen anything at all.

CHAPTER 43
MADAM IN EDEN I'M ADAM

THE NEXT DAY I SAT AT MY DESK WATCHING THE sun outline the paper May basket silhouettes our class had cut from pastel construction paper and taped to the windows. They looked just like last year's and, probably, the year before that and the year before that and on and on until the year Lincoln Elementary was built and somebody like Leon carved the first initials in my desk, "B. T.+ D. C. 1923."

"You're awfully quiet." Mrs. Dahlke was wearing the summer version of her rose wool suit but fortunately re-used her brooches, today the little peacock .

I drew doodles on my spelling list, pretending they were horses.

She erased the spelling words we had covered so far. "How is your mother doing?"

I couldn't even lie with "fine." "You know, your peacock pin is my very favorite."

"I suspected as much."

"Don't you bet it wishes it could fly away?"

"It's pretty heavy with all those rubies and sapphires." She was gentle even in the way she teased me.

"Colored glass is just as heavy."

"Let's consider a few '-sc' words and call it a day. Think of the variations in sound here."

On the board she printed *conscience, conscientious* and *fascination*. I always admired how her fragile hands could be covered with chalk dust and she never got any on her clothes.

This was the perfect time to say, "You left out *unconscionable*."

"Transcendent!" Mrs. Dahlke clapped her hands once, and a little cloud of chalk dust poofed up. "It sounds as if you've been talking to Thelma."

I decided to take a chance. "If Mr. Sprecker fired you, that's what it would be: unconscionable."

She wiped the blackboard with the wet rag which always hung half out of the chalk tray. "We don't know what's going to happen, but it's not for you to worry about."

"That's what grown-ups tell me about the hydrogen bomb."

She paused. "They're right."

She began filling her briefcase with books and our reading tests. I happened to see Leon's paper on top. He printed like a first-grader.

"Edna Vince gave me a new palindrome for you. You might want to write it down as I say it: 'Madam, in Eden I'm Adam'."

"That's wonderful," I said. "Papa discovered one: *plug gulp*."

"Very nice." I couldn't tell if she already knew this palindrome or not, she was so polite.

"And I did, too. All by myself." I hadn't told anyone and didn't know why I was telling Mrs. Dahlke now. "*Live evil*."

She stopped loading her briefcase and held a sheaf of papers in midair. "What made you think of that?"

No matter how much I wanted to, I couldn't tell her about Bobby Clawson and his dog. In fact, I couldn't say anything without lying, so I just shrugged.

"Two very powerful words. Hopefully, not equally powerful."

I looked at the palindromes in my spelling tablet. I had never noticed how you traveled one direction down the words, hit the end and went right back, then hit the beginning and bounced again, until you couldn't tell what was forward and what was backward. Live evil, evil live. Live evil live, to the end of time.

"Jeb, would you consider doing me a favor?"

Would I? Was she joking?

"I have so many books and papers to carry that I need help walking home."

No question about it, Mrs. Dahlke knew exactly how to cheer me up.

On the way downtown, I asked her in very possible way if she would be in Round Prairie next year, but she purposely misunderstood or avoided answering altogether. I knew how that felt.

"No matter what happens, I'll give you a summer study program so you can keep working on vocabulary," she promised.

That wasn't my worry. "My family moves every year."

"Let's make a pact. No matter where we are, you and I will meet at the spelling bee."

"Oh yes." The best: a pact. With Mrs. Dahlke, no less.

It wasn't until after we had admired every struggling daffodil and wild rose and peony bud still tight and round as a shooter marble that I realized which book I had been carrying for her: *Paradise Lost*. "Miss Reynolds told me about this book."

When Mrs. Dahlke smiled, her wire rim glasses rode up on her nose. "Did she recommend that you read it?"

"It has God in it, right?"

"Y-yes."

"But not like the Bible."

"Not exactly."

"Miss Reynolds said Mama should memorize this book instead of 'The Song of Hiawatha'."

"I can hear Thelma say that." Mrs. Dahlke put her hand on my shoulder. "Isn't she a treasure?"

I nodded yes. I could tell her who else was a treasure and that I didn't see how I could survive without her, but you can't just come out and tell your fourth grade teacher that you love her.

By now, we had arrived at the Pawnee Hotel, its windows simultaneously revealing the wood paneled lobby and reflecting elegant Mrs. Dahlke and plain old me.

"This is such a beautiful place, as good as Eddy's Bakery only without the cardboard cake in the window."

"Have you ever been inside?"

"N-never. I've always, always wanted to."

"Today's the day."

With her thumb on the latch of the filigreed brass handle, my teacher opened the heavy glass door, and we glided through as easy and magical as Alice drifted through the looking glass.

Inside the lobby, I got the shock of my life. Mama wouldn't tolerate such a mess for five minutes. Dust covered the floor so thick you could see footprints in it, and everything smelled like dirty socks and burned cooking oil. From somewhere, a person coughed and coughed, a deep, bubbly cough—possibly the opera singer. Lint gathered around the geraniums in the front window, the glass so greasy you could barely see outside. I never needed to worry again that someone might see me peeking in. *Peek/ keep.*

How could Mrs. Dahlke come out of this place every day so clean, so splendid, so opposite to everything inside? Did she come back here every day and think of it as home? Or did she consider every morning an escape from a trap?

Very quietly, Mrs. Dahlke asked, "Was it everything you expected?"

I wished my manners were better or at least that I had learned lies not to hurt people's feelings. With sudden inspiration, I thought of what Mrs. Keindorf would do.

I held out my hand, which Mrs. Dahlke shook solemnly. "Thank you so much for inviting me in. It meant a lot to me."

That, at least, was not a lie.

CHAPTER 44

THE BLUE ELEVATOR

"SCHOOLS' OUT, SCHOOL'S OUT, TEACHER LET THE mules out!" I sang every year, although I liked school much, much more than summer vacation.

At the last school assembly, Sam had won three awards, including straight A's, special recognition for his role in "Why the Bells Rang" and his science project on rockets. If they knew he had almost perfected gunpowder, they would really be impressed. For every one of Sam's honors, I could secretly add a check mark after my name on Sprecker's Blacklist at the front of Mrs. Dahlke's classroom. After the swing episode, I had to admit that Sprecker basically ignored me, but I couldn't ignore my own crimes: continually messing up Doreen's hair, picking fights with Leon on the playground, prying into Jane Englehardt's business, and always, always stretching the truth even when I didn't need to. The worst kind of lying.

Handing out the awards in the assembly, Mr. Sprecker looked so mad at everybody who won, including Mrs. Dahlke as Best Colleague of the Year, that I suddenly realized he didn't just hate me, or even kids in general. He hated school. Really hated it. Somebody should tell him to find a different job. I personally wasn't up to it.

Mama had been too nervous to attend the assembly. Well, "nervous" was Papa's word for it. She stayed in bed a lot these days, letting Papa and us kids eat bread and margarine for breakfast and making Papa pack his own sandwiches for lunch. I liked margarine because we had to stir little capsules of food coloring into it to turn it yellow, a real-life example of coloring a black-and-white world. When I reminded Mama about our coloring the movies, she didn't remember any of it, not even Barbara Stanwyck's purple hair.

At the assembly, I tried to sit beside Jane, who instantly moved to stand behind the back row, but Joe Clary sat in her place and rested his hand on his leg, quite near my leg. He was the only boy I had ever met who never had dirty fingernails. Never.

"I'm filling in for Mama," I explained to him.

He nodded. "My mother said she was sick."

Did people talk about Mama behind our backs? Was she part of the rumor mill, too?

Before I could ask more, Joe said excitedly, "I bet Sam gets a lot of awards. He's so smart. I'm going to clap extra hard for him."

It wasn't the same as having Mama, but Joe and I did make a lot of noise, which spurred everybody else on, and not just the Boy Scouts.

Walking home, I told Sam that "I bust my buttons off," the traditional Wilder expression for feeling proud.

Sam ducked his head. "Thanks, Jeb." To my utter disbelief, he added, "I couldn't have done it without you."

The day after the school assembly, Sam and I cleaned out the fort and held a War Council planning our summer campaigns. An old sleeping bag had appeared in the Inavale storm shelter, so we knew Will Hankins was back in town, although we hadn't spotted him yet. Since Will was one of our most valuable allies, we needed to find a way to leave secret messages for him somewhere closer than the hide-out.

"Jeb? Je-yeb!" From the kitchen window, Mama called across the broomcorn field. Recently, she had started making a diphthong out of my name.

"Oh oh," Sam said. "That's her work voice."

"I did all my chores, even practiced—"

"Je-yeb!"

Neither of us dared ignore her. As I brushed the dust from the fort off my dress, Sam said, "Hurry up. Tell her we're busy."

Mama was waiting in the open trailer door with the look I dreaded, her somewhere-else look, a place nobody else could see and where she lived all alone. She held a library book, but her hair was matted flat in back and on one side where she had been sleeping.

She whispered loudly, "Whenever Richard Cory went down town, we people on the pavement looked at him."

I vaguely remembered the downtown poem Mama had recited the day she saw Dr. Mary ready to jump off the building.

"He was imperially slim. Slim slim slim slim," her voice skidded. "And glittered when he walked. Oh glittered. We don't glitter, do we? Huh? Huh?" She poked me with one finger in my stomach, hard.

"No."

Mama began to sway, to take sliding steps around the living room. "He was rich—richer than a king, and that's g.d. rich, by g-o-d. Rich rich rich and ad-ri-mabely . . ." she sounded out the word, "no: ad-mi-rabe-ly . . . yes! Schooled in . . . what?" She thrust the poem at me and pointed to the line. "In what? What."

I read the answer, "Schooled in every grace." I wondered how much you could change a poem and still have it be the same poem.

"To make us wish . . . that we were . . . something, something. In his place'," she crowed.

She snatched the book from me and threw it on my chair-bed. "That's your fancy-schmancy piano teacher. Her and Dr. Mary. Fellow Travelers." Mama thrust her face into mine. "Fancy name for Commies."

I knew better than to defend Mrs. Keindorf. "Guess what? Sam and I are—"

"Sam schmam. Sam spam. Hahahaha. Guess what happened to Richard Cory," she nodded hard, as if I were agreeing with her. "One calm summer night, caaaalm caaaalm summer night? He went home and put a bullet in his head. Bang! Bang! Bang! BANG!"

She would keep stuttering like a needle caught in a groove on a record unless I could distract her. "Who wrote that poem?" was all I could think of. "Who? Ha ha ha," she said the words, not laughing. "And now get a gander at that." She pointed to empty space in the middle of the living room. "The audacity of bringing that in, right under our noses." She sounded as shiny as the lady at the Hastings fair, the one who sold cleaning solutions.

"Wh-what?"

Mama began touching the walls of an imaginary box filling most of the living room, taller than she, running her hands over smooth surfaces only she could see. "How did they get it in here?"

I strained to see what she was seeing, walking behind her around the box, following her hands with my own, smoothing a surface I couldn't feel.

Suddenly she whirled on me and said, partly angry but mostly scared. "How did you do that?!"

I jerked my hand back. "What?"

She gestured toward the air in front of me. "Opened its door."

I didn't know if I had done a good or a bad thing. "I didn't mean to."

Suddenly suspicious, she asked, "Did they tell you a secret code?"

"N-no."

"They could've brainwashed you while you were asleep."

"The Communists?" At least I knew how to talk to her about Communists.

"In your sleep, they gave you special powers."

I couldn't bear another Special Powers story. "They can't give you Special Powers when you're sleepwalking." This wasn't exactly a lie, because who could know? It sounded reasonable.

"Aggh." Mama sucked in her breath and looked at me as if I were a huge spider.

"Hell's bells," she continued, "the tintinnabulation of hell's bells. Bells bells. You're up in the night as much as I am." Her laugh sounded like a little bell ringing fast. "Haha! Except you're *really* up. Haha!"

Some nights I woke up outdoors now. One minute I would be dreaming about Luther as a full-sized horse, magically changing from a buckskin to a palomino or a pinto, and the next minute I would wake up, barefoot, standing in the fort. One night Mr. Whitaker found me in the barn and carried me to his porch, where he rocked me on his lap until I woke up and he walked me home. It wasn't scary so much as confusing. But what if I walked downtown? In front of a car? What if I wandered into Bobby Clawson's back yard? *Asleep.*

Mama's eyes glistened at whatever she saw in the trailer living room. My curiosity got the best of me. "What is it?" I asked.

Mama's hands dropped to her sides, and she looked down at me. "Silly. Silly girl." Sometimes I wondered if she ever saw me or only an imaginary daughter, like dead Baby Janet grown up. "What does it look like?"

I scanned the piano and bench, the chair-bed with its frayed piping, the kitchen table folded down into the wall. Everything looked normal.

"It looks like . . . " Remembering the way her hands had moved, I guessed, "a big, smooth . . . box."

"Obviously," she said. Until now, I hadn't noticed that her dress was wrinkled and dirty, although I had helped her with the ironing two days ago. "But the doors? And the lights?" She stepped toward the center of the room. "Watch out! The doors open automatically." She turned toward me. "Or did you touch the button again?"

I shook my head no and searched desperately for the door, lights, buttons, anything my mother was seeing.

"I'll go inside if you come with me." She had a strained smile, as if she had false teeth which were too big for her mouth. Her teeth were brown and syrupy all the time now from Nervine.

I tried to manufacture an emergency. "Sam's in trouble–"

"Sam can wait." She wiggled her fingers at me. "If you come inside, you can push the buttons. Won't that be fun?"

Reluctantly, I took hold of Mama's hand and stepped into her elevator. She was looking up at the ceiling, so I could only see the bottom of her chin. "Where does it go?"

"Well, isn't that the million-dollar question? But such a pretty blue. Lapis," she marveled. "Wouldn't you know they'd come up with that?"

"Where does it go?" I repeated.

Mama dropped my hand and started to peer closely at the inside wall of her elevator. "These mirrors—" She moved her face closer to the mirror she saw and put her hand to her cheek. She began rubbing off some rouge, more and more vigorously, harder and harder. "What's that spot? There?" She rubbed so hard I was afraid her cheek would bleed.

"There isn't a spot," I wanted to pull her hand away but didn't dare.

She looked down at me as if she had forgotten I was there. "We're falling too fast! Stop this elevator! STOP IT!"

I began pushing imaginary buttons, slapping the air with my flat palms. Then I remembered slowing my own fall from the sky and looked at the log cabin clock, concentrating on stopping its chimney smoke. Telekinesis. It could happen.

Immediately, Mama lurched and grabbed my shoulders to keep her balance. When I put out my other arm to stay upright, it passed through the wall of the elevator. I could almost feel it.

"You stopped our fall, " she said, pulling a dirty hanky out of her dress pocket and wiping her nose. "How?"

I waved my hand in the air like waving good-bye.

"Of course. The emergency button. You're always saying you can save me, and now you have." She turned to look back at me. "Come out now. I won't let them take you away. It's me they're after."

I stepped across her imaginary line and felt the air change, as if I really were outside a stuffy box and inside the cool of our trailer.

She rubbed her cheek. "What'll we do? To keep it from coming back?"

In spite of myself, I had to ask again, "Where does it go?"

Her hair fell into her eyes, dirty and uncurled, its roots growing out white. "As if you didn't know. I can still escape." She vaguely waved at the inside of the trailer. "Big trap."

"Wh-what trap?"

"The looooney bin. The insane asyyyyylum," she almost sang. "Next to the House of Yesterday, the House of Tomorrow. Hahahaha."

"Mama?"

"Don't Mama me! They sent the elevator to take me to the insane asylum. Don't think I don't know who helped them! Your own mother!"

I knew that protest was useless. "I didn't—"

"Liar." She pointed to the footstool. "Liar liar liar! Sit."

"But, but I haven't—"

"You haven't what? Name thirteen things you haven't done. There's more than thirteen ways of looking at a blackbird, by g-o-d. That's a poem. It's a liar, too. SIT."

I collapsed on the footstool out of shock and sudden hopelessness.

Right then, Sam jerked open the door, "Is Jeb?" He saw me on the footstool and scrunched up his face.

As soon as I saw him, I felt like crying. "I didn't do anything, Sam."

Sam held up his cavalry halt sign to stop me. Crying would only make things worse.

"Sam!" Mama demanded, "What's the fourteenth way of looking at a blackbird?"

"H-how long does Jeb—?" Sam stumbled on the question I was afraid to ask.

"Forever!" Mama trumpeted. "Or until they lock me up. Big fat unbreakable lock. You don't get out the way you get in, that's for g.d. certain."

Sam's mouth turned to a little straight line. Through mental telepathy we both knew: we needed a new battle strategy and quick.

"If you want some of hers, get in here," Mama threatened.

Sam waved the Boy Scout hand signals for "nearby" and "danger," but I think he meant "I, help." He stepped backward and quietly closed the door. I knew that he would stay within shouting distance of the trailer as my reinforcements, and not just with an imaginary B-17 or his experimental rocket launcher.

Mama dropped to her knees out of sight behind the kitchen counter, rummaging under the sink. She could be cleaning, but we had already cleaned the whole trailer today. "Gas, gas," she mumbled at the pipes. "That's the way they get in. To gas us." Her head popped up above the counter, beside the winking cookie jar.

"Don't tell anyone about the gas, Jeb. If they suspect we know their methods, we won't have a chance. It'll be our little secret." She disappeared again and grew quiet. Was she still on her knees or lying down on the kitchen floor?

I tried to remember more about Richard Cory. Why did he put a bullet in his head? When Mama left us for her imaginary world, did she rise through the trailer roof? Could she go and come back whenever she wanted?

Never before had Mama sentenced me to the footstool without a reason. Not that I didn't deserve it for all the rules I had broken without her knowing. It would help if I thought of it that way. The punishment fit my crimes, just not at the right time. Maybe crime and the punishment always existed in two different kinds of time, like play time vs. church time or ticktock time vs. geologic time.

Or maybe time was like Silly Putty, which you could roll into a ball or stretch in different directions, could spread flat like a tablecloth or drape it over the little radio. Then you could press time against the Sunday funnies and lift off the image the way Sam and I copied Dick Tracy and Little Orphan Annie. That way Dick and Annie would stay in paper flat time, as well as in Silly Putty time, rubbery and flexible.

If you could do that with time and the funnies, maybe you could copy and lift real-life events, then play with them. Some events, like the daredevil show or piano lessons or talks with Miss Reynolds, you could keep forever. Others, like bad days with Mama, you could copy, then roll back into the putty and knead it until nothing remained except faint streaks of ink. I could obliterate Mr. Sprecker and Marvin Harkin and Bobby Clawson, or I could copy and preserve spelling lessons with Mrs. Dahlke, romantic reunions in movies, and working on the car with Papa. The good times I could keep whole and safe in time as long as I wanted.

"Jeb." Mama now stood behind the counter twisting the cookie jar's head.

I jumped. Had I said something out loud? Today a longer sentence wouldn't mean anything, since my sentence was forever, anyway. Besides, I wanted to return to my thoughts, as good as a dream.

"Jeb." She looked stern and suspicious. She must have invented a new rule I broke. "Time's up."

Time's *up*: What time? Flat paper time? Silly Putty time? Dead baby time? Dust People time?

"Usually you jump up and tear out of here like a wild animal."

I felt my idea fading like a summer rain and with the same smell, which Sam called ozone.

"What were you doing?" she demanded. "Were you asleep?"

No good: it was gone. But time felt different, not solid like the rags Mama held in her hand.

"Don't ignore me when I'm talking to you," her voice rose. "What were you doing?"

"Thinking." I guessed that's what you would call it.

"You mean, daydreaming."

I still sat on the footstool, suddenly fond of its familiar cracked leather and friendly wheeze as I moved. Out the window, I saw Sam and Jim Hartsock riding their bicycles in slow circles in the street, testing how tight their circles could get before one of them had to put down a foot. Why did it look like slow motion? Had I destroyed everyday time? Maybe Sam would slowly circle in the street forever, never straightening out, never standing on the pedals and pumping in a beeline to a scout meeting or the library or the Inavale hideout. On the other hand, if I moved, maybe I could free him, too.

"Daydreaming about what?" Mom's voice sounded as if she might cry. She leaned over to peer out the window, her cheek next to mine. "What're you looking at?"

She straightened up and pushed her hair out of her eyes. "Tell me what you see."

I lightly slapped my knees and stood up, as I had seen her do so many times. "Well. I guess that's that," I said, unintentionally echoing her.

"Daydreaming about what?" she vaguely threatened.

I couldn't describe it if I wanted to. "Blackbirds," I lied and dreamily walked out the door. She could never use the footstool to punish me again.

CHAPTER 45

THE MISSING ENDING

"How does the story end?" I couldn't even imagine.

"The good guys win," Sam answered me, sharpening a broomcorn spear with his Boy Scout knife.

He carried his knife so much that it was wearing little holes in his front pants pockets. I wished that I could carry Luther like that, although he wouldn't tolerate it. For one thing, he refused to ride on La Cheetah with me, even on a good day. I think he missed living in Hested's window with all that attention from people on the sidewalk. In a way, I missed visiting him there as well. Owning a small bronze horse wasn't all that I thought it would be.

"How do you know the good guys win?" I challenged.

Since I couldn't be trusted with any knife, I was hiding rock-hard dirt clods in shallow cavities we had dug in the walls of the fort. In our last battle, Sam, Jim Hartsock and I had chased Leon Troxel and three of his gang halfway back to the fort behind Eddy's Bakery, stopping at Main Street, No-Man's Land. According to the grapevine, Leon had taken over the bakery fort from the boys who fought with dough balls.

"The good guys always win." Sam used his knife so skillfully that I hoped the Boy Scouts offered a Knifemanship merit badge.

In fact, nobody knew how "Shane" ended. Two nights ago, a small tornado had blown over the drive-in movie screen at Carlinsburg, Kansas, not far across the state line. As if that weren't bad enough, it happened in the middle of the new cowboy movie "Shane," starring Alan Ladd no less, which pitted evil, greedy cattle barons against handsome, hard-working sodbusters.

All evening, Sam and I had been debating what happened to the movie, not just to the happy family and the hired gunslingers, but to the actual images they continued to project through the slicing rain. I argued that each raindrop captured a moment and fell to the ground like a sliver of a broken mirror. Sam maintained that, without a screen to stop it, the movie traveled outward at the speed of light to land on the closest celestial object, probably the moon or Mars.

"Why not Klaatu's home planet?" I countered with what I considered sarcastic flair.

"Don't be dumb. Klaatu's planet is fictional."

It seemed appropriate to me: a reunion of Klaatu and Shane, fake people on an imaginary planet. Heaven only knew what Alan Ladd's real name was.

"We're talking about science. Light."

Light, my foot. Whenever Sam was losing an argument, he deflected me until he could annihilate me later with an obscure fact he had carefully researched, usually during Twenty Questions.

Two could play the deflection game. "Sam. Look."

He ducked deeper into the fort and gazed along my pointing finger. On Mr. Whitaker's porch sat Miss Reynolds and Mr. Whitaker squeezed into rocking chairs, while Papa sat at their feet. They were all drinking iced tea.

Sam whipped off his cowboy hat, transformed into a G-man, and whispered in his sneak-up-and-spy voice, "On the count of three: go."

Faster than you could say "Jack Robinson," we were crouch-running across the field and circling the other side of the house so we could creep close enough to eavesdrop around the corner nearest them. We really needed the periscope Sam was building. He couldn't bear to waste any information he had learned, certainly not about lenses for his Astronomy merit badge.

We heard Miss Reynolds wheeze. "Dr. Mary said I needed more exercise. I. e., more than none at all."

"I'll drive you home if you run out of oomph," Papa offered.

"Thanks. I was out of oomph when I started."

We could hear ice cubes in their glasses. The June evening was humid, but not enough to plaster my dress to my back.

"Where's Edith?" she asked.

"In the trailer," Papa answered. "She sleeps when she can."

"I don't know what that girl's running on," Mr. Whitaker said. "Poor thing. Skinny as a rail."

Papa let out a long breath.

"Is she still taking that ghastly bromide?" Miss Reynolds' rocker creaked in a duet with Mr. Whitaker's. "You know that stuff isn't tested, Frank, or at best on rats and monkeys. And look up the history of Miles' Laboratories if you want your hair to stand on end. Nervine is not a harmless quack remedy."

As we listened, Sam and I stared at each other, doubling the force of what we heard by seeing it reflected in the other's face.

Mr. Whitaker added, "I'd sure talk to Doc Mary if I was you."

"What can she tell me that I don't already know?"

Miss Reynolds attacked. "Gee, Frank, I can't imagine, since you, too, just graduated from medical school in Chicago and know all the latest diagnoses and treatments for nervous disorders. What on earth would a young, smart medical doctor know that you don't?"

"I didn't mean it that way." Papa sounded sad.

"I'm sorry. We're all worried about her. I've read up on bromides, which sometimes intensify the symptoms they're supposed to treat. The 'cure' makes the disease worse." Miss Reynolds paused. "If it's money, I'll loan you—"

Papa interrupted her. "I appreciate that more than I can say, but we'll get by."

"Me, too, Frank." Mr. Whitaker cleared his throat. "Not to change the subject, but McCarthy's finally gone too far. Summbitch—excuse me, Thelma."

"Don't apologize for such a felicitous assessment of McCarthy's parentage."

"I swear, don't you love her words, Frank?"

"They're your words, too, Charlie. I didn't invent them."

"But who can remember all that rigamarole? Anyway, first it's his damned bomb shelters. According to him, we should be sitting in my basement right now."

Sam and I looked at each other bug-eyed. We knew what they would find there. Sam's Greatest Chemistry Experiment of All Time was ready for testing.

Mr. Whitaker continued, "Then it's his—how many?—Commies in the State Department."

"Fifty-seven," Miss Reynolds answered.

Papa added, "He started with 205. Somebody's finally demanding evidence for his accusations."

"Evidence!" she whooped. "Third-hand gossip from some drinking buddy. After attacking Charlie Chaplin and Dashiel Hammet, he should have known better than to tackle Arthur Miller, who simply refused to testify in his kangaroo court. I wouldn't boil McCarthy to make *soup* for Arthur Miller."

"They can only scare people who let themselves be scared." Papa often said this to me.

"Normally, I would agree, Frank, but McCarthy has tapped some vein of paranoia in the country. How else could he make everyone share his insane delusions?

"I ain't never seen anythin' like it, neither," Mr. Whitaker agreed. "Folks reportin' their neighbors—just like Hitler's Germany. Crazy. Plum crazy."

Papa said, "I think McCarthy's overstepped his bounds now. You can't attack the Army under President Eisenhower. Didn't some Senator say to him, 'Have you no sense of decency?'"

"Joseph Welch," Miss Reynolds answered. "Head counsel for the Army."

"You ever take that loyalty oath, Frank?" Mr. Whitaker asked.

"I can be pretty hard to track down on the dam site. With luck, everybody will regain their senses before they miss me."

"Did you hear about Mildred Dahlke?" Miss Reynolds asked.

'Mrs. Dahlke!' I mouthed silently to Sam as if he couldn't hear for himself. He put his index finger to his lips.

"I heard they fired her on some technicality," Mr. Whitaker responded.

"A technicality named Clarence Sprecker."

"That's outrageous," Papa said. "What reason did they give?"

Miss Reynolds spit out, "Sprecker turned her in as a 'liberal.' He cited one of Truman's military intelligence officers: 'A liberal is only a hop, skip and a jump from a Communist. A Communist starts as a liberal'."

I couldn't bear it any longer. I stood up and lurched around the corner, followed by Sam.

"Judith, you have the most unnerving habit of appearing out of nowhere, like the Grim Reaper or Mother Time." Miss Reynolds held her hand to her chest.

Papa frowned. "You better have a good reason for interrupting grown-up conversation."

"Will they put Mrs. Dahlke in jail?" It was worse than I had imagined.

"She's already been hired in Lincoln, where, evidently, they value excellent teaching, not to mention independent thought." Miss Reynolds looked at me, "But she'll come back for the spelling bee. She told me to tell you."

Mr. Whitaker swirled the last of his iced tea in his glass. "That fine lady ain't no Communist. Sprecker's a pissant."

"He kept a Blacklist in our classroom," I volunteered, as if that confirmed he was a pissant.

The grown-ups grew still.

"Mrs. Vince tore down the one he tacked up in our home-room," Sam added.

Mr. Whitaker leaned forward in his rocker toward me. "Whose names was on it?"

Sam answered, "Jeb was on the top of the fourth-grade list. She and Leon Troxel ran neck and neck for first place all year."

Thanks Sam, I thought.

"Well, I'll be–" Papa stopped himself from swearing. "This is the first I've heard about the Blacklist. What did you do for that honor, Jeb?"

Miss Reynolds chuckled. "She refused to kiss . . . up to anybody. Notice our home-grown McCarthyite didn't tackle Edna Vince."

"She scares everybody." Sam added quickly, "But she's the best teacher I ever had."

"Edna has as much blackmail material on everybody in town as I do. Besides, as her dad's only 'son,' she grew up with real farm muscles."

"Can we sit down?" Sam asked Papa.

"*May you* sit down," Miss Reynolds corrected.

"You sure can't," Mr. Whitaker answered, "till you help yourself to the Oreos in the kitchen."

Oreos. O lordy.

"Can–may—we eat them out here?" I didn't want to miss anything.

"You better. I don't want crumbs all over my spotless kitchen." Mr. Whitaker jiggled with his laugh. "Take all you want."

"Only two apiece," Papa called to us. As we walked back outside, he said, "Don't slam the–"

Too late.

Mr. Whitaker defended us. "What kinda kid wouldn't slam the door?"

"Hopefully, mine."

As we sat below him on the porch steps, Mr. Whitaker looked down at us like a Santa Claus in bib overalls with no beard. "I'll take 'em any day you're tired of 'em."

Papa considered this for too long. "Which one do you want?" Sam and I sat still as mice.

I'd had enough. I'd show Papa. "Take me, Mr. Whitaker. Girls are a lot easier to raise than boys."

Miss Reynolds hooted. "Maybe some girls, but none on Sprecker's Blacklist."

In my lap, I carefully separated both of my Oreos so I could eat the frosted halves last. "I have a question."

"Naturally." Miss Reynolds smiled.

"How does 'Shane' end?"

"Judith, that is the least interesting question you have ever asked, at least in eschatological terms."

"What's 'Shane'?" Papa asked.

Mr. Whitaker shook off crumbs from the frosted half-Oreo I had slipped him. "It's the movie from the Carlinsburg drive-in which blew over."

"Hit national news, no less," Miss Reynolds added. "A tornado practically wiped Hebron off the map, a news story that barely made it to the Omaha papers, but some drive-in theater–"

"Don't you imagine the good guys won?" Sam never passed up the chance to campaign for his opinions.

"Doesn't pretty-boy Alan Ladd play the 'good guy,' as you so unimaginatively phrase it?"

Not only could Sam ignore Miss Reynolds' jibes, he never asked how to spell her words. I was still puzzling out *eschatological*. It had to be complex, both in spelling and meaning.

"Yes," Sam answered.

"They aren't about to bloody him up, are they?" She turned to Papa and Mr. Whitaker. "Now there is a boy who really missed his calling. He should have been a . . ." She looked at us kids. "A . . ."

I saw that she needed suggestions. "Real cowboy?"

"Close enough," she answered.

This seemed a good time to ask, "What is Alan Ladd's real name?"

I could see Miss Reynolds trying not to smile. "You won't like it."

I was braced. Any lie was possible in show biz.

"Alan Ladd's real name is . . ." She paused for effect. "Alan Ladd."

Unfair. Sometimes Hollywood lied, and sometimes it didn't. How could you ever know when? "While Judith is digesting that, Sam, calculate all the permutations and combinations for the ending of 'Shane'."

Now Miss Reynolds was singing Sam's song, as Mama would say.

She continued, "Either a) Van Heflin is killed so Jean Arthur can marry Alan Ladd; or b) Alan Ladd is killed, so Jean Arthur can remain faithful to her eminently pedestrian spouse; or c) neither Van Heflin nor Alan Ladd is killed, and since both love Jean Arthur, they must have a gun-fight to win her; or d) both men are killed and Jean Arthur lives happily ever after. I'd go for the last one myself."

"Which is it?" I asked. "A, B, C or D?"

Everyone looked at her expectantly.

"E."

The grown-ups laughed, but Sam and I had no idea why.

CHAPTER 46

$8NI_3NH_3 \rightarrow 5N_2 + 6NH_4 + 9I_2$

THE HAMMER HIT THE MAN BETWEEN HIS EYES SO hard his head jerked back and forward several times, a jack-in-the box on a spring. For a moment, he stared at me, unblinking, as if he had just left his eyes like Mama seeing a vision or like Bobby Clawson beating his dog. Then he slowly fell toward me, stiff and straight as a plank, hitting the floor without a sound. How could he survive this? Would he ever walk or talk again?

Sam always roared at such movie calamities, held his breath while Moe the Stooge picked up a baseball bat to swing at Larry, or Charlie Chaplin walked backwards toward an open manhole. He preferred to watch real people facing disasters but, of course, howled at Yosemite Sam with his eyebrows and mustache burned off or Wile E. Coyote spinning his feet in mid-air just before he dropped into a canyon. At Bugs Bunny and the Roadrunner, his cartoon heroes, Sam laughed until he crumpled over in the movie seat, while I sat beside him without so much as a smile.

If I had to sit through what Sam liked, I preferred the narrow escapes, catastrophes miraculously avoided, and the more dangerous the better—Costello walking under a falling piano, which bounced resoundingly behind him on the sidewalk, or Buster Keaton swinging on a loose ladder behind a fire truck, hanging on for dear life, barely scrambling out of the way of oncoming cars. But escaping the disaster was the key, and the more impossible, the better.

Sam and I often went to the Saturday morning movies for free because he had made friends with Mike Letson, whose father owned the

Avalon Theater. The Boy Scouts were finally good for something, namely boys like Mike Letson, who not only sneaked me into the movie with Sam, but even gave us a sack of popcorn. This boy took the Scout slogan about good deeds seriously. When Mike told me that the ticket lady could eat all the popcorn and candy she wanted, I was ready to exchange my future as a car mechanic for a job at the Avalon Theater. I had given up becoming a desk clerk at the Pawnee Hotel after I went inside with Mrs. Dahlke.

When Sam heard that this Saturday the Avalon would show both the Three Stooges and the Lone Ranger, he decided it was the perfect chance to execute his Greatest Plan of All Time, which he compared to "Thirty Seconds Over Tokyo," "Twelve O'Clock High," and "A Wing and a Prayer" all rolled into one. Over the winter, he had formulated a foolproof battle plan and had solved all his problems with what he called "chemical instabilities."

"The Stooges plus the Lone Ranger will lure every enemy we have in Round Prairie," he said excitedly.

"And environs," I added. I had just learned the word *environs* and used it every chance I could.

The Round Prairie War was just about to become personal: Sam the Lone Mad Scientist would wreak revenge against all his enemies combined, and all at once. The fort and the Formula couldn't hold a candle to it. Friday night, Sam carefully laid out his strategy. He and I would sit through most of the first feature. A few minutes before it ended, I would leave the theater without being seen, walk across the street, and hide in the bushes on the courthouse lawn. From there, I could spy on events and report to Sam afterward the hair-raising details.

Meanwhile, he would leave shortly after I did, sneak into the theater lobby and sprinkle his magic potion all over the carpet. For safe transport, he had dissolved nitrogen triiodide in a pop bottle full of alcohol and had corked it with the sprinkler head Mama used to dampen clothes for ironing, a bottle he would conceal under his jacket. He must be careful to walk backwards into the theater so he didn't step on any of the solution, which would become highly explosive as it dried. To ensure my cooperation and to make up for the fact I was missing the Lone Ranger, Sam promised me the entire bag of popcorn and a box of Jujubes he could trade for a shooter marble. He also reminded me of several unreported playground incidents with Doreen Cavin and other Brownies that he could use for blackmail.

As usual, the movie began with the Movietone News, the earth spinning and the narrator's voice, which sounded like Reverend Harkin praying, only more convincing. Kids bounced in their seats and ran up and down the aisles, all talking at the same time. An American flag rippled across the screen, while the narrator said, "June 14th: the words *under God* have been officially added to the U. S. Pledge of Allegiance."

A chubby lady now smashed a bottle across the nose of an odd boat as it slid into the water. "Groton, Connecticut: First Lady Mamie Eisenhower launches the USS Nautilus, the first nuclear-powered submarine . . . ." I couldn't hear much in the din, but Sam was riveted on this part.

Next came pictures of crowds running in foreign streets with explosions all around them, and the solemn narrator saying, " . . . military coup in Guatemala, triggering a bloody civil war."

His voice brightened during the next film clip, Marilyn Monroe wearing a low-necked dress holding hands with a tall man in a suit: ". . . Monroe and Joe DiMaggio, newlyweds, were spotted at . . . ." I couldn't hear the rest. The man looked sparkly-happy, but her smile never moved, even when she talked, so she looked fake-happy. Mama wouldn't let us see any movies starring Marilyn Monroe.

Finally—I couldn't believe my eyes–a horse race! "High Gun easily wins the Belmont Stakes. The best three-year-old . . . grandson of the legendary Man o' War . . ." I could only hear snippets, but High Gun was so sleek, so stretched out, so effortless, I couldn't wait to tell La Cheetah. Depending on his mood, Luther might be jealous. Except for the horse race, why did they bother to show the news to a bunch of whooping, giggling kids on a Saturday morning? Maybe some handbook required theater owners to show people real news before you showed them fake stuff, especially a comedy.

I sat through an interminable cartoon in which Sylvester the Cat predictably held a firecracker too long and burned his paw, after which he trapped his head in Tweety's birdcage. Sam and Mike laughed uncontrollably. Finally came the Three Stooges posing as plumbers, being drenched with dirty water, hitting each other with pipes, all the usual stupidity.

Taking the popcorn and the box of Jujubes, I left my seat in the dark and, once in the lobby, put on my best spy behavior, plastering myself against the wall and walking sideways. Even though no one was around, I bent over and ran to avoid possible enemy surveillance, shouldered open the swinging door, then straightened up to walk normally across the street to the courthouse lawn.

With the Jujubes in my dress pocket, I sat on a park bench eating the popcorn from the red and white striped sack. I could use this sack as a charming barn for Luther but needed to destroy the evidence. As a girl eating popcorn outside the Saturday morning movie, I looked suspicious enough. The courthouse looked a little like the castles in Mrs. Keindorf's picture of the magic city. Next to it, the jail had straight bars at the windows but nobody's head in sight. I wondered who was in there right now. What crimes had they committed? Unlike the Asylum for the Incurably Insane, they needed a convincing reason to lock people up in jail.

I remembered I should be hiding, so I nestled into a row of big lilacs, my favorite bushes, both for their jolly flowers and their heart-shaped leaves. I had never watched Round Prairie on a Saturday morning, how peaceful it looked. Spots of shade dappled the courthouse lawn, dark and irregular as Appaloosa spots, while people walked in and out of the Rexall drug store, Hawkins Hardware, and Hale's Grocery. Everybody knew and liked everybody else, waving and joking. I wished Mama still shopped for groceries on Saturday morning. Even before Papa took over that job, nobody ever waved at Mama except Charlie Whitaker, Miss Reynolds, and both Harkin brothers. Maxine Harkin would wave and be nice if she realized that Mama were standing in front of her.

Suddenly, I heard little explosions, like faraway gunfire, a hundred cap pistols going off at once. Sam's Greatest Plan of All Time had begun. The theater door slammed open and kids ran out, screaming and pushing each other. Some were so scared they jumped up and down in place and shrieked. Every kid in Round Prairie must have been there today. More and more broke loose outside, some crying, a few smaller ones stumbling and falling. One little boy hit his head on the sidewalk and lay on his back wailing. I ducked further behind the lilac bushes, but every time I looked out, I watched him. No one was paying any attention to him. Now he had curled into a ball, still screaming.

They kept running out, a chaos of shirts and shoes and screams blending into a single cry. The scene looked like a painting in which the colors began to run and sounded like "La Valse," when Ravel's waltz falls apart in the pounding drums and hysterical flutes. Some kids ran into the street, where a farmer in a pick-up quickly stopped and parked sideways to block traffic and jumped out to help. Mr. Hawkins hurried out of his hardware store and put his arms around some of them, meanwhile shouting through the theater doors.

Where was Sam? Why didn't he come out, too? Maybe he'd been crushed by the mob. Or maybe the bottle had partially exploded in his hands. I wanted to go back inside to find him so much that my eyes started to sting. The littlest kids began wailing for their mothers, then a man who must have been Mike's father hurried outside, trying to talk to everybody at once, trying to calm them down. Mr. Hawkins and Mike's father shouted to each other, but I couldn't understand them.

At the back of the pushing crowd, Sam and Mike Letson finally emerged. I could tell from Sam's saunter that he was just pretending to be scared but Mike really was. Mike's dad pointed for him to help with the smaller kids, and he instantly obeyed. Sam followed Mike's lead, pretending to be an innocent Boy Scout in an emergency. Slowly everybody began to disperse, talking with their hands, yelping their memories, and Sam could leave without suspicion. He crossed the street with fake nonchalance.

"Wow!" He grabbed my arm and pulled me toward some bushes further away. "Did you see that?!" He giggled in a high, forced way. "If you thought it was funny out here, you shoulda been inside. Kids were climbing all over each other to escape, practically killing each other, hitting, shoving! And the purple smoke! It was *purple*! They thought they were being gassed. Wow! Did you hear the explosions?"

He bent over and rested his hands on his knees to catch his breath, the bottle under his jacket swinging in front of his stomach. His cheeks were pink all the way to his ears.

"What was it like out here? What happened? I sure wish I coulda been both places at once! Did you see Bobby Clawson? Leon? They were all in there! Screaming!"

Finally he looked at me and realized that I hadn't said anything. "What."

"It was horrible."

He squinted at me for a few seconds, trying to understand my reaction. "It was . . . great. It was amazing. Did you see Doreen Cavin? Or her stupid girlfriends?"

"No."

"She was the first to leave for intermission. I think she was the one who first screamed 'Gas!' Criminy, I sure wish you'd seen her—scared out of her wits! 'Gas! Gas!'" he said nasally, like a squeak toy. "What a baby."

I turned to walk away, but he grabbed my arm again. I let the popcorn fly, sack and all, then pulled the Jujubes out of my pocket and threw those on the grass as well.

"C'mon, Jeb," his voice turned to a plea. "What's the matter?"

I headed across the courthouse lawn toward home. "Everybody was shoving and kids were crying and–"

"Yeah?" Hungry for details, he walked close to my shoulder and bent forward. "Did you see Pat McDonald? Rodney Craig? Curtis Lewis? Who?"

"Nobody."

"Bobby and Leon ran out. You musta seen them."

"They were all mobbed together. One little boy hit his head on the sidewalk—"

He relished. "Wasn't it amazing? I wish I coulda seen Pat McDonald. He thinks he's so smart. And the explosions were beyond my wildest dreams." He punched my arm. "We won!" He punched me again. "We won!"

"The little boy kept crying, and nobody cared, and he had blood—"

"C'mon, Jeb. Don't be such a spoilsport."

Just then, Sheriff Westergaard left the jail and jogged across the street to the Avalon. His pistol slapped against his hip. Sam watched him, sobered.

"When the grown-ups arrived—"

Sam interrupted, instantly on the alert. "What grown-ups?"

"Mr. Hawkins from the hardware store, and a farmer in a truck."

"Wow." As he watched Sheriff Westergaard, Sam markedly lost enthusiasm.

"I guess it was Mike's dad who came out of the theater. All of them were trying to help the kids who were hurt."

"Hurt," Sam repeated.

By tacit agreement, we had increased our pace.

"What're you going to do with the bottle?"

Only then did Sam realize it was genuine, court-of-law evidence against him. "I'll bury it at the fort, then let's bicycle to the hide-out for a full de-briefing."

"Mama will miss her sprinkling bottle when she does the ironing." Hot and hungry, I didn't feel like bicycling all the way to the Inavale storm cellar.

As we neared the trailer house, we saw a man walking quickly toward us on the cross street from the direction of town. It took us both a second to realize it was Papa.

"Jeb! Sam!" He waved to us.

"Uh-oh," Sam said quietly. "Don't say anything." He pulled his jacket more tightly over the bottle hidden inside.

As if I would. I could already see Sam's head at the jail windows. I wondered if they would keep him in Round Prairie or take him to Lincoln.

"Are you all right?" As Papa reached us, he squatted on his haunches and took one of our hands in each of his. "I heard about the ruckus at the theater."

"It wasn't a big deal," Sam slowly pulled his hand out of Papa's. "Everybody just . . . panicked."

"Why? What happened? An accident?" He frowned at Sam, then at me. "Jeb?"

Papa's one good eye could see through lies like x-ray vision, so I never fibbed to him unless it were a matter of life and death. This situation qualified, but I still waffled. "Kids were running everywhere. Outside . . . ."

"What was it?" Papa stood up. He had grease on his hands from working on the fire truck. "At the station, Ed said something about an explosion."

"Cap pistols," Sam downplayed his attack. "But everybody got scared." As he retold it to Papa, Sam lost his dream by the minute. "They panicked. For no reason."

"Was anybody hurt?" Papa looked at me as if I held the secret. "Sugar?"

"I ran outside. I was the first one out." This was pretty good: the truth, but not the whole truth. "One little boy hit his head on the sidewalk."

Papa looked from me to Sam and back several times. "Sam? Sam. Look at me. You didn't have anything to do with this, did you?"

We had reached a crucial point in the conversation. Sam couldn't lie, and certainly not to Papa. He was swallowing so fast I was afraid he would cry. Also, the jacket he was wearing looked pretty suspicious on a hot June day.

I threw him a lifeline. "The sheriff came and some other grown-ups. I don't think the little boy was hurt very much."

I could tell that Papa wasn't deflected very far. Since I had used up all my partial truths, I tried a new approach. "You know what I think?"

Papa still looked at Sam suspiciously. "What?"

"It was the Communists."

I could feel Sam relax a little in the time I bought for him. He shifted the sprinkler bottle under his coat.

I continued, "The Communists don't dare attack grown-ups in Round Prairie yet, but anybody can attack little kids."

"That's true." When Papa pulled us both into a hug, Sam turned slightly so he wouldn't feel the bottle. Even though my nose was mashed hard into Papa's chest, I didn't move so my hug would last as long as possible. His shirt smelled like something baking.

"You kids go home and tell Mama I'll be back in time to cook supper. I wouldn't, uh, mention the theater ruckus. She's having a hard enough day without this."

As Papa walked away, Sam said wistfully, "If those dummies hadn't panicked—"

"I thought that was what you wanted."

"You're just . . . jealous you didn't think of it," Sam added lamely.

I felt sorry to see him go from so excited to so low in such a short time, just like Mama. Then I remembered the little boy with the bloody head curled into a ball. "It was horrible."

Mama didn't hear about the theater incident until evening, when Mr. Whitaker dropped by to check on us kids.

"It was the Communists. Dr. Mary. She's the ringleader," Mama explained to him

Mr. Whitaker stuffed his hands in his overalls and shuffled back home.

"Why would Communists attack a bunch of kids at the movies?" I couldn't believe that Sam was encouraging this conversation.

"Doctor Mary. Doctor Mary. It's exactly what she would do–attack the children to terrify the parents."

It was worth a try for me to say, "It didn't work, Mama. We weren't scared. We were like the kids on 'The Shadow'."

"Mary, Mary, quite contrary, quite contrary, quite contrary–"

Sam's interrupted Mama's stuck-record voice. "Papa, who do you think it was?"

"It doesn't matter." I had seldom seen Papa so worried. "It was a cruel, vicious trick on completely innocent children–"

Sam looked as if Papa had slapped him with each word.

"Who could've been hurt really bad," Papa continued. "They could've been . . . *burned.*"

"But they weren't," Sam said in a tiny voice.

Papa looked into empty space like Mama usually did. "*Burned.* Practical jokes are never funny. Not for the instigator, and sure as hell not for the victim."

I didn't look at Sam. I didn't need to. This was the kind of secret brothers and sisters took to their graves.

*   *   *   *   *   *

Sunday afternoon, I wandered around trying to find Papa, hoping we could fix more brakes or time the Buick again. I heard an odd sound in the barn, where he was probably building something at his work bench.

Using good spy techniques, I tiptoed inside. Through one of the slatted walls, I saw Papa sitting on a stool with his head bent down, his chin almost on his chest, his arms folded across his chest, like he sat in church during the closing prayer. But he was so still, so bent over, as if the Papa I usually saw were a lot larger, and this Papa was all deflated, pulled inside. He had made himself as small as possible, like the little boy on the sidewalk curled into a ball.

Papa took a deep breath and looked up at the shop light overhead and I saw what I had never seen and never, ever expected to see: tears running down Papa's cheeks. My Papa, the strongest and bravest man in the world, was crying. I literally held my breath so he wouldn't know I was there. This wasn't spying, this was something else, and I didn't belong there. I crept out the door, stepping backward in my own footprints.

I didn't know what to do. I wanted to tell Sam, but he couldn't help, either. I decided to ride Maybe out to the Inavale hide-out, stopping to tell Alberta Clipper about High Gun in the Belmont Stakes. Even though neither of us had ever heard of him, it was always nice to share news about a winning horse.

Sure enough, Sam's bicycle lay in the weeds near the storm cellar. In the driveway, he was pouring gasoline on a red ant hill and was just ready to light it. When he noticed me, he concentrated on the ant hill, obviously in no mood to talk to anybody. Since yesterday, he had been as quiet as a prisoner in solitary confinement.

As I walked closer, the flames shot up, blazed wildly for a moment and quickly subsided to little rivers of fire in the sand. The red ants no longer existed even as miniature, incinerated corpses.

"Leave me alone."

"That was pretty impressive." I toed the sand nearby.

"Red ants," he spit out, measuring this feat against his Greatest Triumph at the Avalon Theater.

"I just saw Papa."

"So what?" Little beads of sweat rested on Sam's freckled nose.

"He was in the barn." I watched Sam screw the lid on the gas can. "He was . . . . " It was hard for me to say, "C-crying."

Sam's head jerked up. "He was not. You liar. LIAR."

Sam had never accused me so violently of lying, and certainly not when he suspected I was telling the truth.

"Liar, liar, liar. Get outta here." He shoved my shoulder hard.

"I did see him. In the barn."

"You DID NOT." Sam picked up a handful of sand and threw it in my face. "Get! Unless you want gas on you."

He had never threatened me like that, either.

"You don't scare me." And he didn't. Not for one second. "Why would I lie about Papa? Believe what you want. But I know what I know."

Suddenly Sam tackled me, full force, head on, and we both fell over backward.

That meant war. I scrambled out from under him and tried to get my feet free enough to kick him in the side, but my shoe only grazed his leg. We managed to roll free and stand up again, both covered with dirt and bits of dry weeds.

Sam knew I had only one weapon, my kick, but that could disable him pretty well. On the other hand, he knew all sorts of arm holds from studying jujitsu, which he said he wanted to learn for a merit badge in Personal Fitness. My eye. I knew it was for hand-to-hand combat.

We circled each other like two wrestlers, then he made the first move, jumping around me which indicated a full – or half-nelson. I managed to dodge that, but he grabbed my right wrist and bent my forearm up behind my back, pulling upward, which sent a stab of pain through my elbow and shoulder. He wasn't nearly as strong as Bobby Clawson.

"Say you were lying," he gulped in my ear, "Or I'll break your arm."

I answered like a cowboy. "You and who else?" I struggled to free my arm, meanwhile kicking backward at his legs. Finally, my heel connected with his shin, really hard, and he reflexively stepped back, letting me go.

"I saw Papa cry!" I spit out. "Even if you beat me up, it won't change that."

In a last attempt, Sam rushed me, knocked me over again, and managed to get me on my back in the weeds. Just as he was ready to sit on my stomach and pin my arms with his knees, I saw that we had knocked over the Formula, which was slowly leaking out of its cap.

"Sam! The Formula!"

"Liar."

I jerked my head in its direction. "Look."

Sam knew my technique of trying to divert his attention long enough to blindside him. After all, if Moe the Stooge could do it, it didn't take a genius. But we were both getting hot, tired and too close to the burned red ant hill, so he did look.

"Criminy!" Sam jumped up and grabbed the Formula, now holding it upright.

I slowly stood up and tried to dig out the gravel embedded in fresh scrapes on my elbows. "What'll we do?"

"We could top it up with a little gasoline." He sounded unconvinced.

"Okay."

"Hey!" Will Hankins wiggled his bicycle up the ruts of the driveway. Since we had last seen him, he had grown even taller and wasn't so skinny, but his new overalls still rode above his boot tops.

"Whatchoo fightin' for?"

Almost in perfect unison, Sam and I said "We weren't fighting."

Will looked us up and down. "Huh."

From the kitty cookie jar, I had stolen two of Mama's home-made oatmeal cookies and hidden them in my pockets. She almost never made them anymore. Although they were broken up from the fight, I offered pieces to Will and Sam. Will delicately bit his small piece in two, polite enough even to pass muster with Mama.

"You gonna do another daredevil show?" Will asked. I saw that one of his front teeth had broken off. And that he now had pale fuzz on his cheeks.

"Our Mama is—" I started before I could stop. "Kind of . . . sick." This was the first time I had said anything to anyone. Why Will Hankins?

Will finished his cookie. "What's wrong with her?"

Sam and I looked at each other for a moment, then simultaneously settled on "nerves." Before Will could say anything else, I asked, "Where have you been this year?"

Will was obviously pleased to tell his story. "We harvested all the way up North Dakota and then," he paused, "into Canada. They got sum-mit different wheat, but threshin's the same."

Canada! He might as well have said Russia. How romantic!

"When winter hit at Cardston, I went to school for a coupla months. Enough to get through third grade." He grinned.

"That's neat," Sam said with genuine respect.

Will ducked his head at the compliment. "Wanna shoot some rats at the garbage dump? My old man'll let me use his .22." He considered for a minute. "If he's . . . asleep."

CHAPTER 47
ESCHATOLOGY

MISS REYNOLDS ENTHUSIASTICALLY FILLED IN for Mrs. Dahlke as my summer spelling teacher, proving, she said, that she would make an exceptional teacher if she just didn't hate children. Her words were easier to spell than Mrs. Dahlke's but more grown up in meaning, for example, *eschew* and *umbrage*. We were currently studying '-ology' words, numbering in the hundreds, all rhyming, and meaning "the study of" something. Fortunately, I had outgrown my simple expectations that word endings could be relied upon, remembering those days when I thought that *pious* meant full of pie. Besides, the first syllable of most '-ology' words came from another language, so *geology* didn't concern *geos* any more than *theology* indicated a study of *theos*.

Of course, Miss Reynolds eschewed common words like geology and theology in favor of words she called "friends for life," like *teleology* and *eschatology*. It helped when she used God's Plan as an example of a teleology, although relying on anybody's plan and certainly God's Plan was no way to live a life, in her opinion. No matter how hard I tried, I couldn't understand *eschatology*, let alone what it had to do with the ending of "Shane" after the drive-in movie screen blew over. Miss Reynolds said that if I embraced God's Plan as my teleology, I would inherit an automatic, built-in eschatology and wouldn't need to think for myself the rest of my life. Then she laughed. For the time being, I filed *eschatology* with *exponentially*, words I decided to understand when I had more time, hopefully before I turned twelve.

As I walked home from the library and rounded the corner toward the trailer, I saw Mama sitting in my swing near our front door. That was very odd, since she almost never left the house. Immediately, I wanted to turn around and run, but she had spotted me. To myself, I quickly invented excuses for places where I had to be–a Brownie project, overdue books at the library, an emergency piano lesson.

Then Mama did something she had never done before: she eagerly waved and trotted toward me. She was wearing a crumpled house dress and a dirty butcher's apron, as usual, but for shoes she wore bedroom slippers. She had mashed her hair into a hair net, as if she needed one to go to bed in the middle of the day.

"Jeb! Jeb!" she stumbled a little on the gravel road.

Something was terribly wrong. I looked around hopefully for Sam or Mr. Whitaker, but the block was deserted. She caught my neck in the crook of her arm and dragged me along by my head. When I pushed on her side to pry her loose, I could feel her ribs through her dress and apron. I hadn't touched her for months and didn't realize how skinny she was. If I fought too hard, she would fall down on the ground, which I couldn't bear. Not Mama on the ground.

"Guess what?" she almost shouted in my ear.

I turned my face away from her medicine breath, the familiar smell of molasses and gasoline. "What?" I managed to gag.

"Have I got a surprise for you."

By now we had reached the trailer, lurching along together. The front screen door hung open, letting in flies, askew on its hinges as if someone had tried to kick through it. Mama pushed me up the trailer step ahead of her, scraping my shin.

I looked around warily. The trailer smelled like floor wax and ammonia, signs that Mama had been Deep Cleaning, except the kitchen counter where a bottle of Nervine lay on its side, dripping a brown, sticky pool the size of a quarter.

"Do you see her?" She asked eagerly. "Do you see her?" Mama still stood outside behind me.

"Not yet," I answered feebly. "Maybe she's . . . hiding," I guessed.

"Hiding, schmiding. She's in the middle of the floor." Mama climbed the step and shoved me sideways, stiff as a stick.

"Where is she?! She was right here." Mama pushed me onto the piano bench and, with growing panic, began looking everywhere, ran to the bedroom, throwing open doors and drawers. Back in the kitchen, she opened the refrigerator, peered inside, then slammed it shut. There weren't many places anything could hide in our trailer.

"Don't worry, Mama," I tried to say loudly, but it came out a squeak. "We'll find her." *Who?* Baby Janet? Someone Mama had known in the Olden Days?

Mama looked at me suspiciously. Her pupils had almost taken over her blue eyes, turning them black. "You took her."

"I don't even know–"

"She was DEAD. Dead dead dead dead dead." Mama looked around frantically. "Where does a dead body. A whole dead body? I've been waiting outside to tell you, and she didn't come past me."

I hoped that Mama would stay mad and not turn sad. "We'll find her. Maybe she's in the barn."

"Are you deaf?" She breathed fast now, as if she were trying not to vomit. "She was dead."

"Maybe she wasn't completely dead." I would try anything now.

"The dead should STAY DEAD."

She looked so hopeless that I put my hand on her arm. She yanked it away. "Don't touch me! Go away." She rubbed her arm where I had touched her as if it were burned. "You're not dead. This is the house of the dead." She began to chant,

" . . . see with blinding sight

Blind eyes can blaze like meteors and be gay . . .

Do not go gentle into that good night."

She pointed at the door.

I didn't need a second order and bolted outside.

"I'll clean up this mess," she called behind me.

I ran to the barn to retrieve Maybe. Even with a low tire, she was faster than La Cheetah, although not as much company.

"Jeb! Je-yeb!"

I hadn't been fast enough.

"Guess what?" She lurched toward me so lopsided that she walked out of one of her slippers. She shouted triumphantly, "The dead body? Was ME!"

I kept Maybe between her and me.

Mama twirled like a little girl. "Here I am, risen from the dead. Like Jesus Christ."

She caught my hand and forced it to touch her arm. "Touch me. See? I'm alive. If that's not alive, what is? I who was dead am alive again. First we see through a glass darkly, then face to face."

She shouted loud enough to reach Mr. Whitaker's.

"Do not go gentle into that good night,

Rage, RAGE against the dying of the light!"

She was still shouting as I climbed on Maybe and rode off.

I didn't understand any of it, not *eschatology*, not Mama's poems, not one single thing. And I couldn't ask anybody because I didn't even know what to ask.

CHAPTER 48

PLUG GULP

FTER THE AVALON THEATER RIOT, SAM AND I TAC-
itly agreed that we should lie low for a few days, avoid the fort and
dodge any possibility of combat. Since a lot of kids were on vacation with
their families, it would have been the perfect time to commandeer the bakery fort even with limited troops, but Sam said we needed to regroup, a military exercise more complex than reconnaissance although easier to spell.
Sam's pipe bomb a year ago had blown up a fence we could rebuild; to me,
the movie riot felt more like the maniac with the firecracker who burned
Papa. Although I had vaguely suspected what the nitrogen triiodide would
do, as the mad scientist, Sam must have known how it would explode.
Our famous telepathy sometimes failed, and right now I couldn't tell from
Sam's long silences if he felt guilty or if he were working on a new Greatest
Plan of All Time. As Sam's supply officer, I wasn't exactly innocent.

Meanwhile, we played in the school fire escape, scrambling barefoot
up the steep, hot metal tube, sliding back one step for every two steps forward, finally hoisting ourselves onto the platform two stories high outside
the locked window of Mrs. Vince's classroom. During fire drills, she was
the only teacher strong enough to heave kids out the window one at a
time. From the darkness at the top, the little opening at the bottom looked
blinding bright and the drop looked almost vertical. A grab bar hung over
the platform so you could position yourself before sliding down.

"You first." I needed time to catch my breath from the climb and
to con Sam into slicking the tube with the waxed paper squares we had

sneaked from the trailer to use as seats. We squirmed around each other on the platform, barely large enough to hold both of us.

With an Indian whoop, he let go and instantly changed from full-sized Sam to a rapidly shrinking boy, as if he had drunk Alice's potion, shooting out the bottom into the bright light. He landed on his knees and scrambled sideways out of sight.

Now in the circle of light at the bottom I saw someone else's head. Ono. Was it Marvin Harkin? How would I escape? Where was Sam? As my eyes adjusted, I realized it was Papa. Why was Papa here, on a weekday, when he should be at work on the dam? Maybe he had learned about Sam's causing the movie riot. Maybe Sheriff Westergaard told Papa to turn him in. Since June was nowhere near Christmas or Mamas birthday, it couldn't be a surprise for her. Something was Up.

"Jeb, come on down. I'll catch you."

At the bottom, I hurtled into Papa's hands. He stood me upright.

"Get your shoes and socks, Kids."

Maybe this was a windfall holiday like the blizzard or one of Papa's jokes.

While we put on our shoes, looking expectantly at each other, Papa sat backwards on the picnic table bench leaning over his elbows on his knees. His work shirt had sweat stains around the neck and down his back. He had taken off his khaki baseball cap, and his hair was mushed down and sweaty except around his ears where the cap didn't cover. His neck was sunburned, but his scarred arms stayed mostly white in the sun.

"Come here, Sugar." He looped me in one arm with my back to him. Oh oh. This was no joke—a daytime hug when I wasn't hurt. I warily traced the burn scars on his forearm, like ivy made from bumpy, knotted skin. Sam sat on the grass at his feet.

"I have bad news, Kids."

Sam and I stiffened.

"Are we moving again?" Sam asked, almost hopefully.

I added, "It's okay, Papa. We've moved a lot." But he wouldn't take off work just to tell us that.

"No." Papa ran his hand through his sweaty hair. "It's Mama."

Sam pulled out his Boy Scout knife and began to play mumbly-peg in the grass. Papa and I watched him for a minute.

Papa let out his breath as if he had been holding it a long time. "Mama's having what . . . the doctor calls . . . a nervous breakdown."

I didn't know what that was, but Papa's voice sounded final, as if putting a name on it trapped Mama. It let our secret out of the family, made it something we could no longer control or fight or protect. Not to mention how it would embarrass Mama. I had never felt so much dread, not even when I heard the tornado warning sirens.

"What doctor?" I turned around in Papa's arm and looked at him eye to eye.

"Buchanan."

"What does he know?" I pressed. "You called him a quack."

"Mama's not that bad. We can take care of her," Sam and I overlapped. "We can take turns and–"

"Quit school and just—" I gained energy thinking of possible solutions. In a way, I was relieved that we were finally talking about it, even though I felt like a traitor behind Mama's back.

Sam picked up, "We can go to school at home and–"

"I know you could," Papa's mouth wasn't working right. "But this is something we can't fix by ourselves. Mama needs . . ." His voice sounded as if he had a piece of meat stuck in his throat. "Mama needs . . . to go away for a while."

"Go where? How long? Who says?" Our questions stepped on each other.

Papa tried to swallow the thing in his throat. "I don't know. They want to put her . . . in, uh . . . the State Hospital." For the second time in my life, I saw Papa with tears in his eyes. Both eyes, even his blind one.

I felt like vomiting.

"In Hastings?! For the insane?" Sam was turning red.

I gagged, "Mrs. Dahlke said. It's worse than a prison. People never leave there. Never."

Sam was getting mad. "If they come to get Mama, I'll fight 'em. I can hold 'em off."

"Me too. We know how to fight."

"Calm down," Papa warned with no heart in it.

But I couldn't. We were talking about Mama. Our Mama. "Mrs. Vince and Mrs. Dahlke. I heard them. People put their relatives in there just because . . . they don't like them."

Sam exploded. "That's a lie. Liar. LIAR."

"Mrs. Vince said so. They do experiments on people and give them shots to make them twitch and scream."

"They do not!"

"Mrs. Vince knows somebody in there—"

"Make her stop, Papa!"

"That's enough. Both of you. Sit down and be quiet." We slowly sat cross-legged in the grass at Papa's feet. His work boots had mud caked in all the creases, but the tops were shiny under his pant legs. They were the color of palomino horses.

"We all want the best for Mama," Papa started over.

Sam stabbed the grass again and again with his knife. "What're they gonna do?"

"First of all," Papa took a deep breath, "She and I have to go to . . . Judge Weiss."

"A judge! Why?" I practically shouted. "Like a trial?"

"Will she go to jail?" Sam asked incredulously.

"She didn't do anything, Papa," I pleaded. "She's innocent."

"She is," Sam added.

I plowed on, "Mama can't help it. It's the way she is."

"I know," Papa answered miserably. "I know, I know. Judge Weiss has to . . . determine that she's . . . legally . . . incompetent."

Time slowed. The leaves on the playground trees seemed to hold still.

I tried to figure it out. "If they're trying to make Mama well, they wouldn't put her on trial first." I looked at Sam for help. "Would they?"

"It's not a trial. It's a court order." Papa sighed. "We have to get one, then we have to drive her to Hastings." Papa prodded Sam's knife with the toe of his boot. "I need you kids to help me."

Papa never said that except when he was joking about fixing something complex like a radio.

I wanted to hear a real answer. "What'll they do to her?"

Papa's eyes grew shiny again. "First, they have to . . . calm her down."

"They *electrocute* people there."

"No, they don't. Don't even say that."

"What? How?" Sam and I kept talking at the same time.

"They do something to . . . keep her calm."

"What?" I almost whispered.

Papa stood up and walked around. "I don't know." He rubbed his sunburned neck and looked in the direction of the trailer.

This really scared me, since Papa always knew the answer to things. Sam stabbed the grass harder and harder, closer and closer to his own foot. After a long time, Papa turned back to us and squatted down, bouncing on his heels the way he fixed cars.

"I don't know." He looked from Sam to me. "But we're going to get through this. We're a family, and we've gotten through tough times before, and we'll get through this."

"How long will they keep her?" Sam asked.

"I don't know."

I reached out to pet Papa's boot. "People die in there. That's what Mrs. Dahlke said." "Mama will stay as long as she needs to."

Sam voice grew scratchy. "A week? A month? A . . . year?"

Papa was silent.

I whispered, "Forever?"

"Hopefully not, Sugar."

Hopefully not?! We could be losing Mama forever? Sam and I could be orphans, my worst nightmare.

"She's not that bad, Papa, I promise she's not." Sam and I pleaded.

Papa looked so sad his face was melting. "She might . . . hurt herself. Or you kids."

"She wouldn't hurt us, she wouldn't," I insisted. "I'm around her a lot when we clean and iron and read poetry and sew and she never hurts me. Never." Reason took over. "Except when she makes me sit on the footstool."

Papa's face regained a little of its shape. "That's hard, I know."

He dusted off his pants, although they weren't dirty. "I've got to get back to work. Don't be late for supper. Let's don't upset Mama any more than she already is."

"I love everybody," I called to Papa's back with the old Wilder family refrain, although it didn't feel right, or very protective.

When we couldn't avoid it any longer, Sam and I started walking home the longest way we could invent, overshooting the Methodist Church and Bessinger's Small Engine Repair, circling back near Main

Street, when we saw something that stopped us dead: Papa was walking out of Dr. Mary's office.

Sam and I automatically hid behind the nearest bush.

"Sam!" I whispered fiercely. "Doctor Mary's a Communist. Papa's made a deal with the Communists. Maybe because he wouldn't take the oath, he's turning Mama in."

Sam literally clamped his hand over my mouth. His palm tasted like dirt. "Listen. This isn't make-believe. Papa wouldn't do anything to hurt us or Mama. There's some explanation."

His hand relaxed enough to let me hiss, "We've never gone to Dr. Mary for anything."

"I'll ask Papa. Just give me a chance."

"He'll cover up, he'll lie . . . ." I trailed off.

Sam's eyes squinted to a slit like Gort's melting the Army weapons. "Has Papa ever, EVER lied to us? Lied to anybody?"

I shook my head no. "But Sam. But . . . but." I didn't know what I wanted to say. I had run out of words. It was all too much. I just started to cry, in front of Sam and all.

Reluctantly, Sam put his arm around my shoulders and hugged me, side to side, harder and harder, finally hard enough to make somebody's bones crack. I couldn't tell if they were his bones or mine.

CHAPTER 49
THE ROAD TO MANDALAY

PAPA TOOK THE NEXT DAY OFF WORK, TOO. I SAW him sneaking a sack of Mama's clothes into the car trunk, so this must be The Day.

"Why are you home?" Mama asked him suspiciously, letting the milk from her cereal bubble out through her words. We had eaten corn flakes every day since Mama quit making breakfast.

"It's Saturday," I lied.

"I thought we'd take a ride today," Papa tried to sound casual.

"Where?" Mama looked at all three of us without moving her head. We hadn't taken a ride since we quit going to church two months ago.

"The kids'll do the dishes, and why don't you get dressed?"

"My pajamas are good enough for a ride," she sounded sly, testing.

"Everybody else has to get dressed every day," Sam blurted out.

Papa walked Mama back to their bedroom, while Sam and I set a record for washing and drying dishes. Silently we waited for them in the Buick.

When they came out of the trailer, Mama was wearing a wrinkled but clean dress, her hair was bobby-pinned back of her ears, and she had even put on two bright spots of rouge. She held a bottle of Nervine, about a quarter full.

The wind was blowing hot and strong, as usual in July, spinning little dust devils up from the broomcorn field.

As we drove out of town, Mama mumbled out the open car window. "'For though from out our bourne of time and place the flood may bear me far . . .' Jeb? Jeb, remember that?"

From some footstool episode I miraculously pulled out, "Crossing the Bar."

Sam looked at me wide-eyed.

"That's my girl: yooty-tooty-fruity." She toasted me with a big swallow of Nervine. "'Twilight and evening bell, and after that the dark.' Ain't that the g.d. truth."

"Haven't you had about enough of that?" Papa asked.

"I'll tell you when I've had enough. Of it and you and everything else." She wiped the back of her hand across her mouth.

This must be the way they argued when we couldn't hear them.

"Mama, do 'The Prisoner of Chillon'." If I could get her started, that poem could take up seventeen and half minutes.

"Byron," she answered. Inspecting the label on the Nervine bottle, she added, "By-ron. Buy ron. Is this Ron? Did we buy Ron?"

Papa looked at the road as if it were a railroad track and he were driving a train. The speedometer said 70.

"FIRE!" Mama suddenly screamed.

Papa yanked the steering wheel to miss something he didn't see. "Where?! What?"

"Something's burning. I smell it."

"Nothing," Sam said.

"Oh, it's Frank." As if she just understood what she said, she added, "Frank? Frank's burning!" She grabbed Papa's hand on the steering wheel. "We've got to help Frank!"

Papa shook off her hand. "I'm right here. Everything's fine."

Mama looked bewildered, then turned hard. "You're not Frank. You just look like him."

I didn't want her to worry. "Papa is Frank."

In the rear view mirror, I saw Papa shake his head at me.

Mama turned in her seat and spit out. "Liar! You are such a little *liar*. Liar liar pants on fire, liar liar–"

I had another idea. "Remember? 'Somebody said it couldn't be done, but he with a chuckle replied that maybe it couldn't, but'... what? What, Mama?"

"'He would be one who wouldn't say so 'till he had tried.' But he lied. He lied!"

I started the next stanza, "'So he tackled right in with a grin'—"

"Grin, schmin! Where are you taking me?" Mama cried out. "Fake Frank. You're locking me up, just like Cecil Hauser's wife." She pointed at a road sign. "Hastings! The State Hospital! For the Innn-cur-ably Innn-sane. In. Sane. Sane is in. Insane is out."

"I'm not taking you to the State Hospital." Papa grew quieter as Mama grew louder.

Sam and I looked at each other across the back seat. Papa was lying, actually lying, for the first time in our lives. But I guess he had good reason now.

"For the INN – CURABLY INN – SANE!! Am I in-cur-ably in-sane? Is anybody Curably Insane?" She punched Papa's shoulder with each word. "Huh? Huh? Huh?"

The car swerved each time she hit him.

"Calm down, Edie." Papa defended himself with one hand and drove with the other.

The speedometer now said 80. On every bump, the Buick lifted as if we were taking off in a B-17, a real one this time, with our whole family, but no one knew where we were going or where we would land. A car try-ing to fly, like a flying horse without wings.

"Calm calm. Calm balm." She sang, "There is a balm in Gilead . . . " when her body jerked. "You've been waiting a long time for this, haven't you? Well, I've got news: I won't go."

Suddenly, she yanked the door handle, but Sam was quicker, punch-ing down the door lock button.

She twisted in her seat and threatened, "'Beware the Jabberwock, my son'." She bared her teeth in a nightmare smile. "'The jaws that bite, the claws that catch'." She swung the bottle at Sam, then turned to pull up the lock button.

Again Sam was quicker. Now she pounded the door with her Nervine bottle, aiming at Sam's fingers holding the button down.

"Stop it, Mama! You'll hurt Sam!" I yelled.

"Sam's the man," she said grimly. As she raised the bottle to mash Sam's fingers, I pushed on her head from behind, distracting her long enough for her to change her mind.

"Mama! Mama? How does that poem go? 'So live that when they summons comes to join'—?"

She rapidly mumbled through a few lines to arrive at, "The im-mu-ner-able . . . no. In-num-ber-able'— no. What?"

"Innumerable," I coached, "caravan . . . " I didn't know where the poem went from here until the very last, beautiful line. But Mama did. More and more, she and I used poetry as our own private language, where only we knew the tricks, and everything was a metaphor, both a lie and the truth.

"Good girl!" She continued, "'Which moves to that mysterious realm . . . " she took a long breath and rested her head on the back of the seat. "On a what? A frigate. A frigate? There is no frigate like a . . . what? A whata whata whata—"

"Book," I answered. I felt as if we were going through her personal library of poems before someone burned it.

"No frigate like a book," I finished. "That's one of Miss Reynolds' favorite poems."

Meanwhile, Sam had pulled himself together for the next onslaught. "Jeb's been learning neat words from Miss Reynolds."

Mama snarled, "Like *fat* and *ugly* and *old maid*?"

I was shocked. She might as well have said *white trash*. Nonetheless, I selected words that wouldn't upset her, definitely avoiding *teleology* and *eschatology*. "More like *eschew* and *environs*," I offered without enthusiasm.

"They do palindromes, too," Sam encouraged. "Tell her some palindromes."

"Palindromes are—" I started.

"I know what they are," she snarled. "I'm not an idiot."

"There are simple ones like *racecar* and *deed* and *civic* and *madam*," I explained, "and ones with two words, like *stop pots* and *loop pools*. But the best are whole sentences, like 'Was it a bat I saw?' and 'Borrow or rob' and—"

"In words drown I," Mama interrupted.

I envisioned the words to check if they worked. What a brilliant palindrome. I wondered if Miss Reynolds knew it.

"Wow," Sam said under his breath.

"But the real killer is 'God saw I was a dog'." She hit Papa's shoulder. "Didn't he? You were there. God sees everything. God's Plan. Ask my mother. God saw I was a dog. That's why he could kill my baby. I'm a dog, my baby was a dog. God the Big Dog. WATCH OUT! DOG!"

At that instant, a little white dog ran across the highway in front of the car. Papa yanked the wheel, but we all heard the sickening thump under the rear tire.

Ono. Oh please no. I looked out the back window at the rapidly receding dog, now a flattened scrap of white paper on the pavement. Papa couldn't have missed it, but he didn't even slow down.

"Frank, if I need HELP, take me to Geneva." Mama suddenly pleaded like a child, "Anywhere, Frank, ANYwhere but Hastings. I'll die in there. I'll never see you again. Or the children." She turned in the seat to explain, suddenly calm. "Except Janet. I see her everywhere. I'd see her more in Geneva. She died there." She smiled, her lips smeared with Nervine, a brown lipstick smile like the clown's at the Hastings fair.

"You've had enough of that." Papa tried to grab the bottle from her hand, causing the Buick to veer into the oncoming lane of the two-lane highway.

"My God, you'll kill us!" Mama screamed and hugged the bottle to her chest. "He's trying to kill us all." She stared at Sam and me, her face a savage Halloween mask worse than Dracula or a monster from outer space. Her lips were curled like Bobby Clawson's dog. Sam fell back at the sight.

By now, we had reached the Hastings turn-off but were going too fast. Just as Sam and I braced for a high-speed skid into the State Hospital, we . . . drove straight. Straight ahead. Sam and I looked at each other in disbelief.

"You passed it, you passed it," Mama sang. "A tisket, a tasket, you missed it, you passed it, the crazies, the daisies," she chanted for several miles past the State Hospital. Suddenly sober, she asked, "Where are we going? Where are you taking me?"

"Omaha," Papa said quietly.

"Omaha? What's in Omaha?"

"A new hospital."

"A prison." Mama's voice started to rise in pitch. "Where they kill people. I know what I know. 'I felt a cleavage in my mind, as if my brain had split,' so I could be electrocuted. E-lec-tro-cuted. Fried. Burned. Until smoke comes out my ears. Right, Sam? Our little expert on the electric chair? Smoke comes out their eyes. Burn. Burn. Like Frank." Then, suddenly she cried, "Frank burned. Frank, oh Frank." She sobbed as if Papa weren't sitting right next to her. "Frank burned. My beloved Frank." Lucid again, she looked at Papa. "He was so good to me. I loved him so much. Do you understand?"

In the mirror, I could see Papa's mouth, a straight line like Sam's. The speedometer read 85, we were passing cars and trucks so fast with such narrow escapes from oncoming cars, I thought we would hit them. Each time, their horns blared, first high, then low. I wasn't afraid. I would rather die in a crash right now than live out the future after this day.

"But Frank died." Mama grew angrier.

"Mama," I said in the largest voice I could muster, a squeak, "Frank is Papa." Sam slapped my thigh to shut me up.

She took another swig from the Nervine, looking defiantly at Papa, then me. "Of course, Frank is Papa, you idiot."

She had never called me an idiot before. I didn't have to take this, even from Mama. "I'm not an idiot. Remember 'Build thee more stately mansions, o my Jeb'?" It had become a joke between Mama and me to substitute my name for 'soul'." . Now she answered the questions on my test. "'The Chambered Nautilus.' Oliver Wendell Holmes. 'Let each new temple, nobler than the last . . .'"

I prompted, "'Shut thee from heaven with a dome more vast . . .'" I only knew half of this one stanza.

"'Till thou at length are free . . .'" Mama stopped one line short of the end. She looked at Papa as if she couldn't focus her eyes. "You idiot. That's not Frank. Frank burned."

Out of nowhere, Sam suddenly said, "Does anybody wanna know about sapphires?"

He could have knocked me over with a feather. The airtight secrecy of my brother never ceased to amaze me. Brilliant.

"Believe it or not, sapphires and rubies are the same stone—aluminum oxide. But blue sapphires have a lot of iron in them and rubies don't."

How long had he known this?

"I thought you didn't like geology," was the only response I could muster.

"Star sapphires also have the mineral rutile, which is mostly titanium dioxide."

I felt Mama relax a little.

"And that creates intersecting needle-like structures," he continued.

"How does it turn into a star?" I managed to ask.

"Just with polishing. Because of the needles inside."

I couldn't believe it. "So the stars are buried in the rocks and just have to be brought out."

"Yep. Sometimes jewelry crooks bake them at a very high temperature to deepen the color, but no connoisseur would buy one which has been tampered with."

Sam had performed a miracle. He had brought Mama back from an Extreme State. With science, of all things.

Papa said appreciatively, "We'll certainly watch out for that."

"Can anybody spell *connoisseur*?" I asked.

"You can," Sam acknowledged.

Mama's head lolled back on the seat. "Burned. In the tornado. No. Burned . . . ." she trailed off.

Until the outskirts of Omaha, Mama half-slept, occasionally throwing her head from side to side and muttering. When she woke up, she lifted her Nervine bottle to the light and saw that it was empty. "You never wanted me to drink this. Never. Never anything that would help me. Help me help me help me." Then, sitting up straight, "Where are we?"

"Omaha," Papa answered.

"Where's the prison?"

"It's a hospital."

"That's what they all say. I know what I know. More medicine. If I'm going to be e-lec-tro-cuted, I want more medicine." She began hitting the empty bottle on the seat. A few brown drops spattered her dress.

"More. MORE!" Mama began to hit Papa on the shoulder with the empty bottle. Papa's face looked as if it hurt, but he was trying to drive in traffic.

"Mama, don't," Sam said his first words in a hour. "Don't hit Papa."

She turned on Sam like a witch. "Don't tell me what to do, Sam Wilder. This isn't Papa. It's fake Frank. Taking me to the electric chair." With the bottle, she hit Papa again and again.

From the back seat, I tried to grab her hand, but she wrenched free. She felt as strong as a man. "You little–!" She yelled at me.

The next time she hit Papa, we were at a stop light. He turned sideways in the seat, and I thought he would hit her, but instead he snatched the bottle out of her hands and threw it out the window. The man driving the car next to us called Papa names.

She collapsed and began to cry like a child who has just lost her toy. Papa clenched his teeth and, at that moment, turned into the parking lot of a three-story brick building. He shut off the car and slumped in the seat.

"Where are we?" Mama looked wildly around.

Papa took deep breaths as if he'd been running.

"You won't leave me here." Mama suddenly turned into a beggar. "Don't leave me. Don't take me away from my children." She sobbed, wild and desperate. "Frank. Frank, I know you. I was just pretending to be crazy before. I don't know what comes over me. I can't help it. Do you believe me? I can't help it. I promise not to do it again. Just don't leave me. What will they do to me?"

She frantically tried to climb into the back seat with us, but Papa pulled her back. In their struggle, Papa's elbow hit the horn, which blared on and off, on and off, while he and Mama fought.

At the sound of the horn, two men ran out the back door of the building. They looked like football players, except their uniforms were starched green linen. When Mama saw them, she shrank back, now locking the car door. They tried the handle, then reached through the open window and unlocked it.

"Come on, Mrs. Wilder," one with a little beard coaxed. "We've been expecting you."

"Frank," she pleaded. "Please. Please please please."

When the bigger man reached inside to pull her out, she went limp, worse than fighting. He gently lifted her out like a child, then each man held one of her arms to walk her inside. Mama staggered between them, looking up from one to the other and talking. They looked straight ahead. She pointed back to the car, and I heard her say was "my children."

I felt as if I would never see Mama again.

Suddenly, she fought one of the men off, turned and screamed over her shoulder, "I heard a fly buzz when I died!"

I leaned out of the car window and shouted back, "I did, too, Mama!"

"That's my girl!"

With that, she slumped between the men and let them drag her away.

Holding Mama's sack, Papa stood beside the car. "Lock the doors. If any stranger comes anywhere close, roll up the windows, no matter how hot you get. And stay here. I don't know how long I'll be gone. What did I say?"

We didn't need to repeat what he said. Nothing–*nothing*–could have pried us out of the car.

"Papa?" Sam squeaked.

"What?" Papa was almost crying.

"Mama only had one shoe on."

Papa retrieved her other shoe from the floor of the passenger side. "Thanks, Son. She'll appreciate that." He locked the door and walked into the hospital.

Sam and I slunk down in the seat and didn't look at each other, as if none of this day happened if we didn't see it reflected in the other's face.

After a long time, I asked, "Do you think Mama will be—?"

"They better not hurt her," Sam spit out. "I'll bomb 'em. I'll get a machine gun."

The hospital had bars on the windows, not in tic-tac-toe squares like Hastings or straight bars like the jail in Round Prairie, but bars rolled into flowers and curlicues on all three stories. The grassy back yard was bordered by jumbo marigolds, yellow and orange pom-poms. Mama would like that. If she ever got to see them. I could hear faraway sounds. Screams? I was afraid to ask Sam.

I couldn't think any more and must have fallen asleep, since the next thing I heard was the car door unlock. I jerked awake. It was Papa.

Even sunburned, he looked pale. He slid into the driver's seat and put his hands on the steering wheel but didn't start the car. Motionless, he looked at the back of the hospital as if he were watching a movie on the wall of the Inavale Hotel, trying to choose which story he wanted to follow–one of the real lives behind a window shade, or the huge but chopped-up movie covering the wall.

My training on the footstool occasionally paid off, and I didn't even move on the prickly seat. With puffy eyes, Sam looked from Papa to the marigolds and back several times.

Papa pressed his hands into both of his eyes. Did his glass eye hurt when he pushed on it today, or did he have too many other things to worry about?

Finally, I couldn't stand it. We couldn't get anywhere standing still.

"Papa?" I said in my littlest voice. He jerked as if he had forgotten we were in the car. "Do they have bars on the windows so people won't escape?"

He looked at them. "They might worry that people's families will try to kidnap them and take them back home."

Sam asked, "Will Mama get better in there?"

He shook his head no, but he said, "I hope so. It's the best we can do."

Then he did the funniest thing I had ever seen him do in a car. He put the Buick in gear and turned the wheel to back up, but the engine wasn't running.

"You have to start the motor," I suggested quietly.

"You know what else? I need my kids up here in front with me." Sam and I never got to ride in the front seat, so we scrambled over the back of the front seat and slid into position beside Papa. The old Buick was so wide, there was room enough for yet another person. "Tell me if I make any other mistakes, okay?"

"I'm always Sam's co-pilot, you might want to know."

"She's good, too." Sam was trying to shake off his sadness.

"I didn't have a chance to tell you kids, but this hospital is experimenting with drugs and other things to treat people with nervous breakdowns. They're called 'wonder drugs.' Dr. Mary told me about it yesterday. Just in time. Just before I met with Judge Weiss. Doc Buchanan agreed: anything's better than the State Hospital."

Wonder drugs. I didn't care if Dr. Mary were a Communist if she could keep Mama out of Hastings.

Papa slowly threaded the long, crowded streets out of Omaha, a city with so many streets that, after running through the alphabet and important peoples' names, it resorted to numbers, which Sam said could go to infinity. Did they have an Infinity Street, I wondered.

Just outside Omaha, I had to ask Papa. "Are Sam and I going to be orphans?"

"Of course not. Not as long as you have a mom or a dad."

"Do grandparents count? Jane Englehardt lives with her grandma and grandpa."

Sam made a strangling sound out of the movies. "I'd rather die than live with Grandma Strang,"

"Let's cross that bridge when we come to it," Papa answered.

This didn't qualify as a promise that we wouldn't go to live with Grandma Strang.

Once we got on the country roads, we took a different route.

"Aren't we going past the ice cream factory at Fairmont?"

"I think we've seen enough of Highway 6 for awhile. This will take a little longer, but there's something you like on this road."

Sam sat up straighter. "I know what it is."

Not until we pulled into a long driveway did I remember. A long time ago, we had accidentally seen this corral where four Shetland ponies were already saddled up with their bridles tied to a merry-go-round, just like the Hastings Fair. People could rent a real live pony and ride in a circle until their money ran out.

"I have two extra quarters, so you can both ride."

I gasped.

Sam immediately ran to the fence. "Jeb can have mine." He really meant that he didn't want to ride, but this sounded more like a Boy Scout.

On two of the ponies sat little kids in new cowboy hats with chaps outlined in fringe and shiny six-guns in matching holsters. They were whooping and kicking their ponies, trying to make them go faster, but none of the ponies could walk faster than the slowest one in the circle.

Sam put one foot on the bottom rung of the fence, just like a movie cowboy, except he had to stretch to see between the top two rungs.

"Guess which is my favorite one."

Sam answered, "I already know."

"I'll bet it's that little black and white paint," Papa guessed.

My favorite was actually the miniature palomino, but I said, "You're right."

Sam looked at me with a smirk but didn't say anything. He knew it was the palomino, too.

"How about it, Sugar? I'll go pay."

Faced with riding a real horse for the first time in my life, I suddenly lost heart. It wouldn't change anything or make anybody happier. Besides, riding La Cheetah or Luther was one thing, but a real pony was quite another. Kind of scary. A cowboy outfit would have helped, even Sam's empty holster set.

"I have an idea. Let's pretend," I tried to sound like Roy Rogers, "we've just rounded up a herd of wild horses and locked them in the corral."

"Wild Shetland ponies? Wearing saddles and bridles?" Trust Sam to be literal, especially about horses. "That's pretty stupid."

"Who's calling Jeb stupid?" Papa hoisted me up to sit on the top pole of the fence.

"Not me," Sam clarified, shifting the blame to some invisible person.

The fence scratched the back of my bare legs, but I was so glad to have Papa balancing me that I didn't care. He put his arm around Sam's shoulders.

"Seems to me us cowpokes have put in a hard day's work." Papa looked old enough to be a grandpa.

As I watched the Shetlands plod along on their stubby legs with their bridles tied to the merry-go-round, I wanted to convince myself. "The wild horses will be happier here. They'll get plenty to eat and . . . not have to be afraid. All by themselves, out on the prairie, day and night." I threw in something I had read, "With only the wind for company."

Papa said, "We can sure hope so."

Sam scowled, "I'd like to yank those spoiled brats off and put Jeb up there. They don't even know how to ride."

As if I did. But I would ride a real horse someday, probably not my very own, but you never knew. It could happen.

All the way home, Papa followed county roads with lots of right angle turns, mile after mile with no fences or telephone poles, lined on both sides with ripe wheat the color of butter in the fading light. My favorite kind of country. We drove down the main streets of tiny towns, some hardly more than a grain elevator and weigh station, others with post offices and grocery stores, all with unfamiliar names like Touhy and Ulysses. We even saw a sign leading to Surprise, Nebraska.

At Friend, another fine name for a town, we crossed the highway from the north onto a gravel road. Instead of stopping at Hebron, Papa turned at Alexandria, crossing the railroad his father helped build. Grandpa Wilder could name every single town in order along that fifty-mile stretch. The afternoon sun, the crunchy roads, the wavy ride made me sleepy. Sam was nodding, either fighting sleep or silently talking to an idea, probably one involving gunpowder. He often entertained himself this way.

"Are you sleepy?" I asked Papa.

"A little bit."

"Would you like me to sing a song?"

"No," Sam said quickly.

"I sure would," Papa overrode him.

To myself, I rejected "Blue Skies" and "Happy Trails To You" as not quite right. I suggested, "I could sing the song Mrs. Vince taught the sixth grade."

"That crum-bum thing," Sam muttered. "The only dumb thing she ever did."

"They sang it in the last school assembly where, you might remember, Sam took all the honors."

Papa said, "I sure wish I could've been there. Let's hear it."

I cleared my throat and found an acceptable pitch:

"Ship me somewhere east of Suez

Where the best is like the worst

And there ain't no Ten Commandments

And a cat can raise a thirst . . . ."

By now Sam had covered his ears with his hands, an overreaction, in my opinion. I cleared my throat for the chorus:

"On the road to Mandalay, where the flying fishes play, and the dawn comes up like thunder: outer China 'cross the bay."

After a pause, Papa shook his head. "I must say, I didn't expect that."

"There're a lot of things I don't understand."

"Me, neither," Papa agreed.

"First of all, where's Mandalay?"

Sam answered, "Mrs. Vince said it was somewhere near China. But she didn't have a map to prove it."

"She would know, if anybody would," I defended her. "But how can the dawn come up like thunder?"

"They're probably in the middle of a war," Papa answered.

"Which war?"

"I don't know. There's always a war somewhere."

I could tell by the little sigh under his words that I had room for just one more question. "How can fish fly?"

Papa slowed down for the turn to Deshler, then answered, "With a lot of imagination, Sugar."

That made sense to me, as Papa always did. I moved closer to him and tried to put my arm around his shoulder, but my hand could only reach his neck. It was cool, but cool from being sweaty.

Sam nodded asleep and awake several times before he finally let his head fall onto my shoulder. I held completely still, even after my right foot fell asleep. Somewhere near Guide Rock, my head dropped onto Papa's shoulder and I also fell asleep, but that was all right because we were almost home.

CHAPTER 50

POLYPHONY

IF ANYBODY THOUGHT IT WOULD BE A RELIEF TO have Mama gone, they had another think coming, as Mama herself would say. A huge hole in our lives circled around inside the trailer, a block of silence with constantly changing shapes and different temperatures, playing tricks with the swinging smoke ribbon on the log cabin clock. Every day I played Mama's favorite piano music from earlier John Thompson books, like "Down in the Valley," "You Are My Sunshine," and "The Caissons Go Rolling Along," music she liked to sing and I could play without mistakes. If you're sending someone a song long distance, I figured it better be perfect. Sometimes I played songs from our Methodist hymnal, ones not mentioning God, who Mama might still think was a dog. That left us some great Easter alleluias and Thanksgiving songs of praise. Christmas carols were also safe: Round John Virgin and Deck the Halls with Boston Charlie. I sang them with our private Wilder words to cheer Mama up.

Once a week, Papa and Sam and I wrote her letters which Papa mailed with the warning that they may not let her read them yet. I said that she was too busy to read, a lie meaning that she probably needed to postpone thinking about some things until she was older. I certainly knew how that felt. Every day, I set aside time to talk to Mama silently, telling her about important events—Mrs. Dungan frying another egg on the sidewalk, the golden pyramids of ripe wheat rising beside the grain elevators, Papa's attempts at making waffles. I secretly named them "schwaffles," a cross between "shredded" and "waffles," because they always stuck to the waffle iron and landed on our plates in ragged pieces. Mama's were always perfect.

Without Mama, Sam and I stuck close to home and did everything Papa told us to do, sometimes before he told us. We ate cereal every morning and bread and milk every lunch, but when Papa got home from work, we all pitched in and made a good supper, like boiled hot dogs and sauerkraut. Nobody complained once about eating canned spinach or half-raw macaroni, partly because Papa put a slice of Velveeta on almost everything, but mostly because he looked so tired every night. Maybe he had always looked that way, and I hadn't noticed. Papa hugged us a lot and, in the evenings, read the funnies to us and played Scrabble instead of going out to work on somebody else's car. Like Mama, I usually beat both of them at Scrabble, because they went for easy, cheap words instead of expensive, esoteric ones. Miss Reynolds had just taught me *esoteric*, containing a 4:4 vowel-to-consonant ratio and sounding as if it lacked a final syllable. A crisp word with sharp edges.

Amazingly, Methodist ladies and even some Catholics brought us hamburger casseroles and cold fried chicken, while Mr. Whitaker kept us in cookies and occasional cupcakes from Eddy's Bakery. What a friend. Sometimes he stayed for supper and Papa sent surplus casseroles home with him. Mr. Whitaker would wink at me and pretend to steal the rest of the chicken, fully knowing Sam would kill for the drumsticks. We also had to resume going to church out of gratitude for the ladies who fed us. Papa might have let us sit with Mrs. Keindorf, but she now came late and sat by herself in the back pew, slipping out before she had to talk to anyone or to shake Reverend Harkin's hand. She didn't wear so much jewelry, either.

Every day I practiced my piano lesson a whole hour, pretending that Mama was holding the cardboard over my hands and counting the beats, but I knew it was a figment of my imagination. Sam started coming in from outside to putter around his bedroom while I practiced. We both needed noise, any noise, to fill the silence left by Mama, a silence Papa couldn't fill even if he hadn't been a quiet man to start with. What must orphans feel, when we were only *half*-orphans?

Sam and I never fought, we didn't even argue, and we never, ever talked about Mama. It felt as if we had each lost an arm and a leg and together made one whole kid. Automatically, we re-stocked our dirt clods and broomcorn spears and fought occasional listless skirmishes at the fort, but a lot of kids hadn't returned from vacation, so the undeclared cease-fire was still partially in effect. Sam and I dutifully rode our bikes to the Inavale hide-out to check on his pipe bomb supplies, and we hid the Formula in a new place every day although we knew no one was looking for it. We only saw Will Hankins occasionally in town because he was working so hard in the fields.

In addition to my spelling lessons, Miss Reynolds required us to come in and talk to her at least once a day, so Sam began working on a merit badge in Bookbinding, which says it all. She enrolled us both in a summer reading program from the University of Nebraska which sent out certificates and a gold seal for every ten books you could prove that you read. To prove it, you had to give oral book reports to your local librarian. Our "local librarian" not only assigned our reading but also required written reports which she graded, making school feel like a cakewalk.

To console myself, I re-read *Black Beauty*, the Flicka and Thunderhead books and *Brighty of the Grand Canyon*, but Miss Reynolds wouldn't count re-reading anything for the University of Nebraska program. Without Miss Reynolds' permission, Mrs. Vince brought in her personal non-fiction book for me to read, a biography. Miss Reynolds humphed and I felt the same way until I discovered that it was the biography of a horse—Man o'War!

Reading this book wasn't like reading a novel, but it told the story of one of the greatest horses who ever lived, a "horse of mythic proportions." Soon I was boring Miss Reynolds and the family with facts. Facts from me, if you can imagine. Big Red had a 28-foot stride, lost only one race in his life because of an abscessed tooth, and broke three world records. His jockeys couldn't slow him down even when they stood up in the stirrups and pulled back on his reins. I added *furlong* to my word list, a lovely word containing two full words, and briefly considered renaming Luther Furlong, but he wouldn't come when I called him as it was. Unlike Alberta Clipper, Luther didn't celebrate another horse's victories. I never met such a stubborn pony.

Miss Reynolds pushed me through all the stupid Bobsey twins, the highly flawed Anne of Green Gables books and the insufferable Laura Ingalls Wilder series. At least, Willa Cather offered some challenges, but none like the poetry Miss Reynolds trotted out. While she didn't always have a handle on the right poetry books for my age, she figured any girl who had already faced Richard Cory's suicide and maggots eating people's brains underground was pretty much ready for anything.

The man who wrote Mama's poem about raging against the dying light also wrote a poem called "Fern Hill." I didn't completely understand it, but when Miss Reynolds read it out loud, it sounded like music. Not the words to a song, but music in the words themselves. I especially liked Emily Dickinson, whose poems were short and looked simple but fooled you halfway through. Like Miss Reynolds, she never got married but sounded lonesome. One day Miss Reynolds quoted something Emily Dickinson wrote in a letter to a friend: "There are words to which I lift my hat when I see them sitting on a page." That said it all. A quotation for the rest of my life. I wrote that sentence at the top of every new spelling list and every letter to Mama. One thing was certain: when Mama did come home, we would have wonderful conversations about poetry.

Without talking about it, Sam and I feared that Mama might never return, but we continued to add powerful ingredients to the Formula to protect her wherever she was. Sam put in a few grains of home-made gunpowder and threads from his Safety merit badge, while I stuffed in a scrap of "Abide with Me" from the Methodist Hymnal, and the whole last stanza of "Somebody Said It Couldn't Be Done" from *Tony's Scrapbook*, Mama's own book of poetry:

> There are thousands to tell you it cannot be done,
>
> There are thousands to prophesy failure;
>
> There are thousands to point out to you one by one,
>
> The dangers that wait to assail you.
>
> But just buckle in with a bit of a grin,
>
> Just take off your coat and go to it;
>
> Just start to sing as you tackled the thing
>
> That "cannot be done," and you'll do it.

For my piano lessons, I had learned to play simplified themes and variations by Rachmaninoff but was still struggling with a Bach prelude illustrating a technique called *polyphony*. Of course, I loved that word, both because it employed the ph-for f – trick and it wasn't spelled the way it sounded. Sam, the instant expert on everything I learned, declared Bach the most logical and rational of all composers, although he mispronounced it Polly Phoney, a good nickname for Doreen Cavin.

Polyphony required you to play two independent, equally important melodies at the same time, which Mrs. Keindorf compared to the lives of two people living in the same house like Sam and me or her and Mr. Keindorf. I was working my way toward fugues, which mixed polyphony with themes and variations, sounding more like a chemistry experiment which could blow up in your face than the inspiring, complicated solos Maxine Harkin played in church. Even after I knew what to listen for in a fugue, I always lost track of the melody after its third appearance, buried somewhere in her left hand or even her foot. And she had memorized it all in Braille. Lordy. Her ability to play fugues was one more reason why she should not be married to Marvin Harkin.

Today, as I finished my piano lesson with Bach's polyphonic prelude, I dropped my hands in my lap. "Papa says that sometimes a piano piece is a performance and other times it's an execution."

Mrs. Keindorf smiled broadly. She had drawn dotted lines to show how the thirty-second notes fell between the sixteenths, but in my hands, the notes fell more like Pick-up Sticks.

Because this July was extra hot, Mrs. Keindorf wore a short-sleeved linen dress starched to the eye-teeth. If Mama saw it, she would sniff that Mr. Keindorf was the dry cleaner and could press linen perfectly in his steam press the size of my chair-bed. Her dress was the color of ripe apricots, set off with a coral and pearl necklace, matching ring and peachy lipstick.

"First, tell me what you did right," she reminded me graciously.

"I remembered all the repeats and hit most of the accidentals."

"Good." She finished writing my lesson on her new stationery, monogrammed with a complicated "K" at the top. "Do you have any questions?" She always pronounced 'have' like 'haff.'

For almost a year, I had gazed at the picture of the magical city over her piano, pretending to play for the people living incredibly romantic lives in its tall towers and frilly buildings. I don't know why I waited, but today I finally summoned the courage to ask her about it.

"Is that a real city? Or a picture out of a fairy tale?"

Mrs. Keindorf tucked her hair into her perfect French roll and sat silently for a minute. I must have asked a stupid question, one of my specialties.

She spoke carefully, the way I tiptoed barefoot among the stickers on hot sand in the park. "It's not a picture. It's called an etching."

She looked out the sliding glass door into her back yard, bordered by an empty pasture and a tangled barbed wire fence. "It's where I . . . grew up."

Wow. I never thought of Mrs. Keindorf as a little girl, let alone living in such a splendid place. But that made sense.

"My home." She seemed to look for it beyond the pasture. "Its name is . . . Dresden."

I tried to sound more like Mrs. Dahlke than a girl from a trailer house. "You grew up around *real* castles?"

She swallowed twice. "Yes." She ran her fingers inside her coral necklace to pull it away from her neck and sucked in her plump lips until they almost disappeared. "And real palaces."

No wonder she was so elegant. She might secretly be related to a queen or at least an archduke.

Her voice sounded like a quiet violin. "And the Semperoper and the Schauspielhaus Theatre and the art academy and Katholische Hofkirche and Frauenkirche. A Baroque masterpiece on every block. The showcase of Europe."

I could barely sit on the piano bench. "Did you ever go *inside* a castle?"

"Every public holiday. The Residenzschloss. But the Zwinger Palace was more beautiful. My brother and I played on the grounds all the time." In the clouds billowing over the pasture behind her house, she seemed to see what she was describing. "Every Sunday after church, Johann and I would visit our favorite painting inside the Zwinger–Raphael's 'Sistine Madonna'." She shook her head. "I can barely believe it now. Every Sunday: Raphael's Madonna."

I had no idea who Raphael was but tried to see her memory reflected in her eyes, as I did with Mama's visions. I looked more closely at the picture. "Did you live in one of those towers?"

"Of course not. We lived in . . . ," she tried to clear her throat. "It doesn't . . . exist any more."

I should have known it was too good to be true. "Oh. So the magic city . . . is just your imagination?" To cover my disappointment, I consoled her. "I make up places all the time."

Mrs. Keindorf stood up so fast that she knocked over her chair. "Oh, Dresden existed all right." Her accent deepened. "It was bombed. In the war." Her eyes sparked.

With dread, I asked, "Wh-where is Dresden?"

"Where do you think? Germany." Mrs. Keindorf swallowed faster now.

Oh no. Sam and I had been bombing German cities for years. "There can't be many real castles in the whole world. Why would they bomb—"

"You tell me," she spit out. She spun the coral ring around and around her slender finger. "Not just the castles, Jeb. The cathedral. And art museums. The opera house. Markets, palaces, apartments, the railroad, schools, hospitals . . . ." She sucked in a breath. "All of it. The whole city."

She hugged herself and began walking around the living room, catching her spike heels in the shag carpet. "Everything. EVERYthing. Bombed it to rubble." She put her hand over her mouth as if she were saying something nasty. "The Zwinger alone. A masterpiece full of master-pieces. And our beloved cathedral."

Suddenly B-17s and Messerschmitts were *real*, not just in the mov-ies or on Sunday mornings in Sam's sofa-bed. "But why?"

"No reason. They had no reason to destroy Dresden except a pure hatred of culture. They could not bear to leave anything beautiful. That's how low human beings had descended by 1945. And ordinary bombs weren't enough." She spit out, "They *fire*-bombed Dresden. Bombs making winds of fire stronger than tornadoes. Between the bombs and the fires and the winds, not one. Single. Building was left standing in Old Town." She was drifting away, as Mama did, into a place only she could see.

The afternoon light reflected off the glass in front of the picture in little bursts of light, little explosions.

Her polished fingernails dug into her arm. "February 13, 1945. I had just married Helmut. War bride." She turned on me with the meanest voice she had ever used. "When they were done, Dresden looked like . . . Hebron after the tornado. Twenty Hebrons. Fifty. Miles and miles of rubble."

"Wh-who?"

"*Fifteen* square miles of empty walls and burned bricks. The entire Altstadt, the medieval city. Just . . . piles of bricks."

I tried to imagine the picture turned into a smoking ruin. "Wh-where did the people go?"

Mrs. Keindorf sank into the cowboy sofa. "Where do you think? With the winds of hell burning over their heads?" She was retreating further and further away.

"They b-bombed . . . p-people? They killed–?"

"What do you *think*?" she laughed bitterly. "Thirty thousand dead. Maybe more. How do you count ashes?"

Mrs. Keindorf began rubbing the wooden arm of the sofa, as if she were trying to remove a spot. Mama did that, too. My stomach ached.

"Helmut and I hid in a cellar. It was dark and all of us panicked, tried to escape at the same time. We were pushed upstairs by the people behind us, trampling . . . the slow ones under our feet. Then we saw the burning street, the falling ruins and the terrible firestorm. Explosion after explosion, and so many people horribly burned. Adults shrunk to the size of dogs, people on fire running back and forth, screaming for their children, and fire everywhere, everywhere fire, and all the time the hot wind of the firestorm threw us back into the burning house we were trying to escape from." She covered her face with her hands. "Ogh. Ogh."

As nauseous as I felt, I had to ask one more question. "W-Who did it?"

Mrs. Keindorf looked up at me with tears in her eyes. "The British. The Americans."

Americans?! There must be some mistake. Americans wouldn't kill innocent people.

"People in the street screaming and waving their arms, then suddenly dropping to the ground. The fire tornadoes had burned up all the oxygen. They suffocated and then burnt to cinders. I saw a woman carrying . . . a baby in her arms. She ran, then fell . . . and her baby flew in an arc . . . into the fire."

She couldn't catch her breath. "I cannot forget these terrible things. I can never forget them. I see them in my sleep."

I didn't know what to do. I wanted to put my arm around her, but that might upset her more. I asked in my quietest voice, "Would you like a glass of water?" I couldn't imagine walking into any other part of her house like the kitchen.

"No."

"When Mama cries, sometimes I bring her a glass of water." I hoped where Mama was now that someone would bring her water. "Well, I did, before they put her in the hospital."

When Mrs. Keindorf looked up at me, I saw that her lipstick had left her lips and gone into tiny lines all around her mouth.

"Your mama's little girl." She began to hiccup. I could tell she was trying not to break down crying. "You must be a great comfort to her."

"I couldn't save her." I shouldn't talk about Mama behind her back. "From . . . having a nervous breakdown." Maybe Janet could have kept Mama out of the hospital. Maybe Janet should have lived and not me.

Mrs. Keindorf tried to return to being my teacher. "Oh child, I know. It was too much for her to bear—her dead baby, the Hebron tornado . . . ."

Even Mrs. Keindorf seemed to know about Mama. When Mama was around, nobody cared; now she was gone, she was all they could talk about.

Mrs. Keindorf pulled out a starched handkerchief and touched it to the corner of her eyes, more beautiful, more graceful than any movie star. She swallowed twice. "Dresden makes you think that nothing good will ever happen again. But. Remember 'La Valse'? Ravel? No matter what they do, they can't kill music."

She shivered as if it were cold. "Jeb, I think . . . we need to quit early today. We'll make up the time next week." She pressed her handkerchief to her eyes, but her tears still ran down her cheeks.

I gathered my piano books and tried not to look at the picture or at her. I didn't know how to cheer her up. "I'm sorry if I said something wrong. And played so many mistakes."

She looked at me with big wet eyes "You're beginning to play music and not just notes. No one can teach you to do that."

I didn't want to leave her crying, but I couldn't think of anything else to say. As I closed the door behind me, I saw her standing, silhouetted against the glass doors, hugging herself, with one leg out of line as if she had broken her ankle.

I wanted to say, "I love you." Instead I called out, "See you next week." When the front door clicked shut, I kissed it.

CHAPTER 51

FIRST ECLIPSE

"**S**UGAR! WAKE UP!"

Someone's hand was shaking my shoulder as I tried to swim upward out of sleep.

"M-Mama?" Had she come home? Maybe she never left. Maybe I just dreamed . . . Did she want me to play the piano–?

"Sugar?"

Against the streetlight shining through the window, I saw Papa's outline. What? A tornado! Sam?

Papa's hand rested, heavy and peaceful, on my shoulder. "You kids said you wanted me to wake you up for the eclipse."

"Oh." I shook my head awake. "Oh! Wh-where's Sam?"

Papa chuckled. "Sawing 'em off. So much for our budding scientist: all theory. How about you?"

"No." I threw off my sheet and struggled to get up from the low bed. "I mean, yes."

Sam, Boy Astronomer, stand-in for Tom Swift the Wonder Inventor, was going to miss a total eclipse of the moon? I was thrilled, since my times alone with Papa were so rare.

Papa pulled down the cuffs of my flour-sack pajamas. "Where are your shoes?"

I was still too sleepy to remember.

"I'll carry you." Papa quietly opened the trailer door and bent over at the bottom of the step with his back to me. "Hop on."

Even though I was too old to be carried piggy-back, I wasn't about to pass up this chance. Sticking one leg through each of his waiting arms, I carefully looped my arms around his neck. As a little girl, I would play-fully try to choke him, but I had matured a lot since then. We lurched through patches of moonshade all over the yard, skirted the ditch where I had flown through the air in the daredevil show, heard Tag woofing at us down the alley and stumbled across the broomcorn field to the fort. Here we couldn't see the streetlight at all. Papa carefully let me down on my bare feet, which sank into the warm, dry earth. Crickets rattled the moonlight around us, and the back of Mr. Whitaker's house loomed large and white, a fat, friendly ghost.

"It's about to start. The radio said 2:30 a.m."

In spite of Sam's elaborate lecture on eclipses, delivered in his Public Speaking voice and heavily laced with mumbo-jumbo, Papa's simple draw-ing had explained it perfectly: in one night, the earth and moon passed through every phase in a game of shadows and spirals. Tonight, the moon was almost too bright to look at directly, washing out all but the brightest stars, like the Big Dipper and Lyra-Vega directly overhead, which I still called the Eye.

We sat on the edge of the fort with our feet in the trench.

"You kids have really dug in here. What's that?" Papa pointed to the shadowy end of the fort.

"Our ammo dump." I remembered Mrs. Vince. "I mean, ammuni-tion depot."

"I hope you kids are careful. You know, someone could get hurt pretty bad in your little wars."

"We are careful," I fibbed. Unlike Mama, Papa didn't notice all my scrapes and scuffed knees or Sam's cuts and bruises. When you're covered with burn scars, you don't worry about the little things.

As Mama would say, Papa had no room to talk, having grown up half-wild on the farm with a blind eye and missing fingers to prove it. Sam and I were enthralled by his stories of the Olden Days, like the Halloween he and his buddies stole a Model-T, dismantled it and reconstructed it on top of Belvedere's grain elevator. Or the hot rods he built from scratch, including one with two scrap motors end-to-end, which he thought would make it run twice as fast. Or my personal favorite, when he fell asleep on his second-hand police motorcycle and landed in a haystack. The speedometer had pegged at 98.

Sam's favorite story was about Papa's experiments with his cousin Kenny and an old muzzle loader. They would fill the barrel with powder, a wad, and nails and would pour a little more powder where the "cap" would go, whatever that was. Then Papa would light it with a match. Several times, Sam told me, Kenny would land flat on his back with the explosion. Sam could barely retell the story without choking with laughter.

In the Round Prairie war, we had no rules of combat except the obvious ones: nothing as dangerous as broken glass and no real weapons like knives or guns. The enemy was warned that if they didn't observe these simple rules, Sam could totally demolish their forts with pipe bombs and Molotov cocktails. The most effective weapons on both sides remained subterfuge, superior numbers and surprise attacks. Other kids had tried offering bribes, and we had tried holding hostages for ransom, but neither scheme worked. During the winter, Sam had surreptitiously mapped their tunnels behind Eddy's Bakery, a Tactical Advantage of the first order, especially if Sam were forced to use rotten egg gas.

"Look: it's starting," Papa pointed to the tiny crescent of earth shadow starting across the moon.

I was mesmerized. Slowly, slowly, ever so slowly, the earth's shadow spread across the moon's face like a hand, leaving a smear the color of dried blood. The night shivered, as if the moonlight had been warming it, and the crickets' ratchet-rachet fell silent. Tag trotted up and down his back fence, restless.

In the silent dark, I asked Papa the question I tried not to ask more than once a day. "You sure miss Mama, don't you?"

"I sure do."

"Me, too."

When he reached over to pat my knee, I immediately held his hand, calloused and dry, and felt for the notch where his finger was missing. "Will Mama . . . do you think . . . Will Mama ever come home?"

"We can only hope for the best." At least he didn't add, as he always did, that we should also prepare for the worst. "As soon as they let me visit her, we'll know more."

Mama had been gone over a month.

The night was almost dark now, but a different dark than a moonless night. I had never noticed that darkness came in different degrees.

"They don't hurt her, do they?"

His voice sounded thicker. "They have to do what they have to do. Just like us."

Sometimes you'd rather hear a lie than the truth.

Now the moon was completely covered by the earth's shadow, forming a smoky rose-colored disk surrounded by the stars it had obliterated with its own light.

Papa held my hand in both of his. "I never cease to be amazed at an eclipse. A good reminder that the old earth keeps going and doesn't much care what happens to us. Locked in orbit with that little guy up there, revolving in and out of each other's shadows. Feels like we're going in circles, but we never end up in the same place. It's as beautiful as anything I know."

Papa put his arm around my shoulders. "Getting tired? Want to go in? This takes quite awhile."

I put my arm around his waist and leaned against his side warm and solid through his shirt. "We have to wait till the moon comes back."

"If you say so."

"I love you so much, Papa."

"I love you so much, too, Sugar. I don't know what I'd do without you and Sam."

And so Papa and I sat in that magical July night which would never come back exactly that way again, smack in the middle of a broomcorn field, not even two specks on the earth, but with our arms around each other, and waited for the moon to grow round again.

CHAPTER 52

RECONSTRUCTION

ONE NIGHT WHEN SAM AND I WERE DRYING DISHES, Sam casually mentioned that the Boy Scouts were having a Jamboree in Kansas in two weeks. Long ago, I had recorded *Jamboree* as a good name for a horse, although the Boy Scouts typically wasted it on their huge annual camp-out. It sounded like a glorified picnic in the park until Sam explained they had to cook their own food three times a day–including chopping wood, starting a campfire, and cleaning up afterward. They also had to sleep on the ground with red ants and spiders.

Papa pulled the plug from the dishwater. His hands looked enormous in the trailer's tiny stainless steel sink. "Do you want to go?"

"It costs money."

"How much? Maybe we can afford it."

Sam almost dropped the frying pan he was drying.

I couldn't believe it. We could never cash in our allowance, but Papa was offering an exotic vacation to Sam? Besides, would Papa leave me alone all day for a week? What if something happened to him on the job? Or what if he just left, like Grandpa Strang deserted Mama and Uncle Ralph? Even if I moved in with Mr. Whitaker or Miss Reynolds, I would get awfully lonesome. Although I wouldn't starve.

Sam started talking extra fast. "Mike Letson can't go, and I could take his spot and he'd let me borrow all of his stuff—his sleeping bag and mess kit with one of those knife-fork-spoon tools that hook together. I already have my Boy Scout knife." Realizing that expressing gratitude was in his best interests, he added, "Thanks to Jeb."

Obviously, Sam had thoroughly researched the situation and was way ahead of Papa and me. "But it still costs money. For the food and bus and incidentals."

Incidentals, my eye. All that money was going to Marvin the Larva so he could abuse the very Scouts who paid him. The Boy Scouts had reached a new low, costing money just like church.

"How much?" Papa repeated.

"I found out, under special circumstances I can 'solicit funds' from private citizens."

"Really," Papa said.

"Really." I echoed him.

We both smelled a rat.

Papa lined us up on Sam's sofa-bed for three-fourths of a family council. If Mama were home, we would never have made it to the sofa-bed.

"I, uh . . . already talked to Miss Reynolds," Sam confessed.

"I hope you started by asking how you could repay her."

"Well, but . . . guess what? She said she'd pay my whole way on the condition of absolute secrecy since she didn't want 'every Tom, Dick and Harry to hit her up for travel expenses to pseudo-military exercises using child soldiers'."

Papa laughed out loud and big for the first time since Mama left. "We'll figure out something we can do for her."

Sam looked around Papa to me. "You know what else, Jeb? She asked what she could give you that would be the equivalent."

Now the conversation was getting interesting. I could spend that money as many ways as I spent my fake allowance.

A few days before Sam left, Papa announced that I would stay with Grandma Strang for that whole week.

Grandma Strang! Not only the meanest grown-up I knew, but so old and frail I might knock her over with any sudden movement.

"Not Grandma," I wailed. "I can take care of myself," then hastily added, "as long as you come home every night, Papa."

"I know you can, Jeb, but I would worry about you all day if you didn't have a grown-up around."

"Will Hankins doesn't need a grown-up around. In fact, he could look after me. He could be my new big brother." This was starting to sound good. Will could even drive.

Sam spluttered, "Brother?! Will Hankins?!"

"He could stay here until you came home every day, Papa. He loves our trailer and I could make him bread and butter or leftover church casseroles. He's so skinny, he must always be hungry."

"Mama would never, ever let you do that." Sam must feel desperate if he played this card.

"She wouldn't let you go to the Jamboree, either," I countered.

Papa brought out his Ultimate Weapon. "Sugar, will you stay with Grandma Strang as a personal favor to me?"

I had no defense against this argument. Wilders, especially Papa, were required to do Personal Favors for people all the time.

"If you desert me with Grandma Strang, I'll kill myself."

Papa leaned close to me, which lined up his glass eye with his good one. "If I deserted anyone with Grandma Strang, I'd kill *my*self."

Sunday afternoon before Sam left on the bus, Papa drove us all to Hebron so I could move in with Grandma. Sam called it my "Brownie Jamboree," all the while gleefully separating and rejoining the knife-fork-spoon from Mike Letson's mess kit. At least, I would eat better than he did. For starters, Grandma made great pancakes.

As I stood in Grandma's tiny front yard to wave them off in the Buick, Sam leaned around Papa and smirked, "Don't do anything I wouldn't do," an expression he had heard from some moron like Marvin or Reverend Harkin. Considering the riot at the movie theater, Sam's advice gave me complete freedom short of murder.

Papa suggested, "Better yet, don't do anything that would cost you footstool time." This was serious, realistic advice. I could write the book on those rules. He added, "You know, Grandma has a lot of stories. Get her to tell you some."

Stories? Grandma Strang?

Because we had lived in Hebron during third grade, I knew the town as well as Round Prairie, although gaps where whole city blocks had blown away in the tornado kept confusing me. People had trucked off the wreckage downtown, but in the side streets, piles of bricks and splintered lumber still indicated where houses once stood, now like teetering, lopsided tombstones. The house we had rented had only lost its roof, but across the street, from a gaping hole in the ground, I tried to reconstruct the Fosters' house, especially the screened-in porch where Mrs. Foster let us neighborhood kids play and sometimes fed us warm cookies. How could that big, two-story house just vanish, leaving only an empty basement, a concrete box set into the ground, where we had played with Jimmy Foster's electric trains? Big pieces of their house must be scattered across the prairie where some farmer might use them for repairs, or some kids digging a fort might find Jimmy's green metal dump truck and wonder where it came from. What had happened to Jimmy's family? Where were they now?

Every morning, I watched construction crews pick through the wreckage to reclaim and rebuild what they could, like putting together a puzzle with pieces missing. It would never make the same picture again but might look all right in a different way. The two most interesting ruins were the courthouse, which had lost its central tower, and the Catholic Church, which was now completely flat except for Jesus inside the half-dome. The Catholics still claimed it was a miracle, but in my opinion, a better miracle would have made the tornado skip Hebron altogether.

What could God's Plan be for a tornado? Asking Grandma would be like kicking up a red ant hill, although I wondered what she would say about God choosing to demolish certain houses and leaving others completely alone. Maybe God's Plan was like the Inavale drive-in movie, and people could only figure out what was happening in their hotel room or house but never see the bigger movie projected onto them. I needed to think about this more and couldn't postpone it much longer. Things were piling up for me to think about, no doubt about it.

At Grandma's house, I slept on the living room sofa with the street-light in my eyes, so I felt right at home. The first night, as I tucked myself in, I ventured a question as far from God and his Plan as I could get.

"Do you still have those little painted dolls? The ones which fit into each other, and you take one apart and inside is another one, and another, down to a solid block of wood?"

She answered from her tiny bedroom. "I threw them away." I couldn't believe that I had heard right. "Didn't you know any little girls who needed a toy?" I could nominate one on the spot.

"Little girls don't need toys."

That showed how much she knew, all right. Hebron's ditches and alleys were still littered with broken toys—headless dolls, toy wheels, erector set pieces, Lincoln logs. Somewhere, a little kid was searching for every one of them.

"Besides, those dolls weren't toys," Grandma added. "The Sturdevants gave them to me just to throw it in my face: they were the rich bedbugs, and I did the ironing."

"Didn't Mama have toys when she was a little girl?"

"When you're trying to put food on the table, you don't think about toys. Now go to sleep."

"Mama didn't have *one* toy?" I asked the streetlight outside the window, a short metal pillar with a glass shaped like a big candle flame. Why wasn't it broken in the tornado?

"Oh, she wanted one of those silly monkey dolls, but I didn't have any old work socks to make one. If I remember right, I think I sewed her a stuffed animal."

"What kind of animal? A dog?" Mama had gone to the hospital before she could help me make the little stuffed dog she had promised.

"Go to sleep, Judith Beatrice."

"What about Christmas?" I suddenly missed Luther. Thank goodness, Papa had remembered to send Maybe with me to Hebron.

I heard her sigh. "Christmas. People would bring toys and baskets of food—whole hams and oranges in the middle of winter, if you can imagine."

I was just ready to say how wonderful that was, when Grandma added, "I slammed the door in their faces. Of all the nerve! We weren't charity cases." The light went out under her door. "Now hush up and go to sleep."

After that, I intended to avoid Grandma Strang by playing in the park, climbing the fire escape tube in my old school, and riding Maybe to Rose Hill Cemetery to talk to Janet, where I could also visit the kids who died of the flu in 1918. Nobody ever paid attention to them. When I told Grandma about Mrs. Keindorf's brother, the POW who also didn't have a tombstone, she said something that knocked me off my feet.

"Hebron had a lot of German soldiers. You know, the camp was between here and the river. They marched right by my house after work every night."

In Grandma's back yard!

"Us Methodist women took turns baking bread for them or sour fruit pie, since sugar was rationed. A body would have to have a heart of stone not to feed those boys. They were so thin. Pitiful. And work! Did they know how to work."

After that, she told story after story about individual prisoners she had befriended, as well as men who hitched rides on trains, then walked door to door asking for work. People called them *hoboes*, she said, but that wasn't fair.

One night, Uncle Ralph came over for supper, after which we sat on her tiny front porch, Ralph and I on the step, Grandma in her rocking chair. A square of light through Grandma's screen door lay like a little rug on the porch floor.

Uncle Ralph blew on his coffee. "Mom, did you read that article in the paper about the H-bomb we tested last March? Fifteen megatons. It's about goddam time the U. S. advertised our superiority in the arms race."

"What's a megaton?" I asked.

"A million tons of TNT. Enough to kill everyone in Nebraska and then some. That bomb completely destroyed a whole island. Blasted it off the face of the earth." With his free hand, he threw something invisible into the air. "Phhfft. The Reds can put that in their pipe and smoke it."

Grandma shook her head. "Where's it all going to end." She sat in her small ladies' rocker without arms, squeaking the same porch floorboard each time she rocked. "I'm so glad you're too old to be drafted if we have another war."

"We've got another war. It's called the Cold War."

I had to choose between the Cold War and another pressing question. "Is there more than one kind of hydrogen?"

Ralph stopped with his coffee cup halfway to his mouth. "That depends on what you mean by 'hydrogen.' There are hydrogen ions." His dark hair fell in a wave across his forehead just like Mama's, except his hair wasn't dyed. The roots of Mama's hair had turned white overnight when Papa was in the explosion.

"What's an ion? How do you spell it?"

"I-O-N. It's a hydrogen atom which is missing its electron, a kind of crippled hydrogen. It measures the acidity of a solution."

What a word! Two vowels and one consonant, and meaning crippled hydrogen! I would choose the perfect moment to spring this on Sam, hopefully in front of his Boy Scout buddies.

"You're so smart, Uncle Ralph. You know all about building houses and about stars and about stuff like hydrogen."

"For God's sake, Jeb, it's just high school chemistry."

"I'm a long ways from high school. I'm only nine."

He sipped his coffee and looked at the half-built house across the street. "If you're smart, you'll stay right where you are. Nine is the perfect age."

I couldn't imagine him or Mama nine years old.

"What did they decide to do about the courthouse?" Grandma asked.

"They're going to leave the roof flat. It's too expensive to rebuild the tower."

"What a shame. It was so purdy."

Before the tornado, the courthouse was the most exotic building for miles around. It looked like a small, serious castle.

"Is that what they did in Dresden?" I asked. "Just make flat roofs out of all the missing spires and turrets?"

"Dresden where?"

"Germany. After the firebombs."

"Good God, what are they teaching you in school?"

"My piano teacher told me. She lived in Dresden."

"Oh Jesus." He ran his hand through his hair. "I suspect there wasn't enough left of Dresden to worry about any roofs." He looked at Grandma and shook his head. "They'll be digging that place out for fifty years."

A mosquito whined around my ear in the sudden silence. "I went to your observatory today. Did you put a dome on it because of tornadoes? Sam said domes are strong."

It was odd to talk to the man version of Mama, except Ralph looked right at me. "No. They need domes so they can rotate to observe the whole sky."

In the humid night, Grandma patted her neck with an embroidered hanky. "You must be so tired. Working from dawn to dark."

"I'm lucky to have the work. It's just a goddam shame it has to be on the back of people with such bad luck."

"I wouldn't call it luck, Ralph."

"I know. God knows, I know what you'd call it."

"You must admit—"

"That God decided to wipe out the Shalkas and the Buzecks and the Marquarts? The hardest-working, most honest people you could ever meet?"

"It's not for us to know, Son."

"It sure as hell isn't."

This seemed like a good time to change the subject. "Papa and I watched the lunar eclipse."

Grandma huffed. "Leave it to Frank Wilder to have you out in the middle of the night looking at the moon."

"What did you think?" Uncle Ralph asked.

"It was the most magical thing I ever saw."

"Huh. I haven't watched an eclipse for years and years."

"They have them every once in awhile, you know."

"They do?" Uncle Ralph was actually teasing me.

I swatted a mosquito on my arm. "You should fix up your observatory. It's such a perfect little building, better than a dollhouse. Papa said he'd help fix your telescope."

Instead of exploding as usual, Uncle Ralph sounded sad. "I gave up stargazing a long time ago."

"Miss Reynolds said the same thing, sort of. But, you know, the stars are still out there, whether you look at them or not, just being beautiful."

In the light coming through the screen door, I could see Uncle Ralph's little smile.

"Bunch of nonsense," Grandma said.

"Mama taught me how to wish on stars," I thought this might add weight to my argument.

"I'm sure she did," Grandma said under her breath.

Uncle Ralph said quietly, "Edie and I had some wonderful times looking at stars."

Grandma snorted. "Ridiculous. Out half the night." She paused. "How's the grocery store coming along?"

"We're almost done, then we start on the Western Auto." Ralph gulped down the rest of his coffee and handed Grandma his cup. "I've got to be going, Mom. Thanks for supper." He lightly hit my thigh with the back of his hand like Sam sometimes did. "Thanks for the talk, Jeb."

Even in the middle of "rack and ruin," as Mama called it, Uncle Ralph didn't seem as mad as before, although he still cussed.

Mending was one of the few chores I could do for Grandma Strang, since her eyes had such bad cataracts. She considered an eye operation a waste of good money, but Mama said she couldn't afford one, anyway, and used that excuse to maintain her pride. Grandma wore thick dime store reading glasses and insisted they were good enough, thank you, but they were designed for men and forever rested halfway down her nose. Few things made Papa madder than seeing how Grandma's famous pride had hurt both Mama and Ralph. He said he didn't care what she had done to herself.

Grandma needed a new pair of pajamas and had already bought the material on sale, a red checked cotton. I had never sewn a whole piece of clothing, but she said she would teach me how, since Edith certainly wouldn't.

"Mama has a lot of things on her mind," I argued.

In response, Grandma clicked her false teeth.

First we had to pick apart Grandma's old pajamas to make a pattern, a deliberate destruction before we could create something new. Then oh-so-carefully we cut the new checked material. She guided me with her bony hands, which were spotted like Charlie Whitaker's, but didn't shake. On each knuckle, her skin was so thin and shiny, I could see her bones underneath.

Even in July, Grandma wore three dresses and two aprons on top of each other. I think that was all she owned and was afraid they would accidentally burn up or blow away if she didn't keep them on her body. Electric fans cost too much, so we worked on her front porch from mid-morning until dark every day, with time out for wonderful food like cornbread and ham hocks and beans. Grandma rocked and rocked, shelling peas or peeling potatoes, stirring the capsule of color into a bowl of margarine, sometimes braiding a rag rug if her eyes didn't hurt too much.

I sat at her feet on the splintery porch, sewing her pajamas with the tiniest running stitch I could muster, then turned each seam over to stitch along the same line, but in reverse. Using double thread each direction, I figured the material would disintegrate before the thread gave out. Each morning, she inspected my stitches and decided which needed to be unpicked and re-sewn.

At first, I protested. "It doesn't need to be perfect. Who's going to see you in your pajamas?"

"Nobody but me. But why wouldn't you do the very best job you can? In school, do you aim at being second best?"

She had me there.

She pushed up her glasses, which fell right back down. "I'll wear these pajamas every night for the rest of my life." She smiled, not in her fake way. "I'll probably die in them."

That changed everything. My stitches grew smaller and smaller, almost as neat as machine stitches. While I sewed, she talked, talked more than I had ever imagined she could talk, talked as if she never talked to anybody before and never would again. I soon became so intrigued with Grandma's stories that I started making my own decisions to unpick certain seams to extend my sewing sessions. It was such a strange and happy feeling to do something absolutely right, like playing Bach without missing a single note. I re-set the right sleeve twice and the left one three times even though both had passed her inspection on my first attempt.

One day Grandma began talking about Baby Janet even though I hadn't asked. I held my breath so I wouldn't stop her with a question.

"Such a purdy baby. Even three months premature, she had little wisps of red hair, must've gotten from your father's side. If they would've just had an incubator. Poor little thing. Suffocated to death, right there in my arms."

Until then, I had imagined Janet in every possible way—from perfect Little Girl Blue to a rotting skeleton—but never as a living baby gasping for air in her first and last minutes alive.

Grandma put her paring knife and the potato she was peeling back in the bowl on her lap. "But Edith just fell apart. *Ridiculous.* Almost everybody's lost a child, one time or another. I did. But the way she carried on. And then Frank in that explosion. That was terrible hard, but Edith just gave up. You'd think she was the only person who ever had to face hard times. I didn't teach my children to give up like that."

I remembered that Grandma had lost a baby girl when Grandpa Strang left her, but I couldn't ask about it right now. I hadn't considered that Mama grew up with a dead baby sister just like me.

Grandma began paring the potato again. "Judith Beatrice, you remember this: no matter what your mother says, she didn't have life any harder than anybody else. And it was sure a lot easier than mine, growing up in a sod house in the middle of nowhere."

Her potato peelings were much thicker than she would allow me to make. "When I married Edward, he seemed like such a godsend." She shook her head at the memory. "Inventor. What's an inventor? When he deserted us, if I hadn't had my own dear mother to help me, and her seventy-six years old and half blind and me with two children, trying to earn a living washing and ironing for the rich ladies in town. Ten cents an hour. *Ten cents.*"

Her jaw tightened. "Nobody bargains for a husband leaving you with two children and one on the way. And then losing that one." Her cloudy eyes were magnified behind her thick glasses. "Did I give up? Or break down? Most women don't have time for a 'nervous breakdown,' or whatever they call it. It's disgusting."

I couldn't stay silent any longer. "Mama can't help it, Grandma."

Grandma spit out, "Oh yes she can. It's shameful the way she's carried on."

I accidentally stabbed my finger with my needle. "Stop picking on Mama! She's the best mama I could ever have. She's all I've got."

Grandma stopped rocking, then slowly nodded. "Well, child, that's the God's truth." She stood up slowly, stabilizing herself with her bony hands on the rocker's seat. "Let's have a nice drink of water."

Near her back door, Grandma had a pump which pulled up the sweetest, coldest water in the world, especially if you drank it from the tin cup attached to the handle with a chain.

My last day at Grandma's that summer, when I was hemming her pajama pants, she told me about what happened to her when she was eight years old, almost my age:

I'll never forget that day. Nobody who lived through it ever will: January 12, 1888. For anybody living on the Dakota-Nebraska prairie, that day was a turning point. When we're all on our death-beds, all the days of our lives might be forgotten, but not that one.

Oh, all us homesteaders were used to heavy snowfalls and gale winds and three-day blizzards that buried us inside our soddies. But this blizzard was different than anything anybody had ever seen, before or since.

I loved school, just like you. How I loved school! We lived about a mile and a half from the schoolhouse. Every morning, I hurried through my chores–fed the chickens, gathered eggs, help Pa rake out the barn—so I could run to school. Ma could barely get breakfast down me, and some days I forgot my lunch, I was in such a hurry.

I forgot my lunch that day.

Our teacher was Miss Brinkmeyer. Prettiest thing, I can still see her. Usedta wear a removable velvet collar on her cotton dresses, out of respect for schooling and to distinguish herself from us, you know? Couldn't 'a been more'n sixteen years old, but that made her a year older'n Virgil Voss, the only sixth grader, which was all that mattered.

What fooled us was the unseasonably warm weather that January day. Felt just like spring. Started out so mild, the first break in a terrible cold spell. Forty degrees, and not a breath of wind. Most of us had raced to school with no mittens or even coats. I left my heavy coat home. It was all Miss Brinkmeyer could do to get us inside for our lessons.

It was just about lunchtime when the air inside the schoolhouse turned . . . odd. I don't know how else to describe it. Certainly cold–very cold–all at once, but more like electricity or something. They said later the cold front was like a wall of ice pushing the air in front of it to make static. I remember I was standing at my desk, answering a subtraction problem when I looked up at Miss Brinkmeyer, who was staring out the window, looking puzzled. Puzzled as can be.

"Excuse me, Beatrice," she said and walked to the window. We had two windows across from each other to get cross ventilation on hot days.

All of us–there were fifteen counting her—slowly stood up and followed her to the windows. What we saw didn't make sense. The sky had turned from robin's egg blue to solid black. Not dark grey but coal black. Soot black. If it had been summer, we would've thought a dust storm or a tornado, but this was much bigger and blacker than any tornado. The sky was a wall of darkness as high as you could see. And lightning? Law, the lightning! Racing through that cloud, streaking to earth. It was like the Day of Judgment. The end of the world."

"What is it?" we asked her. It was completely still outdoors, silent, eerie. Nothing stirred. The littlest ones began to whimper.

"I don't know," she answered, knowing she daren't show her own fright. "It must be a storm . . . of some kind."

"Can we go home?" Virgil Voss and some of the older boys were ready to light out on the spot. They lived southeast, the direction opposite to the storm. "We can outrun it."

Miss Brinkmeyer opened the door and stood in it. There was now a light, damp wind. I'll never forget that little woman, barely more than a girl, looking at that immense wall approaching and deciding, for better or worse, to stand her ground and face it head-on.

"No, Virgil, I don't think you can outrun it. I'm responsible for all of you, and we'll outlast it. We'll either hang together . . . or hang separately."

But he wouldn't listen. Virgil bolted out the door before she could say another word.

At that, she told the bigger boys to move the only bookcase in front of the window, which partly covered it. Some of us girls helped her shove her desk to the door, then everybody helped upend it. Pencils and writing slates fell out of the drawers. That left only one window unprotected–the window which still held blue sky.

"Get every piece of clothing you have, and gather in front of the stove," she said, stoking as much wood as it would hold. We did as she told us, but almost no one had brought a coat that day. Luckily, Miss Brinkmeyer kept her dress cape at school, a floor-length circle of lined wool, as well as her full-length winter coat and bonnet. She made sure the littlest children were completely covered, while the rest of us had feet sticking out.

Even though most of us had lived through tornadoes, none of us ever heard a sound like that storm approaching. It wasn't the roar of a loco-motive or an explosion, but as if a door had opened deep inside the earth letting loose all the winds ever made. It was truly hell broke loose. In just a few minutes, the temperature dropped at least twenty degrees and kept going down. And down. And down. And down.

When the wind hit the school house, it sucked the glass out the opposite side and threw in ice crystals as fine and thick as flour dust. Right off, that ice dust sealed our eyes almost shut. That's when you learn how cattle die of suffocation in blizzards.

"What'll we do, Miss Brinkmeyer?" cried Dorie Crandall.

I will never forget our beloved teacher's answer. "We will hold fast to each other, because we are all we have."

We hugged each other and huddled in front of that little heating stove, our heads bent down as the wind raged and the ice stabbed our feet. It was suddenly darker than the darkest night. Miss Brinkmeyer kept cov-ering the smallest children with her cape to save them from frostbite, what with those little toes and fingers.

I don't know how many hours we stayed in that position, but Miss Brinkmeyer kept making us say our names. "Don't go to sleep! Dorie? DORIE? Beatrice! Ernie! Charlie!"

And the temperature kept dropping. Finally, when the fire was going out, and we were all so sleepy, Miss Brinkmeyer stood up, rolling several of us off her. Even inside the schoolhouse, the blowing snow was so thick we could barely see her.

"Help me, Clifford. We have to keep the fire going. Clifford? Someone poke Clifford."

He mumbled and managed to stagger upright. "But . . . but. We're outta wood."

"Desks," she shouted. "We'll burn the desks."

Surely not! Not our desks which our fathers had built with donated wood and borrowed tools and no money.

She had all of us stand up—it was so much colder, worse than putting ice all over your body—to break up the desks. We jumped on them and hacked at them with other desks and threw them on the floor. It was heartbreaking to see those beautiful desks being broken. Then we fed them to the fire, piece by piece.

Even at that, we could only briefly warm up a little in the new heat.

Finally, the last desk was burned. What time was it? The wind was still screaming. It must have been two or three in the morning.

With the fire nearly dead, Miss Brinkmeyer made her last decision. "We will now . . . burn . . . our books."

My heart turned completely cold. The county had bought our books by subscription, asking our parents to contribute what they could, and we had waited for months for them to come by mail.

"But, Miss Brinkmeyer," I managed to say. "How can we have school without books?"

At that, her voice broke. "We can have school . . . as long as . . . anybody wants to learn."

The other picture of her I'll take to my grave is the look on her face as she fed our books into the coal stove. Throughout the rest of the night, she got up from the huddle and burned them, one at a time, opening each one first as if to say good-bye. They didn't offer much heat, but they gave us something more important in that longest, darkest night of our lives. Our burning books gave us hope.

At some time in the night, during one of our roll calls, we just as suddenly heard a new sound—silence. The front had passed, the ice wall had moved on, and the stars burned as cold as ice picks. But it left behind temperatures cold enough to freeze every living thing.

In the morning, if such dim and dismal light even makes a morning, Miss Brinkmeyer was the first to raise her head from our huddle. Enough snow had blown in through the broken window to cover us all in several inches, and the windowpane showing above the bookcase was buried in a snowdrift.

"Roll call," Miss Brinkmeyer said drearily, exhausted. "I know you're cold, but—"

She was cut off by a shout. A shout! From outside!

"Be careful," she warned. "Don't move too fast. We're all so terribly . . . cold and . . . stiff. Take it slow." How could that slip of a girl know that? We later learned that some people who survived the blizzard moved too fast and had heart attacks on the spot.

A man was at the door, trying to push it in, calling, "Miss Brinkmeyer? Anybody in here?"

"We're here. We're alive," she called out. "Come around to the side. The broken window."

And who appeared in the window but Pa. My own dear Pa! He looked in and said in a shaky voice, "B-Bea? Beatrice?"

"I'm here, Pa," I managed to croak. On hearing my voice, he smashed out the rest of the glass. Then he disappeared, only to come back in a few minutes, tossing in cold biscuits and blankets, robes and coats—every warm thing my family owned.

"Others are on their way," he shouted. "Somebody clear the door."

After beating their hands to regain feeling and wolfing down a few biscuits, the two biggest boys pulled down Miss Brinkmeyer's desk, and in stomped my father. He spotted me and almost stepped on the other children to get at me. He lifted me and put his arms around me and pulled me inside his mackinaw and hugged me tighter than I've ever been hugged before or since. And the very strangest thing: my Pa, who had lived through every misery, who'd survived hail and drought and dust storms–everything the Plains can throw at you— my Pa started to cry. He lifted his head from my neck and saw Miss Brinkmeyer wrapping children in blankets and distributing biscuits. He took in the bare walls, the missing desks and books.

"You, Missy," he called out, sternly.

She stopped momentarily and looked up from rubbing Laurie Engstrom's right foot, which had stuck out of the cape and was already turning black with frostbite.

His voice cracked. "You know what temperature it is out there? Our thermometer only goes to 40 below, and it's froze there. You saved these young'uns. You know that?"

She returned to rubbing the frostbitten foot. Laurie set up a wail. "We all saved each other, Mister Stoetzer."

"We found Virgil Voss. Arm sticking up from a snowdrift."

She looked as if my father had slapped her. "Oh no. Please."

"About fifty feet from their farmhouse."

"God help us all."

"There must be scores of dead folks out there. This is the worst storm I ever seen, and I seen some bad ones."

We later learned that the storm had killed hundreds of children, all caught outdoors, all sent home by country teachers who couldn't possibly know what was happening. Children who drifted with the wind and fell, like cattle in the fields. Just around here, the Loontjers lost their teen-aged boy between the barn and the house. And little Emma Sponheimer, and the poor Kaufmanns–all four sons. In Dakota territory, two brothers froze rock hard with their arms around each other and were brought in to thaw near the kitchen stove, so they could be laid out for burial. It was that, or let them lie behind the barn frozen all winter. Their mother began laughing. *Laughing.* That was a woman with reason to lose her mind. Not like Edith."

Grandma took off her heavy glasses and rubbed her eyes. "So many little ones froze to death that people called it the Children's Blizzard."

When Papa and Sam picked me up to drive back home, I hugged Grandma for a long time, feeling all her bones underneath her layers of dresses and aprons. I wasn't the same little girl they had left behind.

"How was it?" Sam felt glitzy, full of Jamboree tales. Underneath his voice was "neener-neener."

I answered, "I'll never forget it. Not even when I'm on my death-bed."

Sam slowed way down, and Papa looked alarmed, but I didn't explain. I would never forget those July days I spent with my grandmother, sitting on her porch until dark, listening to her stories, hearing hammers and saws all over town while Hebron rebuilt itself from the rubble, sewing and unpicking and sewing again my Grandma's last, perfect pair of pajamas. Sam may have learned how to bake potatoes in a campfire, but I learned why I was named Beatrice.

CHAPTER 53
BENIGN ARCHAEOLOGY

IN THE CAR ON THE WAY TO THE HIGH SCHOOL AUDI-
torium, I asked Papa if he had reminded Mama about the tri-county
spelling bee tonight.

"I sure did. I called the hospital from the pay phone at the
Pawnee Hotel."

Wow. Long-distance telephone calls cost so much, Papa must have
thought this was important. My legs were itching from the car seat, and I
kept smoothing my Sunday dress. Patent leather shoes, do your job tonight.

"What did she say?" Sam asked.

"She . . . wished Jeb luck."

Papa was probably stretching the truth, since he knew I wanted to
hear that.

I peeled one of my legs from the car seat. "I'm so nervous I couldn't
spell my own name."

"It's J. E. B." Sam answered helpfully.

"Would it make you less nervous if you sang us a song?"

"Papa! No!" Sam gripped his stomach as if he had been shot.

To torture Sam, it would have been worth a chorus of "The Good
Ship Lollipop," but I felt too strangled even for that.

Thank goodness Papa made our family dress up, since all of the
spellers and most of the audience wore Sunday clothes. There was Mrs.
Dahlke! She said she would take the bus down from Lincoln. It was all

I could do not to run over and hug her, but I had to concentrate. Both she and Miss Reynolds would say so. They stood next to each other and waved from across the hall, as did Mrs. Vince and a few other teachers from Lincoln Elementary. I was shocked to see Joe Clary and some other fourth-graders—not Leon or Doreen Cavin or Jane Englehardt, of course—plus a small platoon of Boy Scouts. And who came in together but Charlie Whitaker and Will Hankins, both in bib overalls, but Will had dressed his up with one of Papa's old work jackets in spite of the heat. It had to be eighty degrees in the hall.

Not until the judges lined us up on stage did I see that the auditorium seats were full and some grown-ups were standing along the back wall. There must have been fifty spellers at least, ranging from third through twelfth grade and from about four to six feet tall. To keep myself from getting sick, I calculated that I was the third shortest person, something Sam would do. Standing on the same stage where we performed "Why the Bells Rang" felt completely different when I couldn't pretend to be somebody else and could only be myself. Since "Wilder" fell near the end of the line, I had to squirm while the contestants ahead of me sat down or remained standing during the first round.

"*Subtle*," the judge called out from across the stage, an easy word which nonetheless eliminated five kids right off. *Scissors, patience, oasis,* and *ancient* whittled the line down to me, where he asked for *rhythm*. Oh goody. This wouldn't be too hard, I thought as I rattled off "*r-h-y-t-h-m*." The second round left me facing all older kids. One tall boy with a white shirt and tie and pimples on his face never paused, no matter how hard his word. As Sam would say, clearly he was the one to take out. I didn't dare look at the audience but merely shuffled my patent leather shoes along in line, silently spelling everyone else's words to stay in practice.

"*Catastrophe.*" Darn, I needed that ph – for f – word, which eliminated three more kids. Some old favorites appeared, like *benign, alignment,* even *physicist*. The judge frowned at me and said, "*excerpt*," which I easily dispatched, bringing us remaining ten contestants to the third round.

Now the words grew harder. *Liaison*, which I also wished were mine, stumped three more kids, while *sovereign*, *archaeology* and *metaphor* reduced our numbers to four— three high school students and me.

The judge handed me *eschatology*. Incredible! I paused for a second, then slowly enunciated, "*E-s . . . c-h-a . . . t-o . . . l-o-g-y.*" In the audience, I heard Miss Reynolds bark.

Two others kids stumbled on *macabre* and *conscientious*, leaving me facing the tall boy with pimples. I felt the crowd shift in their seats.

Juggernaut: he got it, thank goodness, since I had no idea what it meant. *Fractious*: yes! My middle name. Back to him with *reconnaissance*, which he quickly spelled, then to me with *psychic*. I wanted to look at Sam while I spelled that particular word correctly.

The tall boy and I were both having a hard time breathing.

"*Fluorescence*," the judge delivered to the boy, who thought for a minute before slowly spelling "*f-l . .u . . . o-r-e-s . . . c-e-n . . . c-e.*" Lordy. Chance was on my side, since I wouldn't have had a hope on that one, even though it sounded chemical in nature. I momentarily prayed for *triiodide*, but knew I wasn't that lucky. Concentrate, I told myself.

"*Synonymous*," rang out to me. Spared for one more shot, I quickly spelled it.

"*Orrery*," the judge called out.

What? Had I heard him right?

The tall boy played with his tie. "*O-r . . . r-u . . . r-y.*" Clearly, he was guessing.

"That is incorrect."

I let out my breath.

"Young lady?"

"May I ask what it is?" I stalled, as if that would help me.

"A model of the solar system," the judge answered. "*Orrery.*"

What a fine word. Even if I failed tonight, I needed to learn it.

I took a stab, "*O–r . . . r–u . . . r–i–e.*"

"That is also incorrect. It's *o–r–r–e–r–y.* We move on to the next round."

Mimeograph, obfuscate, abyss, surveillance we diced back and forth.

Then came the boy's next word: "*Apocrypha.*"

I couldn't believe my ears. I didn't dare look at Mrs. Dahlke. The teen-aged boy asked, "Would you please repeat the word? Sir?"

"*Apocrypha,*" the judge enunciated.

I knew it wasn't nice to hope that someone else failed, but I couldn't help it. 'Please, please, don't know how to spell it,' I thought and concentrated on the pimples on his chin in case he could read the spelling in my eyes.

"*A . . .*" he began tentatively, followed by, "*p . . . o . . . c . . . r . . . ,*" he paused a long time.

'Don't say *y,*' I kept thinking. I knew that Mrs. Dahlke wasn't small-minded enough to think the same thing.

The boy continued, "*i . . . f . . . a.*" He let out a breath of relief.

"Would you repeat that?" the judge asked, to which the boy answered, this time more quickly, "*A–p–o–c–r–i–f–a.*"

"Is that your final answer?"

Suddenly remembering the ph – for f – trick, the boy suddenly changed his mind. "No. *A–p–o–c–r–i–p–h–a.*"

"That's your final answer?"

"Yes."

Knowing I shouldn't celebrate, I kept looking at the floor, in my imagination jumping up and down in place. My stomach was jumping for me. My toes were jumping inside my patent leather shoes. I could see them. The light was jumping around my shoes. They were dancing without me.

The judge announced, "That is incorrect. On to our remaining contestant. If she also misses the word, we'll proceed to the next round."

I had to glance at Sam, since I so rarely knew something he didn't. He had scrunched up his face in hopelessness.

"Capital *A-p-o-c-r-y-p-h-a*," I quickly spilled out.

There was stunned silence in the hall.

"Would you please repeat that, Miss? More slowly this time?"

I paused between each letter. "Capital *A. P. O. C. R. Y. P. H. A.*"

"Young lady," he said sternly.

I couldn't think what I had said wrong, then added, "Sir," to show respect to the judge.

He paused and looked around at the audience. "Young lady, you have just won the 1954 Nebraska Tri-County Spelling Bee."

The hall erupted. Mrs. Dahlke, Miss Reynolds and Mrs. Vince, plus everyone else from Lincoln Elementary jumped up and clapped. For no reason, Charlie Whitaker was shaking Will Hankins' hand. I could hear Sam cheering, "Yeah Jeb! Yeah Jeb!" which set off the rest of the Boy Scouts. Papa was grinning and clapping, talking and nodding to Miss Reynolds, who stood next to him, her fat positively jiggling up and down. On her other side, Mrs. Dahlke had taken off her glasses and wiped the corner of her eye with a starched hanky. It was better than the cheering on the aircraft carrier when Sam and I miraculously landed our crippled plane.

Over the melee, the judge walked across the stage, shook my hand, said "Congratulations, young lady," and handed me a purple ribbon like the ones they give cows and sheep at the State Fair.

"Thank you, Sir," I said and pointed to the tall teenager. "Does he get something, too?" I could afford to feel a little sorry for him.

"He'll get a certificate," the judge answered.

Mrs. Dahlke was waiting for me at the bottom of the stairs off the stage. As Mama would say, *wonder of wonders*: my teacher put her arms around me and kissed me on each cheek. She smelled like powder.

"Judith Beatrice Wilder, I am so, so proud of you." Her voice sounded as if she had a cold.

"I'm proud of you, too, Mrs. Dahlke." She was wearing the lucky peacock pin on her lapel.

Then, in a gesture I knew I might regret, I held out my purple ribbon. "This really belongs to you."

"That's precious, but you worked very hard to earn it, and you must keep it."

She began to unhook the peacock pin from her lapel. "However. This, my dear, really belongs to you." She held it out to me in her palm. The tiny rubies and sapphires flashed as the little peacock seemed to spread its fan tail, ready to fly to my hand.

To *me*. I've never wanted to take a present so much in my life, but I couldn't imagine wearing something so valuable. More than that, I couldn't imagine Mrs. Dahlke appearing in the classroom without that pin.

"I would . . . love that," I managed to stutter out, "But. Some other little girl will need all its luck to get her through." I looked longingly at the peacock and slowly folded Mrs. Dahlke's fingers over it. "You know?" I kept staring at her closed hand.

"I do know." She hugged me again. "Dear, dear Jeb. Thank you."

For what I didn't know.

Papa, Miss Reynolds and Sam joined us. Papa mashed me into his shirt front, while behind him, Sam repeatedly chanted, "Di-di-di-dah," Morse Code for the V for "victory."

He added, "Papa and I bust our buttons off."

Miss Reynolds rested her folded arms on top of her huge bosom. "*Apocrypha?*" She couldn't stop chuckling. "Mildred Dahlke, what *did* you teach this child?"

"*Eschatology*, Thelma? You have no room to talk," Mrs Dahlke countered.

"But who would have thought *Apocrypha?*"

"It was Jeb's idea. She wanted to know."

Miss Reynolds looked at me. "Of course, she did."

By now, people were leaving the auditorium, but both Joe Clary and Will Hankins hung back and waved at me from across the hall. I waved back, hard, with both hands. Papa thanked all the teachers and the Boy Scouts and everyone within earshot for coming.

Sam had already run outside, while Papa walked out with me, his chewed-up hand on my shoulder.

"You were wonderful, Sugar. I didn't even know what half those words meant."

"Neither did I," I half fibbed. I couldn't help adding, "I wish Mama was here." Then, correcting myself, "*Were* here. Subjunctive mode."

"What on earth is that?"

"A statement expressing a wish or something contrary to fact. You can ask Miss Reynolds if you don't believe me."

"Why wouldn't I believe you? Champion Speller of three counties in Nebraska?"

I petted his beaten-up hand on my shoulder, slipping two fingers in the place where his was missing.

Papa was quiet for a minute, then said, "I'll tell Mama all about it. As soon as they let me see her." He squeezed my shoulder, then began fingering my shoulder bones, partly tickling. "Feel those muscles."

"Sam and I are working on push-ups for his Personal Fitness merit badge. The badge has a beautiful embroidered heart."

"If that boy ever makes Eagle Scout, they better make you one, too."

"Girls can't be Eagle Scouts."

When Papa looked down at me, the lights from the high school windows reflected off his glasses. "If anybody ever earned an Eagle, you certainly have, Sugar."

Sam ran back to walk with us to the car. "I couldn't have spelled any of those words, Jeb," Sam leaped from foot to foot.

Truer words were never spoken, since he couldn't even spell *vegetable*, but this wasn't the time to bring that up.

CHAPTER 54

THE DAY THE EARTH STOOD STILL

*O*RRERY.

As soon as Miss Reynolds heard the word at the spelling bee, she remembered a real live orrery in storage in Round Prairie—in the basement of Lincoln Elementary, no less. Serendipity! I finally learned that word. Miss Reynolds hadn't relaxed for an instant on the spelling lessons, now determined to send me to the state spelling bee. *Serendipity*—a perfect name for a horse—meant chance, fortune, luck, coincidence and accident all rolled into one. She said I should ignore its poor vowel-to-consonant ratio and consider it the perfect substitute for God's Plan. Focus on the larger issues, she had advised, such as the meaning of words. I decided that a word's meaning lived in the spaces between letters, like music lived in the silence between notes. I didn't even attempt to rename Luther Serendipity since he had developed habits I could only describe as intractable. To be fair, he had been through a lot for such a young horse.

Fortunately, Lincoln Elementary was only two blocks from the library, so Miss Reynolds and I could walk there on her lunch hour. She now used a real cane she had bought at the Rexall, trying to hold it stiff against her leg so no one would notice, but she still lurched along. I offered to limp in rhythm with her, and we could both pretend to be wounded gunfighters, a suggestion she rejected, thank you anyway.

Mrs. Vince had loaned us the keys to the school, since she was the unofficial principal for the summer. Miss Reynolds smiled that Edna could get almost anything she wanted, since she was also the unofficial mayor, deputy sheriff and City Council. When I asked how that happened, Miss

Reynolds answered that blackmail beat the electoral process every time. I hoped that when I got as old as Miss Reynolds I would have a friend like Mrs. Vince.

At the school, I pulled open the heavy oak door with the window in it, remembering the day Sam and I stood inside the steamy heat and looked out at the blizzard. Today Miss Reynolds and I escaped the heat pushing against our backs into the cool and echoing halls. To be inside school on a summer day: eerie. At the top of the basement stairs, Miss Reynolds turned on the light below, a bare bulb hanging in the center of the storage room, leaving the corners in shadows. I crept down the shaky wooden stairs first, bracing myself against the spider-webby wall so I could catch her if she fell. Unlike the tomb of the Inavale storm cellar, the basement smelled dry and musty, unopened, unused.

"Well!" At the bottom, Miss Reynolds brushed the dirt off her baggy lilac cotton dress. "An adventure already."

Along one wall loomed the backdrop the sixth graders had painted for the Christmas play, the unconvincing mountain precariously balancing the church with the bell that finally rang, all covered with peeling tan snow. Inexplicably, the picture seemed to drop the temperature in the basement like real snow, causing us both to shiver and Miss Reynolds to rub her bulging bare arms. Although the light bulb wasn't moving, shadows spooked up and down the walls. I suddenly felt the urge to hold Miss Reynolds' hand, a Highly Inappropriate Act, given the fact that I was the scout today, a scout with a wounded pal and no getaway pony in sight.

On the walk to the school, Miss Reynolds had explained that people over the year donated treasures for the House of Yesterday in Hastings, and the only safe storage in the county was the school, where no one entered without coercion. Quite like church, she added. Mentally, I raised my hat to the word *coercion*, as Emily Dickinson had taught me.

"Look," she pointed at a small cement slab holding bones. "It must be the fossil the Heisers donated, a prehistoric horse."

Horse? How could that be? The little pile of bones looked more like a dog skeleton, about twenty inches tall. Huge compared to Luther, but miniscule beside Alberta Clipper.

Maybe someone had donated a human mummy. I peered around cautiously.

As Miss Reynolds contemplated the stacks of books and file folders around the basement, she murmured, "The interminable journals and papers of the long dead, as if anyone cared about Aunt Hattie's diary of pioneer life on the prairie. Remind me that we need to learn the word *soporific*. And promise me that you'll never write a memoir unless it's full of juicy lies."

Since I didn't know what a memoir was, I could safely say, "I promise."

"There it is," she blurted out, causing me to jump. "The orrery."

In the dim light in a corner stood the most delicate mechanism I had ever seen, more a piece of art than a machine. On a brass platform like a small round table stood a merry-go-round of planets and moons. In the center was a golden ball the size of a baseball with brass rods radiating outward, each holding an upright brass rod tipped with a colored marble. The marbles varied proportionally in size to the planets and held their moons on even tinier brass rods, replicating the sun and planets. A brass handle stuck out from the side of the table, the method to crank the solar system into motion.

"You can tell how old the orrery is by its number of planets. Uranus and Pluto hadn't been discovered yet." Her voice stopped my hand in midreach. "We mustn't touch it."

How sad that this solar system couldn't move until someone cranked it to life, a tiny piece of the universe immobilized in time and darkness.

"If we could crank it, could we make it circle really fast? Or really slow? Or even backwards?"

"That's the Judith Wilder I know, all right." Under the bare bulb, her face looked like a Halloween mask, but a friendly one, a marshmallow ghost.

I looked at the cloudy blue marble of the Earth, the only planet with one moon, and thought about the Dust People who at last could have a home, except now they were too large. You just can't win, as Mama would say.

Back at the library, Miss Reynolds pulled off her glasses to hang from her silver chain, a series of small rods and loops like the surveyor's chain Sam and I had used last summer. With her hanky she dabbed at the sweat around her eyes as if she were crying.

"You really know how to give an old woman a work-out, Judith." She collapsed into her chair, her cane falling on the floor.

I picked it up and hung it from an open desk drawer, its new home. "You're not an old woman," I lied.

"You should consider diplomacy, if you don't become a lawyer." She adjusted her whole head of hair like a cap. By now, I had to agree with Mama that her tightly rolled curls must be a wig.

I confided, "I still want to sell candy at the movies."

"A career in diplomacy or movie candy. Actually, they have a lot in common." She chuckled once, then again, although I didn't know why.

"Would you like a glass of water?"

"No, but I would like you to take home the art book Mildred Dahlke donated to the library." She pointed to a book as large as an encyclopedia volume. "It's a beauty. It has several paintings by Raphael, but not the Sistine Madonna Greta told you about."

We had been searching for a print of it as a special treat for Mrs. Keindorf.

"I still don't understand why she's named *Sistine*."

"Her original location. Very exotic, to use your word. We'll look into that later. The book isn't ready to check out. Just take it. But be careful." She waved me out the door, still huffing to catch her breath.

I gingerly cradled the book in Maybe's basket and began pushing her home with yet another flat front tire. Someday, Papa assured me, we would buy a new tire. I would probably be too old to ride her by then. The heat pressed down on my head like a catcher's mitt and the humidity gathered under the trees like thin fog. Slow pushing.

Across the street I heard someone chanting, "–pants, pants, Smarty-pants." Leon Troxel was walking along in parallel motion with me, holding a toy rifle across his chest. I figured I could ignore him at least until I got home.

He veered to prance across the road. "You think you're so smart," he sneered, pointing the gun at the book. He swung the gun back and forth, which I now recognized as a real BB gun, an honest-to-goodness Daisy air rifle like Sam wanted, the one advertised in his Boy Scout manual.

I wobbled Maybe forward on her flat tire, determined not to be sucked into a fight on a public sidewalk. Mama would hear about it all the way to Omaha and would have a fit. I actually hoped so. I would face Mama in one of her fits in a heartbeat, I missed her that much.

"Smart rhymes with—" Leon jumped in front of me on the sidewalk. "Fart. Fart, fart, fart. That's you." He aimed his gun at my stomach like the gunslinger in a cowboy movie. "This is my sidewalk. Get off."

I lunged my bicycle ahead, forcing him to step back.

His scarred upper lip lifted. "Dare ya to cross that crack."

Of course, I crossed it. He kicked Maybe so hard she jerked out of my hands and the beautiful art book somersaulted onto the grass.

"Smarty-Fart. Passes gas. Farty gassy with the looney mommy." He dived to grab the book. "Looney–"

That did it. With my high-pitched Indian yell, I ran straight at him. Startled, he stumbled over backwards, his arms flailing like the legs of an upside down beetle. I kicked him lightly in his ribs, rescued the beautiful book, and high-tailed it for home. I could get Maybe later.

There was no later. As I passed the barn, Sam bolted out of the trailer door. "Bobby Clawson and his gang are headed this way. They started to beat up Jim Hartsock, but he got loose and is hiding in the fort."

I left the art book on the trailer steps and ran after Sam. "Is our ammo–?"

"They didn't raid—" Sam called over his shoulder.

As we scrambled into the trench beside Jim, I took stock of our normal dirt clods and mud dried around rocks, as well as stacks of sharpened broomcorn spears. Near the tips of some of the spears, we had molded mud to give added weight. We were as ready as we would ever be.

"Bobby's got two big kids with him," Jim warned. His John Deere baseball cap was covered in dust.

I added, "Leon Troxel's on my tail with a BB gun. A *real* BB gun. What happened?"

Jim answered, "I spit sunflower shells on Bobby Clawson's lawn."

At that moment, Bobby and two older boys entered the alley near the trailer carrying handfuls of rocks. If this battle turned into hand-to-hand combat, we would be annihilated. Hearing something behind them, they turned to see Leon catching up, shooting his BB gun into the air. As Sam, Jim and I braced for the attack, we heard someone yell from the opposite end of the alley. It was Will Hankins riding his bicycle, oversized as a grown-up on a child's toy, fast and crazy as a true daredevil. He ditched it in the broomcorn stubble, ran toward us and slid into the fort in a cloud of dust.

"I saw 'em. Thought they was headed fer here." Will pulled handfuls of rocks out of his pockets and hunkered down just as the first rounds hit.

We quickly went through all of our broomcorn spears, which were hard to aim and were no match for their rocks, anyway. Although I didn't throw as badly as most girls, my range was pretty short, so I always had to creep close to the enemy to score a hit at all. Today I had no choice but to scramble out of the fort, all the while hearing Leon's BB gun pop-pop.

Now dirt clods were flying in both directions, broomcorn spears were quivering back toward us, combatants were hitting the ground on both sides, the dust was growing thick as smoke. At one point, I heard a strange whoop and saw Bobby Clawson tackle Will Hankins and begin pounding him with his bare fists. They looked about evenly matched, but I had no time to watch.

The rocks which pelted my legs and chest didn't hurt much, but someone caught me at close range on my right cheek with a stinging dirt clod. As I wiped the dust out of my eyes, I saw at the edge of the war zone someone who looked like . . . it couldn't be . . . no, it was . . . Joe Clary. What was he doing here? Momentarily distracted, I felt another dirt clod packed with a rock smack my arm.

"Jeb!" Sam shouted. "Migs at three o'clock!"

I spun a quarter of a turn just in time to duck a broomcorn spear, immediately stooping to gather clods for a return volley. Obviously, all of our spears were in the hands of the enemy now.

"We're running low on ammo!" Jim shouted. Will had left Bobby on the ground and was chasing another big boy. I could hear Leon's BB gun but couldn't see him.

Out of the corner of my eye, I saw a little spotted dog with a rope trailing from his neck start to run across the battlefield with Joe Clary chasing him directly into our crossfire, oblivious of the war in progress.

Automatically, Bobby Clawson began throwing rocks at the dog, narrowly missing its head. Joe waved his arms and shouted something I couldn't hear.

Suddenly I panicked: Joe thought we were just playing. He didn't know it was a battle to the death. I had to warn him. I had to tell him—

"JOE!" I shouted and waved my arms wildly, but before I could yell "STOP," the rocks and broomcorn spears instantly angled toward him, like a flock of birds changing direction in mid-air. I saw it and I didn't see it: in slow motion the broomcorn spear heading for Joe Clary's face, the arc, a movement now in a different dimension; all our bodies slowing, but a relentless momentum still propelling the war furiously forward. I willed time to stop altogether, willed us all to become Dust People I could blow away with my breath. I willed the movie to run backward and the homesteader to get up from the ground, unbloody and unkilled, willed Papa's fiery explosion to suck back into the pile of gunpowder, willed the broomcorn spear to suspend itself in mid-air, like an exhibit at the House of Yesterday.

Instead, there rose an inhuman shriek, the kind no person or animal can fake, so loud and horrible that every one of us froze in place.

I screamed "Joe!" I knew he was hurt before I really knew it, before my legs started running toward him, before I stumbled in the furrows and fell, got up, fell again, on my way toward my friend. "JOE!"

By now, Sam was stumbling toward Joe as well. As soon as they saw Joe might be seriously hurt, Clawson's gang took off in every direction. Will had started running toward us from the distant fence, but I waved him away. He had enough trouble without this.

Joe's hands covered his eyes and blood seeped out between his fingers, making dirty little rivulets through the dust on his face. His eyes, the color of milk chocolate, seemed to be melting and running down his cheek. He kicked us away, screaming then whimpering, "Mama! Mama!" When a boy our age called for his mom, we knew he was really hurt.

Jim Hartsock looked down at Joe writhing in the dirt. "Oh man." Quickly turning, he said, "I'll get Mom." And he was off and running, his long legs leaping the earth furrow, his John Deere cap flying off.

Sam decided, "I'll get Joe's mother. Don't leave him, Jeb." Then he, too, was gone. In less than a minute, I saw Sam pedaling his bicycle furiously toward Joe's house.

Why Joe, why Joe, why Joe, I kept thinking. "Do you want to put your head on my–?"

"NO! Leave me alone!" Joe screeched.

"Can I get you some water–?" I desperately wanted to help, I, who had dreamed of saving the world with the Shadow, the only Man who knew what Evil Lurked in the Hearts of Men.

Joe started to drop his hands. "I can't see. I CAN'T SEE!"

"It's just dirt. It's in your eyes. No, keep your hands there . . ." I held his hands on his face the same way I tried to hold Papa's burned skin on his arms in my nightmares. I was afraid of what I might see if I let go.

I was growing more panicked. Where was Sam? Or Jim's mother? Anybody? I couldn't face this alone.

"Am I gonna die . . . ?" Joe almost whispered.

"No," I said quickly. "Nobody ever dies in a broomcorn war. Besides, you're too little to die." Then I remembered Mrs. Dahlke's little daughter and felt a lurch of nausea.

Just then, Jim Hartsock ran up the alley, closely followed by his mother. "My God, my God," she was calling. Practically in my face, she yelled, "What have you done? *What* have you done *now*?"

Mrs. Hartsock squatted down and circled Joe's shoulder with her arm. "Joe, it's Jim's mom. It's okay, son. We'll get you help."

As soon as he heard Mrs. Hartsock, Joe stopped whimpering.

"Can you walk? If I help you?"

Mrs. Hartsock pulled Joe to his feet, his bloody hands still clamped on his face.

"That's a good boy. Keep your hands over your eyes," she said, with her arm now around his waist, half holding him up.

"Sam . . . went to get . . . Joe's mom–" I managed to gag out.

"You MONSTER!"

My knees buckled, and I sat in the dirt.

"Jim," she rounded on her son. "Tell Mrs. Clary I'm taking Joe to Doctor Mary."

Jim nodded.

Mrs. Hartsock was talking with her teeth clamped shut. "Then you go home and stay there. Do you HEAR ME?"

Jim nodded again, hard and fast.

Half carrying Joe across the field, Mrs. Hartsock disappeared around the trailer.

"We're in trouble, Jeb," Jim said as he slowly backed away from me. "Big trouble."

As I sat in the dirt where Joe had fallen, all the weight, all the horror of the afternoon began to descend. Beat, I lay flat on my back in the dirt, not caring about my dress or filthy hair. I had no Mama to punish me. Overhead, clouds as delicate as the lace Grandma Strang used to crochet, floated in the blue sky. They didn't notice me, or the field, or the war. I might as well live on the little marble Earth in the orrery, not even a speck in the dark basement.

What if Joe died? I knew I didn't do it, I had run out of ammunition, but who would believe me? Would I go to prison? Did they put little kids in jail with grown-ups? I would wait here for them to come and arrest me. Would I ever see Mama again?

My tears ran through the dirt on my face into my ears, making wet trails outlined in mud like Joe's blood.

Between me and the sky, I saw Sam's head, upside down. I thought I was imagining him.

"Jeb?" Sam asked in a tiny voice, then walked around me and turned right side up, my real brother. "Are you hurt?"

"No." I slowly sat up, leaving the sky behind. I wanted to say that I was scared, but I was too proud.

"Your cheek is bleeding."

"Is Joe …?"

"Joe's mom is on her way to Dr. Mary's."

"What did she say?"

"I didn't tell her anything."

"Will we go to jail?"

Sam sat beside me on the edge of the fort, just like Papa had during the eclipse, except that we were two dirty little kids sitting under a blistering sun, a fireball no one could look at for long.

Later that day, Sam and I walked back toward the library to retrieve my bicycle.

"I-I didn't throw the spear," I stammered. I would never lie in such a horrible situation, not to Sam, not to anybody.

"I didn't, either," Sam answered.

"Could one of us have done it accidentally and not know it?"

"Nope." Sometimes I really appreciated Sam's absolute faith in the facts as he saw them. If we didn't do it, why did I feel sick to my stomach, sicker than the day of the Avalon Theater explosion?

"But we're still … " I started. A person could know a lot of words and not know the right one to use. I settled on, "Guilty. Don't you think?"

"It wasn't our fault." Several scratches on his arms were scabbing over, and one sleeve of his shirt had been torn half off.

"It was our fort," I started again.

"If it wasn't our fort, it would've been somebody else's." He sounded like Papa talking about the maniac with the firecracker.

"We sharpened the broomcorn spears."

"Jim started it when he spit sunflower shells on Clawson's lawn."

"But Joe. Was just an innocent bystander. It wasn't his fight."

"That's what happens in war." Sam repeated some stupid thing he had heard a grown-up say, probably Marvin Harkin.

For me, some part was still missing. "It wouldn't have happened . . . without us." While we walked, I purposely stepped on the sidewalk cracks.

Sam fell into step with me, hitting the cracks at the same time.

"Right?" I prodded, but he didn't respond.

My bicycle was still lying on her side where Leon had kicked her over.

"What do you think Papa will do when he finds out?"

Sam lifted Maybe upright. "I dunno."

"We'll deserve it."

"They were looking for a fight, Jeb. And we gave it to them. We didn't do anything wrong."

*   *   *   *   *

Joe was blinded in one eye. Blind for the rest of his life. Forever. I would live to be an old lady like Mrs. Dahlke with two eyes, but Joe would grow into an old man with only one eye. Forever meant your whole life, and then some. Mama must know about forever. And Papa. Before this, I thought you had to be a grown-up to know about forever.

Nobody ever found out for certain who threw the spear. For a long time, I had nightmares that I did it, or sometimes that Sam did. I wanted it to be Leon Troxel or Bobby Clawson, but I could never honestly connect an identifiable hand to the broomcorn spear which sailed so true and sharp through the dust-filled chaos to pierce the eye of my friend Joe Clary.

Mrs. Hartsock absolutely forbade Jim to play with Sam or me ever again. He couldn't even walk across the road or go near the trailer or Mr. Whitaker's or the broomcorn field or go up the alley, not even to catch his dog, Scooter, not even if Scooter might run all the way to the highway and get hit by a car. Not even then.

Papa absolutely forbade any more wars, not with broomcorn or dirt clods or rocks or anything else. He made us fill in the fort, and he stood there and watched every single shovelful of dirt go back in, then we had to stomp it down to make it even with the earth around it as if we had buried a body. After that, we scuffed it up so the site looked exactly like the rest of the broomcorn field, as if it had never existed. Now Sam and I didn't have any protection left except the Formula and the Inavale hideout. Mr. Whitaker sat and watched us from his back porch, shading his eyes with his hand. He hadn't talked to us since the battle, which was all right, because I couldn't bear to face him.

I asked Papa to talk to Joe, since Papa had grown up with only one eye, but Papa said everybody has their own troubles and lots of times they don't want to hear about somebody else's, which wouldn't fit them anyway, like a pair of shoes which might be the same size but have the wrong shape because they've been walked in so long by somebody else's feet. Will Hankins would know what Papa meant, since Will could only wear shoes he found in peoples' garbage cans.

I wanted to talk to Mrs. Hartsock, not for me but because Jim had been one of Sam's best friends, but Papa said it would only make things worse and she might change her mind someday, but probably not soon.

"Time works things out its own way," Papa said. "It doesn't pay attention to what we want." I had to ask, "You know the man who threw the firecracker and gave you such terrible burns? Do you think he ever wanted to talk to you?"

Papa looked at me a long time from both his good eye and his glass one, then answered, "That's a good question, Sugar."

I thought about that lots of times and finally decided it wouldn't have made any difference. As Uncle Ralph would say, the horse was out of the barn.

When I returned the art book with the beautiful Raphael paintings, I waited for a woman carrying a baby to leave the library so I could talk to Miss Reynolds alone.

I sat down at her desk across from her. She took off her glasses, today on the silver chain with ruby buttons, and leaned forward with her chin resting on her fist. When I didn't say anything, she pushed forward the date stamp with her free hand.

"Did you hear about Joe—?"

"How long would it take that story to travel four blocks in Round Prairie, Nebraska?"

"I didn't do it." I lightly touched the date stamper. "Neither did Sam."

"I believe you." I couldn't imagine why I once thought of her eyes as little black pebbles, because they were very bright and very deep and very sorrowful.

"I feel awful."

"You should. It's a tragic situation."

"Do you think–?" I didn't know quite what I meant to ask. I kicked my dangling feet back and forth under the heavy chair. "Do you think this was my punishment for winning the spelling bee?"

She took her fist from her mouth and sat up straight. "Wh-What?"

"That a girl shouldn't get too happy . . . because . . . well, especially when her Mama is–"

"Do you seriously think somebody is watching and just waiting to punish you?" She actually stamped the date on the wooden desktop. "God's plan or Calvin's predestination or the universe's sense of humor. Teleological nonsense! We don't need any help punishing ourselves."

"What can I do for Joe?" I rubbed my fingers along the smooth rubber wheels where Seth Post had cut off the years. "I can't stand to think that Joe woke up that morning with both of his eyes and never even thought about them. Woke up like normal, thinking today would be just like any other summer day with school out. But instead, his whole life changed. His *whole life* in one day. In one *moment*.

"That, my dear, is what happens: one minute, there's a little cloud in the sky, the next minute you're hit by lightning, like George Dahlquist in his wheatfield. Or you're waiting in line at the post office, and you drop dead from a heart attack, like Ettie Rothburg. Or your Pa . . . gets his leg caught in a combine and . . . bleeds to death."

Her voice sounded as if that happened to her father. I didn't dare ask.

"Judith, you can't help Joe. Nobody can help him except Joe. He's an awfully little boy to face what he has to face, but he has no choice. That's how he'll grow up now. Half-blind."

I didn't want to cry in front of Miss Reynolds, but tears began stinging my eyes. "Mrs. Hartsock called me a monster."

Miss Reynolds winced as if she had called her the same name. "Do you think you are?"

"Probably. What should I have done?"

We were both so quiet I could almost hear the sunshine ripple through the tall slag glass windows.

"What would you have done?" I ventured.

"My answer isn't yours, Judith. You have to think it out for yourself."

I flared up. "That's what Papa always says. I'm tired of thinking things out for myself."

I opened and closed the art book again and again, as if my answer lay inside.

"Thinking for yourself is better than any of the alternatives. Believe me."

We grew quiet again. I stared at my dirty hands in my lap. Mama would be mortified at how Sam and I had gone to the dogs. Harem-scarem, she would call us.

"I should have . . . not fought. Should've quit the war. They would've gone on fighting and Joe might still have been blinded, but . . ."

"Yes" was all she said.

"Is that the answer?" I suddenly remembered Papa's duck test. "If you stick around people like Bobby Clawson, you start to act like them."

As Miss Reynolds slipped her glasses back on, the ruby buttons on her chain looked like big drops of blood. I had never seen her so quiet.

"So I should quit fighting. Forever?"

"I doubt that you can," she said slowly. "But, sooner or later, you need to decide what's worth fighting for."

I gently pushed down on the date stamp, not enough to make a mark on the desk. "If only it hadn't been Joe. Bobby Clawson deserved to be blinded."

"You don't mean that."

"Yes, I do. He's evil."

"Judith," she said sharply. "Calling someone *evil*—"

"Bobby beat his dog to death. With a two-by-four. I saw him."

Miss Reynolds recoiled as if she had just slammed her fingers in her drawer.

We sat silently for a while.

"Look at me, child. You can't fix Joe. Or Bobby Clawson."

"Bobby doesn't need fixing."

"Oh yes, he does. More than Joe."

CHAPTER 55

PANDEMIC

O F ALL THE HARD TIME I HAD SERVED ON THE footstool without deserving it, now, when I was involved in a Real Crime, no one was around to punish me. If I understood Miss Reynolds right, I had no other choice. I ate the last ginger snap crumbs in the kitty cookie jar, hid all my music and books, and settled onto the footstool. But I didn't know how long to assign myself. It should be for the rest of my life, or at least until Joe and I were grown-ups, when I would be so crippled I couldn't stand up, let alone play with Sam. Maybe I would know when my time was finished. The log cabin clock said 1:15.

As Grandma Strang would say, I had so many things to puzzle out, I didn't know where to start, and they were all kind of terrible. I wouldn't be in such trouble if I had memorized poems like Mama, especially happy ones like "It Takes a Heap o' Livin' in a House to Make It Home" or thrilling ones like "Invictus." If I closed my eyes, I could hear Mama reciting, "Build thee more stately mansions, O my Jeb." Mama could make anything sound splendid. In the hospital, was she remembering poems? Were they cheering her up? I wished I could recite poetry to her right now to make her time go faster, possibly *Paradise Lost*, although I hadn't read that yet.

Before Joe was blinded, the worst thing I could think about was the riot at the movie theater. For the kids inside, Sam was like the hand throwing the firecracker that burned Papa. Sam. My very own brother. I didn't think that Sam intended to hurt anybody, planning it more like a joke or a cartoon or a Three Stooges movie. But that day, make-believe became real. Like the broomcorn war.

Dresden was different. People dropped real bombs, knowing ahead of time that they would kill thousands of real people and turn all those children into orphans. The Germans couldn't all have been Communists, or even regular bad people like Bobby Clawson. Surely the bomber pilots knew that Dresden contained mostly people like Mrs. Keindorf, beautiful and musical, but they didn't advertise that, I'll bet. Everything felt like a big lie.

Yesterday, Mr. Whitaker had waved me over to sit in his other back porch rocker. I was finally ready to face him. He held out a box of vanilla wafers and told me to take a handful. What a friend. I took six, two each for Papa, Sam and me.

I lunged my body to rock since my feet couldn't reach the porch floor. "Why do some people die and other people don't?"

"What? In tornadoes? War?"

I desperately wanted to ask him about Joe, about what he might have seen during our battle, but I didn't dare. "In the war," I settled on something he liked to talk about.

"What're you botherin' a little girl's head about now? Leave war to the grown-ups. They started it." His cloudy eyes looked over the broom-corn field. "I wish I could tell you I was spared for a reason from the Great War, then from the Second World War." His hand shook as he raised another cookie to his mouth. "But I don't see no reason. No reason for my best friends killed overseas, and so many of 'em with families. Or, for that matter, Edna Vince's brother killed in Hastings, in that terrible explosion nine years ago. No reason a'tall why they're dead, and I'm alive."

He stopped rocking and looked over at me. "What's that brother of yours up to? I ain't heard him going up and down the basement stairs lately."

"I don't know." This was the honest truth. Sam was flying so far under the radar these days that I wouldn't see him for hours at a stretch. "He might still be working on his Personal Fitness merit badge. Or Bookbinding." Somehow, I doubted it.

"He still makin' bombs?"

Ono. Had Mr. Whitaker figured out the Avalon Theater riot?

"Or did blowin' up my fence last summer cure him?"

I let out my breath. In my lap, I separated my vanilla wafers from those I was saving for Papa and Sam.

"You can have more of those, ya know."

"Mama wouldn't let me." I nibbled my first cookie, making it last as long as possible.

"Papa told me I should have stopped Sam."

"Huh. 'Zat why you had to help fix the fence?"

I nodded. "How could I stop Sam? I'm just the little sister."

"Beats the tar outta me." His hand shook as he ate, but not hard enough to drop his vanilla wafer. "Nobody else can stop him."

I couldn't stand it any longer. I had to ask somebody. "Do you think Mama is learning any new poems where she is?"

"It don't matter. You just be damned glad to get her back, however she turns out."

Turns out? Did he know something I didn't?

I tried to rock the same speed as Mr. Whitaker, but I went too fast.

He squinted hard at me. "You need to do somethin' fun, Little One."

"I just got back from the Round Prairie cemetery." It was flat, not like Rose Hill in Hebron, but it had some interesting names.

"You see my folks out there?"

I had noticed Whitaker tombstones, lined up like piano keys, but had never realized they belonged to him.

"Whole row of 'em. Three sisters, my one brother. And my mother," he paused, "God rest her beautiful soul. All of 'em died within two days."

"Wh-what happened?" It had to be in the very very Olden Days, so it couldn't have been the Communists. Maybe it was some other war.

"Influenza. Alive one morning, dead the next night. August 2 and 3, 1918. Died right here in this house."

I had imagined the multiple murders at the Inavale spook house, but I had never thought about people dying in town, and certainly not next door.

"Terrible time. Terrible." He looked across the yard to my swing, past our trailer and the barn, down the gravel street, as if he could see ghosts.

"Killed forty, fifty million people around the world. *Millions.* The big cities run outta coffins, had to bury 'em in mass graves. Some folks thought it was God's punishment for World War I, especially that gas."

I tried not to imagine his family dying in the house behind me. "How did they get the flu?"

"Oh hell, they never did figger it out, or maybe soldiers brought it back from Europe. Only reason Dad 'n me survived was bein' gone. Helpin' my Dad's brother up in South Dakota bring in his wheat harvest."

Mr. Whitaker slid down a little in his chair, even though his bulging sides rested on the wooden arms.

"Got a telegram, the only one in my life and don't need another. I still see that buckboard pullin' up to my uncle's farmhouse. Dust blowin' somethin' fierce that day. They still have terrible dust storms on the South Dakota prairie, you know. And that wagon pullin up to the back door, a good distance away. But you could read "Western Union" on its side. You know fer sure it's bad news. Good news don't come by Western Union."

"Dad 'n me stopped the mules on a turn and watched the driver hand the Missus a paper. And her lookin' at it, turnin' it over in her hands a coupla times and listenin' to the driver. Wind whippin' her hair and her apron."

Even though Mr. Whitaker's eyes had thin clouds over them, he looked as if he could see the whole earth from his back porch.

"And then the Missus shadin' her eyes and lookin' for us, but we was already walkin' toward the farmhouse, my uncle and my dad and me. And she handed Dad the telegram and turned away, and we knowed it was somethin' bad. When my Daddy read it, he … fell down. Right there in the dirt. Just sat there lookin' at the telegram and tryin' to read it agin and agin and shakin' his head and makin' little sounds like an animal caught in a trap."

"I dint know what to do, so I set down beside him and waited and he finally said, 'Oh Charlie, Oh Charlie.' All he could say was 'Oh Charlie.'"

"When I read it, I couldn't take it in, neither. We just set there together, lookin' at the dirt for I don't know how long but my uncle finally walked out and finished the wheat row and come back and unhitched the team."

"It took me I don't know how long to realize that my Mama and my brother and all my sisters was *dead*. My whole family except my Pappy. How could they just die? So fast. And all together. One minute you have 'em, and the next minute, they're gone. They was buried by the time we got the telegram."

I didn't know what to say. I felt so sorry for Mr. Whitaker, for both the young one then and the old one now. His hand was on the wide wooden arm of his rocker, and I put mine on top of it. It twitched, but I knew he wasn't trying to shake me off. I kept my hand there.

"They're still out there," was the only thing I could think to say. "At the cemetery."

He looked at me with a little smile. "Well, I reckon that's a good thing, don't you?" His old eyes had tears under the flaps at the corners. "But like I say, there's no reason why my loved ones are underground, and I'm settin' here." He paused. "Or why one boy gets blinded and the next one don't."

Cookie crumbs stuck in my throat, and I couldn't swallow. "But *Joe*. Wasn't even fighting. It should've been Bobby Clawson or Leon Troxel. Or me."

"You know, Jeb, losin' an eye ain't all bad. It kept your own daddy out of World War II. Might keep the Clary boy from gettin' killed in the next war."

"But it's so unfair."

"Can't worry about fair. Some get blinded, some don't. Some live, some die. " He shook his head. "But the worst is getting' stuck halfway between livin' and dyin'. Helluva note."

Was he talking about Mama?

"Do you think … Sam and I will be … orphans?"

"Sure. Sooner 'r latter, every body's an orphan. Yer daddy. Me. Thelma."

Wow. I had never thought about grown-ups as orphans, only kids like Jane Englehardt.

Mr. Whitaker looked at something across the broomcorn field no one else could see, began eating whole vanilla wafers in one bite, his old, spotted hand in and out of the box, until it was empty.

After a while, the screen door opened, and Sam climbed inside the trailer. He'd been wearing the same shirt for three days and smelled like a wet dog. He sank into my chair-bed.

"What're you doing on the footstool?" He wiped his hand across his mouth, leaving a smudge.

"Thinking."

He looked at me suspiciously. There was no merit badge for thinking. "About what?"

"The Hebron tornado." My answer surprised me. "How one house would be completely demolished, and the house next door wasn't hurt at all. Or Dresden: how some people escaped, but people standing right beside them were burned up."

Sam slid out of the chair onto the floor, where he sat cross-legged. "Yeah." He played with a piece of straw he had tracked in.

"And Joe Clary." I knew that Sam had been thinking about it, too.

"Yeah."

"Mr. Whitaker said it was all chance."

We sat silently for a while. The footstool creaked as if it wanted to be in the conversation, too.

I tried to keep the quiver out of my voice. "Do you think Mama's ever coming home?" Sam and I had a tacit agreement never to talk about Mama, now more than ever.

"She's *got* to." He broke the straw into smaller and smaller pieces. "If she doesn't … I'll attack the hospital. Bomb it. Mount a major offensive … gather every weapon we've ever made and … pipe bombs and …" He began to run down. He knew it was just another Wild Dream.

"Mama's not in the State Hospital," I played our only wild card. "They do let people out of where she is. If they, if they don't … ." I didn't know how to finish this.

Sam answered with his own question, "Do you think Papa would make us live with Grandma Strang?"

I couldn't believe that Sam was asking *me* a question about our future, instead of handing out all the plans and maps and orders. He must feel as scared as I did, even if he would never admit it.

"Papa told me he'd kill himself first."

"Really?" Sam looked as hopeful as I had seen him in weeks.

"When you left me with Grandma while you went to the Scout Jamboree."

"Oh." He deflated. "That was a long time ago."

I took a chance on another forbidden subject. "Do you think Joe will … ever see again?"

Sam pulverized the little pieces of straw under his thumb. "They said his optic nerve was too damaged."

"Maybe he'll grow a new one. He's still a boy."

Sam jumped up. "Don't be stupid. A lotta things don't grow back." He kicked open the screen door, jumped over the steps, and left the door hanging open behind him.

CHAPTER 56

THE SHADOW

SINCE SAM HAD THE ONLY WORKING BICYCLE IN the family, Papa told him to meet me at Hale's to carry groceries home. After the last Round Prairie war, Papa hung it in Sam's throat to watch out for me, so I was surprised that Sam didn't show up. His patrol meeting must have gone overtime, thanks to Marvin the Blowhard. Miss Reynolds said the word *bloviate* was coined to describe the religious and military establishments, both of which were remarkably represented by one family, the Harkins.

To avoid grown-ups with toothy smiles who squeezed our arms and asked about Mama, Sam had drawn a map of the alleys and short-cuts through Round Prairie, especially the quickest route from Main Street to the trailer. It also highlighted other kids' forts, possible stashes for the Formula, emergency hide-outs for temporary safety, and Secret Observation Posts. Since we were no longer enemy combatants, the map served purely defensive purposes. Alleys allowed not only legal spying into people's backyards but also scavenging their trash for possible treasures. Eventually someone would accidentally throw away a diamond ring.

Carrying two heavy sacks of groceries, I realized that I had turned too soon and had already walked halfway down Bobby Clawson's alley. Although I didn't need to worry about his dog any more, I went on alert when I heard strange sounds coming from his back yard. Peeking around the fence at the place where his dog had been tied up, I saw somebody writhing on the ground, with Bobby sitting on his chest, his knees dug into his shoulders. With horror, I realized that the boy on the bottom was

Sam. With one hand, Bobby was slapping Sam's face; in the other, he held a sharpened stick and had already gashed Sam's cheek.

"STOP IT!" I dropped the groceries and ran straight at them.

Bobby paused but, realizing it was me, resumed slapping Sam, harder now, and jabbing at his face with the sharp stick. Sam threw his head from side to side but had no hope of escape. Blood ran out of Sam's nose and down his upper lip.

Bobby prodded the sharp stick ever closer to Sam's eye. "How's that feel, tray-ler boy? Ask Pussy-face Clary."

At his shoulder, I screamed straight in Bobby's ear, "LEAVE HIM ALONE!"

When he didn't stop, I pushed his shoulder as hard as I could. As he pushed back at me, swinging one arm, Sam almost managed to throw him over, but Bobby outweighed him by thirty or forty pounds.

Now Bobby held the sharpened end of the stick right over Sam's eye. Sam squeezed his eyes shut and scrunched up his face.

"Pussy! Say yer old lady's crazy. Nutso." With his face close to Sam's, he hissed, "Say it." Then he spit in Sam's face. "You pussy. SAY IT!"

I grabbed the stick but couldn't wrench it out of Bobby's hand.

"PUSSY!" Bobby screamed in Sam's face.

I took one step back, aimed as if my life depended on it, and, with all the force I could gather, kicked Bobby Clawson in his head, kicked him as hard as I could, right behind his ear.

Time missed a gear, like the moment in the movies when a cowboy hits another one over the head with a whiskey bottle and, for an instant, the victim stands in place before falling over. Bobby dropped the stick, gave a deep sigh, and crumpled sideways off Sam.

Sam slowly stood up, wiping his bloody nose with his dirty hand, leaving smears of blood and dust across his mouth. We watched Bobby slowly struggle to his knees, shake his head like a dog to clear it, then let out a low moan, which cranked up to a howl, loud as a siren.

Behind us, their back door slammed open. In slow motion, we all turned to see a man stomp down their back steps. He might kill us both, but neither Sam nor I would run.

As soon as Bobby saw the man—Bobby Clawson, the meanest bully we had ever known— began to *cry*. "Dad. Dad," he pleaded and stood up, weaving slightly.

"What the hell is going on?" Mr. Clawson was red in the face, maybe from his hot suit or his tight necktie.

"It's my fault," I said to Mr. Clawson. I knew things would go easier for me than Sam. Besides, it was the truth.

"Jeb, don't—" Sam kept sniffing and wiping his nose, which was bleeding harder now. "What is it this time?!" Mr. Clawson shouted at Bobby, who cringed like his dog. He pointed at Sam. "What did he do?"

"I DID IT," I shouted. "It was ME. I kicked him."

Mr. Clawson looked at me as if he had never seen a little girl. I concentrated on Miss Reynolds, thinking this is what a rich, grown-up Visigoth looks like.

Slightly ducking his head, Bobby snuffled, "Y – yeah."

"That little girl kicked you?"

Bobby held his ear and answered with a muffled voice, "In the head."

"A *little girl* kicked you, and you're bawling?"

Bobby nodded.

"I'll give you somethin' to bawl about."

At that—I couldn't believe my eyes—Mr. Clawson wadded up his fist and hit Bobby full force on his mouth. Bobby stumbled backward and sat down hard in the dirt.

"You two," Mr. Clawson turned on Sam and me, "get the hell outta here. And don't ever let me see your sorry asses again!"

We each picked up a sack of groceries and managed not to run until we were out of sight, when we lit out for home and didn't slow down until we skidded into the cool quiet of the trailer. We sat on the linoleum floor, breathing hard for a long time before we even looked at each other. My eyes didn't want to see any more. Of anything.

Slowly I put away the groceries except for the ones on the top shelf, while Sam washed the blood from his face with cold water, then lay down on the sofa with a wet washrag over his nose. It was a good thing Mama wasn't home. Washing blood out of anything always sent her over.

"Want a fig newton?" Papa had added these to the grocery list, even though only Sam liked them.

"You're kidding," Sam said through his swelling lips.

When he could sit up and take away the washrag, Sam took only one and ate it in delicate bites, thoughtfully, just like Mama.

CHAPTER 57

THE HAILSTORM AND
THE RETURN OF SPRING

OUTSIDE CHURCH AND FUNERALS, PAPA NEVER wore a suit, but today was special. The doctor was letting him visit Mama for the first time. The hospital wouldn't allow children, so Papa figured out a safe place to leave Sam and me while he visited her. On top of a hill in Omaha stood an art museum which looked like a Greek temple in the *National Geographic*, except it was pale pink instead of white. I couldn't believe we were in Nebraska, although Omaha was exotic enough to be in a foreign country.

As Papa left us in front of the museum steps, he warned, "Don't touch anything. And don't make any noise." When Papa drilled us with his one good eye, we knew he meant Business and would Find Out if we disobeyed.

"Do we need money?" Sam asked, rather brilliantly, I had to admit.

"It's free on Saturday mornings. I'll be back in a few hours. And don't leave the building." He must have seen me eyeing the cool grassy hill, perfect for rolling down.

By now, an art museum sounded as boring as church. "Do the steps count as part of the building?" At least fifty steps led up to four huge pillars with stone scrolls on top. Any number of Dramatic Moments could be created on this grand staircase.

"Don't leave the *inside* of the building. Sam, I'm putting you in charge. Jeb, what did I say?"

"Why don't you ever put me in charge?"

"Sugar," Papa warned.

For unknown reasons, Papa had also made us wear our Sunday clothes, so at least I could watch the sun dash around my patent leather shoes.

"What did I say about *noise*?" Papa clarified.

Sam volunteered, "I'll keep her quiet."

"I'm never in charge of anything," I complained.

Papa was sweating in his suit, probably from nervousness. He had talked incessantly all the way to Omaha. "You're in charge of keeping Sam in sight. Like a spy." As he climbed back in the Buick, he remembered, "And no running. Nothing faster than a walk. A slow walk." The minute we pulled open the museum's heavy door, all of Papa's warnings became unnecessary. Blocking our entry was a policeman, except he didn't have a gun and had a long white mustache. On his jacket pocket someone had embroidered "**Joslyn Art Museum**." Wow. This place had its own branch of the Omaha police.

"What do you two think you're doing?" He used the voice grown-ups develop to scare children.

That technique never worked with me, but Sam-the-Pseudo-Adult-In-Charge went mute.

I tried to sound like Miss Reynolds. "We came to look at art." For good measure, I added, "You might have noticed, we put on our Sunday clothes on a Saturday."

The old man pulled down on both ends of his mustache, either to look like a movie cowboy or to straighten his smile.

"What kinda art?" The underside of his mustache had tobacco stains.

"Raphael Madonnas and . . . pictures of horses." It never hurt to say what you wanted, and it might actually come true.

"We got plenty of horses."

Oh boy. This place couldn't be a complete waste of time.

He turned on Sam. "What about you?"

Sam was still absorbing my Raphael reference and goggling at the old man's uniform, so I invented, "He's working on his Art merit badge."

The man's eyebrows, furry as his mustache, wiggled upward. "Can't he talk?"

I added, "For Boy Scouts," in case the Omaha police didn't know about merit badges.

Sam stammered, "We . . . we won't make any noise or . . . or . . . ."

"Run or touch anything," I finished, then added, in the interests of accuracy, "except the floor, which we have to walk on."

The guard looked from me to Sam. "I'll be keepin' my eye on both of you." His mouth skewed sideways, definitely an attempt not to laugh. It might be against the rules to laugh in an art museum.

He turned with us as we circled him to enter an indoor courtyard, two stories high. In the middle stood a fountain covered with glistening tiles in sapphire blue, emerald green and shades of turquoise. It bubbled and bubbled, without running over.

"How does it do that?" I whispered.

"I dunno," Sam answered, as mesmerized as I was.

Tiles on the floor had words embedded in them like "Ornat Pictura Ornat Domum" and "Musica Laetificat Musica Domum." Either some-body couldn't spell, or this was a foreign language about something named *domum*. Lights grew out of the walls on golden petals and nearby stood massive gold doors. All that gold wasted on doors. But standing in that courtyard was like standing inside a piece of jewelry. Even with the foun-tain gurgling, the museum created a quiet I had never heard and a kind of safety like a beautiful castle. I couldn't wait to tell Miss Reynolds and Mrs. Keindorf.

Sam whispered, "Do you think they'd care if we stuck our hands in the fountain?"

"Wouldn't that count as *touching* something?" I couldn't believe my brother sometimes.

"It's just water."

"I'll ask the policeman."

"Never mind."

We circled the fountain twice before entering the first room of paintings. Red flowered rugs stretched along the floors as in movie mansions, far too beautiful to walk on, but people were doing it, anyway. If Mama wouldn't let us step on people's lawns, what would she say about this? I wondered if she had ever been here.

Then I saw all the paintings of half-naked people. I was flabbergasted. Sometimes the men were partially wrapped in colorful sheets and held spears or flags over dead people. The half-naked women either lay on their backs in the forest like a camp-out or pleaded with men in armor who didn't seem to notice they were half naked. One lady was completely naked, except her long hair draped over her body, thick as a buffalo rug. I thought she must be Rapunzel, but Sam read a card nearby that called her Magdalene. She was talking to the top half of a tiny angel sticking out of a wall—not a baby, but a full grown-up the size of a doll, as if he had drunk from Alice's potion to grow small. He looked furious and held out a piece of wood to her.

Sam said quietly, "It's a Catholic Communion wafer. Like Methodists eat bread crumbs."

"Why can't we eat Communion wafers?"

"They're too expensive," he answered. "Besides, they taste like cardboard."

"When did you eat one?"

Sam continued to bluff, but with silence.

I was now arrested by a picture of a sick-looking monk with bleeding holes in his palms. Try as I might, I couldn't find anything nearby that could have stabbed him. Over his head, the clouds looked like moldy bread. Near the monk hung a lot of paintings of Mary with Baby Jesus, usually flanked by angels wearing bathrobes and a little boy draped with an animal skin.

"Do you know who that boy is?" Sam pointed.

"Of course," I lied. I had learned the rest of the story about Luther-the-hymn-writer on my own, so Sam could research the boy in fur by himself.

Since this seemed to be a religious room, I looked around for the paintings on our church fans, especially Jesus holding the kids on his lap. Sam explained these people were Catholic heroes, so they wouldn't appear on Methodist fans.

"Besides, Methodists don't have heroes."

"Yes we do," I objected.

"Name one," he challenged.

I pulled out of nowhere, "President Eisenhower."

"Presidents can't be religious," Sam scoffed.

"He added God to the Pledge of Allegiance."

"Okay, but he's not a Methodist," Sam conceded.

"He might be," I finished Sam off with my standard response.

In a long room with skylights hung paintings of rich people wearing yards of changeable velvet and satin so stiff and shiny I could hear it rustle. Every collar and cuff was trimmed with intricate lace that Grandma Strang could have crocheted when her eyes were good. They seemed more real than people in the movies, which was strange because they were flat pictures on a flat wall, but if you looked at them and listened hard, you could hear them whisper. On the other hand, their horses were utterly ridiculous, with curly manes and cow eyelashes, rearing in poses which would break the back legs of a real horse.

However, in the next room, the Indian paintings were chock full of lifelike, sensible horses, mostly appaloosas and pintos charging into battle or running alongside buffalo. With the Boy Scout signal for "come," Sam waved me over to a picture in which several Indians were painting their ponies with war paint. You would think an appaloosa or pinto wouldn't need a fancy paint job and could save the Indians valuable fighting time, but they outlined the natural horse spots with red and drew lightning bolts wherever the ponies didn't have markings.

"Think about this," Sam whispered, his breath hot in my ear. "The Indians are painting horses which are already paints, while the artist is painting them painting their horses."

This sounded deep, but I couldn't quite put my finger on why. "Wow."

In a room called Regionalism, we elbowed each other not to giggle at a painting named "Stone City, Iowa," which showed fake little rounded hills and ping-pong ball trees and matchbox houses and crops which looked like tiny fireworks sprouts. Had this artist ever been to Iowa or seen real corn? Nearby, a painting of a hailstorm sobered us up. Lightning was cracking down near a farmer trying to control his runaway mule, while another farmer was running for cover in exactly the wrong place–under a tree. Even though everything in the painting looked fake, it *felt* like a sudden hailstorm on the prairie. The air in front of the painting actually felt colder, just as it had near the backdrop for the school play in the basement with Miss Reynolds. It was like telling a lie which turned out to be true.

In the last room, Sam stopped dead in front of a painting called "Return of Spring" by a man named Bouguereau, a perfect name containing only three consonants but seven vowels, including three u's. The lady stood completely naked, big as an actual woman, with one knee bent and her arms crossed over her chest. She was being pestered by nine naked little boys with wings, not so much angels as bothersome three-year-olds who thought they were cute. For no reason, the boy directly over her head held a sharp arrow, while the others pulled at her hair and did who knows what behind her. She cocked her head to one side as if she were out of patience, but her partially closed eyes said she was also having fun.

On my fourth return to Sam, I asked, "Why do you keep looking at that lady?" He could have been practicing "freeze."

"I'm not looking at her. I'm trying to figure out how those flimsy wings can hold up a thirty-pound kid."

"That didn't bother you about the angel talking to the hairy Magdalen. He couldn't fly, either."

"He was plastered into a wall."

My very, very favorite painting in the whole museum showed a lady lying in a hammock next to a man sitting at a table drinking tea. He wore a white suit and shirt and tie, even little white coverings over his patent leather shoes, while her pale pink skirt cascaded over the edge of the hammock. He toyed with his teacup handle, while she listened half-asleep, her face partially hidden with her white hand and lace cuff. A tree overhead threw puzzle-shaped shadows around the ground. What would it be like to live in this painting, to see Mama and Papa peacefully talking among spots of sunlight and shade? On second thought, even if our family ever had a real house and yard, we wouldn't own a hammock and a tea set, and Papa wouldn't be caught dead in that white suit.

As we left the museum, Papa thanked the policeman, which was unnecessary, since he hadn't done a darned thing. Papa didn't look exactly happy, but he looked less wound up. For starters, he had taken off his tie.

As soon as we were outside, I asked, "How is Mama?"

"She's . . . different."

Sam pushed, "Better?"

"Well, certainly . . . calmer."

Sam and I overlapped, "Is she coming home? When?"

"I don't know."

I was afraid to ask but had to. "But sometime." Any time would be better than never.

"I think so," he answered.

At the car, Papa took off his suit coat. "What did you think of the art museum?"

I looked back at the pink temple on the hill. "You might want to know that rich people–not rich like the Cavins or Clawsons, but *really* rich people–built this place just for art. It's like a castle."

Sam interrupted, "They let anybody look." He added, "If they're quiet." He wanted to cover our assignment. Neither of us mentioned the naked ladies.

I tried to explain, "Guess what else? The paintings tell stories better than the movies. The people seem more ... real than real people." That wasn't quite right, but it didn't matter. I could tell that Papa had quit listening.

By the outskirts of Omaha, Sam said, "I've decided to work on an Art merit badge."

"Don't do it on my account," I responded. I never felt comfortable when a perfectly good lie came true.

CHAPTER 58

FUGUE

WHEN THE TOWN SIREN SCREAMED, PAPA AND Sam and I all jerked awake, waiting to hear if it signaled a tornado or a fire. If a tornado, we would run for Mr. Whitaker's basement.

A long wail, followed by two shorts: a fire. The sound circled out but didn't fully die before the next howl started, overlapping itself. Was that a round or a fugue, I wondered, half asleep. Mrs. Keindorf would know.

By the end of the first signal, Papa was out of the bedroom, fully dressed and pulling on his boots without even turning on the light.

"You kids," he said, out of breath and dead serious. "Stay here. No matter how long I'm gone. Hear me? Promise. Sam? Jeb?"

Sam and I murmured an answer.

"I'll be back as soon as I can." Papa slammed the door behind him.

In the dim light from the street, Sam stood near my chair bed in his cowboy pajamas. Over the still screaming siren, we heard the Buick start up and spit gravel as Papa raced off to the fire station.

"Wow," Sam sighed. "A real, full-sized fire. We've never seen a real fire. Wonder where it is."

I pulled the sheet up to my chin. "Probably somebody's barn. What time is it?"

He squinted in the dark at the log cabin clock. "One fifteen."

Since Mama left, we never woke up in the middle of the night. I wondered if she were awake right now and what they did to her if she didn't sleep. They probably didn't let her wander around crying or reciting poetry.

Sam paced the trailer, staring out every window, even from the folks' bedroom. "What if it's in town?" he asked wistfully.

The siren dropped in pitch and wound down to silence.

"Must be close, or the siren wouldn't quit," he added.

Without the fort, our opportunities for playing war were severely limited. I began inventing, "It's the perfect time for the enemy to attack."

"Absolutely." Sam now looked like our squadron commander who had just received new orders.

Since it was all make-believe, it couldn't hurt anyone to add, "We haven't practiced night-time maneuvers–"

"We promised Papa," Sam answered tentatively.

"Yeah," I agreed. We both knew how we had mumbled that. "But your Scout oath says to help other people at all times." Even though Sam never obeyed the oath, this excuse could get us to the fire before it burned out.

Sam looked down at me still in bed. "How many chances like this will we ever get to practice reconnaissance during an actual attack?"

I threw back my sheet. "We'll be back before Papa gets home. Nobody will ever know."

We quickly pulled shirts on over our pajama tops and were outside in less than a minute, both wearing shoes without socks. If Mama had seen us, we would have turned to pillars of smoke on the spot, incinerated like Gort's targets. Both Charlie Whitaker's and the Hartsocks' lights flicked on.

"The whole town is under bombardment," Sam used his P-51 Mustang pilot's voice, but with no bombers to escort. "We're the only ones who can save Round Prairie."

"Let's leave the Formula here to protect the trailer." Since Mama had left, we carried the Formula with us everywhere, both for her protection and our own.

"Good idea, Corporal."

A very good idea, since it had instantly promoted me from buck private.

Just then, we heard the siren on the fire truck itself wind up, a mobile version of the town alarm. We were near enough to hear the old truck roar. Papa was probably driving because he was the only one who knew how to double-clutch through its bad gears.

Sam raised his arm in the cavalry "halt" sign, concentrating on the position of the blaring fire truck.

At first, I was afraid that the library was on fire. If the anti-Communists had come to burn books, Miss Reynolds would be patrolling the sidewalk with her shotgun. I would defend her and the library to the death.

"This way," Sam shouted and pointed toward Lincoln Elementary. Surely not the school! We ran in the dark street, zigzagging to avoid enemy machine gun fire from Doreen Cavin's house, brightly lit with people moving inside. All over, people were rushing outdoors to gawk, starting their cars, filling the backs of their pick-ups with neighbors to go see the fire. The movie projected on top of Round Prairie, like on the wall of the Inavale drive-in, was being ripped apart by all the real-life action in the houses and streets.

Sam and I paused to catch our breath and regroup beside the school fire escape. Through the trees lining the playground, we could now see an ominous flickering, while all around us in the dark, dogs were howling. From the direction of Guide Rock, we heard a distant siren racing along the highway.

In spite of the humid night, I felt cold goose bumps on my neck. We skirted the playground to stay in streetlight shadows and then, slowing down, walked toward the fire, now flashing eerie light into the treetops around us. As we rounded the last corner, we stumbled to a halt. I couldn't move. I could barely breathe.

It couldn't be.

It was.

Mrs. Keindorf's house was on fire.

"Sam—" I choked.

"Oh man. Oh man." Sam instinctively grabbed my wrist.

The county's old La France fire truck stood in front of her house, while volunteer firemen shouted and unrolled the hose, flat as snake skin, to connect it to the nearest hydrant. The fire engine kept a steady, throaty beat under the chaos of men running every direction. Mr. Hawkins from the hardware store and Mike Letson's father and—of all people—Mr. Sprecker were putting on hard hats and heavy coats. Mr. Sprecker a fireman. I would never have guessed that. The men suddenly transformed into strangers in their uniforms, exotic as movie stars. I couldn't see Papa anywhere.

Smoke rolled out the windows dark as soot, but laced with flashes of unexpected blue and emerald, as if we were seeing her jewelry burn.

"Wow." Sam was transfixed.

"It's Mrs. Keindorf's house," I repeated, trying to convince myself while hoping this was a nightmare or even a hallucination like Mama's blue elevator.

Suddenly, the fire pierced through the roof, and the crowd gave a little ahhh, as if they were looking at fireworks. Flames began to chew the shingles and rafters like teeth, spitting huge sparks into the sky. The air smelled like burning hair.

With growing panic, I remembered Mrs. Keindorf. "Sam! She could be inside! We've got to save her!"

"No!" Sam twisted my wrist behind my back in a loose half-nelson. In the jumping firelight, his face looked pale and sweaty. "If she's in there, it's too late."

"But it's *Mrs. Keindorf,*" I pleaded. "She could be burning alive." I remembered her story about climbing out of the basement while Dresden burned. The harder I tried to pry loose, the higher up my back Sam pulled my arm, his death grip.

"It's TOO LATE!" Sam's voice had the high, frenzied pitch I only heard once before, in our last broomcorn war. "I'll pin you down right here in the street and sit on you until Papa finds us."

Sam kept staring at the popping, spurting flames. It was deafening, more violent and destructive than his wildest dreams while building pipe bombs or planning the Avalon Theater riot, greater than any Greatest Plan of All Time he could ever imagine.

He talked more to himself than to me. "How did it start? How would you get a whole house to catch fire at once?"

I couldn't believe what was happening until I found the words that fit. "This isn't a trick or a joke or a movie. It's a real fire, the kind that burns all your treasures and kills people."

I watched a fireman checking hose connections for a few seconds before I realized it was Papa. As in my nightmare, his body was silhouetted against the flames, cutting his own shape out of the fire wherever he moved.

I elbowed Sam.

He had seen him, too. "Sh-h-h!"

"If Papa gets burned—" I couldn't finish the sentence. Could burn scars burn twice? What if Papa were killed? Sam and I would be complete orphans without a mother or father.

A woman, tall as Mrs. Vince and wearing a man's shirt and pants, walked quickly among the firemen, ignoring the fire and smoke, closely looking into their faces and listening to what they said. From her back pocket I saw a stethoscope dangling. This must be Dr. Mary!

The pumper dropped in pitch under the work load as it began throwing a weak stream of water onto Mrs. Keindorf's perforated roof. By now, people had filled the street, the women with their hair tied in rags or crimped in bobby pins, all strangely silent, tying and re-tying their robes, staring. Everyone's face looked distorted in the firelight, like Halloween masks or the clown at the Hastings fair, and they moved like zombies, heavy and slow. In contrast, the yelling firemen seemed to run even faster, as if they lived in a different time frame, as if Mrs. Keindorf's metronome were set at Largo while the pianist played Presto.

"Sam! Judith!" We turned to see Miss Reynolds with her cane limping and swaying down the road in a loose dress and her bedroom slippers. I had never seen her move so fast. As she caught up with us, she was breathing hard. "I knew you two would be here. Shame on you!"

"Papa," I said feebly, "could be hurt."

Sam loosened his grip on my arm, which was starting to cramp.

"I'll tell you who'll be hurt!" She shouted above the deafening sound of the fire engine, people arriving in cars, and the Guide Rock fire truck siren, now close. I didn't know she could shout.

"It's Mrs. K-Kein—" Now that a grown-up was around, I felt like crying.

"Your father would be furious if he knew you were here." The flames reflecting off her glasses gave her fire for eyes, like a powerful figure out of a fairy tale.

"She could be inside." I pulled on Miss Reynolds' bare arm, which felt soft and cool. "Doesn't anybody *care*?" I was feeling sick.

"We all care," she yanked her arm out of my hand. "But we can't help now. Do you *hear* me?"

"Where is Mrs. Keindorf?" Sam asked.

"I don't know. But Greta's not. In there." Her cheeks shook. "They're not about to do that."

"Do what?" Sam asked breathlessly.

"They might play with arson, but they wouldn't gamble with manslaughter."

"Who?" Sam now used his G-man's voice.

"Whoever did this," Miss Reynolds answered with her teeth closed.

I felt sicker and sicker. "On purpose? Somebody burned her house on purpose?" It still might be a trick that got out of hand, like Sam's at the Avalon Theater. But whose Greatest Plan of All Time would burn down a house and possibly kill innocent people?

At that moment, who but Marvin Harkin walked in front of the crowd, waved his arms and shouted for everyone to move back. Even at this hour, he wore his Scoutmaster's shirt, which pulled at the buttons across his stomach and hung out of his pants. His bald head looked shiny in the firelight.

Sam and I ducked out of sight behind Miss Reynolds, who snorted at him, "What are you doing here, Marvin?"

"Crowd control." His grin looked as wide and painted on as the clown's at the county fair.

"How big a crowd were you expecting?"

"Real funny, Thelma."

He started to take her arm, but she yanked back.

"Don't you touch me." While he walked off but could still hear her, she added, "Nitwit."

Across the crowd, I briefly glimpsed Will Hankins, who held both his hands over his mouth as if he would scream if he let go. I wondered how many fires he had seen, not counting campfires or fires in garbage drums.

As Marvin went down the line, a man yelled, "BETTER! DEAD! Than RED!" A few people echoed, "Red . . . Dead . . ." Some people around him nodded, but others shied away.

The less I understood, the more frantic I felt. "Who's dead? They said dead. And who's red? What does that mean?"

Miss Reynolds' voice rose over the chaos. "Some brilliant barbarian deduced the Keindorfs were Communists."

"But . . . but she wasn't—" I defended her.

"Of course not! All it took was one rumor. Like a match in a powder keg."

Sam reluctantly looked away from the exploding fire long enough to ask, "Who?"

Miss Reynolds stared at three men standing with their arms folded and their legs wide apart. "I don't know, but I'll bet they do."

The men looked at the burning house as if they were judging cattle at the county fair.

I immediately recognized Bobby Clawson's father, but not the man standing beside him. I had seen the third man but couldn't remember where. He kept pulling up his pants.

"Bobby Clawson's dad!" I gasped.

"Your friend and mine," Miss Reynolds answered.

Sam pressed, "Why would those guys know who did it?"

As Miss Reynolds looked at the men, the muscles in her cheek moved, as if she were chewing something she couldn't swallow. "They know everything that happens. Sometimes before it happens."

Something within the house exploded, sending flames and cinders into the street. The crowd fell back then resurged like a musical crescendo.

The fat under Miss Reynolds' chin quivered. "How fortunate that you two can witness firsthand the savages at work."

Visigoths, I thought.

"And all the rest of us dead little souls," she waved her cane in a vague gesture, "Even the 'innocent' ones are thanking our miserable gods it's the Keindorfs and not ourselves." Her voice rattled. "Civilization collapses, one person at a time." She sounded as if she were about to cry.

With another small explosion, the roof over the living room dropped all at once, engulfing Mrs. Keindorf's piano and the wall behind her piano, the wall holding the Archduke Franz Ferdinand and the picture of Dresden. Her lovely blonde piano burning. A piano wasn't like a regular piece of furniture, not even the cowboy furniture that she hated.

"Dresden," I murmured. I imagined the picture of the magic city falling with the wall, the glass shattering, the print itself curling at the edges then floating upward in ashes as delicate as antique lace. Dresden burning, again.

I suddenly felt that the collapse of her living room crushed time as well, all the time she and I had spent there—my piano lessons, her playing for me, the waltzes and lullabies, the themes and variations–were smashed on the floor. My music. My memories. My teacher.

"Mrs. Keindorf's records—" I choked, remembering those thin ebony plates she had brought from Germany.

Sam answered, "They've melted. They're just plastic." The firelight jumped in his eyes.

I wanted my brother, not the Boy Wonder Scientist. "They're Rachmaninoff and *La Valse* and fugues."

Miss Reynolds said, "Greta may have had time to save something. But she and Helmut probably felt lucky just to escape with their lives." Miss Reynolds kept taking deep breaths. "For the second time. Or third time, or tenth time. Those poor, poor people."

"Are you sure she escaped?" I rested my hand on her arm.

"Oh, child." This time Miss Reynolds put her hand over mine. "Child, child."

The fire was growing smaller, but the smoke rolled out thicker, causing onlookers to retreat to neighboring yards.

"Is this the most terrible thing that ever happened in Round Prairie?" I asked.

"Yes, Judith. It is."

Sam always wanted to establish scale. "Worse than the Hebron tornado?"

"People didn't cause the tornado."

I felt the need to clarify, "Sam didn't have anything to do with this." For once, I could be his alibi without lying.

"Cross my heart," he said solemnly, but without sounding completely relieved to be out of the competition.

She looked Sam for a long moment. "I would certainly hope not," she responded, then decided, "Time's up. You go straight home right now, and I won't tell your father that I saw you here tonight."

Sam admitted, "He said he would skin us alive if he ever caught us chasing a fire and gawking at someone's tragedy."

"That's because your father's a civilized human being. Unlike most of us in Round Prairie."

We took one last, long look.

"Let me phrase it differently," Miss Reynolds added, now impatient. "If you don't go home on your own volition, right now, I will personally accompany you there and stay until Frank comes home."

"We're leaving," Sam answered quickly.

"Judith, I'm putting you in charge."

What?

"I'm trusting you to make sure that Sam gets home."

I couldn't believe my ears. How was I supposed to do that?

Watching Sam's reaction, she added, "And Judith, I'm putting you on your honor to tell me if Sam doesn't go directly home."

Sam finally looked away from the fire and up at her.

"What is the vulgar colloquialism for that?" She continued, "*Ratting? Squealing?*"

"Yeah," he answered.

"Promise me, Judith."

"I promise."

As we walked away, Miss Reynolds' last words to me were, "Remember, Judith, you're in charge."

Sam led the way, although our line of command had shifted, if only temporarily.

As Sam and I reached the back of the crowd, we saw Sheriff Westergaard walk over to the little group of men now including Marvin Harkin. I motioned for us to snake around and hide behind a huge snowball bush to eavesdrop.

"Town council meeting? At this hour?" the Sheriff asked.

"Evenin,' Sheriff," the stranger said.

"Whatchoo doin' here, Cavin?"

Now I recognized him from the birthday party: Doreen's father!

"Terrible thing," he answered.

"Terrible, terrible," they all echoed, shook their heads and looked at the ground. Any idiot could see they didn't mean it.

"Any idea how it started?" Marvin asked. His eyes jerked from the Sheriff to each man in turn.

The Sheriff rested his hand on the butt of the revolver at his waist. "Keindorf's Dry Cleaners was broken into earlier tonight."

"Izzat so?" Mr. Clawson asked.

"Good God," Mr. Cavin responded. "What a coincidence."

"Maybe so, maybe not," the Sheriff answered. "Somebody took a lotta chemicals outta there."

The other men grunted, "Huh."

"Flammable chemicals." The Sheriff added, "Splashed them around inside as if they were gonna burn that building, but then changed their mind."

"That's good, anyway," Mr. Cavin said.

Marvin added, "That woulda burned halfa downtown." He nodded at everyone around the circle as if he needed their agreement that burning half of Main Street would be a bad idea.

Mr. Clawson nudged the grass under his toe. "Whadda you know."

"Not much," the Sheriff answered. "How 'bout you, Clawson?"

"Less every day."

"Ain't that the truth?" Mr. Cavin echoed.

"Looks like arson," the Sheriff slowly looked from one man to the next. "Keep your eyes open, Councilmen. Once arson gets started, it could burn any of us." The Sheriff ambled off, his arms folded across his chest.

Sam and I practiced "freeze" until they moved away, then we practically tiptoed away from the scene.

Sam kept looking over his shoulder at the fire, the last house fire we were ever likely to see, and throwing out facts about A-bombs and H-bombs.

"This sure was more powerful than a pipe bomb."

"*Exponentially* more powerful." I had finally learned what that word meant.

Attempting to regain command, Sam used his B-17 pilot's voice, more boomy than the Mustang pilot's and way boomier than his Hardy Boys detective voice. "They probably used a pipe bomb to start it."

As we turned the corner to cross the playground and head for home, I seized my chance. "Do you think Marvin Harkin helped start the fire?"

"Don't be stupid."

I used my new authority to echo Papa, "Who are you calling stupid?"

"The Scoutmaster wouldn't do something illegal."

"I wouldn't count on it." Sounding like Mama, I added mysteriously, "I know what I know."

"Which isn't much."

In the case of Marvin Harkin, it was considerably more than Sam knew.

Mostly to irritate him, I asserted my temporary authority from Miss Reynolds to call a halt at the fire escape. He knew I would squeal on him in this special circumstance.

For no reason, Sam half-whispered, "Did you see how weird the people acted who were watching? Like zombies."

"Do you think they were brainwashed? By the Communists?"

"Who knows?"

"Mama would know."

"No, she wouldn't. Or, at least, not anymore. I hope she's given up on the Communists."

I wasn't in the mood for Sam's realism. By now, we had lived through so many events without Mama that I always included her whenever I could, keeping her alive as long as possible.

Before walking on home, we looked back across the dark playground. Trees obscured everything but sparks and ashes climbing the night sky, flying up like torn musical notes trying to make the stars pay attention.

CHAPTER 59
STUFFY

MAMA NEVER DID COME BACK.

Near the end of summer, we drove to Omaha, past the Insane Asylum and fairgrounds at Hastings, past the various standpipes like candy sticks and coffee pots, past the turn-off to the little ponies probably still trudging around their circle, last of all past the grand temple of the Joslyn Art Museum. As we drove by, I waved hello to the paintings of the woman in the hammock, the angel stuck in the wall holding out the Communion wafer, and the farmers running from the hailstorm. But not to the three-year-olds teasing the naked lady.

In the hospital parking lot, Sam and I waited, quieter than in church, too nervous to play Twenty Questions or even toy cars. On the ground floor, the hospital windows had curlicue jail bars behind iron flower boxes spilling out pink and white petunias.

For today, Sam had braided my stupid hair into two stubs sticking out of my head at different levels, tidier than Papa's daily attempts, but, after all, Sam had ten complete fingers and extensive practice braiding Boy Scout latigo. While Mama was gone, I had lost two front teeth, right in the middle, looking like the reverse of Bugs Bunny. Sam called me "Sgub Ynnub," the only time he had ever indulged in backward spelling.

After a long time, a woman who vaguely resembled Mama walked out, smiling, with her hand through Papa's arm. He opened the car door for her, and she climbed in to ride home with us. But it wasn't Mama. For starters, her hair was snow white with dark brown tips, and it had no waves at all. This lady was chubby, an inflated balloon rounded out, but not enough to pop. If this were Mama, what had they blown into her? And what had they sucked out?

At the first corner, she slowly twisted in the seat and said, "Hello, children." Her metronome was barely moving. Slower than Lento. I wouldn't let myself think about my beautiful, missing teacher Mrs. Keindorf, and certainly not now.

Sam and I silently nodded hello.

This lady's mouth sounded dry, but at least her teeth were white and her dress, a green cotton sack tied at the waist, was starched so stiff it didn't move when she did. Her eyelids drooped, and her eyes moved slowly, taking extra time to refocus when they stopped. She looked at the passing buildings as if she had never seen a city.

On the drive home, like Mama, she looked out the car window but remarked on fancy new tractors and fields of summer fallow, not just deserted farmhouses or crops with hail damage. Papa agreed with everything she said, talking incessantly as if he were afraid that silence might rip holes in the air in the car, and we might suffocate. Since he was incapable of pretending, Papa must be happy, happier than I had ever seen him, although in a glittery way, like Christmas decorations. Occasionally, the lady turned halfway around to ask us questions about the spelling bee, the Scout Jamboree, and new merit badges. Sam and I nodded like two ventriloquist dummies without anyone to run us.

"How's your stick horse, Jeb? What's its name?" she asked with a thick tongue. She sounded like one of the church ladies inquiring how our 'dear mother' was, acting polite to cover up being nosy.

"La Cheetah," I spit out through the hole between my front teeth.

Sam and I looked at each other, unblinking, and answered the rest of her questions with a plain yes or no. Soon we fell into sign language and tapped Morse code on each other's leg, then silently counted cows and cemeteries, although we knew every cemetery and most of the cows on the road home.

As the days passed, she did some things I always wanted Mama to do, like hold my hand or kiss me good-night, but now it felt creepy. I wanted my Mama, not some stranger. Even if my old Mama scared the tar out of me, even if she ignored me or made me cry, she was still *mine*. I saw no way of getting her back now.

This woman sewed three flowered dresses for herself, wore the right amount of rouge on both cheeks and shopped for groceries on Saturday morning, one of my former dreams come true. Now I couldn't remember why I wanted it. In Hale's Grocery, she discovered that we had forgotten to buy Volumes 12, 13 and 14 of Funk and Wagnall's Encyclopedia while she was in the hospital. Instead of flying off the handle, she laughed. If you can imagine. Laughed. I had to admit that I liked her laugh. When Mama One had laughed, it was worse than crying: high-pitched and hysterical, more like flailing her arms. Mama Two's laugh was raspy as a spring on a screen door which hadn't been opened for years, causing people around her to laugh as well.

She also walked across the street to talk to people on the opposite sidewalk, which embarrassed me no end. Sam and I had perfected so many methods of dodging people, had created so many secret maps and trails through town, that suddenly navigating Round Prairie like everybody else felt like a lie. Just because she wanted to be normal didn't mean that I did. She actually told people we met that I was shy, the last word my original mother would ever have used for me. Besides, everybody in town knew better, although, amazingly, they played along with her. For starters, they tried to pat my head. What liars.

It felt as if our original Mama were a house hit by a tornado, now looking safe from the outside, but once you climb through a window, you see the tilting walls and sagging ceilings, floors caved in all the way to the basement, beams and rafters ripped apart and fallen like Pick-up sticks. I listened for sounds from her like those in the Inavale spook house—whispered memories, old piano music, screams thin and high as a wire. Silence.

Could anybody find and reassemble all her missing pieces like a complex puzzle? Or would she be like the reconstructed houses after the Hebron tornado, new and livable, with almost no resemblance to the original mansions they once were, no memory of their wide wraparound porches and intricate gingerbread trim? Or the county courthouse, now safe and solid but with a flat roof, missing all its magic turrets and spires?

After supper one evening, Sam and I were stacking the dishes to dry them when she said that we didn't need to help.

"Hot dog!" Sam was out the door before she could change her mind.

"Why?" I asked suspiciously. "We've always dried the dishes."

"That's right, she said uncertainly.

"Don't you remember?" Instead of feeling glad, my eyes began to sting.

She gestured for me to sit back down at the table, cleared except for the dirty silverware. She had a new habit of tucking her white hair behind her ears, even though it wasn't escaping. Deep down, I knew that the roots of her hair had turned white overnight when Papa was in the explosion. All the color had drained out, a Technicolor movie turned black and white. I knew that all my life her hair had been actually white, white as piano keys, white as Joe Clary's hair, just waiting to show itself in the next terrible event. Like a nervous breakdown.

But I didn't want to know what I knew. I didn't want to look at Mama's true hair. I wanted her to have dark brown waves like Uncle Ralph's, even if it were a lie. I wanted her to be skinny and to scream at me and push me down on the footstool when I broke a rule I didn't know existed.

"Sam and I have always dried the dishes," I objected. "For years and years and years."

Over her shoulder the cookie jar winked at me.

"Did you?"

I could understand her forgetting La Cheetah's name, but not an everyday thing like doing the dishes. Next it would be ironing and sewing and cleaning. Who was this woman? What had they done to her?

I couldn't stand it. "You're not my Mama!"

She played with one of the dirty knives on the table. "I'm not the woman who left here, that's for sure." She paused. "They call it 'being out of your mind' for a reason, Jeb. I was out of my mind."

I didn't know how to ask it. "Are you in your mind now?"

When she smiled, her chubby cheeks made her blue eyes smaller, although not as small as Miss Reynolds'. "Most of the time."

"So the person you are now? That's who you will be? Forever?" Or until one of us dies, I silently added.

"There's no such thing as forever. The Wilder family should know that by now. Tornadoes, explosions, nervous breakdowns all make sure of that." She sighed. "But I know this: I was too hard on you kids."

What was she doing now? Trying to erase Mama One, like a Magic Slate? "No you weren't."

"Making you be quiet, working all the time, the footstool. I expected you to act like adults." She pushed down on the knife as if she wanted to carve some message in the tabletop, not just her initials like those carved in my school desk.

"In other words, just like Grandma Strang raised me."

Immediately, I wanted to defend Grandma, to tell her about sewing her pajamas and listening to stories about the POWs and the Children's Blizzard, but this didn't seem like the right time. She probably already knew. If she hadn't forgotten that, too. I also wanted to ask how someone could grow up "too soon": was growing up a brand-new kind of time? I took the easy way out and decided not to think about it yet.

"Can I, *may* I, go outside and play with Sam?" A pure lie. I didn't feel like playing with Sam or anybody else.

She nodded yes and kept pushing the knife into the tabletop, tracing words only she could understand.

As the days passed, I began to worry about the poetry. I casually started by testing her with old and easy poems, reciting from memory "The Children's Hour" and "Little Boy Blue" and "Somebody said it couldn't be done." She looked at me as if I were speaking in tongues, an expression I had overheard in the grocery store. It seemed to me that all speech was speaking in tongues, but this had something to do with the Church of the Spirit or the Church of the Lamb or the Church of the New Day or something like that. Most likely in Kansas, where they conducted church differently than in Nebraska.

Maybe she would remember the harder poems. I trotted out "Richard Cory" and the brains of men eaten by maggots, I recited "I heard a fly buzz when I died" from memory, then read aloud other Emily Dickinson, like "I felt a cleavage in my brain" and "Hope is a thing with feathers." No luck. She stared at me with a slack jaw, as if she were asleep with her eyes open.

I grew so desperate that one day, to make her hopping mad, I sang Brahms' "Lullaby" in German. She merely hummed along with her eyes closed, rocking her head from side to side.

"Remember 'The Bells'? 'The Bells, the bells, the tintinnabulation of the bells . . .'?"

She began tentatively, "The bells, the bells . . . ."

Oh good. This would work.

Then I watched her walk down the bookshelves in her mind, watched her search for bells, bells, bells. And saw reflected in her eyes that all those shelves were empty.

She blinked fast a few times. "Jeb, if you tell me I used to recite all those poems by heart, I must have done it. You wouldn't lie. But I. Can't. Remember."

"Why would the hospital steal your poems?" I asked incredulously.

"Poems must have made me crazy in the first place." How? How could *poems* do that?

She put her open palms on her cheeks and pulled her mouth downward into an upside-down smile. "Humpty-Dumpty."

I didn't have the heart to ask if she remembered "Humpty-Dumpty." I had one idea left. A few days later, I cranked up my courage and asked if she remembered the flying horses or the jumper on the ledge downtown, the blue elevator or the dead body in the trailer.

She looked at me a long time, then slowly shook her head no. She looked so sad I almost put my arm around her. Maybe Papa had secretly married Mama's chubby twin or Grandma Strang's baby who hadn't really died but had grown up in secret somewhere. How else could I explain this woman who slept all night, who bought extra ice cream, who never screamed, who didn't clean the trailer when it was already spotless, and who sometimes stared at Sam and me as if she had never seen us before?

Huddled in candlelight in the Inavale storm cellar, I continually tried to talk to Sam about her, but he was no help.

"You gotta admit, she's a lot easier to get along with than before," Sam pointed out cheerfully while he sharpened his Boy Scout knife on a special stone he had bought with extra allowance.

"She's forgotten all the poems."

"So? Now she's normal."

"Is that what you want?"

"Yep."

Thinking of Miss Reynolds, I asked, "You want that on your tombstone? *Sam Wilder Was Normal?*"

"Yep." He was just trying to make me mad, I could tell. I refused to let him do that.

"Why can't you go along to get along?" Sam plagiarized some stupid grown-up.

Plagiarize was a new and beautiful 'z' word, meaning a particular kind of lie, no less.

"You sound like Marvin the Cretin." "Bet you can't spell *plagiarize*."

Naturally, Sam ignored that taunt. "When things are going good, why rock the boat?" He felt the edge on his knife with his thumb. "Like Papa says."

"Just because you and Papa and everybody else signs the Duck Test doesn't mean I have to." I wasn't quite sure how that fit, but it sounded authoritative enough for Sam to look impressed.

To help reconstruct Mama One, I added two powerful ingredients to the Formula, a tiny nick from Miss Reynolds' date stamp at the library and my precious keychain reins from Luther. Of course, Luther was thrilled. He had always hated that bridle and the fancy bronze saddle I couldn't remove. I had to admit that he was a wild horse at heart. Someday I would have to let him go. When I pleaded with Sam, he reluctantly tore off a tiny corner from his Warren Spahn baseball card and stuck it inside the old Nervine bottle.

But nothing seemed to help. As Sam constantly repeated, we were no worse off than before: we had learned to navigate our first mother's version of things, and we could do it again. But now I wanted to know which version was the real one. And which was a lie.

The hardest thing to accept was that Papa liked Mama Two better than Mama One. Sometimes he would kiss her in front of us kids. And she would kiss him back. Sam said it was like committing *adulteration*, a word he had learned in Scouts. At least, Sam hadn't been dishonorably discharged from Scouts over Joe Clary's eye, and Jim Hartsock had started playing with him again, although on the sly.

One day, Sam and I were buying jawbreakers in Hested's dime store with our allowance which was no longer imaginary and now routinely turned into real pennies and nickels.

Sam stuffed my three pennies' change into his left pocket and his three pennies into his right.

"Mama would never let us do this." He paused. "Remember the days of fake allowance and no candy?"

I talked around the jawbreaker in my mouth. "Maybe this Mama is just a figment of our imagination."

Sam replied, "Maybe that one was."

"Do you think Mama One was brainwashed?"

"Definitely."

"By the Communists?" I asked, almost hopefully.

"Nope. Chemistry. They washed out her brain with chemicals."

"That's a lie."

"Papa told me so. They drugged her."

"He didn't tell me that." I was always the first to be left out of any interesting conversation.

"He said you were too young to understand."

"He did not."

What an insult. Papa had never said anything like that to me.

"He just wants us to give her a chance."

Although I knew Sam wasn't lying, I repeated, "He did not say I was too young."

I hit Sam in the shoulder and braced myself for a full-scale leg wrestling match, right here on Main Street. That would bring Mama One running and shrieking if anything would.

Sam simply shrugged.

Where had his fight gone?

"I'll ask Mama Two." When insults failed, threats always worked.

The brim of Sam's cowboy hat had disintegrated so much that big patches of sun ran across his freckles when he moved his head."Suit yourself."

He climbed on his bicycle and pedaled off, saying he needed to work on his Art merit badge. On page 456, the famous Boy Scout manual actually required a sketch of "some Scout equipment grouped together." What a joke. Sam had recently abandoned the Personal Fitness badge because as a prerequisite, you had to go to the dentist. No matter what he called them, all of his merit badges were euphemisms for building bombs. I treasured the word *euphemism*, not only an elegant word for lying but a friend for life, right up there with *teleology* and *Apocrypha*. He wasn't fooling me.

At home, I found Mama sitting on my chair-bed, reading a magazine called *Better Homes and Gardens* she had borrowed from the library.

I blurted out, "In the hospital, did they make you take drugs?"

She smoothed the pages of her magazine and considered for a minute. "They called them 'wonder drugs.' You must admit, they worked wonders."

I sat on the piano bench. Obviously, she didn't think I was too young to understand. "Did they hurt?"

"Not exactly. They did something called insulin coma. And a lot of new drugs." When she looked at me, her eyes focused much more quickly than when she first came home. "With big names you would like, but I don't remember them. We were all guinea pigs."

She closed her magazine and rested her hands on its cover, a picture of a mansion and back yard like in the museum's painting of the lady in the hammock.

"When I first got there, I was tied into a straightjacket and locked in a padded cell. They told me later. I don't remember any of those days."

I didn't know what a straightjacket was, but it sounded awful. How sad. My very own Mama. I had to ask, no matter how hard the answer would be. "Did they ever put you in the electric chair?"

She paused, playing with her thin wedding ring, still missing the pinhead diamond. Her finger had grown too fat to take it off. "They called it electric shock therapy." She added quickly, "It doesn't hurt . . . exactly. It confuses you . . . terribly . . . for awhile."

Maybe that was when they stole her poems and other parts of her real self.

"Everyone was terrified of it. The straps and . . . they'd scream." I saw her start to drift away like Mama One. What a relief. But she pulled herself back. "Remember, Papa in his work taught me a lot about electricity."

I could almost hear the screams in the hospital corridors.

"But guess what, Jeb? I thought of you. And I wasn't afraid."

"M-Me?"

"Judith Beatrice. My brave little girl. Remember the girl on 'The Shadow'? The one who said she would save her mother?"

I nodded.

"She did. *You* did." Her voice stalled. "I had to get back to you. I knew that much. You and Sam and dear, dear Frank."

*   *   *   *   *   *

I continued to practice the last pieces Mrs. Keindorf had assigned me until we could find a new piano teacher. One day, Mama Two sat on the chair-bed to hold the cardboard over my hands.

"I don't need that anymore," I announced abruptly. "I haven't needed it for a long time."

"Oh. Of course." She slowly put the cardboard on top of the piano. "I always loved doing that." Her heavy eyes flicked up. "Didn't I?"

I wanted to lie and deny it, but she looked so sad, I had to nod yes.

She nodded, too. "It felt as if you and I were playing a duet."

This was as good a moment as any for the Ultimate Test, so I plunged ahead. "You know, while you were gone? Mrs. Keindorf's house burned down."

"Papa told me."

"And nobody has seen her or her husband since." I waited for Mama to be thrilled that one of her conspiracy theories had come true.

She slowly stood up. "It's tragic. Both for the Keindorfs and Round Prairie."

Tragic? That was the second time this summer I had heard that word. Was Mrs. Keindorf's tragedy worse than Joe's? Or better?

I tried to regain momentum. "It had to be Communists. Marvin Harkin or Bobby Clawson's dad or the Catholics, led by Dr. Mary."

"Jeb!" Her voice slashed out like Mama One's. "Dr. Mary saved my life. Get that straight. She was the one who knew about the hospital in Omaha. Without her, I would have ended up in the insane asylum. I would have *died* in Hastings."

I backed up. "But you always said the Communists—"

"Jeb, don't say that. Please." She put her hands on my shoulders and turned me on the bench to push her face close to mine.

I squirmed out of her hands. "You said–"

"I was confused. I was wrong. Do you hear me?"

"But now you're right?"

She straightened up.

I had to get something straight. "About everything?"

"No."

"Some things?"

"Yes."

"Which things?" This was getting worse and worse.

"I . . . don't know."

Then she began to laugh, her new laugh, like a screen door spring, so loud and banging that I had to smile back.

I finally decided that I would stay confused forever, or until I had a nervous breakdown when someone could explain to me how I had been wrong, and how I had been right, and often both at the same time.

* * * * * *

Sam figured he could deal with Mama Two quickest if he worked on a merit badge for Citizenship in the Home. A little overdue, I pointed out. Since I couldn't bear to talk to Mama Two about poetry, I wondered if we could at least still sew together.

Grandma Strang had given me the scraps from her pajamas, enough pieces of red checked cotton to sew the stuffed dog Mama One had promised during the January blizzard. I drew the outline of a dog with a rounded head and stubby tail, figuring I would add ears later. Mama Two left me alone while I cut it out and hand-stitched its two pieces together, leaving an open seam along its chest where I could stuff it.

Then came the big day when I carefully poked granulated foam into its head and tail, down its legs, finishing with its body. It was only when I held it up that I realized my mistake: I had stuffed the *outline* of a dog, not a three-dimensional one. My dog had only two legs.

The more I tried not to cry, the more Mama Two tried not to laugh.

She kept saying, "It's the sweetest little dog I ever saw."

"You're lying."

"Have I ever lied to you?"

I thought, that would depend upon what you called hallucinations, but I answered out loud, "It only has two legs."

"Any dog can have four legs. This is a Jeb Wilder dog. What'll we name him? Stuffy."

"It can't even stand up." I began to pull out the stuffing so I could start over.

She held my hand. "Don't hurt his feelings that way."

I tried to pull away. "I want him to be perfect."

She held both my hands in hers and looked steadily at me. "This is how he turned out."

Tears started down my cheeks.

"Stuffy needs you to love him the way he is."

*   *   *   *   *   *   *   *

I often saw Papa talking to Mr. Whitaker, although they fell silent when I came around, the sure sign of a Grown-Up Conversation. I wondered if Papa were breaking the old Wilder rule about Keeping Family Secrets in the Family. Or maybe that rule had changed, too. Well, two people could play that game, and I started visiting Mr. Whitaker every chance I got. He didn't think I was too young to understand things.

Because of my missing teeth, I couldn't eat Mr. Whitaker's cookies or candy, which he refused to eat in front of me, I noticed. Such a gentleman.

Today we sat on his front porch, side by side on a dilapidated wicker sofa with water-stained cushions, what he called his "family" furniture as opposed to his "company" rockers on the back porch facing the broom-corn field.

"Did the tooth fairy come?" He swirled the ice in his tea. He knew I hated tea so hadn't offered me a glass.

"She left me a dime. An actual dime, not an IOU."

"Wanna double that dime? You could pull my honest-to-god radishes before they grow into softballs like they did last year." He chuckled. "I can still see you kids trying to sell those radishes."

I rocked back and forth even though the sofa stayed still. "I don't know if Mama Two will let me."

He looked down at me sideways. From below, I could count three chins. "I hope you don't call her Mama Two to her face. Or anywhere else, for that matter."

"She's so different from my real Mama."

"She is your real Mama. And she's a lot easier on yer Pa, that's fer damned sure." He waved to a woman shaking out a rug on her front porch across the street. "He's had enough grief for several lifetimes, an' don't you ferget it."

I rocked harder in place to make the wicker squeak. "Papa says that her snoring is the sweetest sound he ever heard."

"Damned right. Darned right." When Mr. Whitaker smiled, one of his chins disappeared. "Plenty o' kids would give their eye teeth to have yer Mama, just like she is." He paused. "Fer starters, Will Hankins."

Sam and I had hardly seen Will all summer, and certainly not since Mama Two had arrived. I had noticed Papa welding on Will's bicycle in the barn, probably trying to make it taller. That much was back to normal: Papa fixing things for everybody but us. I sounded like Mama One.

"Mama could recite a jillion poems by heart. Mama Two doesn't remember a single one. Not one." Every time I said an 's,' too much air escaped from the hole between my front teeth, making me sound like a leaky balloon. I couldn't even take myself seriously.

"She must not need pomes anymore." He pronounced it *pomes*, sounding like a grandfather clock chime.

The idea of *needing* a poem had never occurred to me. "I need them."

"Yer hands ain't tied: go dig 'em up. Anybody who knows all those big words should be able to learn her own pomes." He shook his glass so hard some tea jumped out in little beads. "You and Thelma. I swear."

I had been dying to ask this for over a year and realized I might never have another chance. "Have you ever considered marrying her?"

He was so shocked his bib overalls didn't breathe. "What. Who?"

"Miss Reynolds."

"Marry Thelma?" He began to laugh and laugh, his lap poofing up and down, and couldn't stop and then began to cough. When he could finally quit, he wiped his eyes and said, "Thank you, Little One. I haven't laughed that hard in a month of Sundays."

"You're both orphans, and I worry about you."

He looked down at me again. "Don't waste yer time worryin' about things you can't change. Not the orphans, or the dead babies, or yer Mama, or any of it. It'll all work out. Not the way you expect, but it's up to you to make it good or bad."

I really wanted to pat his tummy, he was so much like a huge stuffed bear. Instead, I put my hand on his leg, almost as big around as my whole body. "I hope nothing ever happens to you, Mr. Whitaker."

"Well I sure as hell don't. I mean heck. If nothin' ever happens to ya, yer dead."

"I mean, I hope you don't get sick and . . . die."

"My family's waitin' fer me in the Round Prairie cemetery. Has been fer years—in that slot between my Mama and my kid sister. I'm ready to crawl in."

Was he fibbing, at least a bit? The folds hanging under his eyes held little tears. The size of the diamonds in Mrs. Keindorf's rings.

CHAPTER 60

GONE WITH THE WIND

"**I** WANT TO VISIT MISS REYNOLDS," I ANNOUNCED.

Mama Two stopped peeling carrots into the sink. "That's not a good idea."

"Is that a 'no'?" I pushed this new mother as far as I could every chance I got.

She had dyed her hair to look more like Mama One, but she looked directly at me, a dead giveaway that she was an impersonator. "It's a suggestion. Miss Reynolds is very sick."

"I know how to talk to sick people."

"She isn't the same."

"Neither are you," I lashed out. "Miss Reynolds is my friend. She and Sam are the best friends I ever had."

She put down her paring knife and rubbed her eyes, leaving a tiny carrot peel on her cheek. "Then you should go."

That was another thing different about Mama Two: she actually listened to me. I didn't have to make up reasons. I couldn't get used to it.

I walked up the sidewalk to the Republican Valley Rest Home, carrying the grocery sack which Mrs. Vince and I had filled yesterday. Mrs. Vince was the unofficial librarian but said she didn't have the patience to fill in for Miss Reynolds long.

"Give me sixth-graders over the general public any day. They're so much more mature," she had said.

The rest home was built of cinder blocks painted turquoise and had pink ruffled curtains at each window. Some of the windows were lined with knickknacks, little angels and pink kittens, or cowboy salt and pepper shakers.

Last Friday, Miss Reynolds had a stroke and was living here for now. Sam said she would never get out, but he could be a *cynic*, my latest substitute word for *realist*. Too bad he still couldn't see through Marvin Harkin.

Stroke was a funny word, like a golf stroke, or a stroke of genius, or a stroke of luck. If it were the past tense of *strike*, when a miners' strike was over, why wasn't it a stroke? Or the end of a lightning strike? Mama Two said that in a stroke, a blood vessel in your brain bursts and floods everything, like the Republican River, only on a small scale and with blood. I guess your brain is the farmland near the river, and some of your crops are drowned and can't grow again.

Inside, the rest home looked like a little hospital, except sitting outside almost every door was a person in a wheelchair. Funny sounds came from somewhere inside, moans and yelps and chirps, like trapped puppies and birds. When the wheelchair people saw me, they raised their hands as if we were in school and I was the teacher, and each one had the answer but I didn't have any questions. One very old lady was curled over her lap, where she hid a little doll. It wasn't wearing any clothes and looked as if someone had chewed on its hair. She kept saying "help me, help me, help me" to her doll, but no one paid any attention.

The nurse pointed to Miss Reynolds' door and told me to walk in, but I knocked. As Mama One would have said, I wasn't raised in a barn. After a minute, I didn't hear any sound, so I slowly opened it. Miss Reynolds was squeezed into a wheelchair looking out the window at Walnut Street.

"Hello?" I called. I knew that Miss Reynolds wouldn't answer. She couldn't talk or even move.

In her room, Mrs. Vince had mercifully taken down the pink ruffled curtains and had lined her windowsill with books, including a fat dictionary. Her walls had framed pictures of old cities full of arches and domes and broken stone columns, cities older than Dresden, maybe Rome. Nothing religious or half-naked, but all very distinguished and probably famous. They must have come from her house.

"It's me. Jeb." I walked around to face her and pulled up a metal folding chair so we could look directly at each other. Her eyes were still glittery, but her mouth drooped on one side and her body held still in an odd way, a little like a dead person or a statue.

"Mrs. Vince told me that you could talk by blinking your eyes. That one blink means *yes* and two blinks mean *no*."

Miss Reynolds blinked once: *yes*.

"Oh good. It works." I pawed through the sack of things I had brought. "Mrs. Vince and I decided on some things you might want."

I pawed through the sack and pulled out Miss Reynolds' glasses attached to my favorite necklace, the one with marble-sized pearls. "She said that you couldn't hear without these, but that was a joke."

I carefully draped the necklace over Miss Reynolds' head and let the glasses rest on her bosom. Even though she couldn't read, she looked more like herself now.

"They're just as pretty as real pearls," I said.

Miss Reynolds blinked *no*.

With a person who can't talk, it was only fair to say out loud what she would have said. "No they're not. That's what you're saying."

Miss Reynolds blinked *yes*.

"You know, when Sam and I are spies captured by the enemy, we blink Morse code with our eyes. I could teach you Morse code. With short blinks for dots and long blinks for dashes."

I illustrated with one short blink followed by one long one. "That's a dot and a dash, an *a*." Inspired, I leaned forward in the metal chair. "This is what your name—*Miss Reynolds*— would look like." All the way from the two dashes for the *M* to the last three dots for the final *s*, I blinked through her name.

"Before I leave today, I'll teach you how to blink *Jeb*."

Miss Reynolds distinctly blinked *no*.

I backed up. "You'd rather learn how to blink *Judith*."

She blinked *yes*.

I looked at her big, lifeless body stuffed into the wheelchair and searched for consolation. "It's as if somebody has assigned you to sit on the footstool. Do you remember Mama One and the footstool?"

She blinked *yes*.

"On the footstool, I learned a lot, like how to travel in time and space without moving a muscle. You know, I wasn't supposed to move. Or make a peep."

Miss Reynolds blinked *yes*, but I had the feeling she wanted to say more.

"I'll bet you're thinking that was a good thing," I filled in for her.

She blinked *yes*.

"For the time being, you'll have to do that, too. Except you'll be so much better at it than me."

Miss Reynolds began blinking rapidly. Something was wrong.

"Are you all right? Should I get the nurse?"

She distinctly blinked *no*.

I looked at her a minute, then backed up in our conversation. Better than me .. "Oh. Better than *I*. That's it. Wrong case or something like that."

She blinked *yes*.

If I thought Miss Reynolds couldn't correct my English any more, I now realized that it was worse than ever: I had to figure out what I had done wrong all by myself and then correct it.

"You'll be better at the footstool than *I* because you know so much more and have been so many more places and are so much smarter than I am."

From the sack I now pulled a stack of books. "I know you hate children, but I could read to you."

She gave no response except following my hands with her eyes.

"I would be better than nothing."

Miss Reynolds blinked three times.

"Did you mean I would be or wouldn't be better than nothing? Or was that just an ordinary blink?"

She *yes*, slowly and deliberately.

"Oh good! I was thinking that you might want to hear some poems, but poems are hard to read, and I'm not very good at reading them, and I might actually hurt them. You know? I think poets, even dead poets, have feelings like composers, and when I louse up a piece of piano music, I can feel the composer cringe. Do you know what I mean?"

Miss Reynolds blinked wildly.

What was it? *Louse*. "I didn't mean *louse up*, I meant when I made mistakes."

She blinked *yes* twice.

"Isn't this wonderful? Here we are, having a lovely conversation."

"I figured we needed a long book, because it might take you awhile to get well, so I asked Mrs. Vince for suggestions. She said *Brighty of the Grand Canyon*, but I've never considered you a fan of horses or burros."

She blinked *no*.

I touched her hand, which felt cold. "If you ever change your mind, let me know, and I'll teach you how to blink *Brighty*."

She blinked *yes*.

"Mrs. Vince said that if I read something by J. Edgar Hoover, it would make you so mad you'd get up from your wheelchair. Would that be a good idea?"

Miss Reynolds just stared at me, very deliberately, which I knew was a big *NO*.

"Good. Hoover's so boring. So Mrs. Vince got these from the library. I hope that she checked them out properly, since she's still so new at your job. The first one is called *The Seven Pillars of Wisdom*, by T. E. Lawrence. She said it takes place in the desert. On camels. Camels might be fun."

Miss Reynolds blinked a definite *no*.

"This one is long, but it has huuuge names in it: *War and Peace?*"

I could have sworn that Miss Reynolds smiled. At least her eyes smiled. Then she blinked *no*.

Mrs. Vince mentioned the poem you said Mama should memorize while I'm on the footstool. Remember *Paradise Lost*? But I couldn't even read the first page. That is a really grown-up book."

When I looked at her, her eyes were smiling again.

I pulled the last book out of the sack. "Mrs. Vince said you read this a long time ago, but you might like to hear me read it out loud. It's called *Gone with the Wind*."

Miss Reynolds blinked *yes*, waited and blinked *yes* again.

"Oh goody." I sat Indian-style on her bed and opened the book, which smelled like old dust mixed in with the floor oil in the library. "*Gone with the Wind*, by Margaret Mitchell. New York: the Macmillan Company, 1936." I turned pages. "To J. R. M. Part I. Chapter I. Scarlett O'Hara was not beautiful, but men seldom realized it when caught by her charm as the Tarleton twins were . . . ."

Two pages later, I was lost, completely absorbed in Scarlett O'Hara and Ashley Wilkes, Tara and Ft. Sumter and talk of war. Before I knew it, an hour and a half had flown by.

"Oh oh. Mama Two said I can only visit you an hour a day, because I wear people out."

Miss Reynolds blinked *no*.

I carefully balanced *Gone with the Wind* on top of the dictionary in her windowsill.

"Before I leave, would you like me to sing you a song?"

She blinked *yes*.

"Would you like 'Blue Skies'?"

No.

"'The Road to Mandalay'?"

No.

"How about 'When You Wish Upon a Star'?"

A blink *yes*.

I sang it all the way through to the end:

"Fate steps in and sees you through; when you wish upon a star, your dreams come true."

I realized that tears were running down her cheeks. I didn't know what to do until I saw her hanky in her curled-up, paralyzed hand. I carefully pulled it out and dabbed her tears. "Remember, Miss Reynolds: Never let them see you cry. *Never.*"

CHAPTER 61

TRAP PART

ALISTERING WIND BLEW THROUGH THE WALLS of the Inavale spook house, where Sam and I were homesteaders fighting the evil cattle barons trying to run us off our land. "Shane" couldn't hold a candle to us today. Since the movie hadn't yet arrived at the Inavale drive-in, we still had time to make up our own ending.

The spook house wasn't much protection, given its missing wall, the ceiling bowed halfway to the floor in the living room, and the floor itself a latticework over the dirt basement. It was hard enough to duck and balance along the disintegrating floorboards, let alone to shoot from the broken windows. Today I not only heard faint honky-tonk music coming from the broken-down piano but also saw its curled, furry keys wiggle slightly, like dead fingers coming to life. If I told Sam, he would call this my overactive imagination, an insult left over from the Days of Mama One. Since it kept Mama One alive in a way, I egged him on to say it whenever I felt especially homesick for her.

Sam shouted. The cattlemen had just brought in reinforcements and any minute would surround us completely, like Chesty Puller in Korea. Using the crude wooden rifle he and Papa had cut from a one-by-four, Sam was picking them off one by one, but he was running out of ammo. I had brought my finger pistol, a short-barreled revolver which required constant reloading and was accurate only at close range. In spite of the bad guys I knew I dropped, only Sam's score counted, and he said we were fatally outnumbered, unable to hold out much longer. As soon as this gunfight was over, I would protest his body count. I was tired of letting Sam grab all the points, win all the toy car races and make all the important decisions by himself.

Suddenly the wind stopped. Stopped as if someone had turned off a powerful fan in the sky. Both of us noticed it instantly. More than that, the air in the house changed, grew thick with humidity and an odd tingling. Without saying anything, Sam and I quit fighting and, balancing along a few creaking floorboards, walked outside.

A cloud like a massive black fist was swinging toward us, grabbing the blue sky in fistfuls the size of small towns. The cows in the pasture nearby were growing restless, moaning and bumping against each other, turning in small circles. We had seen enough storms to know this would strike fast and drench everything in its path. Automatically, we looked for a funnel hanging below it but didn't see one. Closer now, the cloud looked like a huge drum, a giant tire skidding on its side.

"Shall we run for home?" An explosion of thunder buried my shout.

The wind, suddenly coming back, hit like a train locomotive at full speed, stripping leaves from the old cottonwoods and dropping the temperature. Now lightning ripped the rolling black drum from top to bottom. Pounded by the wind, Sam and I were nonetheless riveted by the sky directly overhead—sickly green and beginning to swirl. Around its large churning spiral were smaller eddies, little spinoff whirlpools. At the same time, over the wind we heard sirens go off in Round Prairie and, seconds later, in Inavale. Long, overlapping wails: a tornado had been spotted close by.

"–storm cellar!" Sam yelled, already running toward the gaping stairs leading into the earth.

Stumbling behind him, I remembered the Formula and ran back to scoop it out of my bicycle basket.

The hail hit like a barrage of icy gravel, while lightning splintered and thunder rolled overhead. Our clothes were sopped all the way through in seconds, even our socks. The last I saw, the cows were huddled with their tails to the wind, their fur soaked black and shiny, unprotected from the battering hail.

Sam and I slipped down the stairs, slick with dead leaves and now a small waterfall, and landed at the bottom on our seats. Rain and hail poured in behind us. I propped the Formula bottle beside the stairs.

"—close the door!" Sam shouted above the din.

Shoulder to shoulder we climbed back into the turbulence, almost blinded by the horizontal rain, our wet clothes whipped by the wind and my hair unbraided into wild strings. We managed to heave the sodden, slatted door upright, get underneath it and slip down three steps with it on our shoulders, before the wind caught it and slammed it shut with us underneath.

Instantly it was quieter. As we sat panting on the dark stairs, rain drizzled on our heads through the slats in the door.

Since I had never been inside the storm cellar with the door closed, I didn't realize how dark it would be. Following Sam, I groped down the stairs along the rough cement wall, then shuffled awkwardly along the dirt floor, hands sweeping in front of me to find the candles and matchbook we had stored in the shelves on the back wall. Maxine Harkin had to live this way all the time. I couldn't imagine.

Sam lit a candle, then dripped wax onto a paint can lid to stand it upright on the floor. We sat cross-legged in the dirt for a long time, staring at the wobbling flame, listening to the wind howl and the hail hammer on the heavy door.

"Boy, are we lucky," I said, hugging myself. My wet dress stuck to my back like a cold towel.

Sam didn't answer, silently taking inventory of the gasoline, bottles of chemicals, sections of pipe and rusty tools he had stockpiled, partly as a Boy Scout, mostly as a Mad Scientist waiting for his next Great Idea.

My treasured cowbell rested in one corner next to Will Hankins' bedroll wrapped with Papa's old jacket. Just seeing Papa's jacket cheered me up.

Sam idly passed a piece of straw through the candle flame, watching it flare to life and die. "Wanna play dive bomber? We could fly a Dauntless, back to back."

Unexpectedly I decided, "I want my own plane."

He looked at me in surprise. "A P-38? Spitfire? What?"

"A Curtiss Helldiver." I liked its name because it let me say "hell" with impunity, even if no one cared enough to punish me anymore. Grown-ups must feel free to cuss all the time, especially Uncle Ralph, Mr. Whitaker and the characters in *Gone with the Wind*, where Miss Reynolds and I had discovered the word *impunity*. I was constantly amazed at how much she could say without saying one word.

Sam shrugged, then immediately decreed that we were both flying Helldivers when we were machine-gunned and went down in flames, fortunately not before we had dive-bombed an enemy destroyer in the Philippine Sea. I went along with his version for a while before I pointed out that if we hadn't made it back to our aircraft carrier, we would be bobbing on the open ocean, pretty inconvenient since neither of us could swim. In spite of myself, I occasionally yielded to brief attacks of realism.

Sam stood up and walked out of the candlelight. "I was the only kid at the Jamboree who didn't know how to swim."

"Swim? Swim where?"

"We camped in a park near the city pool."

Park? City pool? I thought that Scouts went to Jamborees to learn survival skills like identifying non-poisonous mushrooms in the woods or trapping small birds to cook over their flint-sparked campfire. Instead, Sam had spent the week in competitions for maintaining the neatest campsite, tying the most exotic knots, and building the fastest fire to burn a string stretched three feet overhead. Not exactly survival. Who dreamed up these inane tests? The Boy Scouts must be full of Marvin Harkins.

"My favorite was the orientation contest," Sam continued. "Without maps. I used Mike Letson's compass to get a bearing on the target, a wooden stake in the ground about a football field away. Then they blindfolded me so I could peek only at the compass, and I had to find the target."

"Did you?" I wondered if they were on an actual football field.

"I, uh . . . yeah."

Clearly he wasn't telling me the whole story. "So you won?"

With his straight line mouth, he answered, "I . . . got a badge. Next year we'll learn Advanced Survival Skills."

Survival in a city park, I wanted to emphasize. "While you were gone, Grandma Strang told me stories about the Olden Days, the German POWs in Hebron and the Children's Blizzard."

"What blizzard?"

Until now, the Children's Blizzard had been my cherished secret, but I figured that Sam needed it now, if for no other reason than to lord it over Marvin the Moron when he transformed into the expert on Advanced Survival. As I told Sam about the lowest recorded barometric pressure in history, the 80-degree drop in temperature, the ice finer than flour, he didn't believe me. But when I described how Grandma's teacher had burned their books to save their lives, he was convinced. He knew I wouldn't lie about burning books.

I lingered over each child discovered frozen in a snowdrift or within a few yards of their back door and took an especially long time describing the dead brothers who had to be thawed out in the kitchen before they could be buried. I must admit, I was tempted to add a few grisly details of my own, like how their eyes had frozen open, but the truth was bad enough. Worse than anybody could make up.

"Wow," Sam kept saying. "Forty below. Grandma Strang. Wow."

Before long, we both grew bored and began to circle the cellar. Rain still poured through the door and down the stairs.

"How long do you think we've been in here?" My dress had dried enough to feel clammy instead of soaked.

"I don't know. We'll head for home as soon as it quits."

Over the sound of the rain and thunder, we suddenly heard a series of loud cracks. Maybe the spook house was collapsing, or one of the half-dead cottonwoods nearby had been split.

Almost at the same moment, something heavy thudded across the cellar door, bouncing once before settling. It sounded like a huge branch or a small tree.

Sam looked at me with wide eyes. "It's okay," he said.

We both knew it wasn't okay. But as long as we didn't say it out loud, as long as we observed Wilder Rules and didn't admit feeling afraid, we would be all right.

Now we sat as quietly as if we were both on footstools, watching the candle burn, waiting for the storm to pass. Time expanded to fill the cellar, lighter than the clammy air, slowly curled in the candle's black ribbon of tallow-scented smoke before floating like ashes to the damp floor. If we were down here long enough, I would teach Sam how to play with time, imagining a metronome like Mrs. Keindorf's, or the Geologic Clock in the House of Yesterday, or best of all, Silly Putty. I stood the Formula upright near the candle. By now, the Nervine bottle was an old friend. At least we had seven candles and some stubs.

We waited.

And waited.

A long time later, the wind quit as suddenly as it had started. Without a word, reading each other's minds, Sam and I slowly climbed the stairs to push open the door. We tried first pushing with our arms straight over our heads.

Sam directed, "One, two, three, heave!"

The door might as well have been the ceiling in the spook house. It didn't budge.

"We need to use our legs more," he decided.

We squatted next to each other three steps from the top, our heads to one side so we could push with our shoulders. The wet splintered wood quickly soaked our backs.

"One, two, three, heave!"

Even if nothing lay across it, the door was sodden with water, twice its normal weight. Sam briefly tried to gain an inch or two by propping it with our broken axe handle. Still no luck. We couldn't see anything through the slits between the heavy boards. How could rain come in, but not light? Was it night already?

"We mustn't panic," Sam said in a weak imitation of his Public Speaking voice.

I tried to sound cheerful. "Boy, they really knew how to build a storm cellar, huh."

"It probably saved our life."

"Yeah," I agreed without adding, 'If it doesn't kill us.'

We sat back down by the candle.

"Wanna tell ghost stories?" he suggested.

"No." The last thing I needed was a ghost story, since the Inavale house harbored a whole family of ghosts, including a piano player.

"How about palindromes?" I counter-offered.

"I don't know very many," Sam sulked. "You always win."

"You get first try, and I won't say one until you've thought of the next one." I made up a nice new rule impromptu, still the best word for "on the spot."

"Racecar, level, kayak," he grabbed the easiest ones first.

"Rotor, civic, redivider," I answered. I could tell that *redivider* shocked him.

He considered for a minute, "Stack cats."

"Star rats," I instantly responded.

"Tar rat," he unimaginatively subtracted s'es from my words.

"Loop pool."

"Sloop pools." Now he characteristically added s'es.

"Wolf flow."

From there, we quickly went through deer-reed and loot-tool, straw-warts and stop-pots, until I could tell that Sam was losing interest. Perhaps it would help to move on to sentence-length palindromes.

"Miss Reynolds' favorite is 'Dogma: I am God'."

He looked at me suspiciously, obviously spelling it backwards in his head. "I quit."

"She told me that dogma had something to do with teleology." I didn't quite know what I was talking about and certainly couldn't define *dogma*. "Want to know what teleology is?"

"Nope."

That didn't surprise me. Scientists didn't need to think about such things as design in the universe. "Guess what. Miss Reynolds found a palindrome just for Mrs. Vince."

"So what?"

Here I was, trying to keep our minds off our situation, and this was the thanks I got. "The palindrome is 'Too far, Edna, we wander afoot'." I waited for his response. "Isn't that wonderful?" In case he had forgotten, I reminded him, "Mrs. Vince's name is Edna."

Sam scraped the floor with the bent spoon. "I said I quit."

In spite of Sam's clear warnings, I continued, "Remember on the way to the hospital in Omaha when Mama One came up with 'God saw I was a dog'?"

Now he stabbed the floor with the spoon. "Palindromes are stupid. They just go around and around in circles you can't escape, like a trap. "

I had thought about palindromes as circles but never as traps. "Trap," I repeated, then discovered, "trap part."

"Part trap," Sam reversed it. I hope he didn't think that counted as a new palindrome.

"I miss Mama One," I said wistfully. She left holes like missing puzzle pieces all around my life.

"Could you ever go one whole day without saying that? Have you forgotten all the awful stuff? Like when we'd get home from school and find her taking everything out of the cupboards—again—to see where the Communists had put in new gas lines? Or scrubbing the pipes under the trailer—again?"

I hadn't forgotten, but it didn't matter to me. "One day, in the living room," I had never told anyone about Mama's visions. "Mama saw an elevator."

Sam picked up pieces of pipe, one by one, looking down some like a telescope, others like a microscope.

"A blue elevator. She said it had come to take her away." I felt like a traitor, betraying our secrets like this.

Sam pretended to ignore me.

"At first, I thought it was for her to escape, but—"

Escape what, I suddenly thought. The trailer? Us kids? Papa? Mama must have felt just like me today in the storm cellar: trapped, with growing dread, and no way out. I wished I could tell her that right now. Or that I could convey messages to Mama One through Mama Two. But that would be like talking to someone who was there and not there at the same time.

"But what?" Sam asked impatiently.

"She said they sent the elevator to take her to the insane asylum." As I told him, I saw it. "It was all blue. Lapis. And had shiny walls and a bunch of push buttons."

Sam spit out, "You sound just like her. If you keep talking like that, I'm gonna stop talking to you."

This was a very serious threat.

I said feebly, "I miss her. I can't help it. She was my Mama."

His mouth turned down at the corners. "She was mine, too." He put down the piece of pipe he was turning in his hands. "Papa said we've got to try to be nicer to Mama Two."

"He didn't tell me."

"He tells me a lotta stuff he doesn't tell you."

That must be true, odd as it seemed. It was hard to imagine that Sam and Papa had a whole life together without me.

"Papa asked us to be nice as a personal favor to him."

"I hate that." It was Papa's most unfair argument.

When Sam looked straight at me, I could almost hear Papa talking. "But then he said something different. 'Don't do it for her sake. Do it for *your* sake. Because you've got to live with yourself the rest of your life'."

There was so much to think about, I wouldn't finish by my twelfth birthday. If I had a twelfth birthday, that is.

After a while, I must have dozed off because I found myself lying on the ground and couldn't remember where I was. "Papa?" I panicked. "Sam?!"

Curled on his side with his back to me, Sam made sleepy sounds. The candle was about an inch high, standing in a pool of its own wax on the paint can lid.

It all came back to me. We could die here. And not be found for years and years, when some stranger would dig us up, two piles of rags and skeletons, just like the mummy in the House of Yesterday or the *National Geographic*. All those years I had tried to get Mama's sympathy, and now I would have it, and she would be sorry, but I would be dead. And it would be the wrong Mama.

"Sam!" I pushed his arm. I refused to think these thoughts all alone. "We'll turn into mummies."

"They'll find us," he answered sleepily. "When we don't show up at home—"

"We already haven't shown up at home."

He turned toward me on his side. "Papa and Mama will tell Sheriff Westergaard."

"They won't know where to look. They don't even know the hide-out exists."

"Yeah they do." His tone said that he hadn't thought about that.

"Nobody will ever move the tree, not in our lifetimes." I felt like crying, which would only make things worse and would be just like a girl.

Sam sat up. "There'll be a huge manhunt. After a tornado, they look everywhere."

"Round Prairie could be flattened. Worse than Hebron. *Gone*."

This prospect hadn't occurred to me until I said it out loud.

"C'mon, Jeb," he finally answered. "Don't borrow trouble." Papa's motto, a version of Don't Rock the Boat.

Then the worst thought of all occurred to me. "What if Papa and Mama Two . . . are dead? The trailer would be the first thing to blow away." We'd be orphans. Real live orphans like Jane Englehardt."

Sam interrupted before I could get on a roll. "Be rational." *Rational* was his new favorite science word. "Chances are just as good that it was a small tornado that missed Round Prairie altogether. Calculate the odds."

For once, mathematics might be useful. "How do we do that?"

"I . . . dunno."

"Mr. Whitaker says everything depends on chance."

"That's exactly what I mean," Sam quickly agreed.

I might as well say everything terrible at once. "I'm thirsty. I've never been so thirsty."

My tongue felt twice its normal size. For a moment, I wished that we had filled Mason jars with water during Mr. Sprecker's Civil Defense bomb shelter period, but I would still hate to give him the satisfaction of being right. Even if he were a volunteer fireman and had tried to save Mrs. Keindorf's house, even if he saved me from Marvin Harkin, he still fired Mrs. Dahlke. That put him on my blacklist forever.

"I am, too. Try not to think about it." He lit another candle from the burning stub and balanced it upright. We had burned four of our seven candles.

"At least we have the Formula with us." I cradled the old Nervine bottle in my arms, a precious souvenir of Mama One.

Sam was quiet for a long time.

"I could ring the cowbell," I finally suggested. "In case there's somebody . . . ."

"Somebody what?" Sam snapped.

"Nearby. Walking past. By chance."

I was trying to remember ways Grandma's teacher kept everybody's spirits up during the Children's Blizzard. Roll call didn't seem very useful, since there were only two of us.

"Remember the eight first-magnitude stars? And the constellations? Lyra-Vega, the Big Eye?"

Sam refused to play.

"Maybe Uncle Ralph will rebuild his observatory. When he finishes Hebron."

"So?"

"He told me about H-bombs." I paused for effect. "And the different kinds of hydrogen, like ions."

Sam's eyes flickered with interest, but he was too proud to ask me for any factual information, least of all about chemistry.

"I've got an idea for getting out of here," he said.

Oboyoboy. I knew if Sam just had enough time, he would figure out something brilliant.

He pointed to the gasoline, the bedding and the matches. "We can burn down the door."

Even I, who had very low expectations of Sam's practical skills, did not expect this.

I pointed out, "The door is sopping wet."

"Yeah, but–"

"A fire would fill the cellar with smoke."

"We can—"

"And burn up all the oxygen."

He looked at me with distrust. Obviously, I had more than one piece of new scientific information.

I decided to share my second cherished secret, Mrs. Keindorf's story about Dresden. I couldn't remember the German names of the castles and palaces which were destroyed, but that didn't matter.

"Thousands and thousands of people burned, but she said more people died from suffocation than from the fires."

Sam didn't move. "Dresden. What Dresden?"

"Germany. She and her husband climbed out of the basement and saw people turning to ashes."

"Why was it burning?"

"Fire bombs."

If Sam had never heard of fire bombs, he wasn't letting on. "Wh-Whose fire bombs?"

"Americans. And English."

"That can't be. That's a lie."

"Mrs. Keindorf wouldn't lie. She barely escaped alive."

"When did she tell you? Why didn't you tell me?"

"I know a lot of stuff you don't know."

"Tell me the rest."

"I'm too tired. It's a long story. Tragic."

"Promise to tell me later."

"I will. If there is a later."

Sam looked around the cellar more despondently.

"You can't burn down the door, Sam. It's just not feasible."

Sam got lower and lower. Except for the days right after we put Mama One in the hospital, I had never seen him so low.

"Can I tell you the thing I miss most about Mama One? And then I'll be quiet."

He started tearing paper into tiny scraps and throwing them at the candle. When they hit the flame, they flared briefly and went out.

"Her poems. She recited poems to me on the footstool to make the time go faster."

"Why would she want to make your time go faster?"

I modified my theory, "Or to make me feel better."

That couldn't be right, either. The footstool was a punishment. Why *did* she recite poems to me? Mama Two couldn't tell me why because poems made Mama One crazy in the first place. Miss Reynolds would know the answer but couldn't talk, Mrs. Dahlke had moved to Lincoln, and Mrs. Vince read only non-fiction. Who could help me now?

"Want to hear a poem? I memorized a bunch to surprise Mama when she came home."

"Do you know a short one?"

"Yes." This could cheer us up.

I recited "Because I could not stop for Death, he kindly stopped for me," a personal favorite by Emily Dickinson.

Sam frowned. "Try another one."

I went through "There's been a death in the opposite house" and started "A long long sleep" until I remembered it ended in a "little hut of stone" not too different from the storm cellar. I quit in the middle.

"Is that the end?"

"Yes," I lied.

"Weird."

"I know another one by her:

"I felt a funeral in my brain,

And mourners, to and fro,

Kept treading, treading, till it seemed

That sense was breaking through."

I decided to skip the next verse and went to

"And then I heard them lift a box,

And creak across my soul

With those same boots of lead,

Then space began to toll . . . "

This didn't seem quite right, so I skipped to the end:

"And then a plank in reason, broke,

And I dropped down and down—

And hit a world at every plunge,

And finished knowing—then—"

"Then what?"

"That's the end." It really was.

Sam had actually listened. "Are they all about death?"

I had never thought about it. "Mostly."

I could tell he was growing restless again. "Want to hear some poems about World War One?"

"They're also about death, right?"

He had a point.

"Okay. How about one for kids?" I went straight to one we already knew—"The Duel," a.k.a. "The Gingham Dog and the Calico Cat."

When I finished, Sam was thoughtful. "I never really listened to Mama One recite that. The dog and cat ate each other up."

I hadn't realized it either, and I had memorized the words.

"Do you know any more?"

By now I was reduced to poems Mama One had recited, but I could only remember the first or last lines.

"When to the sessions of sweet, silent thought . . . ." I started.

After a minute, Sam asked, now almost politely, "What happens?"

"I don't remember."

I started another, "So live that when thy summons comes to join . . . the something something caravan–"

"Caravan of what?" Sam was growing interested.

"Camels," I made up.

I stumbled through bits and pieces of "Little Boy Blue" and "Richard Cory," but I really wanted to remember the last verse of "The Chambered Nautilus."

"Build thee more stately mansions, O my soul, as the swift seasons roll . . ."

So far, so good. Then I lost track. "Something . . . shut thee from heaven with a dome more vast."

I couldn't remember it and was growing increasingly frustrated because the words

were so beautiful, but I plowed ahead:

"At length thou art free, leaving thine outgrown shell

by life's unresting sea."

I walked in small circles, defeated and discouraged. If I survived the storm cellar, I needed to memorize whole books of poems to get me through the rest of my life.

"I wish I knew some poems," Sam sounded envious.

"I just butchered some of the world's greatest poems. Like I butcher Bach and Rachmaninoff and everybody else."

"You sound good to me."

"I mess up everything." I was approaching tears again. "Who would sew a stuffed dog with only two legs?"

"Stuffy? Stuffy's great."

Sam had stopped me cold. I could tell he was serious.

"He's the greatest little dog I ever saw." Even in the candlelight, I could see Sam's smile bunch up his freckles a little. "I wish we had him here."

We sat in silence for a long time, watching our fifth candle.

I waited as long as I could stand it before I asked, "Now how long do you think we've been here?" It felt as if time had died in the cellar. "Do you think it's night?"

No light filtered through the slats in the door.

"Could be."

"The first night? Or the second?"

"How would I know?"

"I'm hungry." Once I said it, I was starving. It seemed like a week since we had eaten breakfast and ridden to the spook house on our bicycles.

"Don't talk about it. You know, we could try to sleep."

"I'm not sleepy."

"It would kill some time."

I had always hated that expression.

Sam unrolled Will Hankins' bedding, which was big enough for both of us, and let me cover up with Papa's jacket.

As we lay on our backs staring up through the dark, I asked, "Do you want me to sing us to sleep?"

"No."

"Not even Brahms' 'Lullaby'?"

"Just hum it."

Which I did, thinking of the words Mrs. Keindorf translated from German for me: 'If God wills it, I will wake again . . .'

Turning over with our backs to each other, Sam and I slowly fell asleep. Sleep peels.

I was still in the storm cellar but sitting on the footstool, now covered with camouflage material to look like the boulder it had been in the Christmas play. Light as smoke, I drifted off the footstool, up the stairs and through the slats in the cellar door.

Immediately, the wind yanked me upward and pulled me into its spiral, peppering my arms and legs with dirt clods, blinding me with fine dust. My stomach churned worse than being trapped on the merry-go-round with someone else spinning it. Every time I tried to breathe, I coughed. Slowly, slowly, the wind died down and I opened my eyes in little slits, expecting to see Round Prairie or at least Nebraska. Instead, the whole Earth turned below me, a blue ball partially covered with swirling white clouds. Would I fly so far up that I could finally see the whole movie projected on top of our heads, understand the big plot, watch real life all over earth break into the story just as it did at the Inavale drive-in?

I now cartwheeled off into space, a Dust Person blown out among the planets. The solar system looked like a huge orrery and all the planets like cold marbles orbited by tiny pebble moons. This orrery spun so fast that a year happened in a minute, and all the moons in the solar system raced in and out of eclipses in a blur, swirling like the eddies Sam and I had seen in the green sky.

What made the huge orrery turn so fast? What was cranking the handle, churning the brass wheels, hurling the planets and moons in such quick circles? Was I dead? Maybe death wasn't lying in the dark ground, but floating, smaller than a Dust Person among the stars forever. Would I meet Janet out here?

Should I try to return to Earth, not the beautiful blue shooter marble, but real Earth, windstorms and all? Should I return to ticktock time held firm and predictable by the log cabin clock? But what if the trailer—? What if the clock—? Papa and Mama—?

"Jeb! JEB!"

I was standing in the middle of the storm cellar, and Sam was shaking my shoulders.

"You were sleepwalking." He looked scared. "And twirling in circles and making creepy sounds. Calm down," he ordered, plagiarizing Papa again.

Dizzy, I felt my legs buckle, and I sat down. "We're going to die in here."

"Not if I can help it." Sam sounded older.

While I had been asleep or gone wherever I was, he had organized all his equipment.

"We're going to die like all the thousands of little kids in the Children's Blizzard and in tornadoes around the world and babies like Janet and Grandma Strang's baby, and Mrs. Vince's brother and Mr. Whitaker's whole family and all the thousands and thousands of people in Dresden—" I ran out of breath.

"Here's my idea."

Maybe Sam the Wonder Boy Scientist could save us this time.

"We have enough matches, gunpowder and pipe . . . to build a pipe bomb."

"What?"

"To blow open the door."

"Are you crazy?" Maybe I was still dreaming.

"I have home-made powder, even though it isn't very reliable. If I use twice as much, it might work."

"Sam, this isn't a chemistry experiment. It's *us*. You could blow us up."

"It's our only chance. Do you have a better idea?"

"We can wait for help. Like the kids in the Children's Blizzard."

"Until we starve."

He could always hit me where it hurt. I felt famished, which meant *really* hungry.

He hesitated. "We're burning our last candle. After that, we only have a few stubs left."

"Have you ever set off a bomb inside a little space like this?"

Sam paused while pouring out the powder.

"Have you?"

"No."

"So this bomb could kill us, or at least blind or deafen us."

Sam threw his supplies to the ground. "What do you wanna do? Wait until we're both so weak we can't even call for help or make a bomb? Or run out of candles and die in the dark?"

I had always been afraid of the dark, and Sam knew it.

"You can't do it unless I agree. It's my life, too."

He reluctantly admitted, "That's true."

This gave me new hope.

"What do you wanna do? Flip a coin?" Sam suggested.

"Coin, schmoin. I don't want my whole life to depend upon the toss of a coin." Besides, we didn't have a coin.

He thought for a moment. "I gotta better idea, anyway. Let's fight for it. Leg wrestle. Whoever wins decides about the pipe bomb."

I flared, "Why do we always have to fight? I'm tired of fighting."

"Leg wrestling isn't fighting."

I thought of Miss Reynolds. Maybe this was the time I should decide to fight. Leg wrestling at least gave me a chance. Sam had the advantage of strength, but my shorter legs were harder to throw. If I caught him off-guard, before he was fully braced with his back flat on the ground, I could win about a fourth of the time.

"Okay," I agreed.

We cleared a space, carefully moving the candle to the wall, and lay down on our backs, head to foot, on the cellar floor. I made sure that Sam was on my right side, my stronger leg.

"On the count of three," Sam said, as if we hadn't done this since I was five years old.

"One, two—"

Before he could say "three," I hooked his leg and threw all my weight and remaining strength into my right leg, pushing his leg as hard as I could back toward his body.

"Cheat!" he groaned. "You cheated!"

I kept pushing, trying to make him somersault over backwards, or at least to give up with his leg sideways, scissored between mine. I felt his thigh muscles tense as he gathered his strength and slowly, slowly brought both of our legs upright.

With that, I knew I was a goner. In seconds, he had bent my leg back to my chest, and I shouted "Uncle!" before getting thrown completely over.

We unhooked our legs and lay there catching our breath.

"You cheated," he repeated.

"I'm not the Boy Scout."

Having a plan, even a stupid one, energized us. I had to admit that dying while making our own bomb beat dying in the dark. It was almost romantic: a satisfying, if violent, ending to the movie being projected onto our heads. As Sam made final preparations, I began to clang the cowbell, my own black-up plan. Even swung just a little bit, it hurt our ears in such an enclosed space.

First , we had to push over the shelf and stand it on its side so we would have some protection from the blast.

"It won't protect our ears," I objected.

"From the shrapnel," Sam admitted.

For old times' sake, I would have asked if he could spell *shrapnel*, but I already knew the answer. We had both seen shrapnel fly sky high when Sam blew up Mr. Whitaker's picket fence—pieces of pipe, dirt clods and splintered fence posts flying higher than a house roof.

"*Shrapnel* was named after a guy in the English army in the Very Olden Days," I volunteered to keep up our spirits. "I mean a *man*."

Normally, Sam would have objected to any military fact I offered, but he was too focused on the bomb.

"Hold your finger over the little hole in the side of the pipe."

I looked more closely at the hole, which would have required a drill. "When did you make this one?"

"Last summer. Papa helped me."

"Papa! Made a pipe bomb?"

"We made a couple before the fence explosion." Sam carefully poured powder down the pipe. "But that was with store-bought powder. All I have left is home-made."

Why hadn't I known this before now? Because I was a girl? Or too young? A lying Brownie instead of an honest Boy Scout?

"Wh-Where did you get store-bought powder?" I felt like moving my finger and letting it all dribble onto the floor.

"Papa brought it from the dam site. He didn't exactly tell me *not* to use it. Only to be careful."

This sounded like a new kind of lie. What Sam wasn't saying was bigger and more important than what he was saying. There must be a special word for this.

"Papa." I repeated with disbelief. "Papa made pipe bombs with you."

"Well, he showed me how to make them. And drilled the holes which are really hard to do in a rounded surface like a pipe."

In the candlelight jumping along the cellar walls, Sam finished filling the pipe with his home-made powder, then tamped it down inside with a stick. He carefully screwed on the pipe cap and tightened it with his hands.

The pipe was now completely closed except for the tiny hole Sam and Papa had drilled in its side earlier.

"Will this be like the fence bomb?" My throat constricted.

"Not that big, because I used a lot bigger pipe and a pound of real powder." Sam clamped his tongue between his front teeth as he gave the pipe a final twist.

"That's about it." He wiped his hands on his pants just like Papa. "We can't get it any tighter without a pipe wrench."

From a dark corner behind the upended shelf, Sam brought out a small piece of newspaper and began rolling it like a cigarette, except filled with powder instead of tobacco. He tightly twisted both ends of the paper.

I felt sick to my stomach, not just because I was hungry. This might be the last thing I see in my whole life: Sam making a fuse for the pipe bomb which would blow us to smithereens. What would it be like to be dead, I wondered. I wished that Janet could appear to tell us it was fine, but she was such a tiny baby, she couldn't talk. Emily Dickinson could certainly describe it. In fact, she probably already had in her poems, but I didn't understand.

"Get behind the shelf." Sam sounded like a cross between Mr. Sprecker and a B-17 pilot. "Put your arms over your head. Bury your face. Cover yourself with Papa's coat."

"Klaatu barada nikto," I chanted as I followed his directions, tripping in the half dark. I hugged the Formula.

Sam carefully laid the pipe bomb on the top step and said, "I'm gonna light the fuse, then run down to where you are. Cover us both with Papa's coat. Get ready? Get set—"

My thumping heart drowned out the rest.

He struck the match, lit the fuse and scrambled down the stairs to half somersault behind the shelf next to me. I threw the coat over him and we plugged our ears. Under Papa's coat, it was totally dark. Sam's breath was hot and fast.

We listened. Listened hard. No sound, not even of the fuse burning.

After what seemed like five minutes, I ventured, "Do you think—?"

"Shhh-hh!" His voice was muffled by the coat. "One hundred one, one hundred two," Sam counted all the way to fifty very slowly.

Finally deciding it was safe to investigate, he walked around the shelf and climbed the stairs.

He called down to me, "The fuse burned out but didn't catch the powder inside."

I didn't realize I had been holding my breath until I let it out.

After that, Sam grew quieter and quieter.

"I failed," he finally said. "The only time it really mattered—all my research and chemistry experiments and home-made powder . . ."

I wanted to say that failure in this case might be a blessing.

"I'm not a scientist, I'm not a Boy Scout, I'm not anything."

"But you already blew up Mr. Whitaker's fence. You proved—"

"I can't do anything. Not *anything*." Sam threw a piece of pipe across the cellar, and it bounced off the shelf.

To my utter disbelief, I saw tears in Sam's eyes. My brother, my big brother was *crying*. It was horrible. Sam never cried, not because he was brave or a boy, but because he wasn't the kind of person who cried.

"Sam, you can do everything. You can invent daredevil shows, you can make nitrogen triiodide, you're brilliant. Smarter than Tom Swift, smarter than—"

"I cheated, Jeb."

Time stopped. Even the candle flame didn't wobble.

"Ch-cheated?" I couldn't have heard him right.

He hurried to finish before he changed his mind. "At the Boy Scout Jamboree. In the compass contest. I . . . lifted my blindfold to find the target."

It was like a death-bed confession.

"I wanted to win more than . . . ." Tears ran down his cheeks.

I didn't know what to say. "Don't tell me anymore."

He paced outside the candlelight for a long time.

For no reason, I finally said, "Papa shouldn't have given you the gunpowder."

Sam sat beside me, leaning against the upended shelf, where we watched our last candle get shorter by the hour.

"Papa used to like explosions, too."

That couldn't possibly be true, not after he was burned by the maniac with the firecracker.

"Did he ever tell you the story about the railroad torpedoes?" Sam tossed little pebbles at the candle.

"Torpedoes?" Had I heard right?

"Railroads use 'torpedoes,' little dynamite charges to stop a train in an emergency. They fasten three of them on the track, and when the train hits them, they're so loud the engineer can hear them, even over the sound of the locomotive. Three in a row means an emergency, like a bridge out ahead."

I was starting to feel queasy. If I had to hear this story, or at least I wanted to hear Papa's version, not Sam's.

"Anyway, one day Papa broke into the railroad storage shed at Belvedere and put three torpedoes along the track when he knew a freight train was coming, then hid in the bushes. Sure enough: the three explosions were deafening, and the engineer instantly *locked up all the wheels*, screeching to a sliding stop about a half mile down the track."

This had to be a lie. Papa wouldn't do that.

"The engineer jumped out, looked as far as he could see down the track, and began running. He headed for the nearest farmhouse to phone or get a ride back to Belvedere, to find out what had happened and to warn the trains behind him that he was stopped on the track."

I was horrified. "That's a lie."

"Everything worked out fine," Sam shrugged it off like Papa's other adventures.

"Trains could've been coming up the tracks behind the stopped one and there could've been train wrecks and people killed."

"But there weren't," Sam objected. "Don't be such a kill-joy, Jeb."

I kept swallowing a sour taste. "It would've been Papa's fault."

"Accidents happen."

"But this wasn't an accident."

I couldn't believe that my father, my peace-loving, gentle father, could even think of something so cruel, much less do it. And after he had lectured us about hurting innocent people. Almost every time Mama One and I talked about Papa, she would say, "Remember: nobody's perfect." Often she would add, "No matter what high horse they're riding." She must have known about the railroad torpedoes. And probably a lot more.

I knew that I was a liar and a loud-mouth, and I showed off too much and got under people's skin on purpose, but I always thought that Sam was a better person and Papa was, well, perfect. If Sam could cheat and Papa could almost kill people with railroad torpedoes, I didn't want to go on living. I never felt so low in my whole life, not even when Bobby Clawson killed his dog or when Joe Clary was blinded.

I swallowed and swallowed, although I didn't have any spit left to swallow.

"Jeb?" Sam finally asked, but I didn't answer.

A while later, he tried again, "Jujube?"

"Don't tell me any more secrets" was all I could say.

If Sam kept sharing secrets, we were sure to die. His secrets were like bricks sealing us in here forever, cutting off what little oxygen we had. Already, we could never go back. Never. No matter what happened, we could never be the same little kids we were when the cellar door dropped shut over our heads.

I lay down on my side with my arm bent under my head and stared at the sputtering candle and thought and thought. From this position I noticed that pale light came through the door slats, but I didn't care. I watched Sam inspect the pipe bomb which had fizzled.

My dry mouth and throat made my voice hoarse. "Mama One is gone. All gone. Huh. As if she were dead. Not even parts of her will grow back. Mama One is like Papa's eye or Joe Clary's eye."

"Yep," Sam answered.

A few minutes later, he added, "But I'll tell you one thing." He sounded like Papa. "Mama Two is out looking for us right now. Her and Papa. Mama One wouldn't have noticed we were missing for a week."

That was true. Truly true. I had to admit it.

His voice sounded thick. "She's our mom, Jeb. She's all we've got."

This was also true.

Sam weighed the old pipe bomb in his hand. "I have one last idea. If we wedge this hard against the door, all its force will blast upward. Think we should try it? You didn't agree to a second try." He looked at me as if he wanted me to say no.

I stood up, picking up the cowbell in one hand and the Formula in the other. "Why not." What difference did it make now?

He carefully carried the bomb up the stairs and packed it with rocks and rags as tightly as he could under the door.

As a reminder, I had to ask, "This could kill us, right?"

He stopped pushing the bomb with his foot. "Yeah. Really and truly." He paused. "Do you want to wait longer?"

I shook my head no and began clanging the cowbell softly.

I hunkered behind the shelf as before, looking out only enough to see him light the fuse, which sparked brightly.

He tumbled down beside me, I threw Papa's coat over him, and we waited for the last explosion of our lives.

"Good-bye, Sam," I whispered.

"Good-bye, Jeb."

"I love everybody." It couldn't hurt to use the oldest Wilder good-night.

"Me too."

With our ears plugged, we waited for the fuse to burn all the way into the pipe.

We waited.

And waited.

Finally, we peeked around the shelf and saw that the fuse had burned perfectly, but the powder hadn't caught.

We threw off Papa's coat and walked toward it slowly.

As we started up the stairs toward the pipe bomb, we heard a strange sound.

"Watch out!" Sam warned. "It might still blow. Get back behind the shelf."

As we tumbled backward, I listened harder. "No. Sam, wait."

The sound was outside. *Above the door.*

We both listened and–yes–something was near the door. Maybe a cow had gotten out of the pasture. For just a minute, I considered that it might be Bobby Clawson, who would not only finish burying us alive but also steal our bicycles.

"HELP!" I shouted anyway. "C'mon, Sam!"

We both shouted, "MAYDAY! MAYDAY!"

And then–miracle of miracles–we heard a faint shout back. A *shout*.

I clanged the cowbell until my arm ached, and Sam shouted and then there was a lot of scraping on the door, and long, long minutes of someone moving the branch, and "HELP" we shouted again and again, "WE'RE ALIVE!" and shouts came back and then the door creaked open. Open! To a slot of clouds pink as cotton candy.

Who peeked over the opening but Will Hankins! He might as well have been god or Santa Claus.

"WILL!" Sam and I shouted and stumbled up the stairs, awkward and stiff.

"I figgered you'd be here," he was grinning to beat the band, as Grandma Strang would say. "They come an' found me workin' at Dagendorf's."

Then we realized that Will was not alone.

It was Papa and Mama. Papa and Mama and Will, all there, waiting in the open, wide air, waiting with their faces hurting and their arms open. "JEB! SAM!" everybody shouted at once. Mama grabbed me, and I hugged her back, while Sam hugged Papa, who had his other arm around Will. We pulled each other into a big circle hug, Will so surprised he stumbled, causing us kids to fall down in a heap, laughing. Mama and Papa were as radiant and glittering as the cottonwood leaves, and so relieved that their knees gave way and they sat down in the long weeds. Will kept looking at us all sideways, shyly, and I knew how much he wished he belonged to us.

It wasn't the movies, the long, slow-motion, loping reunions I had dreamed for so many years. It was better. Better than making friends with dead baby Janet, better than sewing Grandma's perfect pajamas, better than winning the spelling bee. It was better than finding a pony tied to the trailer door on Christmas morning. It was Mama and Papa and Sam and Will Hankins and me living out the happiest moment of my life.

CHAPTER 62

THEME AND VARIATIONS

INSIDE THE TRAILER, THE LIGHT OF THE EARLY September evening slid along the seamless oak walls and over the tube-like roof, slick and warm as melted butter. Papa had called a Family Council, which always made Sam and me nervous. I sat on the piano bench, kicking my feet. Mama sat on the sofa-bed beside Sam, who was exercising Stuffy by stretching his two legs apart. After a few minutes, she gently took Stuffy away and petted him on her lap. She had started dying and curling her hair again, so she looked more like our original mother, although a chubby version.

Papa sat on my footstool, as he always did, with his elbows on his knees, looking at his hands loosely folded and hanging between them. "You kids have probably guessed. I've been transferred, and it's time to move again."

Sam and I exchanged wary glances. What had happened? They couldn't have finished the dam that fast. Was this about Sam's pipe bombs? The riot in the Avalon Theater? Or Joe Clary's eye?

I had to ask, "Are you trying to keep us out of jail?"

Sam rolled his eyes until they were half white.

On the alert, Papa looked up. His new glasses caught the light and made it hard to see his eyes. "What have you done now?"

Sam tried to cover for me. "It's a joke." He looked at me threateningly. "A dumb kid's joke."

"It won't be jail, but it will be . . . Kansas." Papa looked at Mama and grinned.

"Not far: just across the border," she added.

"But we have good news." He bounced his clasped hands up and down as if he were holding a magic trick. "We're going to sell the trailer and rent a house. A real house."

I should have felt *ecstatic*, one of my new favorite words, although having nothing to do with static. But I suspected this move had to do with our new mother. "Why?"

Clearly disappointed, Papa answered, "I thought you wanted to live in a house, Sugar."

"That's when I was younger. I'm going to be in fifth grade."

"What a waste of time," Sam said. "You already know everything in fifth grade." With his new Citizenship in the Home voice, Sam tried to sound diplomatic. "We could move to Kansas and keep the trailer, just as we've always done."

"Frank," Mama said. "Tell them the truth."

We were going to jail. I knew it.

She turned Stuffy over to pet his other side. "We need to sell the trailer to pay for my doctor bills."

Paying bills was the argument which always ended the discussion, and I should have let it drop, but something didn't make sense.

"Before, we had to sell our real house and buy the trailer to finish paying Papa's doctor bills. From his burns."

"That's true." Papa answered.

I pressed on. "So sometimes we have to *buy* a trailer to pay doctors' bills, and sometimes we have to *sell* one to pay doctors' bills."

"That about sums it up." When Papa smiled full-sized, the white creases in his sunburned face disappeared, and he was all red.

"Can we go out and play?" This was Sam's way of calling our own Kids' Council.

On our way out, Mama started to say, "Don't slam–" but Sam was already closing it quietly. We had learned a thing or two while she was gone.

From Mr. Whitaker's lawn, Sam and I looked at the trailer–a friendly little toaster, two-toned, freckled with evening light and shade. The trailer, which I had blamed for everything from Mr. Sprecker to Doreen Cavin and the Brownie nation, which had felt like something between a cage and a circus wagon, now looked like a suit of armor just big enough for four people, for our family. A perfect, self-contained fort.

Sam sensed that I needed cheering up. "In a house, you'll probably get your own room."

"I don't want my own room." I couldn't imagine not sleeping in the living room, in everybody's way, under everybody's feet, with every new town's streetlight in my face, and the log cabin chimney smoke clicking off seconds, and the cookie jar winking at me, and hearing Sam in the night mumble with a nightmare, and myself carefully turning over in place like a sausage so I wouldn't fall off the chair-bed, especially now that I had to sleep with Stuffy.

"I don't want my own room," I repeated. "You know what happened to the Prisoner of Chillon?"

"Who?"

"A man in a poem Mama One used to recite to me on the footstool. Seventeen-and-a-half minutes long. When they came to let him out of prison, he didn't want to leave. I wish I could remember it all, but I know how it ends."

Taking the same pose I held at the ending of "Why the Bells Rang," I tried to imitate Mama One's poetry voice. "My very chains and I grew friends, so much a long communion tends."

"Communion?" Sam interrupted. "Like church?"

"I guess so."

"With chains?"

"And spiders and mice and other things." I wasn't sure about these additions.

"That is totally irrational."

"It's a poem. By Lord Byron. I mostly remember the last lines."

I was growing quite *adept*, another new favorite, at swamping his objections with more words, as long as they didn't involve anything scientific. If I had been explaining rocket fuel, for example, I wouldn't have made it through the first sentence.

I resumed. " A long communion tends to make us what we are: even I regained my freedom with a sigh."

"Huh." Clearly my word swamping mechanism was working. "Who was this guy?"

"I don't know."

"Why was he in prison?"

I created on the spot, "He was on the wrong side."

"Why'd they set him free?"

Once you start a lie, you have to finish. "His side won the war."

Sam concluded, "Oh: release of POWs."

Every once in a while now, Mama would ask me to recite a poem to her, if you can imagine. I was trying to memorize brand new ones, happy ones, none about death.

We looked at our Buick in the driveway. In the barn sat Mrs. Vince's old Ford panel truck which Papa was fixing so she could safely drive to Hastings to visit her dead brother's family or to Lincoln to see Mrs. Dahlke. Papa was also figuring out how to modify it so she could take Miss Reynolds with her, wheelchair and all.

"We can still run away, Sam."

"Yeah," he agreed half-heartedly.

"We're still young enough–" I didn't know where to go with this thought.

Sam put his arm completely around my neck, the old stranglehold, but loose. "We'll be all right, Jujube. Trust me."

Trust a Boy Scout with fourteen merit badges, including useless Firemanship, disastrous Chemistry and potentially fatal Electricity. At least he couldn't do too much damage with Art.

No one ever found out who almost blew up the Avalon Theater, or put out Joe Clary's eye, or burned down Mrs. Keindorf's house.

The day before we left Round Prairie, Sam and I buried the Formula deep in the site of the old fort, so they could share a grave. Mr. Whitaker waved to us from his back porch, not realizing the Formula would protect him as long as he lived. We built a fort in our new town in Kansas, but it turned into a tree house, where Sam and his friends pulled up the rope ladder so I couldn't get in. Sam still taught me the formula for every complex thing, and I taught him all the exotic words I learned, which, I kept reminding him, were actually ideas. I grew out of my patent leather shoes but learned to play all of Rachmaninoff's variations on Paganini's theme. We never filled in Volumes 12-14 of the Funk and Wagnall's Encyclopedia, but after a while, we didn't even miss them. Instead, we made a game out of inventing the missing information, outdoing each other with crazier and crazier imaginary facts.

Our new mother held firm, warm and full of wonder, and Papa grew glad watching our family spiral in and out of light and darkness, never returning exactly to the same place, just as he had promised in my first eclipse.